KING OF RPGs

ALSO BY JASON THOMPSON

Manga: The Complete Guide
Clark Ashton Smith's Hyperborea

KING OF RPGs

VOLUME 1

STORY BY
JASON THOMPSON

ILLUSTRATIONS BY
VICTOR HAO

DEL REY

BALLANTINE BOOKS • NEW YORK

A Del Rey Manga Trade Paperback Original

Published in the United States by Del Rey, an imprint of The Random House Publishing Group, a division of Random House, Inc., New York.

DEL REY is a registered trademark and the DEL REY colophon is a trademark of Random House, Inc.

Illustrations and lettering by Victor Hao

ISBN 978-0-345-51359-5

Printed in the United States of America

www.delreybooks.com

9 8 7 6 5 4 3 2 1

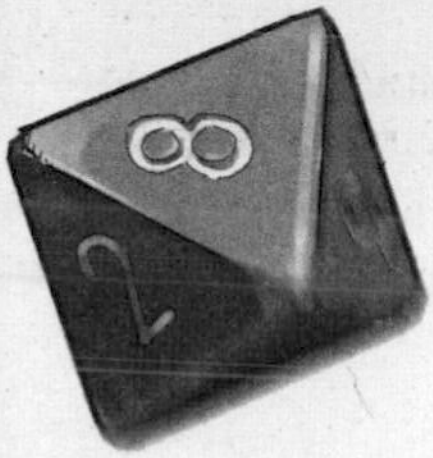

CONTENTS

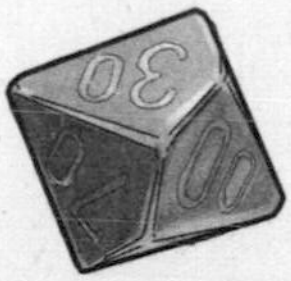

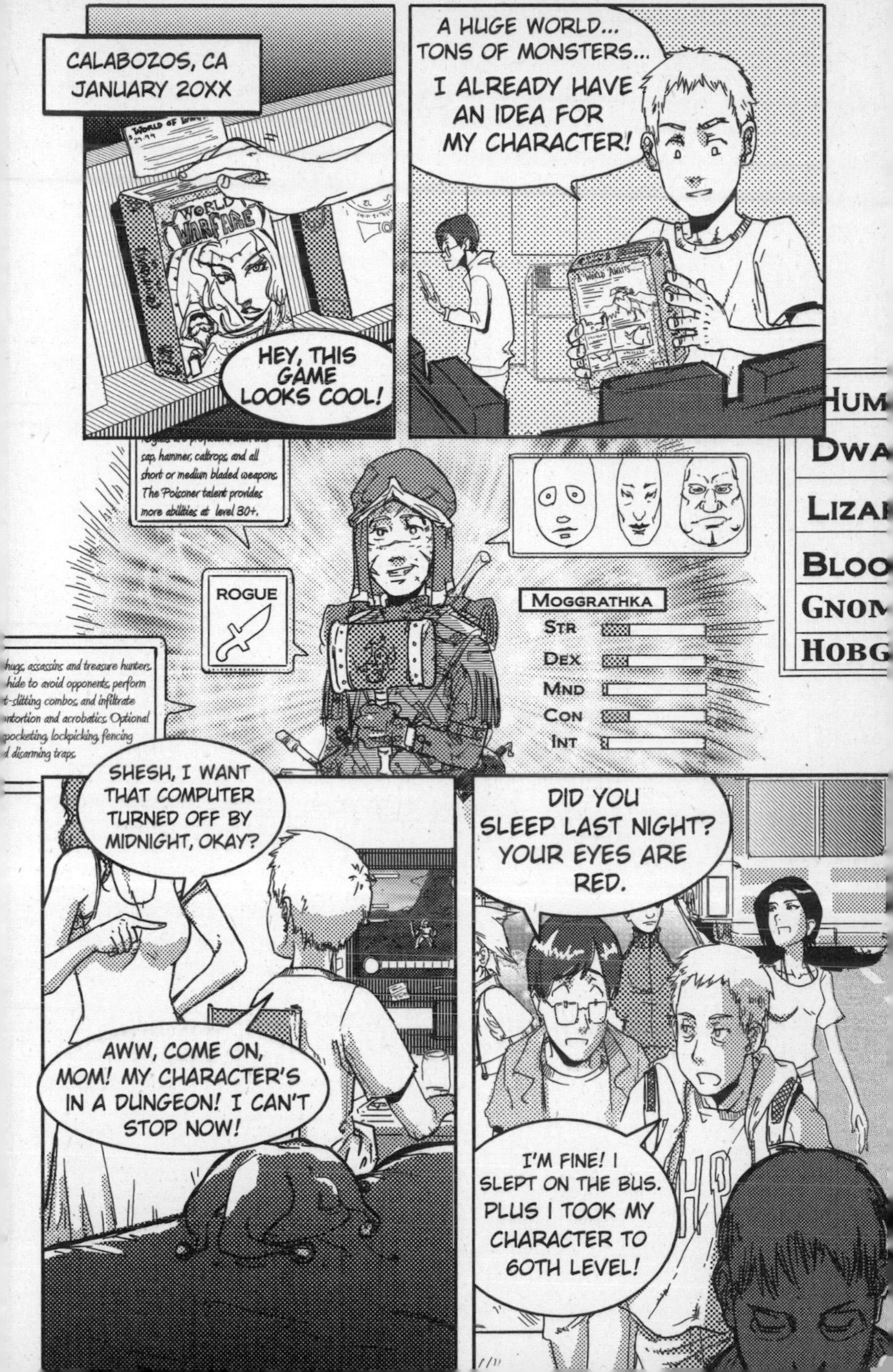
CALABOZOS, CA JANUARY 20XX
WORLD OF WARFARE
HEY, THIS GAME LOOKS COOL!
A HUGE WORLD... TONS OF MONSTERS...
I ALREADY HAVE AN IDEA FOR MY CHARACTER!
A WORLD AWAITS
sap, hammer, caltrops, and all short or medium bladed weapons. The Poisoner talent provides more abilities at level 30+.
ROGUE
hugs, assassins and treasure hunters. hide to avoid opponents, perform t-slitting combos, and infiltrate ontortion and acrobatics. Optional pocketing, lockpicking, fencing d disarming traps.
MOGGRATHKA
STR
DEX
MND
CON
INT
HUM
DWA
LIZA
BLOO
GNOM
HOBG
SHESH, I WANT THAT COMPUTER TURNED OFF BY MIDNIGHT, OKAY?
AWW, COME ON, MOM! MY CHARACTER'S IN A DUNGEON! I CAN'T STOP NOW!
DID YOU SLEEP LAST NIGHT? YOUR EYES ARE RED.
I'M FINE! I SLEPT ON THE BUS. PLUS I TOOK MY CHARACTER TO 60TH LEVEL!

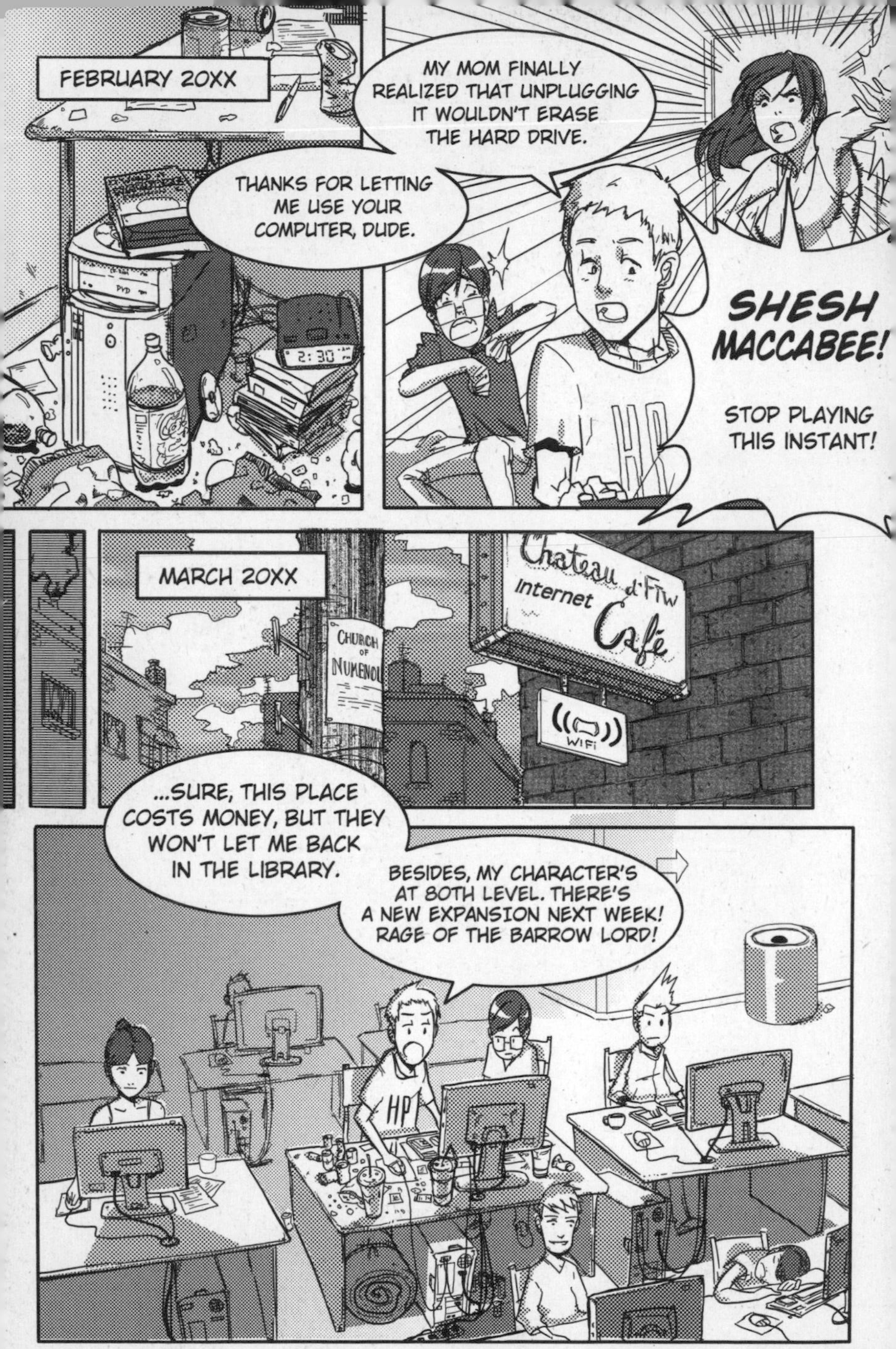
FEBRUARY 20XX
THANKS FOR LETTING ME USE YOUR COMPUTER, DUDE.
2:30
MY MOM FINALLY REALIZED THAT UNPLUGGING IT WOULDN'T ERASE THE HARD DRIVE.
SHESH MACCABEE!
STOP PLAYING THIS INSTANT!
MARCH 20XX
CHURCH OF NUMENOL
Chateau d'Ftw Internet Café
WiFi
...SURE, THIS PLACE COSTS MONEY, BUT THEY WON'T LET ME BACK IN THE LIBRARY.
BESIDES, MY CHARACTER'S AT 80TH LEVEL. THERE'S A NEW EXPANSION NEXT WEEK! RAGE OF THE BARROW LORD!
HP

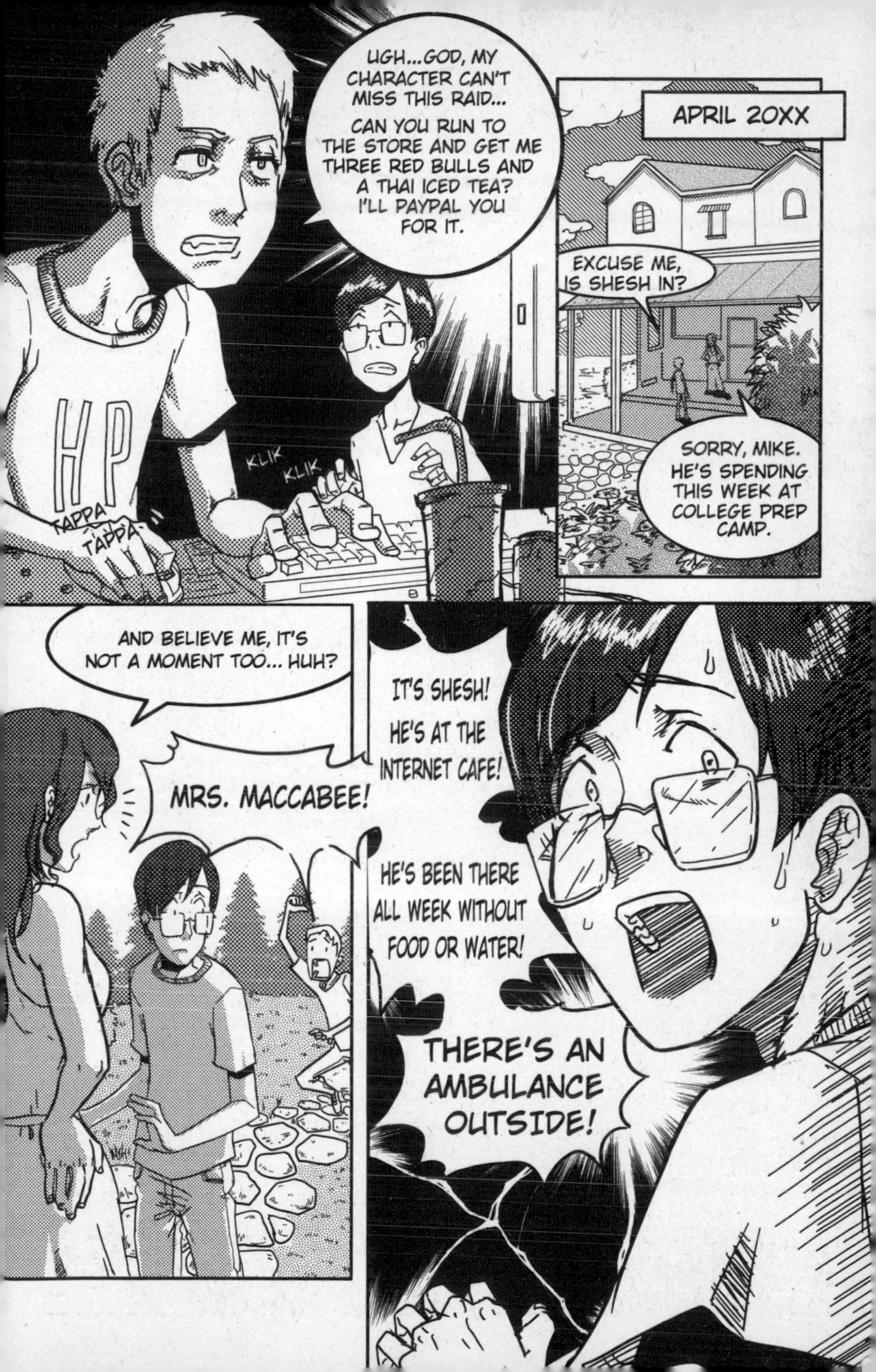
UGH...GOD, MY CHARACTER CAN'T MISS THIS RAID...
CAN YOU RUN TO THE STORE AND GET ME THREE RED BULLS AND A THAI ICED TEA? I'LL PAYPAL YOU FOR IT.
KLIK KLIK
TAPPA TAPPA
APRIL 20XX
EXCUSE ME, IS SHESH IN?
SORRY, MIKE. HE'S SPENDING THIS WEEK AT COLLEGE PREP CAMP.
AND BELIEVE ME, IT'S NOT A MOMENT TOO... HUH?
MRS. MACCABEE!
IT'S SHESH!
HE'S AT THE INTERNET CAFE!
HE'S BEEN THERE ALL WEEK WITHOUT FOOD OR WATER!
THERE'S AN AMBULANCE OUTSIDE!

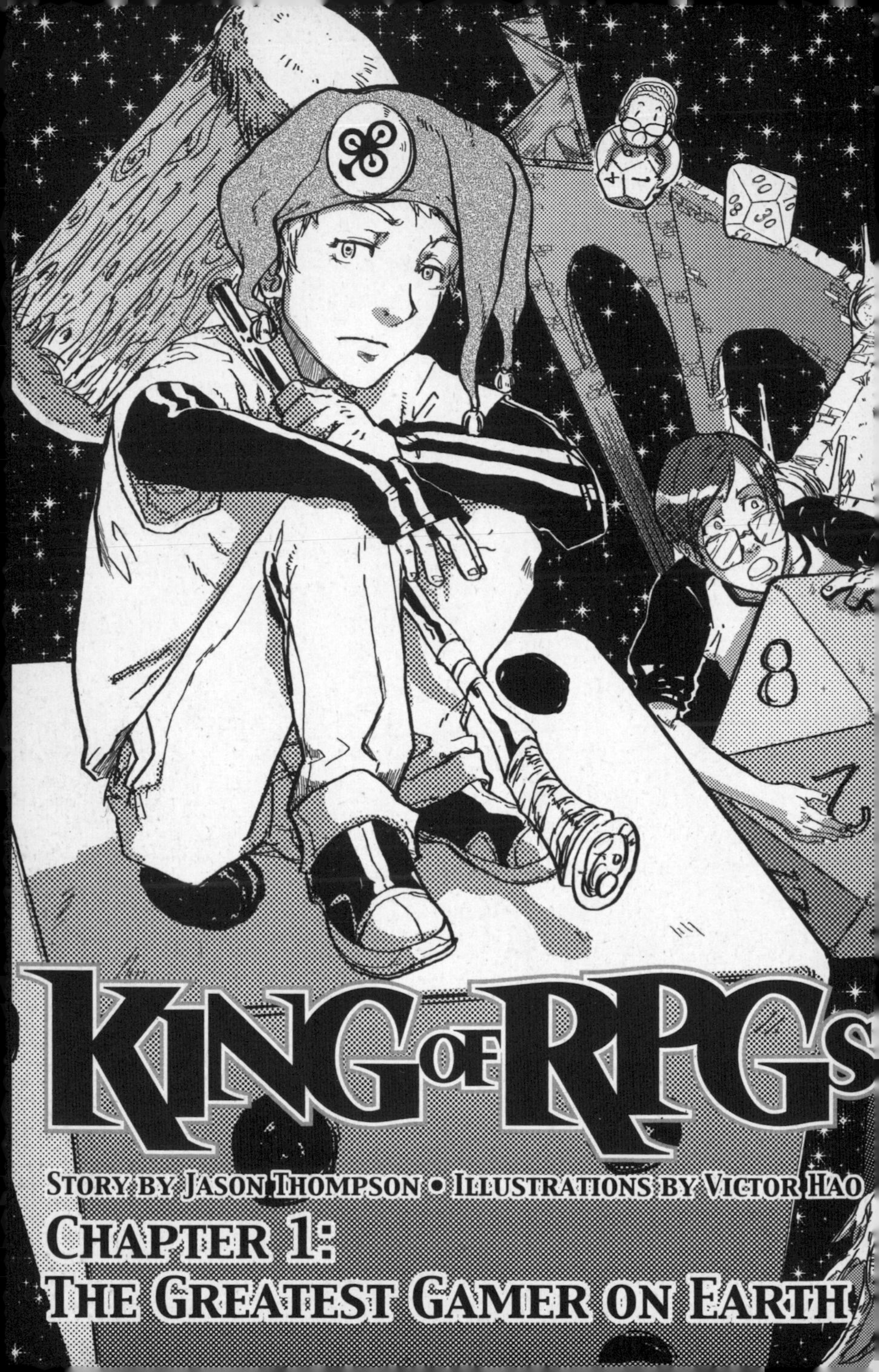
KING OF RPGs
STORY BY JASON THOMPSON • ILLUSTRATIONS BY VICTOR HAO
CHAPTER 1:
THE GREATEST GAMER ON EARTH

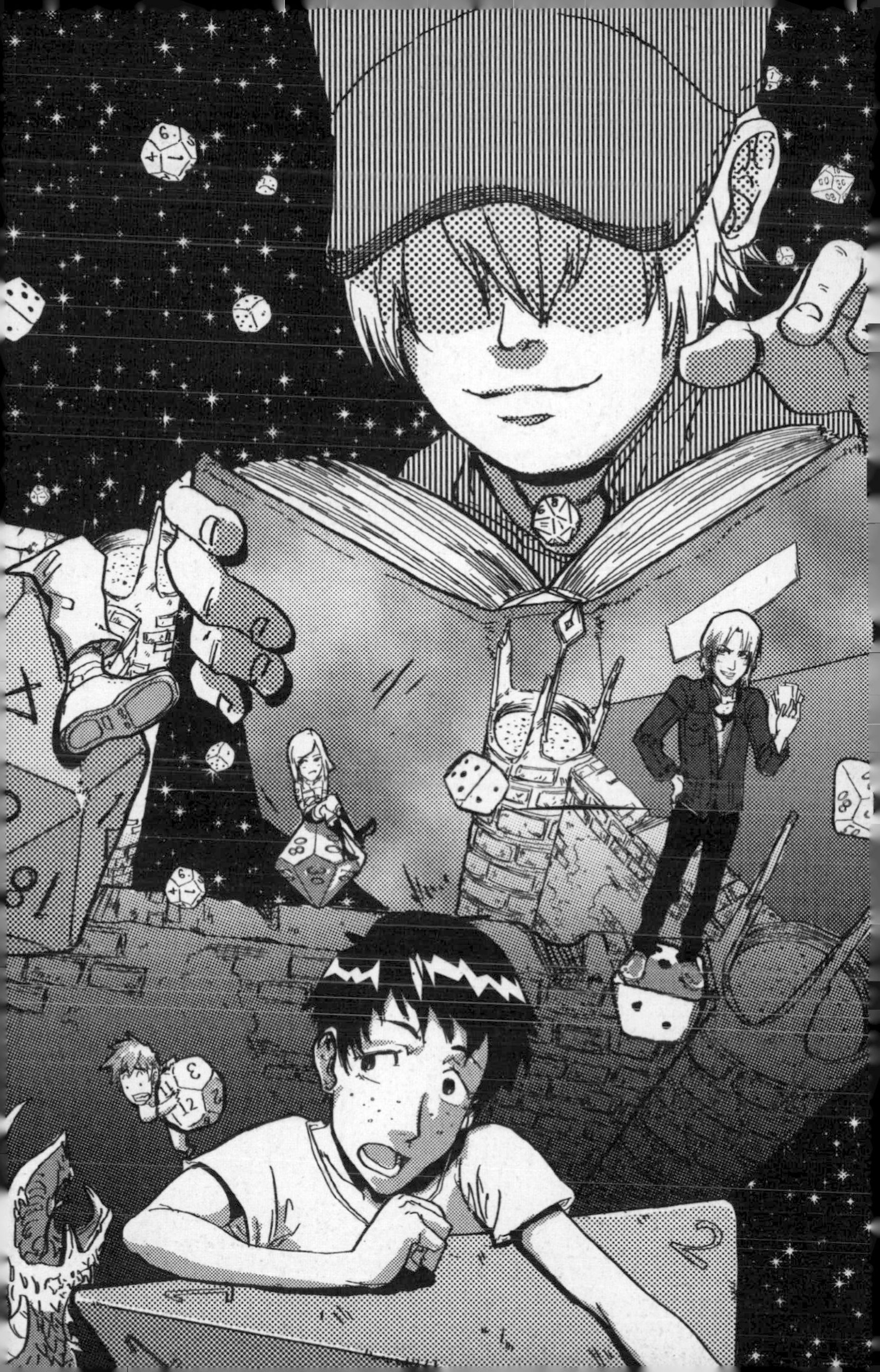

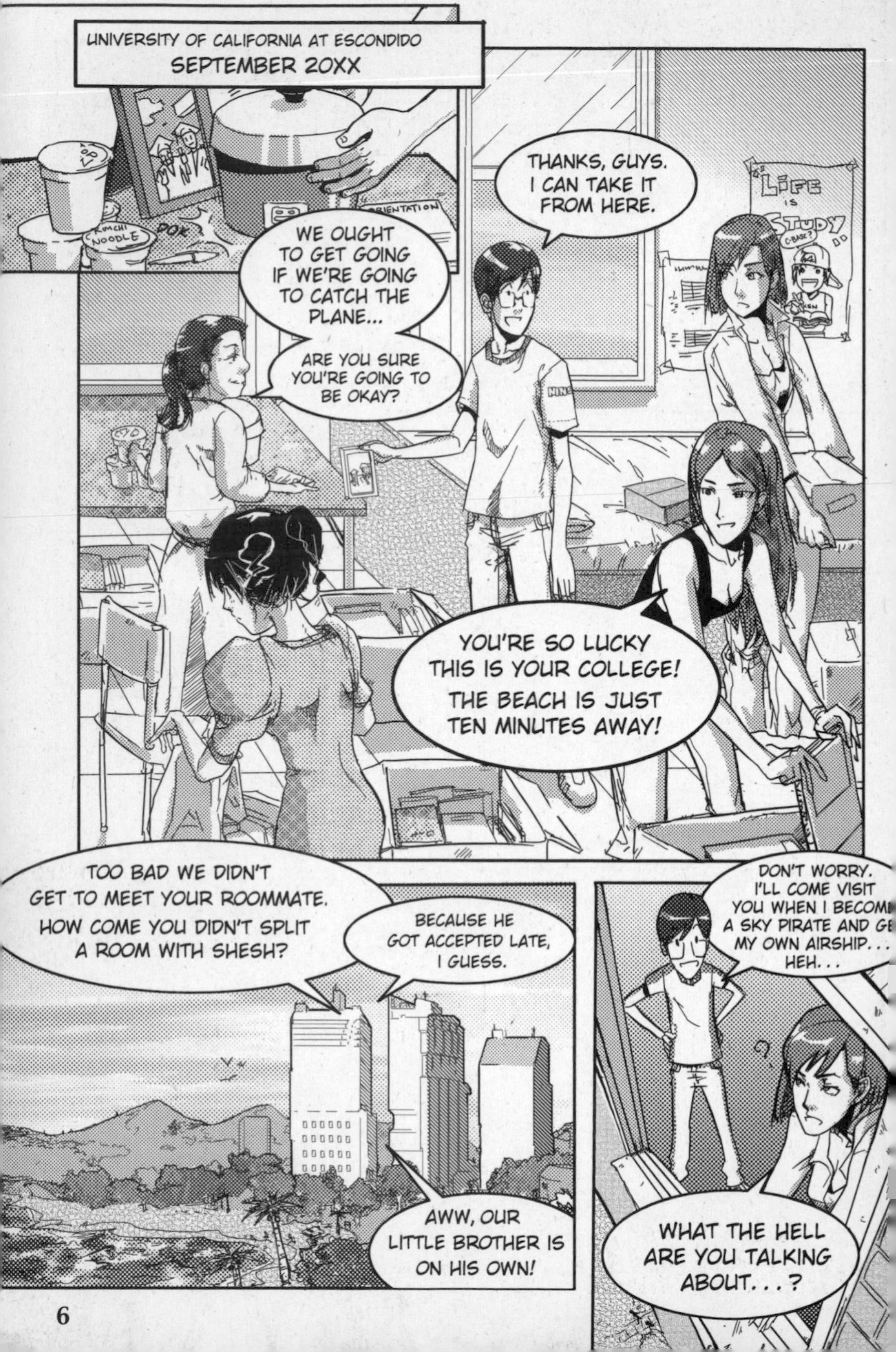
UNIVERSITY OF CALIFORNIA AT ESCONDIDO
SEPTEMBER 20XX
KIMCHI NOODLE
ORIENTATION
THANKS, GUYS. I CAN TAKE IT FROM HERE.
WE OUGHT TO GET GOING IF WE'RE GOING TO CATCH THE PLANE...
ARE YOU SURE YOU'RE GOING TO BE OKAY?
LIFE IS STUDY
YOU'RE SO LUCKY THIS IS YOUR COLLEGE!
THE BEACH IS JUST TEN MINUTES AWAY!
TOO BAD WE DIDN'T GET TO MEET YOUR ROOMMATE.
HOW COME YOU DIDN'T SPLIT A ROOM WITH SHESH?
BECAUSE HE GOT ACCEPTED LATE, I GUESS.
AWW, OUR LITTLE BROTHER IS ON HIS OWN!
DON'T WORRY. I'LL COME VISIT YOU WHEN I BECOM A SKY PIRATE AND GE MY OWN AIRSHIP. . . HEH. . .
WHAT THE HELL ARE YOU TALKING ABOUT. . . ?

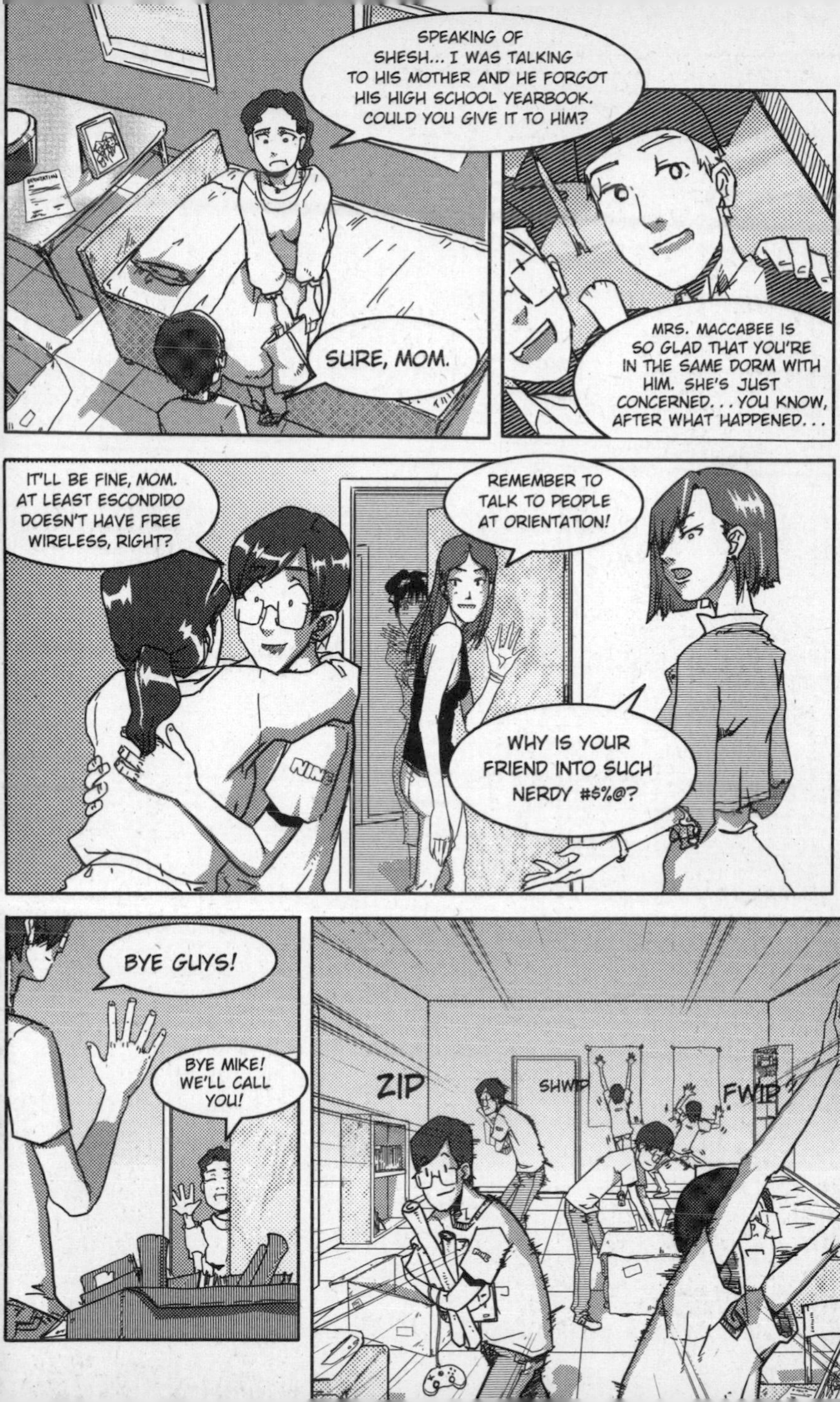
SPEAKING OF SHESH... I WAS TALKING TO HIS MOTHER AND HE FORGOT HIS HIGH SCHOOL YEARBOOK. COULD YOU GIVE IT TO HIM?
SURE, MOM.
MRS. MACCABEE IS SO GLAD THAT YOU'RE IN THE SAME DORM WITH HIM. SHE'S JUST CONCERNED. . . YOU KNOW, AFTER WHAT HAPPENED. . .
IT'LL BE FINE, MOM. AT LEAST ESCONDIDO DOESN'T HAVE FREE WIRELESS, RIGHT?
REMEMBER TO TALK TO PEOPLE AT ORIENTATION!
WHY IS YOUR FRIEND INTO SUCH NERDY #$%@?
BYE GUYS!
BYE MIKE! WE'LL CALL YOU!
ZIP
SHWP
FWIP

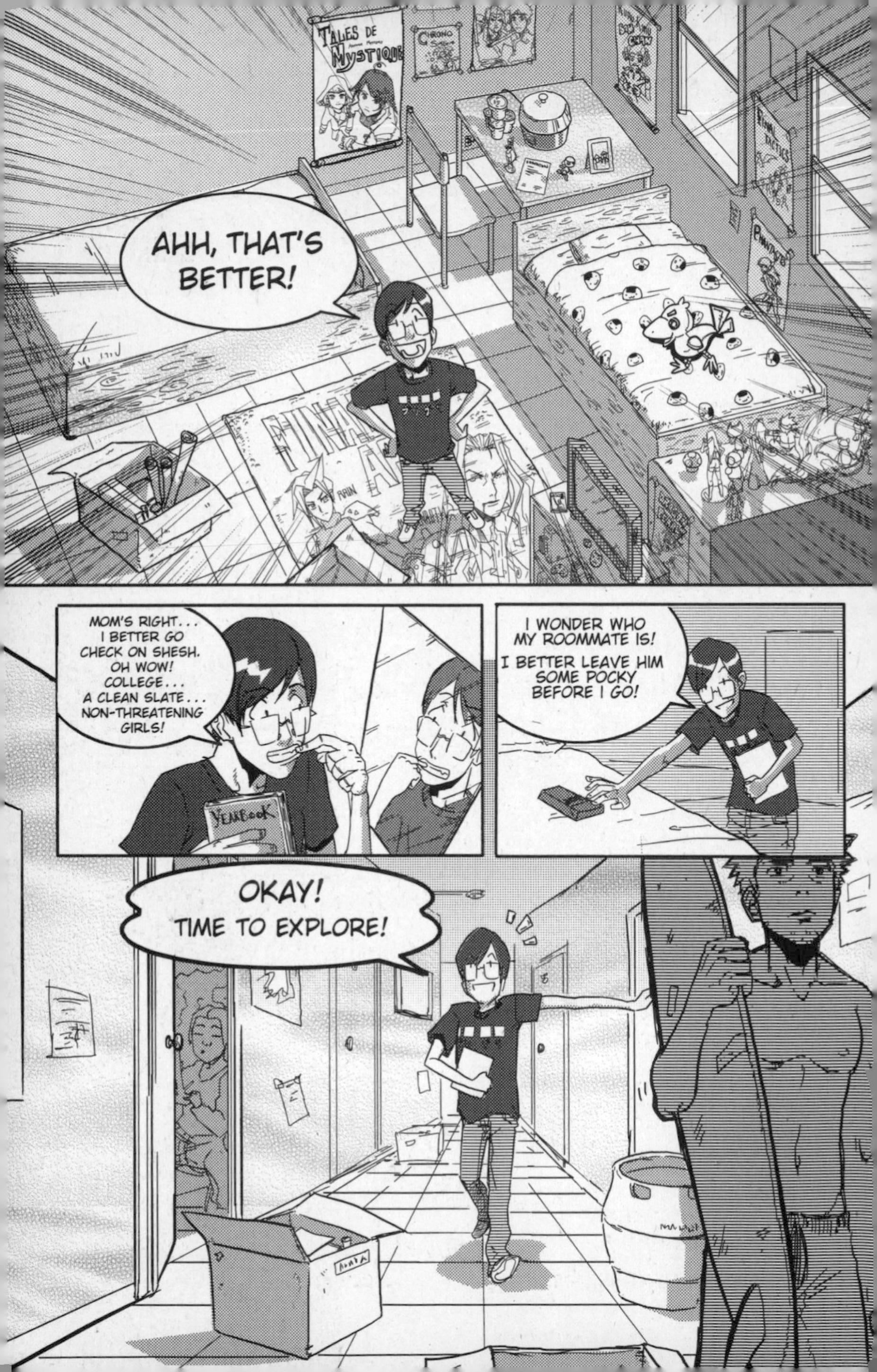
TALES DE MYSTIQUE
AHH, THAT'S BETTER!
MOM'S RIGHT... I BETTER GO CHECK ON SHESH. OH WOW! COLLEGE... A CLEAN SLATE... NON-THREATENING GIRLS!
YEARBOOK
I WONDER WHO MY ROOMMATE IS!
I BETTER LEAVE HIM SOME POCKY BEFORE I GO!
OKAY! TIME TO EXPLORE!

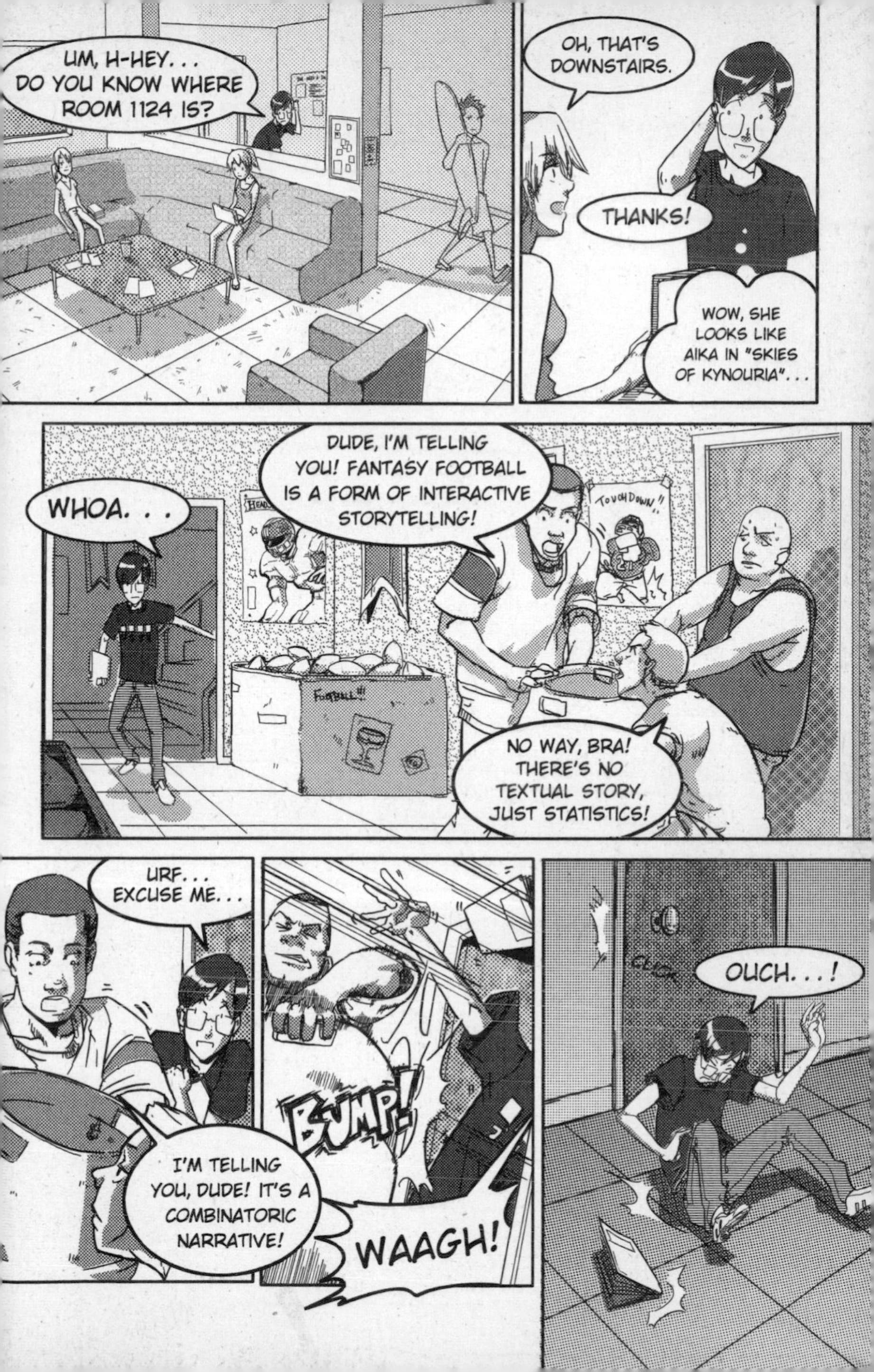
UM, H-HEY. . . DO YOU KNOW WHERE ROOM 1124 IS?
OH, THAT'S DOWNSTAIRS.
THANKS!
WOW, SHE LOOKS LIKE AIKA IN "SKIES OF KYNOURIA". . .
WHOA. . .
DUDE, I'M TELLING YOU! FANTASY FOOTBALL IS A FORM OF INTERACTIVE STORYTELLING!
TOUCHDOWN!!
FOOTBALL!!!
NO WAY, BRA! THERE'S NO TEXTUAL STORY, JUST STATISTICS!
URF. . . EXCUSE ME. . .
BUMP!
I'M TELLING YOU, DUDE! IT'S A COMBINATORIC NARRATIVE!
WAAGH!
CLICK
OUCH. . .!

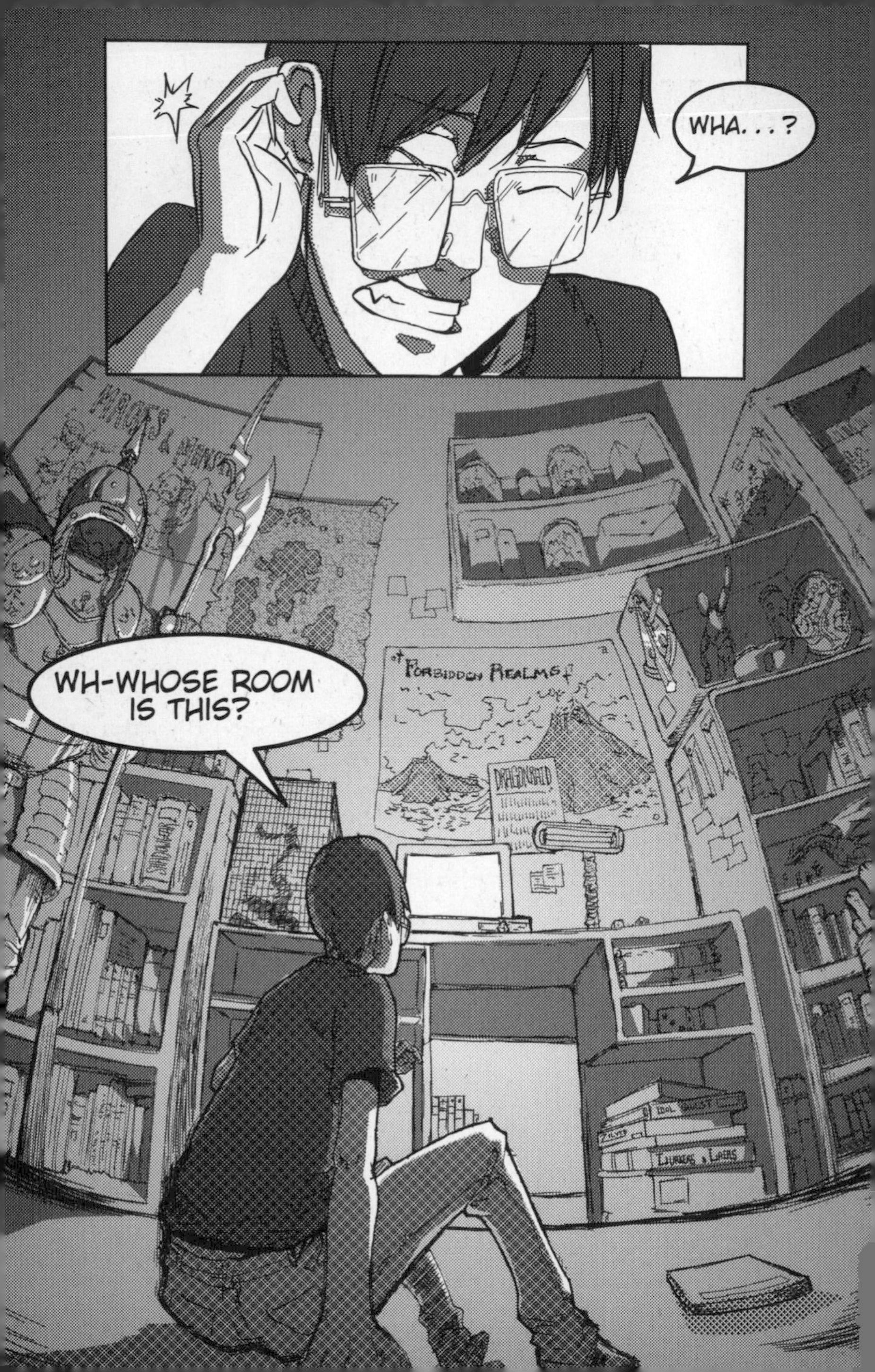
WHA. . . ?
WH-WHOSE ROOM IS THIS?
FORBIDDEN REALMS

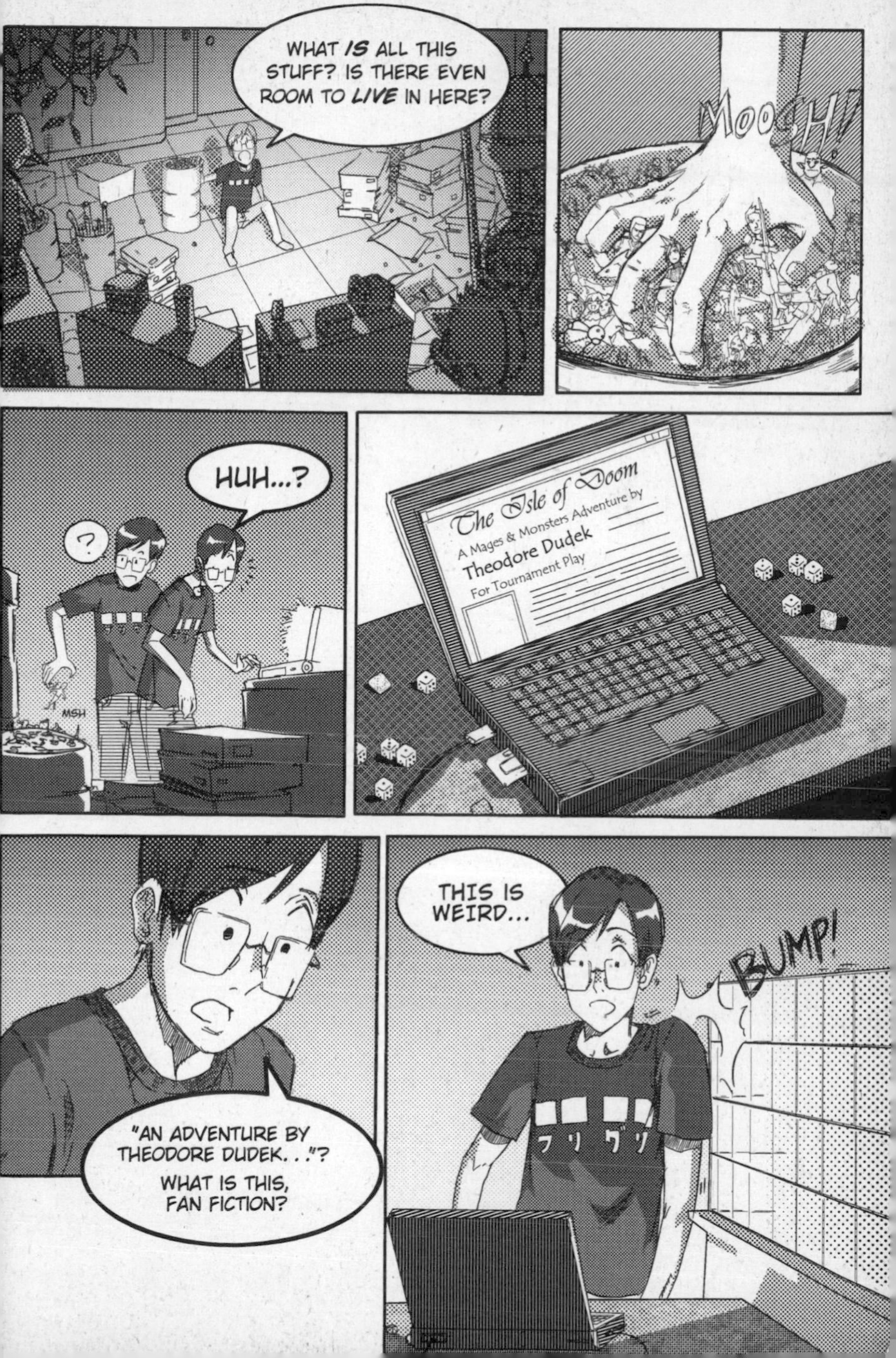
WHAT *IS* ALL THIS STUFF? IS THERE EVEN ROOM TO *LIVE* IN HERE?
MOOSH!
?
HUH...?
MSH
The Isle of Doom
A Mages & Monsters Adventure by
Theodore Dudek
For Tournament Play
"AN ADVENTURE BY THEODORE DUDEK. . ."? WHAT IS THIS, FAN FICTION?
THIS IS WEIRD...
BUMP!

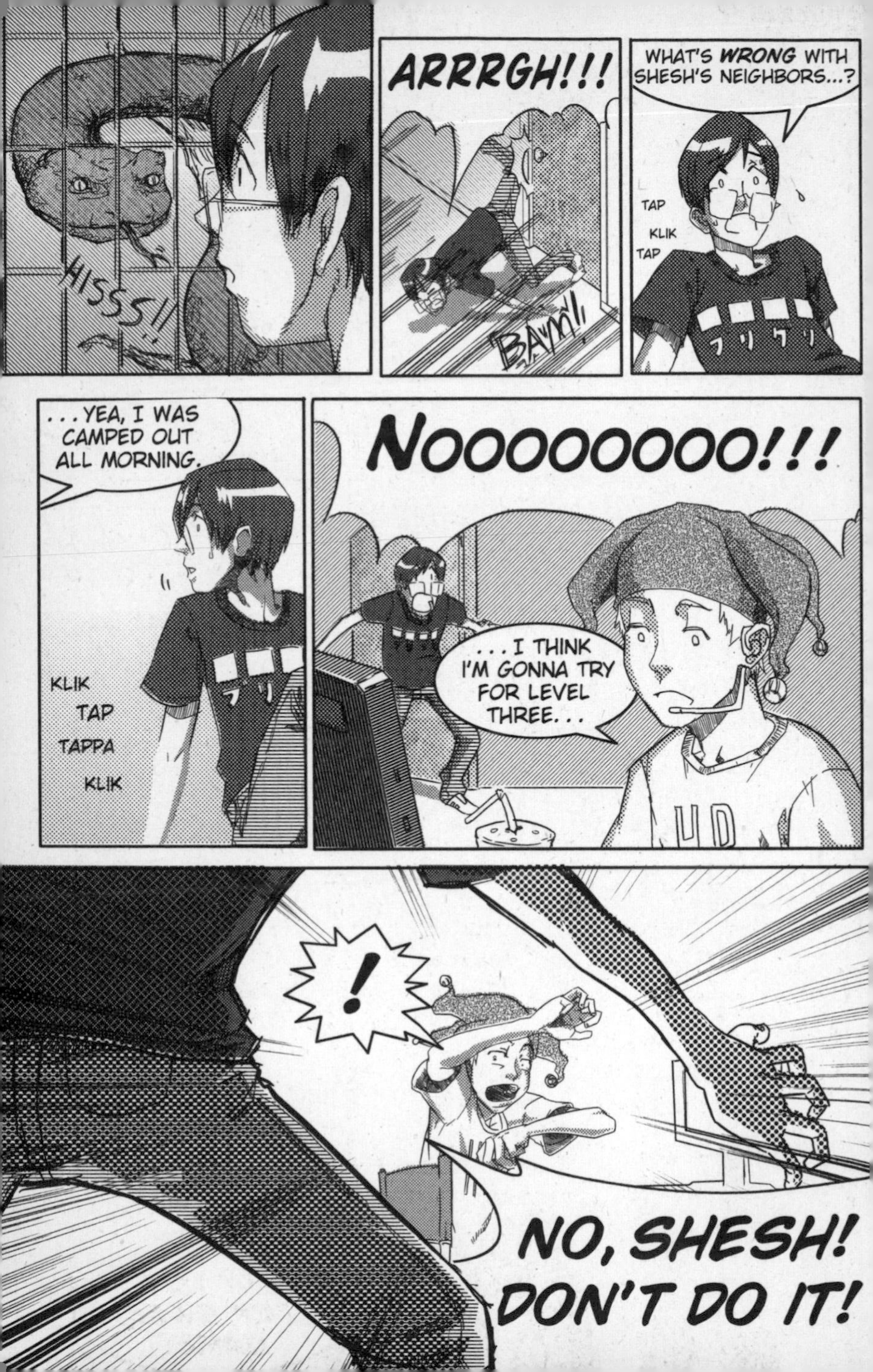
HISSS!!
ARRRGH!!!
BAM!!
WHAT'S WRONG WITH SHESH'S NEIGHBORS...?
TAP
KLIK
TAP
. . . YEA, I WAS CAMPED OUT ALL MORNING.
KLIK
TAP
TAPPA
KLIK
NOOOOOOOOO!!!
. . . I THINK I'M GONNA TRY FOR LEVEL THREE. . .
!
NO, SHESH! DON'T DO IT!

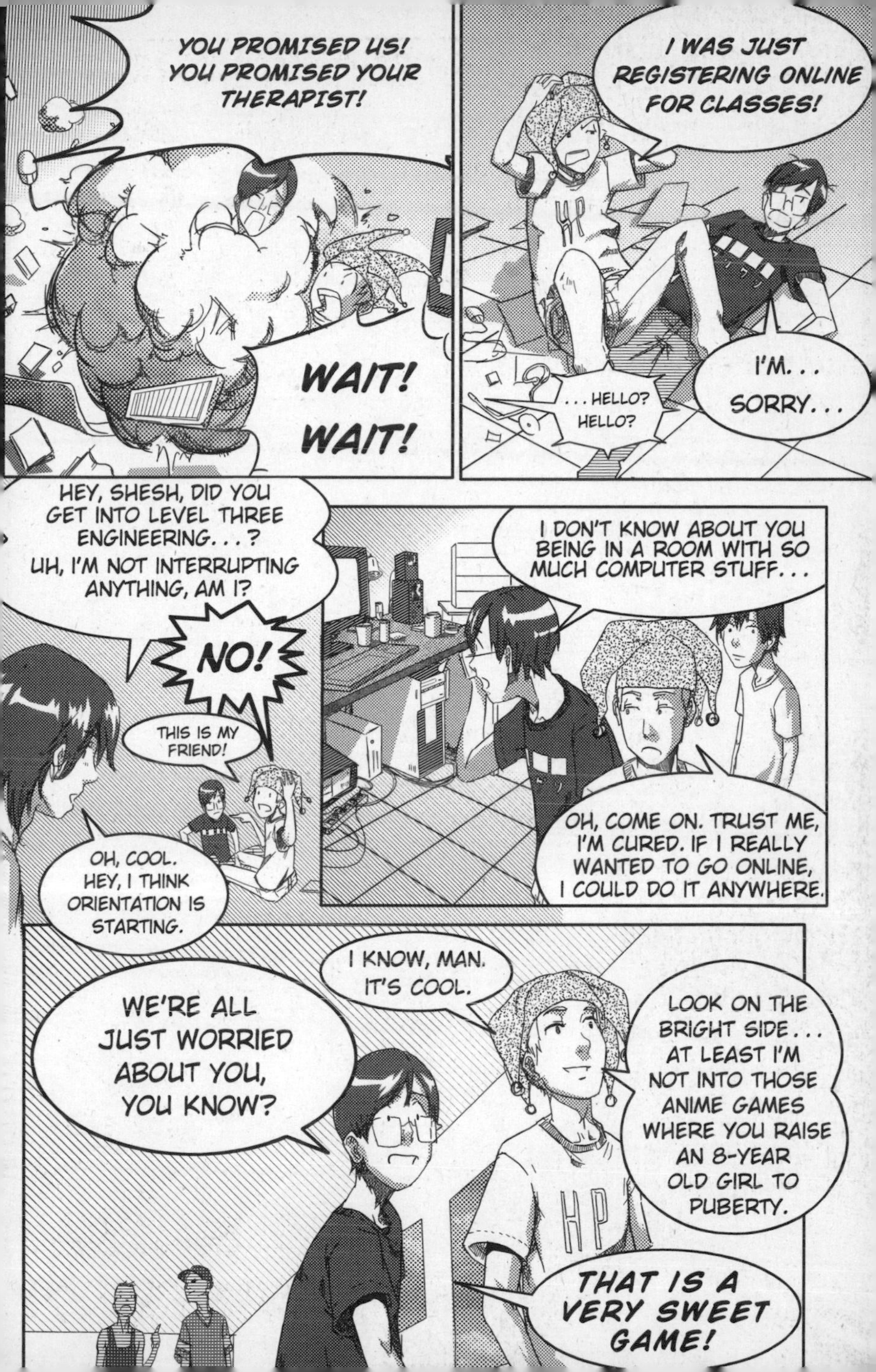
YOU PROMISED US! YOU PROMISED YOUR THERAPIST!
WAIT!
WAIT!
I WAS JUST REGISTERING ONLINE FOR CLASSES!
. . . HELLO? HELLO?
I'M. . . SORRY. . .
HEY, SHESH, DID YOU GET INTO LEVEL THREE ENGINEERING. . . ? UH, I'M NOT INTERRUPTING ANYTHING, AM I?
NO!
THIS IS MY FRIEND!
OH, COOL. HEY, I THINK ORIENTATION IS STARTING.
I DON'T KNOW ABOUT YOU BEING IN A ROOM WITH SO MUCH COMPUTER STUFF. . .
OH, COME ON. TRUST ME, I'M CURED. IF I REALLY WANTED TO GO ONLINE, I COULD DO IT ANYWHERE.
WE'RE ALL JUST WORRIED ABOUT YOU, YOU KNOW?
I KNOW, MAN. IT'S COOL.
LOOK ON THE BRIGHT SIDE . . . AT LEAST I'M NOT INTO THOSE ANIME GAMES WHERE YOU RAISE AN 8-YEAR OLD GIRL TO PUBERTY.
THAT IS A VERY SWEET GAME!

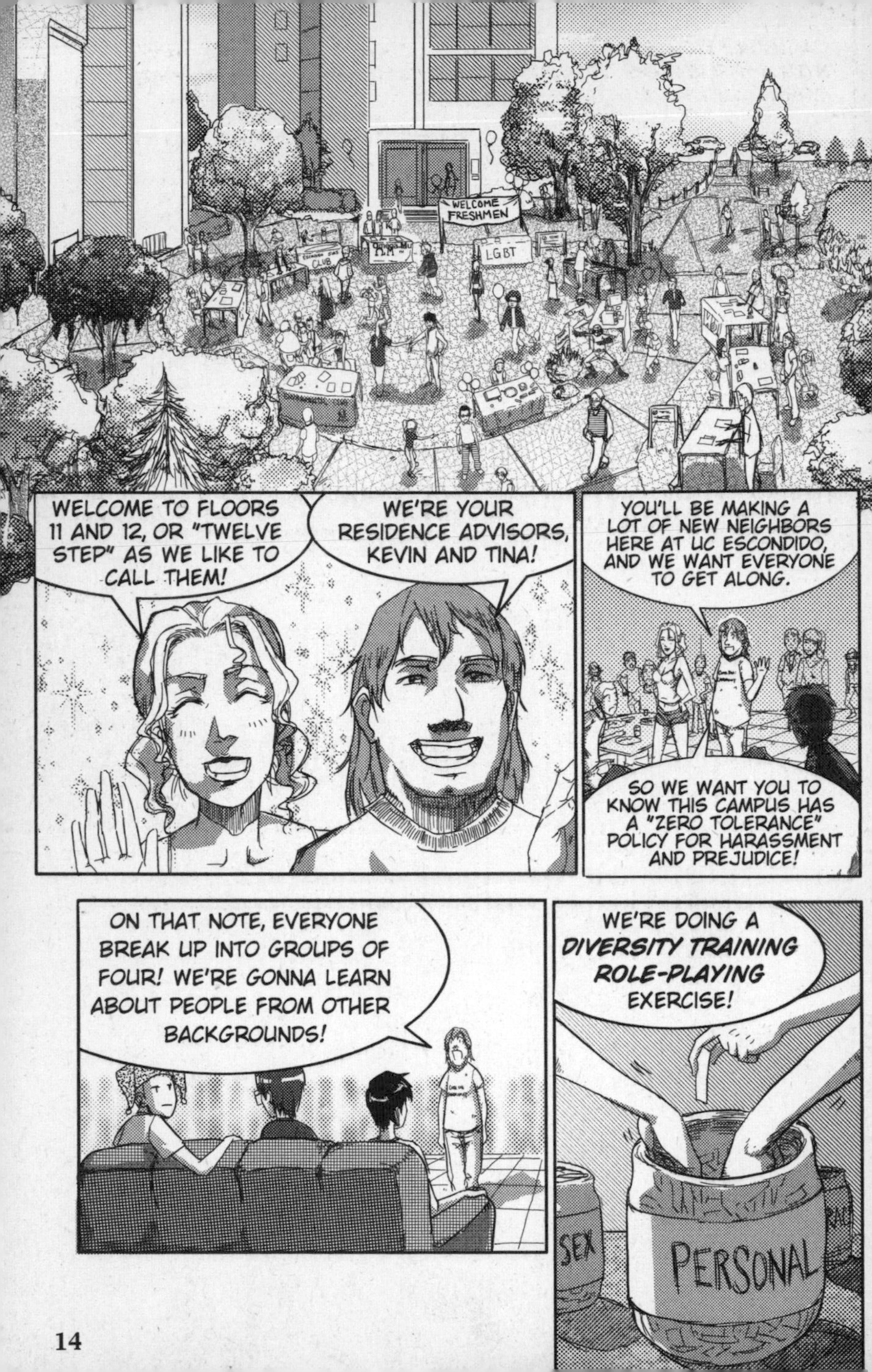

WELCOME FRESHMEN
LGBT
WELCOME TO FLOORS 11 AND 12, OR "TWELVE STEP" AS WE LIKE TO CALL THEM!
WE'RE YOUR RESIDENCE ADVISORS, KEVIN AND TINA!
YOU'LL BE MAKING A LOT OF NEW NEIGHBORS HERE AT UC ESCONDIDO, AND WE WANT EVERYONE TO GET ALONG.
SO WE WANT YOU TO KNOW THIS CAMPUS HAS A "ZERO TOLERANCE" POLICY FOR HARASSMENT AND PREJUDICE!
ON THAT NOTE, EVERYONE BREAK UP INTO GROUPS OF FOUR! WE'RE GONNA LEARN ABOUT PEOPLE FROM OTHER BACKGROUNDS!
WE'RE DOING A *DIVERSITY TRAINING ROLE-PLAYING* EXERCISE!
SEX
PERSONAL

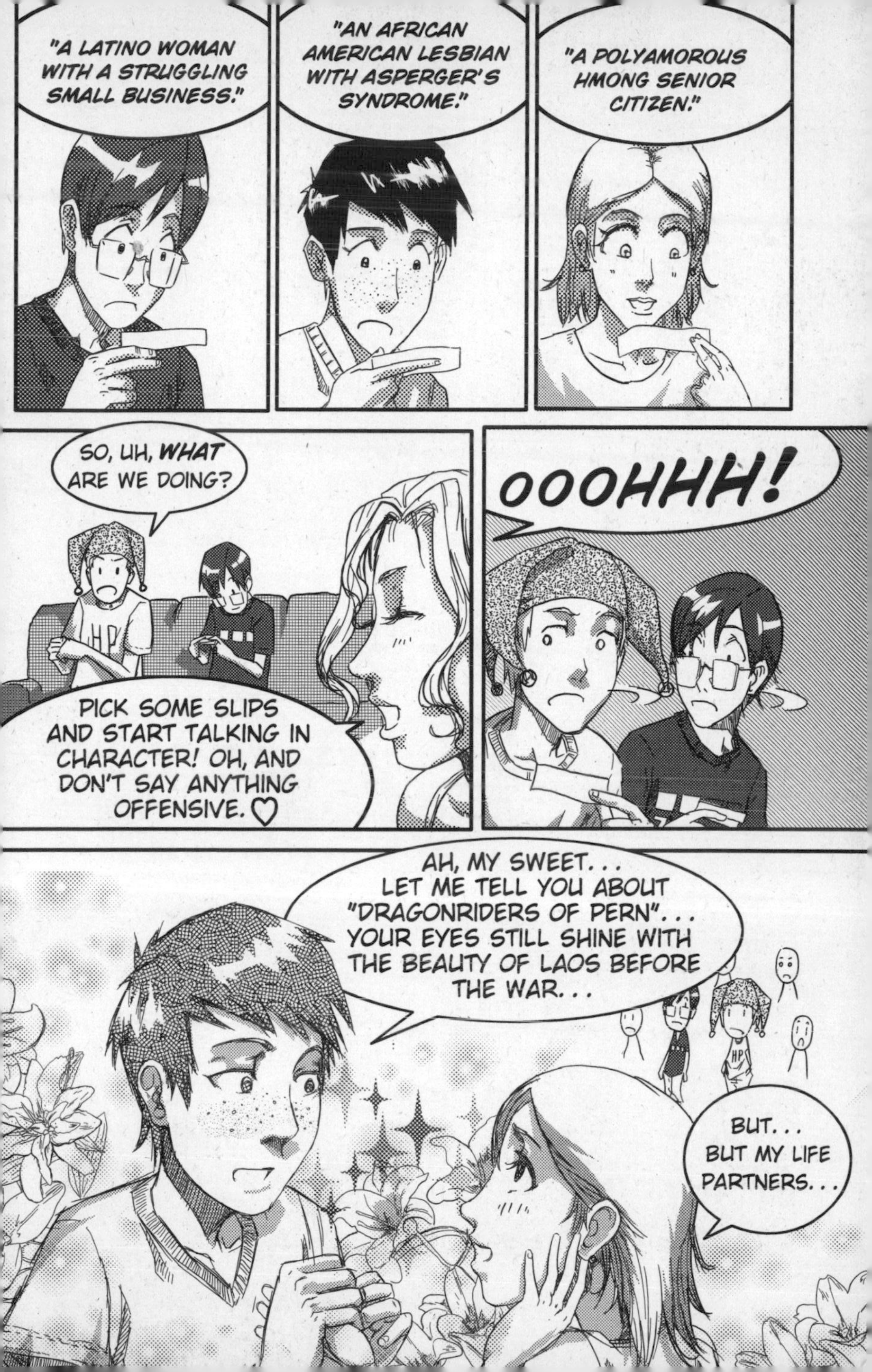
"A LATINO WOMAN WITH A STRUGGLING SMALL BUSINESS."
"AN AFRICAN AMERICAN LESBIAN WITH ASPERGER'S SYNDROME."
"A POLYAMOROUS HMONG SENIOR CITIZEN."
SO, UH, WHAT ARE WE DOING?
PICK SOME SLIPS AND START TALKING IN CHARACTER! OH, AND DON'T SAY ANYTHING OFFENSIVE. ♡
OOOHHH!
AH, MY SWEET... LET ME TELL YOU ABOUT "DRAGONRIDERS OF PERN"... YOUR EYES STILL SHINE WITH THE BEAUTY OF LAOS BEFORE THE WAR...
BUT... BUT MY LIFE PARTNERS...

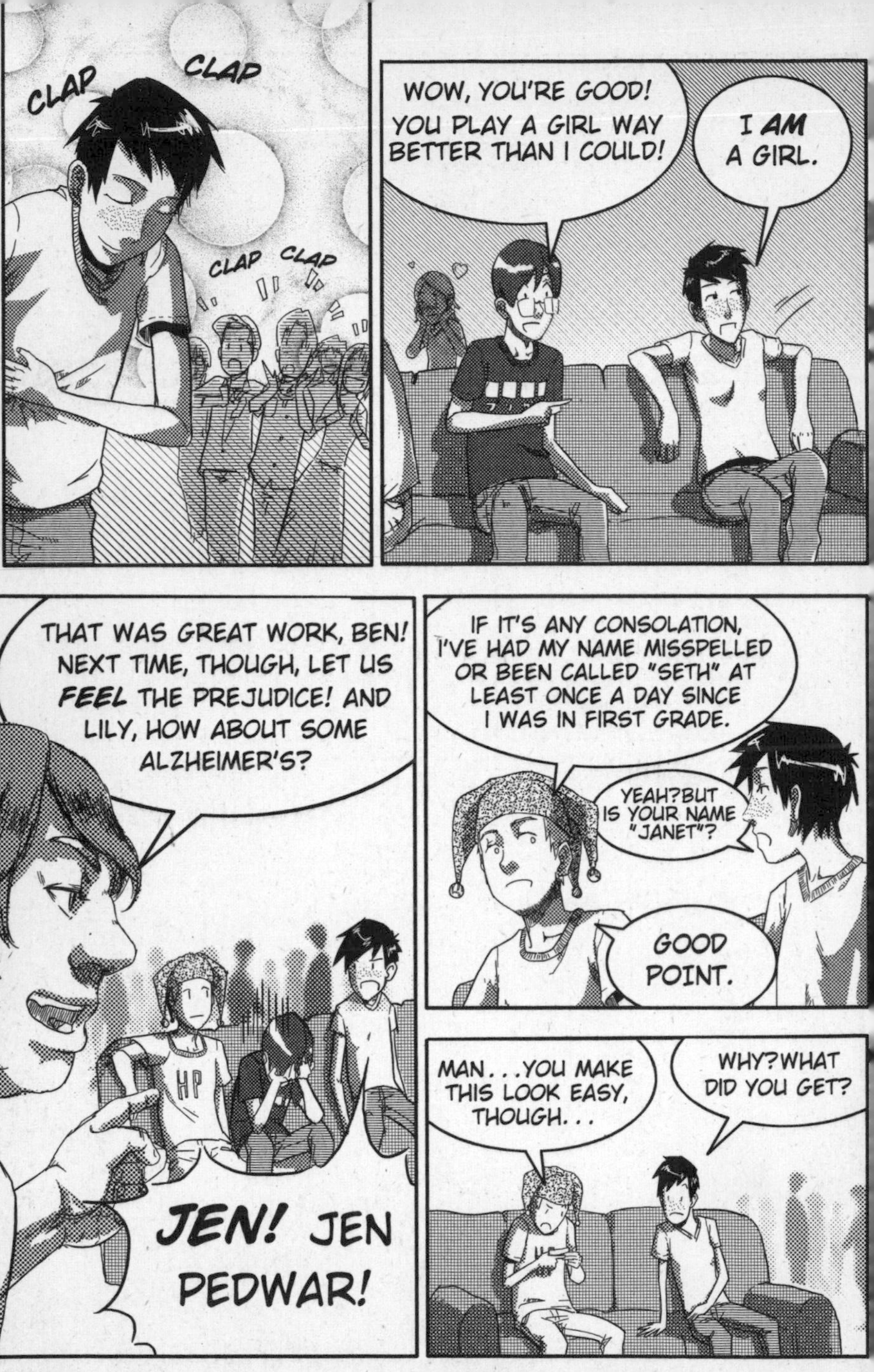
CLAP
CLAP
CLAP CLAP
WOW, YOU'RE GOOD! YOU PLAY A GIRL WAY BETTER THAN I COULD!
I AM A GIRL.
THAT WAS GREAT WORK, BEN! NEXT TIME, THOUGH, LET US FEEL THE PREJUDICE! AND LILY, HOW ABOUT SOME ALZHEIMER'S?
JEN! JEN PEDWAR!
IF IT'S ANY CONSOLATION, I'VE HAD MY NAME MISSPELLED OR BEEN CALLED "SETH" AT LEAST ONCE A DAY SINCE I WAS IN FIRST GRADE.
YEAH?BUT IS YOUR NAME "JANET"?
GOOD POINT.
MAN. . .YOU MAKE THIS LOOK EASY, THOUGH. . .
WHY?WHAT DID YOU GET?

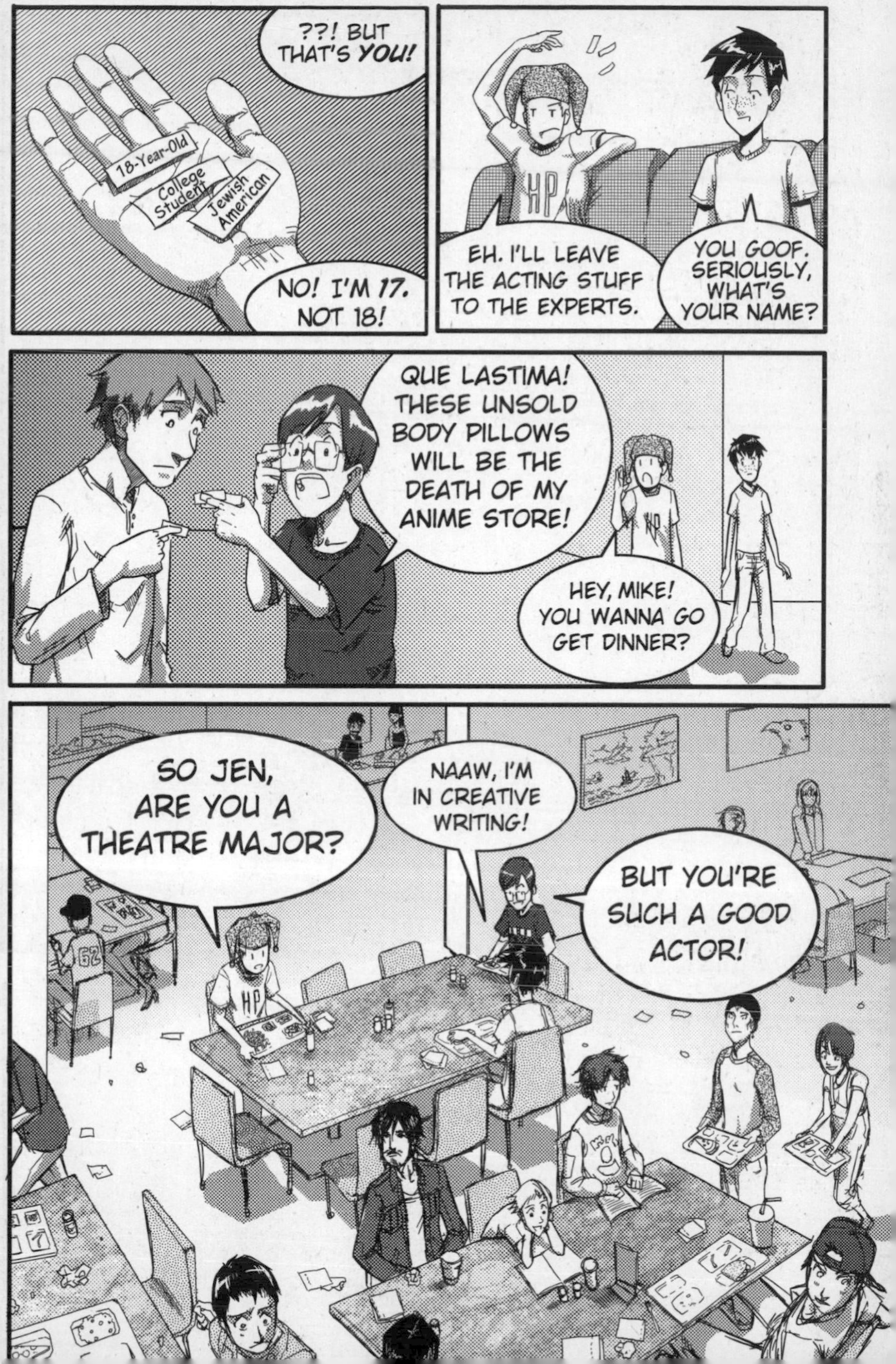
??! BUT THAT'S YOU!
18-Year-Old
College Student
Jewish American
NO! I'M 17. NOT 18!
EH. I'LL LEAVE THE ACTING STUFF TO THE EXPERTS.
YOU GOOF. SERIOUSLY, WHAT'S YOUR NAME?
QUE LASTIMA! THESE UNSOLD BODY PILLOWS WILL BE THE DEATH OF MY ANIME STORE!
HEY, MIKE! YOU WANNA GO GET DINNER?
SO JEN, ARE YOU A THEATRE MAJOR?
NAAW, I'M IN CREATIVE WRITING!
BUT YOU'RE SUCH A GOOD ACTOR!

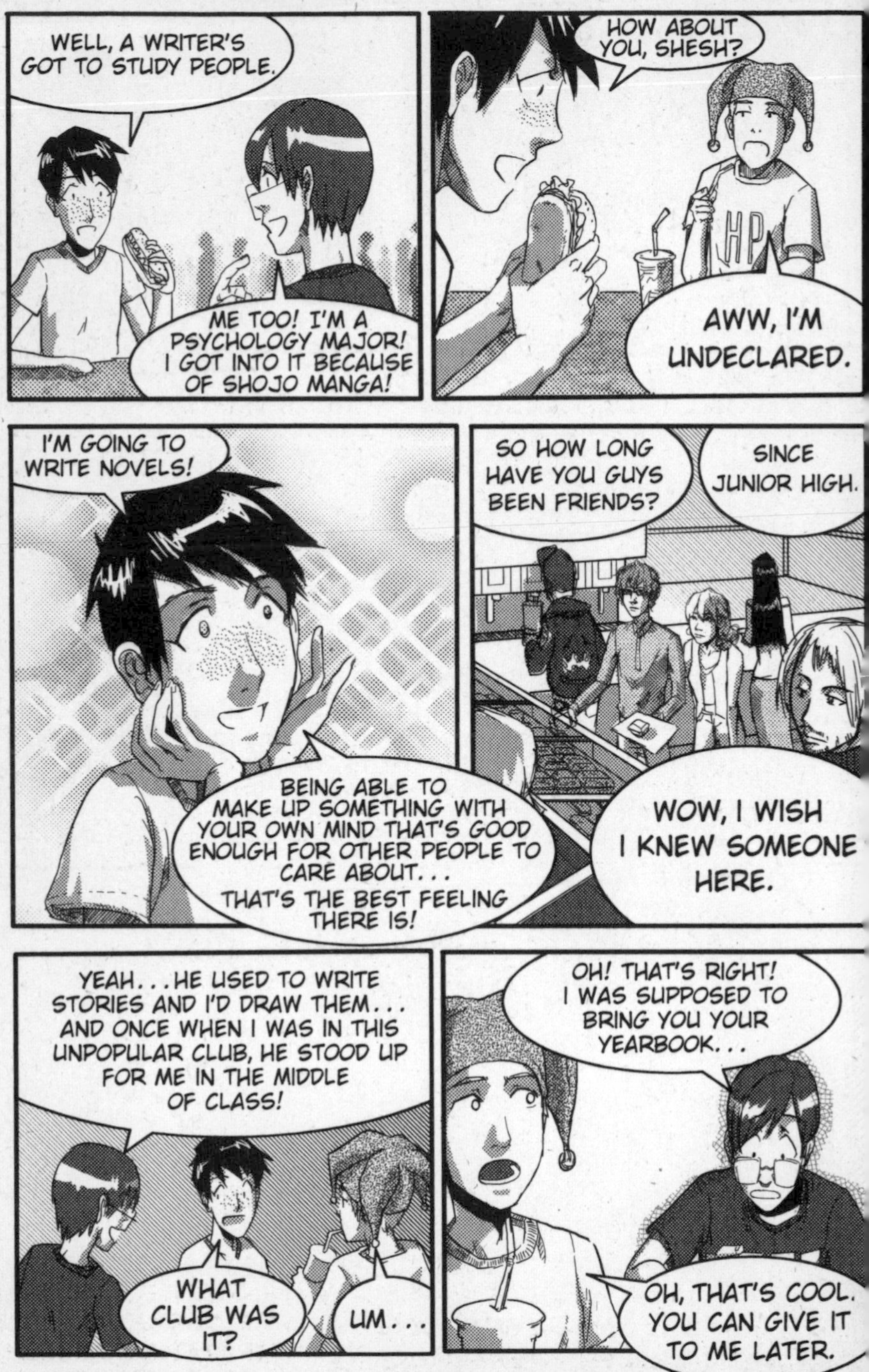
WELL, A WRITER'S GOT TO STUDY PEOPLE.
ME TOO! I'M A PSYCHOLOGY MAJOR! I GOT INTO IT BECAUSE OF SHOJO MANGA!
HOW ABOUT YOU, SHESH?
AWW, I'M UNDECLARED.
I'M GOING TO WRITE NOVELS!
BEING ABLE TO MAKE UP SOMETHING WITH YOUR OWN MIND THAT'S GOOD ENOUGH FOR OTHER PEOPLE TO CARE ABOUT...
THAT'S THE BEST FEELING THERE IS!
SO HOW LONG HAVE YOU GUYS BEEN FRIENDS?
SINCE JUNIOR HIGH.
WOW, I WISH I KNEW SOMEONE HERE.
YEAH...HE USED TO WRITE STORIES AND I'D DRAW THEM... AND ONCE WHEN I WAS IN THIS UNPOPULAR CLUB, HE STOOD UP FOR ME IN THE MIDDLE OF CLASS!
WHAT CLUB WAS IT?
UM...
OH! THAT'S RIGHT! I WAS SUPPOSED TO BRING YOU YOUR YEARBOOK...
OH, THAT'S COOL. YOU CAN GIVE IT TO ME LATER.

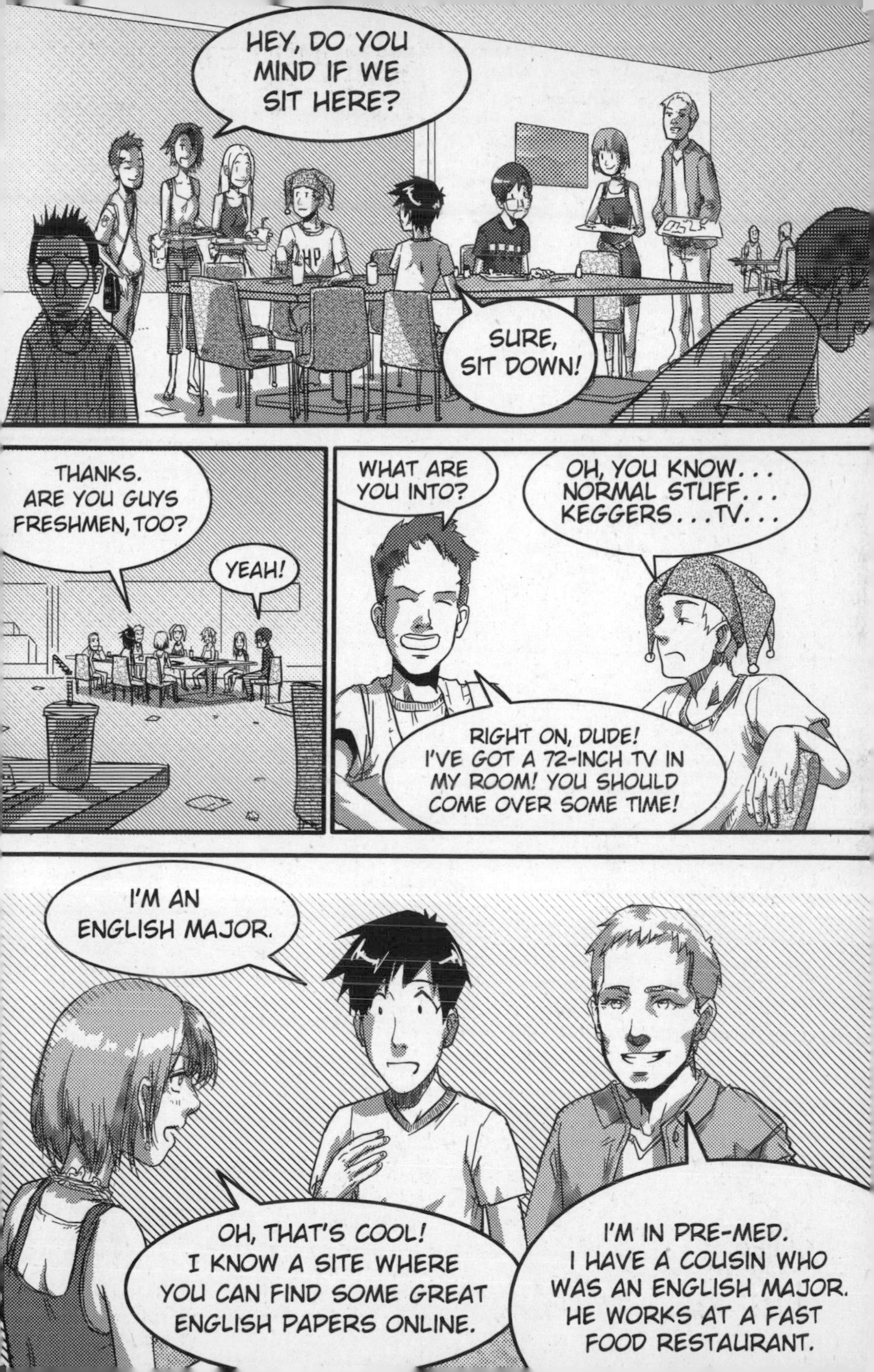
HEY, DO YOU MIND IF WE SIT HERE?
SURE, SIT DOWN!
THANKS. ARE YOU GUYS FRESHMEN, TOO?
YEAH!
WHAT ARE YOU INTO?
OH, YOU KNOW... NORMAL STUFF... KEGGERS...TV...
RIGHT ON, DUDE! I'VE GOT A 72-INCH TV IN MY ROOM! YOU SHOULD COME OVER SOME TIME!
I'M AN ENGLISH MAJOR.
OH, THAT'S COOL! I KNOW A SITE WHERE YOU CAN FIND SOME GREAT ENGLISH PAPERS ONLINE.
I'M IN PRE-MED. I HAVE A COUSIN WHO WAS AN ENGLISH MAJOR. HE WORKS AT A FAST FOOD RESTAURANT.

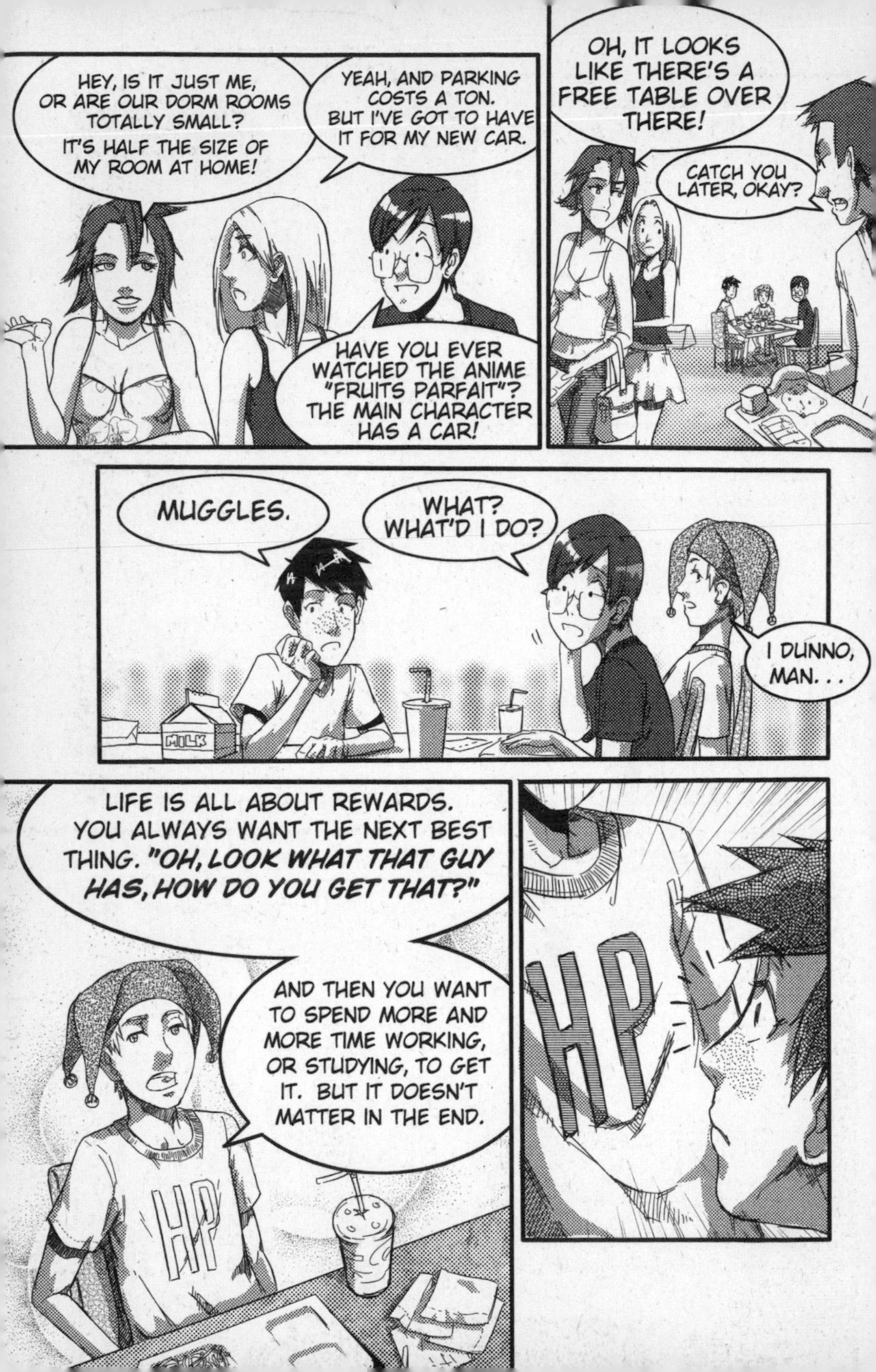
HEY, IS IT JUST ME, OR ARE OUR DORM ROOMS TOTALLY SMALL?
IT'S HALF THE SIZE OF MY ROOM AT HOME!
YEAH, AND PARKING COSTS A TON. BUT I'VE GOT TO HAVE IT FOR MY NEW CAR.
HAVE YOU EVER WATCHED THE ANIME "FRUITS PARFAIT"? THE MAIN CHARACTER HAS A CAR!
OH, IT LOOKS LIKE THERE'S A FREE TABLE OVER THERE!
CATCH YOU LATER, OKAY?
MUGGLES.
WHAT? WHAT'D I DO?
I DUNNO, MAN. . .
MILK
LIFE IS ALL ABOUT REWARDS. YOU ALWAYS WANT THE NEXT BEST THING. "OH, LOOK WHAT THAT GUY HAS, HOW DO YOU GET THAT?"
AND THEN YOU WANT TO SPEND MORE AND MORE TIME WORKING, OR STUDYING, TO GET IT. BUT IT DOESN'T MATTER IN THE END.
HP
HP

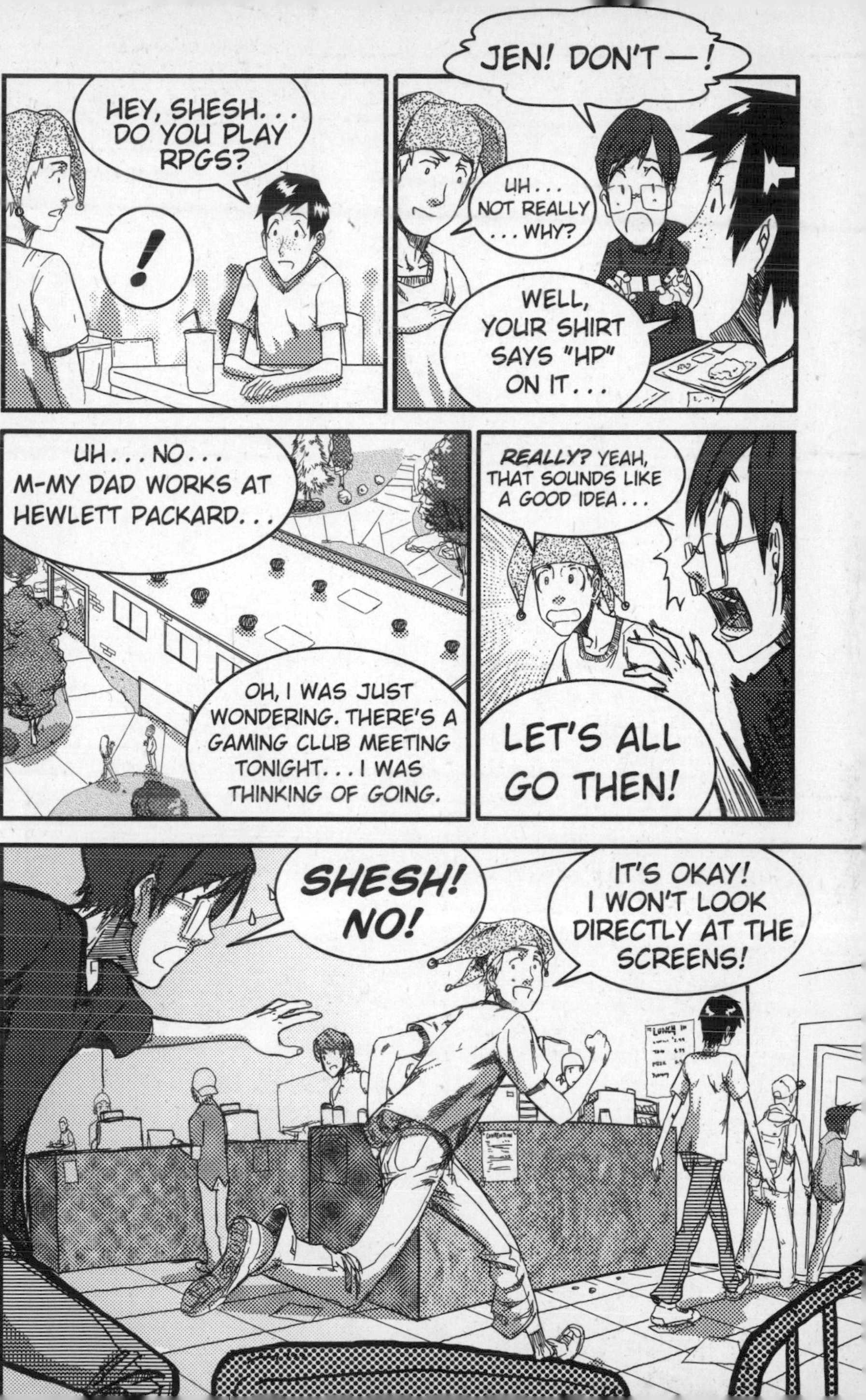
HEY, SHESH... DO YOU PLAY RPGS?
!
JEN! DON'T—!
UH... NOT REALLY ...WHY?
WELL, YOUR SHIRT SAYS "HP" ON IT...
UH...NO... M-MY DAD WORKS AT HEWLETT PACKARD...
OH, I WAS JUST WONDERING. THERE'S A GAMING CLUB MEETING TONIGHT... I WAS THINKING OF GOING.
REALLY? YEAH, THAT SOUNDS LIKE A GOOD IDEA...
LET'S ALL GO THEN!
SHESH! NO!
IT'S OKAY! I WON'T LOOK DIRECTLY AT THE SCREENS!

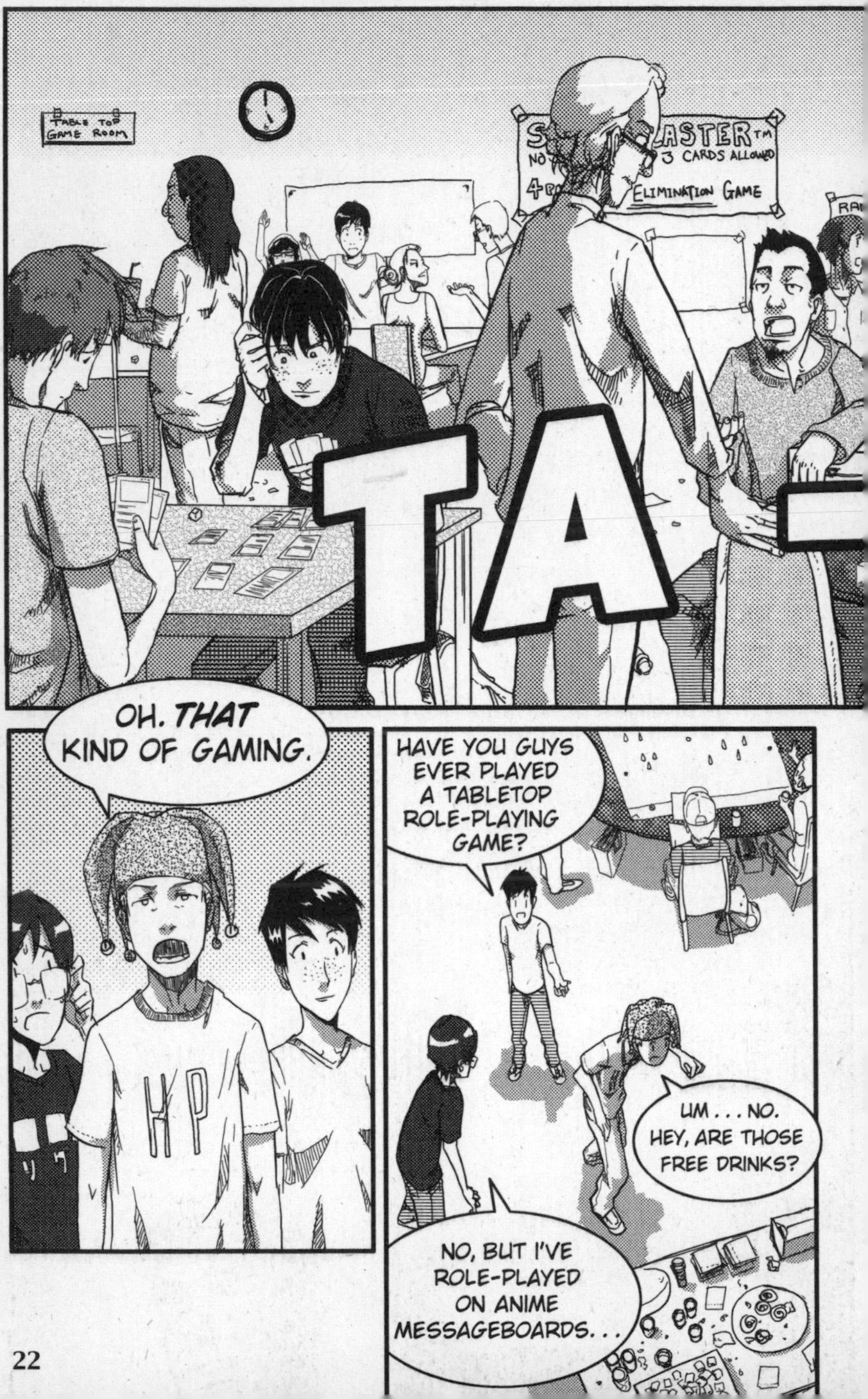
TABLE TOP GAME ROOM
ELIMINATION GAME
TA-
OH. THAT KIND OF GAMING.
HAVE YOU GUYS EVER PLAYED A TABLETOP ROLE-PLAYING GAME?
UM . . . NO. HEY, ARE THOSE FREE DRINKS?
NO, BUT I'VE ROLE-PLAYED ON ANIME MESSAGEBOARDS. . .

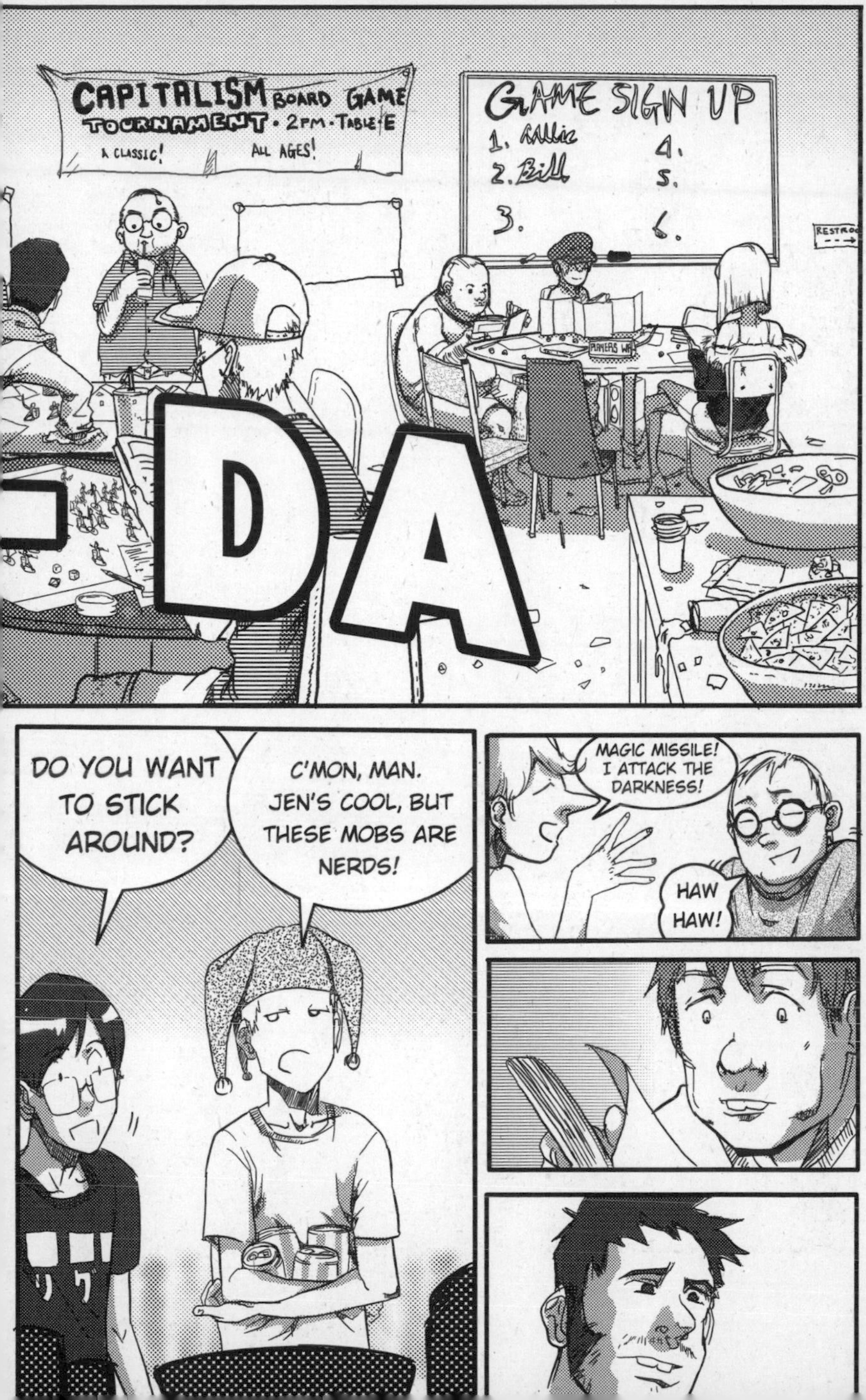
CAPITALISM BOARD GAME
TOURNAMENT • 2PM • TABLE E
A CLASSIC!
ALL AGES!
GAME SIGN UP
1.
2. Bill
3.
4.
5.
6.
DA
DO YOU WANT TO STICK AROUND?
C'MON, MAN. JEN'S COOL, BUT THESE MOBS ARE NERDS!
MAGIC MISSILE! I ATTACK THE DARKNESS!
HAW HAW!

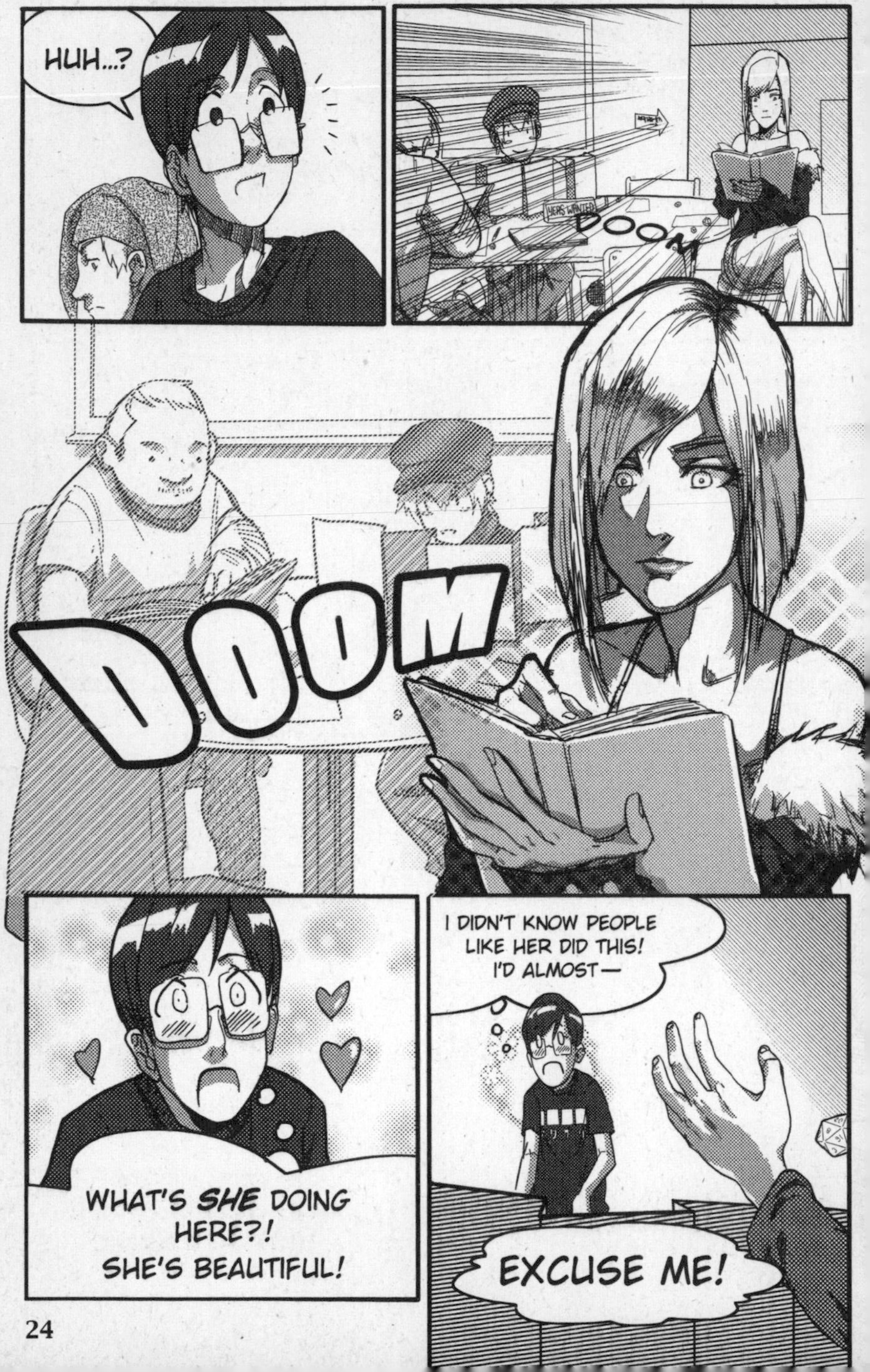
HUH...?
DOOM
DOOM
WHAT'S *SHE* DOING HERE?! SHE'S BEAUTIFUL!
I DIDN'T KNOW PEOPLE LIKE HER DID THIS! I'D ALMOST—
EXCUSE ME!

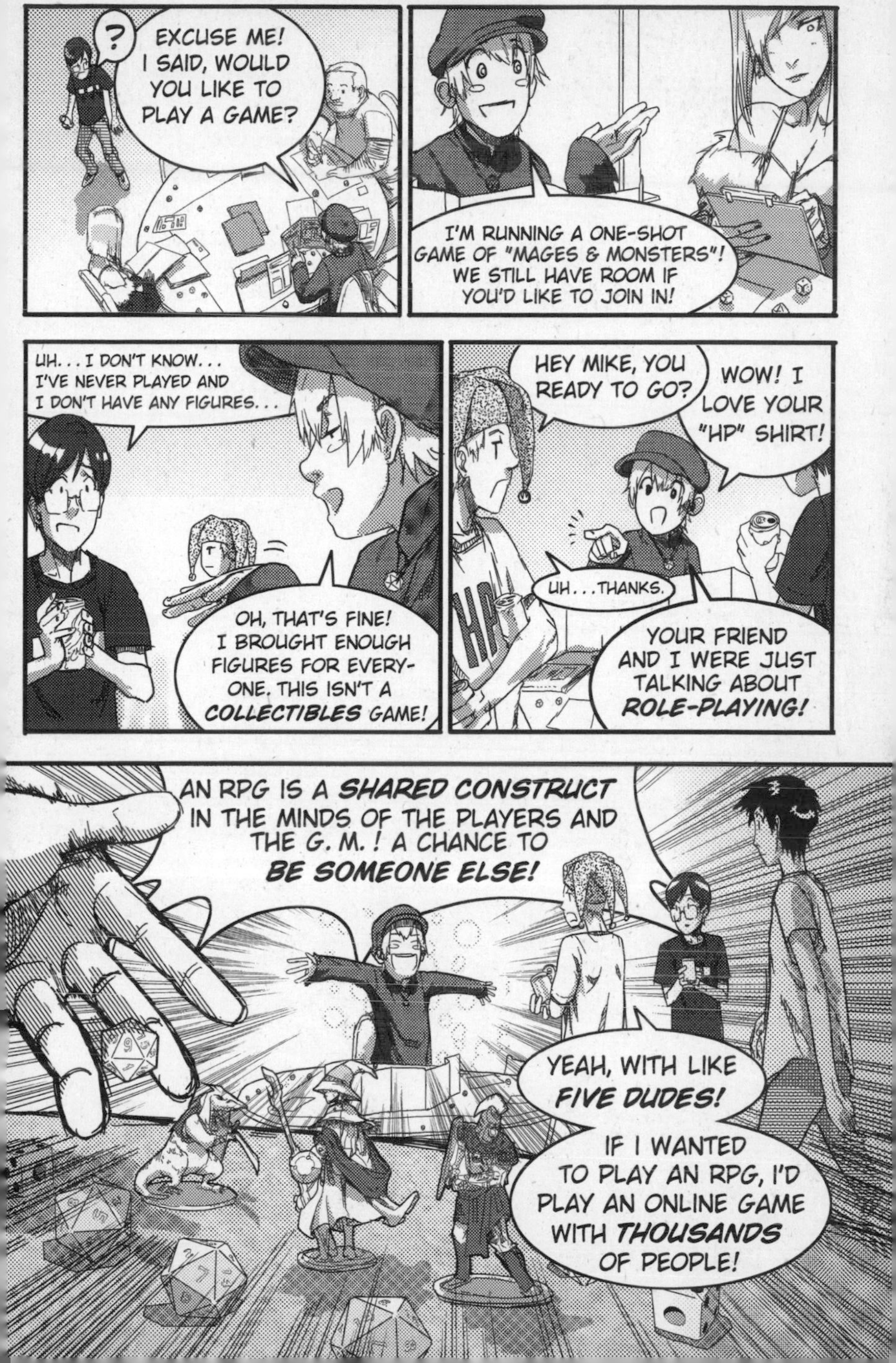
?
EXCUSE ME! I SAID, WOULD YOU LIKE TO PLAY A GAME?
I'M RUNNING A ONE-SHOT GAME OF "MAGES & MONSTERS"! WE STILL HAVE ROOM IF YOU'D LIKE TO JOIN IN!
UH. . . I DON'T KNOW. . . I'VE NEVER PLAYED AND I DON'T HAVE ANY FIGURES. . .
OH, THAT'S FINE! I BROUGHT ENOUGH FIGURES FOR EVERY-ONE. THIS ISN'T A *COLLECTIBLES* GAME!
HEY MIKE, YOU READY TO GO?
WOW! I LOVE YOUR "HP" SHIRT!
UH. . .THANKS.
YOUR FRIEND AND I WERE JUST TALKING ABOUT *ROLE-PLAYING!*
AN RPG IS A *SHARED CONSTRUCT* IN THE MINDS OF THE PLAYERS AND THE G. M. ! A CHANCE TO *BE SOMEONE ELSE!*
YEAH, WITH LIKE *FIVE DUDES!*
IF I WANTED TO PLAY AN RPG, I'D PLAY AN ONLINE GAME WITH *THOUSANDS* OF PEOPLE!

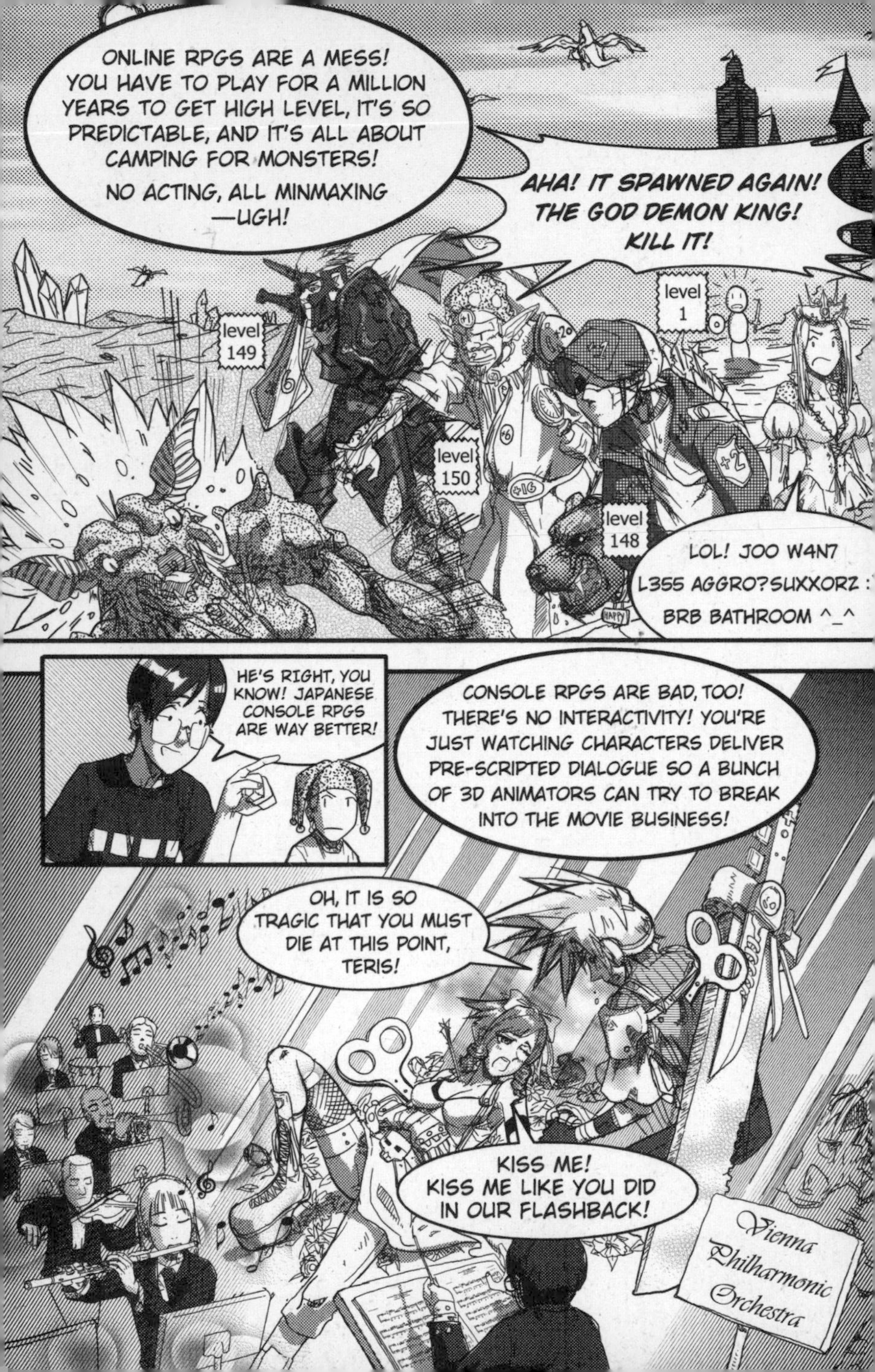
ONLINE RPGS ARE A MESS! YOU HAVE TO PLAY FOR A MILLION YEARS TO GET HIGH LEVEL, IT'S SO PREDICTABLE, AND IT'S ALL ABOUT CAMPING FOR MONSTERS!
NO ACTING, ALL MINMAXING —UGH!
AHA! IT SPAWNED AGAIN! THE GOD DEMON KING! KILL IT!
level 1
level 149
level 150
level 148
LOL! JOO W4N7 L355 AGGRO?SUXXORZ : BRB BATHROOM ^_^
HE'S RIGHT, YOU KNOW! JAPANESE CONSOLE RPGS ARE WAY BETTER!
CONSOLE RPGS ARE BAD, TOO! THERE'S NO INTERACTIVITY! YOU'RE JUST WATCHING CHARACTERS DELIVER PRE-SCRIPTED DIALOGUE SO A BUNCH OF 3D ANIMATORS CAN TRY TO BREAK INTO THE MOVIE BUSINESS!
OH, IT IS SO TRAGIC THAT YOU MUST DIE AT THIS POINT, TERIS!
KISS ME! KISS ME LIKE YOU DID IN OUR FLASHBACK!
Vienna Philharmonic Orchestra

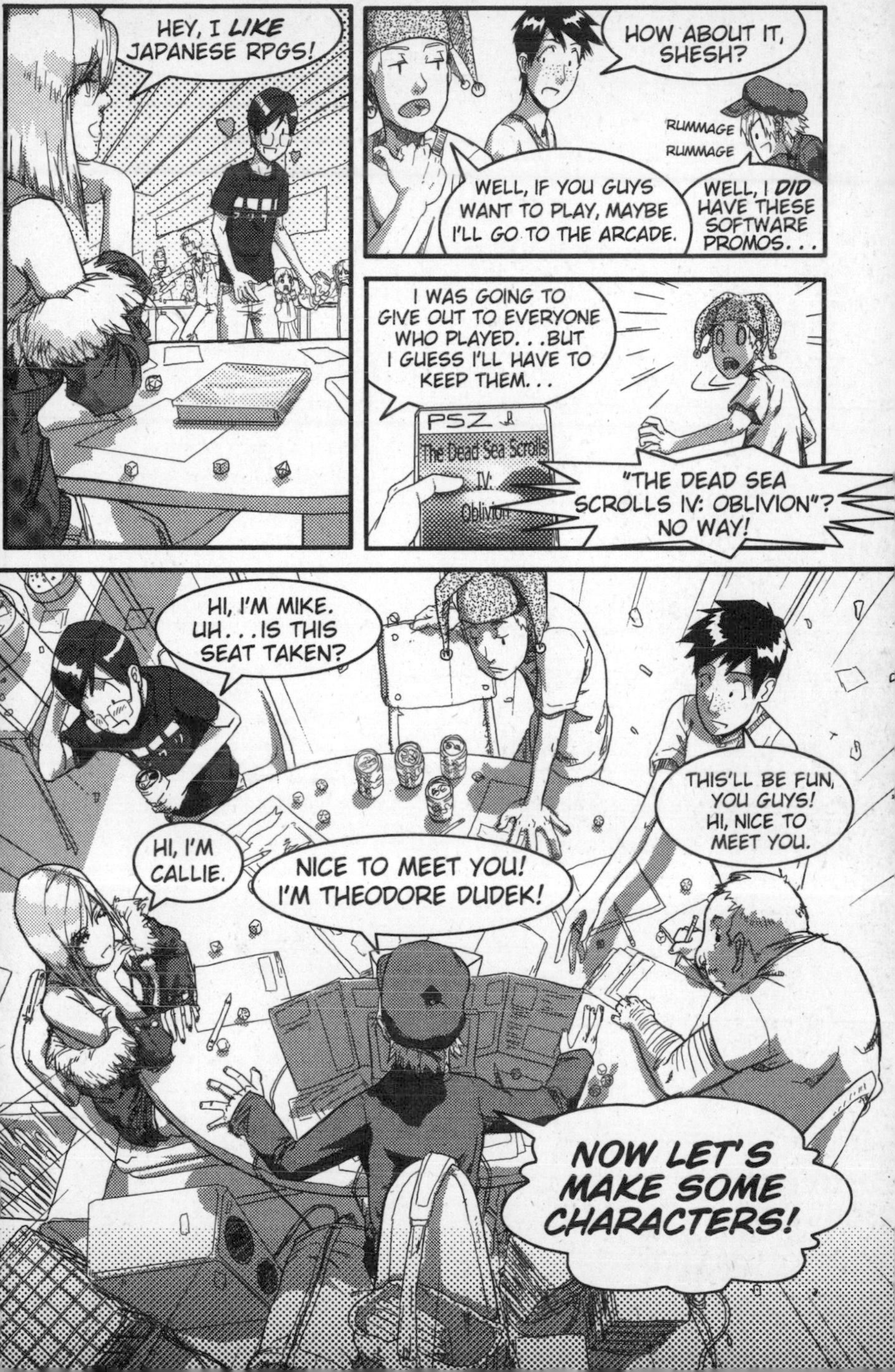
HEY, I *LIKE* JAPANESE RPGS!
HOW ABOUT IT, SHESH?
RUMMAGE
RUMMAGE
WELL, IF YOU GUYS WANT TO PLAY, MAYBE I'LL GO TO THE ARCADE.
WELL, I *DID* HAVE THESE SOFTWARE PROMOS. . .
I WAS GOING TO GIVE OUT TO EVERYONE WHO PLAYED. . .BUT I GUESS I'LL HAVE TO KEEP THEM. . .
PSZ
The Dead Sea Scrolls IV: Oblivion
"THE DEAD SEA SCROLLS IV: OBLIVION"? NO WAY!
HI, I'M MIKE. UH. . .IS THIS SEAT TAKEN?
THIS'LL BE FUN, YOU GUYS! HI, NICE TO MEET YOU.
HI, I'M CALLIE.
NICE TO MEET YOU! I'M THEODORE DUDEK!
NOW LET'S MAKE SOME CHARACTERS!

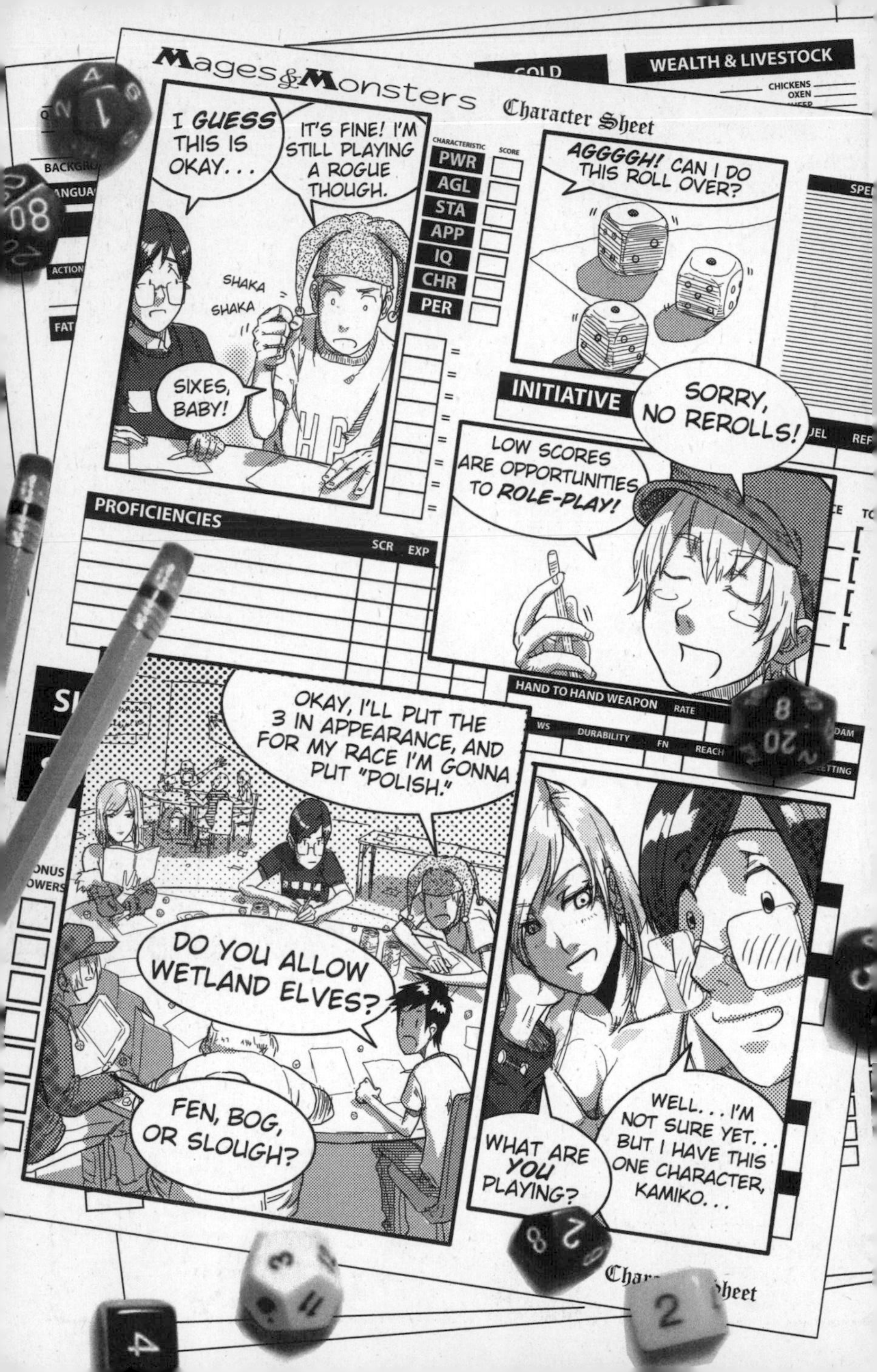

Mages & Monsters
Character Sheet
I GUESS THIS IS OKAY. . .
IT'S FINE! I'M STILL PLAYING A ROGUE THOUGH.
SHAKA
SHAKA
SIXES, BABY!
AGGGGH! CAN I DO THIS ROLL OVER?
SORRY, NO REROLLS!
LOW SCORES ARE OPPORTUNITIES TO ROLE-PLAY!
OKAY, I'LL PUT THE 3 IN APPEARANCE, AND FOR MY RACE I'M GONNA PUT "POLISH."
DO YOU ALLOW WETLAND ELVES?
FEN, BOG, OR SLOUGH?
WHAT ARE YOU PLAYING?
WELL. . . I'M NOT SURE YET. . . BUT I HAVE THIS ONE CHARACTER, KAMIKO. . .

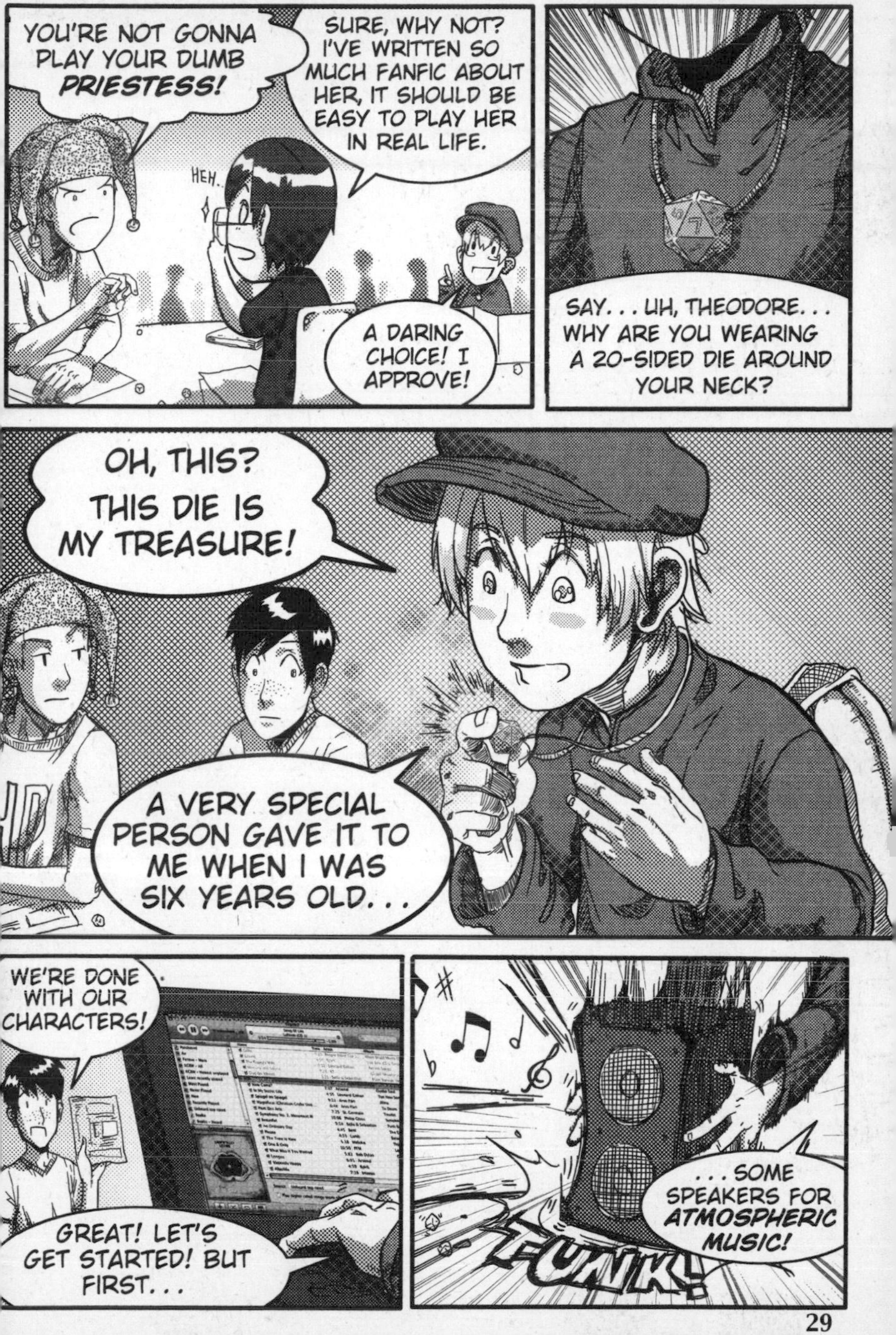
YOU'RE NOT GONNA PLAY YOUR DUMB PRIESTESS!
SURE, WHY NOT? I'VE WRITTEN SO MUCH FANFIC ABOUT HER, IT SHOULD BE EASY TO PLAY HER IN REAL LIFE.
HEH..
A DARING CHOICE! I APPROVE!
SAY. . . UH, THEODORE. . . WHY ARE YOU WEARING A 20-SIDED DIE AROUND YOUR NECK?
OH, THIS? THIS DIE IS MY TREASURE!
A VERY SPECIAL PERSON GAVE IT TO ME WHEN I WAS SIX YEARS OLD. . .
WE'RE DONE WITH OUR CHARACTERS!
GREAT! LET'S GET STARTED! BUT FIRST. . .
. . . SOME SPEAKERS FOR ATMOSPHERIC MUSIC!
CHUNK!

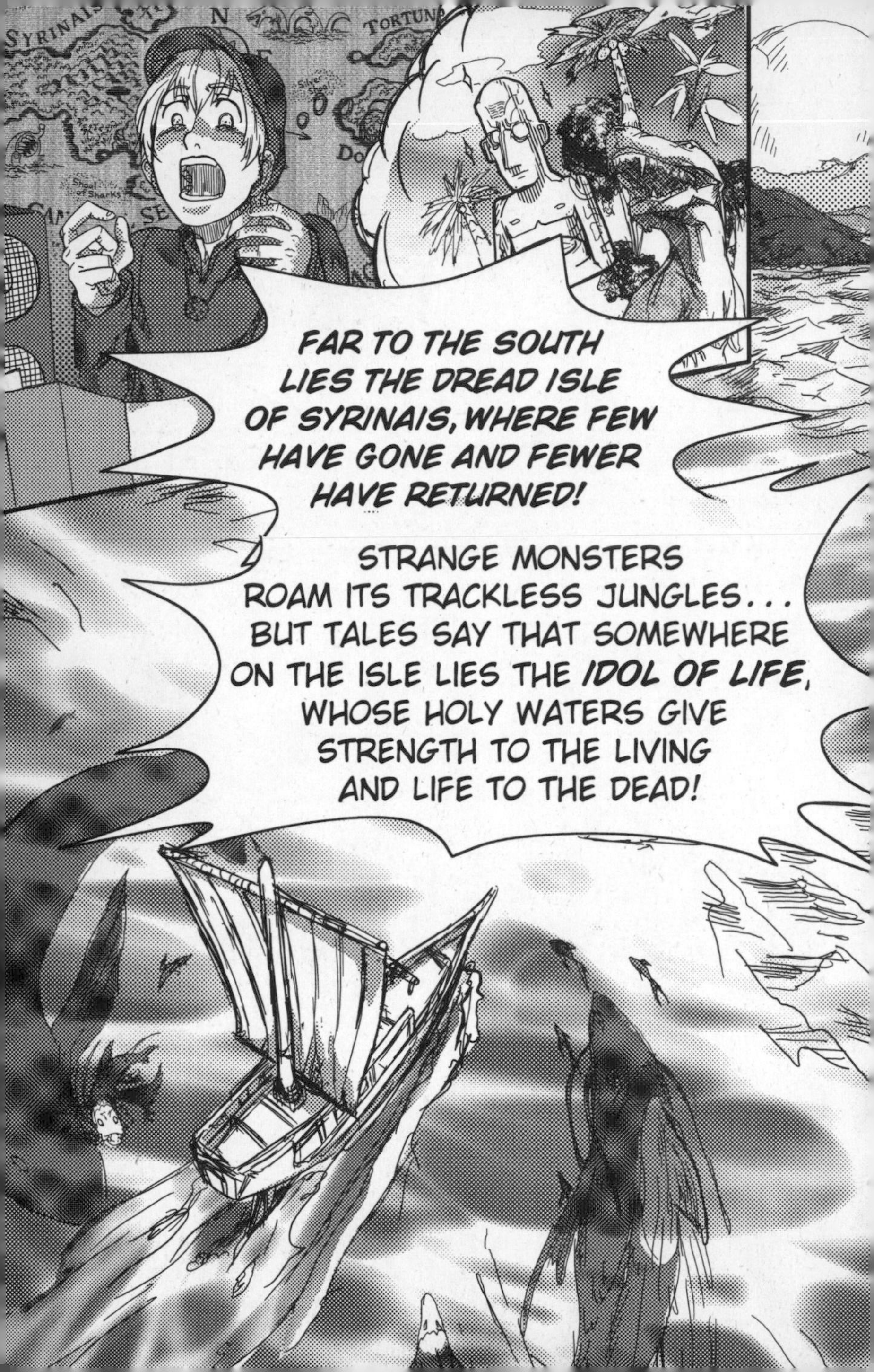
SYRINAIS
N
Shoal of Sharks
FAR TO THE SOUTH LIES THE DREAD ISLE OF SYRINAIS, WHERE FEW HAVE GONE AND FEWER HAVE RETURNED!
STRANGE MONSTERS ROAM ITS TRACKLESS JUNGLES... ...BUT TALES SAY THAT SOMEWHERE ON THE ISLE LIES THE *IDOL OF LIFE*, WHOSE HOLY WATERS GIVE STRENGTH TO THE LIVING AND LIFE TO THE DEAD!

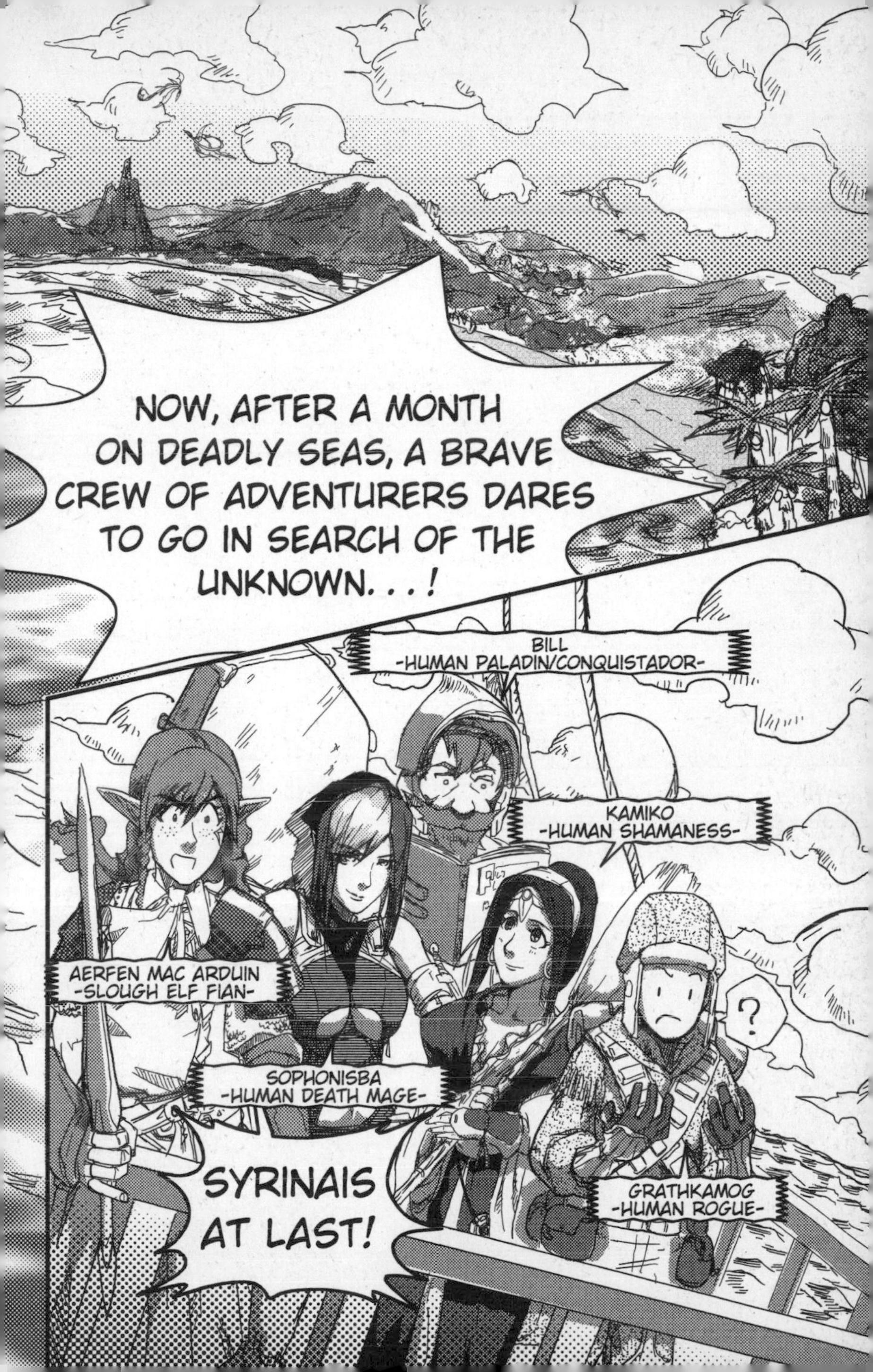
NOW, AFTER A MONTH ON DEADLY SEAS, A BRAVE CREW OF ADVENTURERS DARES TO GO IN SEARCH OF THE UNKNOWN. . . !
BILL -HUMAN PALADIN/CONQUISTADOR-
KAMIKO -HUMAN SHAMANESS-
AERFEN MAC ARDUIN -SLOUGH ELF FIAN-
?
SOPHONISBA -HUMAN DEATH MAGE-
SYRINAIS AT LAST!
GRATHKAMOG -HUMAN ROGUE-

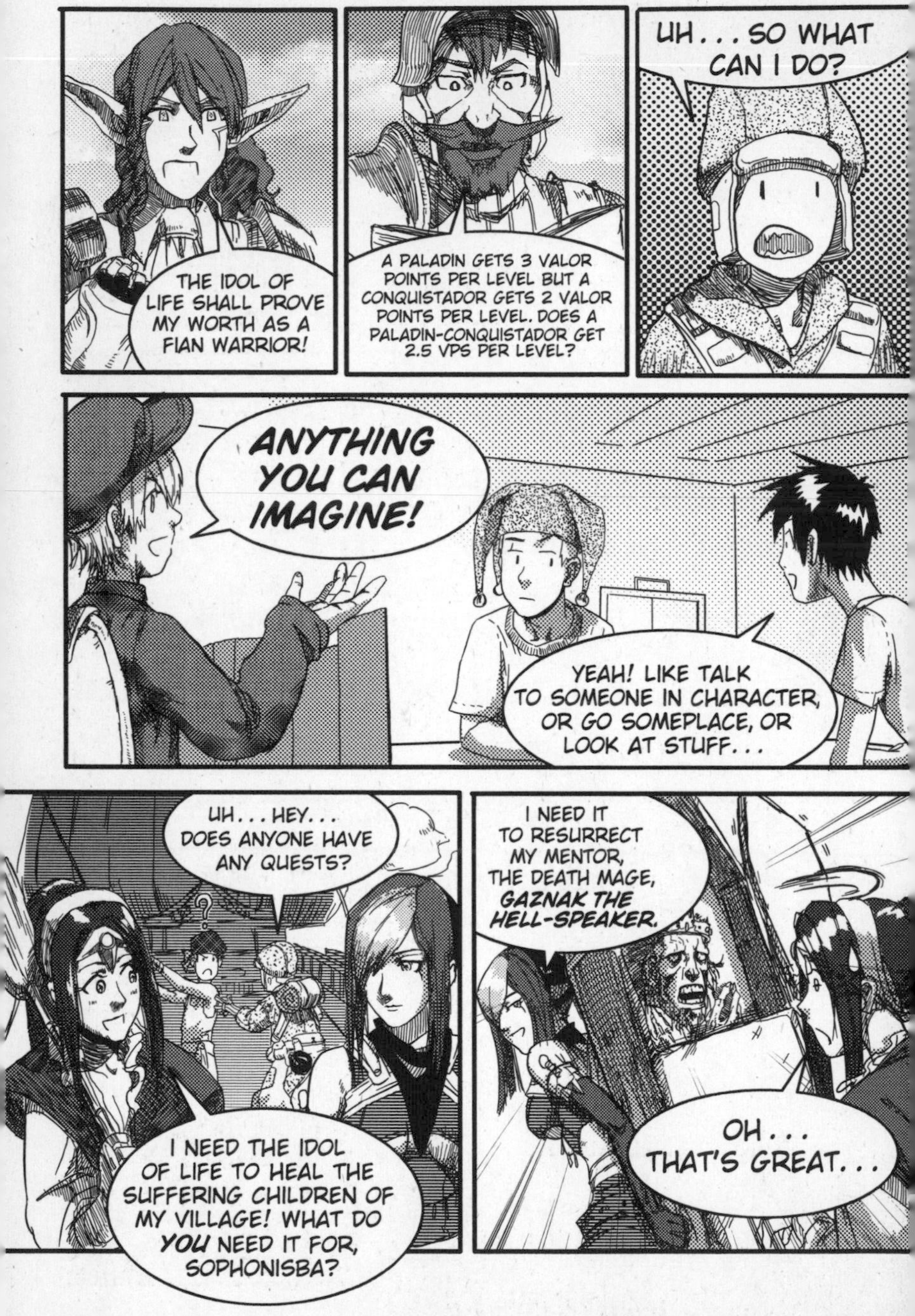
THE IDOL OF LIFE SHALL PROVE MY WORTH AS A FIAN WARRIOR!
A PALADIN GETS 3 VALOR POINTS PER LEVEL BUT A CONQUISTADOR GETS 2 VALOR POINTS PER LEVEL. DOES A PALADIN-CONQUISTADOR GET 2.5 VPS PER LEVEL?
UH . . . SO WHAT CAN I DO?
ANYTHING YOU CAN IMAGINE!
YEAH! LIKE TALK TO SOMEONE IN CHARACTER, OR GO SOMEPLACE, OR LOOK AT STUFF . . .
UH . . . HEY . . . DOES ANYONE HAVE ANY QUESTS?
I NEED THE IDOL OF LIFE TO HEAL THE SUFFERING CHILDREN OF MY VILLAGE! WHAT DO *YOU* NEED IT FOR, SOPHONISBA?
I NEED IT TO RESURRECT MY MENTOR, THE DEATH MAGE, *GAZNAK THE HELL-SPEAKER.*
OH . . . THAT'S GREAT . . .

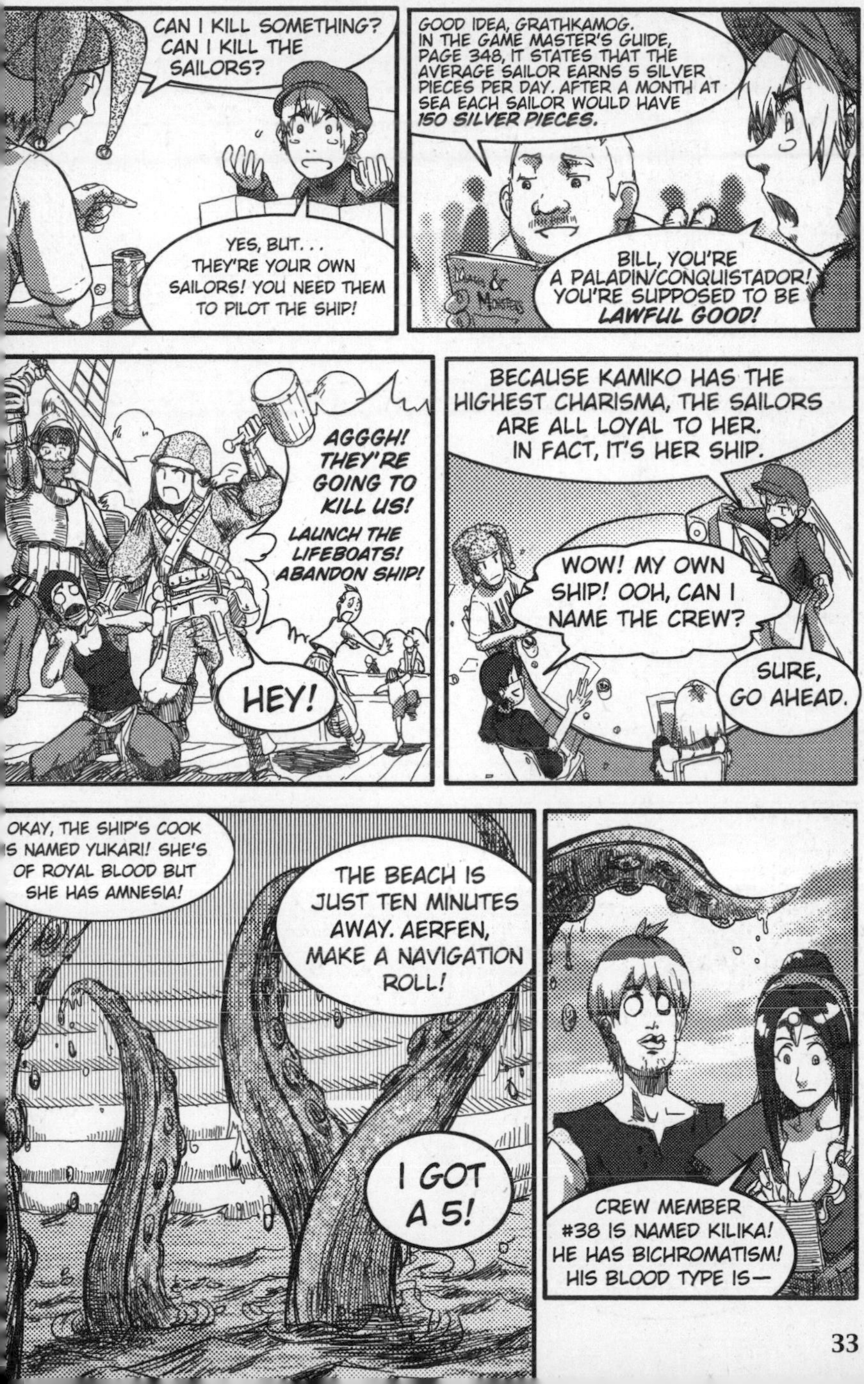
CAN I KILL SOMETHING? CAN I KILL THE SAILORS?
YES, BUT. . . THEY'RE YOUR OWN SAILORS! YOU NEED THEM TO PILOT THE SHIP!
GOOD IDEA, GRATHKAMOG. IN THE GAME MASTER'S GUIDE, PAGE 348, IT STATES THAT THE AVERAGE SAILOR EARNS 5 SILVER PIECES PER DAY. AFTER A MONTH AT SEA EACH SAILOR WOULD HAVE 150 SILVER PIECES.
BILL, YOU'RE A PALADIN/CONQUISTADOR! YOU'RE SUPPOSED TO BE LAWFUL GOOD!
AGGGH! THEY'RE GOING TO KILL US!
LAUNCH THE LIFEBOATS! ABANDON SHIP!
HEY!
BECAUSE KAMIKO HAS THE HIGHEST CHARISMA, THE SAILORS ARE ALL LOYAL TO HER. IN FACT, IT'S HER SHIP.
WOW! MY OWN SHIP! OOH, CAN I NAME THE CREW?
SURE, GO AHEAD.
OKAY, THE SHIP'S COOK IS NAMED YUKARI! SHE'S OF ROYAL BLOOD BUT SHE HAS AMNESIA!
THE BEACH IS JUST TEN MINUTES AWAY. AERFEN, MAKE A NAVIGATION ROLL!
I GOT A 5!
CREW MEMBER #38 IS NAMED KILIKA! HE HAS BICHROMATISM! HIS BLOOD TYPE IS—

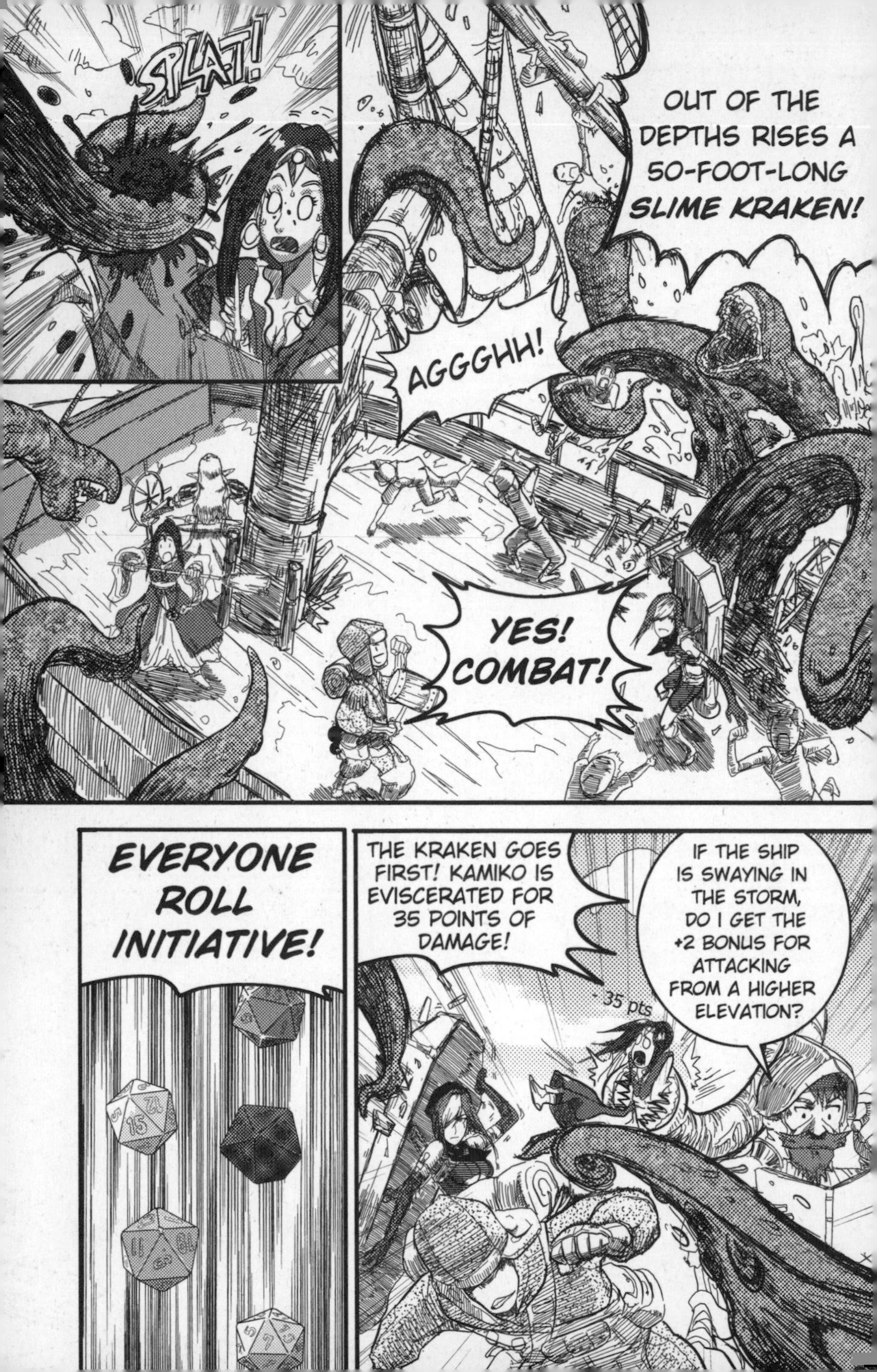
SPLAT!
OUT OF THE DEPTHS RISES A 50-FOOT-LONG SLIME KRAKEN!
AGGGHH!
YES! COMBAT!
EVERYONE ROLL INITIATIVE!
THE KRAKEN GOES FIRST! KAMIKO IS EVISCERATED FOR 35 POINTS OF DAMAGE!
35 pts
IF THE SHIP IS SWAYING IN THE STORM, DO I GET THE +2 BONUS FOR ATTACKING FROM A HIGHER ELEVATION?

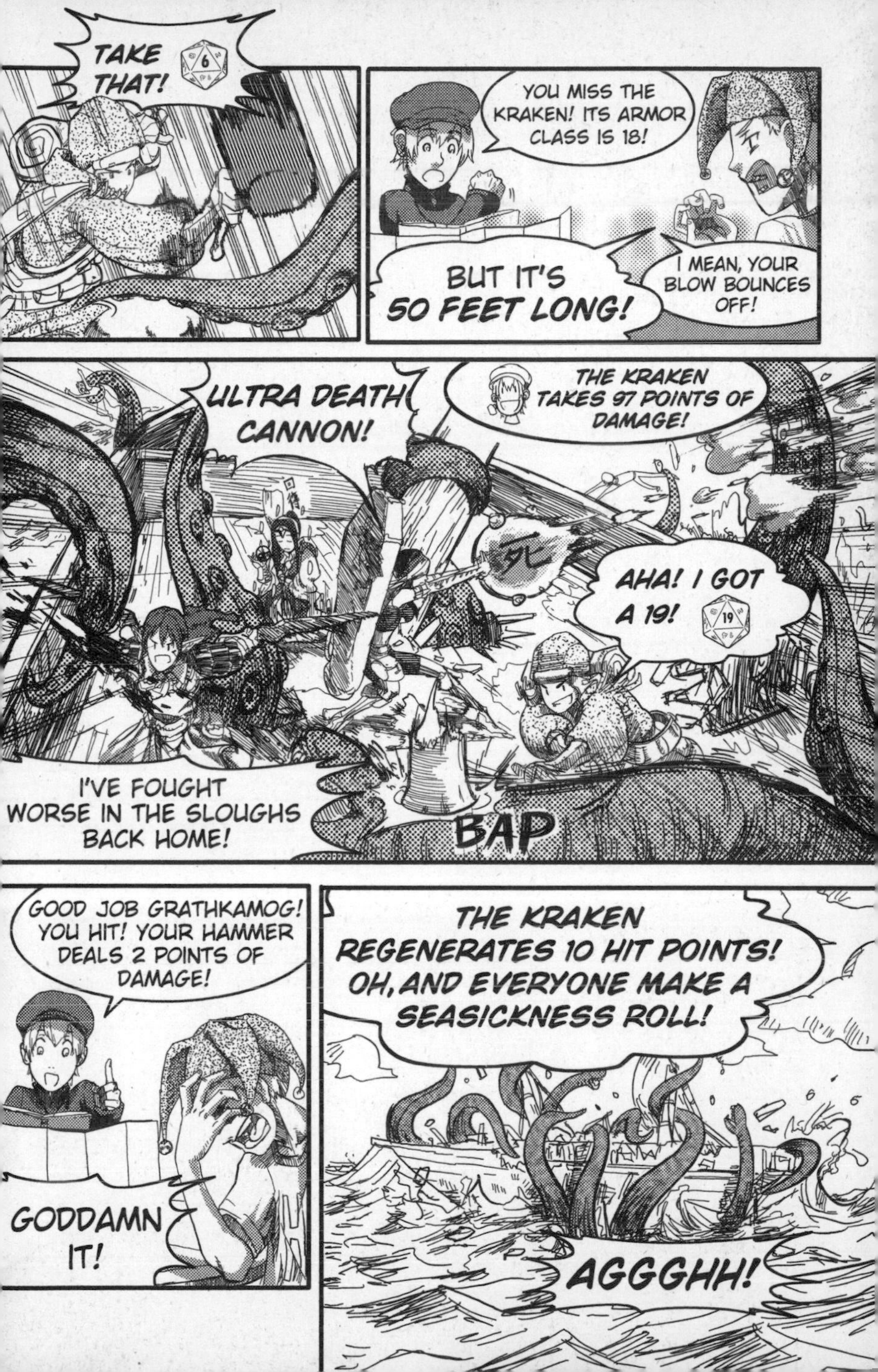
TAKE THAT!
YOU MISS THE KRAKEN! ITS ARMOR CLASS IS 18!
BUT IT'S 50 FEET LONG!
I MEAN, YOUR BLOW BOUNCES OFF!
ULTRA DEATH CANNON!
THE KRAKEN TAKES 97 POINTS OF DAMAGE!
AHA! I GOT A 19!
I'VE FOUGHT WORSE IN THE SLOUGHS BACK HOME!
BAP
GOOD JOB GRATHKAMOG! YOU HIT! YOUR HAMMER DEALS 2 POINTS OF DAMAGE!
GODDAMN IT!
THE KRAKEN REGENERATES 10 HIT POINTS! OH, AND EVERYONE MAKE A SEASICKNESS ROLL!
AGGGHH!

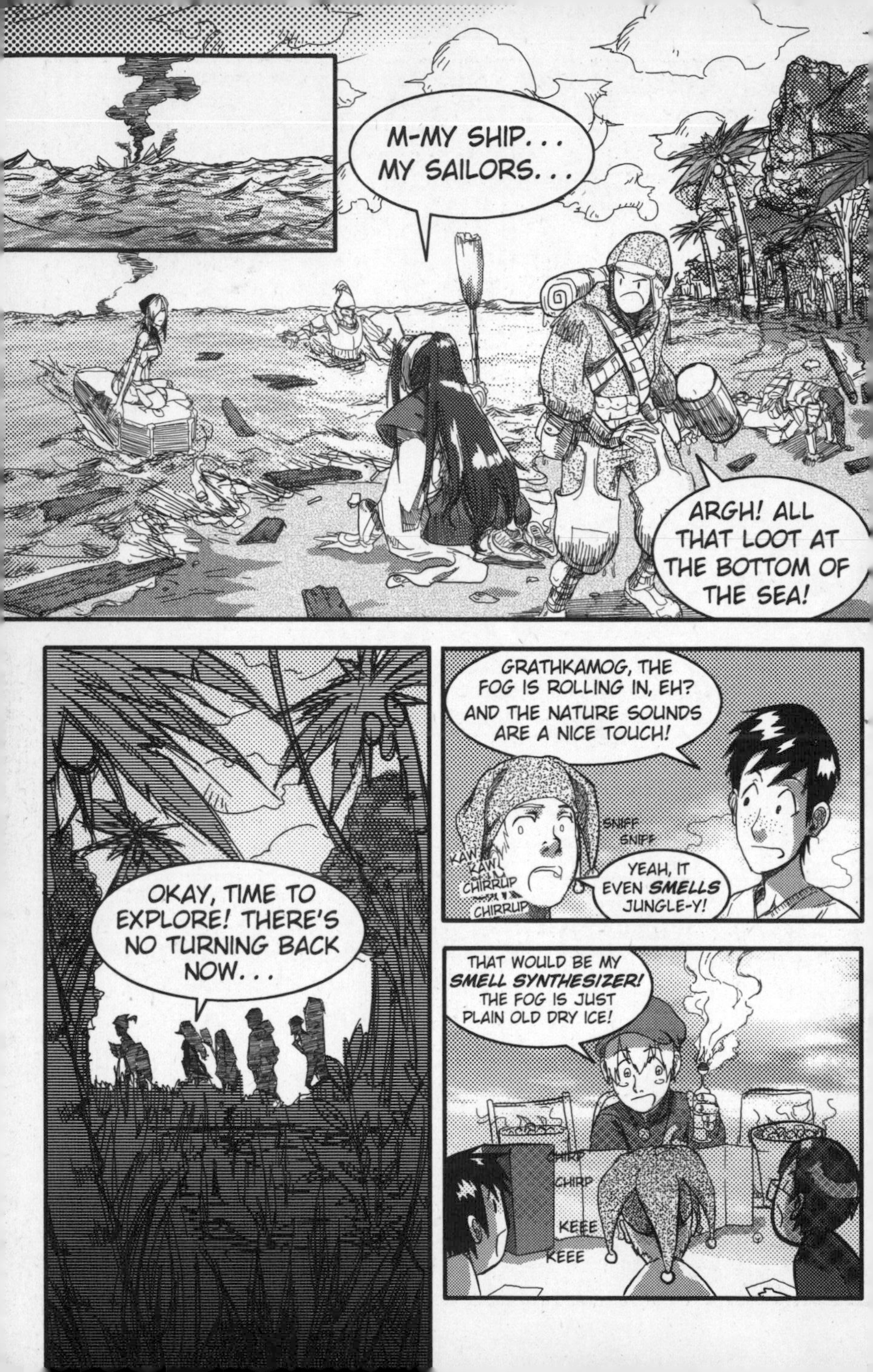
M-MY SHIP... MY SAILORS...
ARGH! ALL THAT LOOT AT THE BOTTOM OF THE SEA!
OKAY, TIME TO EXPLORE! THERE'S NO TURNING BACK NOW...
GRATHKAMOG, THE FOG IS ROLLING IN, EH? AND THE NATURE SOUNDS ARE A NICE TOUCH!
SNIFF SNIFF
KAW KAW CHIRRUP CHIRRUP
YEAH, IT EVEN SMELLS JUNGLE-Y!
THAT WOULD BE MY SMELL SYNTHESIZER! THE FOG IS JUST PLAIN OLD DRY ICE!
CHIRP CHIRP
KEEE KEEE

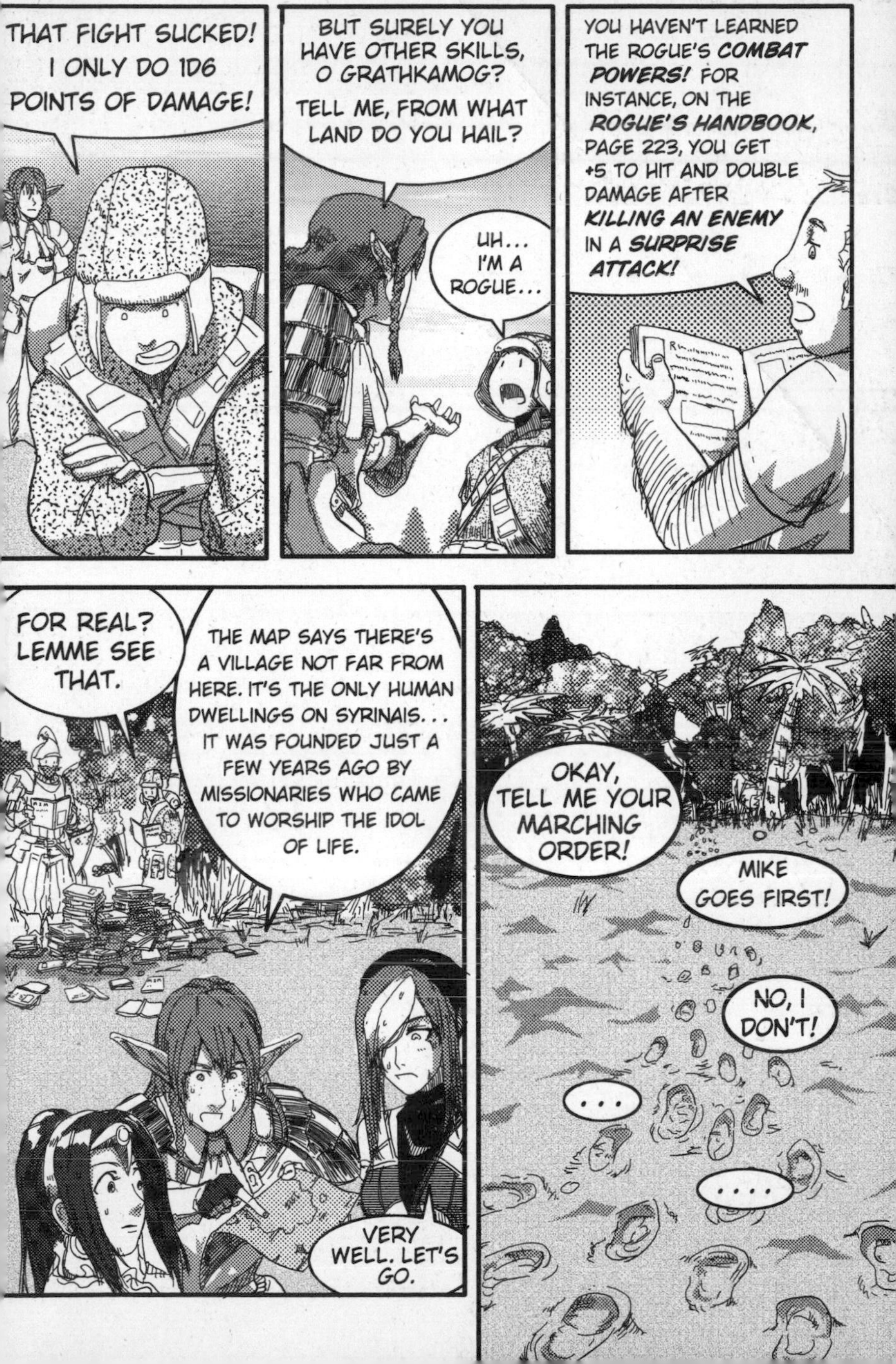
THAT FIGHT SUCKED! I ONLY DO 1D6 POINTS OF DAMAGE!
BUT SURELY YOU HAVE OTHER SKILLS, O GRATHKAMOG?
TELL ME, FROM WHAT LAND DO YOU HAIL?
UH... I'M A ROGUE...
YOU HAVEN'T LEARNED THE ROGUE'S COMBAT POWERS! FOR INSTANCE, ON THE ROGUE'S HANDBOOK, PAGE 223, YOU GET +5 TO HIT AND DOUBLE DAMAGE AFTER KILLING AN ENEMY IN A SURPRISE ATTACK!
FOR REAL? LEMME SEE THAT.
THE MAP SAYS THERE'S A VILLAGE NOT FAR FROM HERE. IT'S THE ONLY HUMAN DWELLINGS ON SYRINAIS... IT WAS FOUNDED JUST A FEW YEARS AGO BY MISSIONARIES WHO CAME TO WORSHIP THE IDOL OF LIFE.
VERY WELL. LET'S GO.
OKAY, TELL ME YOUR MARCHING ORDER!
MIKE GOES FIRST!
NO, I DON'T!
...
....

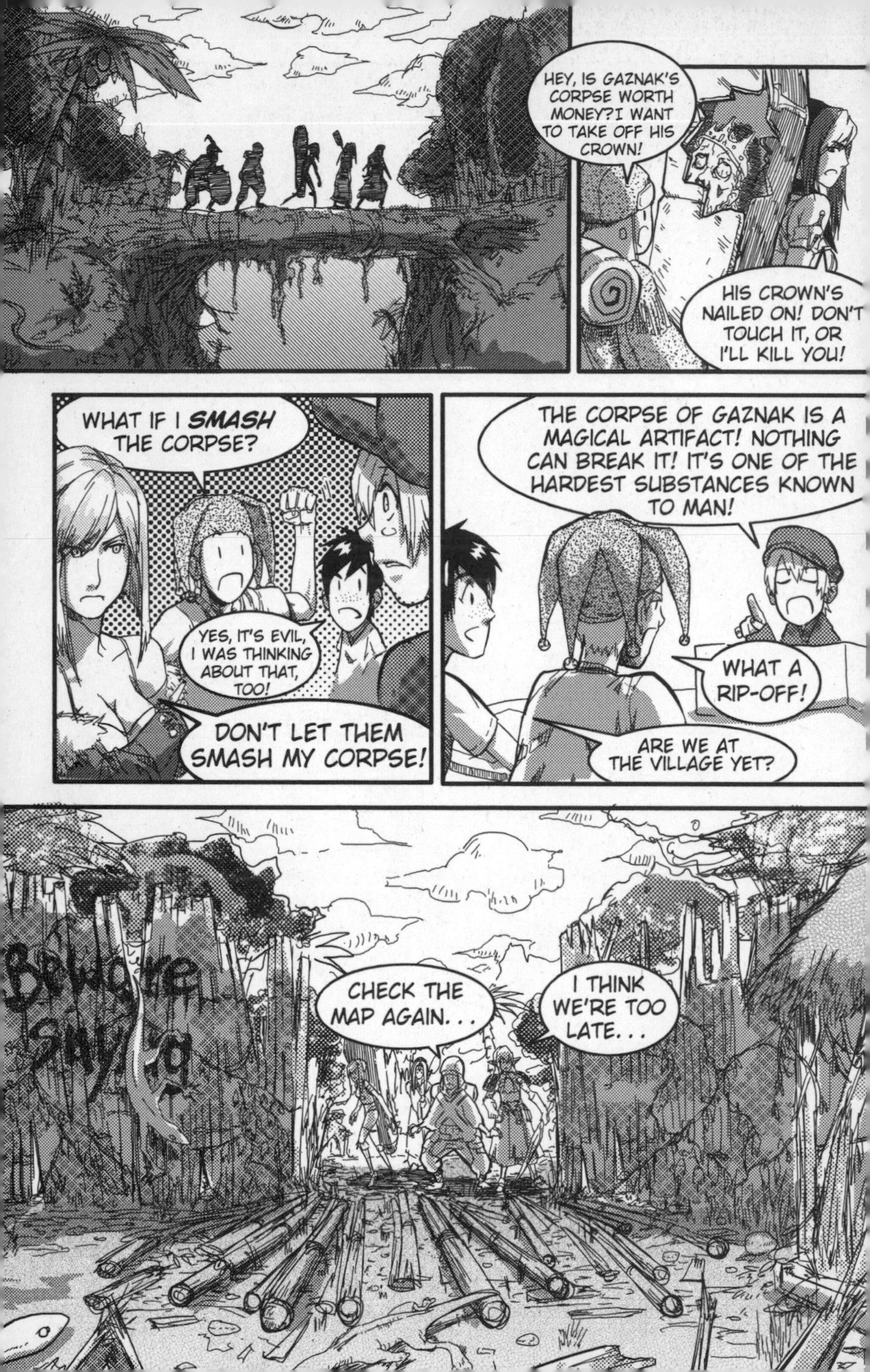
HEY, IS GAZNAK'S CORPSE WORTH MONEY?I WANT TO TAKE OFF HIS CROWN!
HIS CROWN'S NAILED ON! DON'T TOUCH IT, OR I'LL KILL YOU!
WHAT IF I ***SMASH*** THE CORPSE?
YES, IT'S EVIL, I WAS THINKING ABOUT THAT, TOO!
DON'T LET THEM SMASH MY CORPSE!
THE CORPSE OF GAZNAK IS A MAGICAL ARTIFACT! NOTHING CAN BREAK IT! IT'S ONE OF THE HARDEST SUBSTANCES KNOWN TO MAN!
WHAT A RIP-OFF!
ARE WE AT THE VILLAGE YET?
CHECK THE MAP AGAIN. . .
I THINK WE'RE TOO LATE. . .

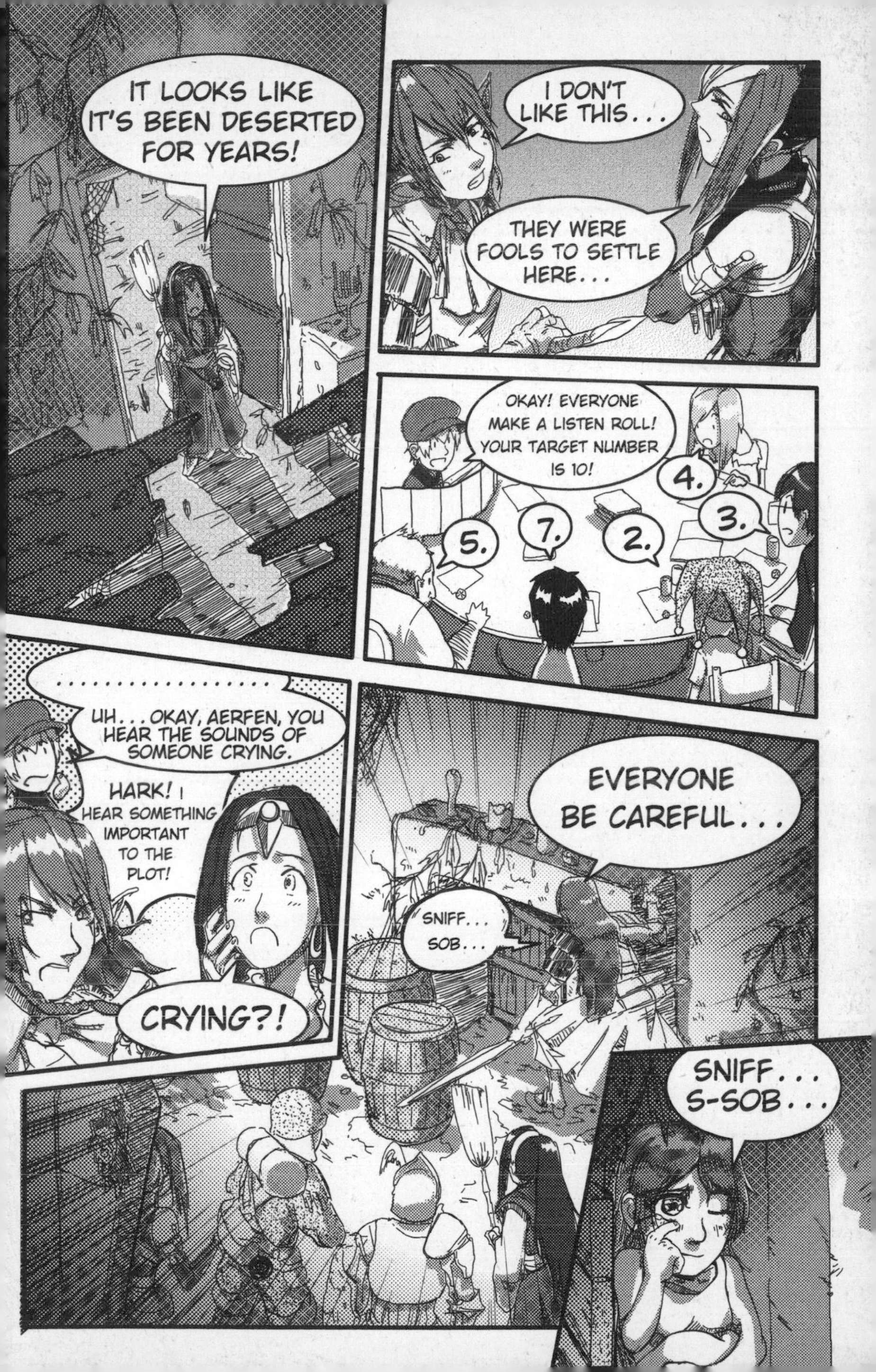
IT LOOKS LIKE IT'S BEEN DESERTED FOR YEARS!
I DON'T LIKE THIS...
THEY WERE FOOLS TO SETTLE HERE...
OKAY! EVERYONE MAKE A LISTEN ROLL! YOUR TARGET NUMBER IS 10!
5.
7.
2.
4.
3.
....
UH...OKAY, AERFEN, YOU HEAR THE SOUNDS OF SOMEONE CRYING.
HARK! I HEAR SOMETHING IMPORTANT TO THE PLOT!
CRYING?!
EVERYONE BE CAREFUL...
SNIFF... SOB...
SNIFF... S-SOB...

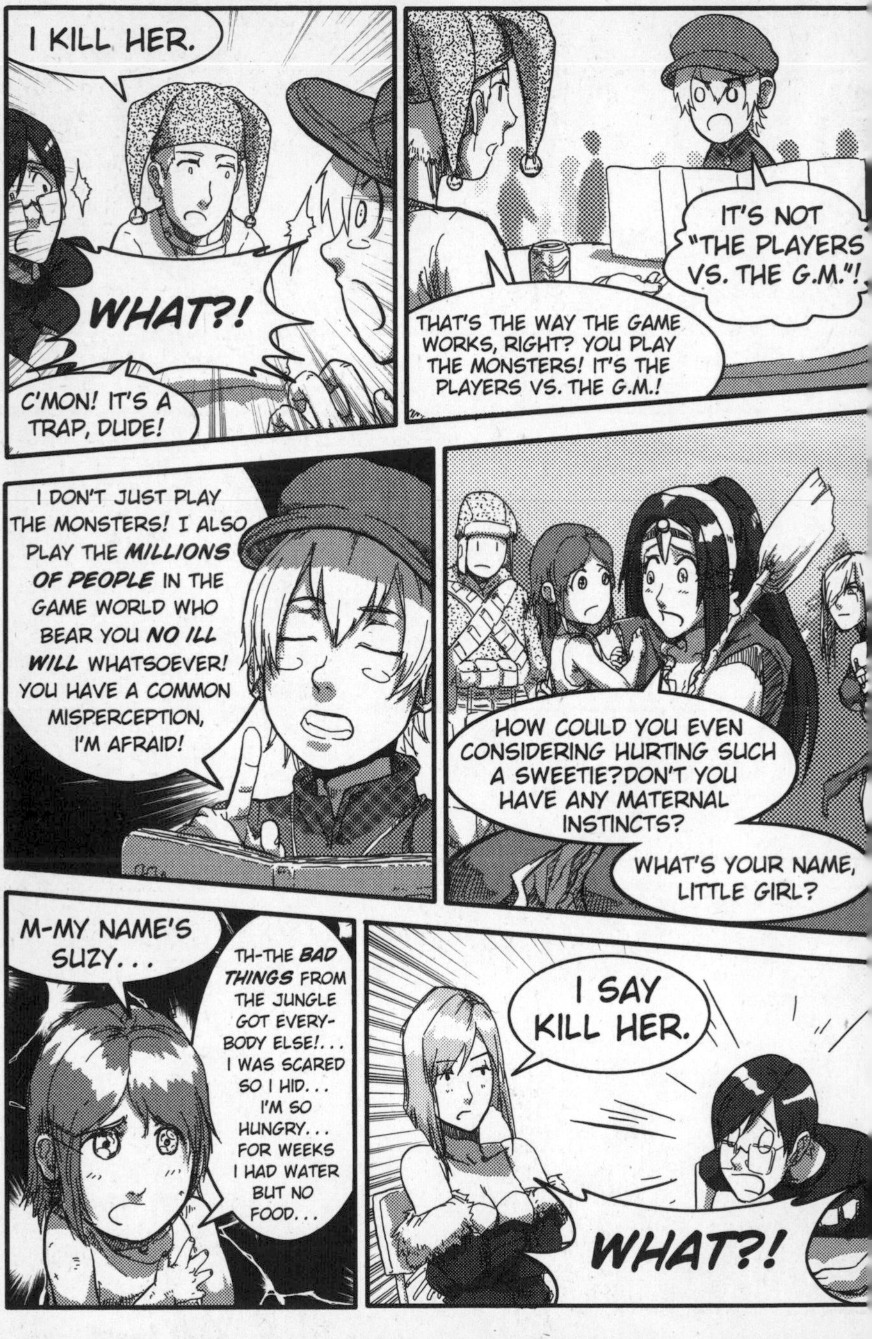
I KILL HER.
WHAT?!
C'MON! IT'S A TRAP, DUDE!
THAT'S THE WAY THE GAME WORKS, RIGHT? YOU PLAY THE MONSTERS! IT'S THE PLAYERS VS. THE G.M.!
IT'S NOT "THE PLAYERS VS. THE G.M."!
I DON'T JUST PLAY THE MONSTERS! I ALSO PLAY THE *MILLIONS OF PEOPLE* IN THE GAME WORLD WHO BEAR YOU *NO ILL WILL* WHATSOEVER! YOU HAVE A COMMON MISPERCEPTION, I'M AFRAID!
HOW COULD YOU EVEN CONSIDERING HURTING SUCH A SWEETIE?DON'T YOU HAVE ANY MATERNAL INSTINCTS?
WHAT'S YOUR NAME, LITTLE GIRL?
M-MY NAME'S SUZY...
TH-THE *BAD THINGS* FROM THE JUNGLE GOT EVERY-BODY ELSE!... I WAS SCARED SO I HID... I'M SO HUNGRY... FOR WEEKS I HAD WATER BUT NO FOOD...
I SAY KILL HER.
WHAT?!

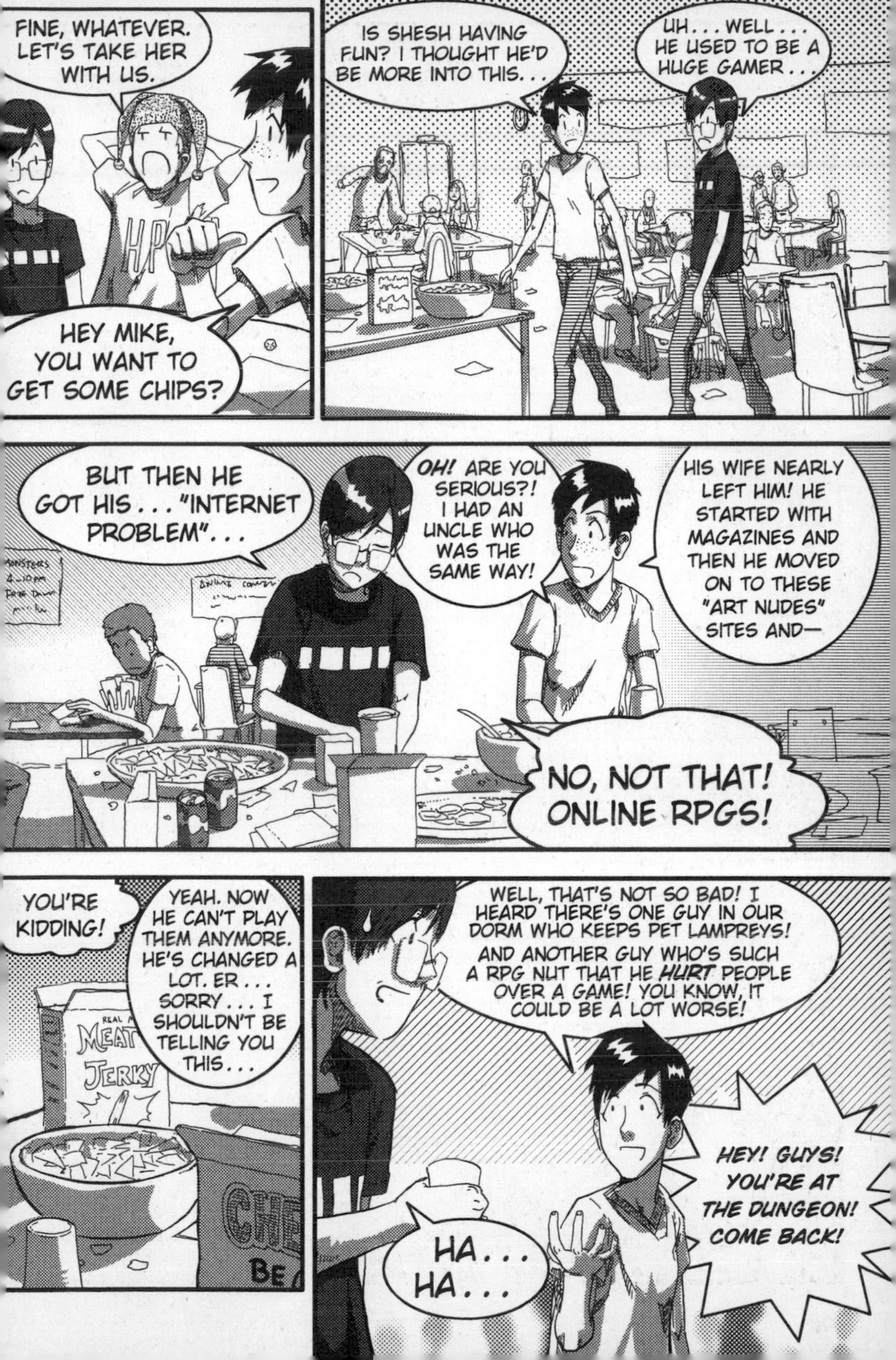
FINE, WHATEVER. LET'S TAKE HER WITH US.
HEY MIKE, YOU WANT TO GET SOME CHIPS?
IS SHESH HAVING FUN? I THOUGHT HE'D BE MORE INTO THIS...
UH... WELL... HE USED TO BE A HUGE GAMER...
BUT THEN HE GOT HIS... "INTERNET PROBLEM"...
OH! ARE YOU SERIOUS?! I HAD AN UNCLE WHO WAS THE SAME WAY!
HIS WIFE NEARLY LEFT HIM! HE STARTED WITH MAGAZINES AND THEN HE MOVED ON TO THESE "ART NUDES" SITES AND—
NO, NOT THAT! ONLINE RPGS!
YOU'RE KIDDING!
YEAH. NOW HE CAN'T PLAY THEM ANYMORE. HE'S CHANGED A LOT. ER... SORRY... I SHOULDN'T BE TELLING YOU THIS...
MEAT
JERKY
WELL, THAT'S NOT SO BAD! I HEARD THERE'S ONE GUY IN OUR DORM WHO KEEPS PET LAMPREYS! AND ANOTHER GUY WHO'S SUCH A RPG NUT THAT HE *HURT* PEOPLE OVER A GAME! YOU KNOW, IT COULD BE A LOT WORSE!
HA... HA...
HEY! GUYS! YOU'RE AT THE DUNGEON! COME BACK!

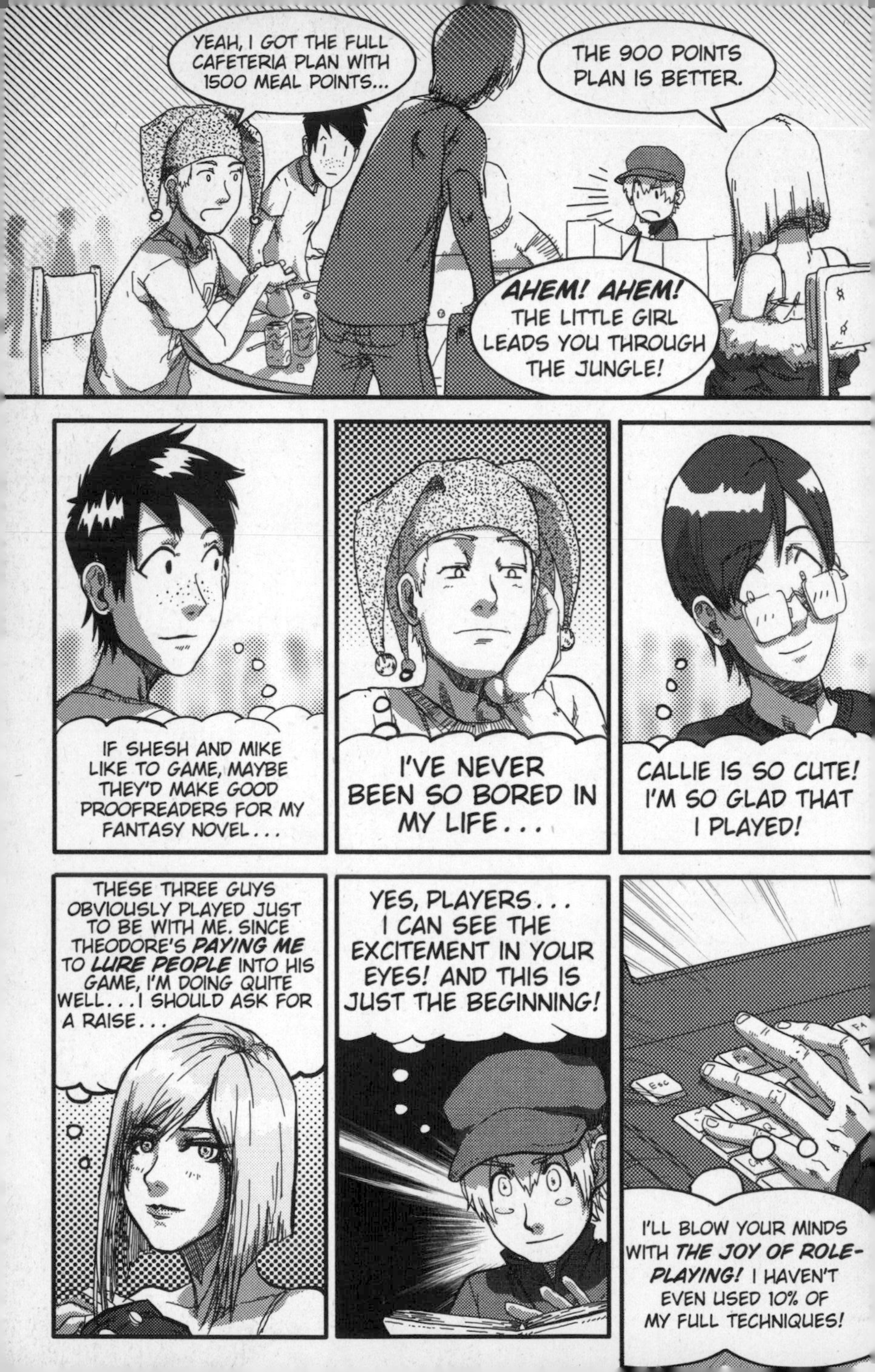

YEAH, I GOT THE FULL CAFETERIA PLAN WITH 1500 MEAL POINTS...
THE 900 POINTS PLAN IS BETTER.
AHEM! AHEM! THE LITTLE GIRL LEADS YOU THROUGH THE JUNGLE!
IF SHESH AND MIKE LIKE TO GAME, MAYBE THEY'D MAKE GOOD PROOFREADERS FOR MY FANTASY NOVEL...
I'VE NEVER BEEN SO BORED IN MY LIFE...
CALLIE IS SO CUTE! I'M SO GLAD THAT I PLAYED!
THESE THREE GUYS OBVIOUSLY PLAYED JUST TO BE WITH ME. SINCE THEODORE'S *PAYING ME* TO *LURE PEOPLE* INTO HIS GAME, I'M DOING QUITE WELL...I SHOULD ASK FOR A RAISE...
YES, PLAYERS... I CAN SEE THE EXCITEMENT IN YOUR EYES! AND THIS IS JUST THE BEGINNING!
I'LL BLOW YOUR MINDS WITH *THE JOY OF ROLE-PLAYING!* I HAVEN'T EVEN USED 10% OF MY FULL TECHNIQUES!

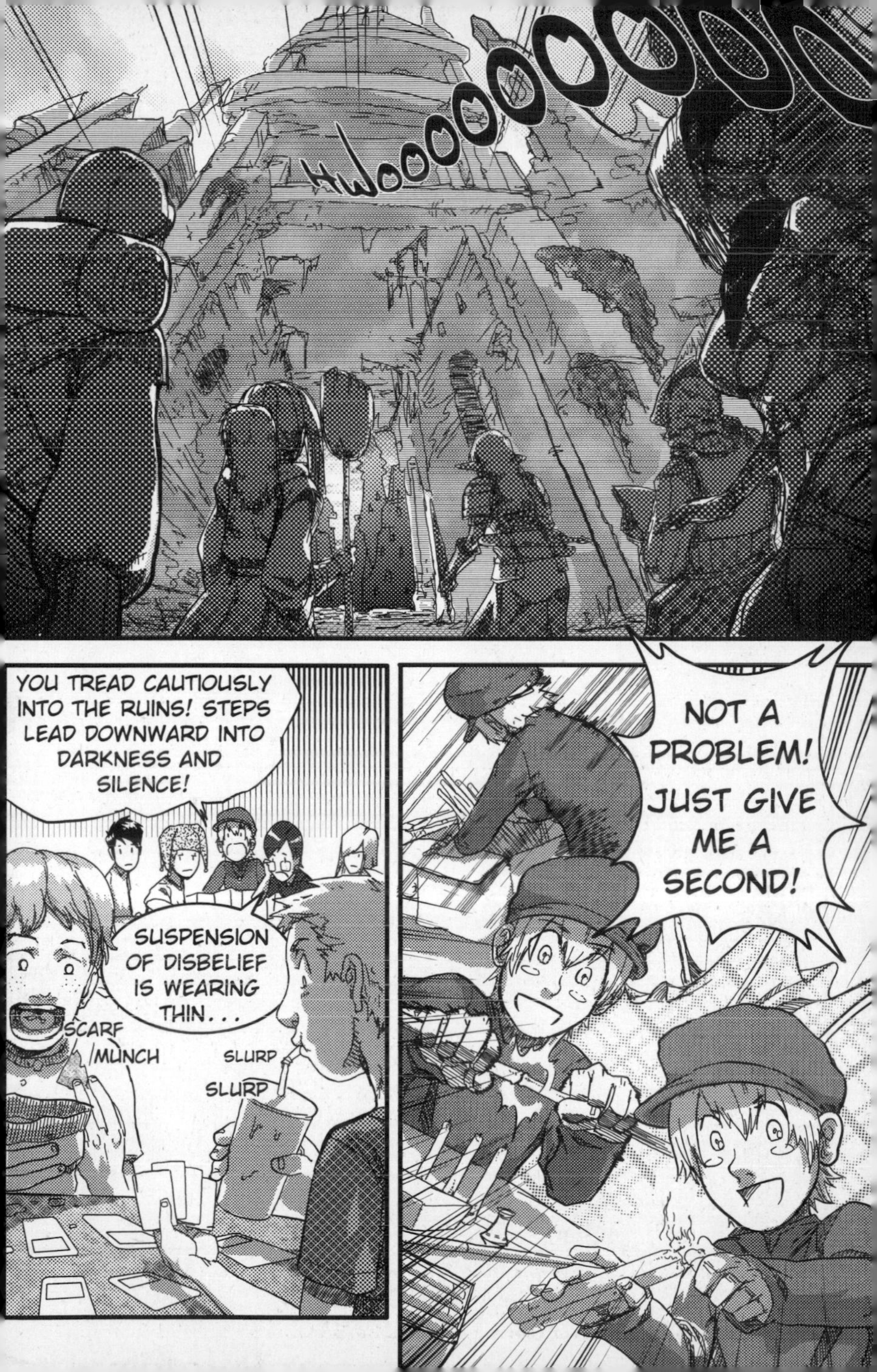
HWOOOOOOOOOO
YOU TREAD CAUTIOUSLY INTO THE RUINS! STEPS LEAD DOWNWARD INTO DARKNESS AND SILENCE!
SUSPENSION OF DISBELIEF IS WEARING THIN. . .
SCARF /MUNCH
SLURP
SLURP
NOT A PROBLEM! JUST GIVE ME A SECOND!

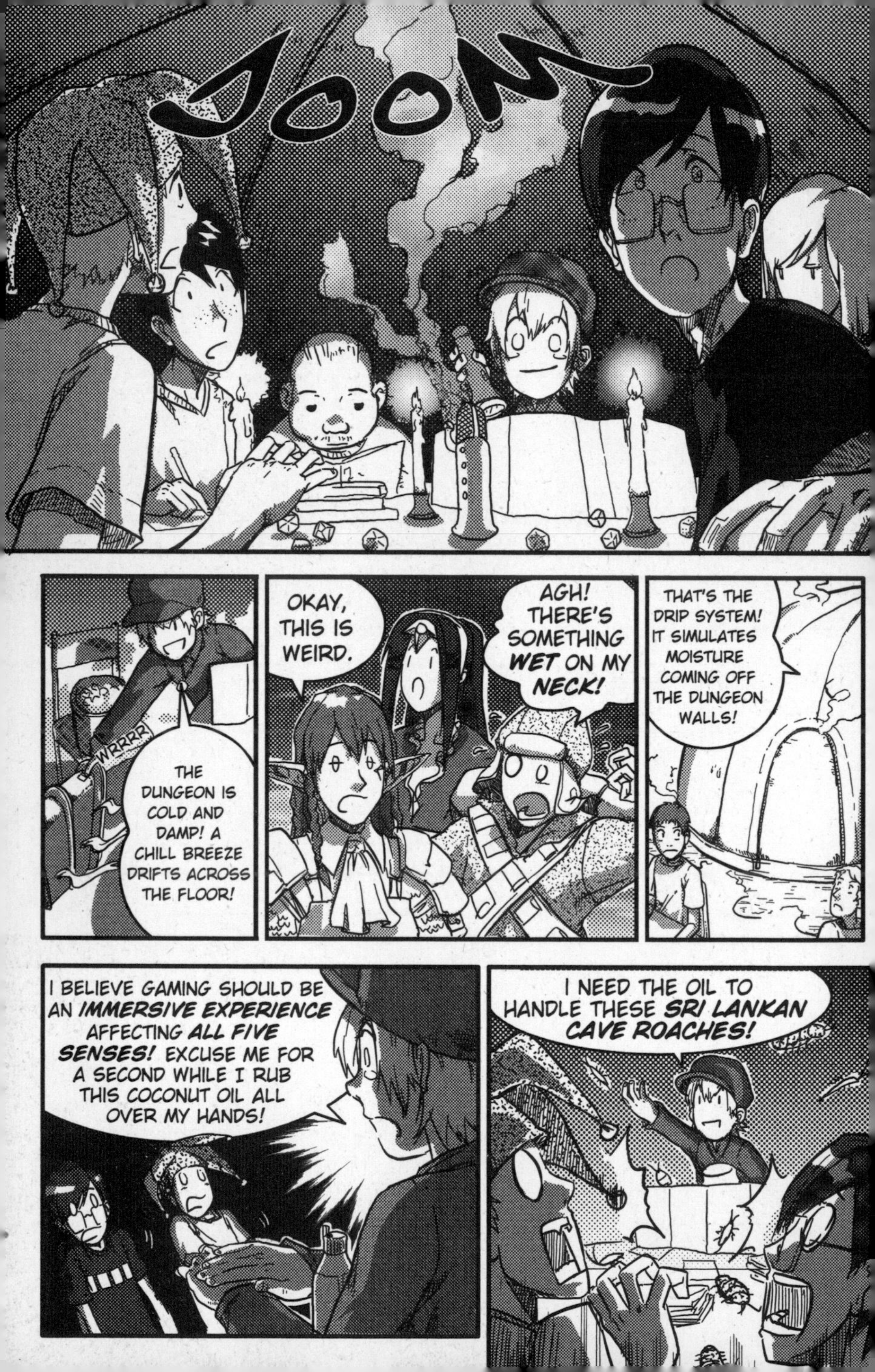
DOOM
THE DUNGEON IS COLD AND DAMP! A CHILL BREEZE DRIFTS ACROSS THE FLOOR!
WRRRR
OKAY, THIS IS WEIRD.
AGH! THERE'S SOMETHING *WET* ON MY *NECK!*
THAT'S THE DRIP SYSTEM! IT SIMULATES MOISTURE COMING OFF THE DUNGEON WALLS!
I BELIEVE GAMING SHOULD BE AN *IMMERSIVE EXPERIENCE* AFFECTING *ALL FIVE SENSES!* EXCUSE ME FOR A SECOND WHILE I RUB THIS COCONUT OIL ALL OVER MY HANDS!
I NEED THE OIL TO HANDLE THESE *SRI LANKAN CAVE ROACHES!*

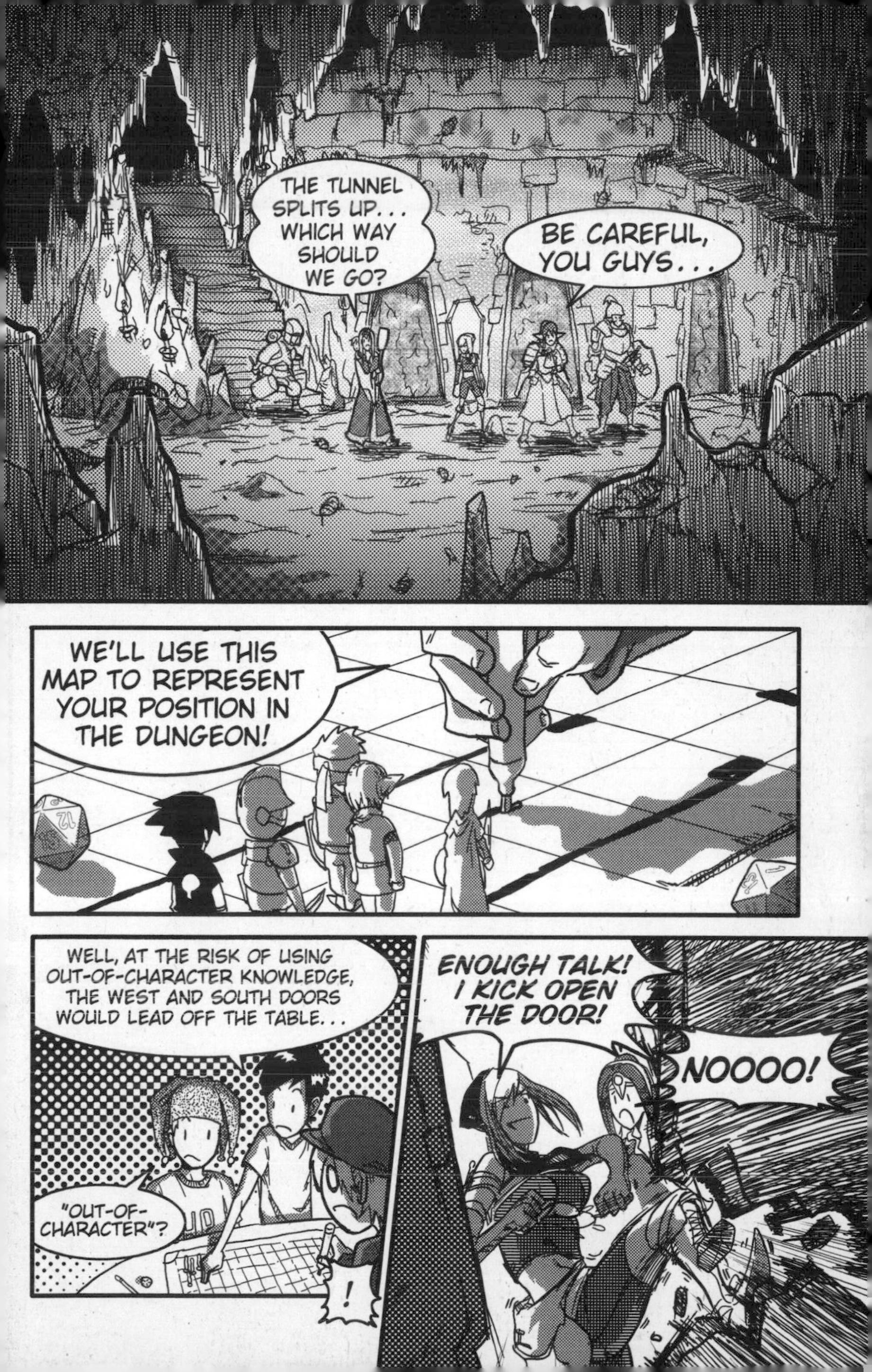
THE TUNNEL SPLITS UP... WHICH WAY SHOULD WE GO?
BE CAREFUL, YOU GUYS...
WE'LL USE THIS MAP TO REPRESENT YOUR POSITION IN THE DUNGEON!
WELL, AT THE RISK OF USING OUT-OF-CHARACTER KNOWLEDGE, THE WEST AND SOUTH DOORS WOULD LEAD OFF THE TABLE...
"OUT-OF-CHARACTER"?
!
ENOUGH TALK! I KICK OPEN THE DOOR!
NOOOO!

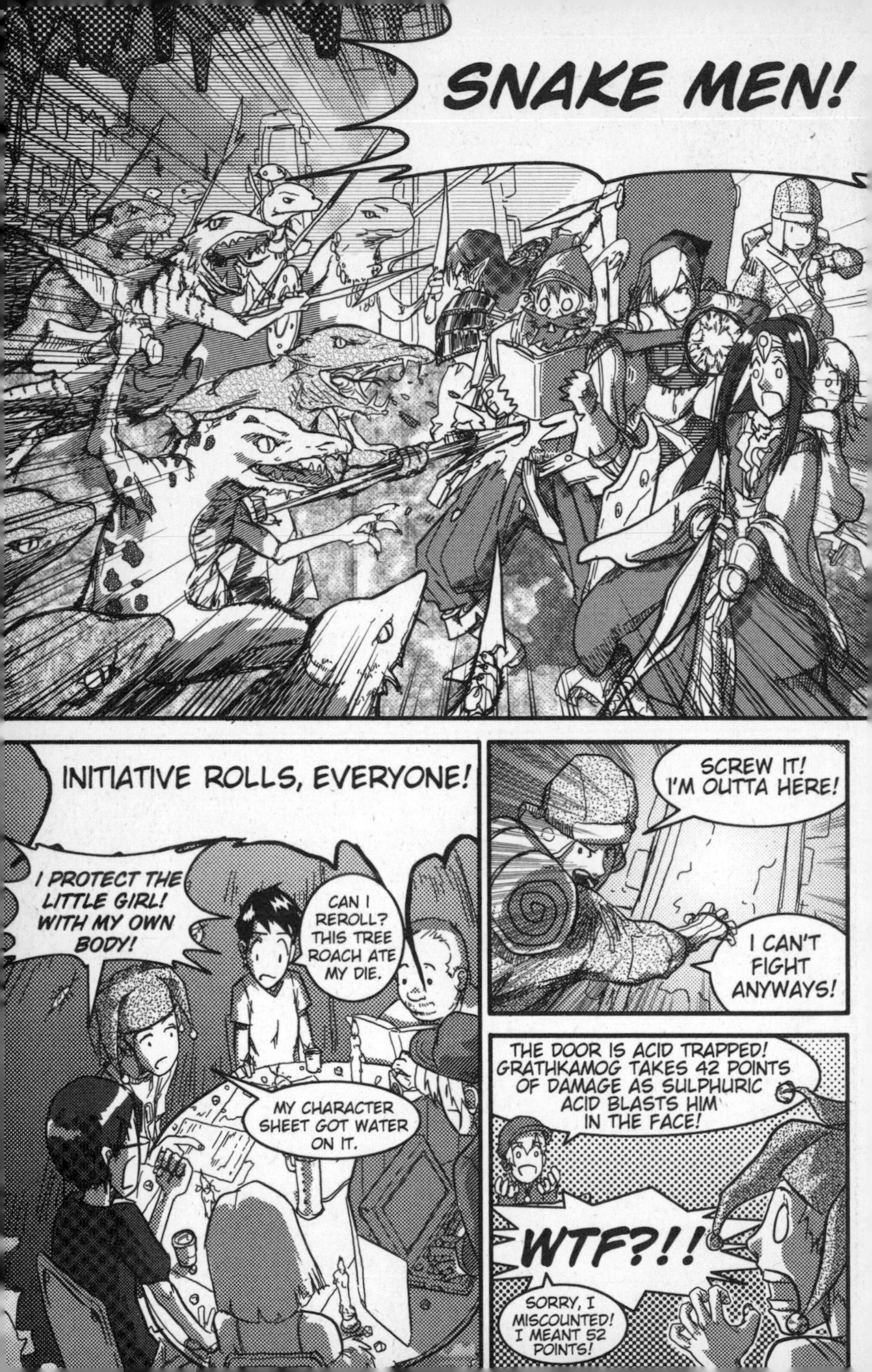
SNAKE MEN!
INITIATIVE ROLLS, EVERYONE!
I PROTECT THE LITTLE GIRL! WITH MY OWN BODY!
CAN I REROLL? THIS TREE ROACH ATE MY DIE.
MY CHARACTER SHEET GOT WATER ON IT.
SCREW IT! I'M OUTTA HERE!
I CAN'T FIGHT ANYWAYS!
THE DOOR IS ACID TRAPPED! GRATHKAMOG TAKES 42 POINTS OF DAMAGE AS SULPHURIC ACID BLASTS HIM IN THE FACE!
WTF?!!
SORRY, I MISCOUNTED! I MEANT 52 POINTS!

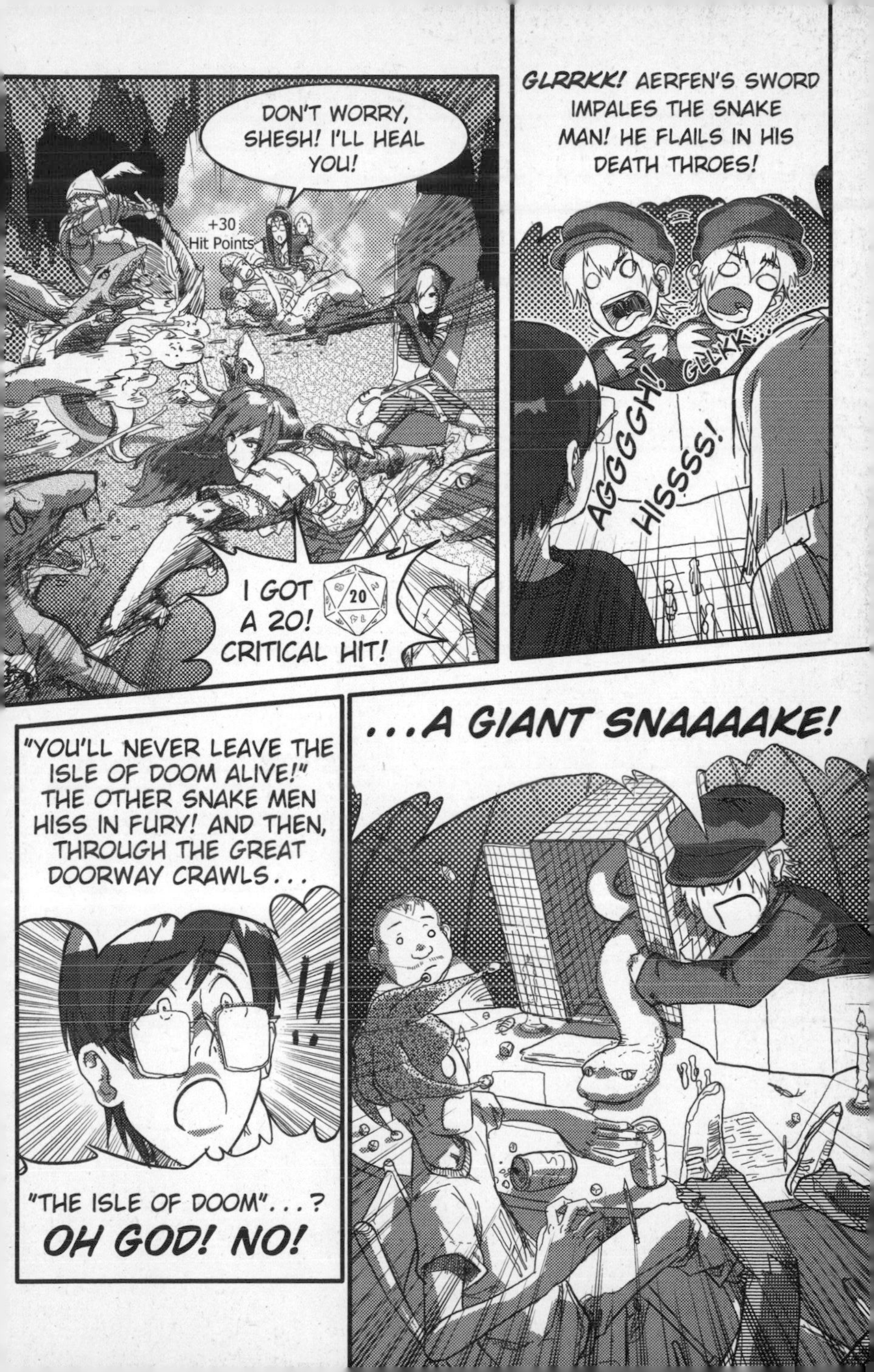
DON'T WORRY, SHESH! I'LL HEAL YOU!
+30 Hit Points
I GOT A 20! CRITICAL HIT!
20
GLRRKK! AERFEN'S SWORD IMPALES THE SNAKE MAN! HE FLAILS IN HIS DEATH THROES!
AGGGGH!
HISSSS!
GLLKK...
"YOU'LL NEVER LEAVE THE ISLE OF DOOM ALIVE!" THE OTHER SNAKE MEN HISS IN FURY! AND THEN, THROUGH THE GREAT DOORWAY CRAWLS...
!!
"THE ISLE OF DOOM"...?
OH GOD! NO!
...A GIANT SNAAAAKE!

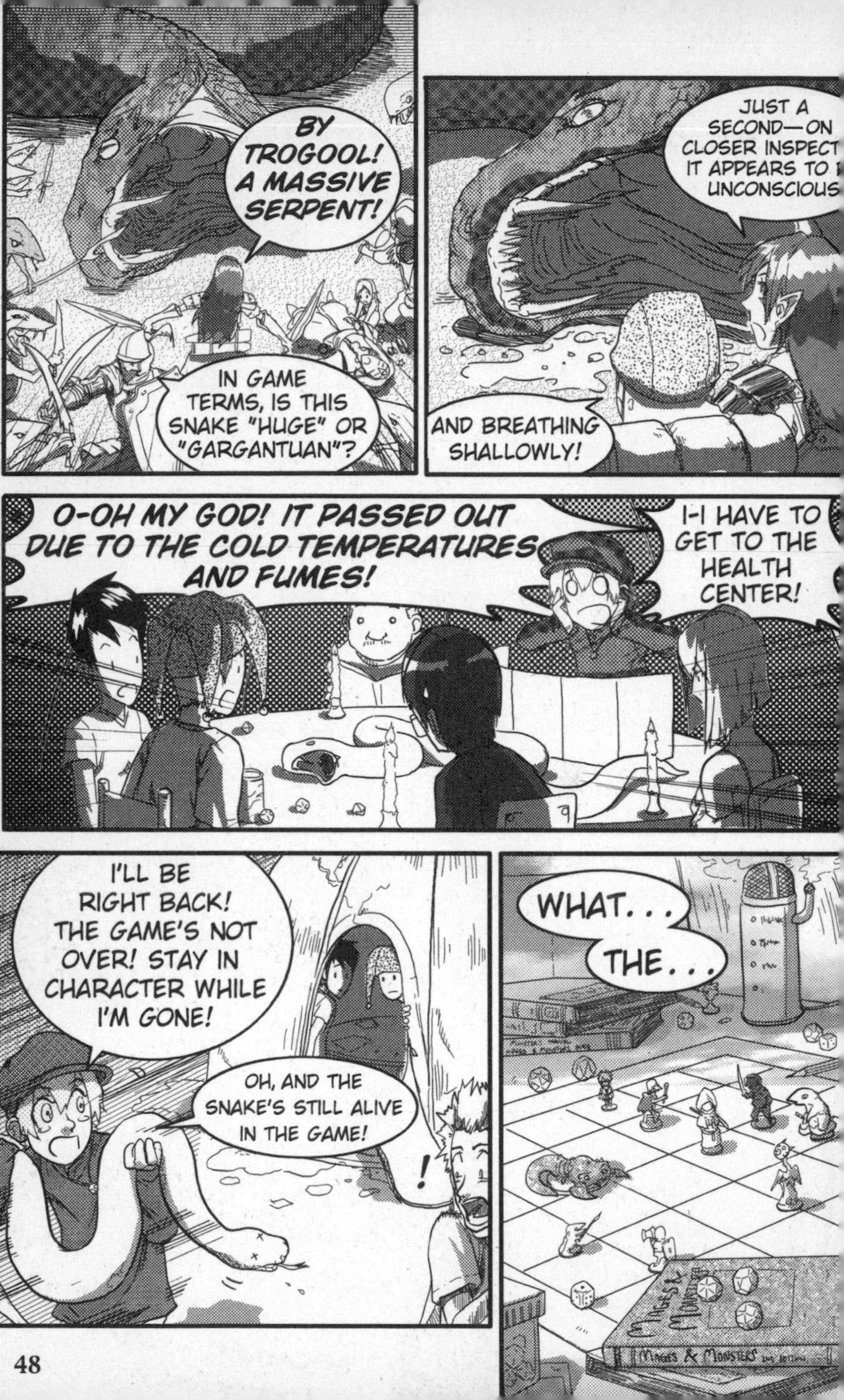
BY TROGOOL! A MASSIVE SERPENT!
IN GAME TERMS, IS THIS SNAKE "HUGE" OR "GARGANTUAN"?
JUST A SECOND—ON CLOSER INSPECT
IT APPEARS TO
UNCONSCIOUS
AND BREATHING SHALLOWLY!
O-OH MY GOD! IT PASSED OUT DUE TO THE COLD TEMPERATURES AND FUMES!
I-I HAVE TO GET TO THE HEALTH CENTER!
I'LL BE RIGHT BACK! THE GAME'S NOT OVER! STAY IN CHARACTER WHILE I'M GONE!
OH, AND THE SNAKE'S STILL ALIVE IN THE GAME!
!
WHAT. . .
THE. . .
MAGES & MONSTERS

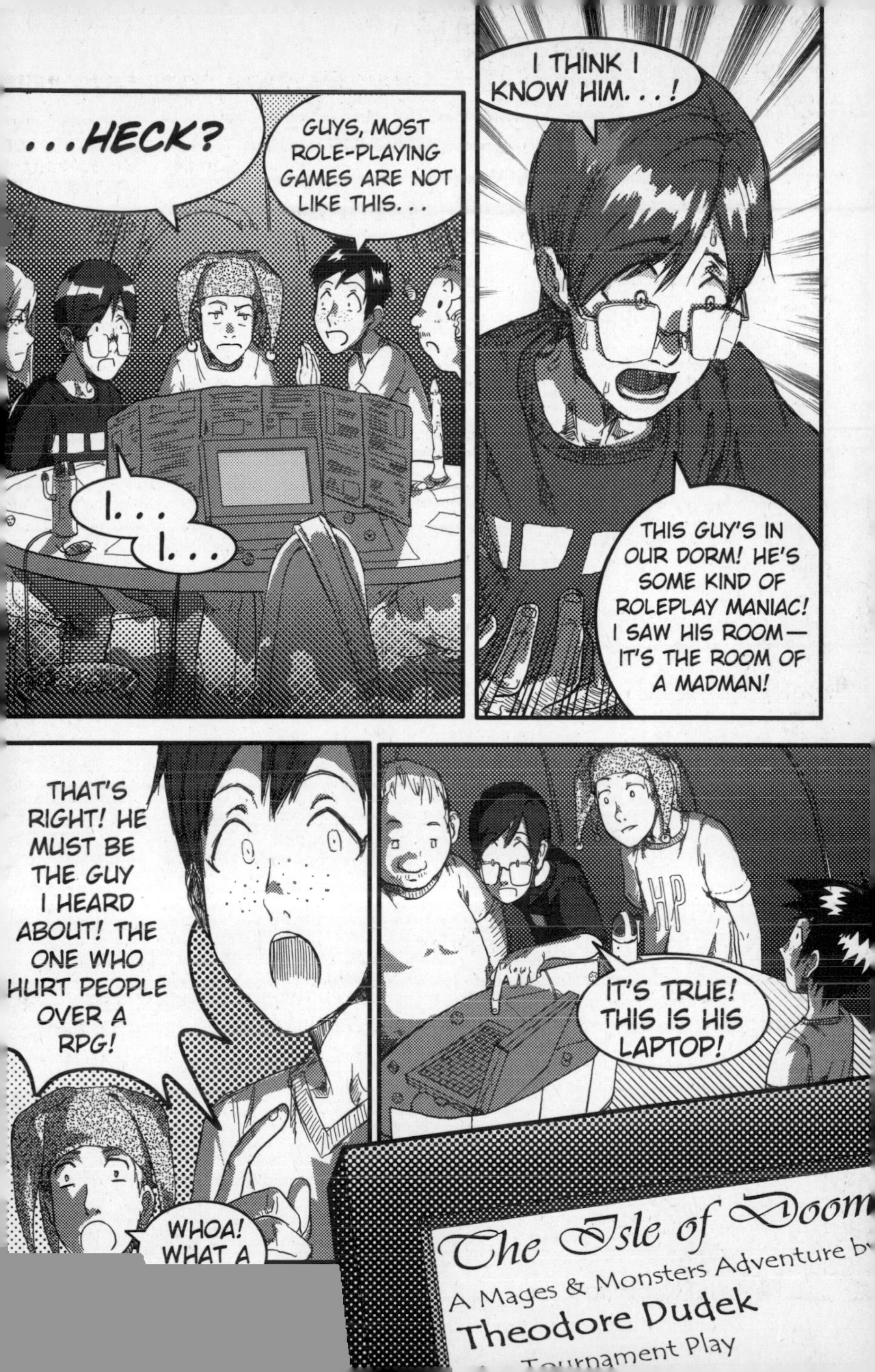

...HECK?
GUYS, MOST ROLE-PLAYING GAMES ARE NOT LIKE THIS...
I... I...
I THINK I KNOW HIM...!
THIS GUY'S IN OUR DORM! HE'S SOME KIND OF ROLEPLAY MANIAC! I SAW HIS ROOM—IT'S THE ROOM OF A MADMAN!
THAT'S RIGHT! HE MUST BE THE GUY I HEARD ABOUT! THE ONE WHO HURT PEOPLE OVER A RPG!
WHOA! WHAT A
IT'S TRUE! THIS IS HIS LAPTOP!
The Isle of Doom
A Mages & Monsters Adventure by
Theodore Dudek
Tournament Play

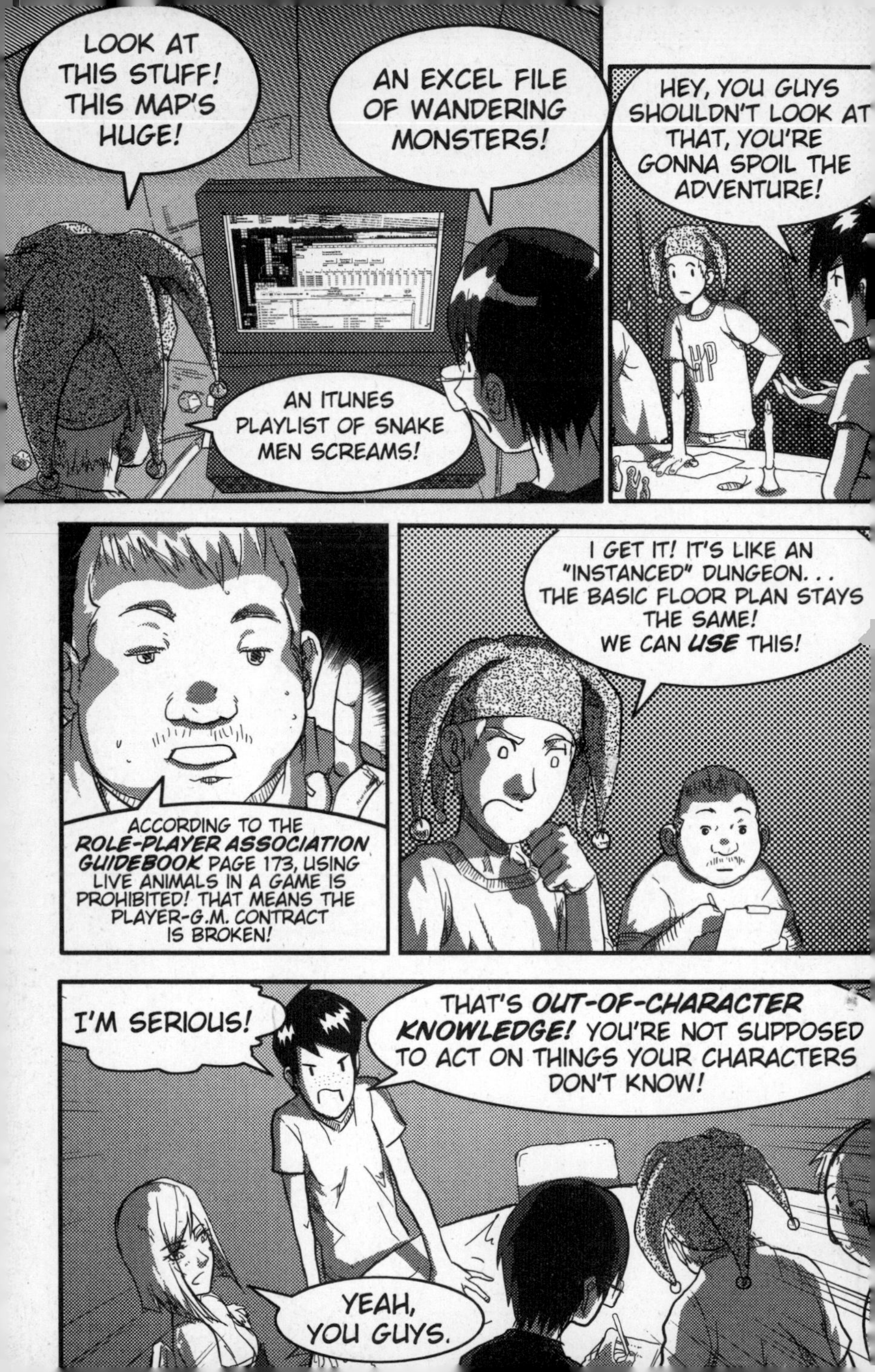
LOOK AT THIS STUFF! THIS MAP'S HUGE!
AN EXCEL FILE OF WANDERING MONSTERS!
AN ITUNES PLAYLIST OF SNAKE MEN SCREAMS!
HEY, YOU GUYS SHOULDN'T LOOK AT THAT, YOU'RE GONNA SPOIL THE ADVENTURE!
ACCORDING TO THE *ROLE-PLAYER ASSOCIATION GUIDEBOOK* PAGE 173, USING LIVE ANIMALS IN A GAME IS PROHIBITED! THAT MEANS THE PLAYER-G.M. CONTRACT IS BROKEN!
I GET IT! IT'S LIKE AN "INSTANCED" DUNGEON. . . THE BASIC FLOOR PLAN STAYS THE SAME! WE CAN *USE* THIS!
I'M SERIOUS!
THAT'S *OUT-OF-CHARACTER KNOWLEDGE!* YOU'RE NOT SUPPOSED TO ACT ON THINGS YOUR CHARACTERS DON'T KNOW!
YEAH, YOU GUYS.

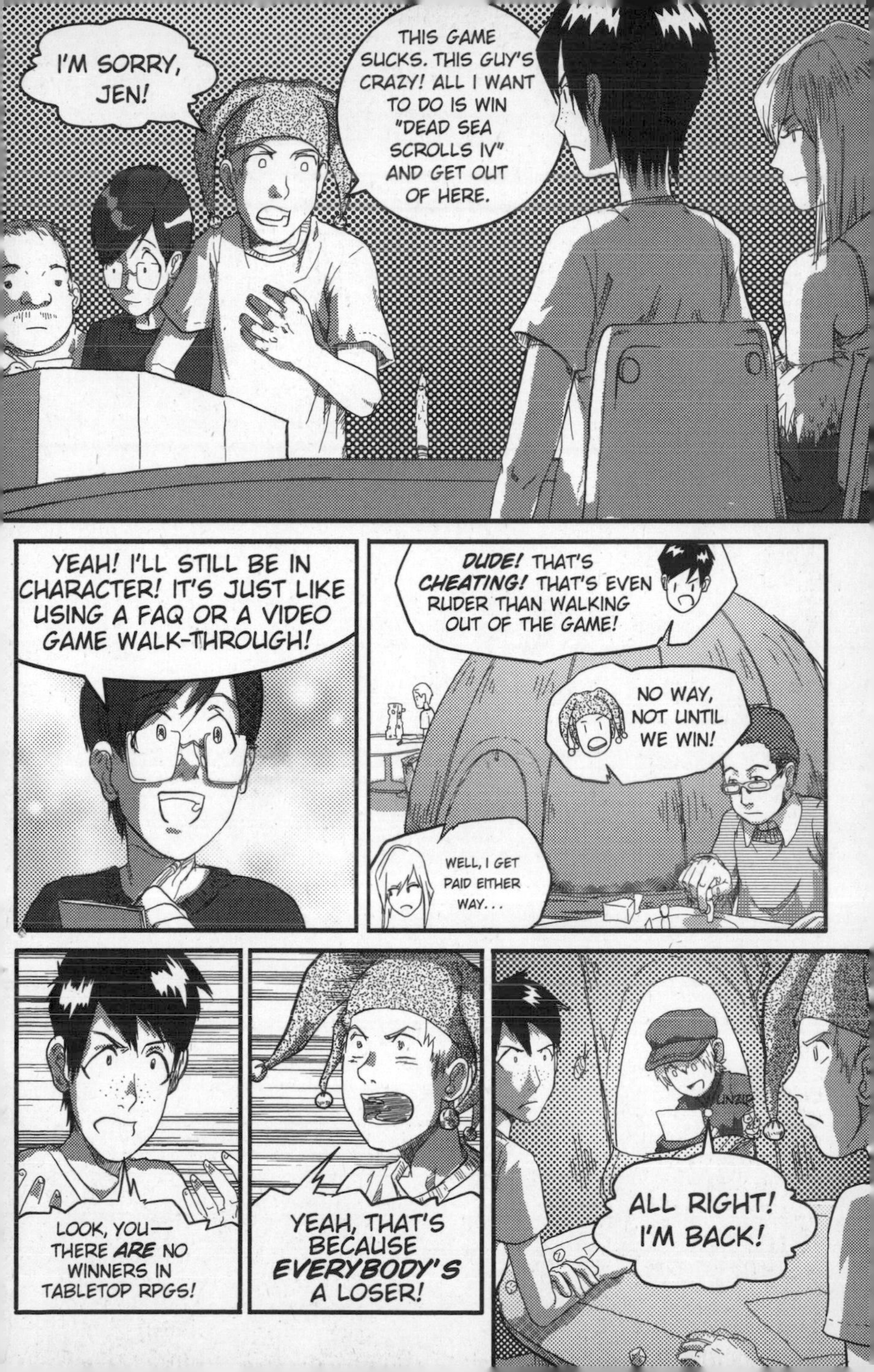
I'M SORRY, JEN!
THIS GAME SUCKS. THIS GUY'S CRAZY! ALL I WANT TO DO IS WIN "DEAD SEA SCROLLS IV" AND GET OUT OF HERE.
YEAH! I'LL STILL BE IN CHARACTER! IT'S JUST LIKE USING A FAQ OR A VIDEO GAME WALK-THROUGH!
DUDE! THAT'S CHEATING! THAT'S EVEN RUDER THAN WALKING OUT OF THE GAME!
NO WAY, NOT UNTIL WE WIN!
WELL, I GET PAID EITHER WAY...
LOOK, YOU— THERE ARE NO WINNERS IN TABLETOP RPGS!
YEAH, THAT'S BECAUSE EVERYBODY'S A LOSER!
ALL RIGHT! I'M BACK!

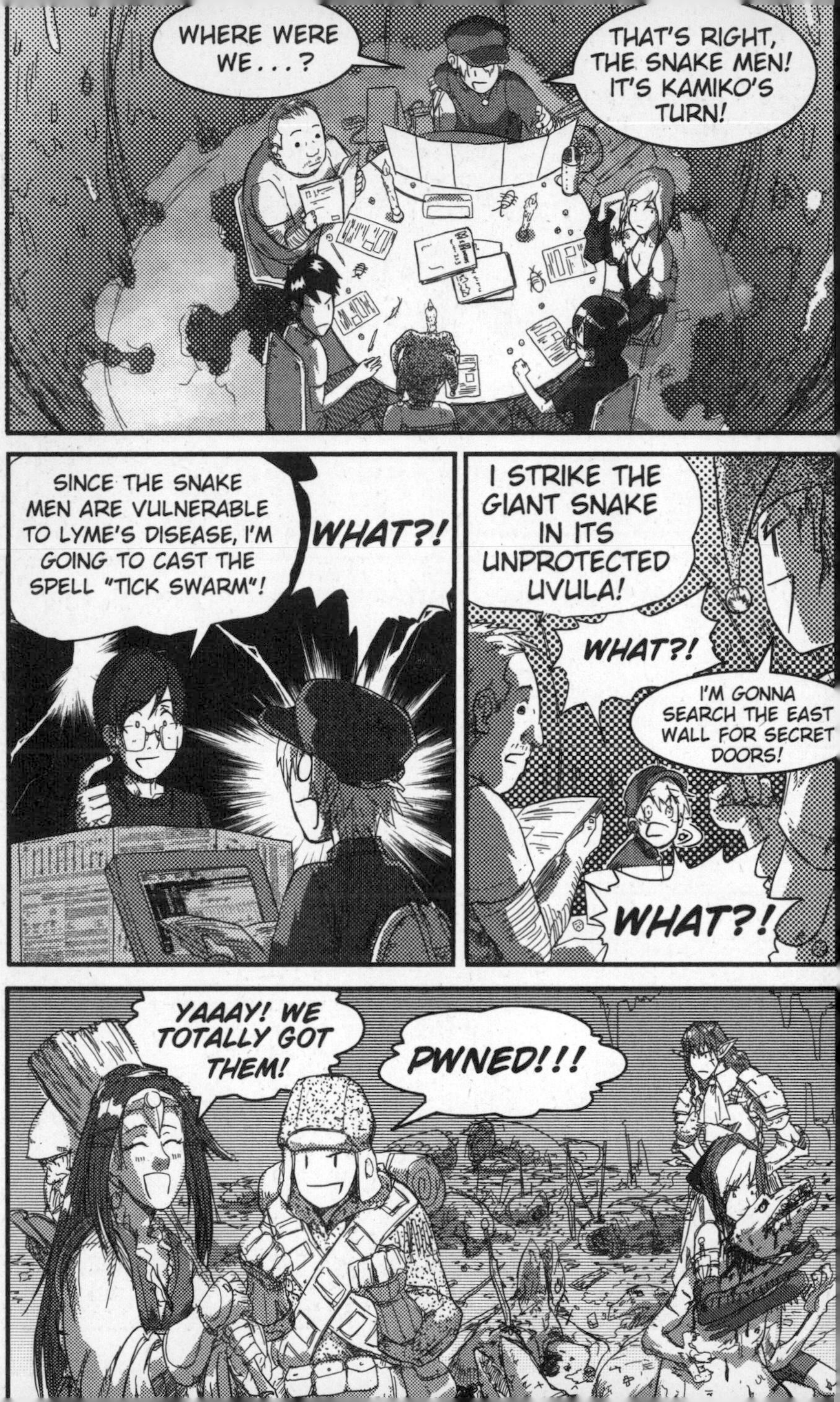
WHERE WERE WE . . . ?
THAT'S RIGHT, THE SNAKE MEN! IT'S KAMIKO'S TURN!
SINCE THE SNAKE MEN ARE VULNERABLE TO LYME'S DISEASE, I'M GOING TO CAST THE SPELL "TICK SWARM"!
WHAT?!
I STRIKE THE GIANT SNAKE IN ITS UNPROTECTED UVULA!
WHAT?!
I'M GONNA SEARCH THE EAST WALL FOR SECRET DOORS!
WHAT?!
YAAAY! WE TOTALLY GOT THEM!
PWNED!!!

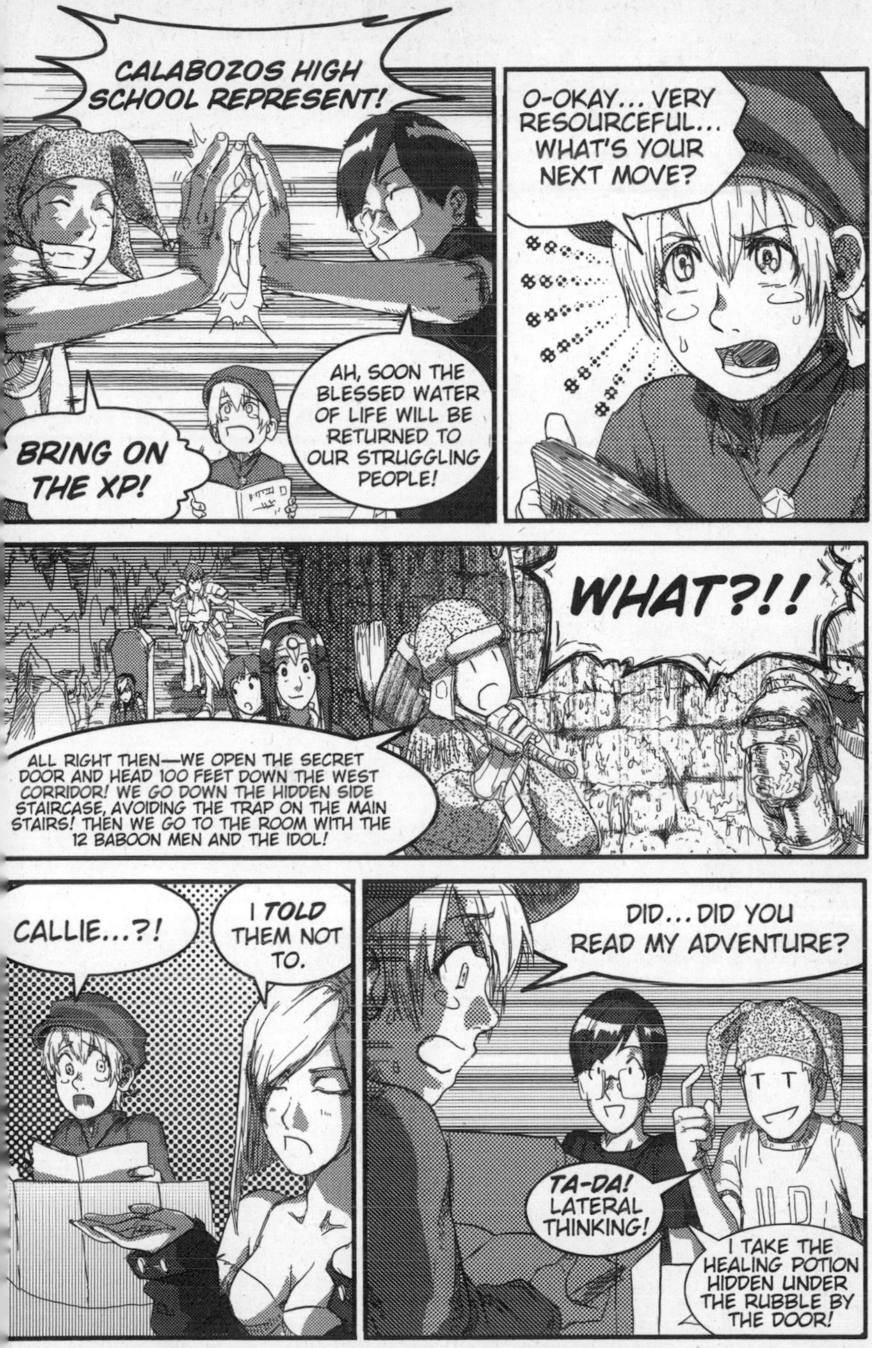
CALABOZOS HIGH SCHOOL REPRESENT!
BRING ON THE XP!
AH, SOON THE BLESSED WATER OF LIFE WILL BE RETURNED TO OUR STRUGGLING PEOPLE!
O-OKAY... VERY RESOURCEFUL... WHAT'S YOUR NEXT MOVE?
ALL RIGHT THEN—WE OPEN THE SECRET DOOR AND HEAD 100 FEET DOWN THE WEST CORRIDOR! WE GO DOWN THE HIDDEN SIDE STAIRCASE, AVOIDING THE TRAP ON THE MAIN STAIRS! THEN WE GO TO THE ROOM WITH THE 12 BABOON MEN AND THE IDOL!
WHAT?!!
CALLIE...?!
I TOLD THEM NOT TO.
DID... DID YOU READ MY ADVENTURE?
TA-DA! LATERAL THINKING!
I TAKE THE HEALING POTION HIDDEN UNDER THE RUBBLE BY THE DOOR!

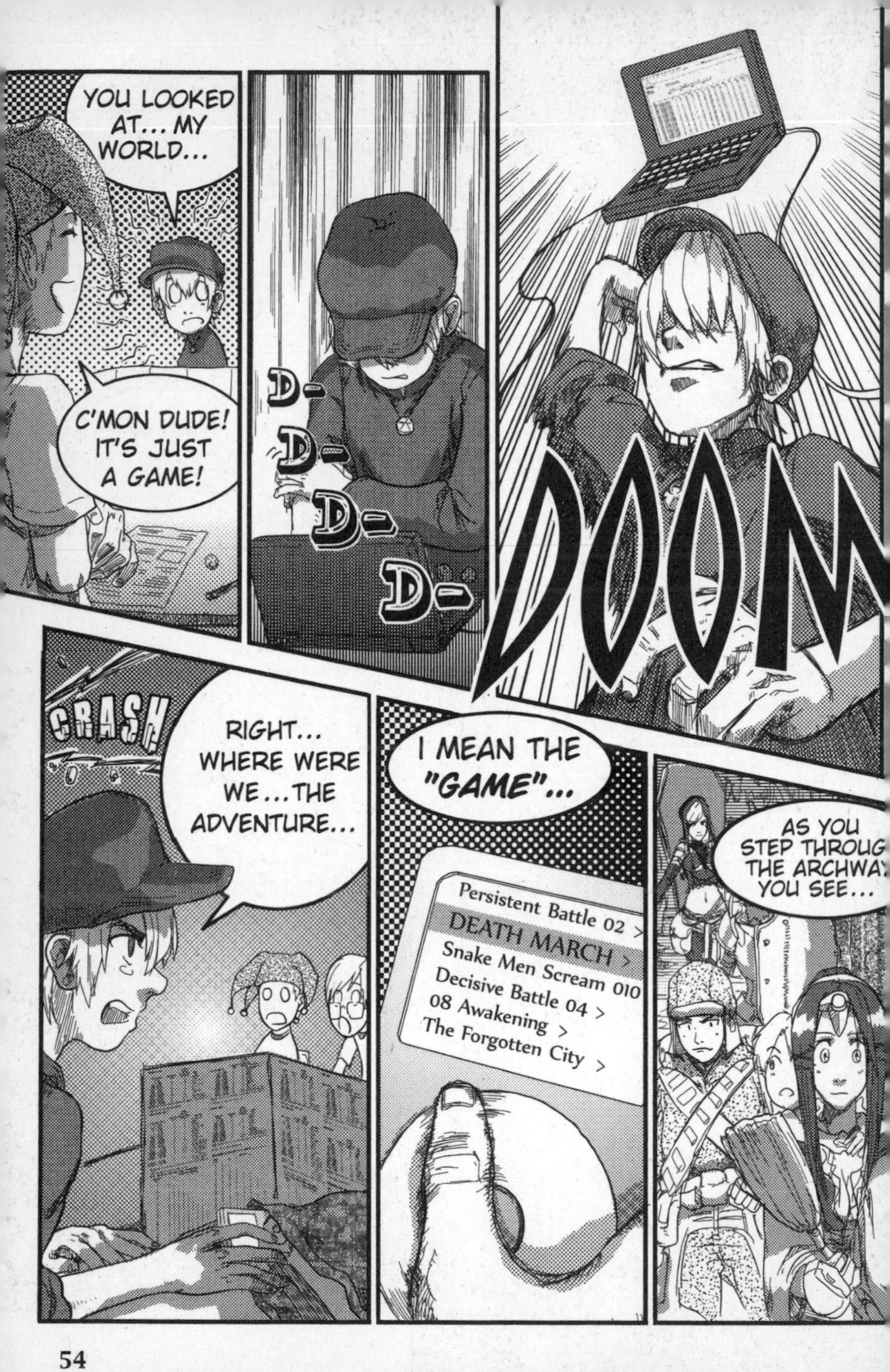
YOU LOOKED AT... MY WORLD...
C'MON DUDE! IT'S JUST A GAME!
D-
D-
D-
D-
DOOM
CRASH
RIGHT... WHERE WERE WE... THE ADVENTURE...
I MEAN THE "GAME"...
Persistent Battle 02 >
DEATH MARCH >
Snake Men Scream 010
Decisive Battle 04 >
08 Awakening >
The Forgotten City >
AS YOU STEP THROUG THE ARCHWA YOU SEE...

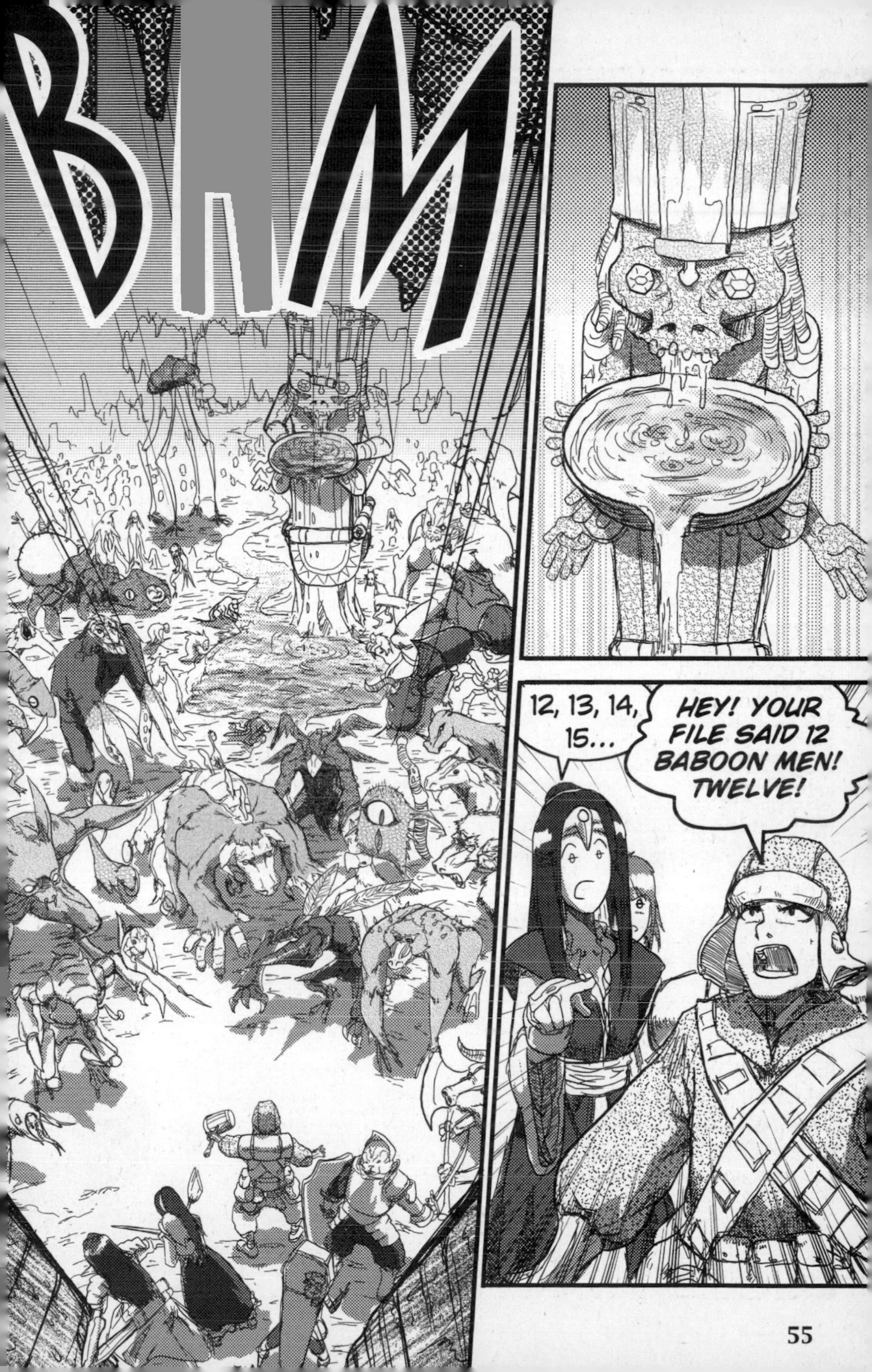
12, 13, 14, 15...
HEY! YOUR FILE SAID 12 BABOON MEN! TWELVE!

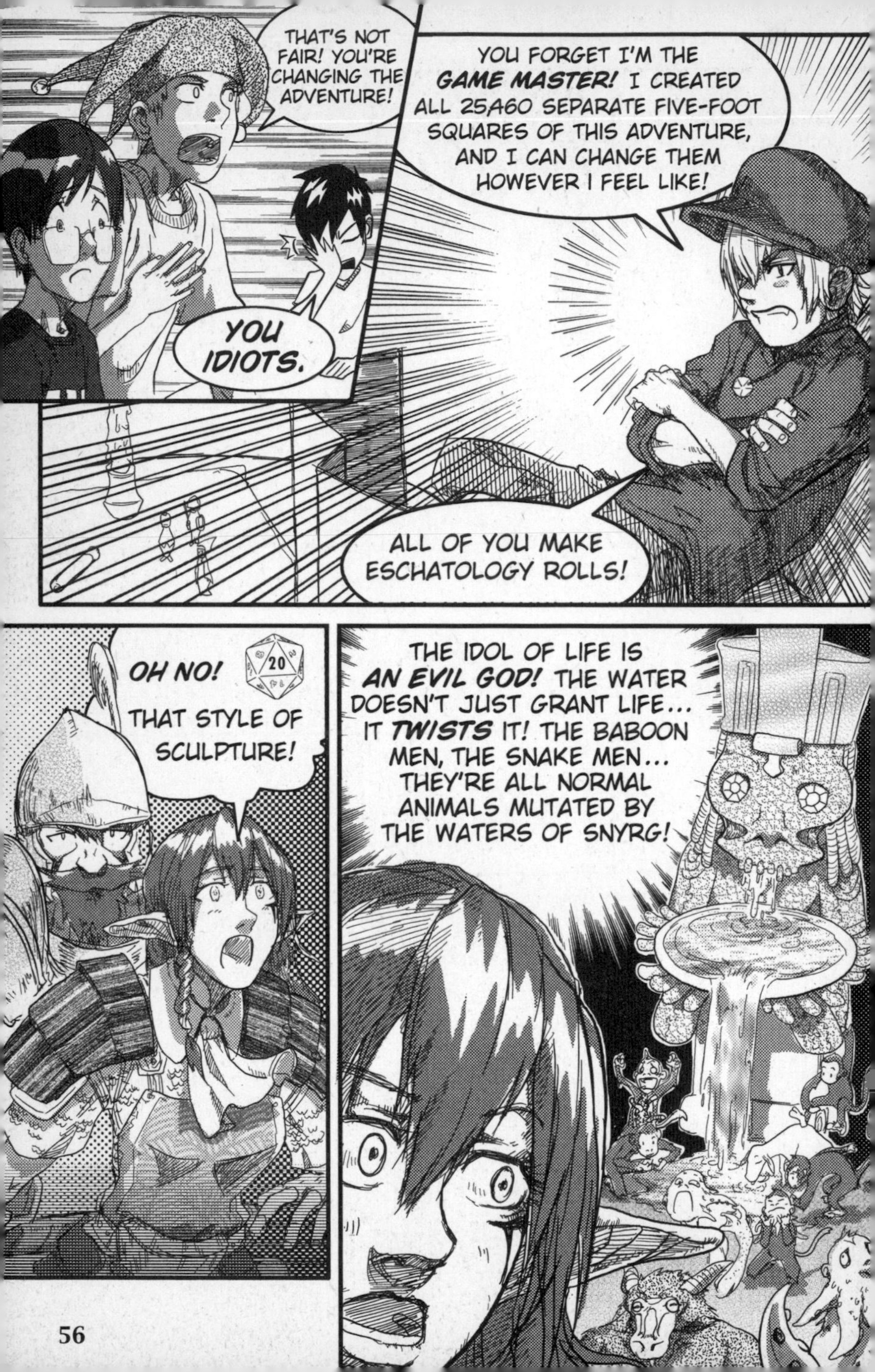
THAT'S NOT FAIR! YOU'RE CHANGING THE ADVENTURE!
YOU IDIOTS.
YOU FORGET I'M THE *GAME MASTER!* I CREATED ALL 25A60 SEPARATE FIVE-FOOT SQUARES OF THIS ADVENTURE, AND I CAN CHANGE THEM HOWEVER I FEEL LIKE!
ALL OF YOU MAKE ESCHATOLOGY ROLLS!
20
OH NO! THAT STYLE OF SCULPTURE!
THE IDOL OF LIFE IS *AN EVIL GOD!* THE WATER DOESN'T JUST GRANT LIFE... IT *TWISTS* IT! THE BABOON MEN, THE SNAKE MEN... THEY'RE ALL NORMAL ANIMALS MUTATED BY THE WATERS OF SNYRG!

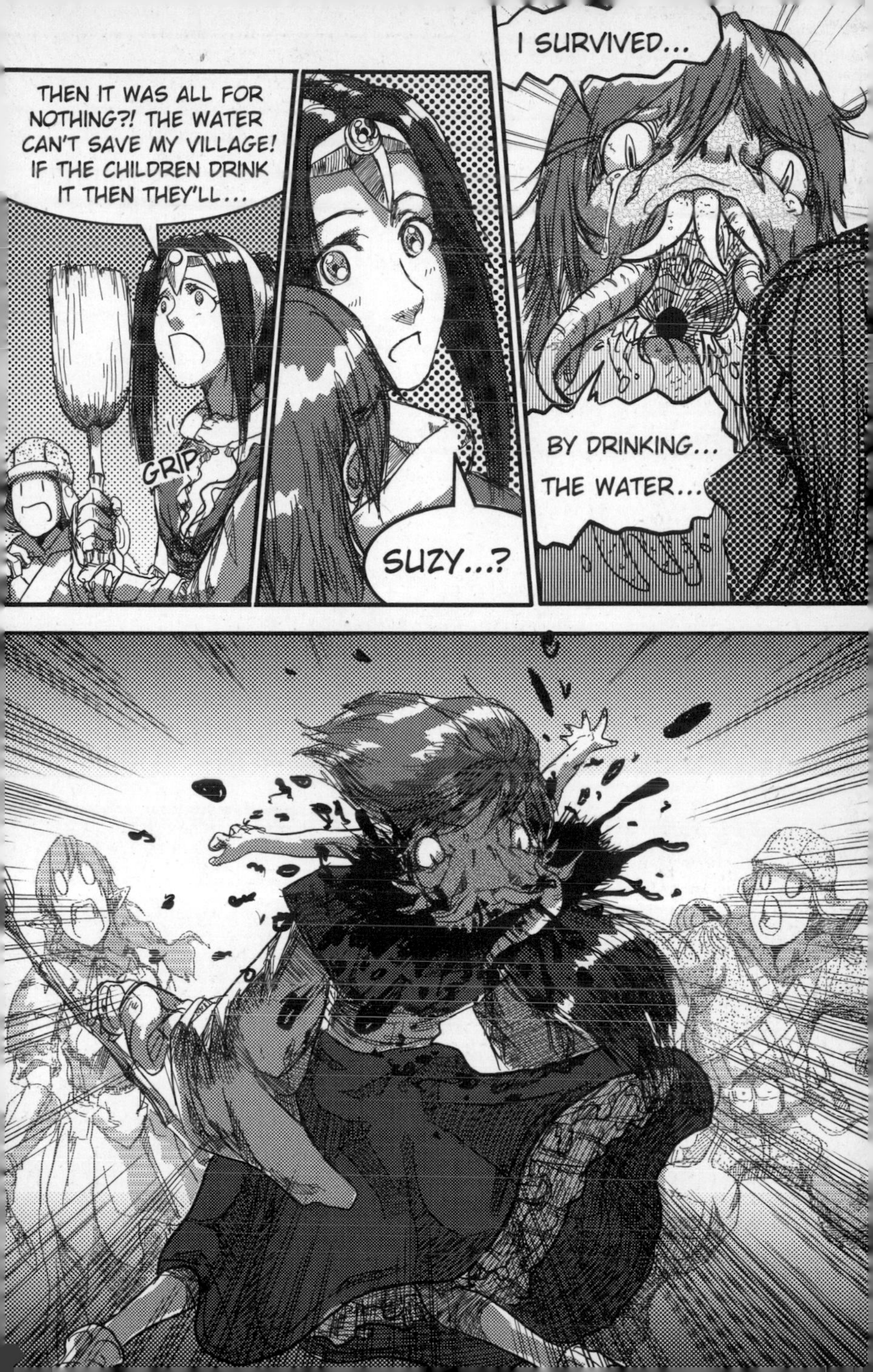
THEN IT WAS ALL FOR NOTHING?! THE WATER CAN'T SAVE MY VILLAGE! IF THE CHILDREN DRINK IT THEN THEY'LL...
GRIP
SUZY...?
I SURVIVED...
BY DRINKING... THE WATER...

MMM... EYEBALLS...

SPLTHUNK

SLURP MUNCH

RIP CRIP

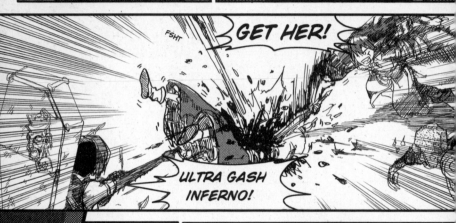

FSHT

GET HER!

ULTRA GASH INFERNO!

FSHT

!

SO SLOW...

EAT YOU... UNTAINTED MEAT SO TASTY... YOUR BONES AND GRISTLE MAKE *SACRIFICE* TO SNYRG!

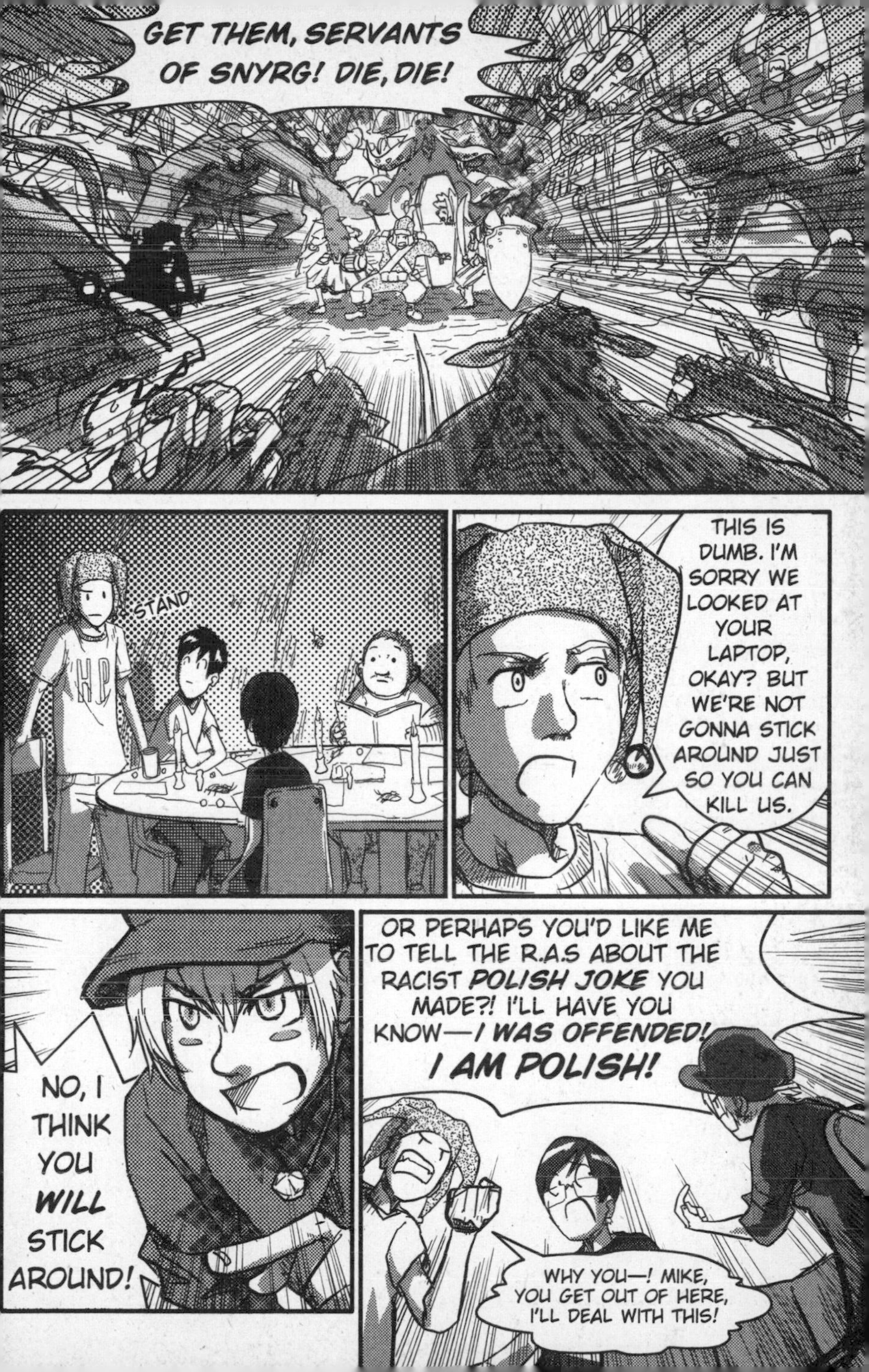
GET THEM, SERVANTS OF SNYRG! DIE, DIE!
STAND
THIS IS DUMB. I'M SORRY WE LOOKED AT YOUR LAPTOP, OKAY? BUT WE'RE NOT GONNA STICK AROUND JUST SO YOU CAN KILL US.
NO, I THINK YOU WILL STICK AROUND!
OR PERHAPS YOU'D LIKE ME TO TELL THE R.A.S ABOUT THE RACIST POLISH JOKE YOU MADE?! I'LL HAVE YOU KNOW—I WAS OFFENDED! I AM POLISH!
WHY YOU—! MIKE, YOU GET OUT OF HERE, I'LL DEAL WITH THIS!

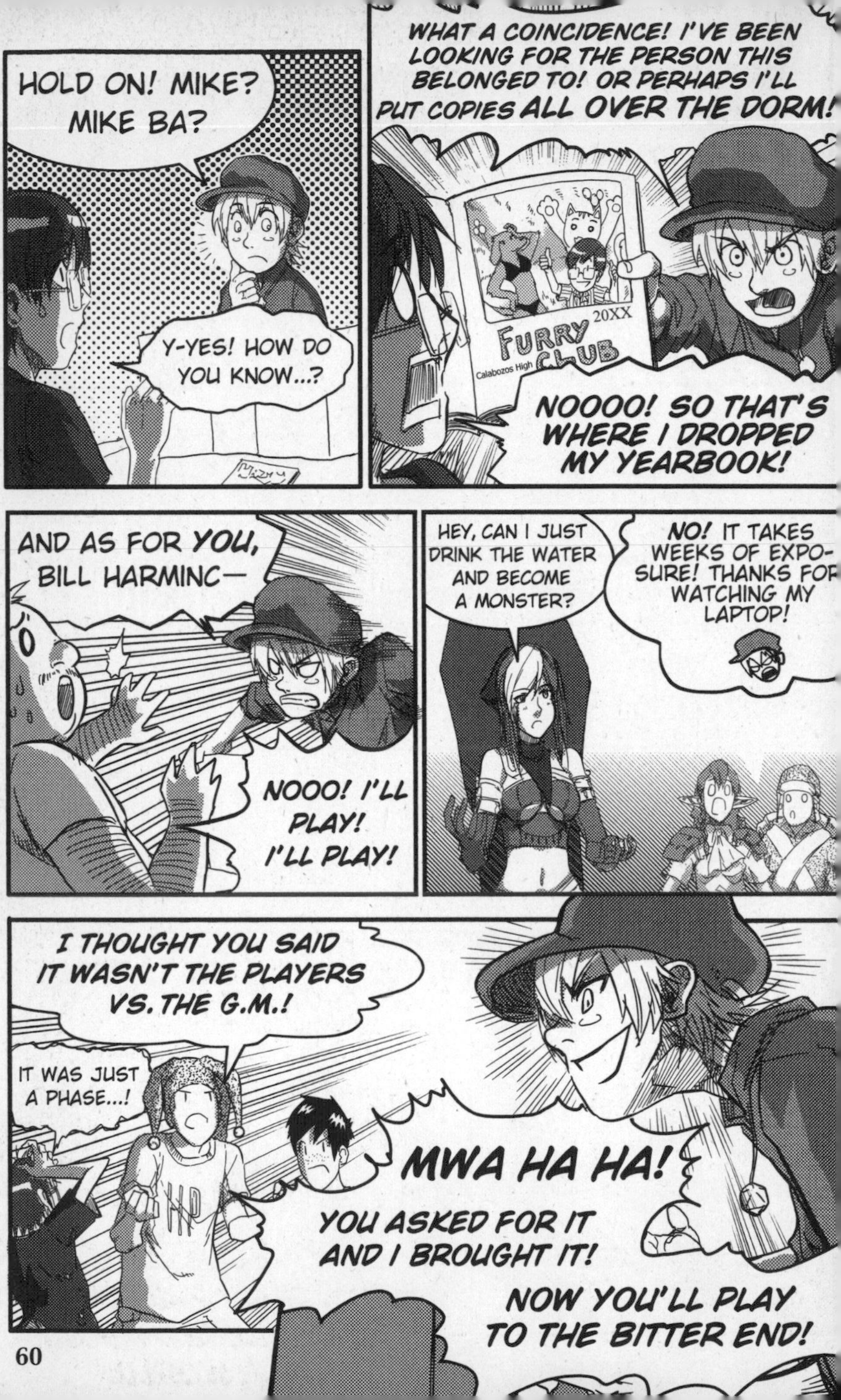
HOLD ON! MIKE? MIKE BA?
Y-YES! HOW DO YOU KNOW...?
WHAT A COINCIDENCE! I'VE BEEN LOOKING FOR THE PERSON THIS BELONGED TO! OR PERHAPS I'LL PUT COPIES ALL OVER THE DORM!
20XX
FURRY CLUB
Calabozos High
NOOOO! SO THAT'S WHERE I DROPPED MY YEARBOOK!
AND AS FOR YOU, BILL HARMINC—
NOOO! I'LL PLAY! I'LL PLAY!
HEY, CAN I JUST DRINK THE WATER AND BECOME A MONSTER?
NO! IT TAKES WEEKS OF EXPO-SURE! THANKS FOR WATCHING MY LAPTOP!
I THOUGHT YOU SAID IT WASN'T THE PLAYERS VS. THE G.M.!
IT WAS JUST A PHASE...!
MWA HA HA!
YOU ASKED FOR IT AND I BROUGHT IT!
NOW YOU'LL PLAY TO THE BITTER END!

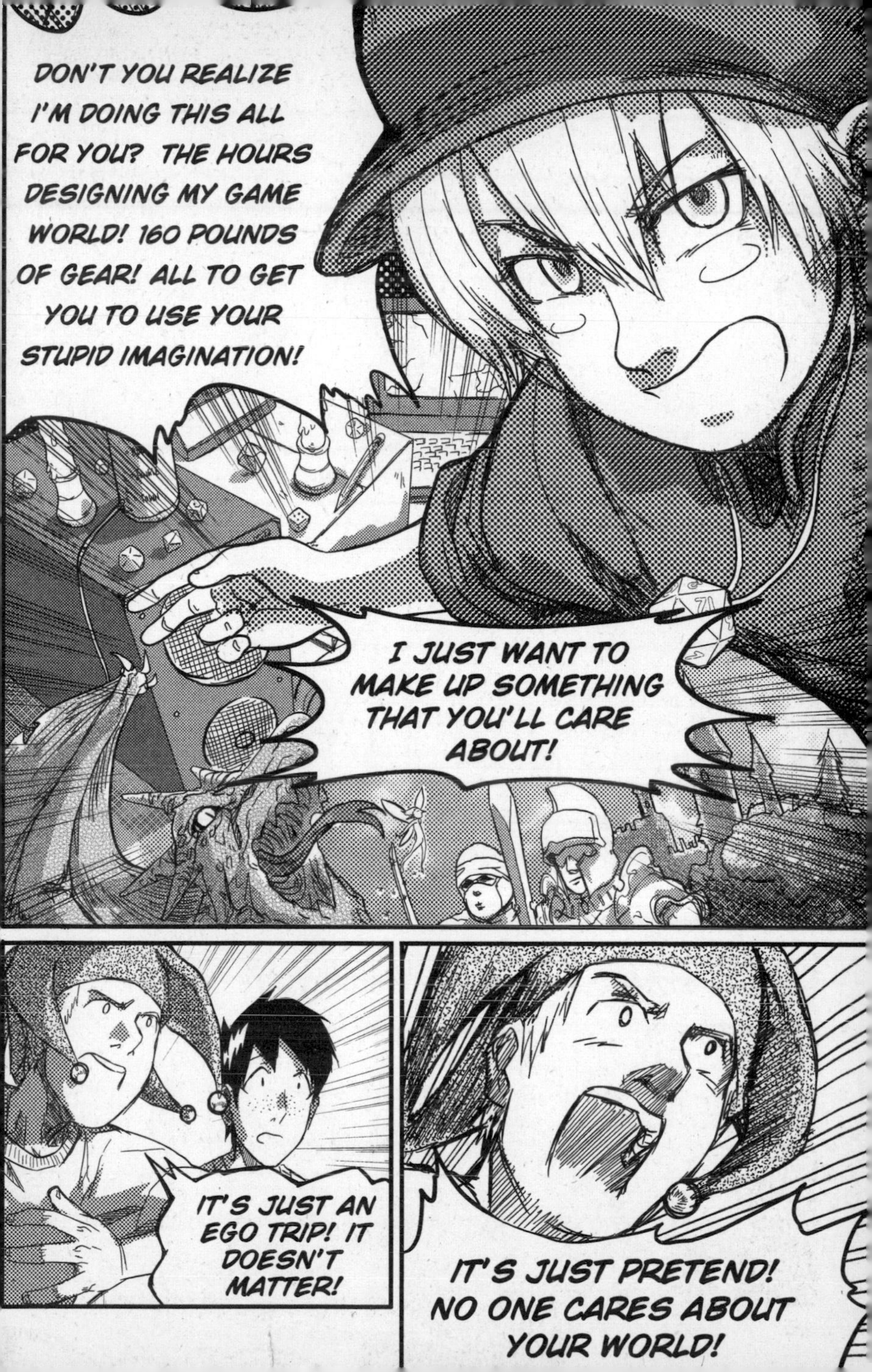
DON'T YOU REALIZE I'M DOING THIS ALL FOR YOU? THE HOURS DESIGNING MY GAME WORLD! 160 POUNDS OF GEAR! ALL TO GET YOU TO USE YOUR STUPID IMAGINATION!
I JUST WANT TO MAKE UP SOMETHING THAT YOU'LL CARE ABOUT!
IT'S JUST AN EGO TRIP! IT DOESN'T MATTER!
IT'S JUST PRETEND! NO ONE CARES ABOUT YOUR WORLD!

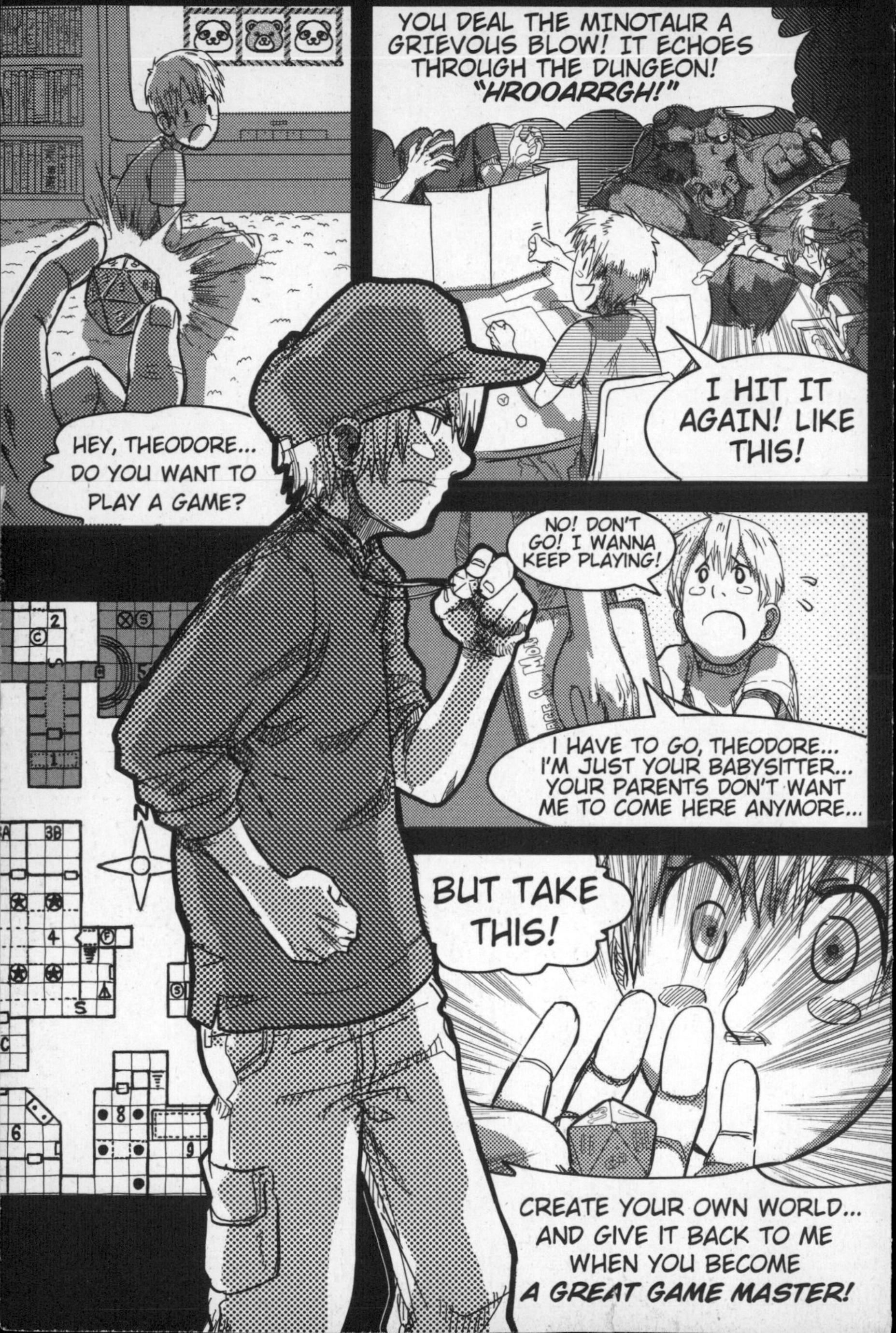
HEY, THEODORE... DO YOU WANT TO PLAY A GAME?
YOU DEAL THE MINOTAUR A GRIEVOUS BLOW! IT ECHOES THROUGH THE DUNGEON! "HROOARRGH!"
I HIT IT AGAIN! LIKE THIS!
NO! DON'T GO! I WANNA KEEP PLAYING!
I HAVE TO GO, THEODORE... I'M JUST YOUR BABYSITTER... YOUR PARENTS DON'T WANT ME TO COME HERE ANYMORE...
BUT TAKE THIS!
CREATE YOUR OWN WORLD... AND GIVE IT BACK TO ME WHEN YOU BECOME A GREAT GAME MASTER!

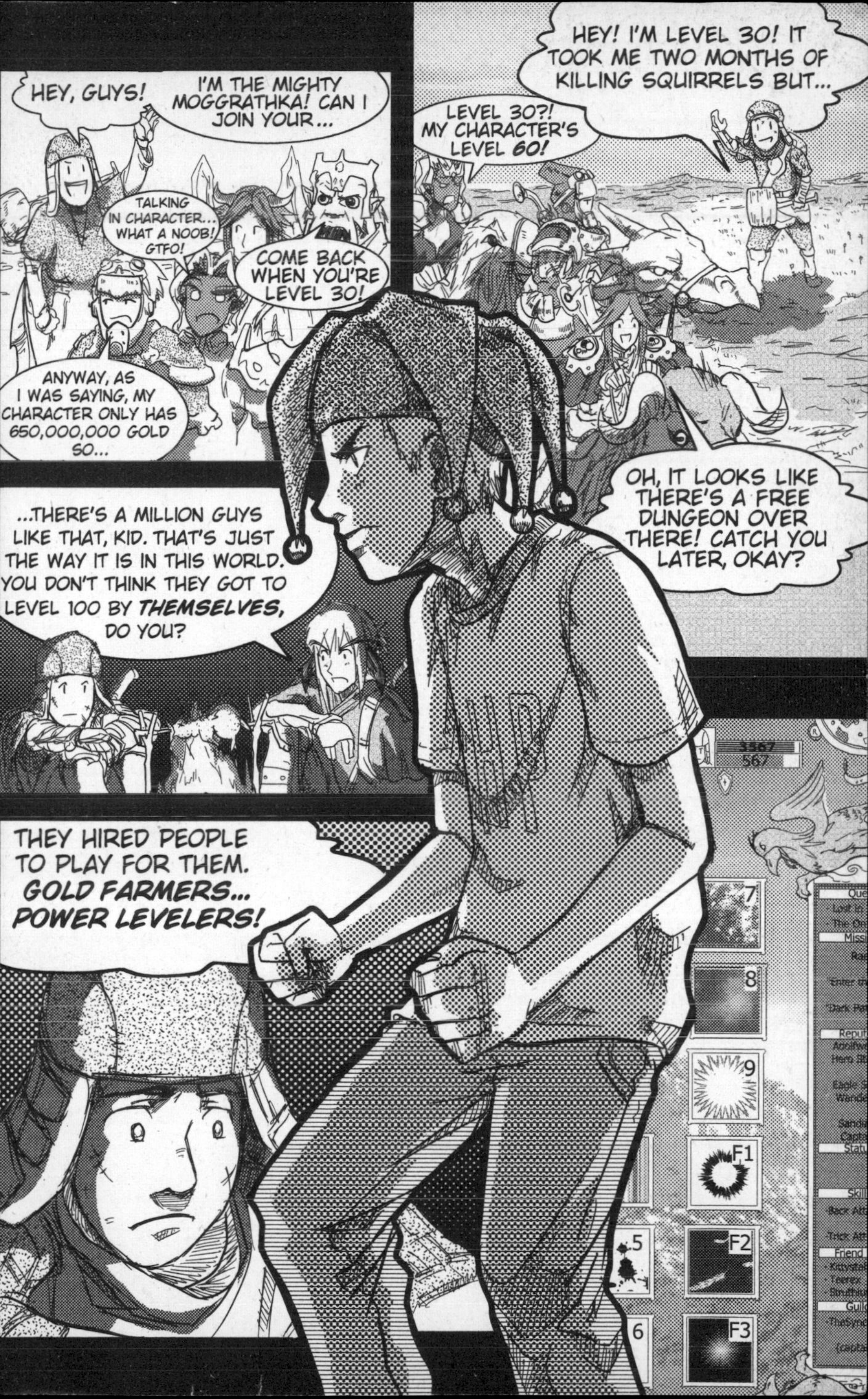
HEY, GUYS!
I'M THE MIGHTY MOGGRATHKA! CAN I JOIN YOUR...
TALKING IN CHARACTER... WHAT A NOOB! GTFO!
COME BACK WHEN YOU'RE LEVEL 30!
ANYWAY, AS I WAS SAYING, MY CHARACTER ONLY HAS 650,000,000 GOLD SO...
HEY! I'M LEVEL 30! IT TOOK ME TWO MONTHS OF KILLING SQUIRRELS BUT...
LEVEL 30?! MY CHARACTER'S LEVEL 60!
OH, IT LOOKS LIKE THERE'S A FREE DUNGEON OVER THERE! CATCH YOU LATER, OKAY?
...THERE'S A MILLION GUYS LIKE THAT, KID. THAT'S JUST THE WAY IT IS IN THIS WORLD. YOU DON'T THINK THEY GOT TO LEVEL 100 BY THEMSELVES, DO YOU?
THEY HIRED PEOPLE TO PLAY FOR THEM. GOLD FARMERS... POWER LEVELERS!

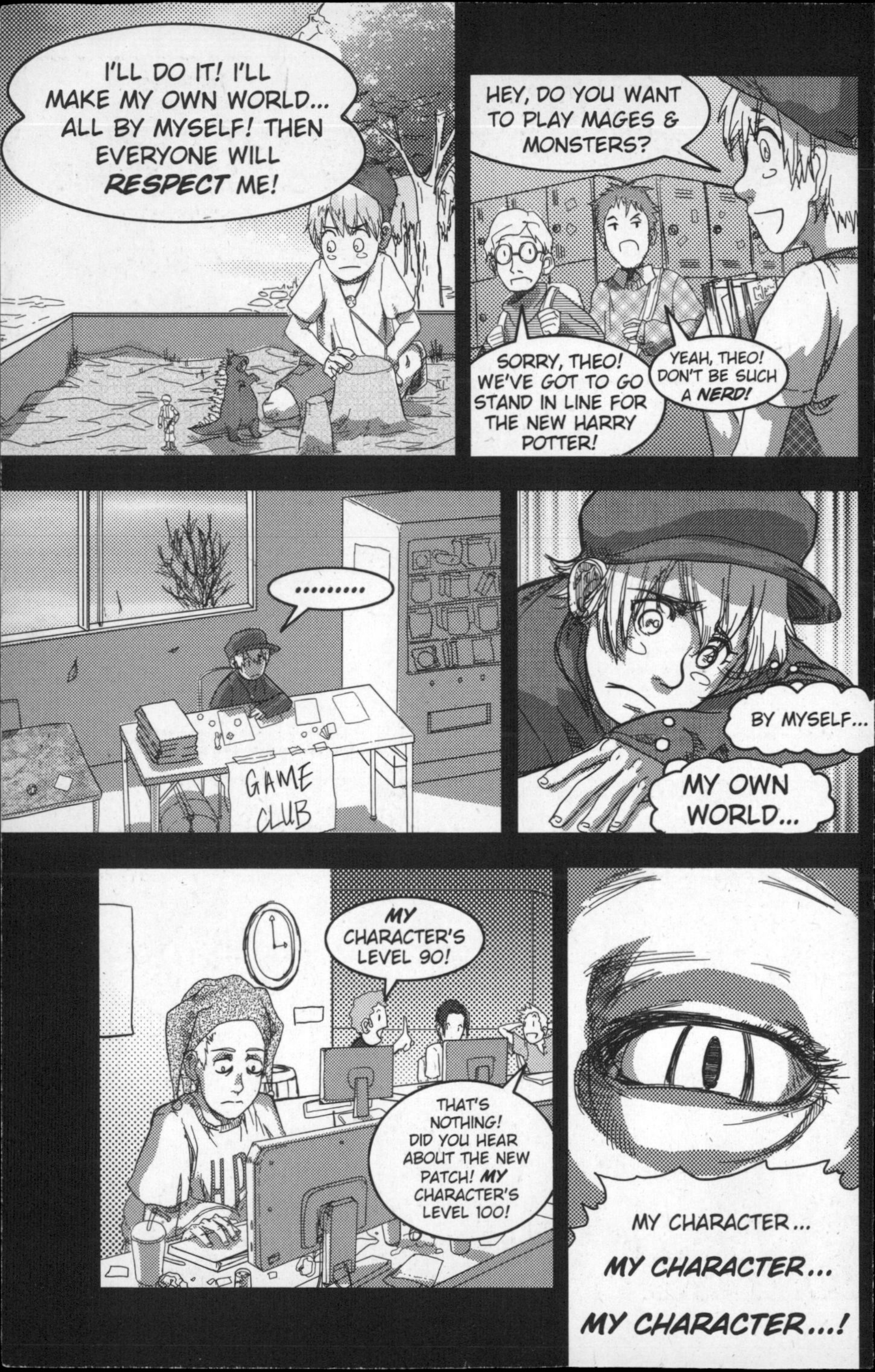
I'LL DO IT! I'LL MAKE MY OWN WORLD... ALL BY MYSELF! THEN EVERYONE WILL ***RESPECT*** ME!
HEY, DO YOU WANT TO PLAY MAGES & MONSTERS?
SORRY, THEO! WE'VE GOT TO GO STAND IN LINE FOR THE NEW HARRY POTTER!
YEAH, THEO! DON'T BE SUCH A ***NERD!***
....
GAME CLUB
BY MYSELF...
MY OWN WORLD...
MY CHARACTER'S LEVEL 90!
THAT'S NOTHING! DID YOU HEAR ABOUT THE NEW PATCH! ***MY*** CHARACTER'S LEVEL 100!
MY CHARACTER...
MY CHARACTER...
MY CHARACTER...!

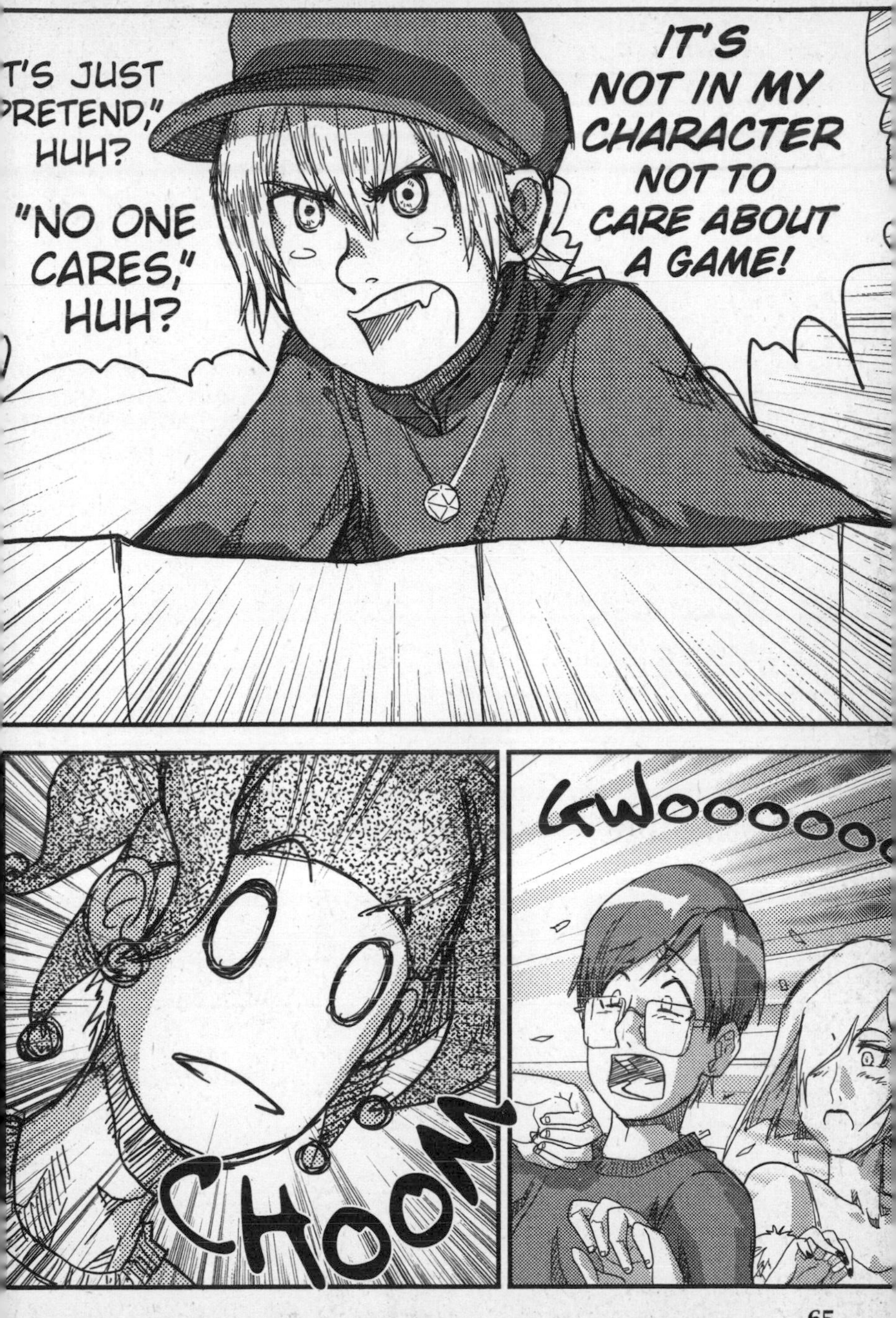
T'S JUST
RETEND," HUH?
"NO ONE CARES," HUH?
IT'S NOT IN MY CHARACTER NOT TO CARE ABOUT A GAME!
CHOOM
GWOOOOOO

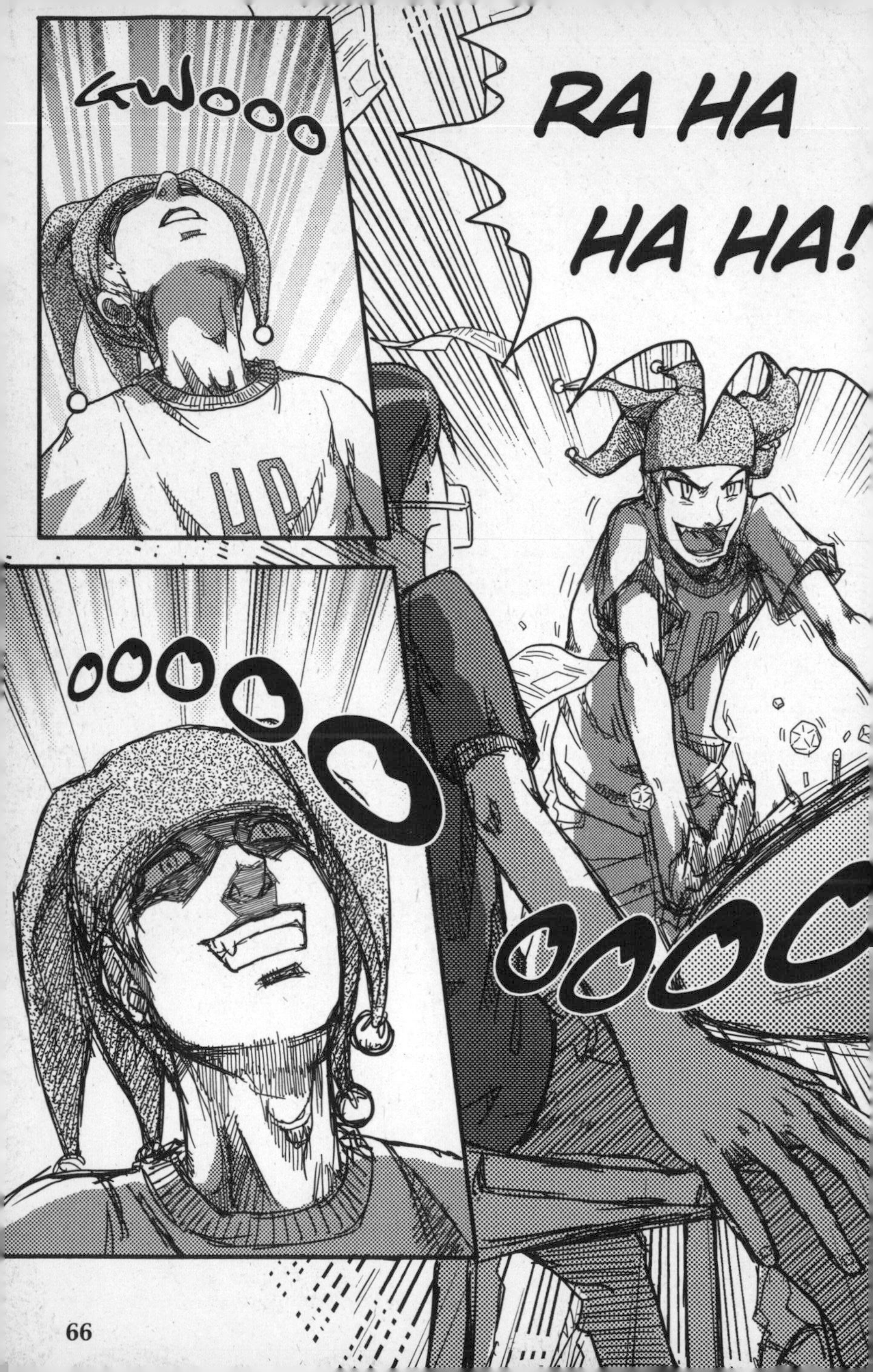
GWOOO
OOOOOO
RA HA HA HA!
OOOC

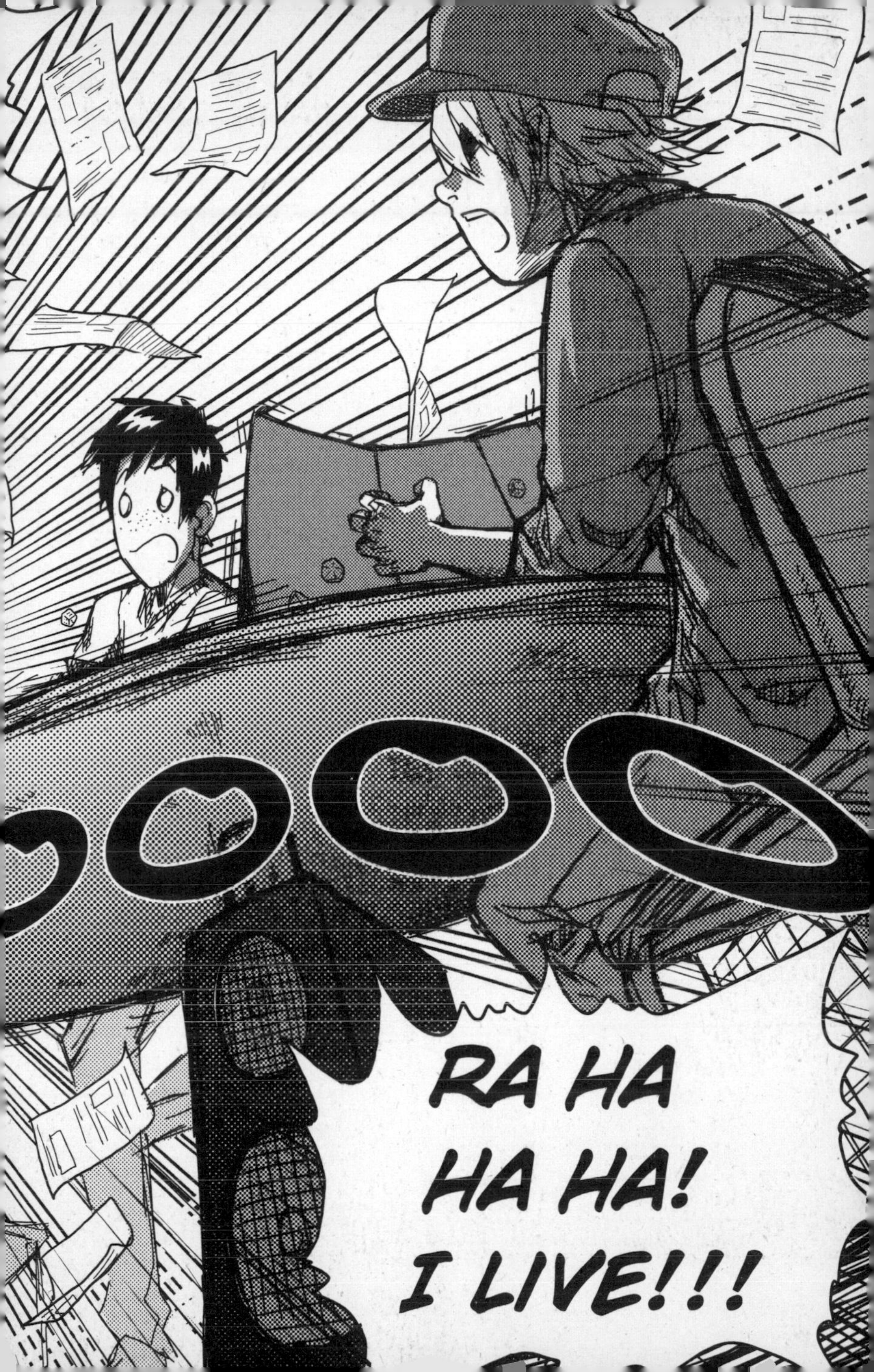
RA HA HA HA! I LIVE!!!

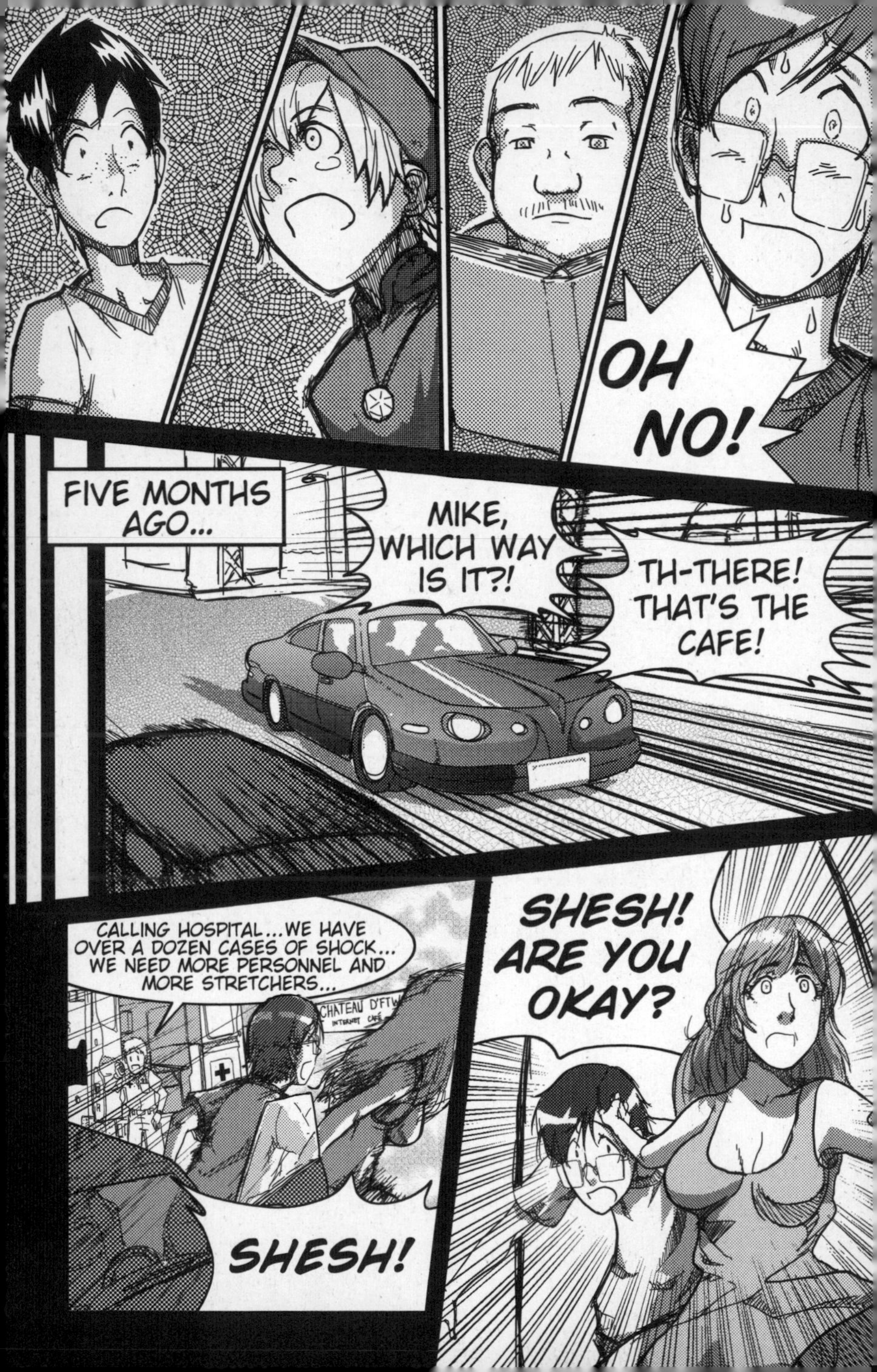
OH NO!
FIVE MONTHS AGO...
MIKE, WHICH WAY IS IT?!
TH-THERE! THAT'S THE CAFE!
CALLING HOSPITAL...WE HAVE OVER A DOZEN CASES OF SHOCK... WE NEED MORE PERSONNEL AND MORE STRETCHERS...
CHATEAU D'FTW
INTERNET CAFÉ
SHESH!
SHESH! ARE YOU OKAY?

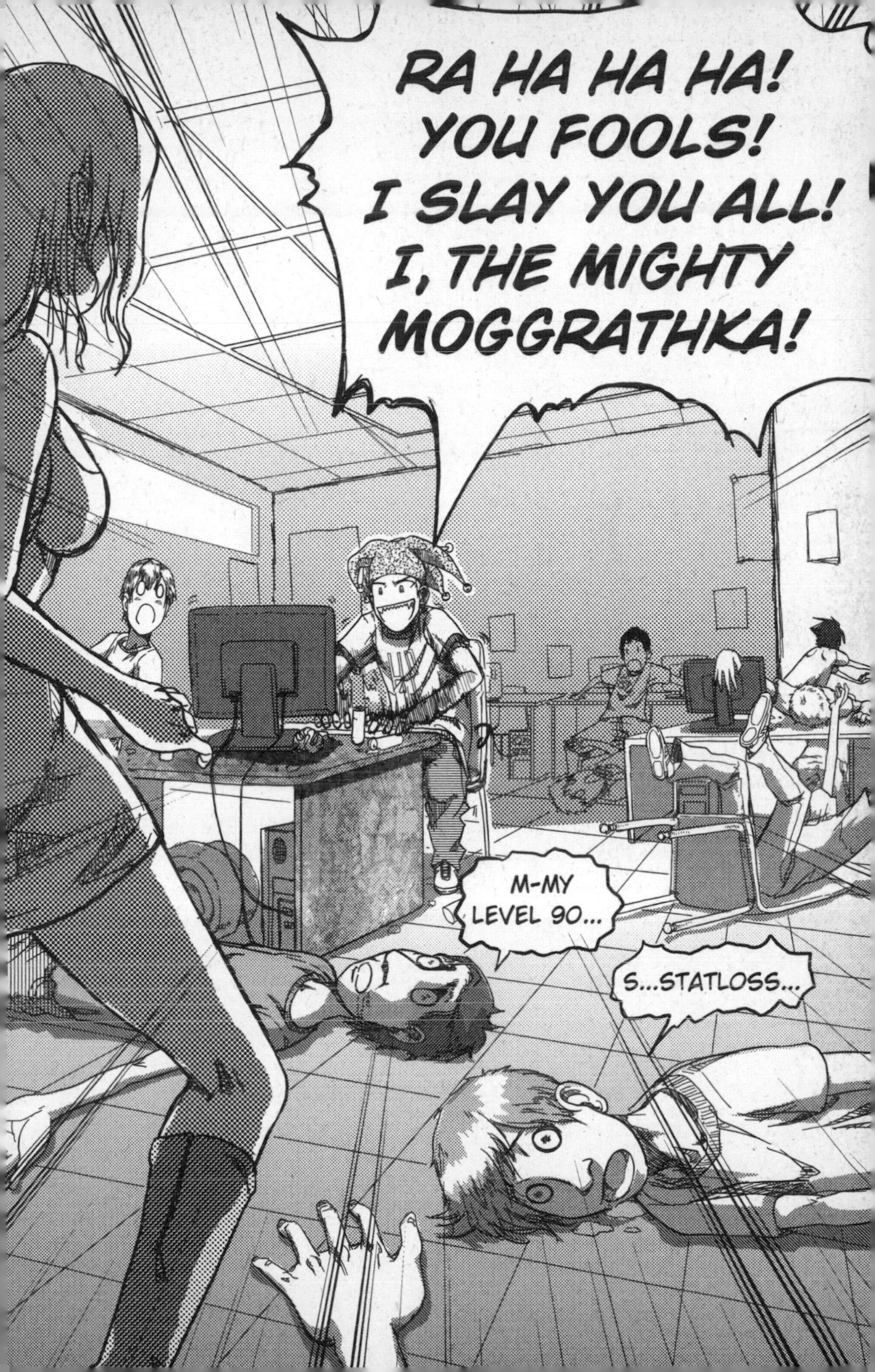
RA HA HA HA! YOU FOOLS! I SLAY YOU ALL! I, THE MIGHTY MOGGRATHKA!
M-MY LEVEL 90...
S...STATLOSS...

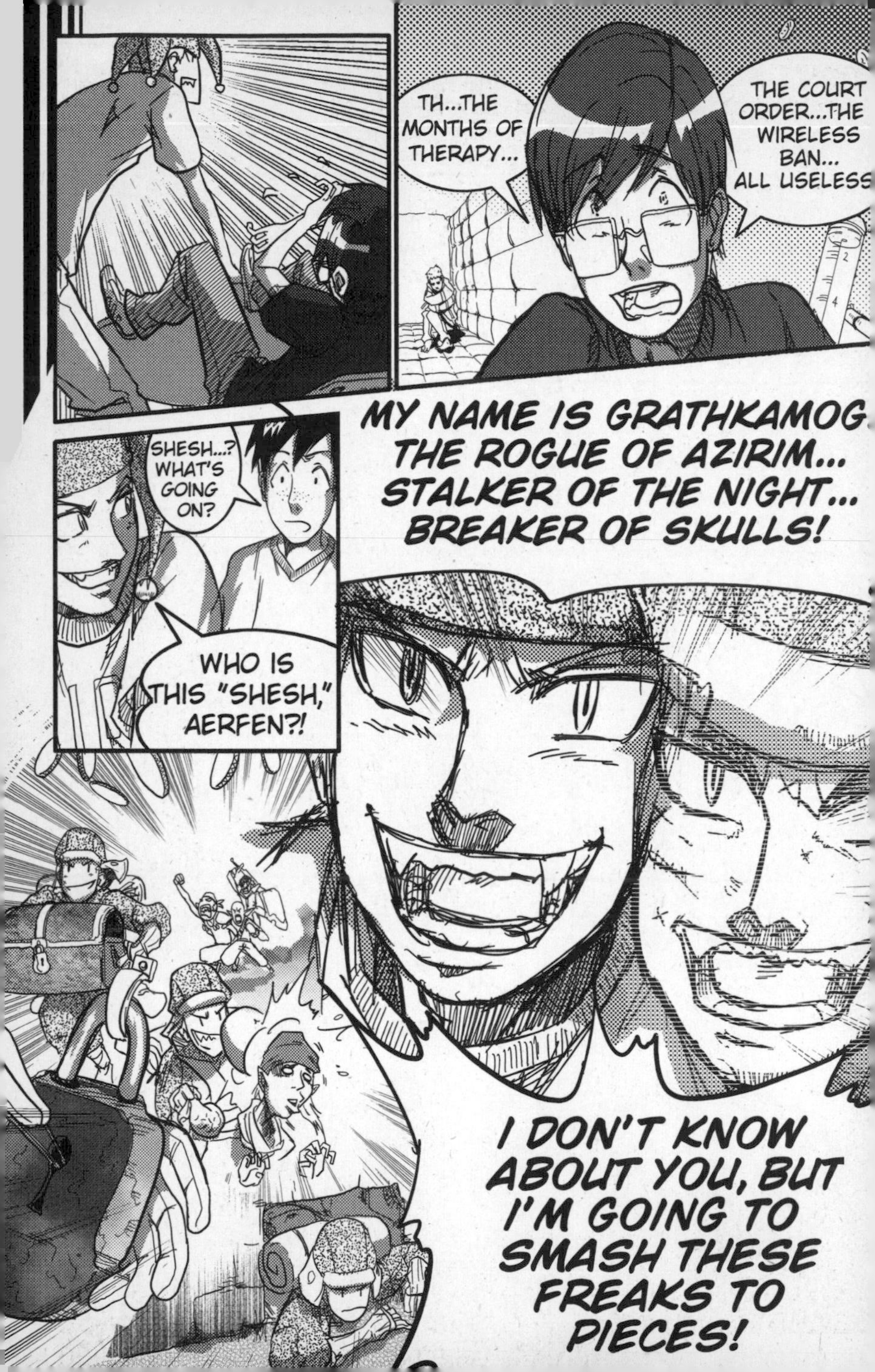
TH...THE MONTHS OF THERAPY...
THE COURT ORDER...THE WIRELESS BAN... ALL USELESS
SHESH...? WHAT'S GOING ON?
WHO IS THIS "SHESH," AERFEN?!
MY NAME IS GRATHKAMOG. THE ROGUE OF AZIRIM... STALKER OF THE NIGHT... BREAKER OF SKULLS!
I DON'T KNOW ABOUT YOU, BUT I'M GOING TO SMASH THESE FREAKS TO PIECES!

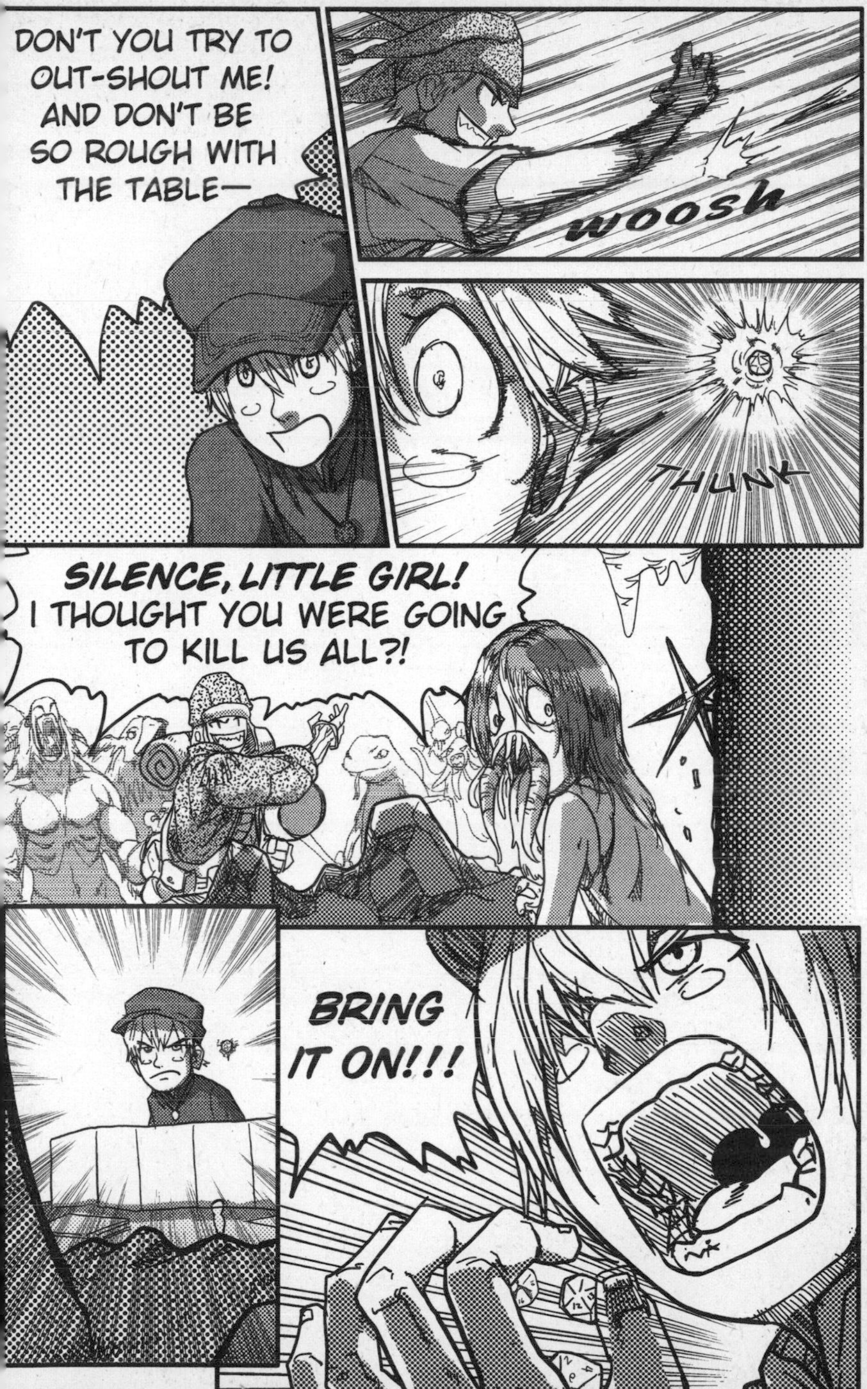
DON'T YOU TRY TO OUT-SHOUT ME! AND DON'T BE SO ROUGH WITH THE TABLE—
WOOSH
THUNK
SILENCE, LITTLE GIRL! I THOUGHT YOU WERE GOING TO KILL US ALL?!
BRING IT ON!!!

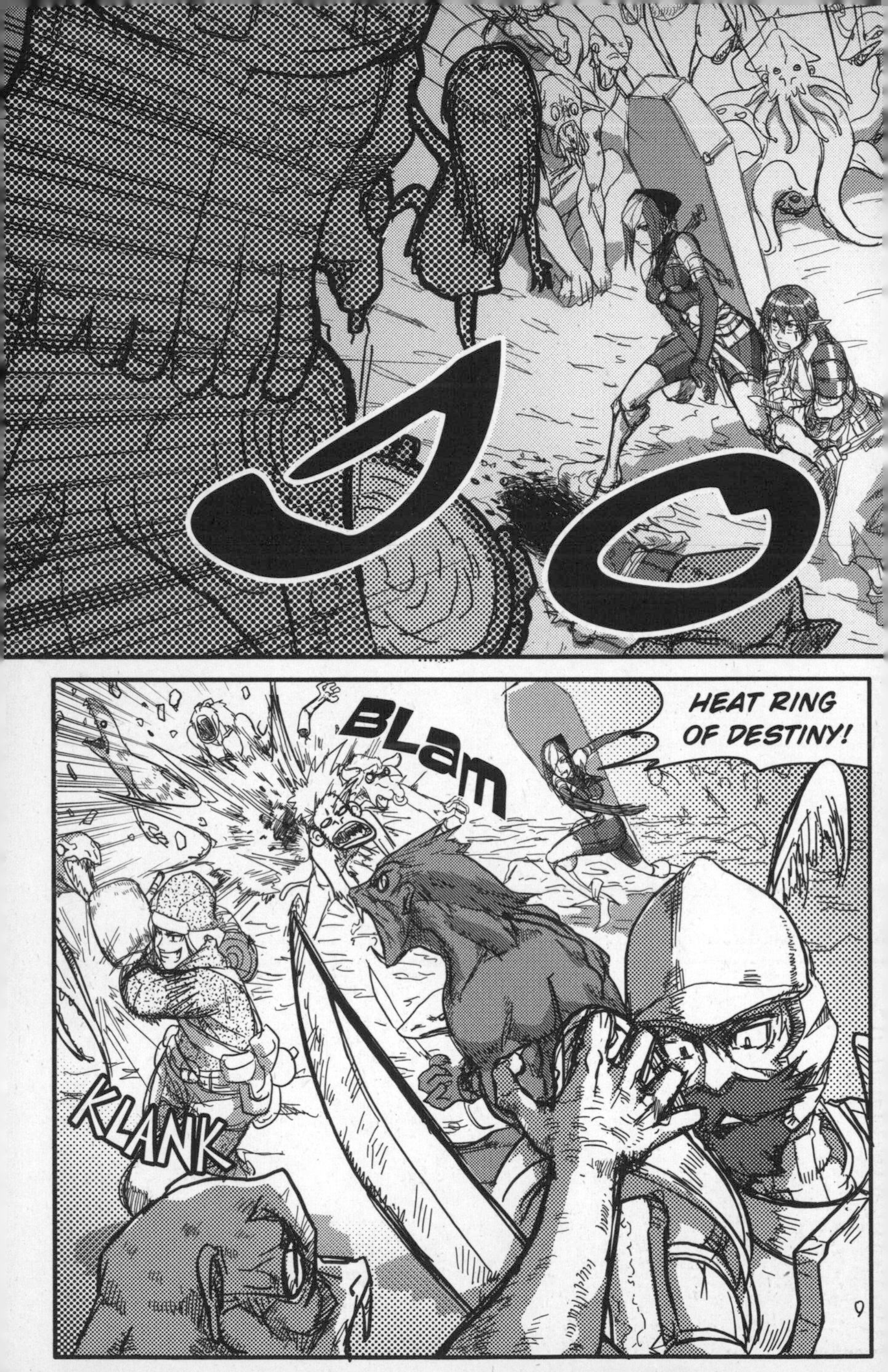
BLAM
HEAT RING
OF DESTINY!
KLANK

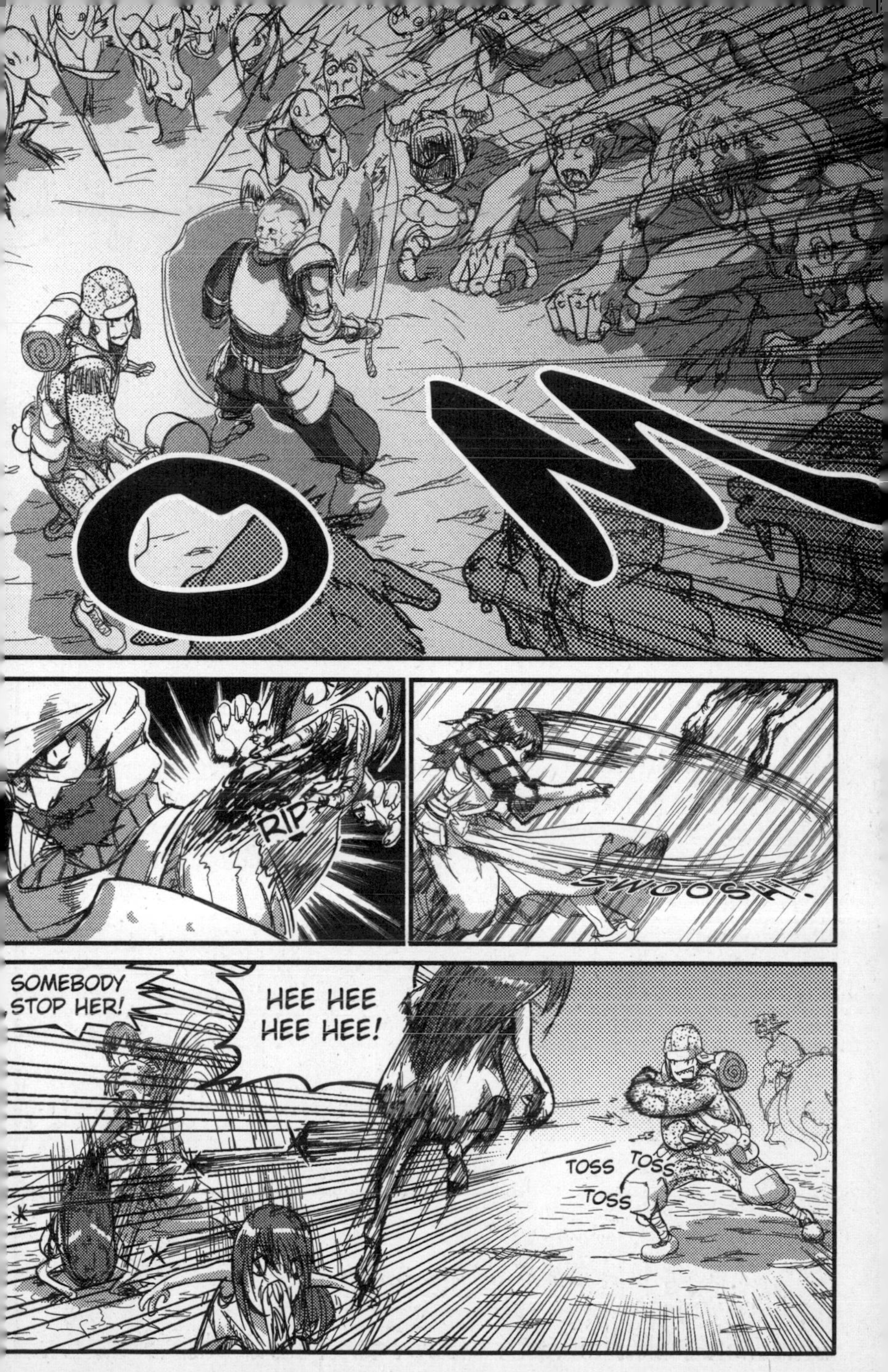
OM
RIP
SWOOSH
SOMEBODY STOP HER!
HEE HEE HEE HEE!
TOSS
TOSS
TOSS

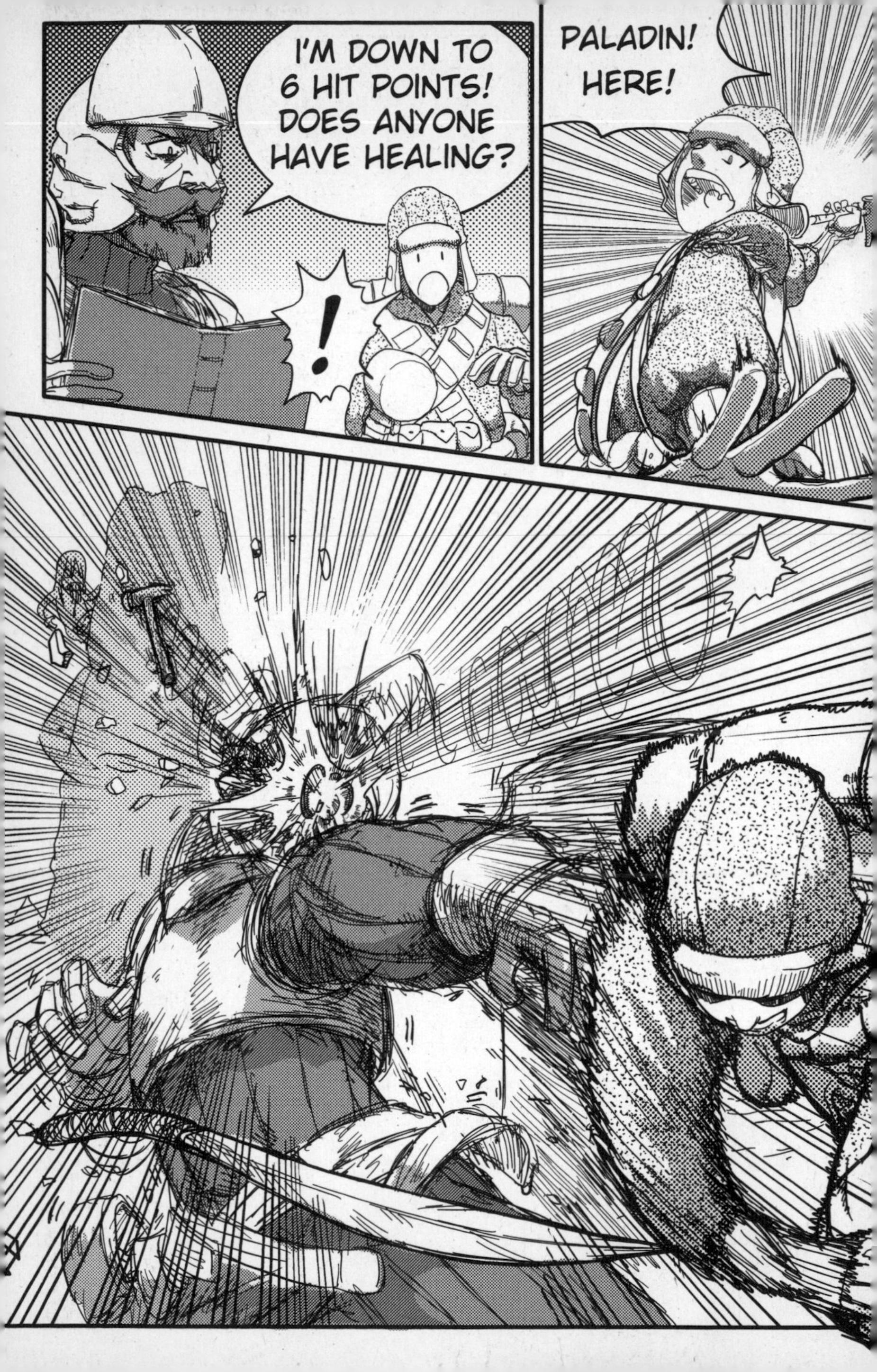
I'M DOWN TO 6 HIT POINTS! DOES ANYONE HAVE HEALING?
!
PALADIN! HERE!

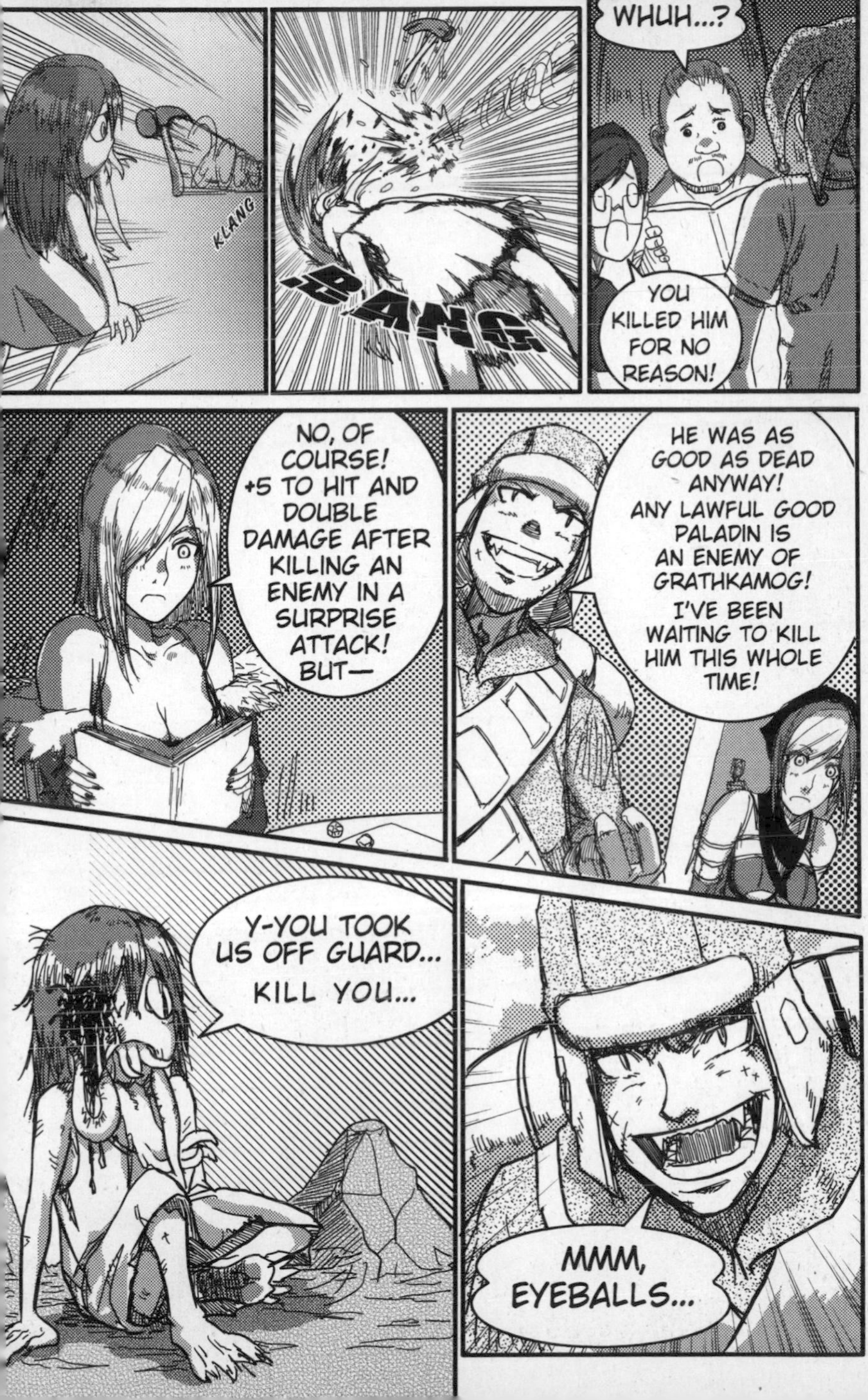
KLANG
BANG
WHUH...?
YOU KILLED HIM FOR NO REASON!
NO, OF COURSE! +5 TO HIT AND DOUBLE DAMAGE AFTER KILLING AN ENEMY IN A SURPRISE ATTACK! BUT—
HE WAS AS GOOD AS DEAD ANYWAY! ANY LAWFUL GOOD PALADIN IS AN ENEMY OF GRATHKAMOG!
I'VE BEEN WAITING TO KILL HIM THIS WHOLE TIME!
Y-YOU TOOK US OFF GUARD... KILL YOU...
MMM, EYEBALLS...

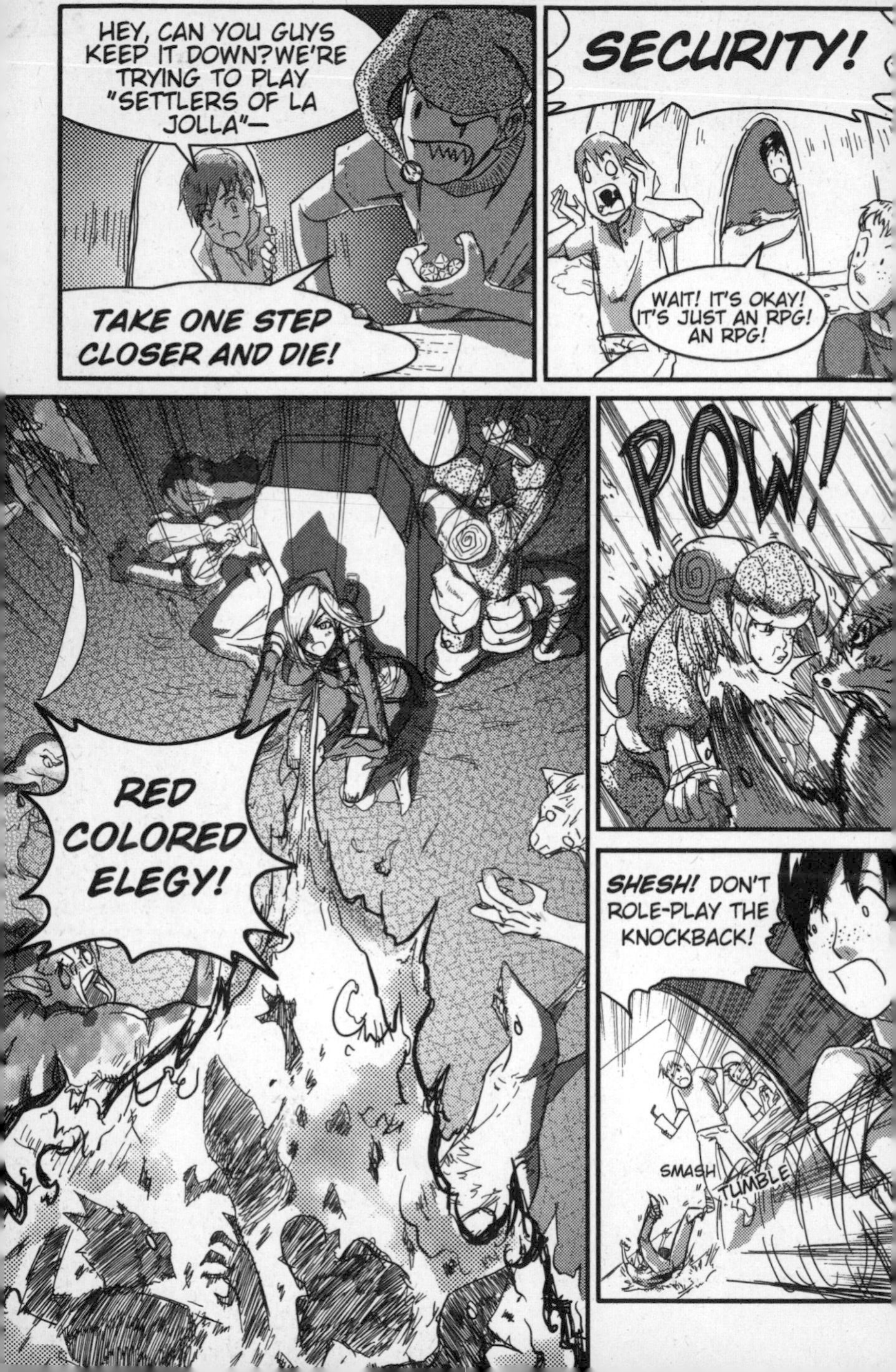
HEY, CAN YOU GUYS KEEP IT DOWN? WE'RE TRYING TO PLAY "SETTLERS OF LA JOLLA"—
TAKE ONE STEP CLOSER AND DIE!
SECURITY!
WAIT! IT'S OKAY! IT'S JUST AN RPG! AN RPG!
RED COLORED ELEGY!
POW!
SHESH! DON'T ROLE-PLAY THE KNOCKBACK!
SMASH
TUMBLE

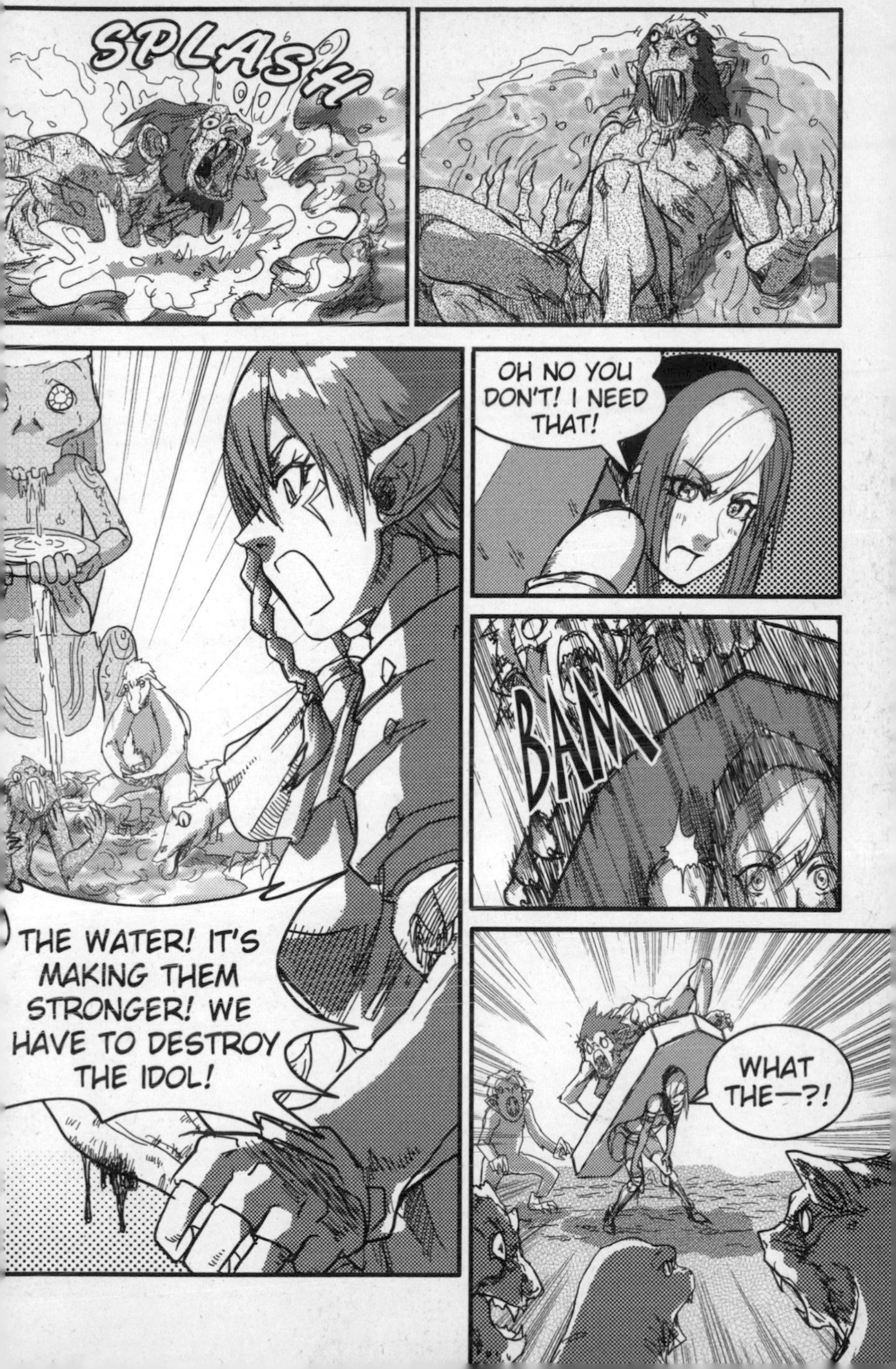
SPLASH
THE WATER! IT'S MAKING THEM STRONGER! WE HAVE TO DESTROY THE IDOL!
OH NO YOU DON'T! I NEED THAT!
BAM
WHAT THE—?!

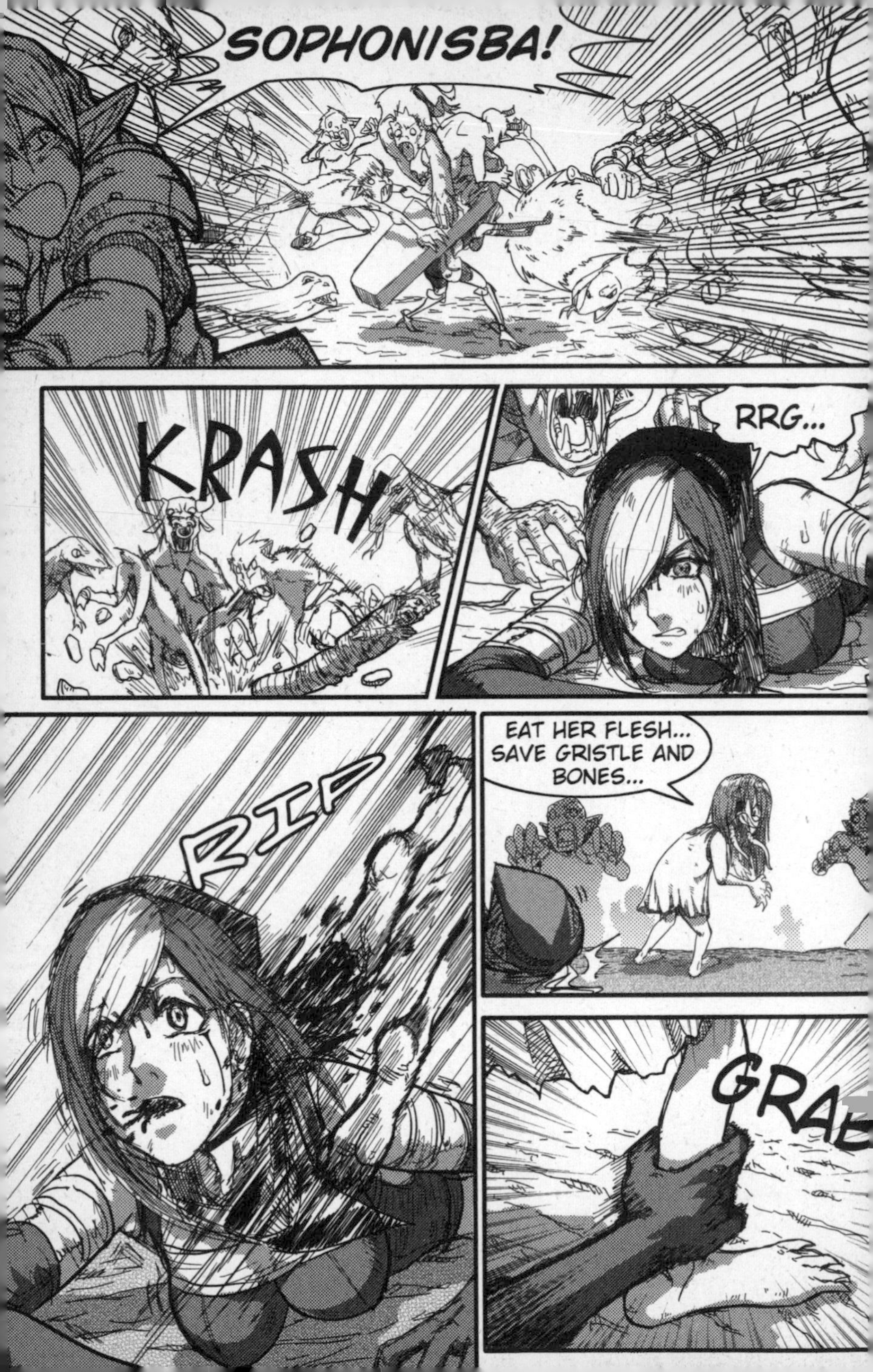
SOPHONISBA!
KRASH
RRG...
RIP
EAT HER FLESH... SAVE GRISTLE AND BONES...
GRAB

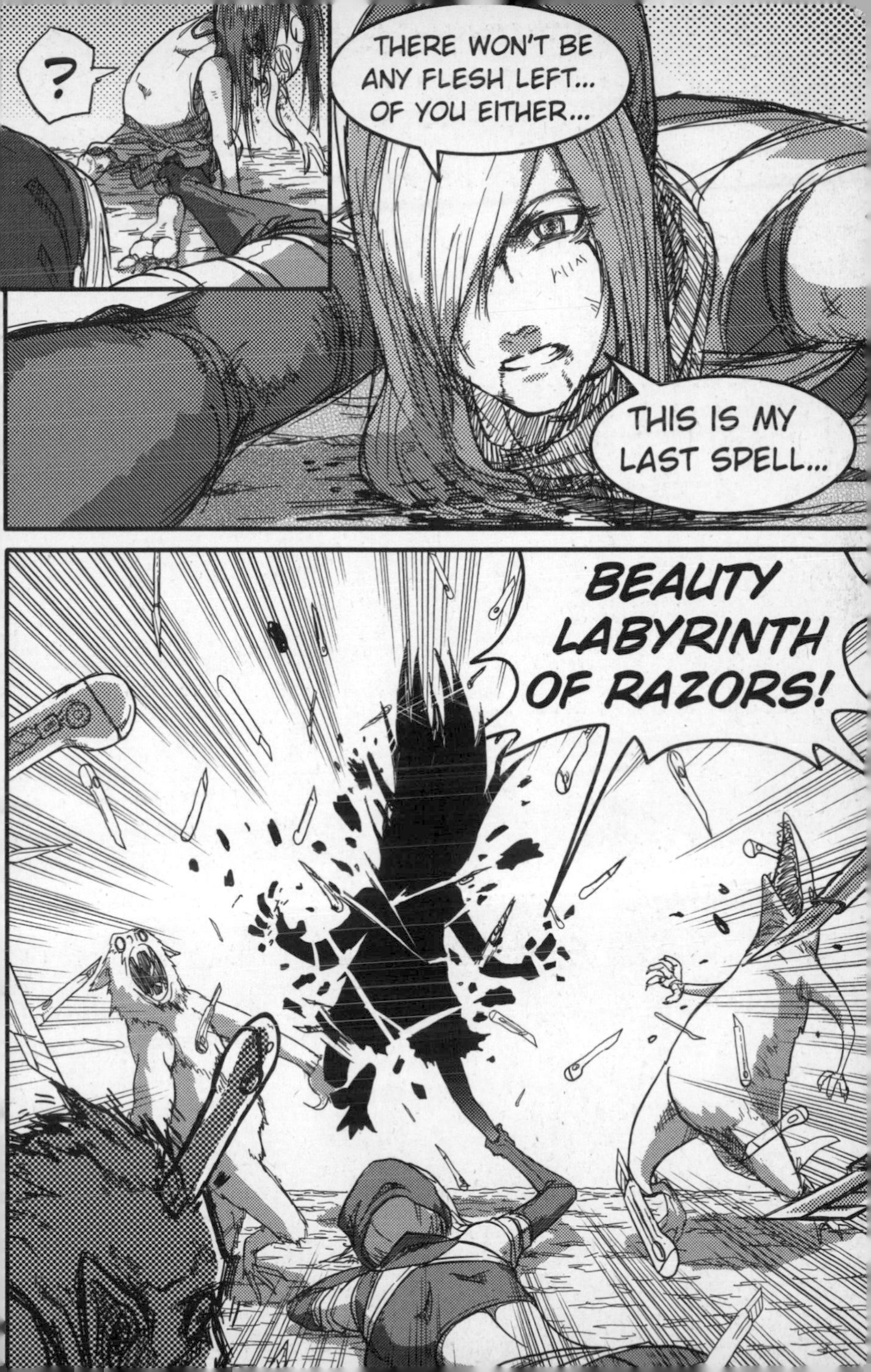
?
THERE WON'T BE ANY FLESH LEFT... OF YOU EITHER...
THIS IS MY LAST SPELL...
BEAUTY LABYRINTH OF RAZORS!

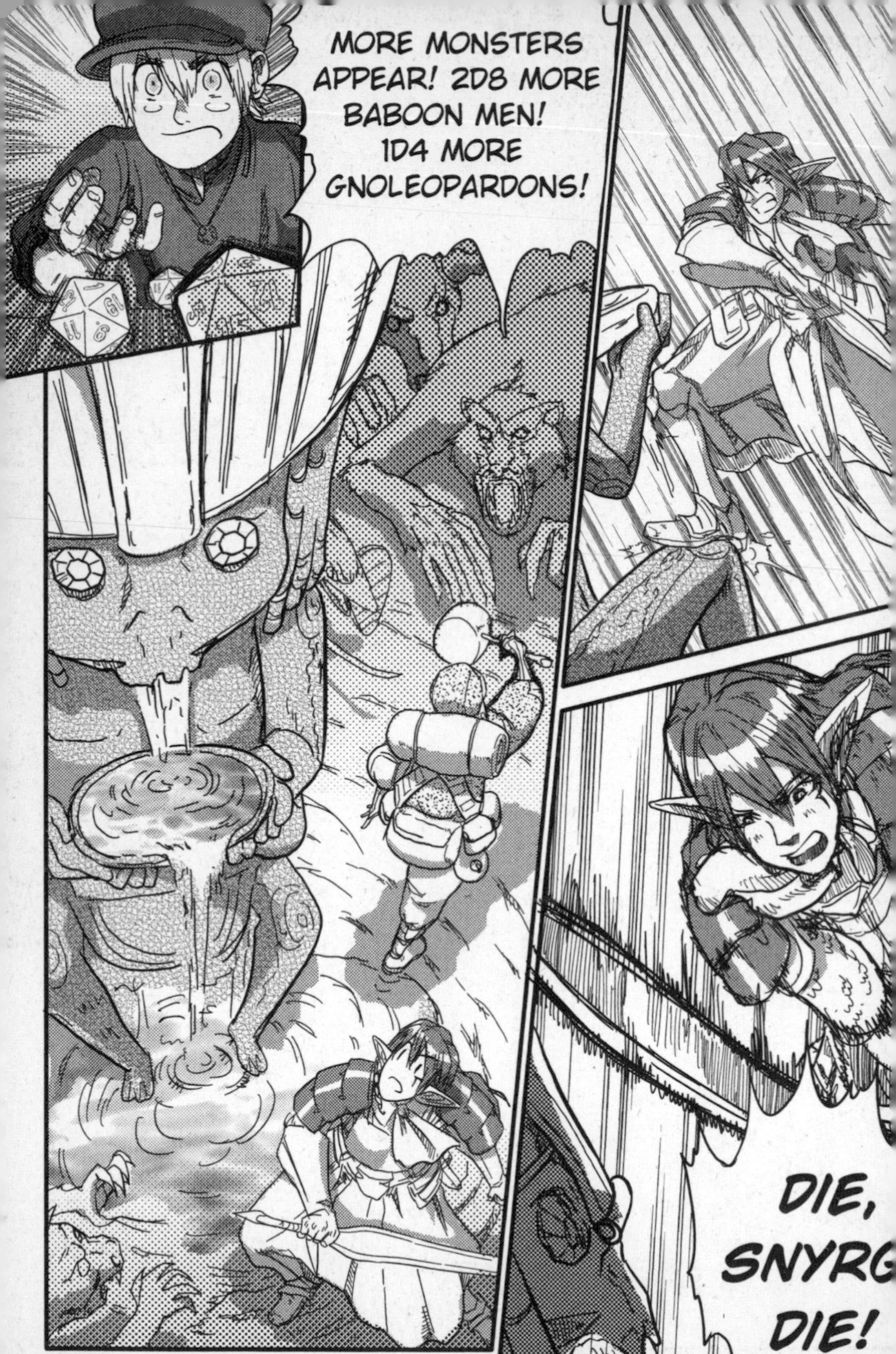
MORE MONSTERS APPEAR! 2D8 MORE BABOON MEN! 1D4 MORE GNOLEOPARDONS!
DIE, SNYRG DIE!

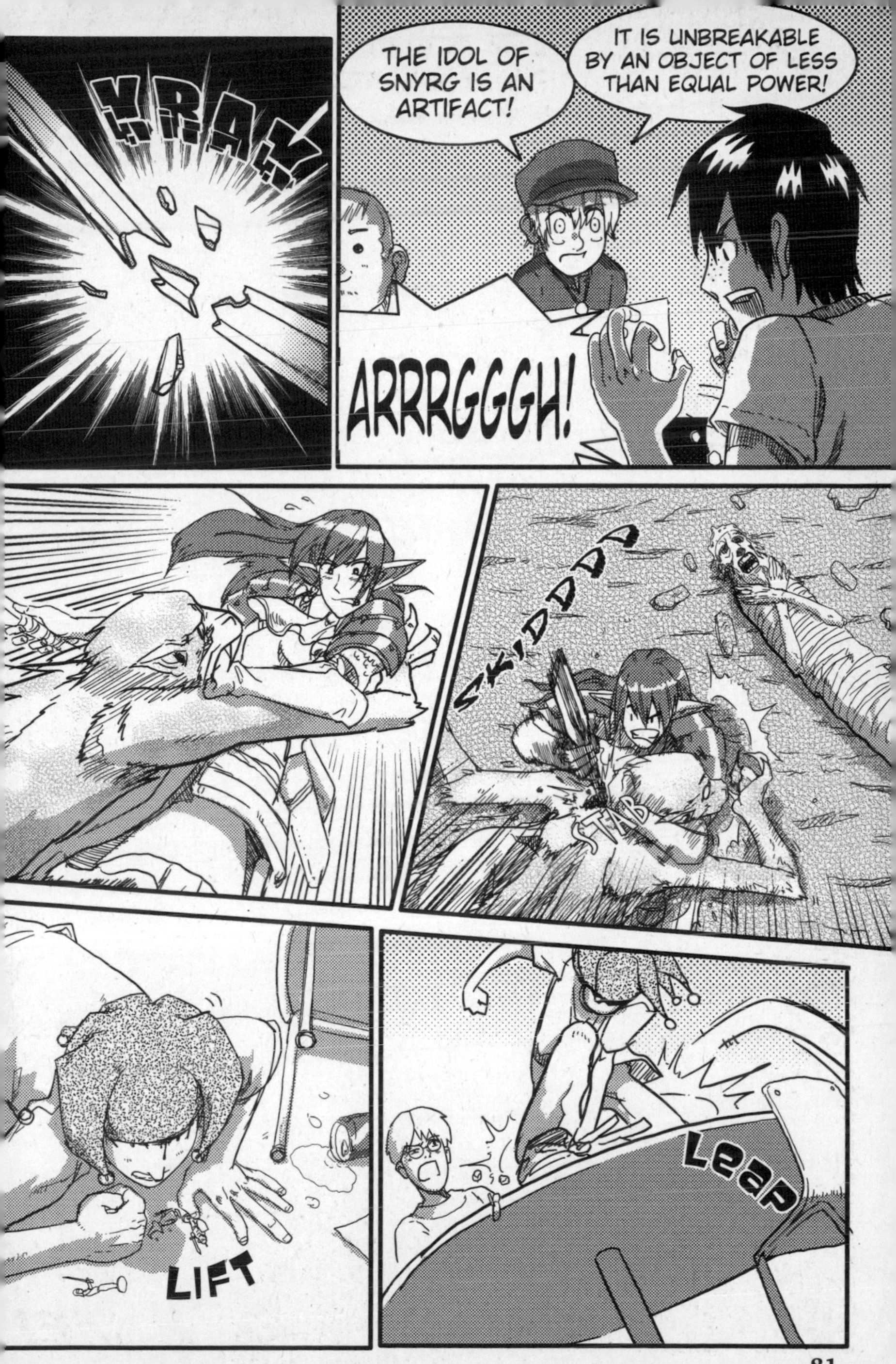
KRAK
THE IDOL OF SNYRG IS AN ARTIFACT!
IT IS UNBREAKABLE BY AN OBJECT OF LESS THAN EQUAL POWER!
ARRRGGGH!
SKIDDDD
STAB
LIFT
Leap

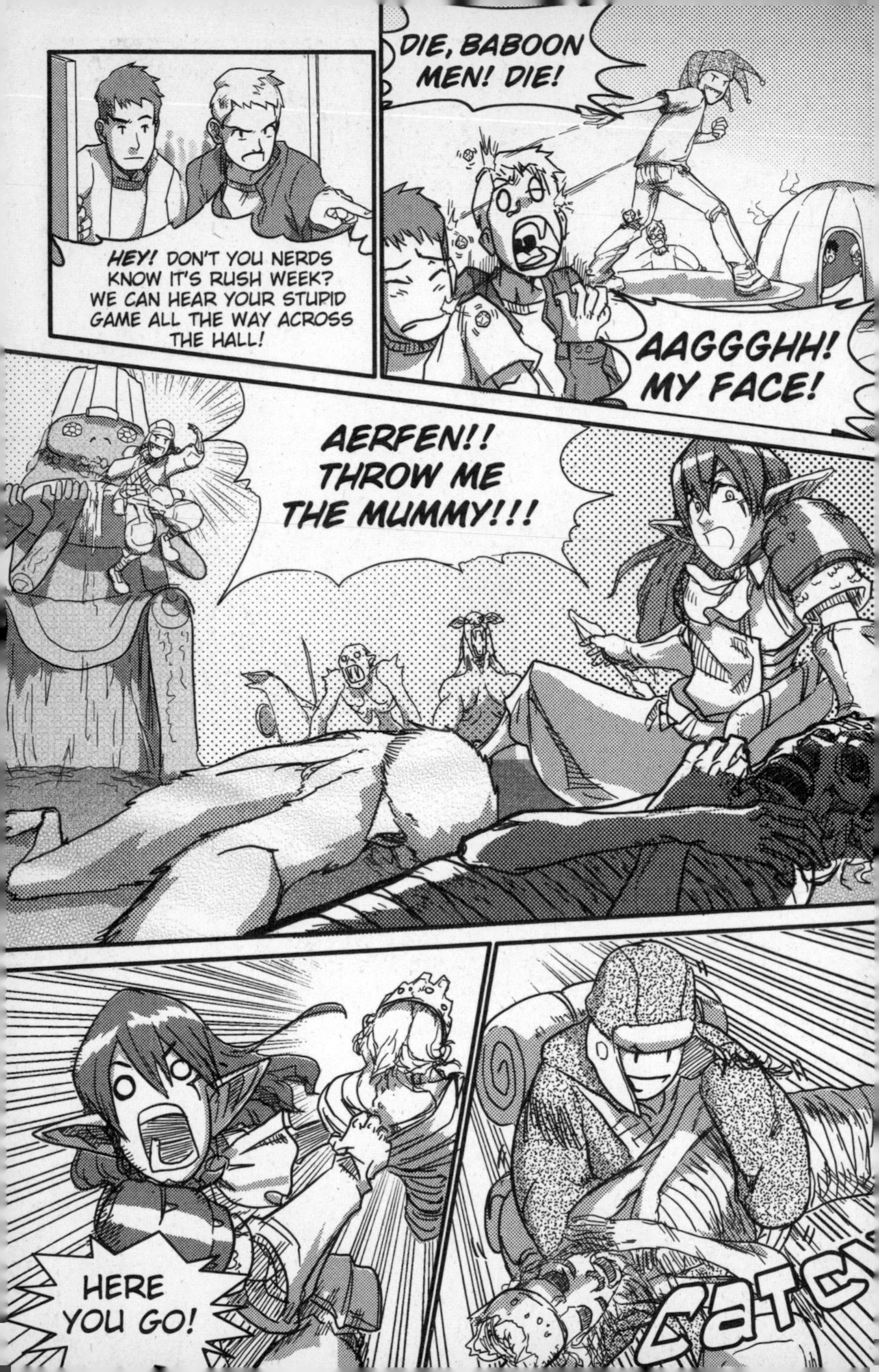
HEY! DON'T YOU NERDS KNOW IT'S RUSH WEEK? WE CAN HEAR YOUR STUPID GAME ALL THE WAY ACROSS THE HALL!
DIE, BABOON MEN! DIE!
AAGGGHH! MY FACE!
AERFEN!! THROW ME THE MUMMY!!!
HERE YOU GO!

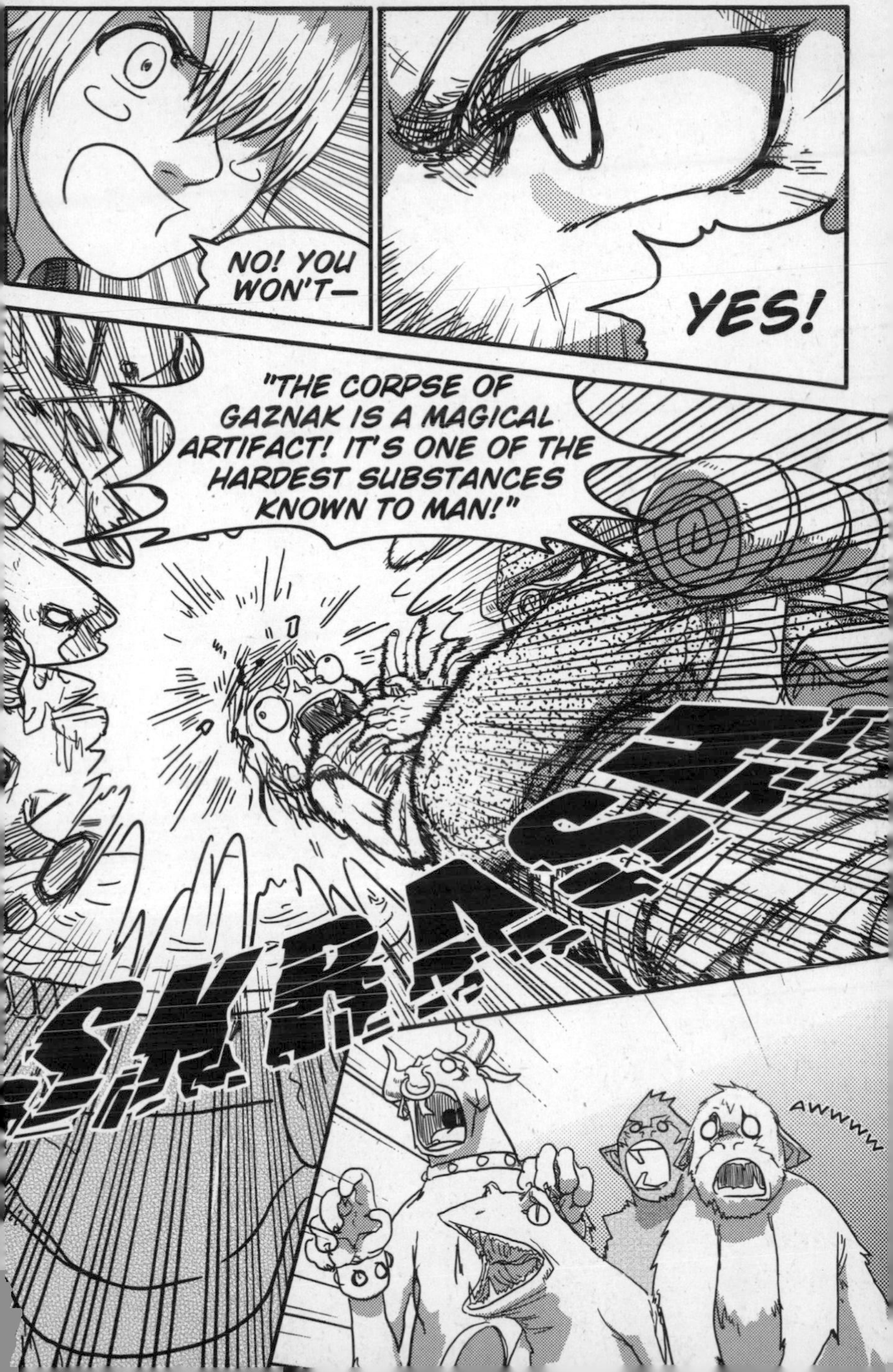
NO! YOU WON'T—
YES!
"THE CORPSE OF GAZNAK IS A MAGICAL ARTIFACT! IT'S ONE OF THE HARDEST SUBSTANCES KNOWN TO MAN!"
SKRASH!!
AWWWW

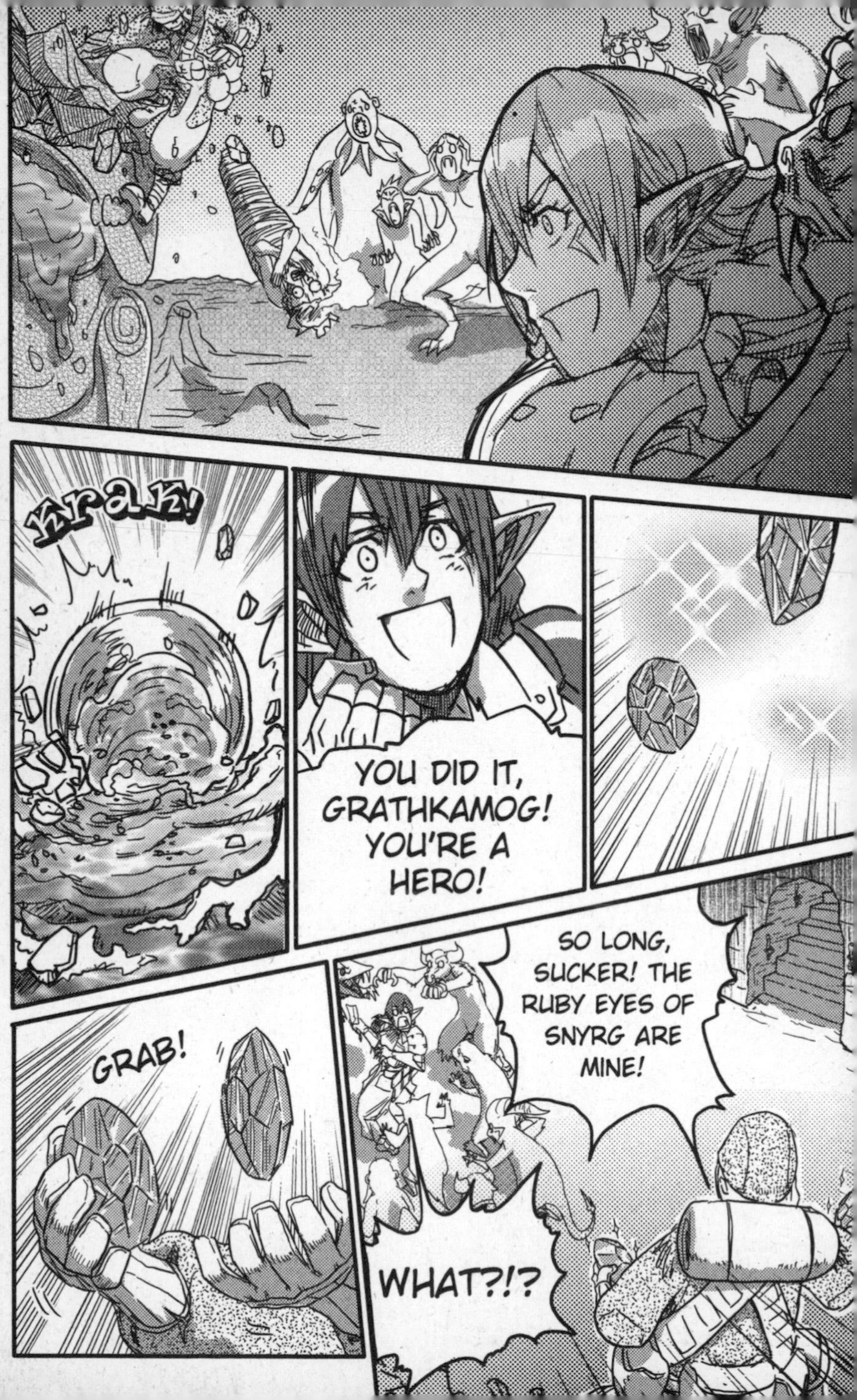
KRAK!
YOU DID IT, GRATHKAMOG! YOU'RE A HERO!
GRAB!
SO LONG, SUCKER! THE RUBY EYES OF SNYRG ARE MINE!
WHAT?!?

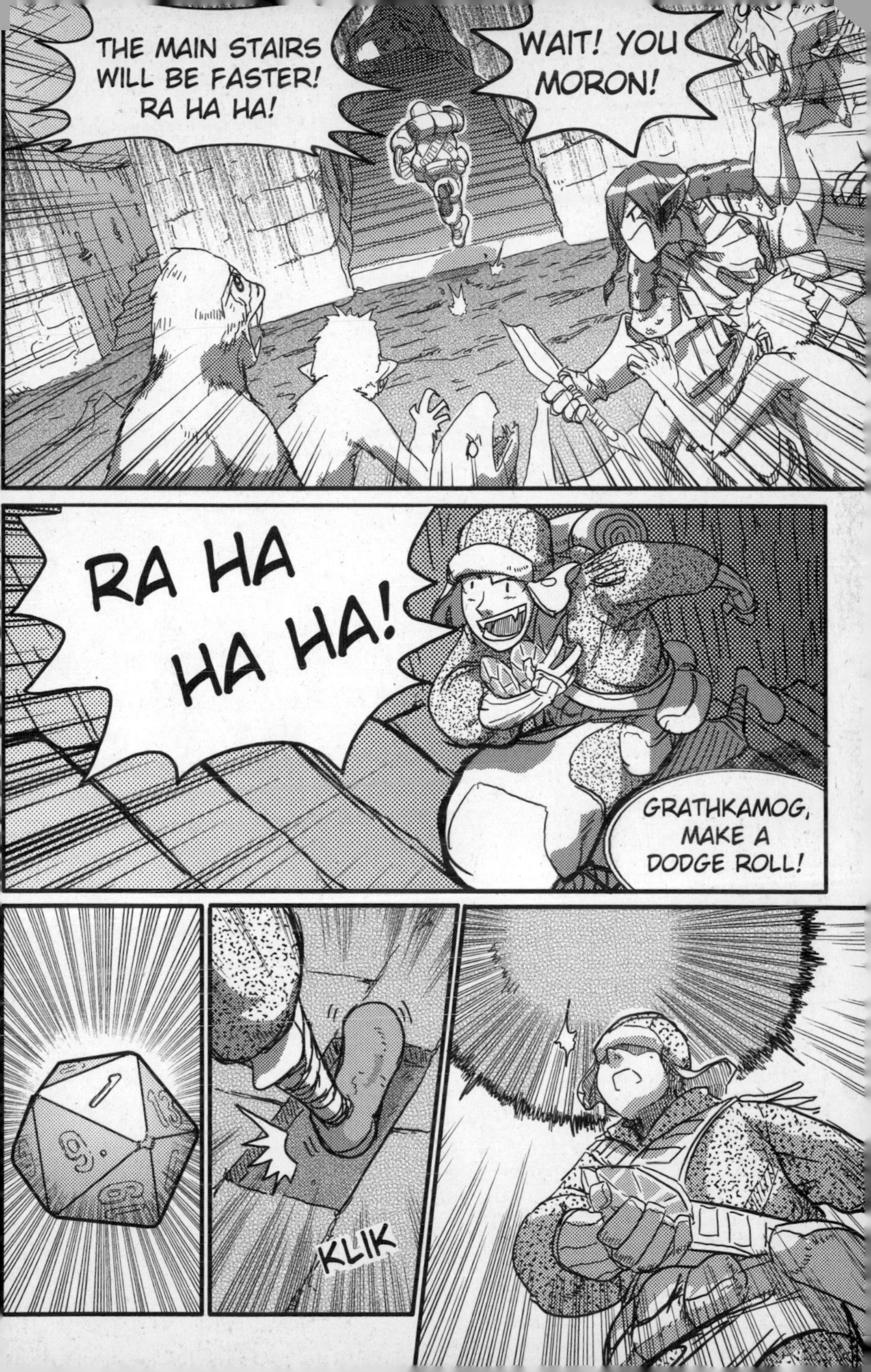
THE MAIN STAIRS WILL BE FASTER! RA HA HA!
WAIT! YOU MORON!
RA HA HA HA!
GRATHKAMOG, MAKE A DODGE ROLL!
KLIK

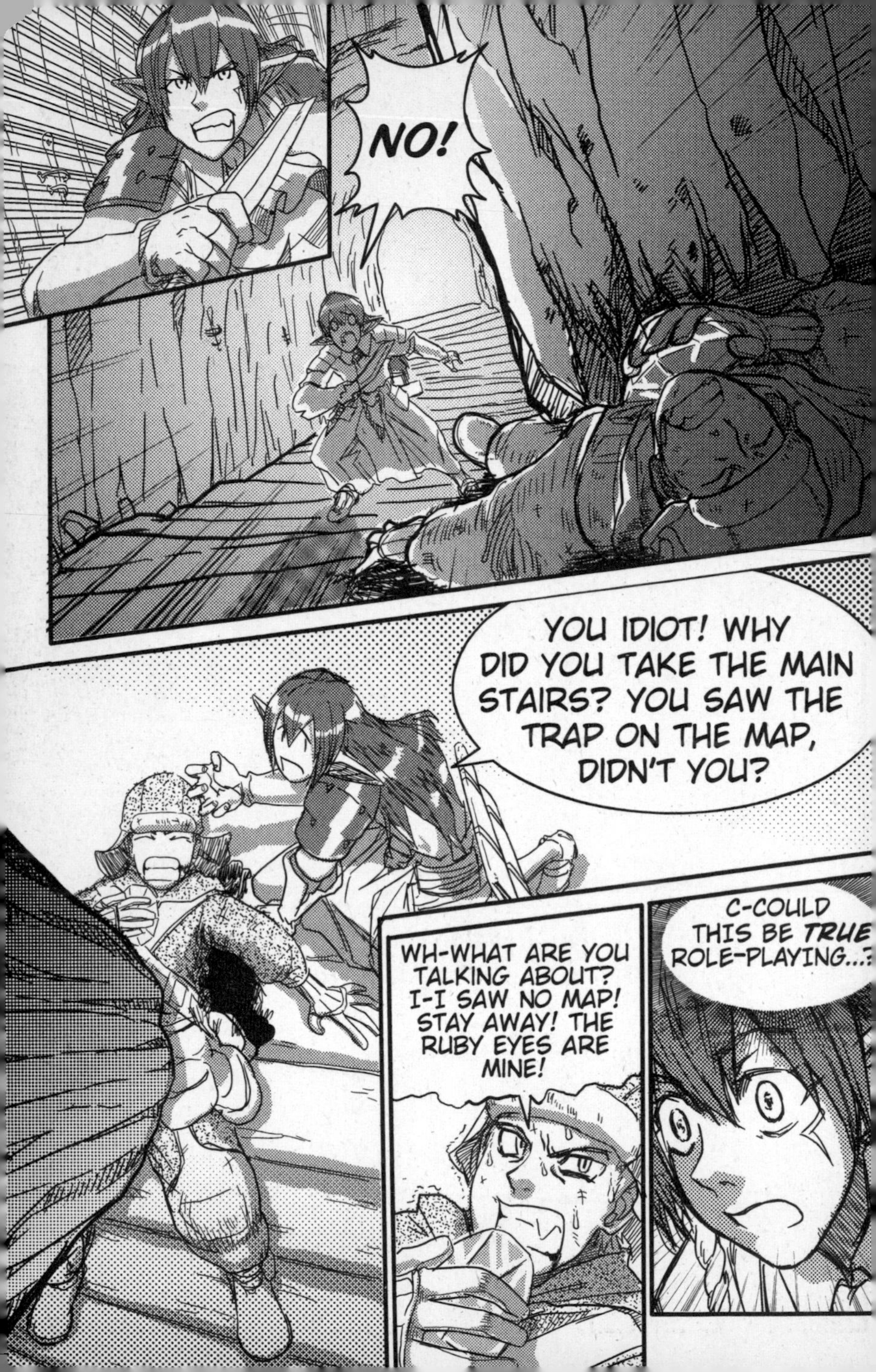
NO!
YOU IDIOT! WHY DID YOU TAKE THE MAIN STAIRS? YOU SAW THE TRAP ON THE MAP, DIDN'T YOU?
WH-WHAT ARE YOU TALKING ABOUT? I-I SAW NO MAP! STAY AWAY! THE RUBY EYES ARE MINE!
C-COULD THIS BE *TRUE* ROLE-PLAYING...?

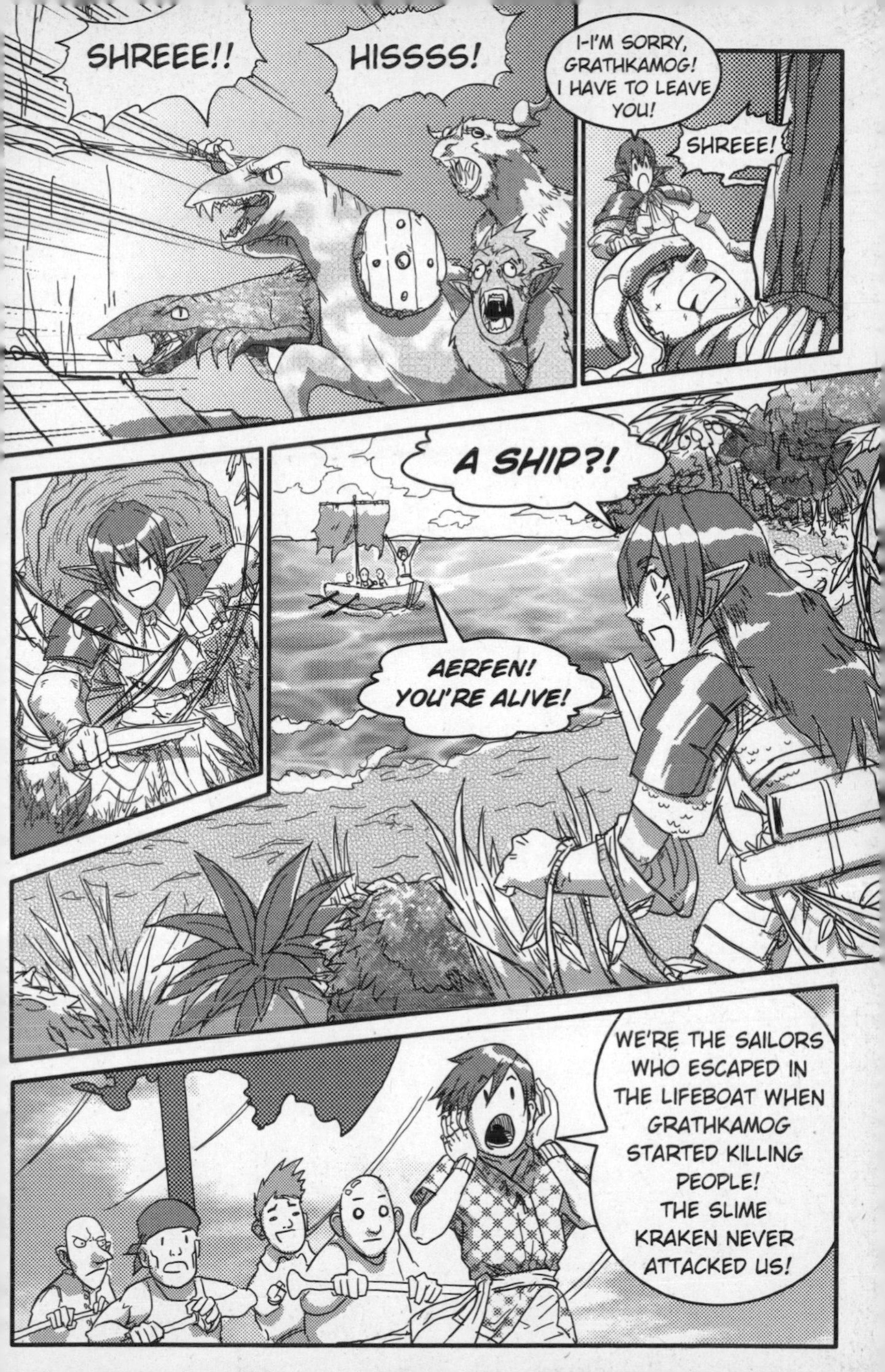
SHREEE!!
HISSSS!
I-I'M SORRY, GRATHKAMOG! I HAVE TO LEAVE YOU!
SHREEE!
A SHIP?!
AERFEN! YOU'RE ALIVE!
WE'RE THE SAILORS WHO ESCAPED IN THE LIFEBOAT WHEN GRATHKAMOG STARTED KILLING PEOPLE! THE SLIME KRAKEN NEVER ATTACKED US!

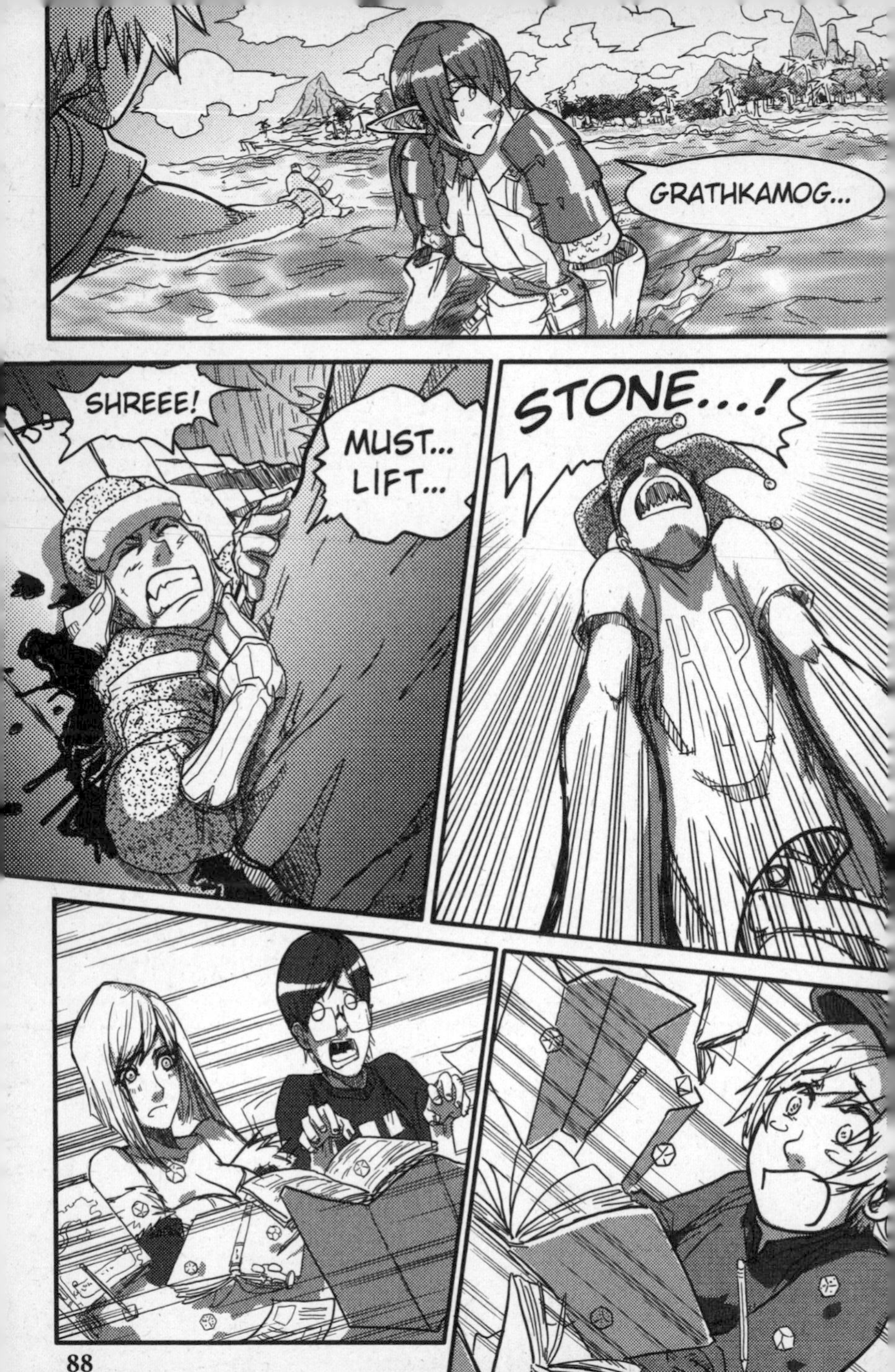
GRATHKAMOG...
SHREEE!
MUST... LIFT...
STONE...!

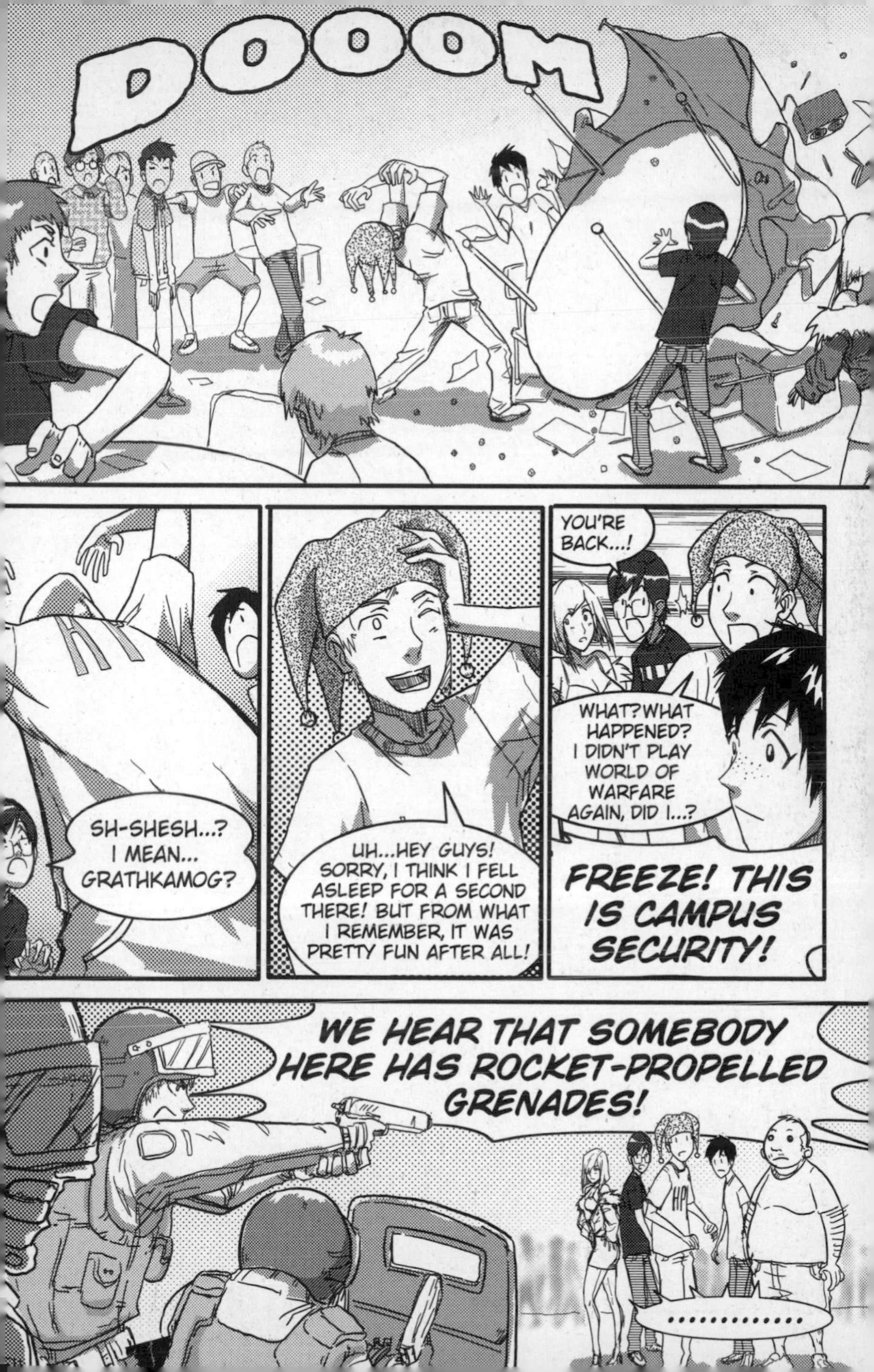
DOOOM
SH-SHESH...? I MEAN... GRATHKAMOG?
UH...HEY GUYS! SORRY, I THINK I FELL ASLEEP FOR A SECOND THERE! BUT FROM WHAT I REMEMBER, IT WAS PRETTY FUN AFTER ALL!
YOU'RE BACK...!
WHAT? WHAT HAPPENED? I DIDN'T PLAY WORLD OF WARFARE AGAIN, DID I...?
FREEZE! THIS IS CAMPUS SECURITY!
WE HEAR THAT SOMEBODY HERE HAS ROCKET-PROPELLED GRENADES!
....

SO...I GUESS YOU THINK I'M "BEATEN"...

ALL MY PROPS... ALL MY GAMING TECHNIQUES... YOU SURPASSED THEM ALL...

H-HEY MAN! I DIDN'T MEAN TO BREAK YOUR STUFF! THINGS JUST GOT OUT OF CONTROL!

YOU'RE THE BEST ROLE-PLAYER I'VE EVER MET! YOU WERE SO INTO IT!

THAT WAS AWESOME!

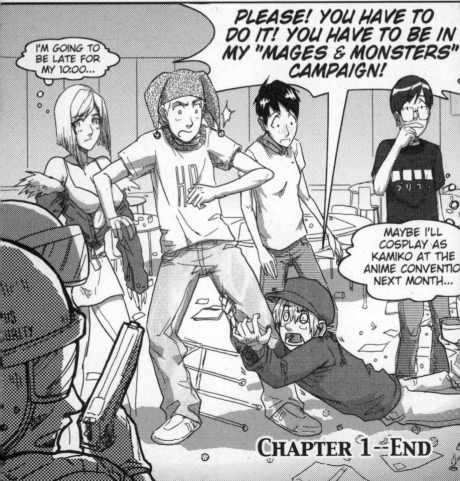

PLEASE! YOU HAVE TO DO IT! YOU HAVE TO BE IN MY "MAGES & MONSTERS" CAMPAIGN!

I'M GOING TO BE LATE FOR MY 10:00...

MAYBE I'LL COSPLAY AS KAMIKO AT THE ANIME CONVENTION NEXT MONTH...

CHAPTER 1—END

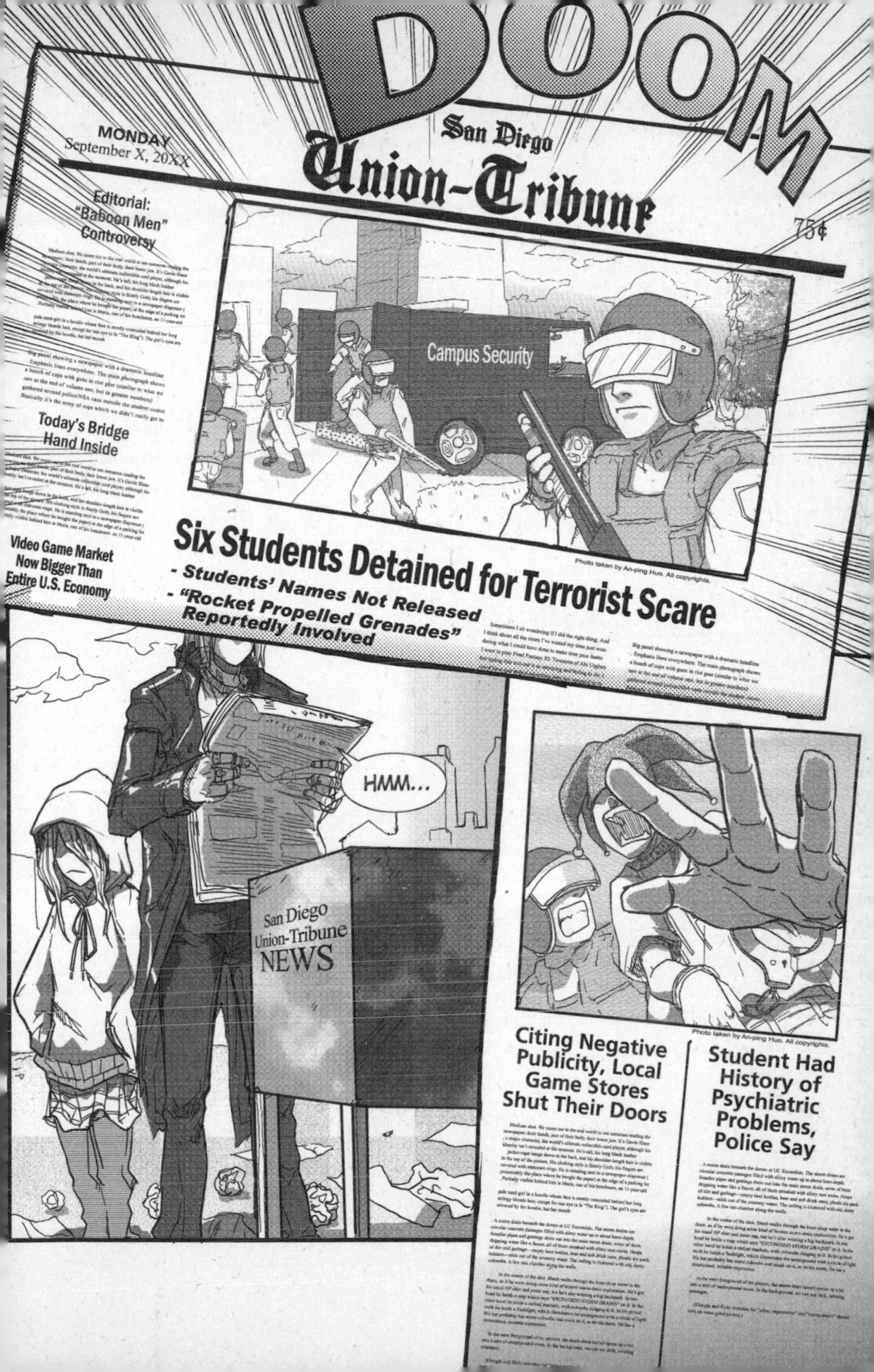
DOOM
MONDAY
September X, 20XX
San Diego
Union-Tribune
75¢
Editorial:
"Baboon Men"
Controversy
Today's Bridge
Hand Inside
Video Game Market
Now Bigger Than
Entire U.S. Economy
Campus Security
Photo taken by An-ping Huo. All copyrights.
Six Students Detained for Terrorist Scare
- Students' Names Not Released
- "Rocket Propelled Grenades"
Reportedly Involved
HMM...
San Diego
Union-Tribune
NEWS
Photo taken by An-ping Huo. All copyrights.
Citing Negative
Publicity, Local
Game Stores
Shut Their Doors
Student Had
History of
Psychiatric
Problems,
Police Say

CHAPTER 2:
DON'T HATE THE PLAYER

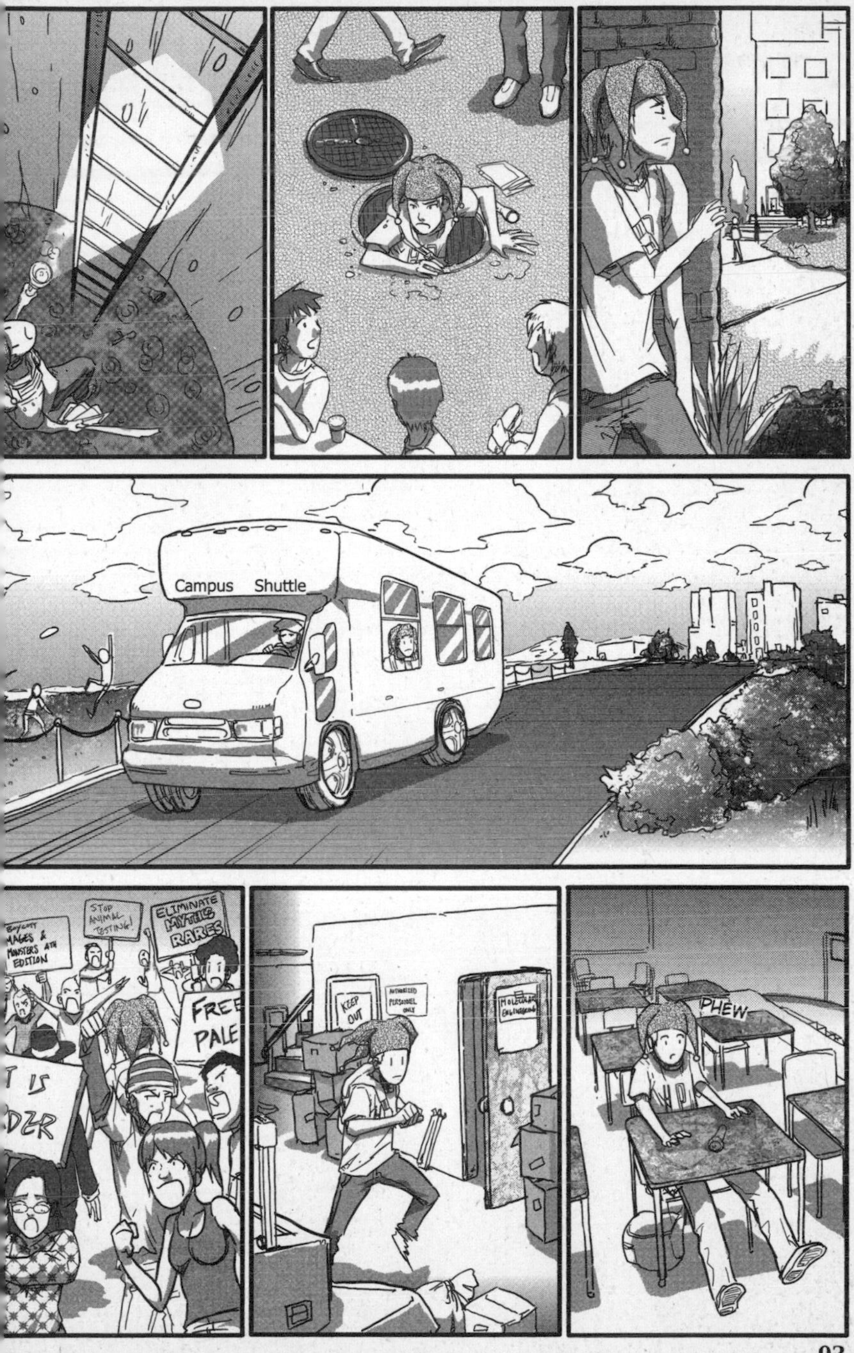

Campus Shuttle
Boycott MAGES & MONSTERS 4TH EDITION
STOP ANIMAL TESTING!
ELIMINATE MYTHIC RARES
FREE
KEEP OUT
AUTHORIZED PERSONNEL ONLY
PHEW

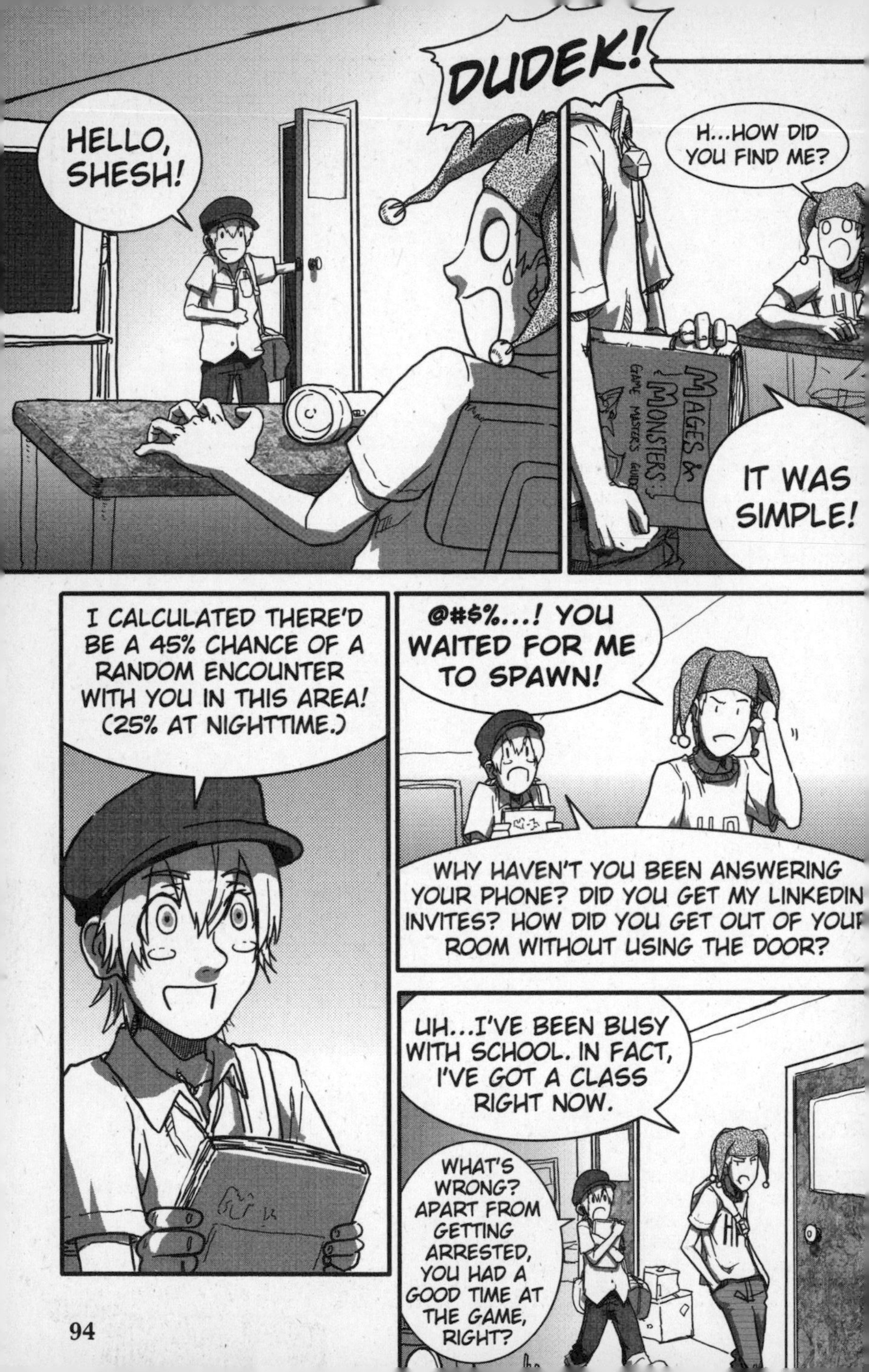
DUDEK!
HELLO, SHESH!
H...HOW DID YOU FIND ME?
IT WAS SIMPLE!
MAGES & MONSTERS GAME MASTER'S GUIDE
I CALCULATED THERE'D BE A 45% CHANCE OF A RANDOM ENCOUNTER WITH YOU IN THIS AREA! (25% AT NIGHTTIME.)
@#$%...! YOU WAITED FOR ME TO SPAWN!
WHY HAVEN'T YOU BEEN ANSWERING YOUR PHONE? DID YOU GET MY LINKEDIN INVITES? HOW DID YOU GET OUT OF YOUR ROOM WITHOUT USING THE DOOR?
UH...I'VE BEEN BUSY WITH SCHOOL. IN FACT, I'VE GOT A CLASS RIGHT NOW.
WHAT'S WRONG? APART FROM GETTING ARRESTED, YOU HAD A GOOD TIME AT THE GAME, RIGHT?

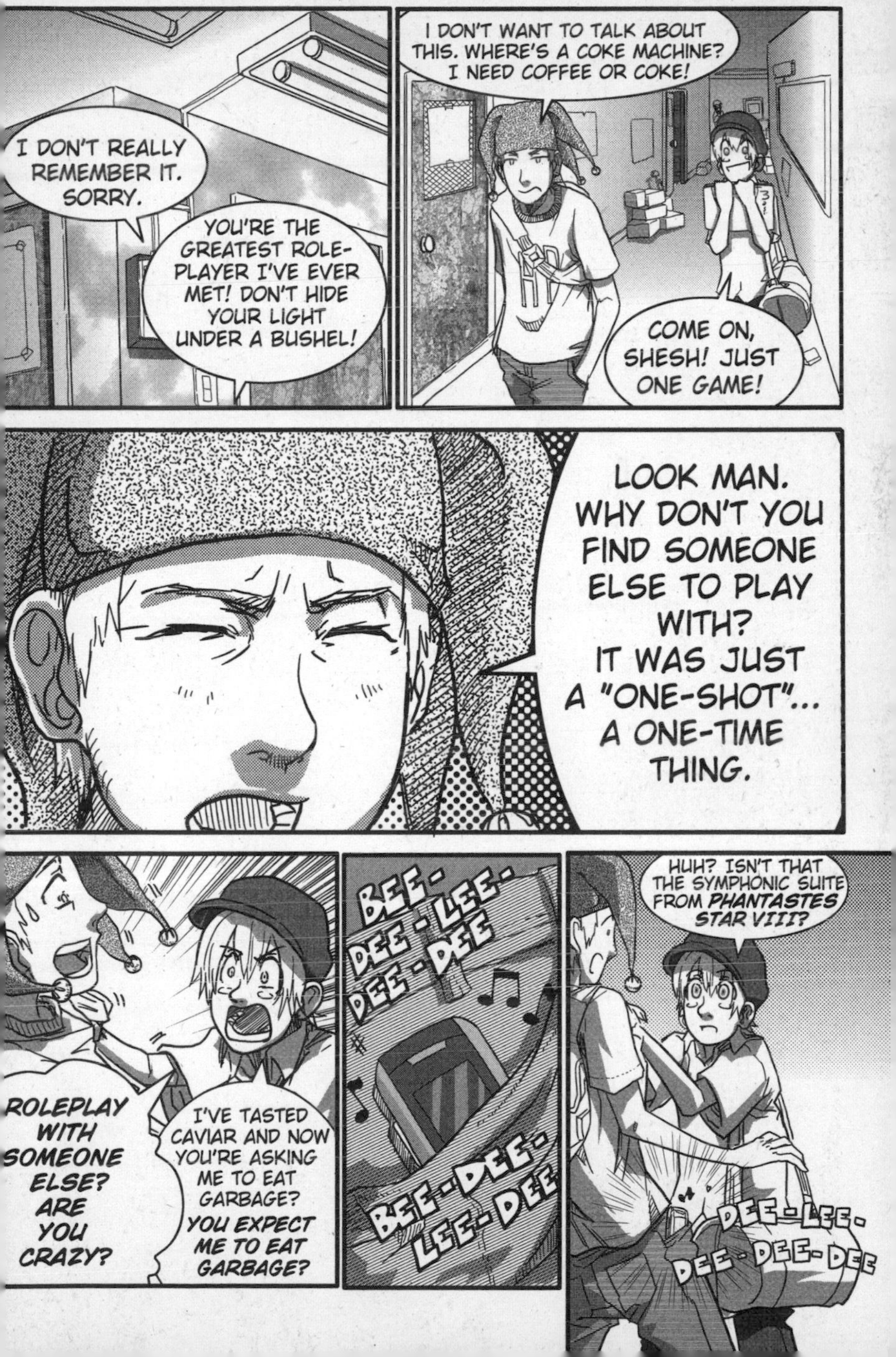
I DON'T REALLY REMEMBER IT. SORRY.
YOU'RE THE GREATEST ROLE-PLAYER I'VE EVER MET! DON'T HIDE YOUR LIGHT UNDER A BUSHEL!
I DON'T WANT TO TALK ABOUT THIS. WHERE'S A COKE MACHINE? I NEED COFFEE OR COKE!
COME ON, SHESH! JUST ONE GAME!
LOOK MAN. WHY DON'T YOU FIND SOMEONE ELSE TO PLAY WITH? IT WAS JUST A "ONE-SHOT"... A ONE-TIME THING.
ROLEPLAY WITH SOMEONE ELSE? ARE YOU CRAZY?
I'VE TASTED CAVIAR AND NOW YOU'RE ASKING ME TO EAT GARBAGE? YOU EXPECT ME TO EAT GARBAGE?
BEE-DEE-LEE-DEE-DEE
BEE-DEE-LEE-DEE
HUH? ISN'T THAT THE SYMPHONIC SUITE FROM *PHANTASTES STAR VIII*?
DEE-LEE-DEE-DEE-DEE

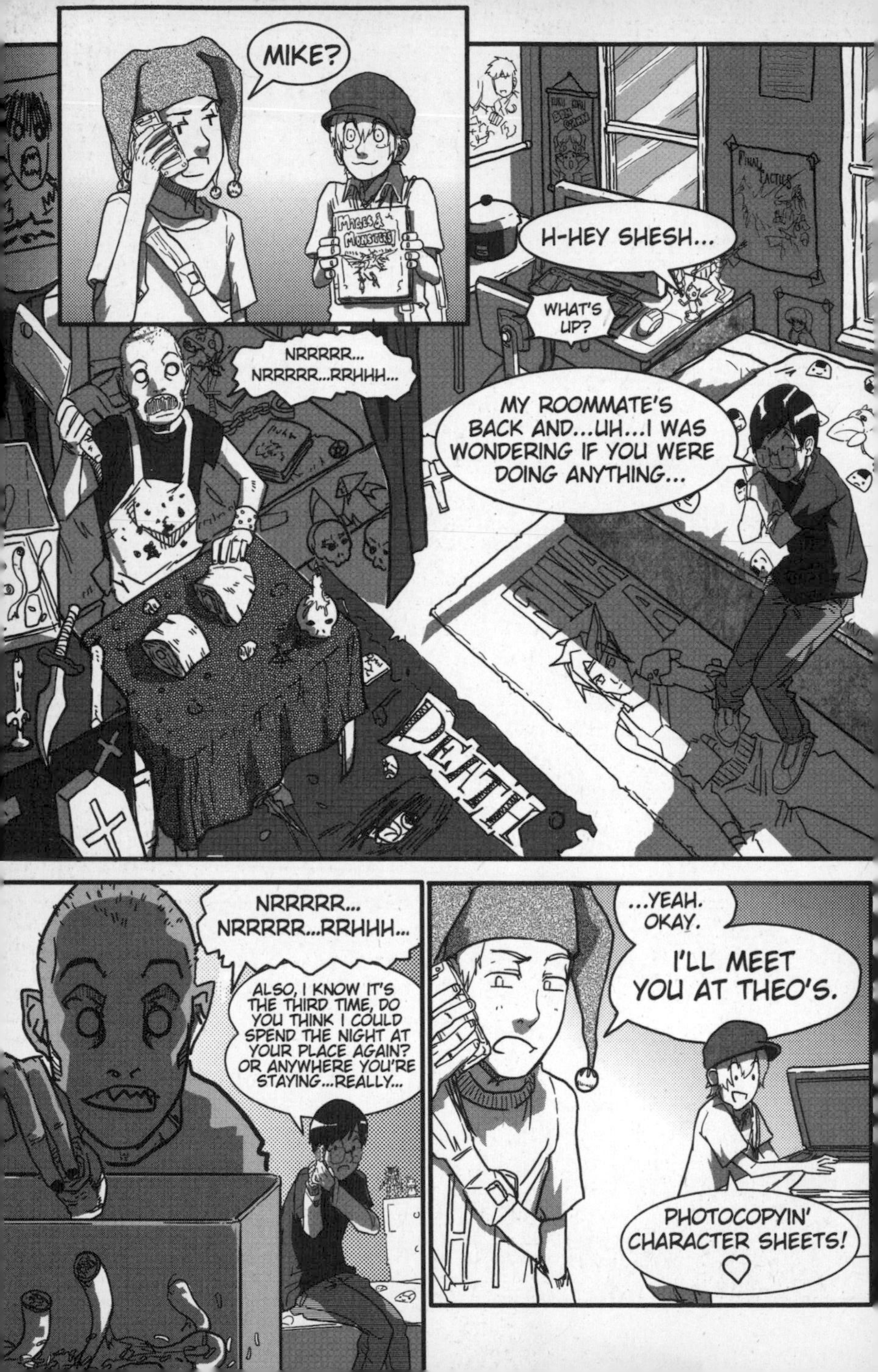
MIKE?
MAGES & MONSTERS
H-HEY SHESH...
WHAT'S UP?
FINAL TACTICS
NRRRRR... NRRRRR...RRHHH...
MY ROOMMATE'S BACK AND...UH...I WAS WONDERING IF YOU WERE DOING ANYTHING...
DEATH
NRRRRR... NRRRRR...RRHHH...
ALSO, I KNOW IT'S THE THIRD TIME, DO YOU THINK I COULD SPEND THE NIGHT AT YOUR PLACE AGAIN? OR ANYWHERE YOU'RE STAYING...REALLY...
...YEAH. OKAY.
I'LL MEET YOU AT THEO'S.
PHOTOCOPYIN' CHARACTER SHEETS!

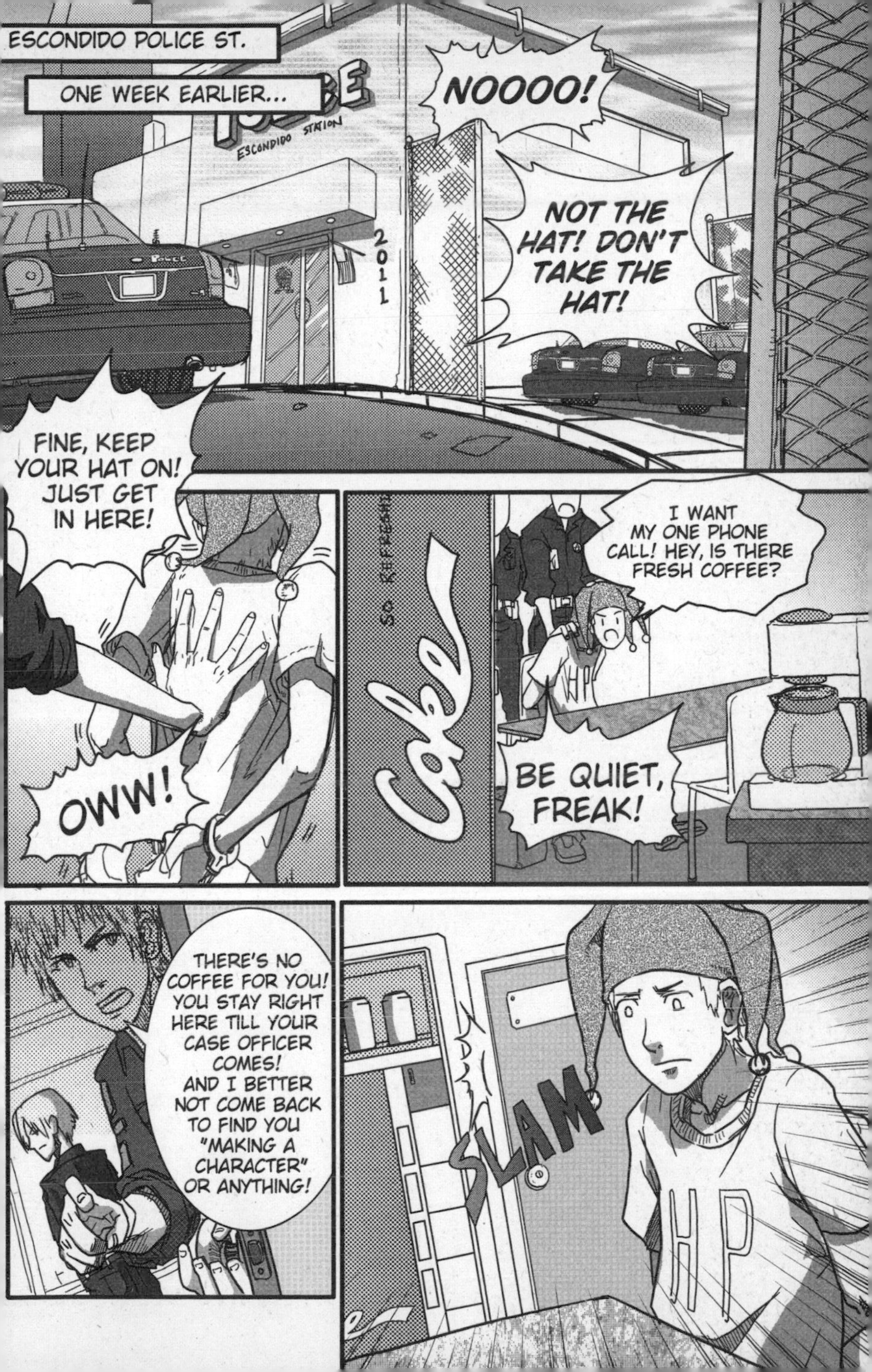
ESCONDIDO POLICE ST.
ONE WEEK EARLIER...
ESCONDIDO STATION
2011
NOOOO!
NOT THE HAT! DON'T TAKE THE HAT!
FINE, KEEP YOUR HAT ON! JUST GET IN HERE!
OWW!
Coke
I WANT MY ONE PHONE CALL! HEY, IS THERE FRESH COFFEE?
BE QUIET, FREAK!
THERE'S NO COFFEE FOR YOU! YOU STAY RIGHT HERE TILL YOUR CASE OFFICER COMES! AND I BETTER NOT COME BACK TO FIND YOU "MAKING A CHARACTER" OR ANYTHING!
SLAM

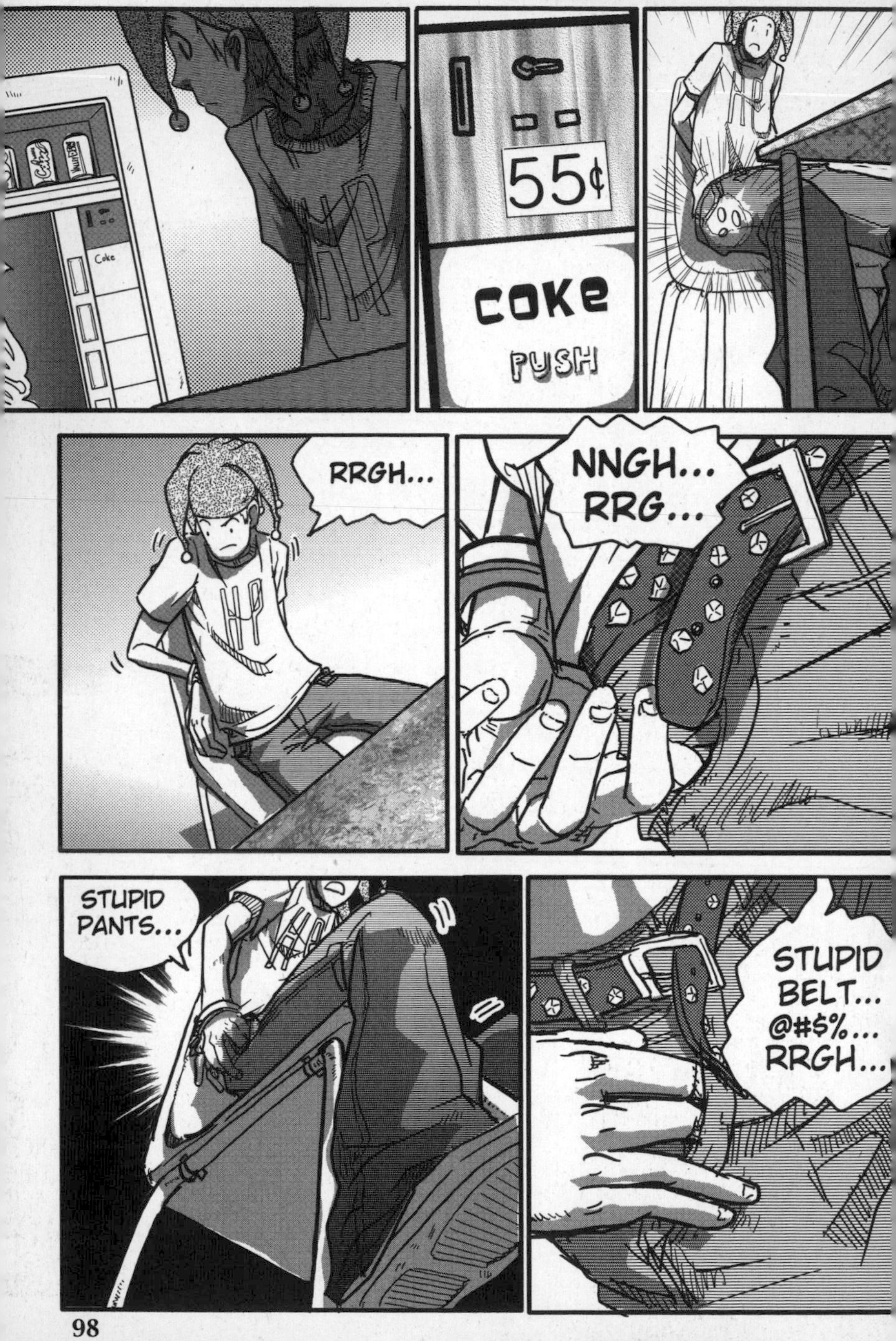

Coke
Coke
55¢
COKE
PUSH
RRGH...
NNGH... RRG...
STUPID PANTS...
STUPID BELT... @#$%... RRGH...

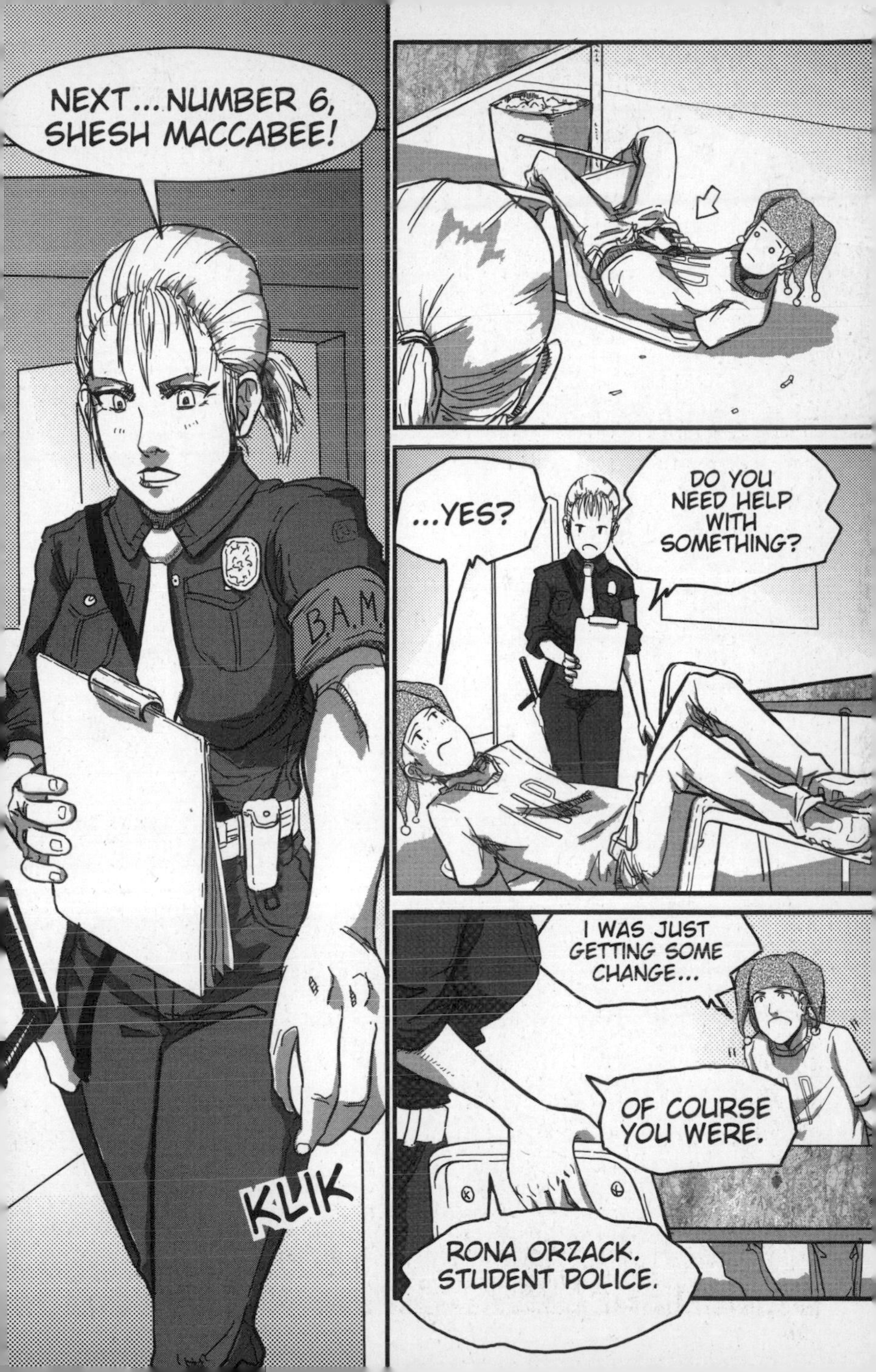
NEXT.... NUMBER 6, SHESH MACCABEE!
B.A.M.
KLIK
...YES?
DO YOU NEED HELP WITH SOMETHING?
I WAS JUST GETTING SOME CHANGE...
OF COURSE YOU WERE.
RONA ORZACK. STUDENT POLICE.

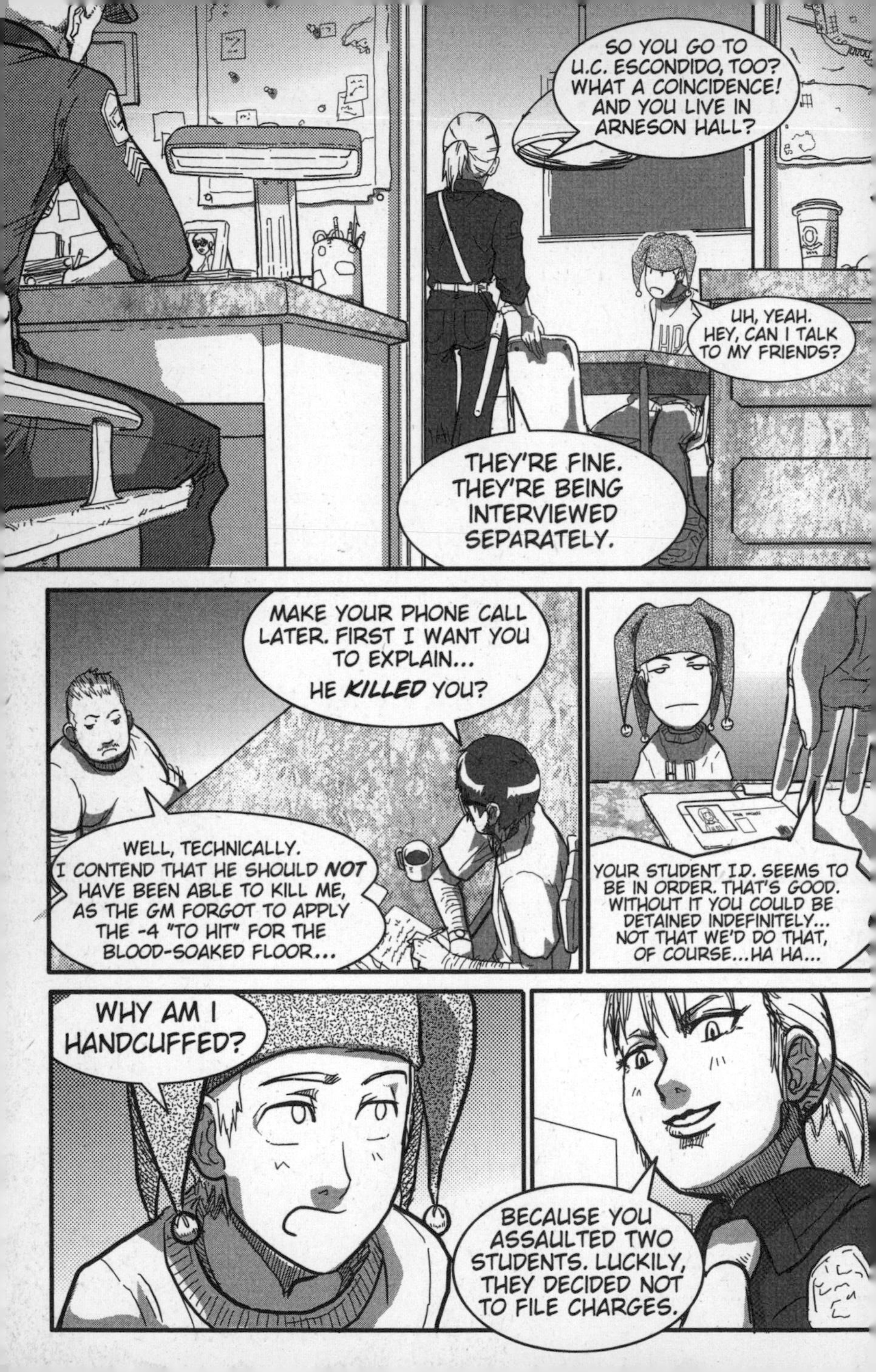
SO YOU GO TO U.C. ESCONDIDO, TOO? WHAT A COINCIDENCE! AND YOU LIVE IN ARNESON HALL?
UH, YEAH. HEY, CAN I TALK TO MY FRIENDS?
THEY'RE FINE. THEY'RE BEING INTERVIEWED SEPARATELY.
MAKE YOUR PHONE CALL LATER. FIRST I WANT YOU TO EXPLAIN...
HE KILLED YOU?
WELL, TECHNICALLY. I CONTEND THAT HE SHOULD NOT HAVE BEEN ABLE TO KILL ME, AS THE GM FORGOT TO APPLY THE -4 "TO HIT" FOR THE BLOOD-SOAKED FLOOR...
YOUR STUDENT I.D. SEEMS TO BE IN ORDER. THAT'S GOOD. WITHOUT IT YOU COULD BE DETAINED INDEFINITELY... NOT THAT WE'D DO THAT, OF COURSE...HA HA...
WHY AM I HANDCUFFED?
BECAUSE YOU ASSAULTED TWO STUDENTS. LUCKILY, THEY DECIDED NOT TO FILE CHARGES.

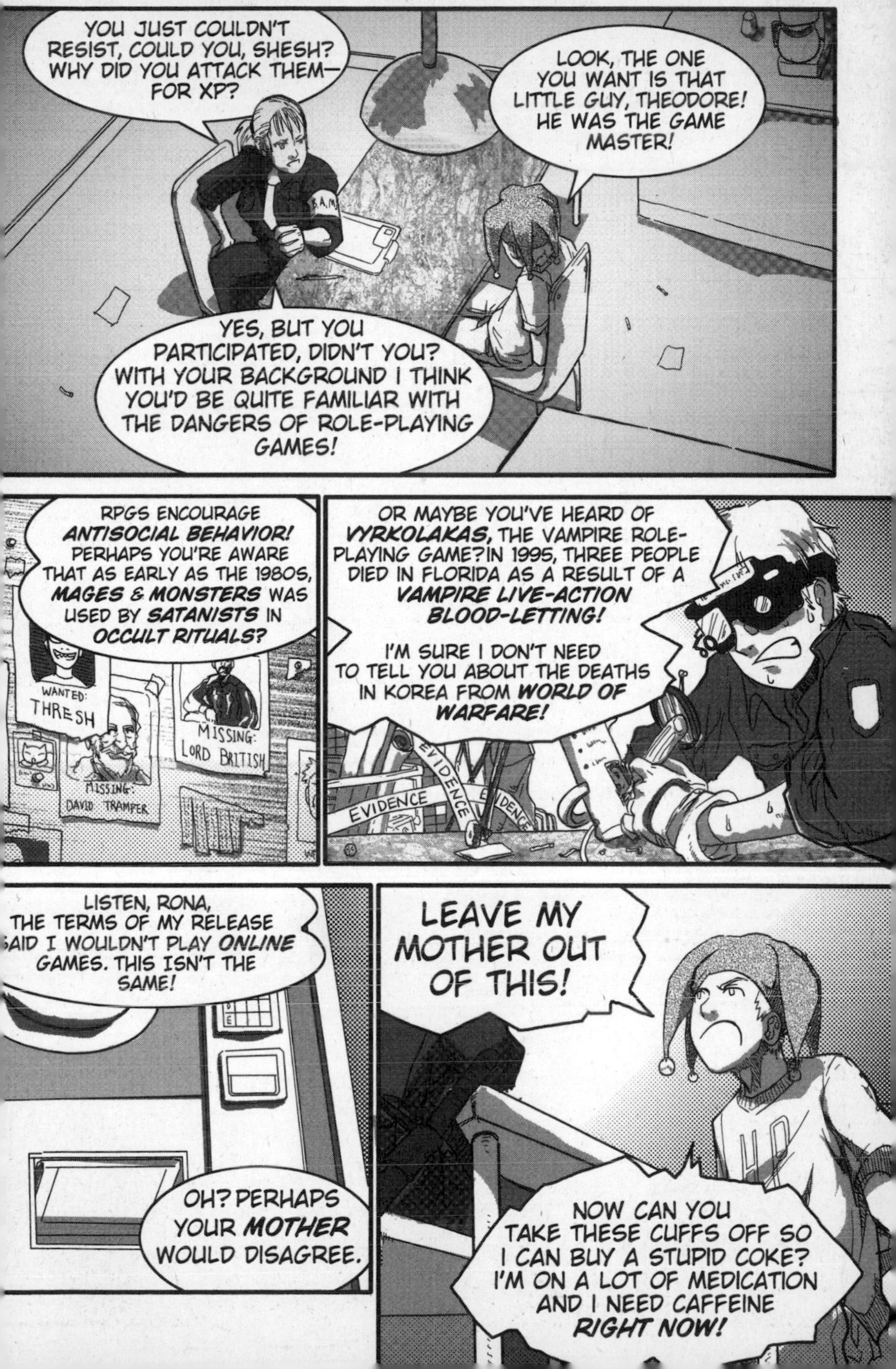
YOU JUST COULDN'T RESIST, COULD YOU, SHESH? WHY DID YOU ATTACK THEM—FOR XP?
LOOK, THE ONE YOU WANT IS THAT LITTLE GUY, THEODORE! HE WAS THE GAME MASTER!
B.A.M.
YES, BUT YOU PARTICIPATED, DIDN'T YOU? WITH YOUR BACKGROUND I THINK YOU'D BE QUITE FAMILIAR WITH THE DANGERS OF ROLE-PLAYING GAMES!
RPGS ENCOURAGE ***ANTISOCIAL BEHAVIOR!*** PERHAPS YOU'RE AWARE THAT AS EARLY AS THE 1980S, ***MAGES & MONSTERS*** WAS USED BY ***SATANISTS*** IN ***OCCULT RITUALS?***
WANTED: THRESH
MISSING: LORD BRITISH
MISSING: DAVID TRAMPER
OR MAYBE YOU'VE HEARD OF ***VYRKOLAKAS,*** THE VAMPIRE ROLE-PLAYING GAME? IN 1995, THREE PEOPLE DIED IN FLORIDA AS A RESULT OF A ***VAMPIRE LIVE-ACTION BLOOD-LETTING!***
I'M SURE I DON'T NEED TO TELL YOU ABOUT THE DEATHS IN KOREA FROM ***WORLD OF WARFARE!***
EVIDENCE
EVIDENCE
EVIDENCE
LISTEN, RONA, THE TERMS OF MY RELEASE SAID I WOULDN'T PLAY ***ONLINE*** GAMES. THIS ISN'T THE SAME!
OH? PERHAPS YOUR ***MOTHER*** WOULD DISAGREE.
LEAVE MY MOTHER OUT OF THIS!
NOW CAN YOU TAKE THESE CUFFS OFF SO I CAN BUY A STUPID COKE? I'M ON A LOT OF MEDICATION AND I NEED CAFFEINE ***RIGHT NOW!***

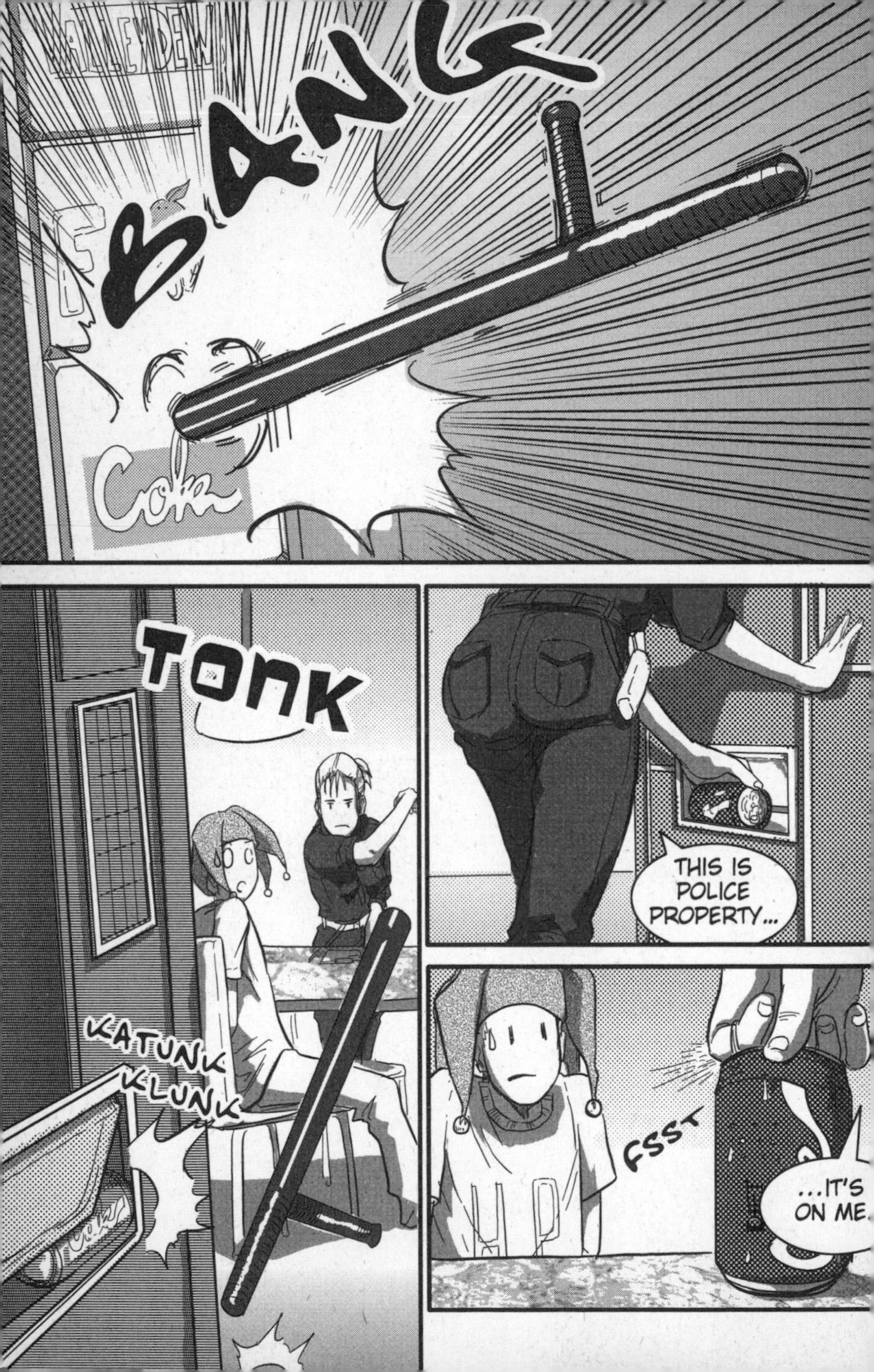
BANG
TONK
KATUNK
KLUNK
THIS IS POLICE PROPERTY...
FSST
...IT'S ON ME.

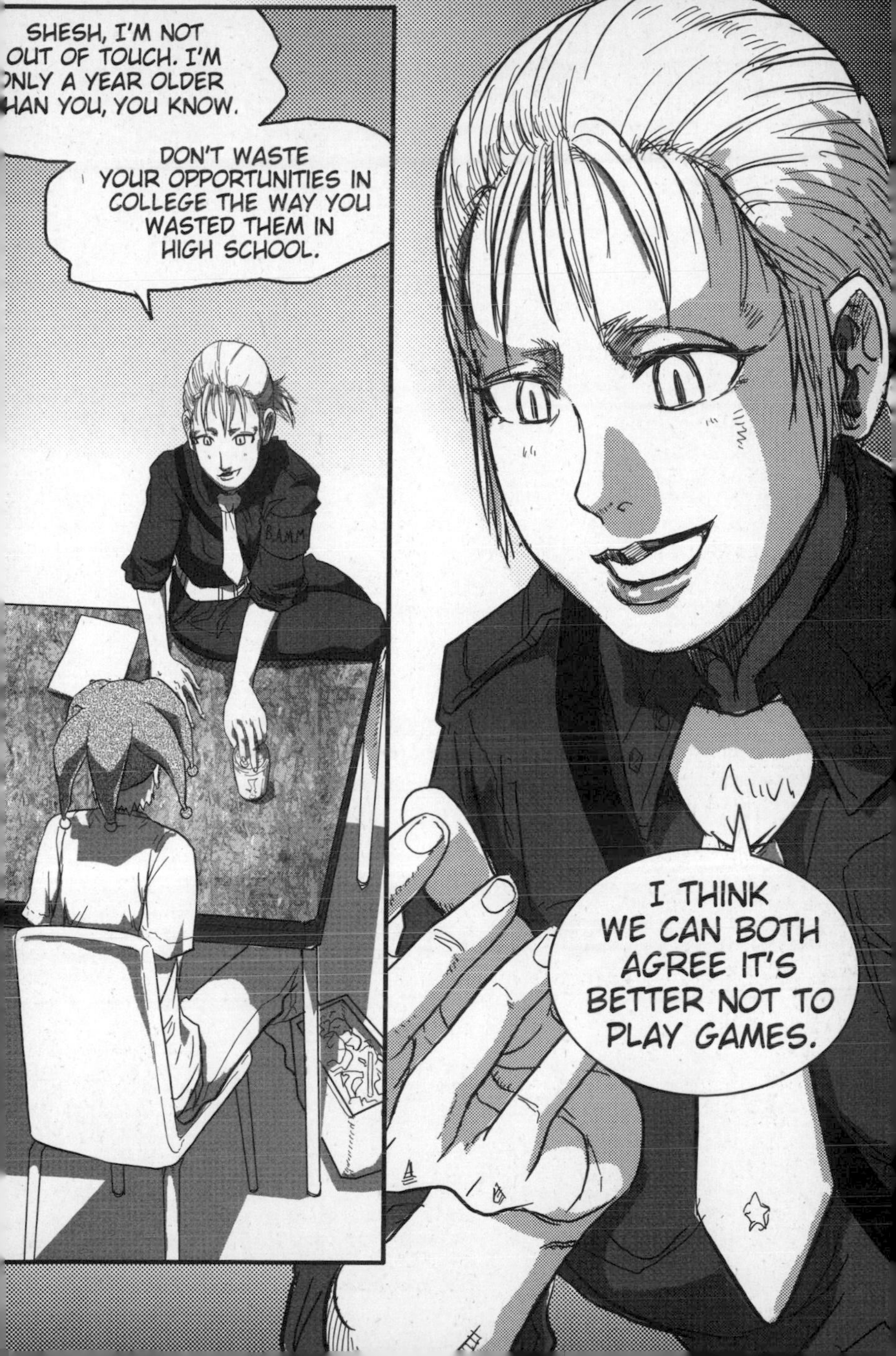
SHESH, I'M NOT OUT OF TOUCH. I'M ONLY A YEAR OLDER THAN YOU, YOU KNOW.
DON'T WASTE YOUR OPPORTUNITIES IN COLLEGE THE WAY YOU WASTED THEM IN HIGH SCHOOL.
I THINK WE CAN BOTH AGREE IT'S BETTER NOT TO PLAY GAMES.

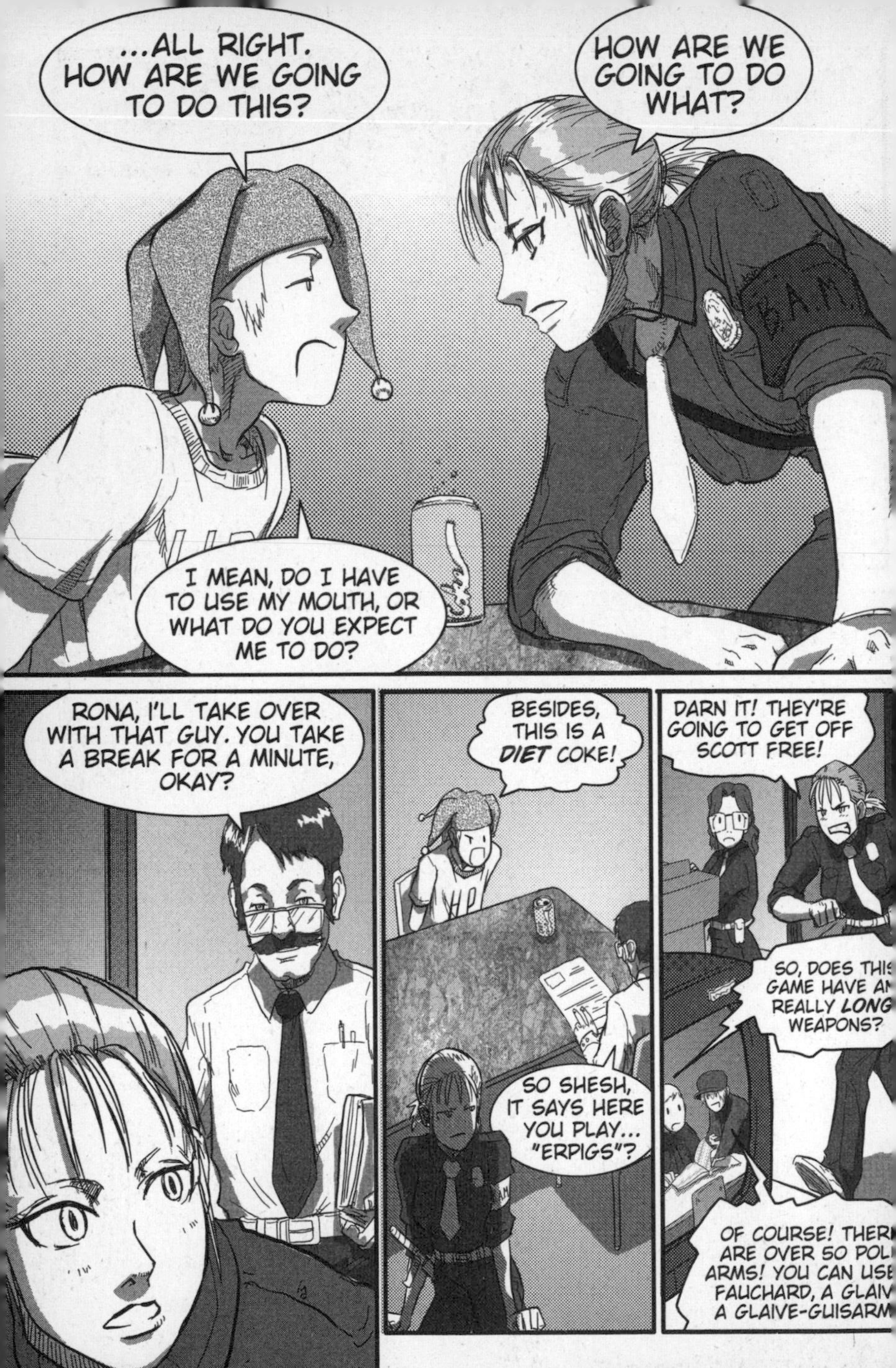
...ALL RIGHT. HOW ARE WE GOING TO DO THIS?
HOW ARE WE GOING TO DO WHAT?
I MEAN, DO I HAVE TO USE MY MOUTH, OR WHAT DO YOU EXPECT ME TO DO?
RONA, I'LL TAKE OVER WITH THAT GUY. YOU TAKE A BREAK FOR A MINUTE, OKAY?
BESIDES, THIS IS A *DIET* COKE!
SO SHESH, IT SAYS HERE YOU PLAY... "ERPIGS"?
DARN IT! THEY'RE GOING TO GET OFF SCOTT FREE!
SO, DOES THI GAME HAVE A REALLY *LONG* WEAPONS?
OF COURSE! THER ARE OVER 50 POL ARMS! YOU CAN USE FAUCHARD, A GLAIV A GLAIVE-GUISARM

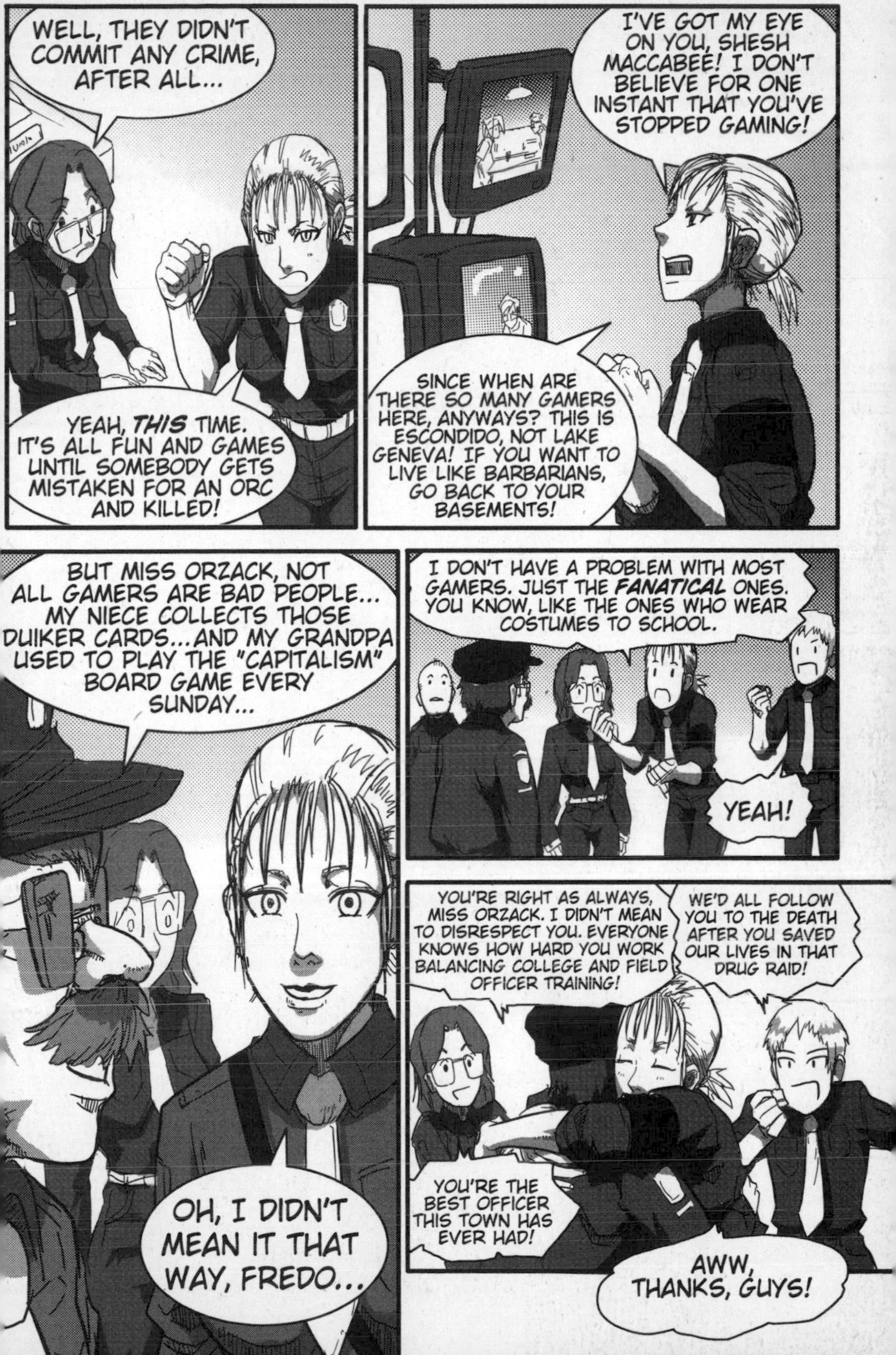
WELL, THEY DIDN'T COMMIT ANY CRIME, AFTER ALL...
YEAH, *THIS* TIME. IT'S ALL FUN AND GAMES UNTIL SOMEBODY GETS MISTAKEN FOR AN ORC AND KILLED!
I'VE GOT MY EYE ON YOU, SHESH MACCABEE! I DON'T BELIEVE FOR ONE INSTANT THAT YOU'VE STOPPED GAMING!
SINCE WHEN ARE THERE SO MANY GAMERS HERE, ANYWAYS? THIS IS ESCONDIDO, NOT LAKE GENEVA! IF YOU WANT TO LIVE LIKE BARBARIANS, GO BACK TO YOUR BASEMENTS!
BUT MISS ORZACK, NOT ALL GAMERS ARE BAD PEOPLE... MY NIECE COLLECTS THOSE DUIKER CARDS...AND MY GRANDPA USED TO PLAY THE "CAPITALISM" BOARD GAME EVERY SUNDAY...
OH, I DIDN'T MEAN IT THAT WAY, FREDO...
I DON'T HAVE A PROBLEM WITH MOST GAMERS. JUST THE *FANATICAL* ONES. YOU KNOW, LIKE THE ONES WHO WEAR COSTUMES TO SCHOOL.
YEAH!
YOU'RE RIGHT AS ALWAYS, MISS ORZACK. I DIDN'T MEAN TO DISRESPECT YOU. EVERYONE KNOWS HOW HARD YOU WORK BALANCING COLLEGE AND FIELD OFFICER TRAINING!
WE'D ALL FOLLOW YOU TO THE DEATH AFTER YOU SAVED OUR LIVES IN THAT DRUG RAID!
YOU'RE THE BEST OFFICER THIS TOWN HAS EVER HAD!
AWW, THANKS, GUYS!

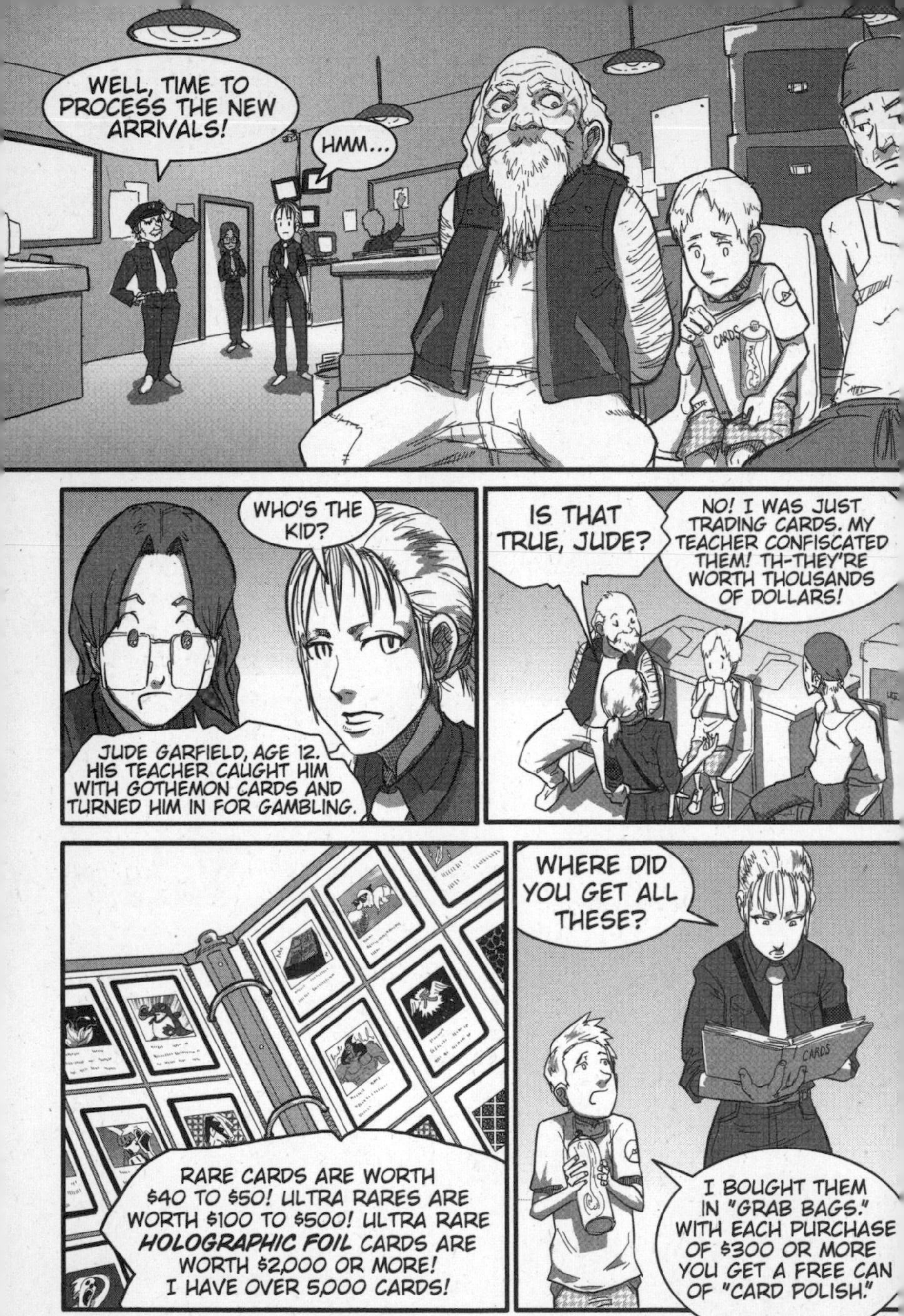
WELL, TIME TO PROCESS THE NEW ARRIVALS!
HMM...
WHO'S THE KID?
JUDE GARFIELD, AGE 12. HIS TEACHER CAUGHT HIM WITH GOTHEMON CARDS AND TURNED HIM IN FOR GAMBLING.
IS THAT TRUE, JUDE?
NO! I WAS JUST TRADING CARDS. MY TEACHER CONFISCATED THEM! TH-THEY'RE WORTH THOUSANDS OF DOLLARS!
RARE CARDS ARE WORTH $40 TO $50! ULTRA RARES ARE WORTH $100 TO $500! ULTRA RARE *HOLOGRAPHIC FOIL* CARDS ARE WORTH $2,000 OR MORE! I HAVE OVER 5,000 CARDS!
WHERE DID YOU GET ALL THESE?
I BOUGHT THEM IN "GRAB BAGS." WITH EACH PURCHASE OF $300 OR MORE YOU GET A FREE CAN OF "CARD POLISH."

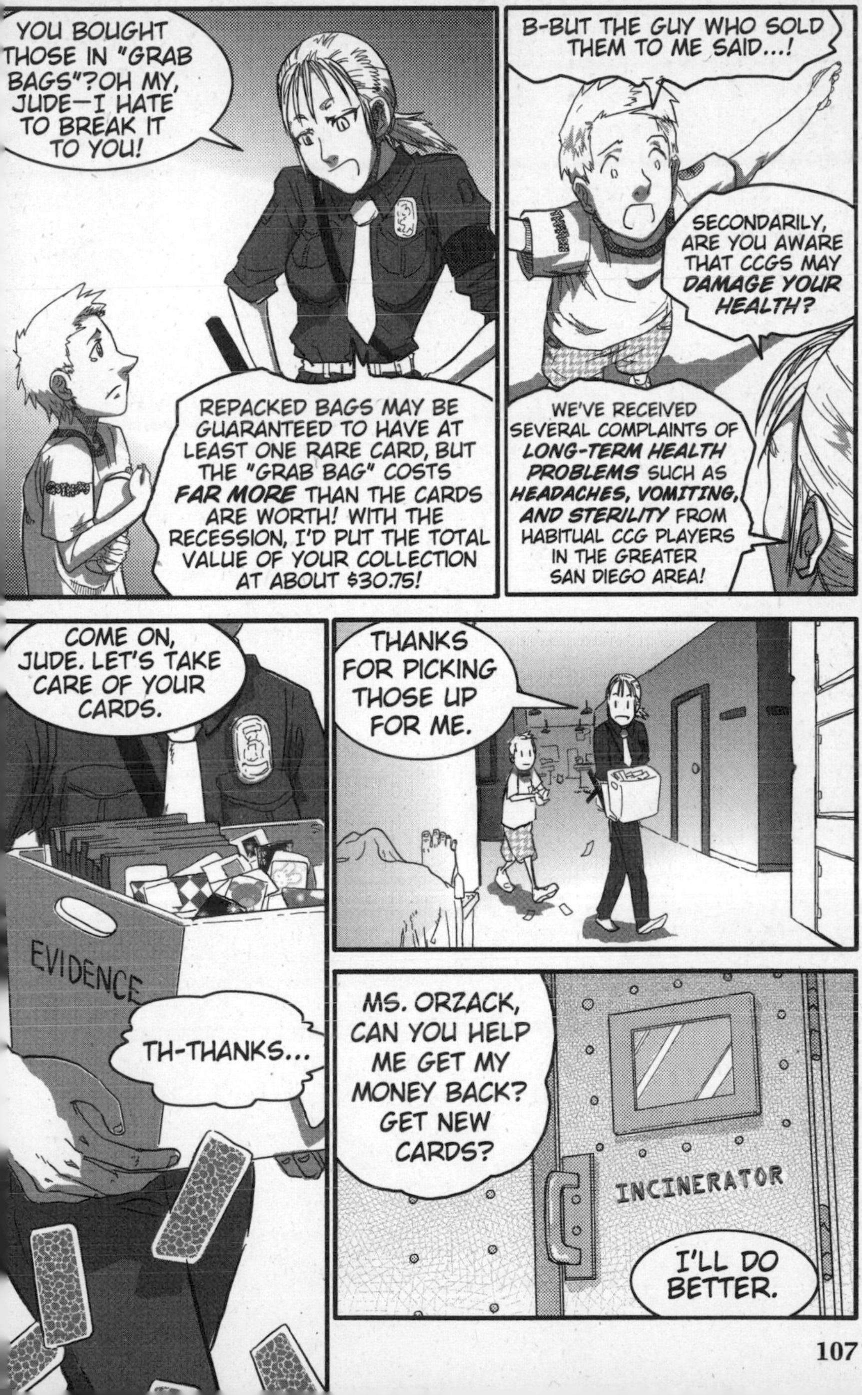
YOU BOUGHT THOSE IN "GRAB BAGS"?OH MY, JUDE—I HATE TO BREAK IT TO YOU!
REPACKED BAGS MAY BE GUARANTEED TO HAVE AT LEAST ONE RARE CARD, BUT THE "GRAB BAG" COSTS FAR MORE THAN THE CARDS ARE WORTH! WITH THE RECESSION, I'D PUT THE TOTAL VALUE OF YOUR COLLECTION AT ABOUT $30.75!
B-BUT THE GUY WHO SOLD THEM TO ME SAID...!
SECONDARILY, ARE YOU AWARE THAT CCGS MAY DAMAGE YOUR HEALTH?
WE'VE RECEIVED SEVERAL COMPLAINTS OF LONG-TERM HEALTH PROBLEMS SUCH AS HEADACHES, VOMITING, AND STERILITY FROM HABITUAL CCG PLAYERS IN THE GREATER SAN DIEGO AREA!
COME ON, JUDE. LET'S TAKE CARE OF YOUR CARDS.
EVIDENCE
TH-THANKS...
THANKS FOR PICKING THOSE UP FOR ME.
MS. ORZACK, CAN YOU HELP ME GET MY MONEY BACK? GET NEW CARDS?
INCINERATOR
I'LL DO BETTER.

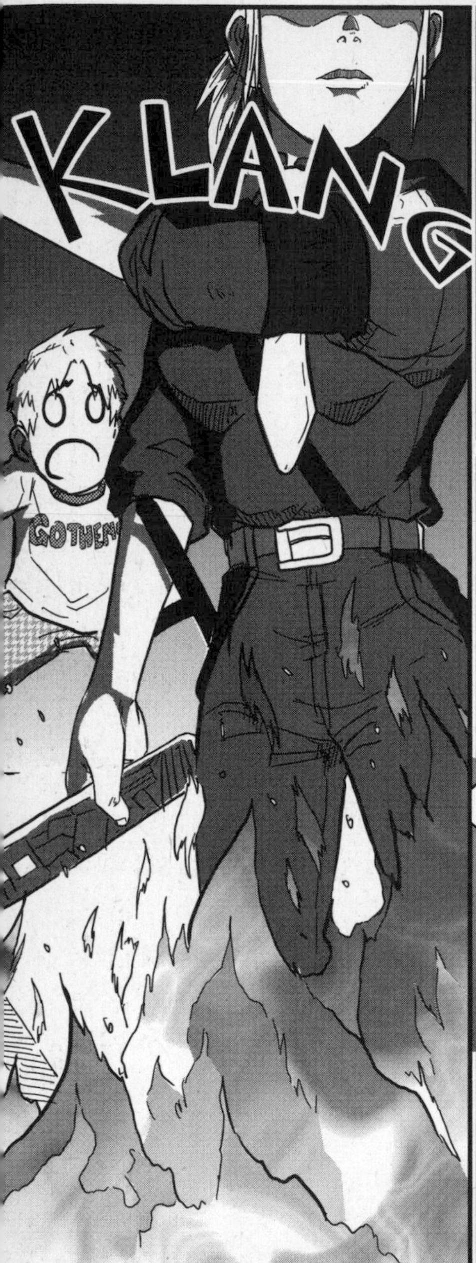
KLANG

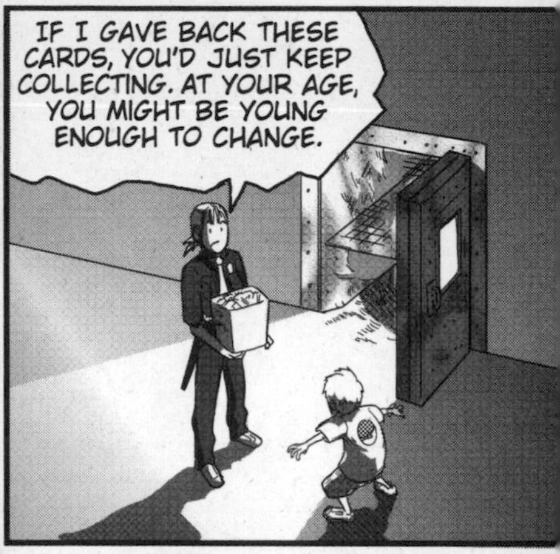
IF I GAVE BACK THESE CARDS, YOU'D JUST KEEP COLLECTING. AT YOUR AGE, YOU MIGHT BE YOUNG ENOUGH TO CHANGE.

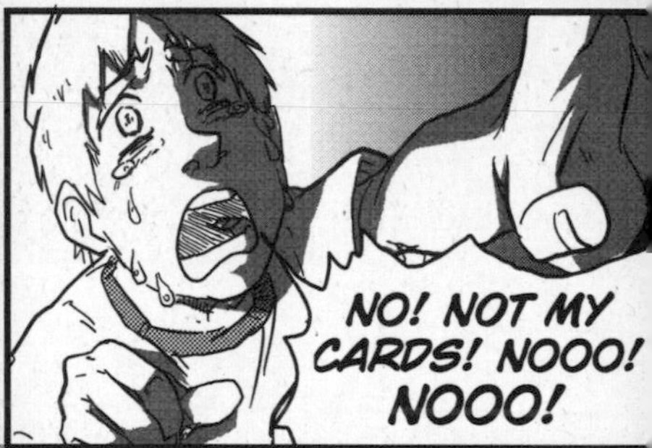
NO! NOT MY CARDS! NOOO! NOOO!

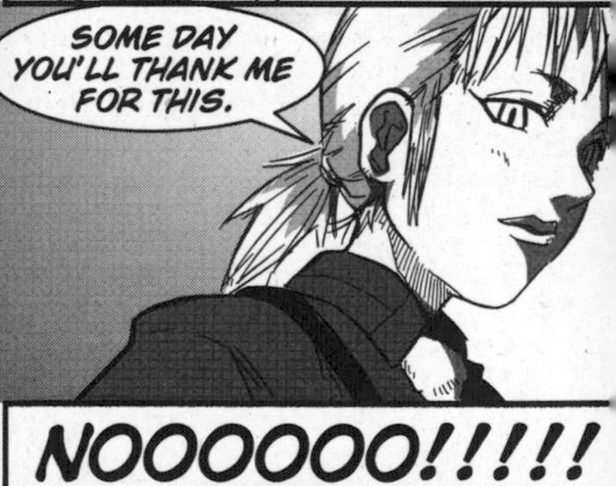
SOME DAY YOU'LL THANK ME FOR THIS.

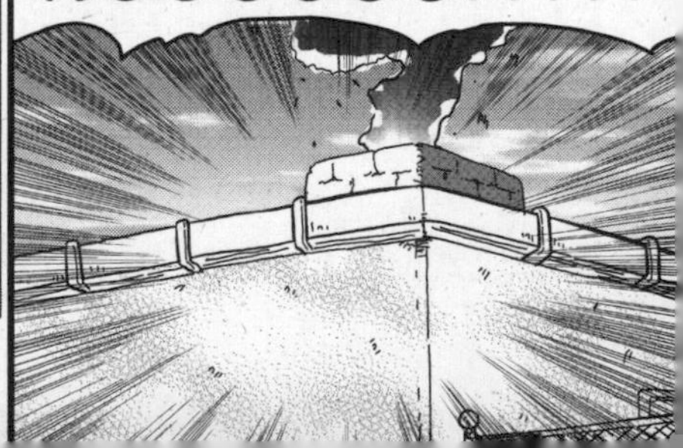
NOOOOOO!!!!!

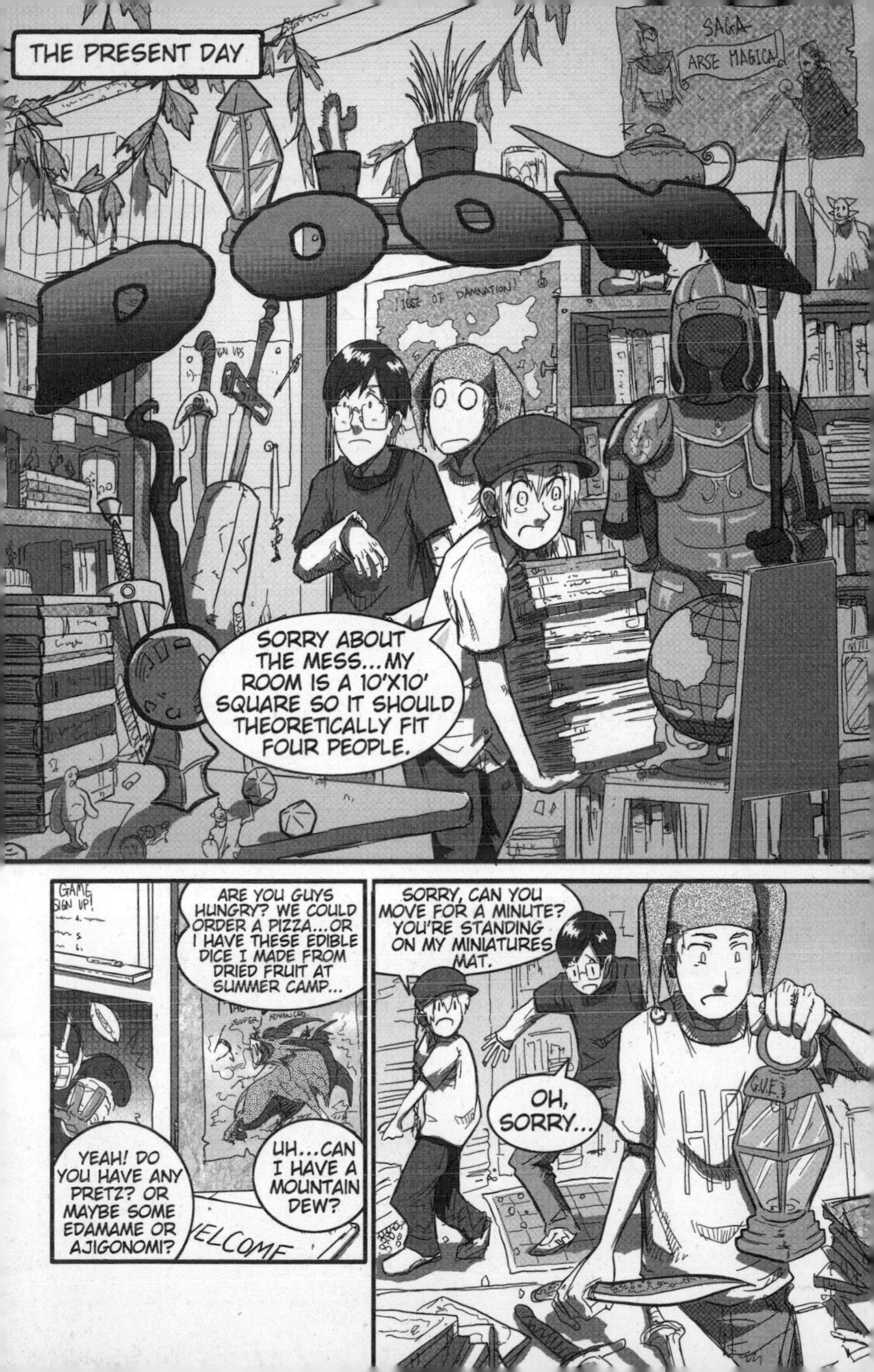
THE PRESENT DAY
SAGA
ARSE MAGICA
SORRY ABOUT THE MESS...MY ROOM IS A 10'X10' SQUARE SO IT SHOULD THEORETICALLY FIT FOUR PEOPLE.
GAME SIGN UP!
ARE YOU GUYS HUNGRY? WE COULD ORDER A PIZZA...OR I HAVE THESE EDIBLE DICE I MADE FROM DRIED FRUIT AT SUMMER CAMP...
YEAH! DO YOU HAVE ANY PRETZ? OR MAYBE SOME EDAMAME OR AJIGONOMI?
UH...CAN I HAVE A MOUNTAIN DEW?
SORRY, CAN YOU MOVE FOR A MINUTE? YOU'RE STANDING ON MY MINIATURES MAT.
OH, SORRY...

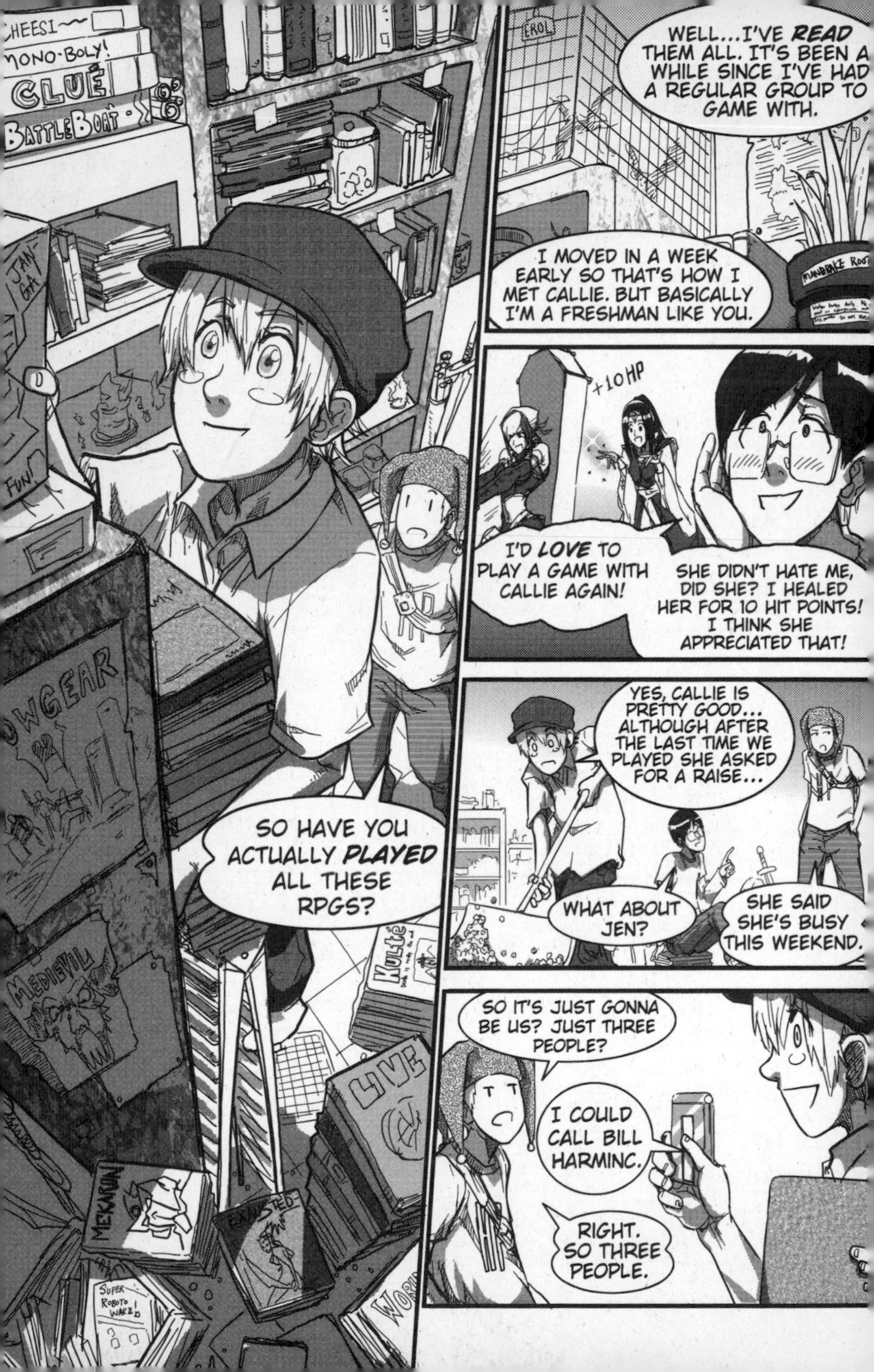
CHEESI~~
MONO-BOLY!
CLUÉ
BATTLEBOAT
FUN!
MEDIEVIL
SO HAVE YOU ACTUALLY *PLAYED* ALL THESE RPGS?
Kulté
LIVE
MEKARUN
SUPER ROBOTO WARZ D
EROL
WELL…I'VE *READ* THEM ALL. IT'S BEEN A WHILE SINCE I'VE HAD A REGULAR GROUP TO GAME WITH.
I MOVED IN A WEEK EARLY SO THAT'S HOW I MET CALLIE. BUT BASICALLY I'M A FRESHMAN LIKE YOU.
MANDRAKE ROOT
+10HP
I'D *LOVE* TO PLAY A GAME WITH CALLIE AGAIN!
SHE DIDN'T HATE ME, DID SHE? I HEALED HER FOR 10 HIT POINTS! I THINK SHE APPRECIATED THAT!
YES, CALLIE IS PRETTY GOOD… ALTHOUGH AFTER THE LAST TIME WE PLAYED SHE ASKED FOR A RAISE…
WHAT ABOUT JEN?
SHE SAID SHE'S BUSY THIS WEEKEND.
SO IT'S JUST GONNA BE US? JUST THREE PEOPLE?
I COULD CALL BILL HARMINC.
RIGHT. SO THREE PEOPLE.

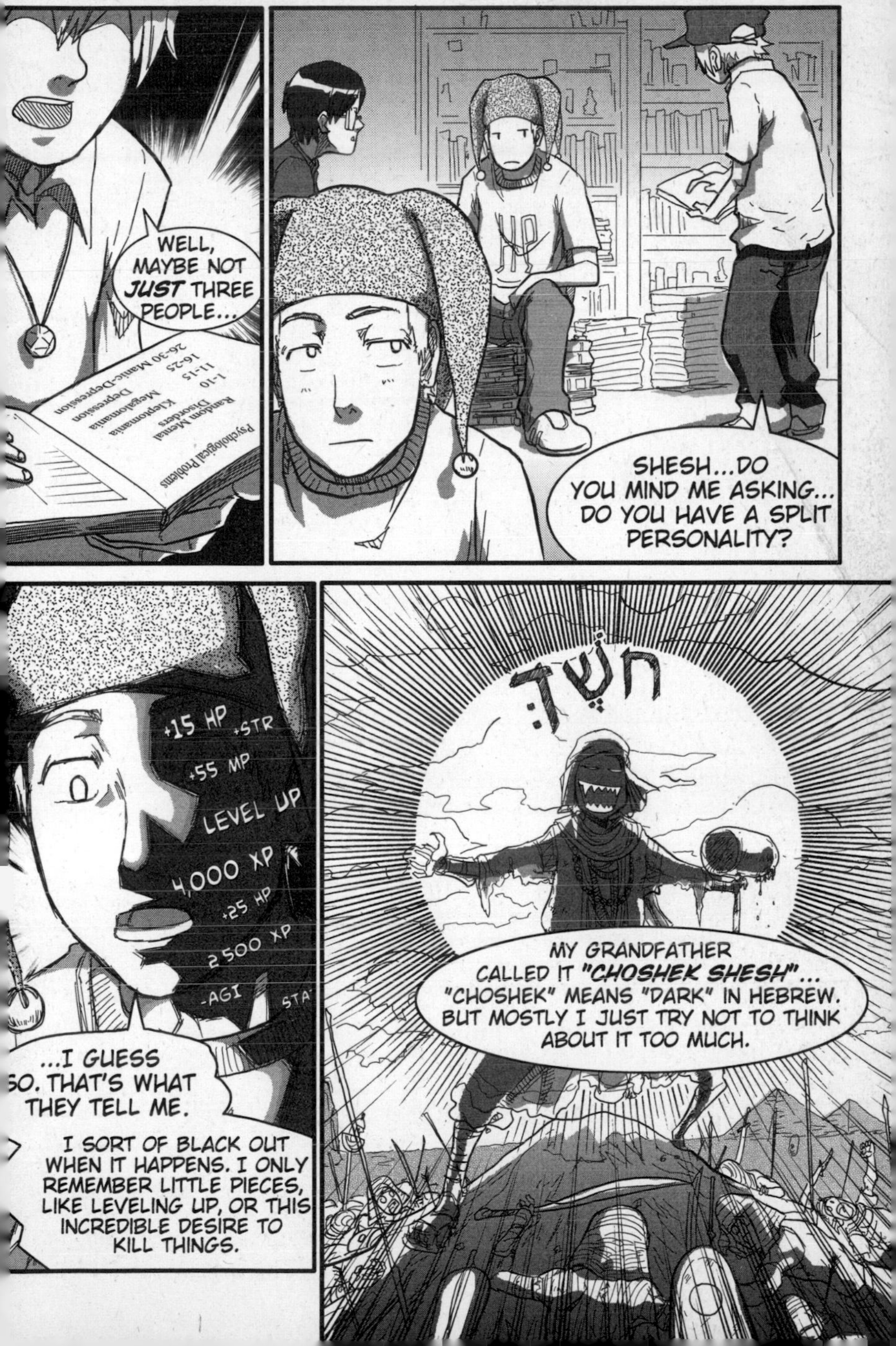
WELL, MAYBE NOT ***JUST*** THREE PEOPLE...
Psychological Problems
Random Mental Disorders
1-10 Kleptomania
11-15 Megalomania
16-25 Depression
26-30 Manic-Depression
SHESH...DO YOU MIND ME ASKING... DO YOU HAVE A SPLIT PERSONALITY?
+15 HP
+STR
+55 MP
LEVEL UP
4,000 XP
+25 HP
2,500 XP
-AGI
...I GUESS SO. THAT'S WHAT THEY TELL ME.
I SORT OF BLACK OUT WHEN IT HAPPENS. I ONLY REMEMBER LITTLE PIECES, LIKE LEVELING UP, OR THIS INCREDIBLE DESIRE TO KILL THINGS.
חֹשֶׁך
MY GRANDFATHER CALLED IT ***"CHOSHEK SHESH"***... "CHOSHEK" MEANS "DARK" IN HEBREW. BUT MOSTLY I JUST TRY NOT TO THINK ABOUT IT TOO MUCH.

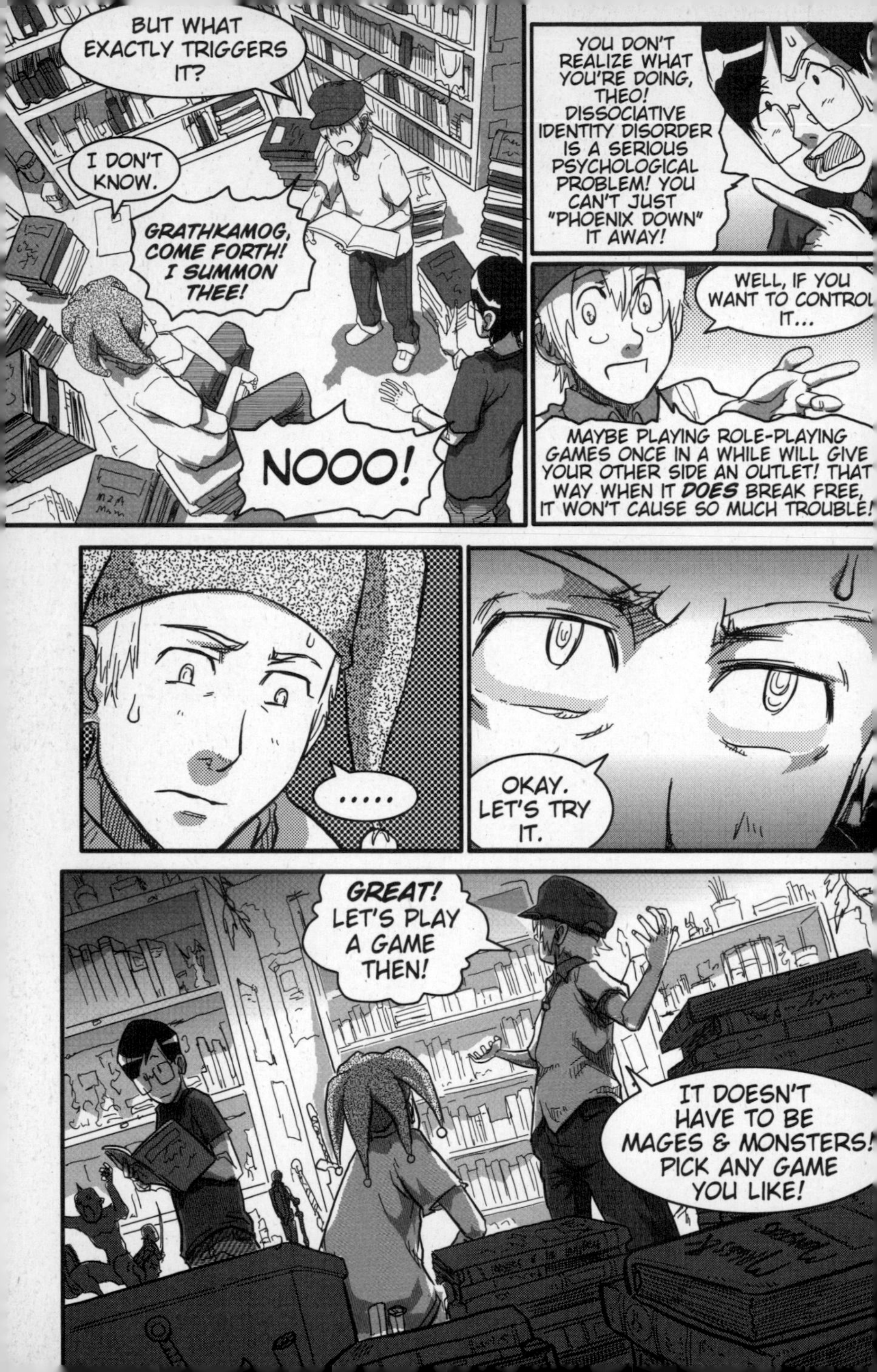
BUT WHAT EXACTLY TRIGGERS IT?
I DON'T KNOW.
GRATHKAMOG, COME FORTH! I SUMMON THEE!
NOOO!
YOU DON'T REALIZE WHAT YOU'RE DOING, THEO! DISSOCIATIVE IDENTITY DISORDER IS A SERIOUS PSYCHOLOGICAL PROBLEM! YOU CAN'T JUST "PHOENIX DOWN" IT AWAY!
WELL, IF YOU WANT TO CONTROL IT...
MAYBE PLAYING ROLE-PLAYING GAMES ONCE IN A WHILE WILL GIVE YOUR OTHER SIDE AN OUTLET! THAT WAY WHEN IT DOES BREAK FREE, IT WON'T CAUSE SO MUCH TROUBLE!
.....
OKAY. LET'S TRY IT.
GREAT! LET'S PLAY A GAME THEN!
IT DOESN'T HAVE TO BE MAGES & MONSTERS! PICK ANY GAME YOU LIKE!

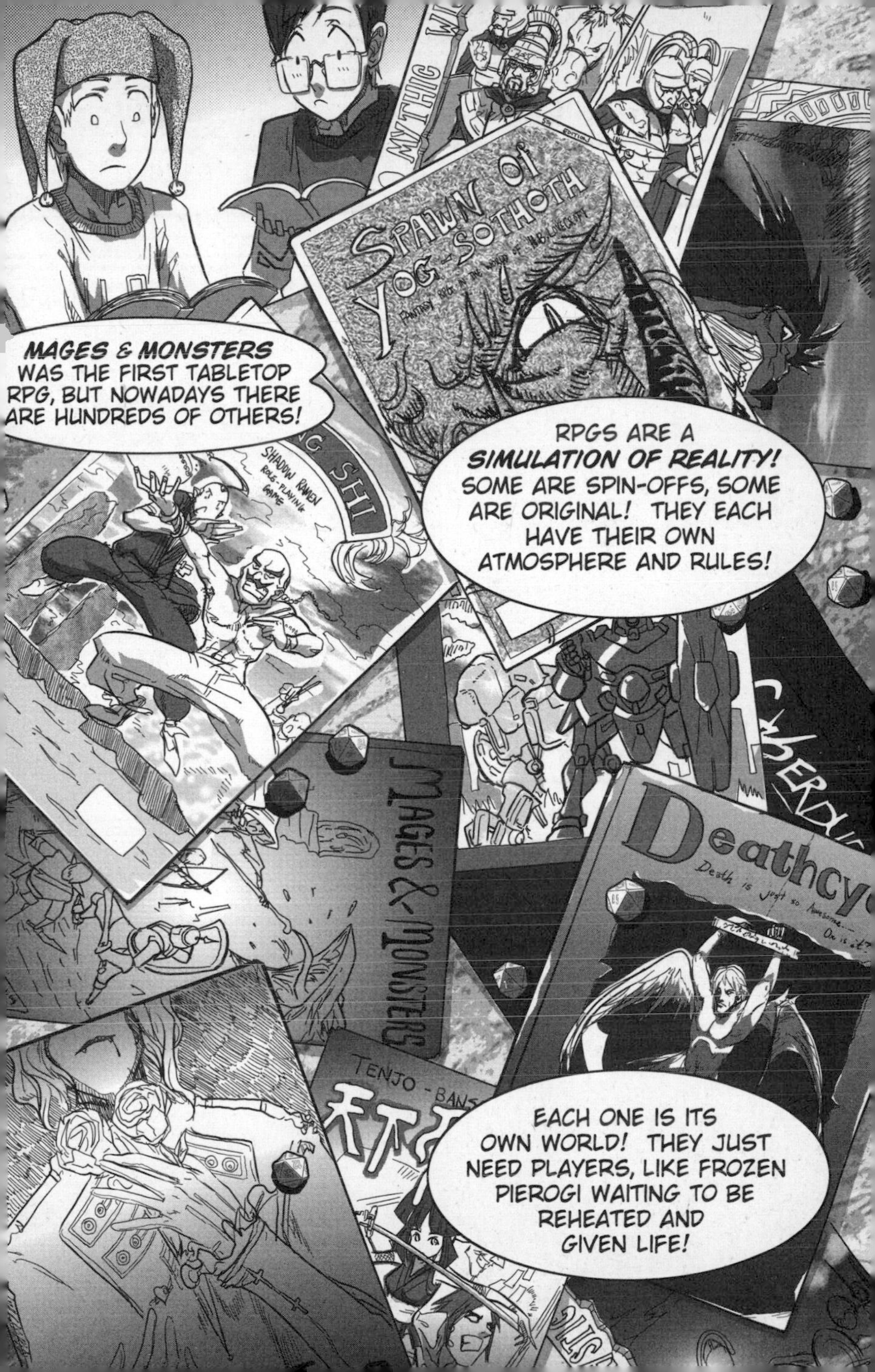
MAGES & MONSTERS WAS THE FIRST TABLETOP RPG, BUT NOWADAYS THERE ARE HUNDREDS OF OTHERS!
RPGS ARE A SIMULATION OF REALITY! SOME ARE SPIN-OFFS, SOME ARE ORIGINAL! THEY EACH HAVE THEIR OWN ATMOSPHERE AND RULES!
EACH ONE IS ITS OWN WORLD! THEY JUST NEED PLAYERS, LIKE FROZEN PIEROGI WAITING TO BE REHEATED AND GIVEN LIFE!
SPAWN OF YOG-SOTHOTH
SHADOW RAMEN ROLE-PLAYING GAME
MAGES & MONSTERS
Deathcy
TENJO-BANS

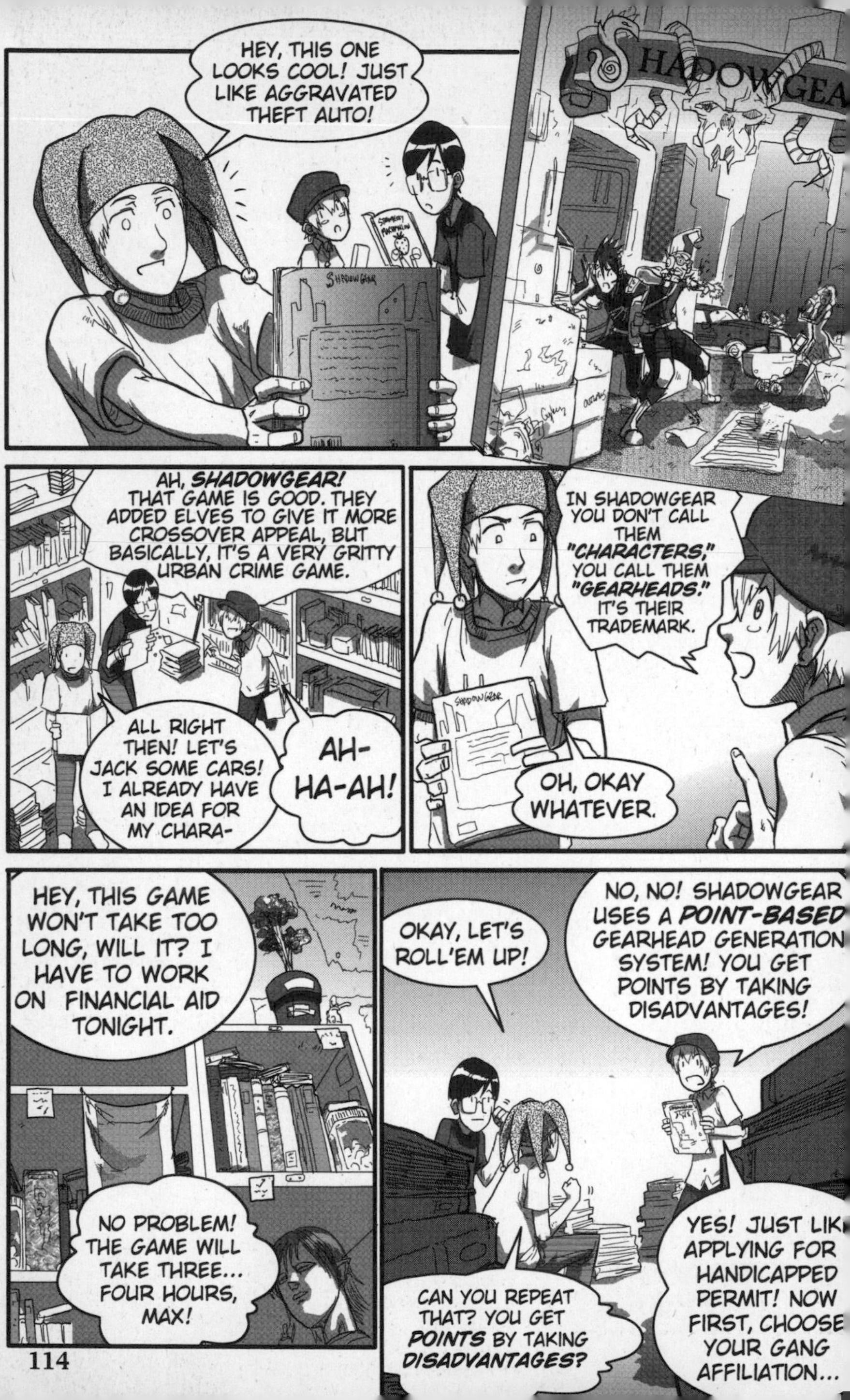

HEY, THIS ONE LOOKS COOL! JUST LIKE AGGRAVATED THEFT AUTO!
AH, ***SHADOWGEAR!*** THAT GAME IS GOOD. THEY ADDED ELVES TO GIVE IT MORE CROSSOVER APPEAL, BUT BASICALLY, IT'S A VERY GRITTY URBAN CRIME GAME.
ALL RIGHT THEN! LET'S JACK SOME CARS! I ALREADY HAVE AN IDEA FOR MY CHARA-
AH-HA-AH!
IN SHADOWGEAR YOU DON'T CALL THEM ***"CHARACTERS,"*** YOU CALL THEM ***"GEARHEADS."*** IT'S THEIR TRADEMARK.
OH, OKAY WHATEVER.
HEY, THIS GAME WON'T TAKE TOO LONG, WILL IT? I HAVE TO WORK ON FINANCIAL AID TONIGHT.
NO PROBLEM! THE GAME WILL TAKE THREE... FOUR HOURS, MAX!
OKAY, LET'S ROLL'EM UP!
NO, NO! SHADOWGEAR USES A ***POINT-BASED*** GEARHEAD GENERATION SYSTEM! YOU GET POINTS BY TAKING DISADVANTAGES!
CAN YOU REPEAT THAT? YOU GET ***POINTS*** BY TAKING ***DISADVANTAGES?***
YES! JUST LIK APPLYING FOR HANDICAPPED PERMIT! NOW FIRST, CHOOSE YOUR GANG AFFILIATION...

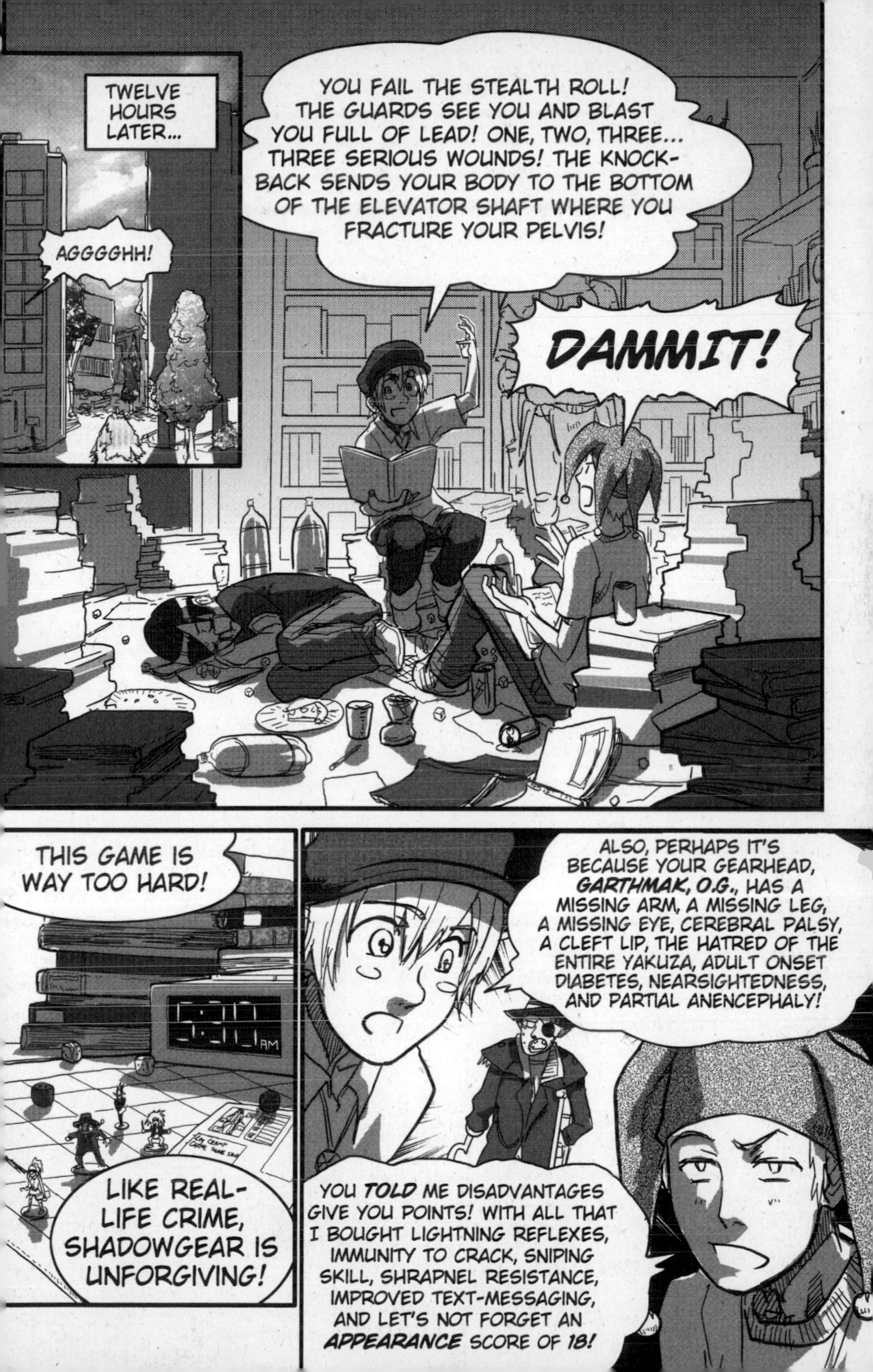
TWELVE HOURS LATER...
AGGGGHH!
YOU FAIL THE STEALTH ROLL! THE GUARDS SEE YOU AND BLAST YOU FULL OF LEAD! ONE, TWO, THREE... THREE SERIOUS WOUNDS! THE KNOCK-BACK SENDS YOUR BODY TO THE BOTTOM OF THE ELEVATOR SHAFT WHERE YOU FRACTURE YOUR PELVIS!
DAMMIT!
THIS GAME IS WAY TOO HARD!
5:30 AM
LIKE REAL-LIFE CRIME, SHADOWGEAR IS UNFORGIVING!
ALSO, PERHAPS IT'S BECAUSE YOUR GEARHEAD, GARTHMAK, O.G., HAS A MISSING ARM, A MISSING LEG, A MISSING EYE, CEREBRAL PALSY, A CLEFT LIP, THE HATRED OF THE ENTIRE YAKUZA, ADULT ONSET DIABETES, NEARSIGHTEDNESS, AND PARTIAL ANENCEPHALY!
YOU TOLD ME DISADVANTAGES GIVE YOU POINTS! WITH ALL THAT I BOUGHT LIGHTNING REFLEXES, IMMUNITY TO CRACK, SNIPING SKILL, SHRAPNEL RESISTANCE, IMPROVED TEXT-MESSAGING, AND LET'S NOT FORGET AN APPEARANCE SCORE OF 18!

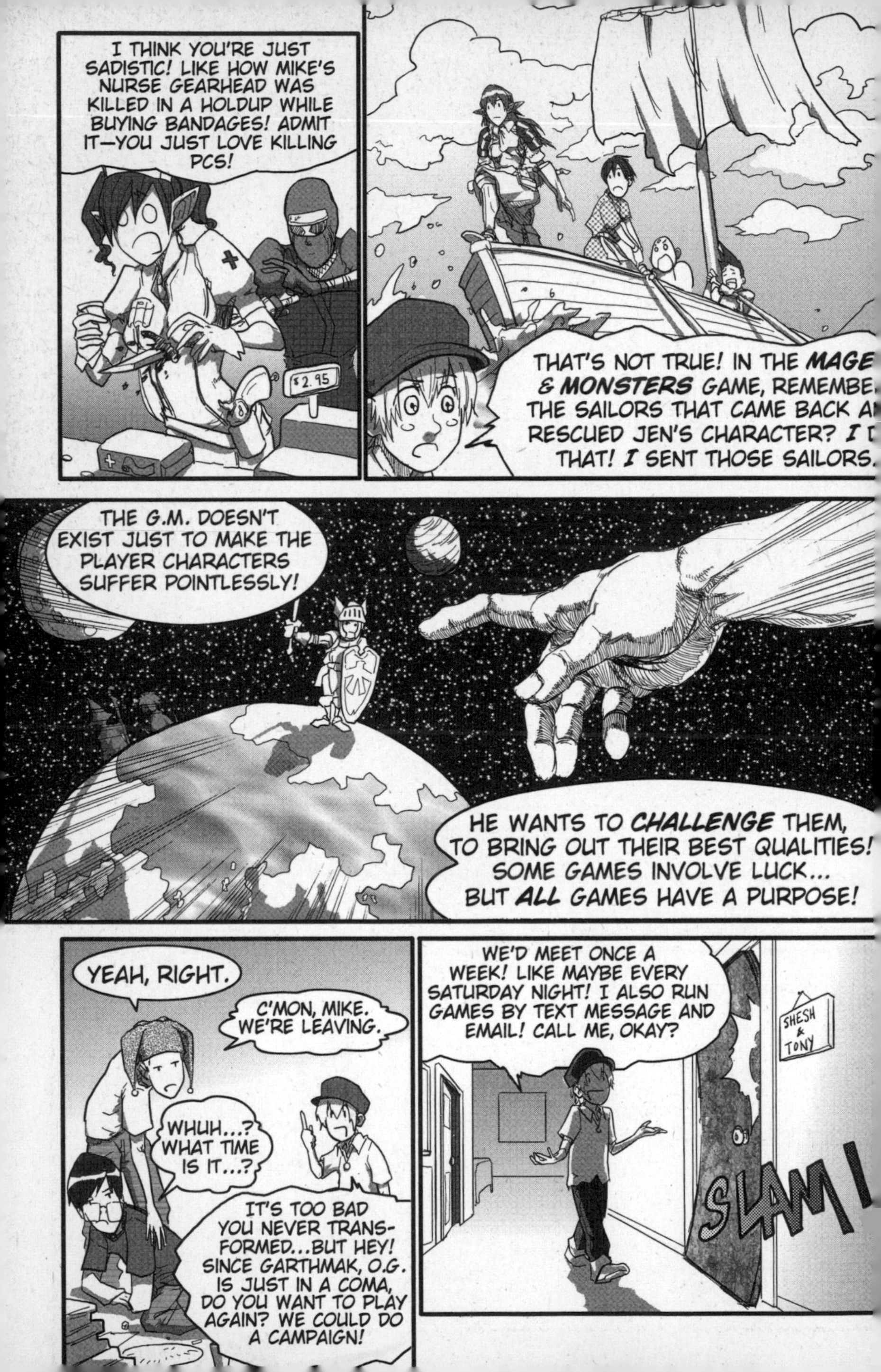
I THINK YOU'RE JUST SADISTIC! LIKE HOW MIKE'S NURSE GEARHEAD WAS KILLED IN A HOLDUP WHILE BUYING BANDAGES! ADMIT IT—YOU JUST LOVE KILLING PCS!
$2.95
THAT'S NOT TRUE! IN THE MAGE & MONSTERS GAME, REMEMBE THE SAILORS THAT CAME BACK A RESCUED JEN'S CHARACTER? I D THAT! I SENT THOSE SAILORS.
THE G.M. DOESN'T EXIST JUST TO MAKE THE PLAYER CHARACTERS SUFFER POINTLESSLY!
HE WANTS TO CHALLENGE THEM, TO BRING OUT THEIR BEST QUALITIES! SOME GAMES INVOLVE LUCK... BUT ALL GAMES HAVE A PURPOSE!
YEAH, RIGHT.
C'MON, MIKE. WE'RE LEAVING.
WHUH...? WHAT TIME IS IT...?
IT'S TOO BAD YOU NEVER TRANS-FORMED...BUT HEY! SINCE GARTHMAK, O.G. IS JUST IN A COMA, DO YOU WANT TO PLAY AGAIN? WE COULD DO A CAMPAIGN!
WE'D MEET ONCE A WEEK! LIKE MAYBE EVERY SATURDAY NIGHT! I ALSO RUN GAMES BY TEXT MESSAGE AND EMAIL! CALL ME, OKAY?
SHESH & TONY
SLAM!

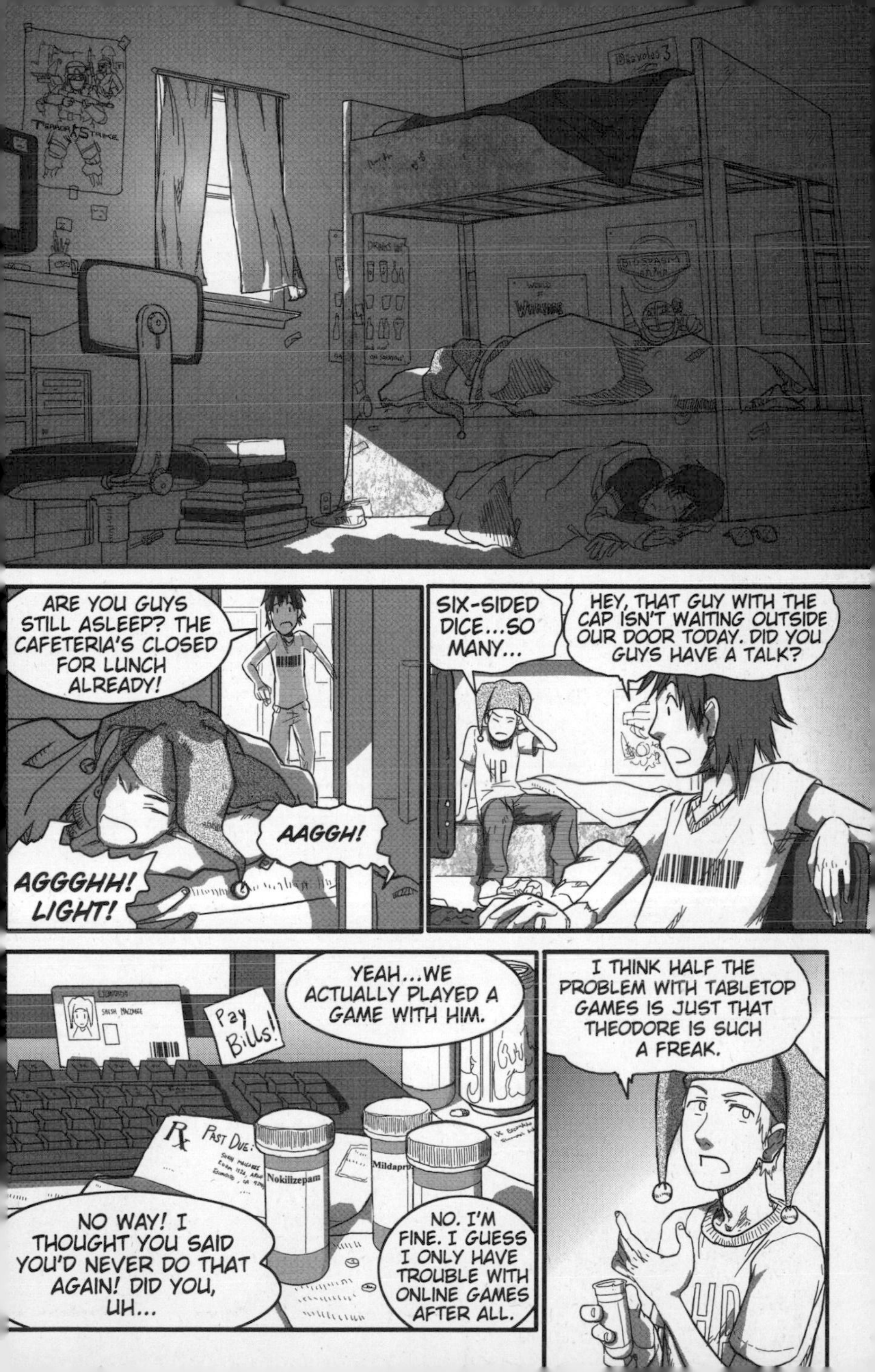
ARE YOU GUYS STILL ASLEEP? THE CAFETERIA'S CLOSED FOR LUNCH ALREADY!
AAGGH!
AGGGHH! LIGHT!
SIX-SIDED DICE...SO MANY...
HEY, THAT GUY WITH THE CAP ISN'T WAITING OUTSIDE OUR DOOR TODAY. DID YOU GUYS HAVE A TALK?
Pay Bills!
YEAH...WE ACTUALLY PLAYED A GAME WITH HIM.
Past Due:
Nokilizepam
NO WAY! I THOUGHT YOU SAID YOU'D NEVER DO THAT AGAIN! DID YOU, UH...
NO. I'M FINE. I GUESS I ONLY HAVE TROUBLE WITH ONLINE GAMES AFTER ALL.
I THINK HALF THE PROBLEM WITH TABLETOP GAMES IS JUST THAT THEODORE IS SUCH A FREAK.

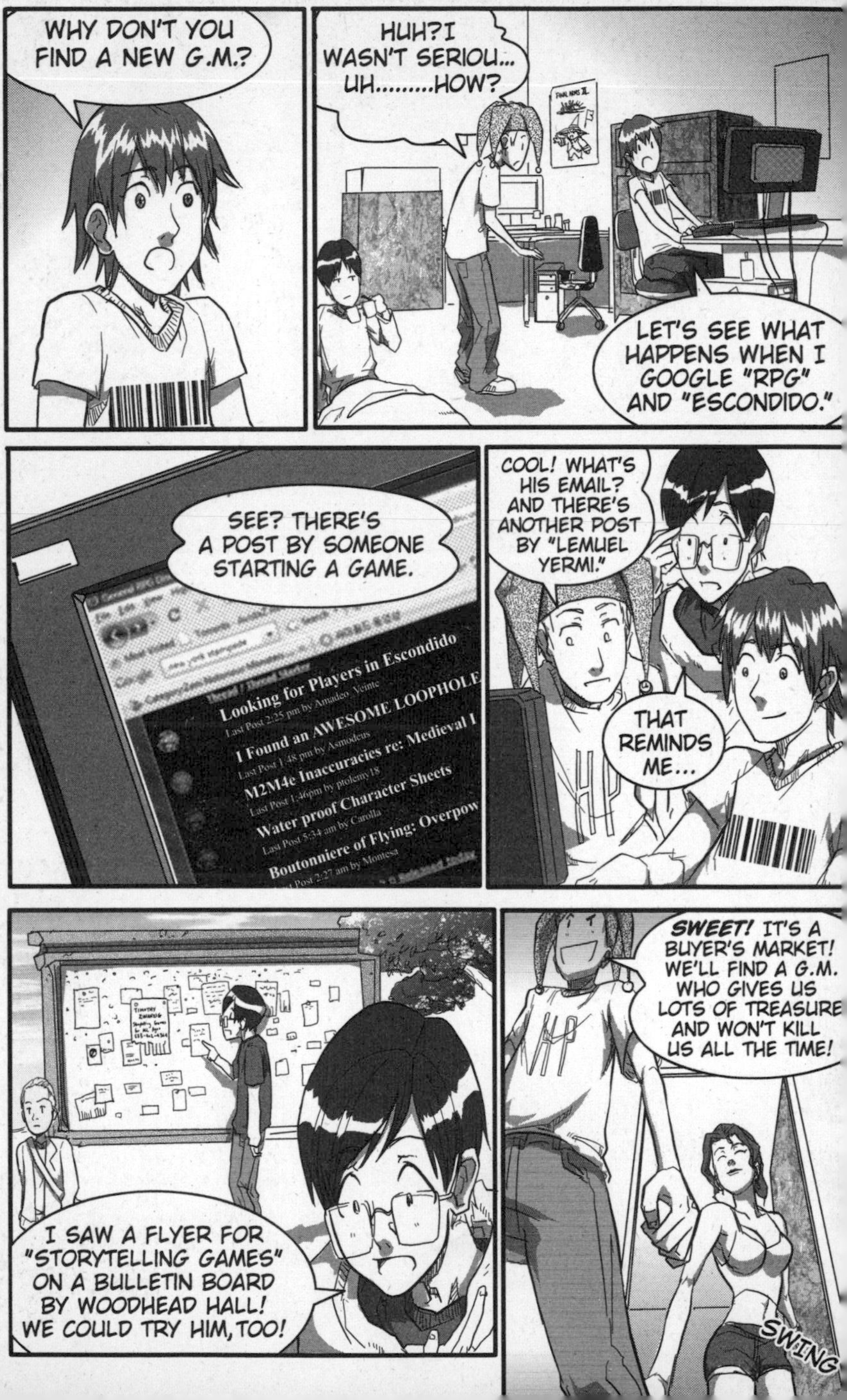
WHY DON'T YOU FIND A NEW G.M.?
HUH?I WASN'T SERIOU... UH.........HOW?
LET'S SEE WHAT HAPPENS WHEN I GOOGLE "RPG" AND "ESCONDIDO."
SEE? THERE'S A POST BY SOMEONE STARTING A GAME.
Looking for Players in Escondido
Last Post 2:25 pm by Amadeo_Veinte
I Found an AWESOME LOOPHOLE
Last Post 1:48 pm by Asmodeus
M2M4e Inaccuracies re: Medieval I
Last Post 1:46pm by ptolemy18
Water proof Character Sheets
Last Post 5:34 am by Carolla
Boutonniere of Flying: Overpow
Last Post 2:27 am by Montesa
COOL! WHAT'S HIS EMAIL? AND THERE'S ANOTHER POST BY "LEMUEL YERMI."
THAT REMINDS ME...
I SAW A FLYER FOR "STORYTELLING GAMES" ON A BULLETIN BOARD BY WOODHEAD HALL! WE COULD TRY HIM, TOO!
SWEET! IT'S A BUYER'S MARKET! WE'LL FIND A G.M. WHO GIVES US LOTS OF TREASURE AND WON'T KILL US ALL THE TIME!
SWING

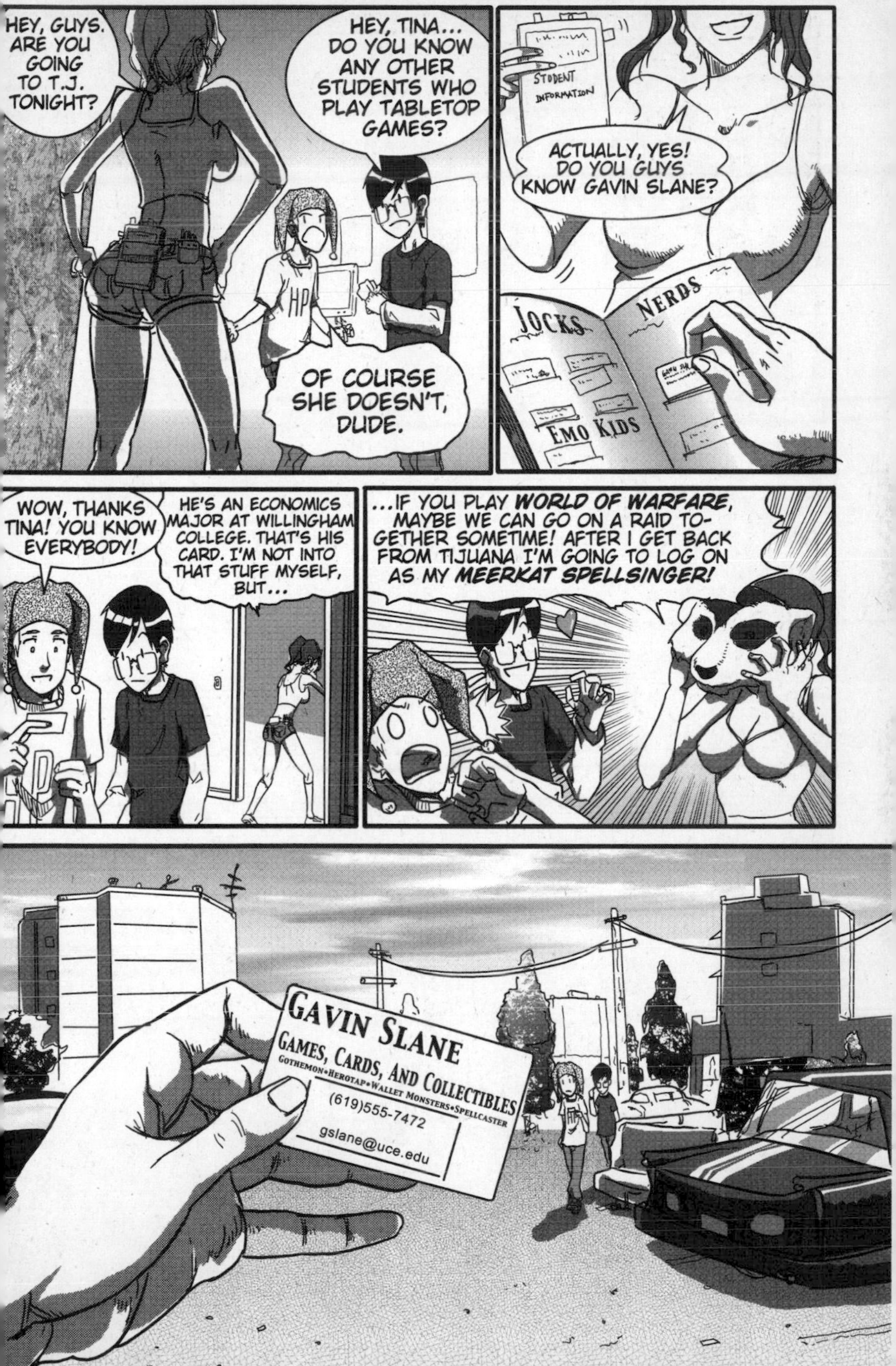
HEY, GUYS. ARE YOU GOING TO T.J. TONIGHT?
HEY, TINA... DO YOU KNOW ANY OTHER STUDENTS WHO PLAY TABLETOP GAMES?
OF COURSE SHE DOESN'T, DUDE.
STUDENT INFORMATION
ACTUALLY, YES! DO YOU GUYS KNOW GAVIN SLANE?
JOCKS
NERDS
EMO KIDS
WOW, THANKS TINA! YOU KNOW EVERYBODY!
HE'S AN ECONOMICS MAJOR AT WILLINGHAM COLLEGE. THAT'S HIS CARD. I'M NOT INTO THAT STUFF MYSELF, BUT...
...IF YOU PLAY ***WORLD OF WARFARE***, MAYBE WE CAN GO ON A RAID TOGETHER SOMETIME! AFTER I GET BACK FROM TIJUANA I'M GOING TO LOG ON AS MY ***MEERKAT SPELLSINGER!***
GAVIN SLANE
GAMES, CARDS, AND COLLECTIBLES
GOTHEMON•HEROTAP•WALLET MONSTERS•SPELLCASTER
(619)555-7472
gslane@uce.edu

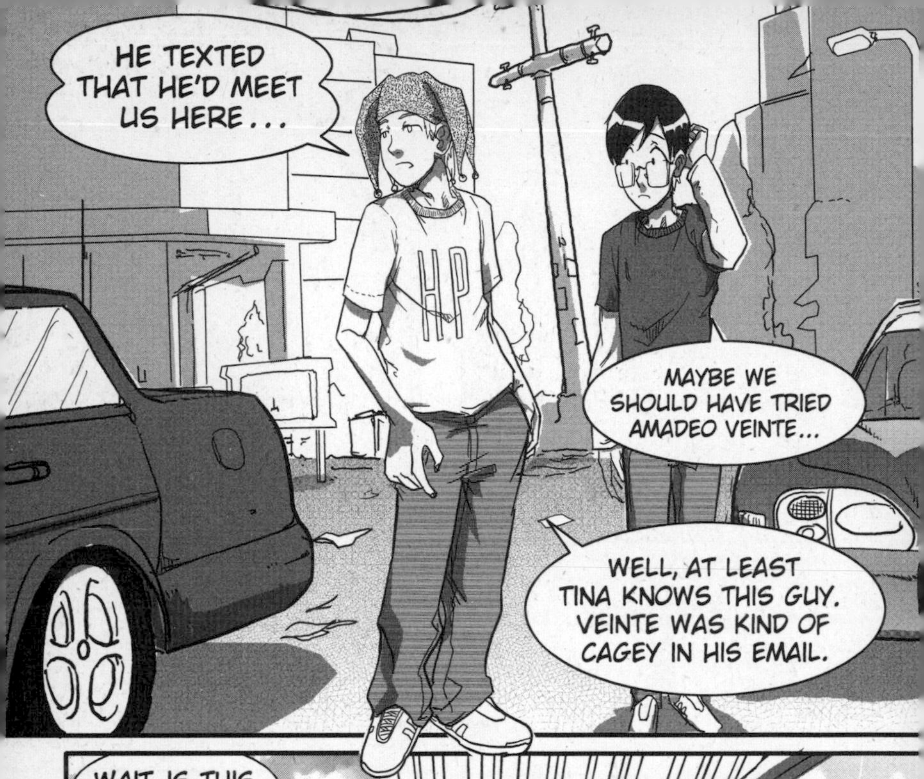
HE TEXTED THAT HE'D MEET US HERE...
MAYBE WE SHOULD HAVE TRIED AMADEO VEINTE...
WELL, AT LEAST TINA KNOWS THIS GUY. VEINTE WAS KIND OF CAGEY IN HIS EMAIL.

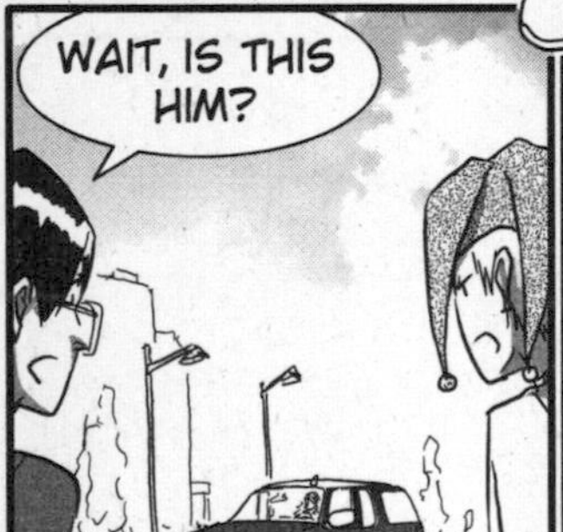
WAIT, IS THIS HIM?
NO WAY THAT'S A GAMER'S CAR!

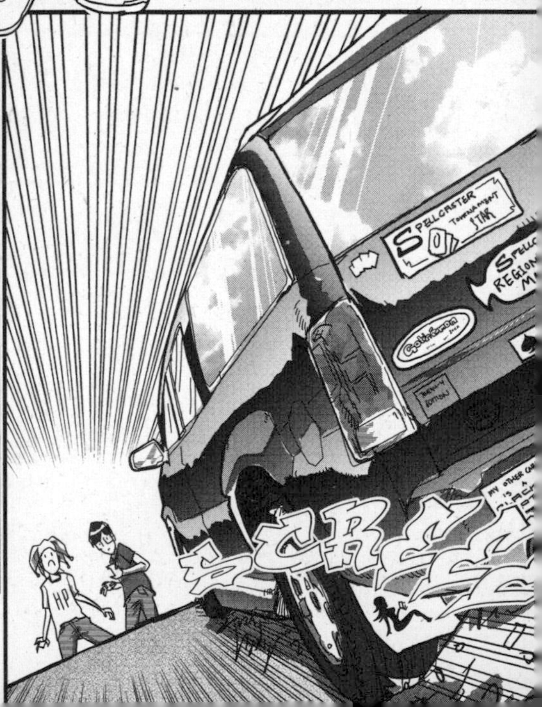

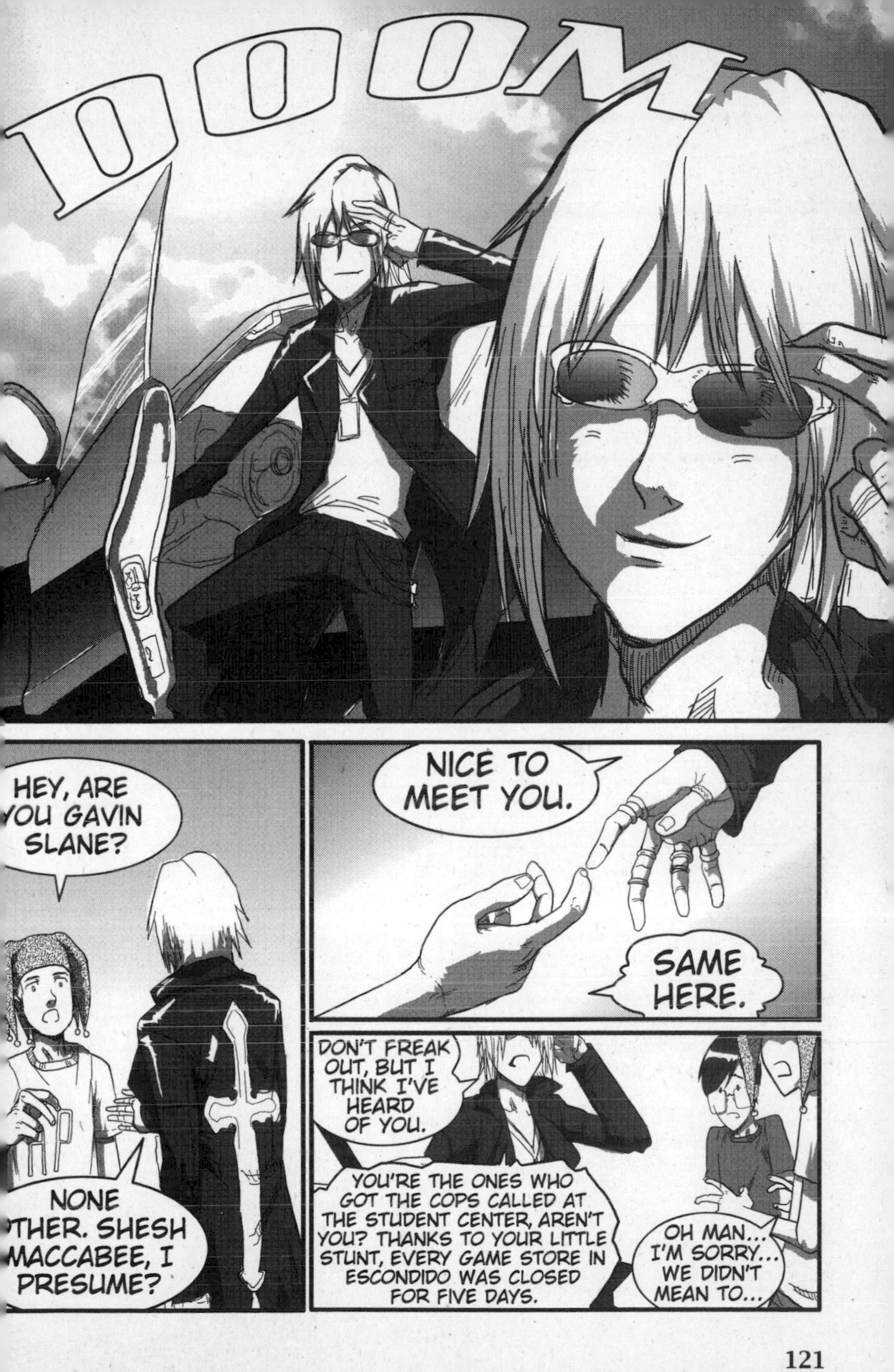
DOOOM
HEY, ARE YOU GAVIN SLANE?
NONE OTHER. SHESH MACCABEE, I PRESUME?
NICE TO MEET YOU.
SAME HERE.
DON'T FREAK OUT, BUT I THINK I'VE HEARD OF YOU.
YOU'RE THE ONES WHO GOT THE COPS CALLED AT THE STUDENT CENTER, AREN'T YOU? THANKS TO YOUR LITTLE STUNT, EVERY GAME STORE IN ESCONDIDO WAS CLOSED FOR FIVE DAYS.
OH MAN... I'M SORRY... WE DIDN'T MEAN TO...

NO, IT'S FINE! IN FACT, I OWE YOU ONE!

THE GOTHÉMON EXPANSION *"TENEBROUS SHADOW OF DARK UMBRA"* WAS SUPPOSED TO COME OUT THAT WEEK! BECAUSE NONE OF THE LOCAL STORES WERE OPEN, I DROVE UP TO L.A., BOUGHT 1,000 PACKS OF BOOSTERS, AND BROUGHT THEM DOWN HERE TO ESCONDIDO!

GOTHÉMON

TONIGHT: TAPIOCA PUDDING & SPECIAL INVESTMENT SPEAKER

SOLD EVERY ONE OF THEM FOR $5.99 PER PACK! MALLS, JUNIOR HIGHS, GROUP HOMES...THE HYPE FOR THIS RELEASE WAS *TREMENDOUS!*

GOTHÉMON CARDS $2.99 & UP NEW REL

OF COURSE, I INVESTED ALL MY PROFITS IN THE NEW EXPANSION, *"SACRIFICE TO DEMON GOD BELIAL"*...

...EXCUSE ME, I FORGOT, IN THE U.S. THEY'RE CALLING IT *"TRIBUTE TO MAMODO BERIA."* TOO OCCULT-SOUNDING, YOU KNOW.

YOU SELL CARDS AS A HOBBY?

NOT A HOBBY. A *BUSINESS.*

WE HAVE WALLET MONSTERS

COLLECTIBLE CARDS AND MINIS ARE A *20 BILLION DOLLAR A YEAR* INDUSTRY!

THE FIRST GENERATION OF *WALLET MONSTERS* PLAYERS ARE JUST STARTING TO MOVE ON TO MORE SOPHISTICATED GAMES. GAMING IS ALL ABOUT *PRODUCT!*

122

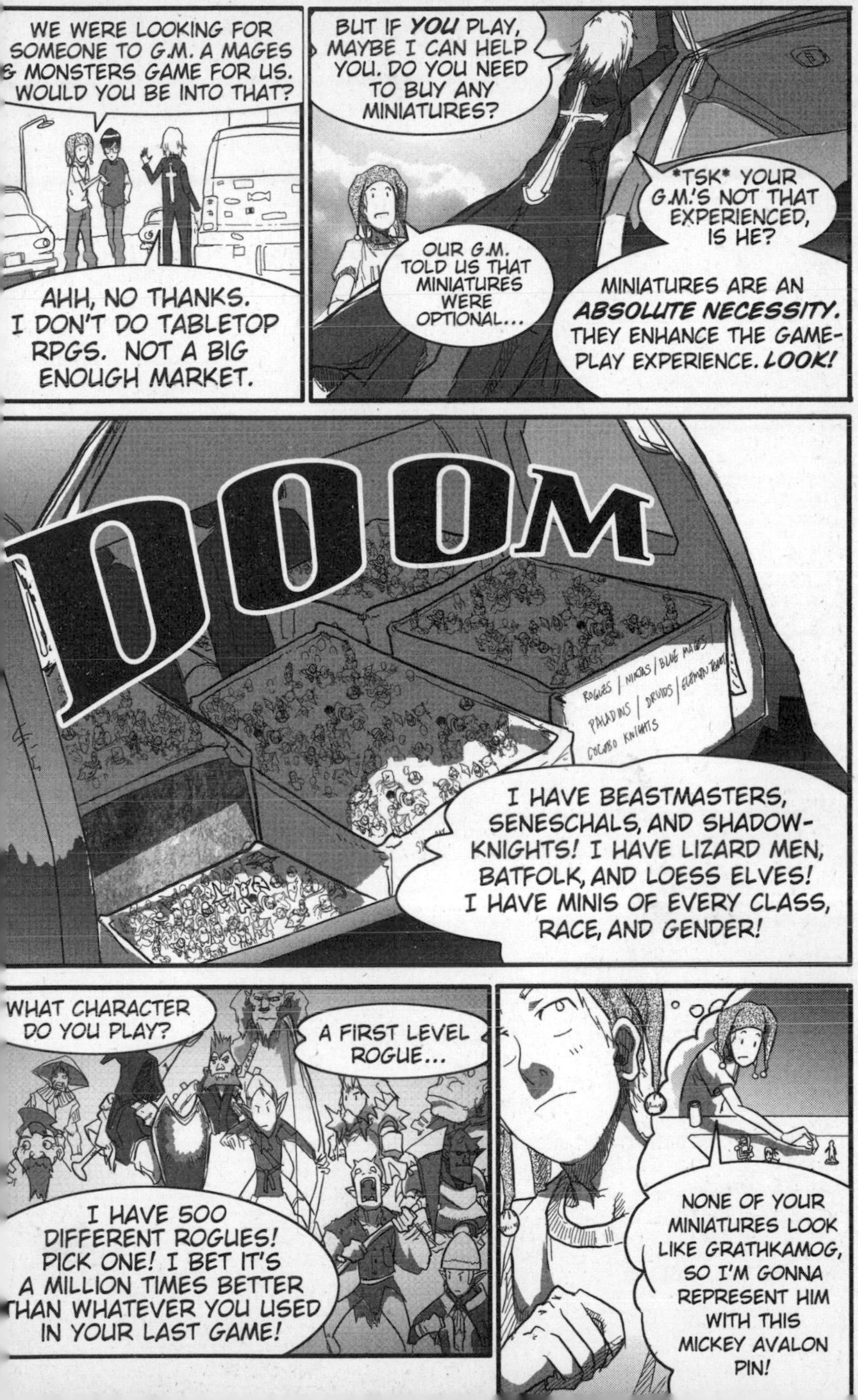
WE WERE LOOKING FOR SOMEONE TO G.M. A MAGES & MONSTERS GAME FOR US. WOULD YOU BE INTO THAT?
AHH, NO THANKS. I DON'T DO TABLETOP RPGS. NOT A BIG ENOUGH MARKET.
BUT IF YOU PLAY, MAYBE I CAN HELP YOU. DO YOU NEED TO BUY ANY MINIATURES?
OUR G.M. TOLD US THAT MINIATURES WERE OPTIONAL...
TSK YOUR G.M.'S NOT THAT EXPERIENCED, IS HE?
MINIATURES ARE AN ABSOLUTE NECESSITY. THEY ENHANCE THE GAME-PLAY EXPERIENCE. LOOK!
DOOM
ROGUES / NINJAS / BLUE MAGES
PALADINS / DRUIDS /
COCOBO KNIGHTS
I HAVE BEASTMASTERS, SENESCHALS, AND SHADOW-KNIGHTS! I HAVE LIZARD MEN, BATFOLK, AND LOESS ELVES! I HAVE MINIS OF EVERY CLASS, RACE, AND GENDER!
WHAT CHARACTER DO YOU PLAY?
A FIRST LEVEL ROGUE...
I HAVE 500 DIFFERENT ROGUES! PICK ONE! I BET IT'S A MILLION TIMES BETTER THAN WHATEVER YOU USED IN YOUR LAST GAME!
NONE OF YOUR MINIATURES LOOK LIKE GRATHKAMOG, SO I'M GONNA REPRESENT HIM WITH THIS MICKEY AVALON PIN!

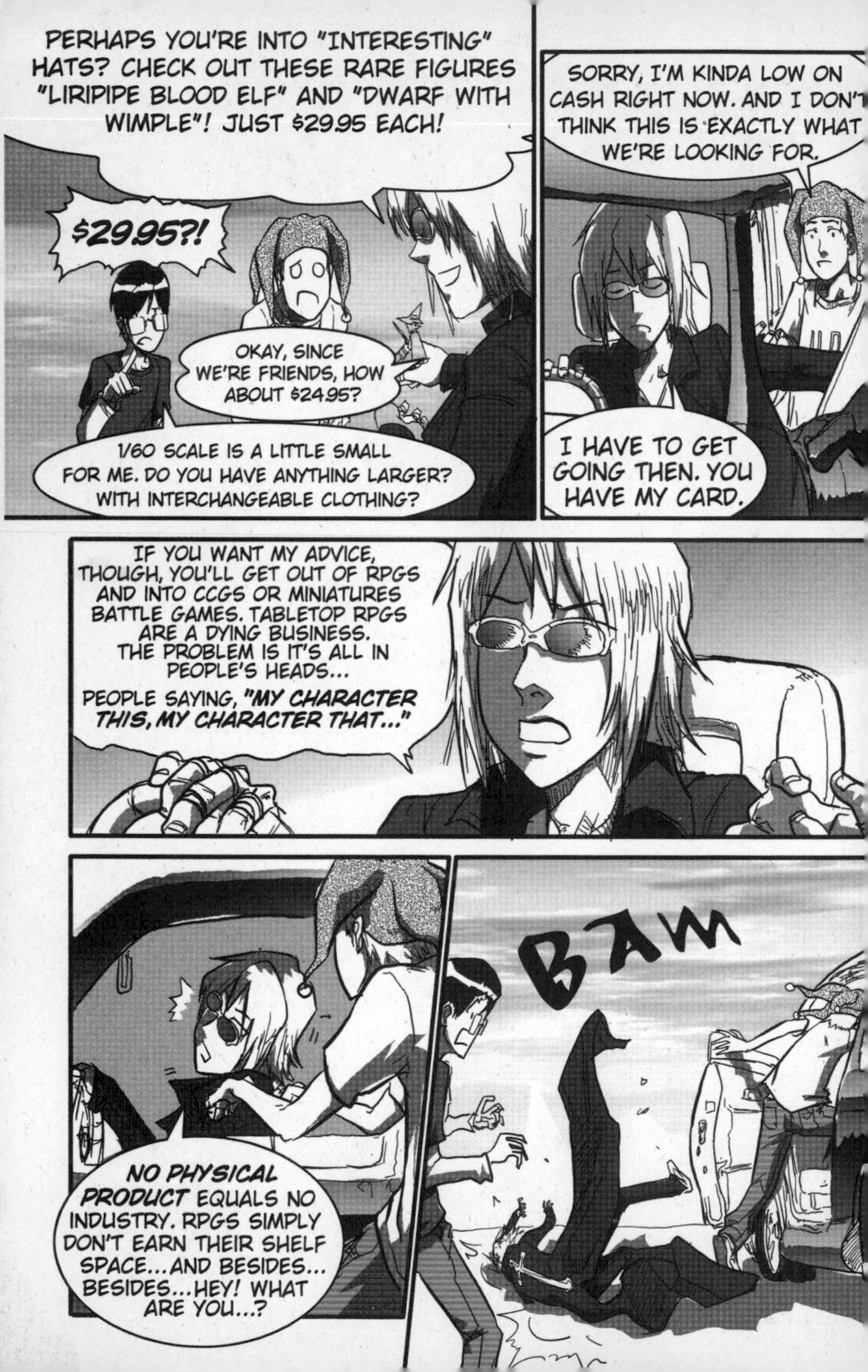
PERHAPS YOU'RE INTO "INTERESTING" HATS? CHECK OUT THESE RARE FIGURES "LIRIPIPE BLOOD ELF" AND "DWARF WITH WIMPLE"! JUST $29.95 EACH!
$29.95?!
OKAY, SINCE WE'RE FRIENDS, HOW ABOUT $24.95?
1/60 SCALE IS A LITTLE SMALL FOR ME. DO YOU HAVE ANYTHING LARGER? WITH INTERCHANGEABLE CLOTHING?
SORRY, I'M KINDA LOW ON CASH RIGHT NOW. AND I DON'T THINK THIS IS EXACTLY WHAT WE'RE LOOKING FOR.
I HAVE TO GET GOING THEN. YOU HAVE MY CARD.
IF YOU WANT MY ADVICE, THOUGH, YOU'LL GET OUT OF RPGS AND INTO CCGS OR MINIATURES BATTLE GAMES. TABLETOP RPGS ARE A DYING BUSINESS. THE PROBLEM IS IT'S ALL IN PEOPLE'S HEADS...
PEOPLE SAYING, *"MY CHARACTER THIS, MY CHARACTER THAT..."*
NO PHYSICAL PRODUCT EQUALS NO INDUSTRY. RPGS SIMPLY DON'T EARN THEIR SHELF SPACE...AND BESIDES... BESIDES...HEY! WHAT ARE YOU...?
BAM

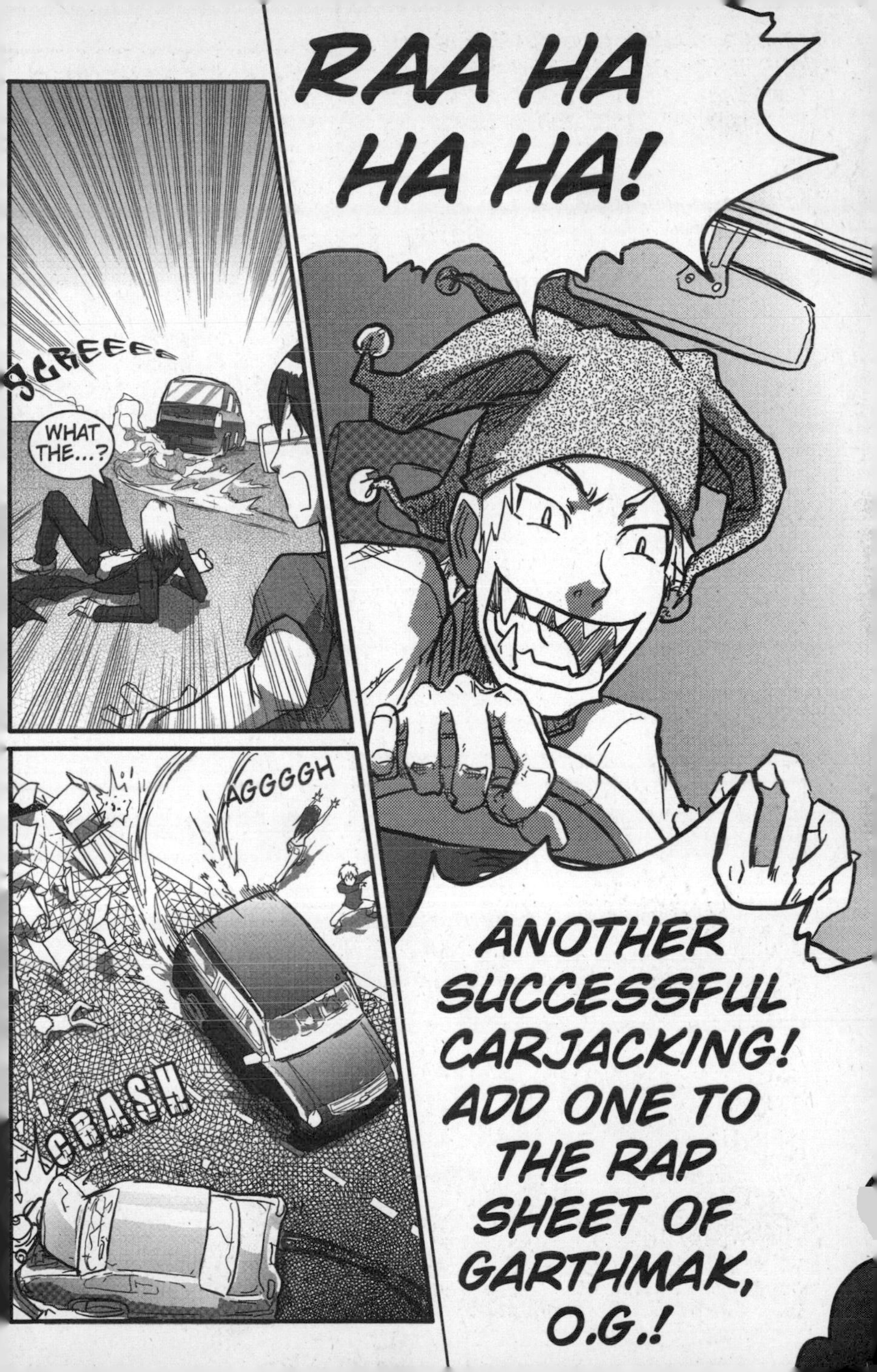
SCREEEE
WHAT THE...?
AGGGGH
CRASH
RAA HA HA HA!
ANOTHER SUCCESSFUL CARJACKING! ADD ONE TO THE RAP SHEET OF GARTHMAK, O.G.!

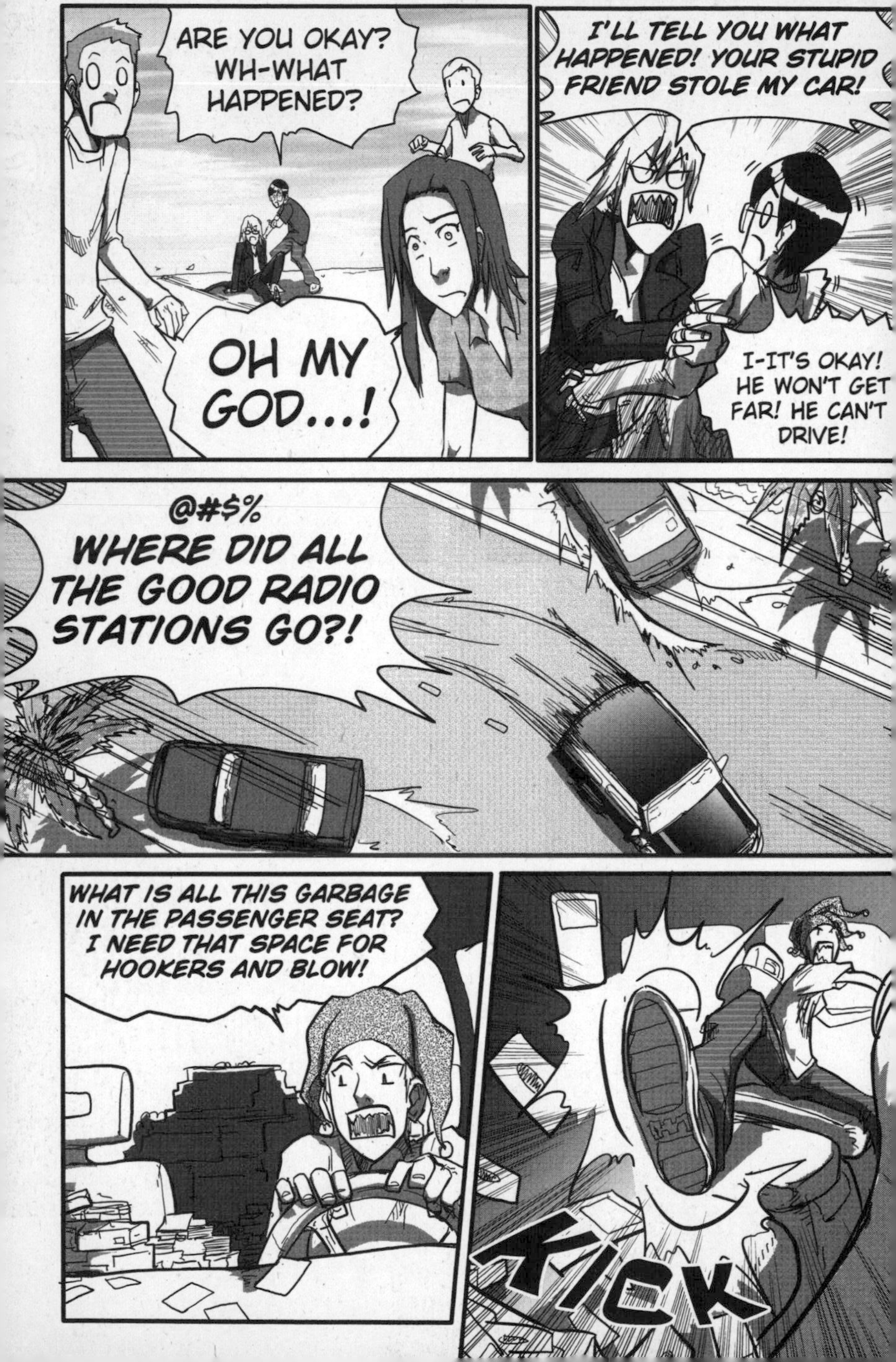
ARE YOU OKAY? WH-WHAT HAPPENED?
OH MY GOD...!
I'LL TELL YOU WHAT HAPPENED! YOUR STUPID FRIEND STOLE MY CAR!
I-IT'S OKAY! HE WON'T GET FAR! HE CAN'T DRIVE!
@#$% WHERE DID ALL THE GOOD RADIO STATIONS GO?!
WHAT IS ALL THIS GARBAGE IN THE PASSENGER SEAT? I NEED THAT SPACE FOR HOOKERS AND BLOW!
KICK

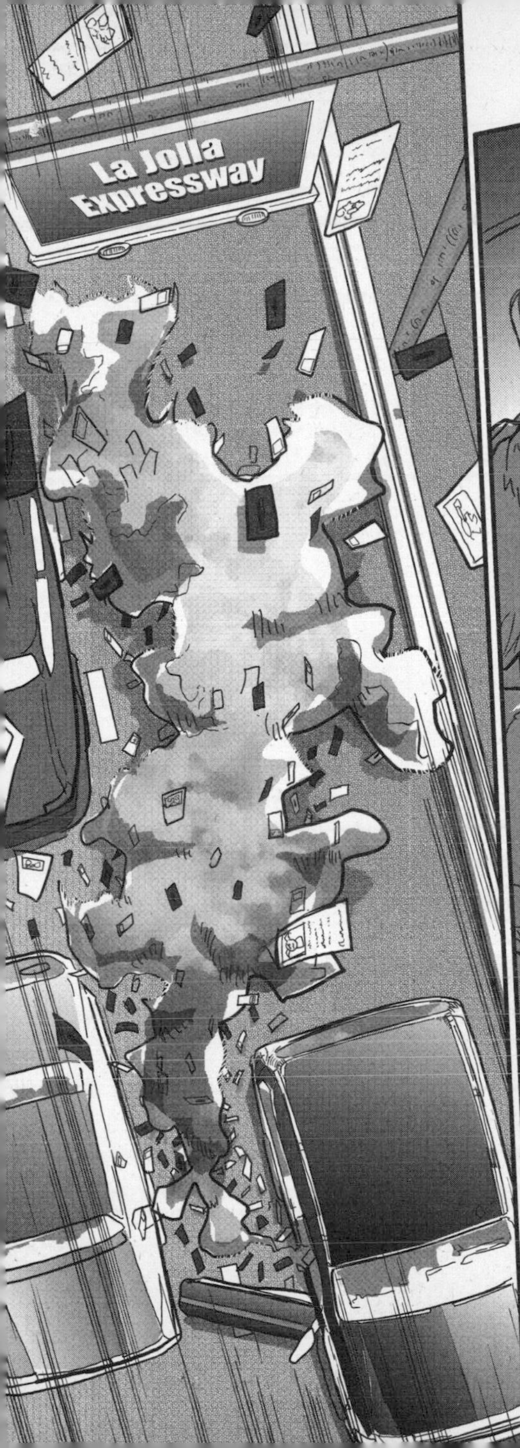
La Jolla
Expressway
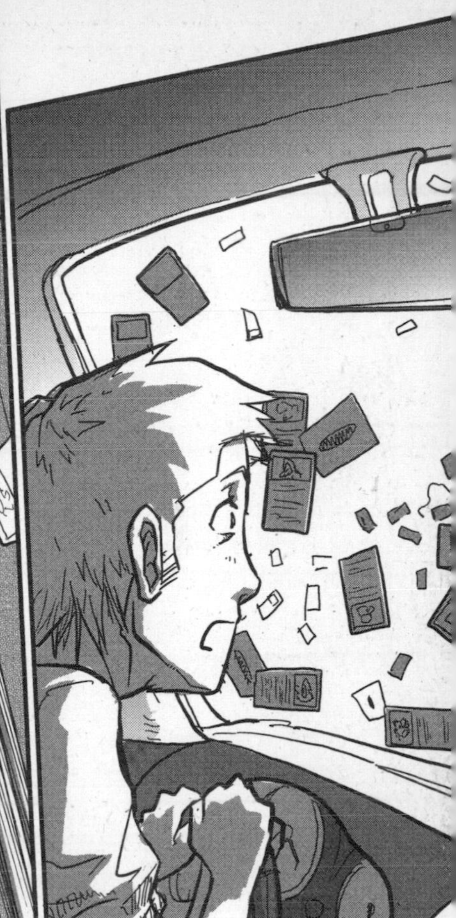

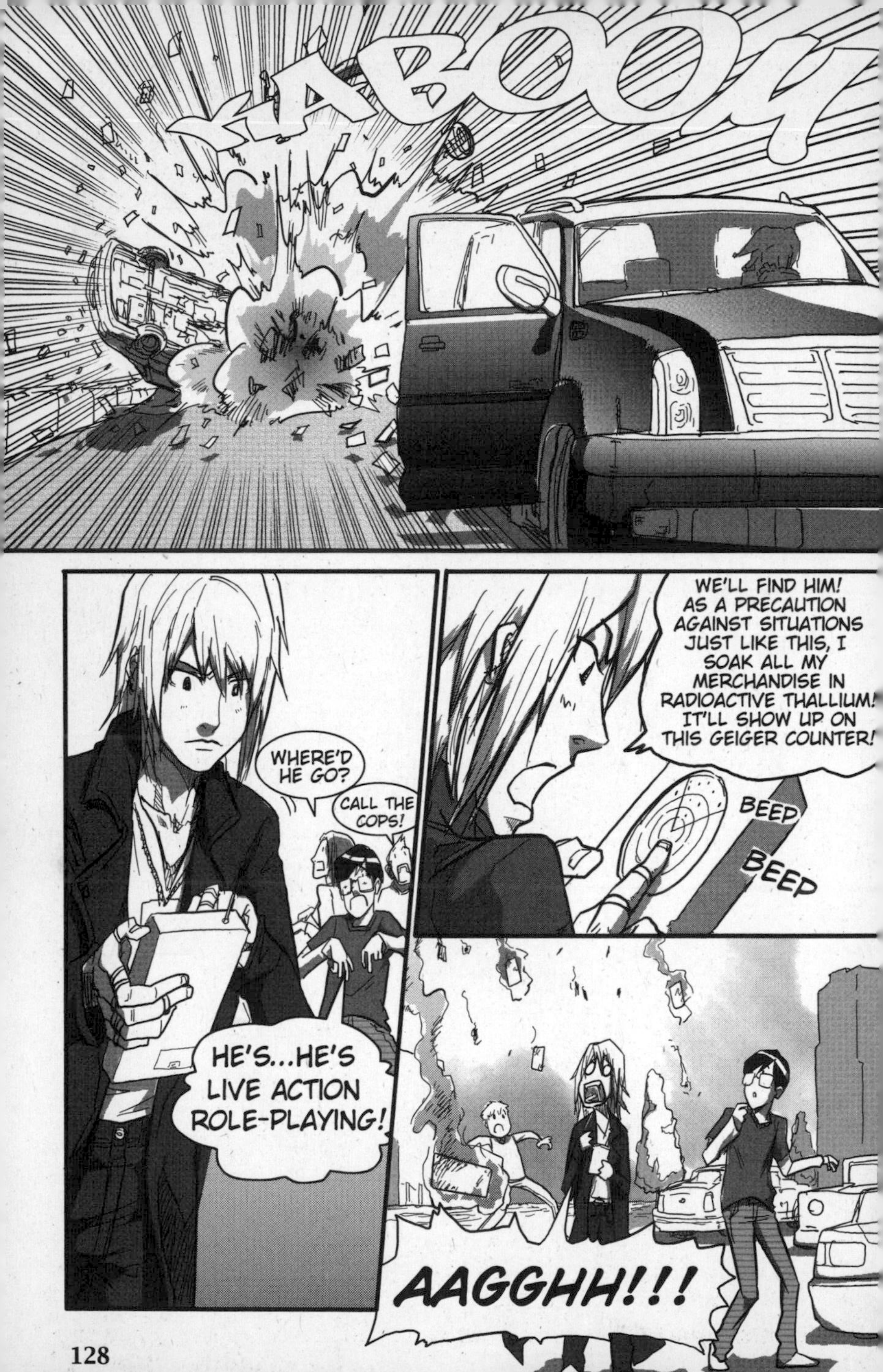
KABOOM
WHERE'D HE GO?
CALL THE COPS!
HE'S...HE'S LIVE ACTION ROLE-PLAYING!
WE'LL FIND HIM! AS A PRECAUTION AGAINST SITUATIONS JUST LIKE THIS, I SOAK ALL MY MERCHANDISE IN RADIOACTIVE THALLIUM! IT'LL SHOW UP ON THIS GEIGER COUNTER!
BEEP
BEEP
AAGGHH!!!

CURSE YOU, SHESH MACCABEE! I'LL NEVER FORGIVE YOU FOR THIS!

MAYBE—

POLICE

91·1

THEO? ARE YOU THERE?

HELLO, THEODORE DUDEK SPEAKING?

MIKE?! WHAT'S GOING ON?

THEO! I NEED YOUR HELP! SHESH IS ON A RAMPAGE! HE THINKS HE'S STILL IN YOUR GAME!

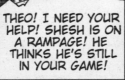

YEAH! I SEE IT! DON'T WORRY, I'LL STOP HIM!

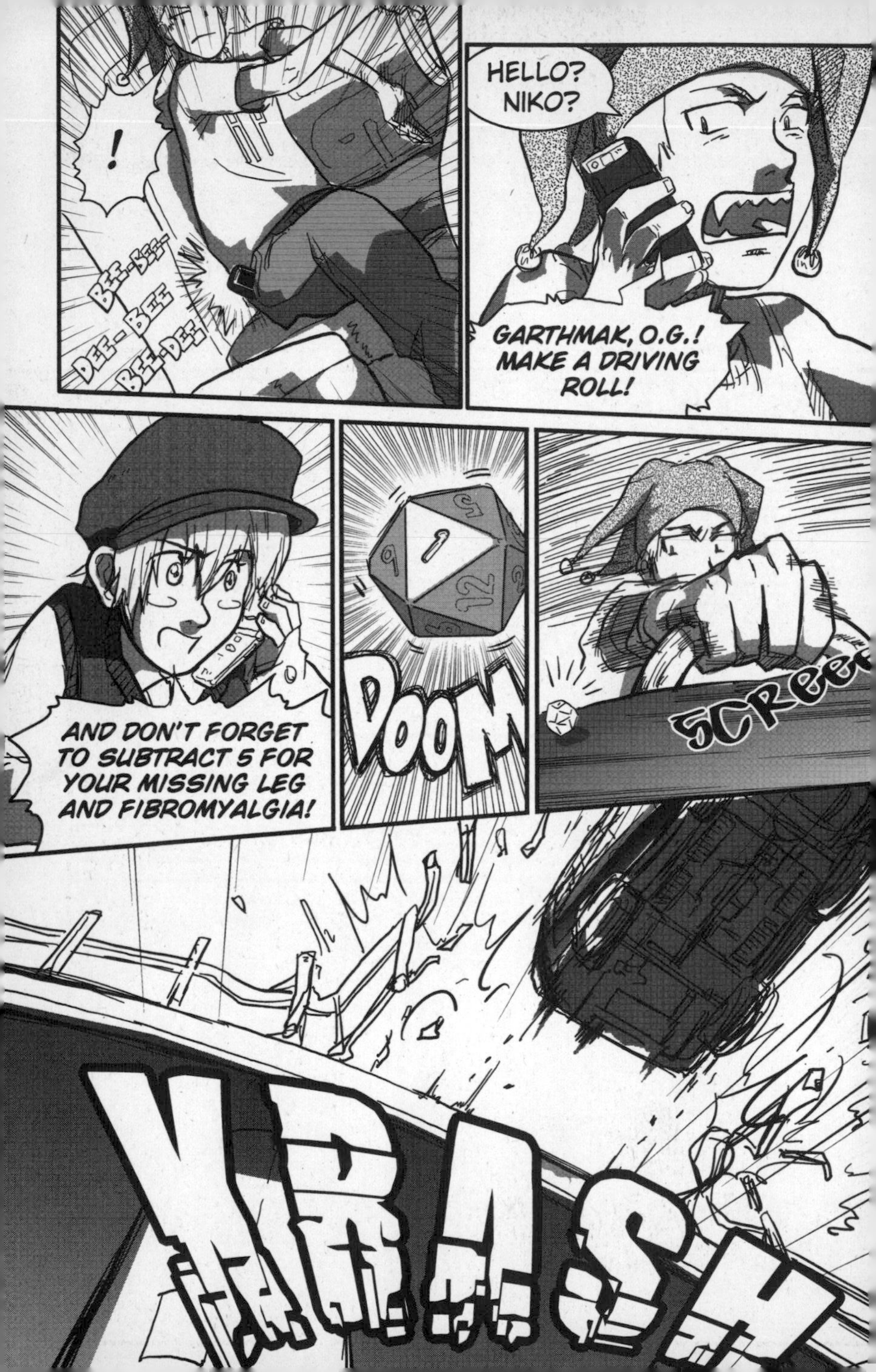
!
BEE-BEE-DEE-BEE-BEE-DEE
HELLO? NIKO?
GARTHMAK, O.G.! MAKE A DRIVING ROLL!
AND DON'T FORGET TO SUBTRACT 5 FOR YOUR MISSING LEG AND FIBROMYALGIA!
DOOM
SCREEE
KRASH

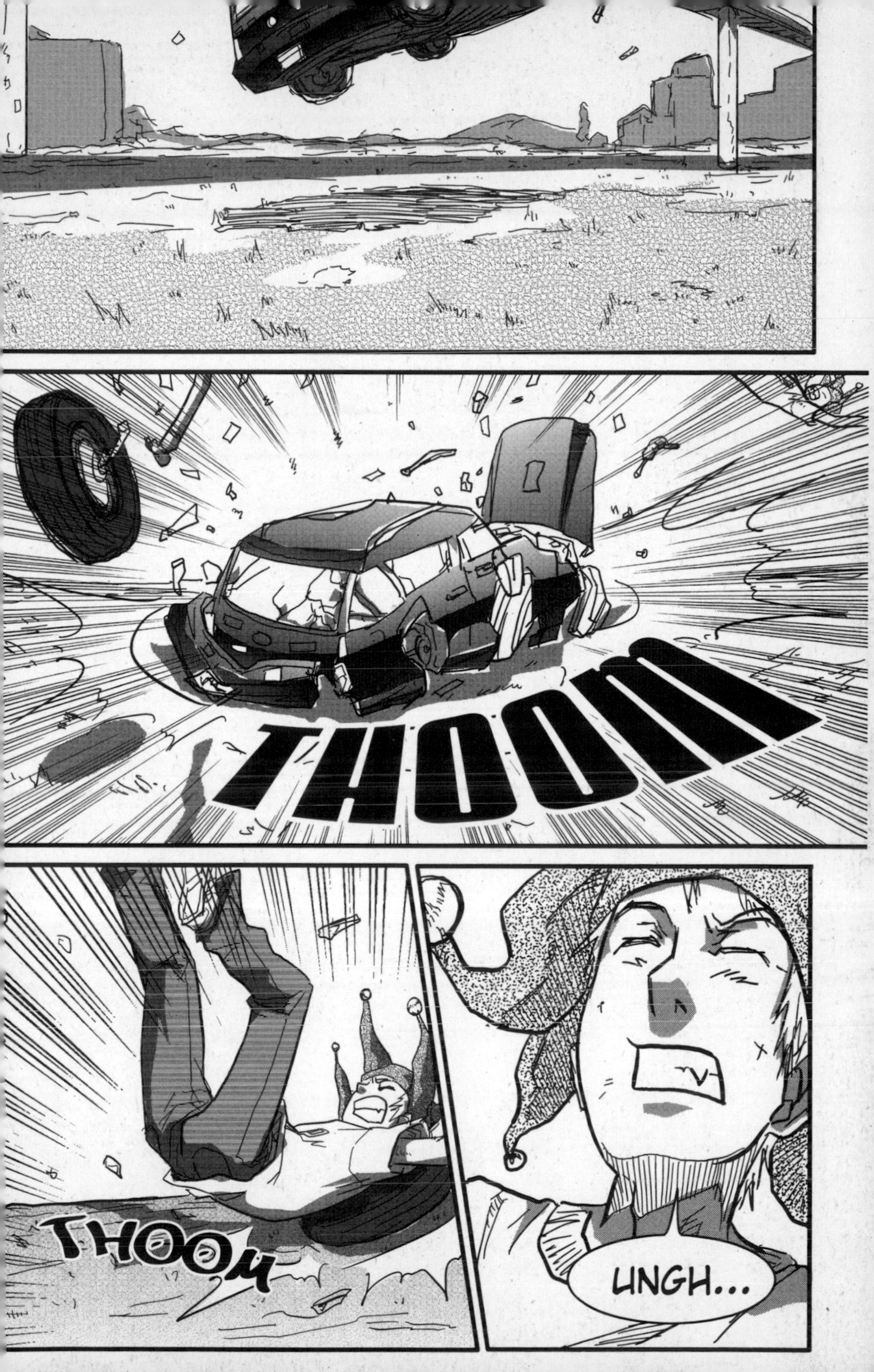
THOOM
THOOM
UNGH...

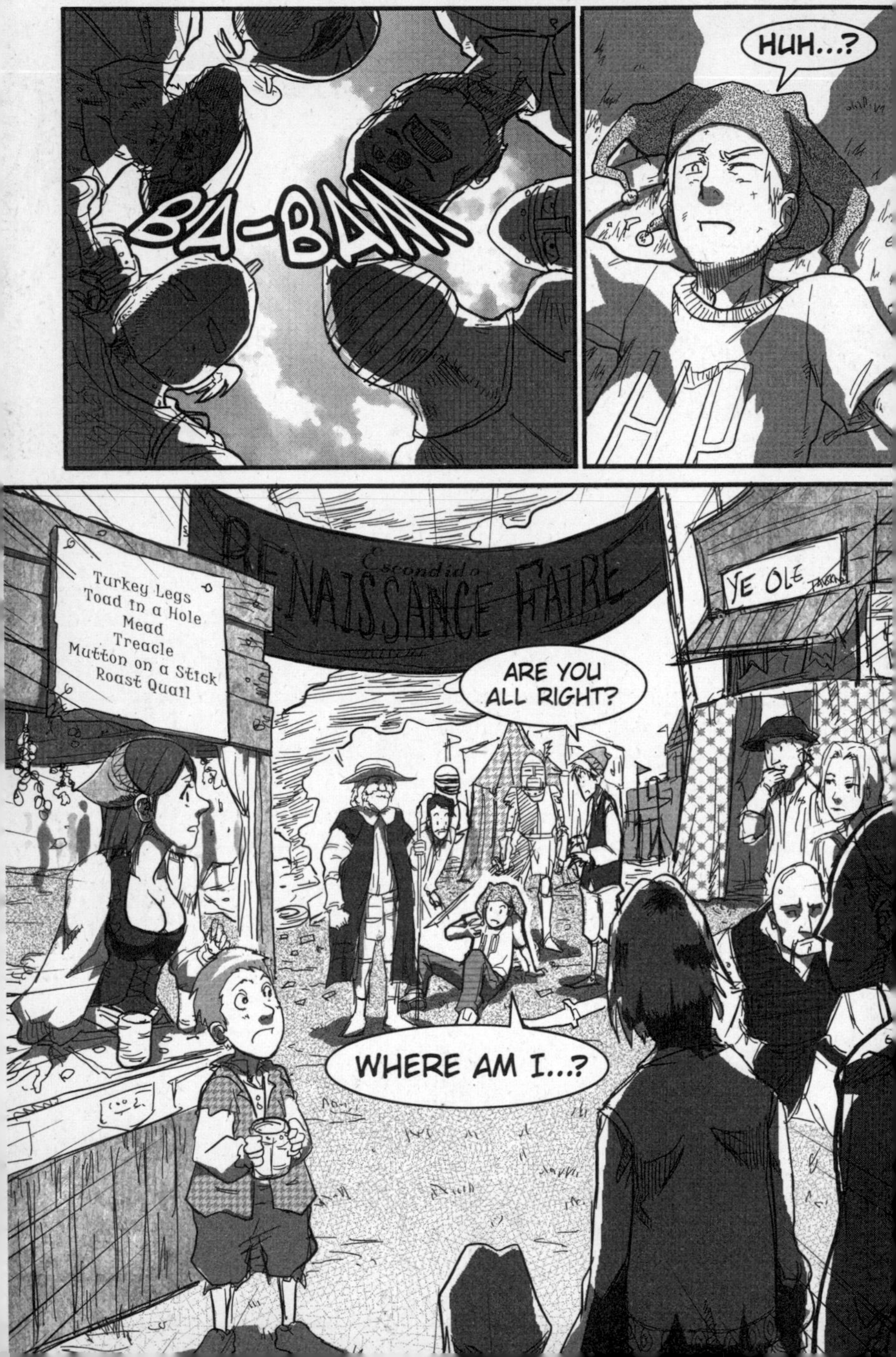
BA-BAM
HUH...?
Turkey Legs
Toad in a Hole
Mead
Treacle
Mutton on a Stick
Roast Quail
Escondido
RENAISSANCE FAIRE
YE OLE
ARE YOU ALL RIGHT?
WHERE AM I...?

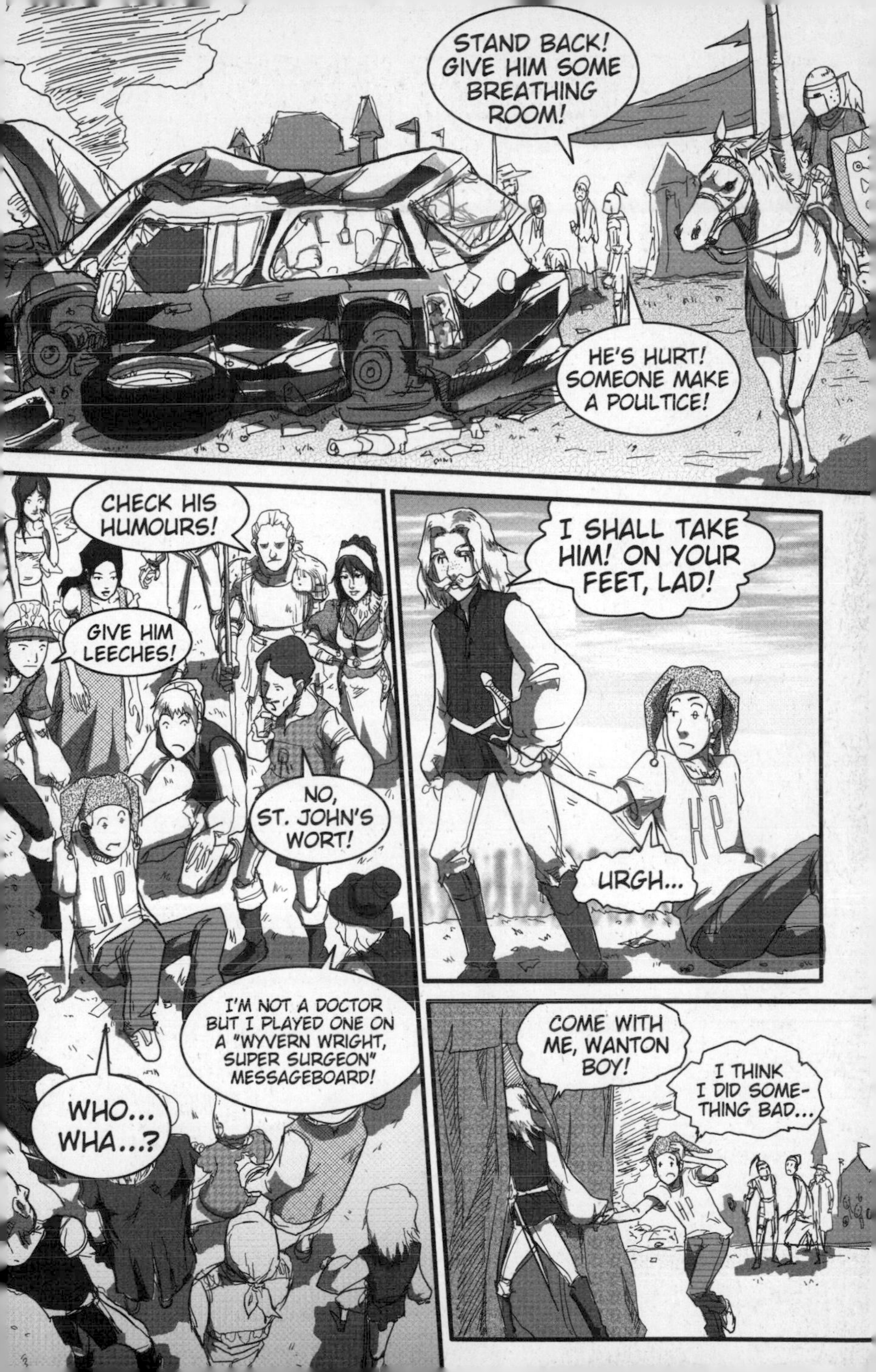
STAND BACK! GIVE HIM SOME BREATHING ROOM!
HE'S HURT! SOMEONE MAKE A POULTICE!
CHECK HIS HUMOURS!
GIVE HIM LEECHES!
NO, ST. JOHN'S WORT!
I'M NOT A DOCTOR BUT I PLAYED ONE ON A "WYVERN WRIGHT, SUPER SURGEON" MESSAGEBOARD!
WHO... WHA...?
I SHALL TAKE HIM! ON YOUR FEET, LAD!
URGH...
COME WITH ME, WANTON BOY!
I THINK I DID SOMETHING BAD...

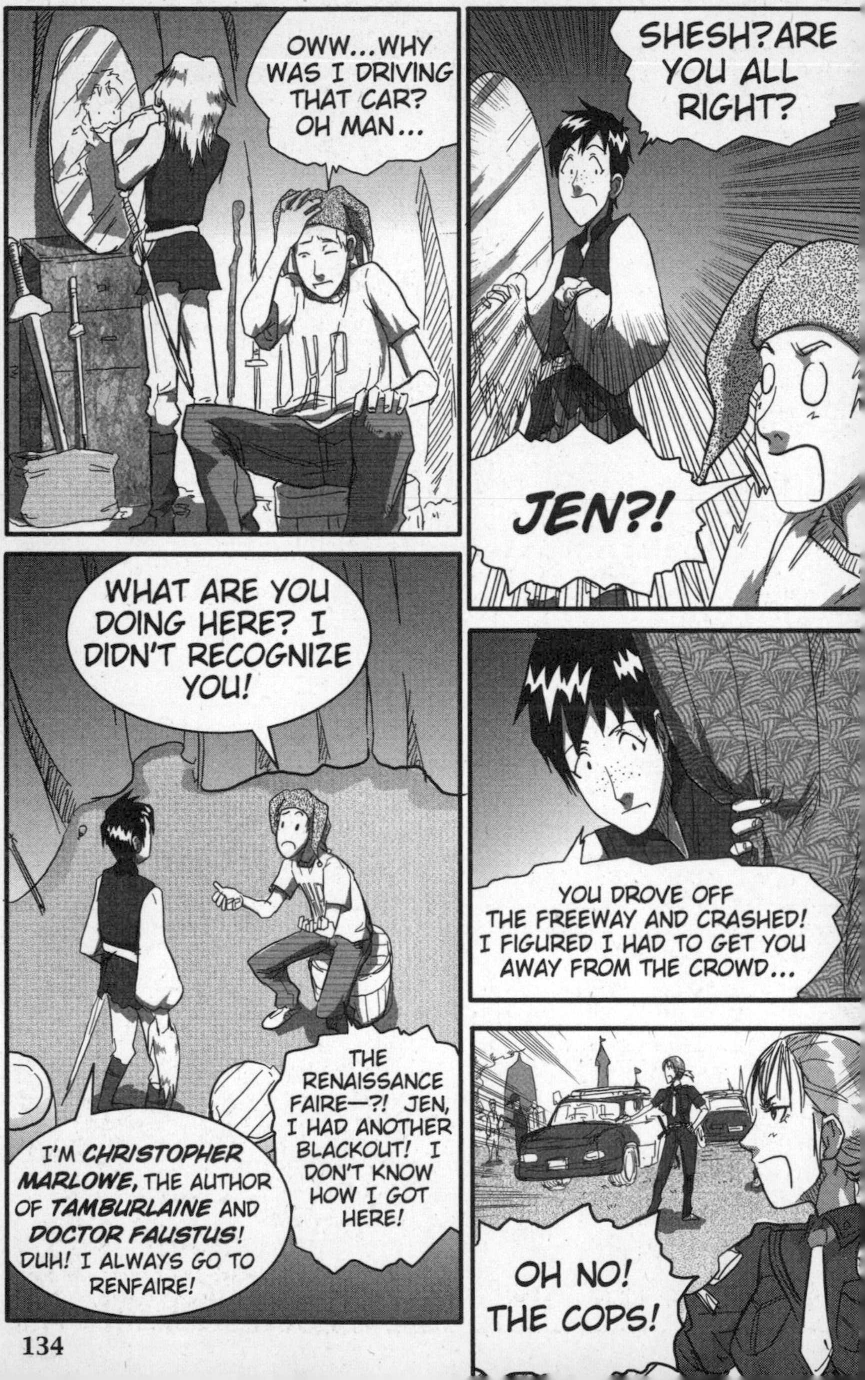
OWW...WHY WAS I DRIVING THAT CAR? OH MAN...
SHESH?ARE YOU ALL RIGHT?
JEN?!
WHAT ARE YOU DOING HERE? I DIDN'T RECOGNIZE YOU!
I'M *CHRISTOPHER MARLOWE,* THE AUTHOR OF *TAMBURLAINE* AND *DOCTOR FAUSTUS*! DUH! I ALWAYS GO TO RENFAIRE!
THE RENAISSANCE FAIRE—?! JEN, I HAD ANOTHER BLACKOUT! I DON'T KNOW HOW I GOT HERE!
YOU DROVE OFF THE FREEWAY AND CRASHED! I FIGURED I HAD TO GET YOU AWAY FROM THE CROWD...
OH NO! THE COPS!

RONA!!!

YOU KNOW HER?

WHAT ARE YOU DOING WITH THAT GUTENBERG BIBLE?

THIS ISN'T A BIBLE! IT'S MY LAPTOP! SINCE I'M WORKING FAIRE IT HAS TO HAVE A RENAISSANCE THEME!

PLUS IT HAS A FILTER SO IT CAN ONLY ACCESS THE *RENAISSANCE INTERNET!* BUT ANYWAY... LEMME CHECK THE NEWS!

WHY ARE THEY AFTER ME? WHAT DID I DO?

Ye Googelle

Webb Bookes Maps Tidings Wares

escondido carjacking

IMAGE RESULTS:
Image Resultes for escondido carjacking - Reporte Images

RESULTS:
Subject Sought in *Escondido Carjacking*
Police have still not identified the man responsible for the 12 car pileup on the La Jolla Freeway ...
unionsandiego.com/news/42312514.html

Minute Coverage

LET'S GO! LET'S GO!

HE CAN'T HAVE GOTTEN FAR!

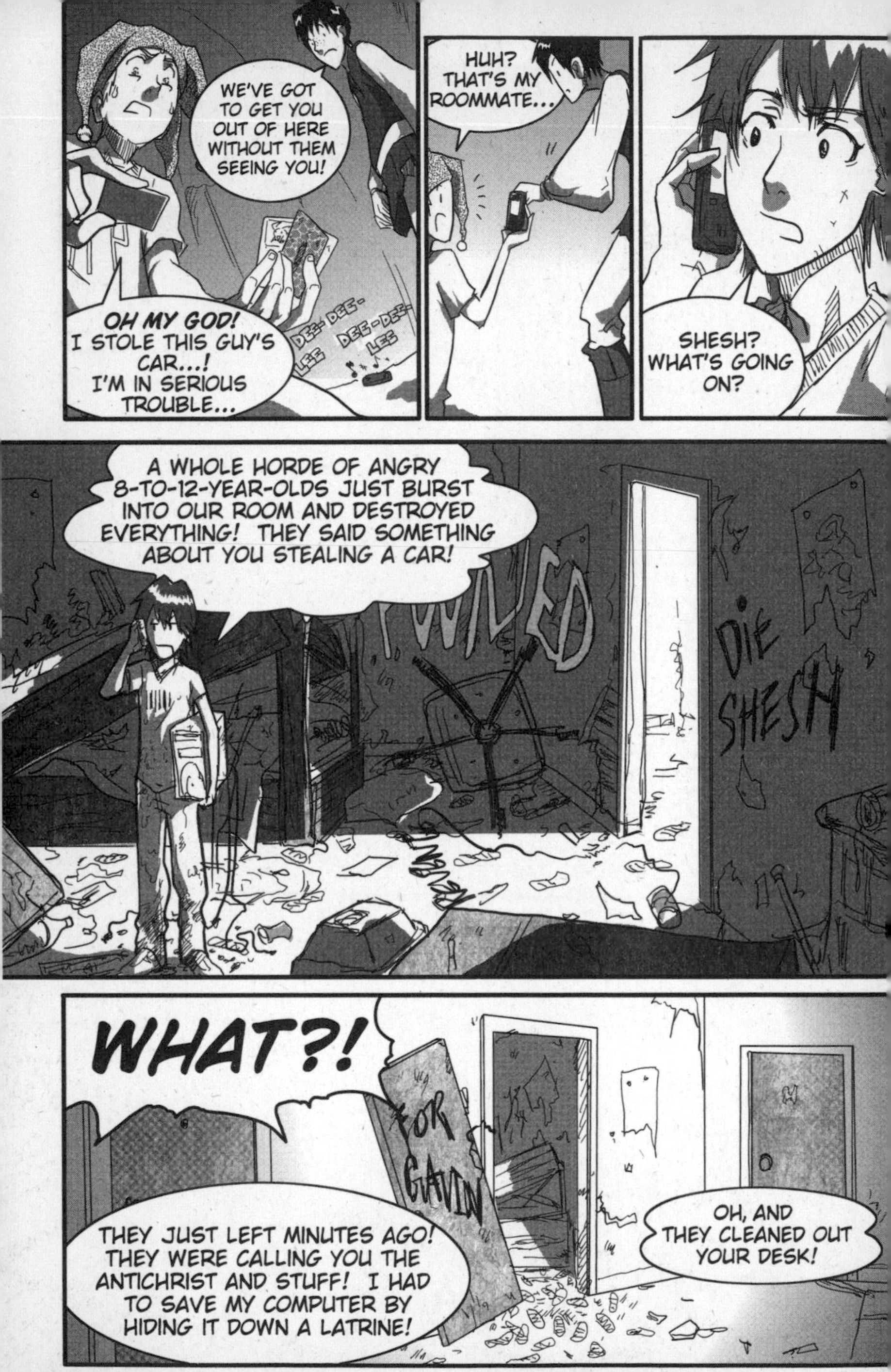
WE'VE GOT TO GET YOU OUT OF HERE WITHOUT THEM SEEING YOU!
OH MY GOD! I STOLE THIS GUY'S CAR...! I'M IN SERIOUS TROUBLE...
DEE-DEE-LEE DEE-DEE-LEE
HUH? THAT'S MY ROOMMATE...
SHESH? WHAT'S GOING ON?
A WHOLE HORDE OF ANGRY 8-TO-12-YEAR-OLDS JUST BURST INTO OUR ROOM AND DESTROYED EVERYTHING! THEY SAID SOMETHING ABOUT YOU STEALING A CAR!
PWNED
DIE SHESH
WHAT?!
FOR GAVIN
THEY JUST LEFT MINUTES AGO! THEY WERE CALLING YOU THE ANTICHRIST AND STUFF! I HAD TO SAVE MY COMPUTER BY HIDING IT DOWN A LATRINE!
OH, AND THEY CLEANED OUT YOUR DESK!

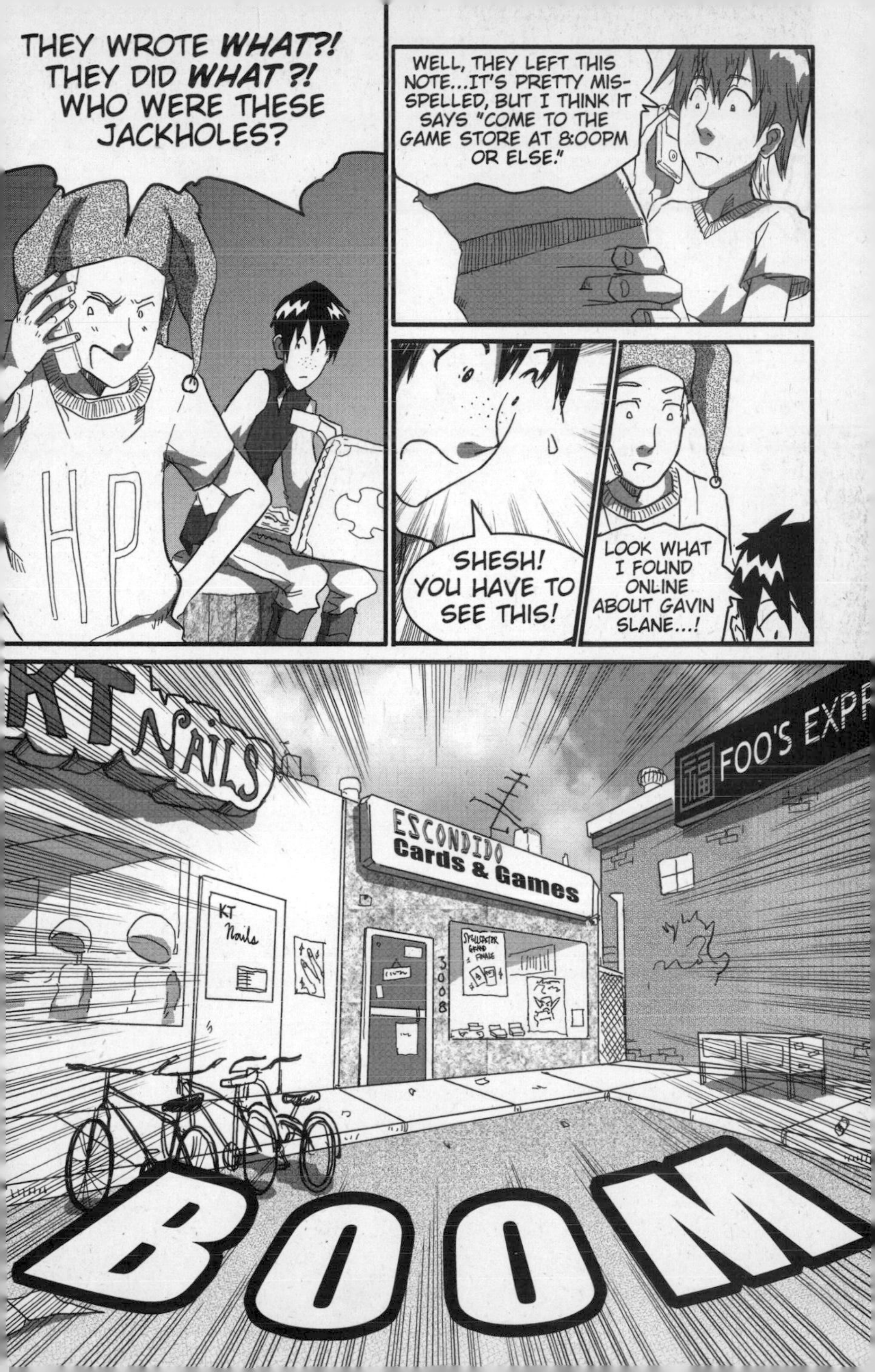
THEY WROTE WHAT?! THEY DID WHAT?! WHO WERE THESE JACKHOLES?
HP
WELL, THEY LEFT THIS NOTE...IT'S PRETTY MIS-SPELLED, BUT I THINK IT SAYS "COME TO THE GAME STORE AT 8:00PM OR ELSE."
SHESH! YOU HAVE TO SEE THIS!
LOOK WHAT I FOUND ONLINE ABOUT GAVIN SLANE...!
KT Nails
FOO'S EXPR
ESCONDIDO Cards & Games
KT Nails
3008
BOOM

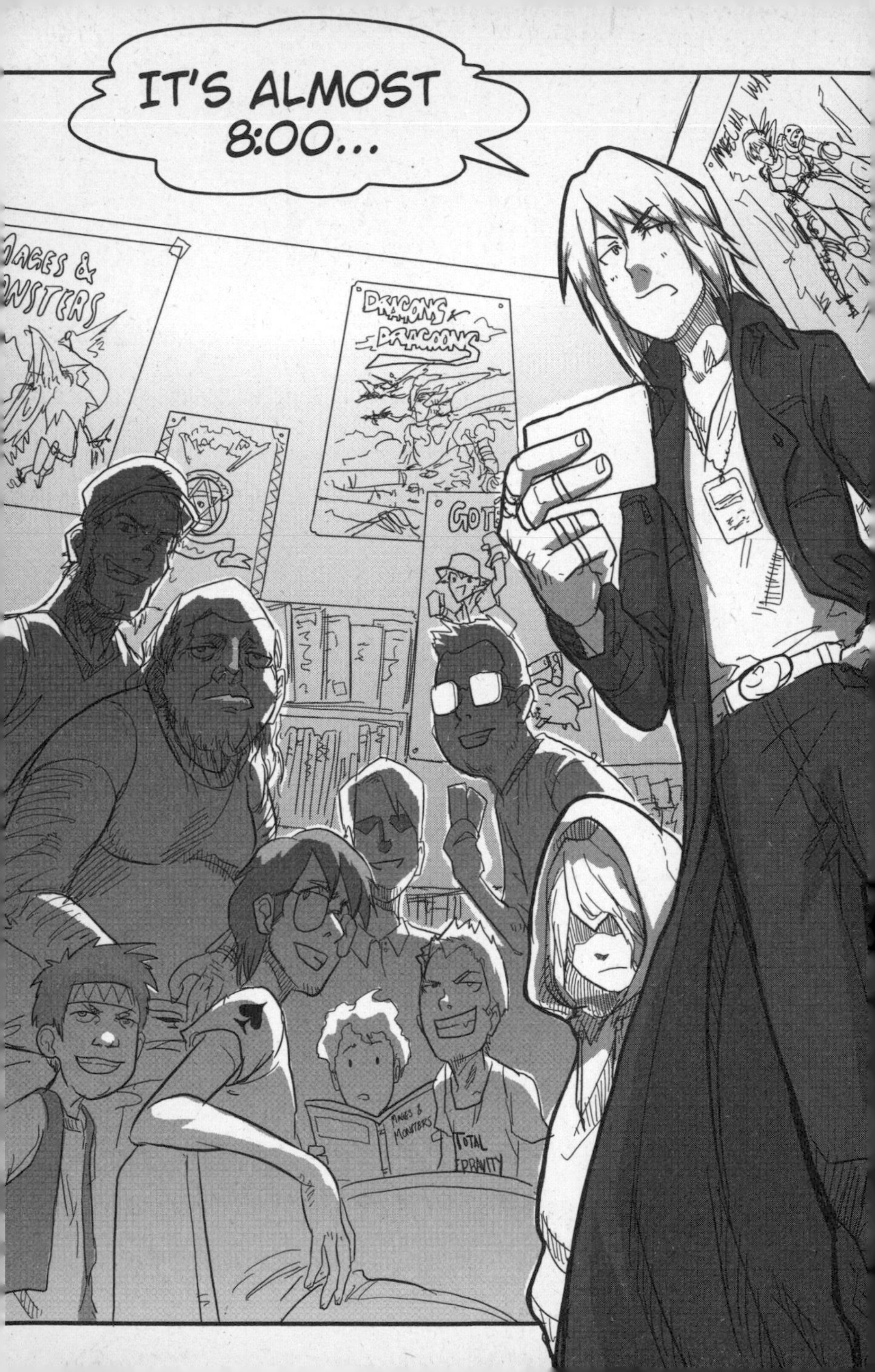
IT'S ALMOST 8:00...
DRAGONS & DRAGOONS
MAGES & MONSTERS

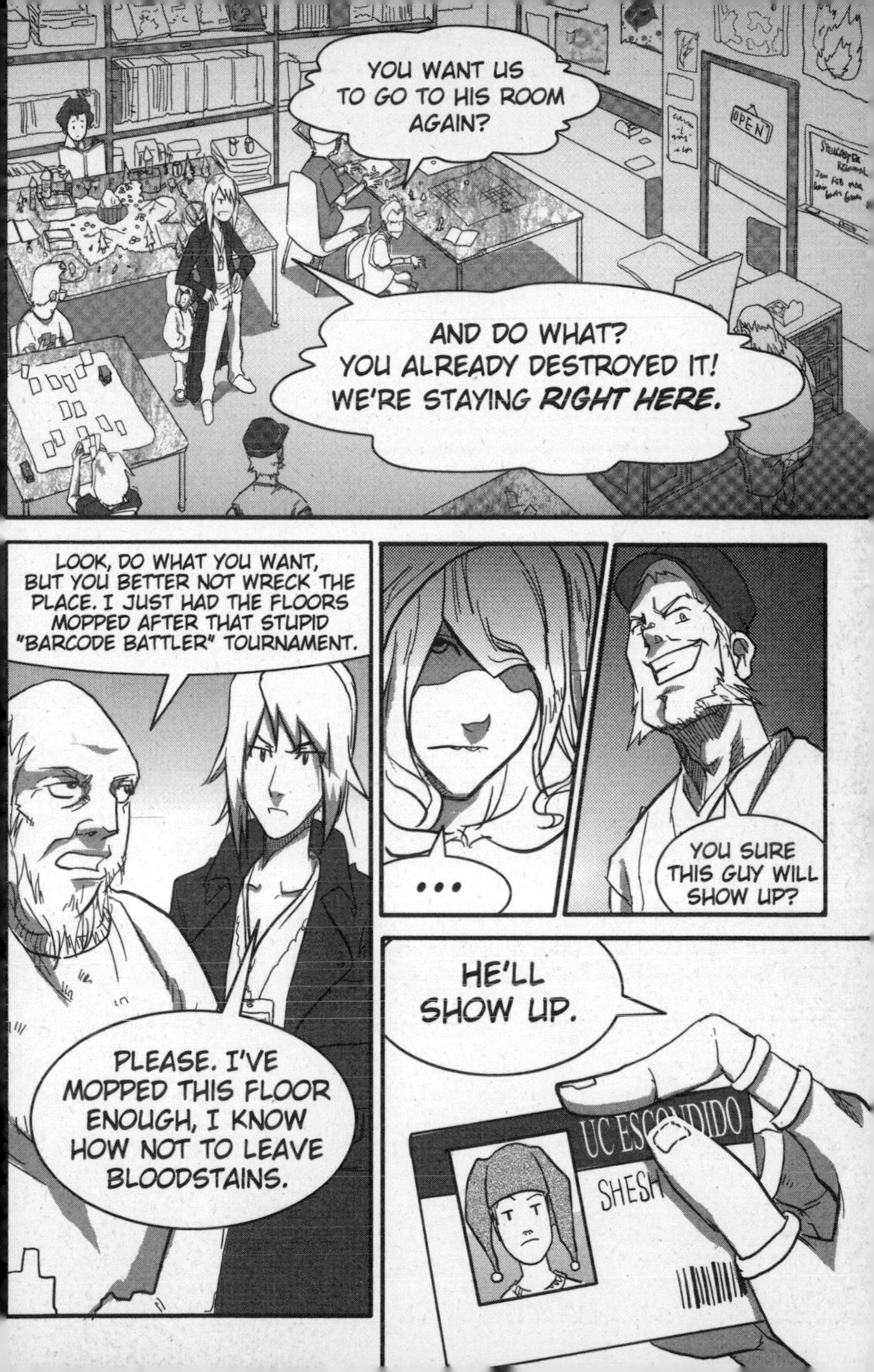
YOU WANT US TO GO TO HIS ROOM AGAIN?
AND DO WHAT? YOU ALREADY DESTROYED IT! WE'RE STAYING *RIGHT HERE.*
LOOK, DO WHAT YOU WANT, BUT YOU BETTER NOT WRECK THE PLACE. I JUST HAD THE FLOORS MOPPED AFTER THAT STUPID "BARCODE BATTLER" TOURNAMENT.
PLEASE. I'VE MOPPED THIS FLOOR ENOUGH, I KNOW HOW NOT TO LEAVE BLOODSTAINS.
...
YOU SURE THIS GUY WILL SHOW UP?
HE'LL SHOW UP.
OPEN
UC ES
DIDO
SHESH

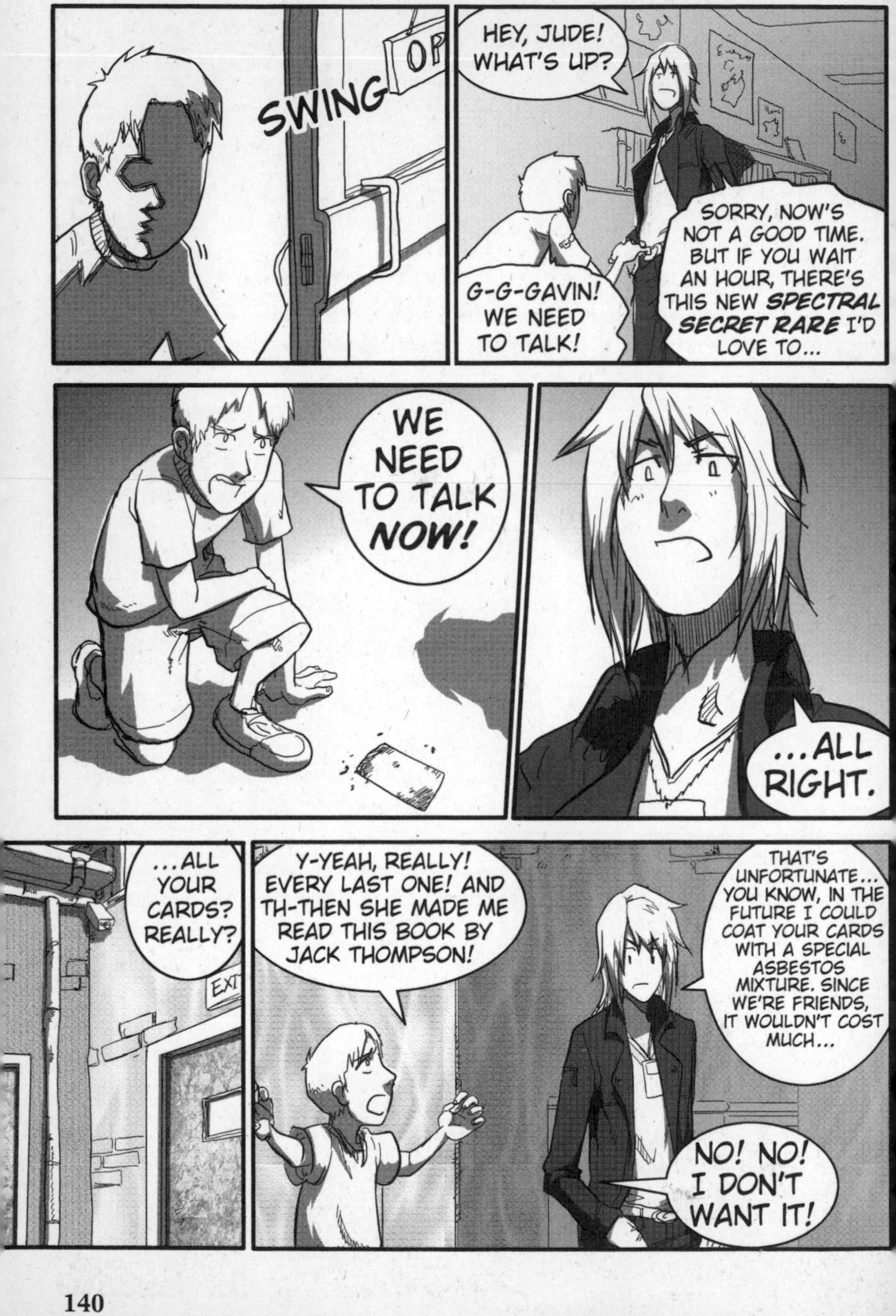
OP
SWING
HEY, JUDE! WHAT'S UP?
G-G-GAVIN! WE NEED TO TALK!
SORRY, NOW'S NOT A GOOD TIME. BUT IF YOU WAIT AN HOUR, THERE'S THIS NEW ***SPECTRAL SECRET RARE*** I'D LOVE TO...
WE NEED TO TALK ***NOW!***
...ALL RIGHT.
...ALL YOUR CARDS? REALLY?
EXIT
Y-YEAH, REALLY! EVERY LAST ONE! AND TH-THEN SHE MADE ME READ THIS BOOK BY JACK THOMPSON!
THAT'S UNFORTUNATE... YOU KNOW, IN THE FUTURE I COULD COAT YOUR CARDS WITH A SPECIAL ASBESTOS MIXTURE. SINCE WE'RE FRIENDS, IT WOULDN'T COST MUCH...
NO! NO! I DON'T WANT IT!

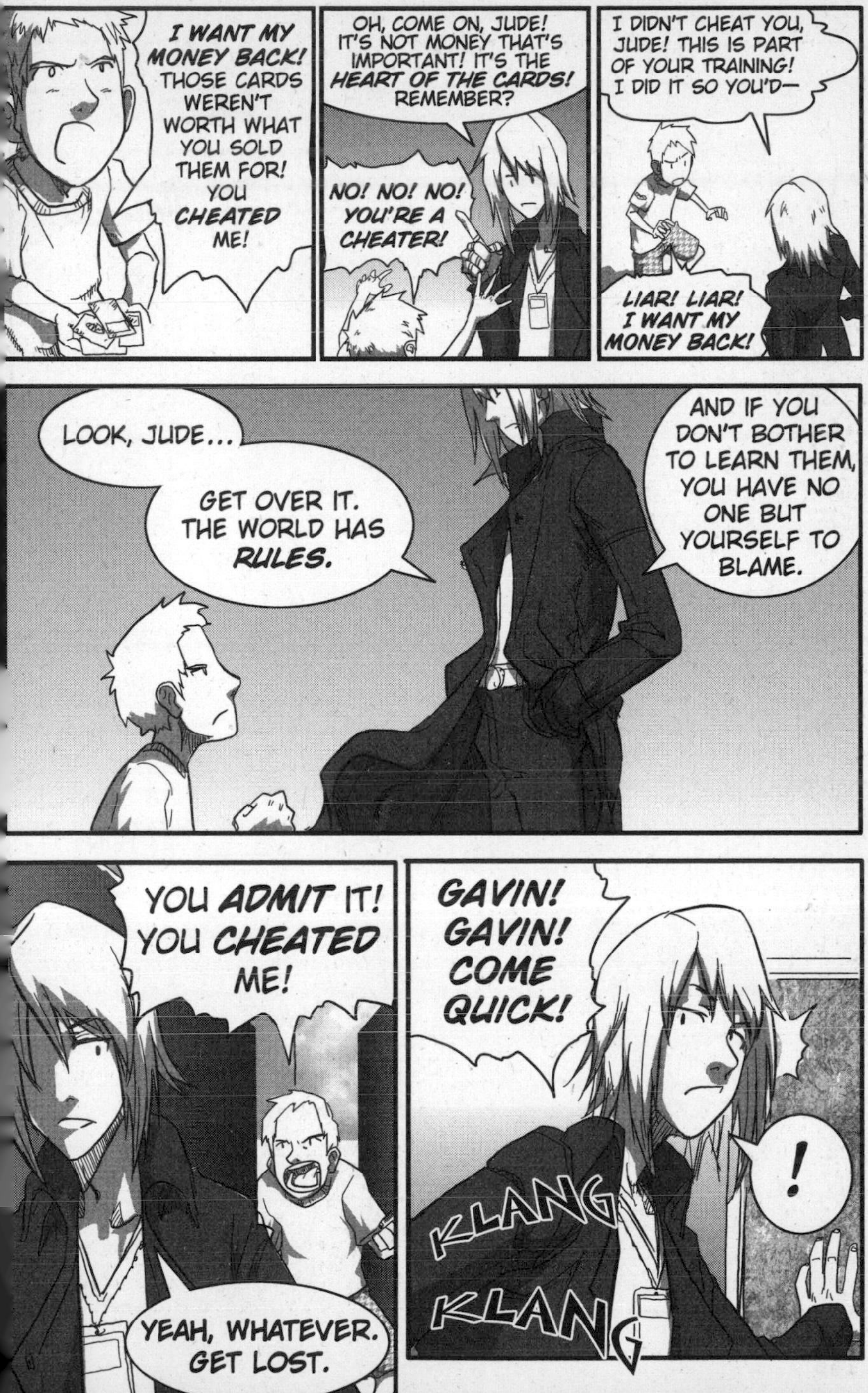
I WANT MY MONEY BACK! THOSE CARDS WEREN'T WORTH WHAT YOU SOLD THEM FOR! YOU CHEATED ME!
OH, COME ON, JUDE! IT'S NOT MONEY THAT'S IMPORTANT! IT'S THE HEART OF THE CARDS! REMEMBER?
NO! NO! NO! YOU'RE A CHEATER!
I DIDN'T CHEAT YOU, JUDE! THIS IS PART OF YOUR TRAINING! I DID IT SO YOU'D—
LIAR! LIAR! I WANT MY MONEY BACK!
LOOK, JUDE...
GET OVER IT. THE WORLD HAS RULES.
AND IF YOU DON'T BOTHER TO LEARN THEM, YOU HAVE NO ONE BUT YOURSELF TO BLAME.
YOU ADMIT IT! YOU CHEATED ME!
YEAH, WHATEVER. GET LOST.
GAVIN! GAVIN! COME QUICK!
!
KLANG
KLANG

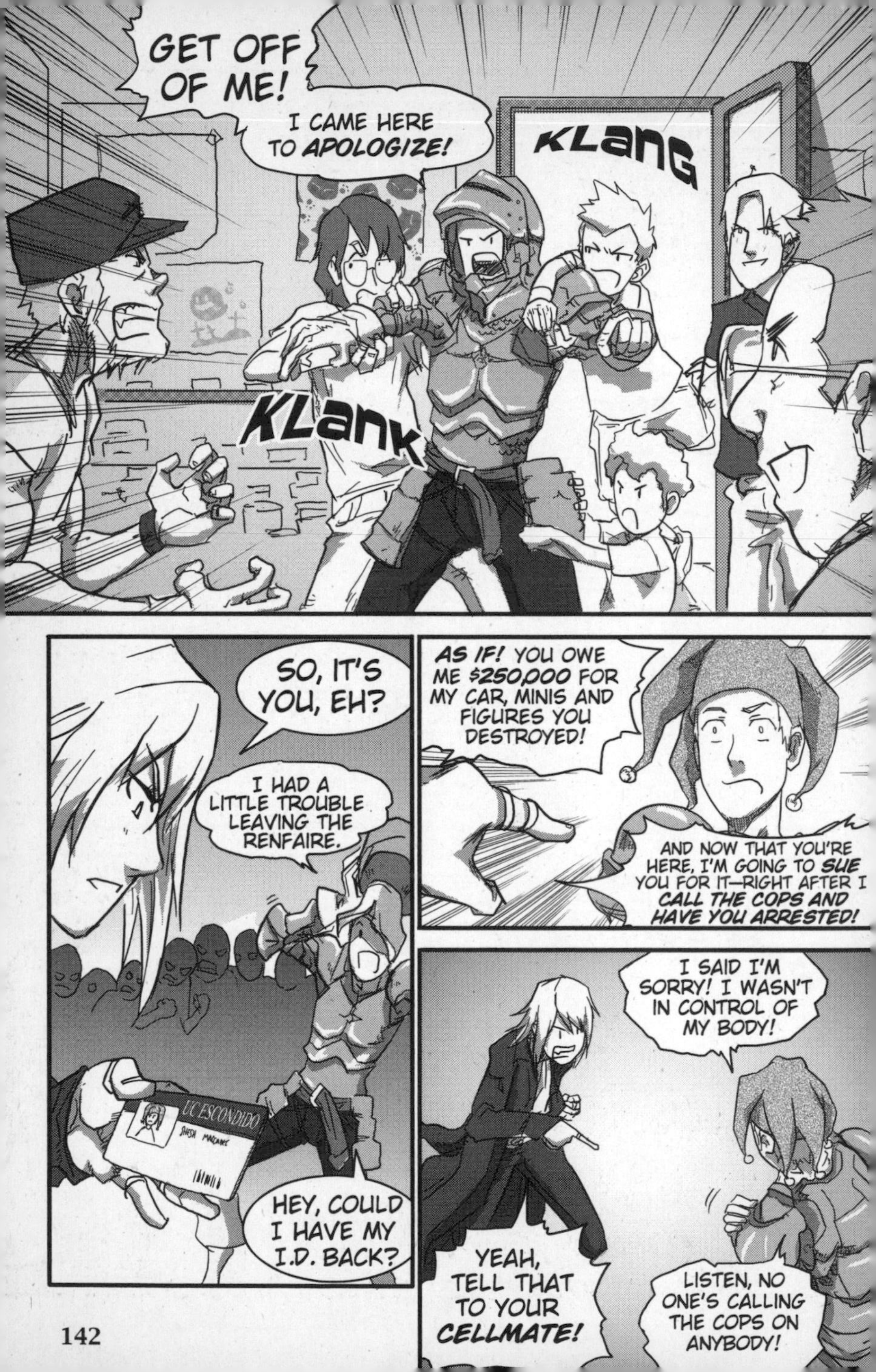
GET OFF OF ME!
I CAME HERE TO *APOLOGIZE!*
KLANG
KLANK
SO, IT'S YOU, EH?
I HAD A LITTLE TROUBLE LEAVING THE RENFAIRE.
UC ESCONDIDO
HEY, COULD I HAVE MY I.D. BACK?
AS IF! YOU OWE ME *$250,000* FOR MY CAR, MINIS AND FIGURES YOU DESTROYED!
AND NOW THAT YOU'RE HERE, I'M GOING TO *SUE* YOU FOR IT—RIGHT AFTER I *CALL THE COPS AND HAVE YOU ARRESTED!*
I SAID I'M SORRY! I WASN'T IN CONTROL OF MY BODY!
YEAH, TELL THAT TO YOUR *CELLMATE!*
LISTEN, NO ONE'S CALLING THE COPS ON ANYBODY!

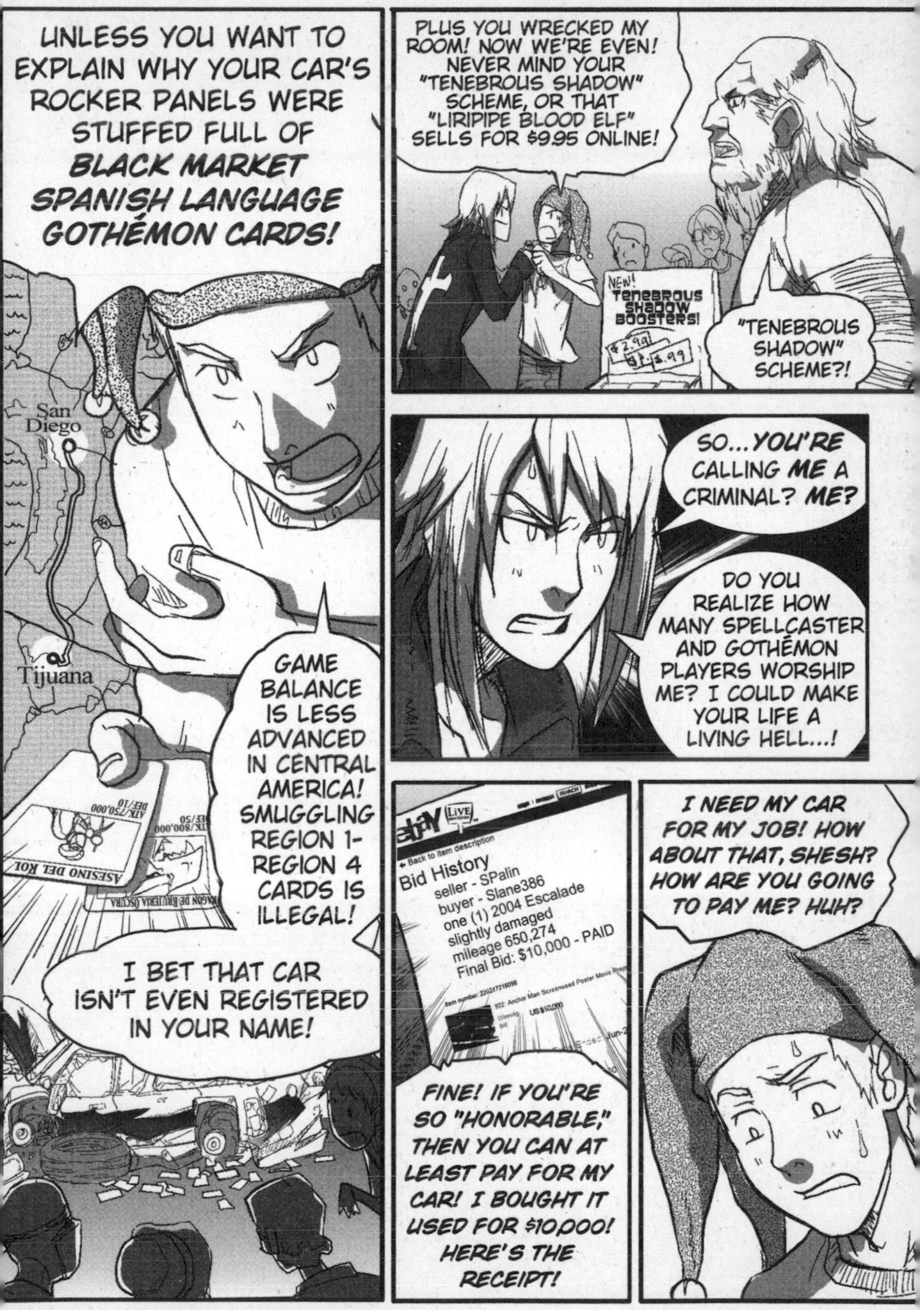
UNLESS YOU WANT TO EXPLAIN WHY YOUR CAR'S ROCKER PANELS WERE STUFFED FULL OF BLACK MARKET SPANISH LANGUAGE GOTHÉMON CARDS!
San Diego
Tijuana
GAME BALANCE IS LESS ADVANCED IN CENTRAL AMERICA! SMUGGLING REGION 1-REGION 4 CARDS IS ILLEGAL!
I BET THAT CAR ISN'T EVEN REGISTERED IN YOUR NAME!
PLUS YOU WRECKED MY ROOM! NOW WE'RE EVEN! NEVER MIND YOUR "TENEBROUS SHADOW" SCHEME, OR THAT "LIRIPIPE BLOOD ELF" SELLS FOR $9.95 ONLINE!
NEW! Tenebrous Shadow Boosters!
$2.99
"TENEBROUS SHADOW" SCHEME?!
SO...YOU'RE CALLING ME A CRIMINAL? ME?
DO YOU REALIZE HOW MANY SPELLCASTER AND GOTHÉMON PLAYERS WORSHIP ME? I COULD MAKE YOUR LIFE A LIVING HELL...!
Bid History
seller - SPalin
buyer - Slane386
one (1) 2004 Escalade
slightly damaged
mileage 650,274
Final Bid: $10,000 - PAID
FINE! IF YOU'RE SO "HONORABLE," THEN YOU CAN AT LEAST PAY FOR MY CAR! I BOUGHT IT USED FOR $10,000! HERE'S THE RECEIPT!
I NEED MY CAR FOR MY JOB! HOW ABOUT THAT, SHESH? HOW ARE YOU GOING TO PAY ME? HUH?

TOOM

THEO?!

WHO THE—?!

I'LL HANDLE THIS! THE WHOLE THING IS MY FAULT!

HEY! YOU CAN'T TAKE ALL THAT IN HERE! CAN'T YOU READ?

ALL BAGS MUST BE LEFT ON THE COUNTER!

20 MINUTES LATER...

ALL BAGS MUST BE LEFT ON THE COUNTER!

ENOUGH! THIS IS TAKING TOO LONG! WHY ARE YOU HERE?

I'M HERE TO PAY SHESH'S DEBT!

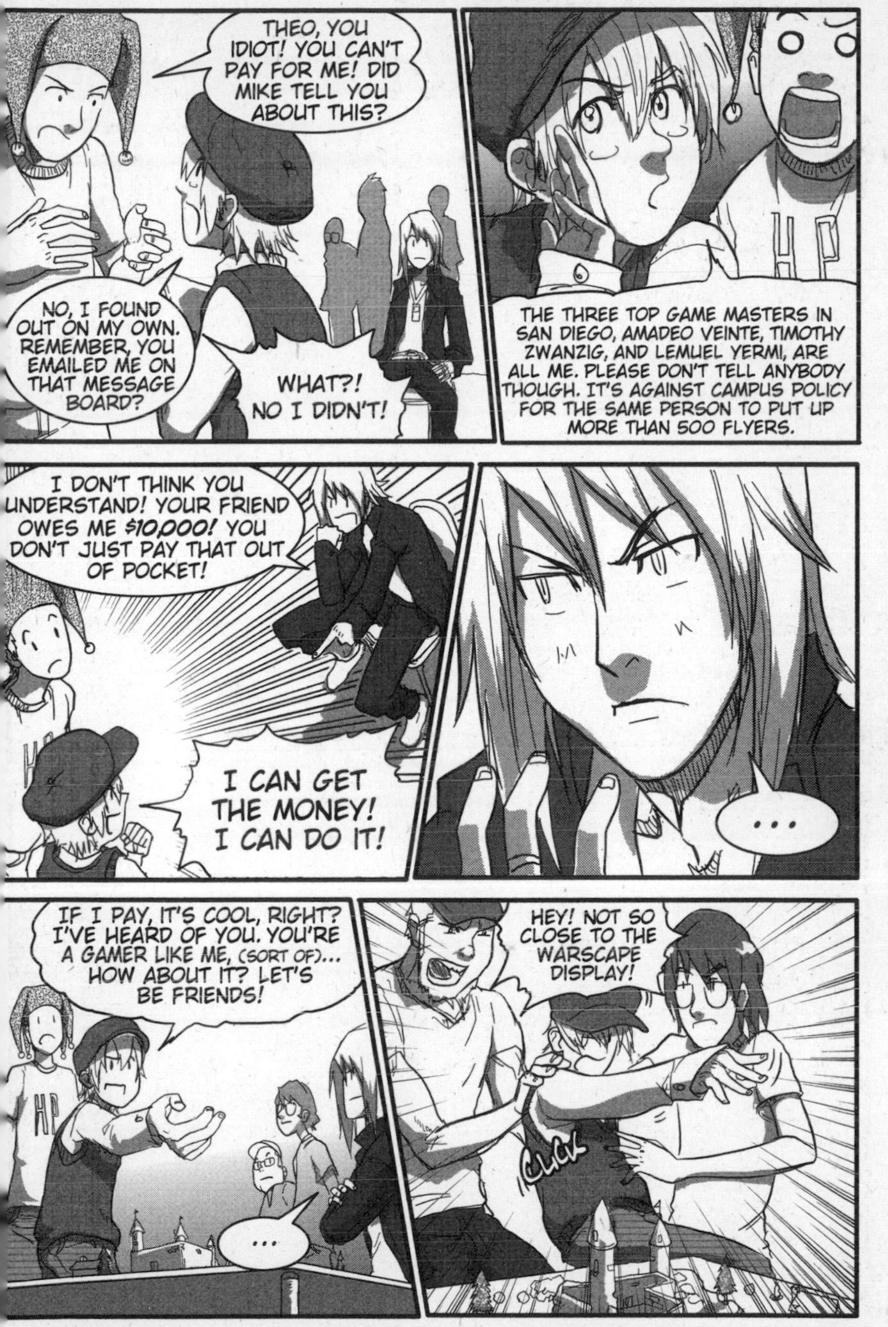
THEO, YOU IDIOT! YOU CAN'T PAY FOR ME! DID MIKE TELL YOU ABOUT THIS?
NO, I FOUND OUT ON MY OWN. REMEMBER, YOU EMAILED ME ON THAT MESSAGE BOARD?
WHAT?! NO I DIDN'T!
THE THREE TOP GAME MASTERS IN SAN DIEGO, AMADEO VEINTE, TIMOTHY ZWANZIG, AND LEMUEL YERMI, ARE ALL ME. PLEASE DON'T TELL ANYBODY THOUGH. IT'S AGAINST CAMPUS POLICY FOR THE SAME PERSON TO PUT UP MORE THAN 500 FLYERS.
I DON'T THINK YOU UNDERSTAND! YOUR FRIEND OWES ME $10,000! YOU DON'T JUST PAY THAT OUT OF POCKET!
I CAN GET THE MONEY! I CAN DO IT!
...
IF I PAY, IT'S COOL, RIGHT? I'VE HEARD OF YOU. YOU'RE A GAMER LIKE ME, (SORT OF)... HOW ABOUT IT? LET'S BE FRIENDS!
...
HEY! NOT SO CLOSE TO THE WARSCAPE DISPLAY!
CLICK

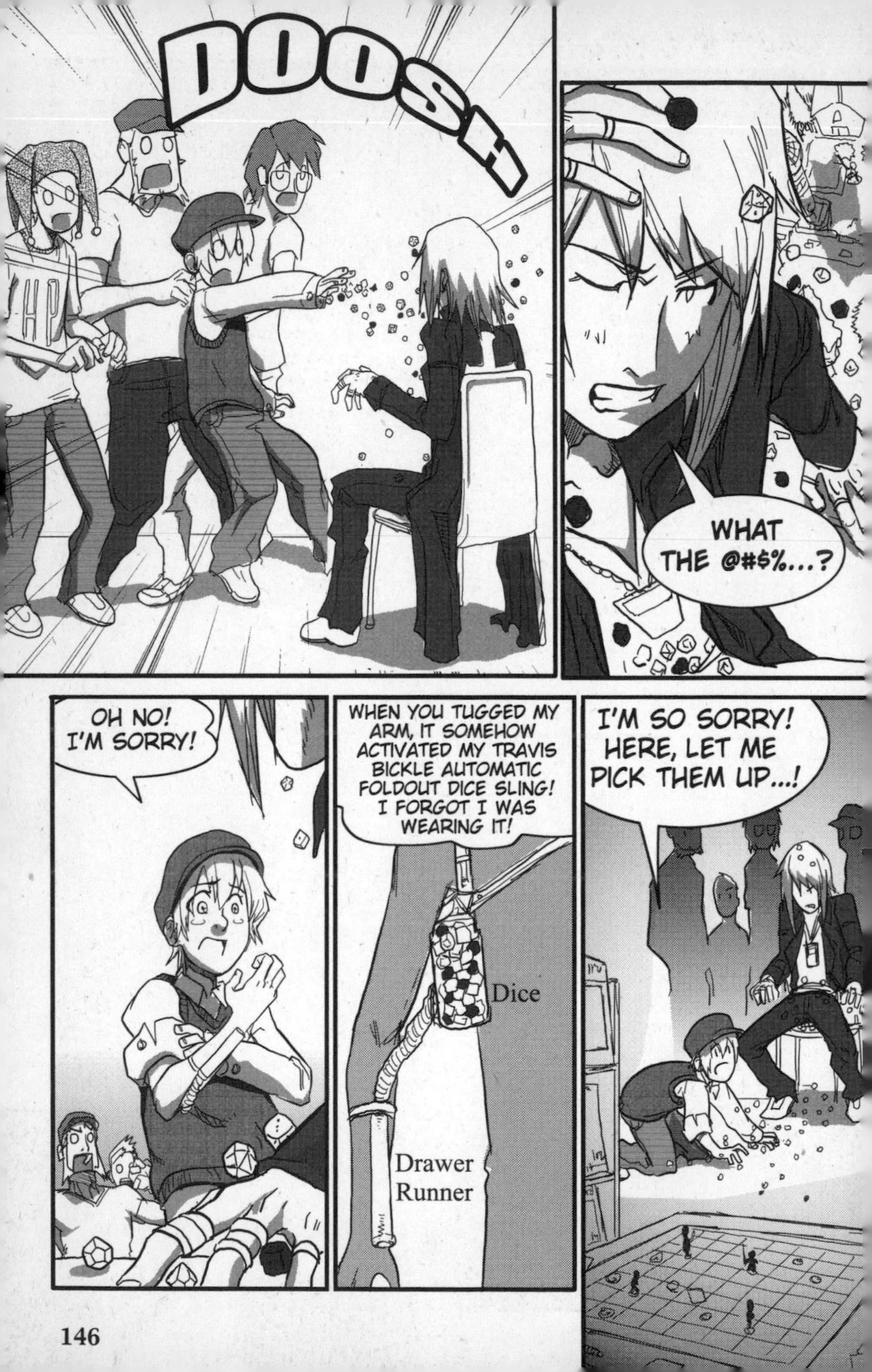
DOOSH
WHAT THE @#$%...?
OH NO! I'M SORRY!
WHEN YOU TUGGED MY ARM, IT SOMEHOW ACTIVATED MY TRAVIS BICKLE AUTOMATIC FOLDOUT DICE SLING! I FORGOT I WAS WEARING IT!
Dice
Drawer Runner
I'M SO SORRY! HERE, LET ME PICK THEM UP...!

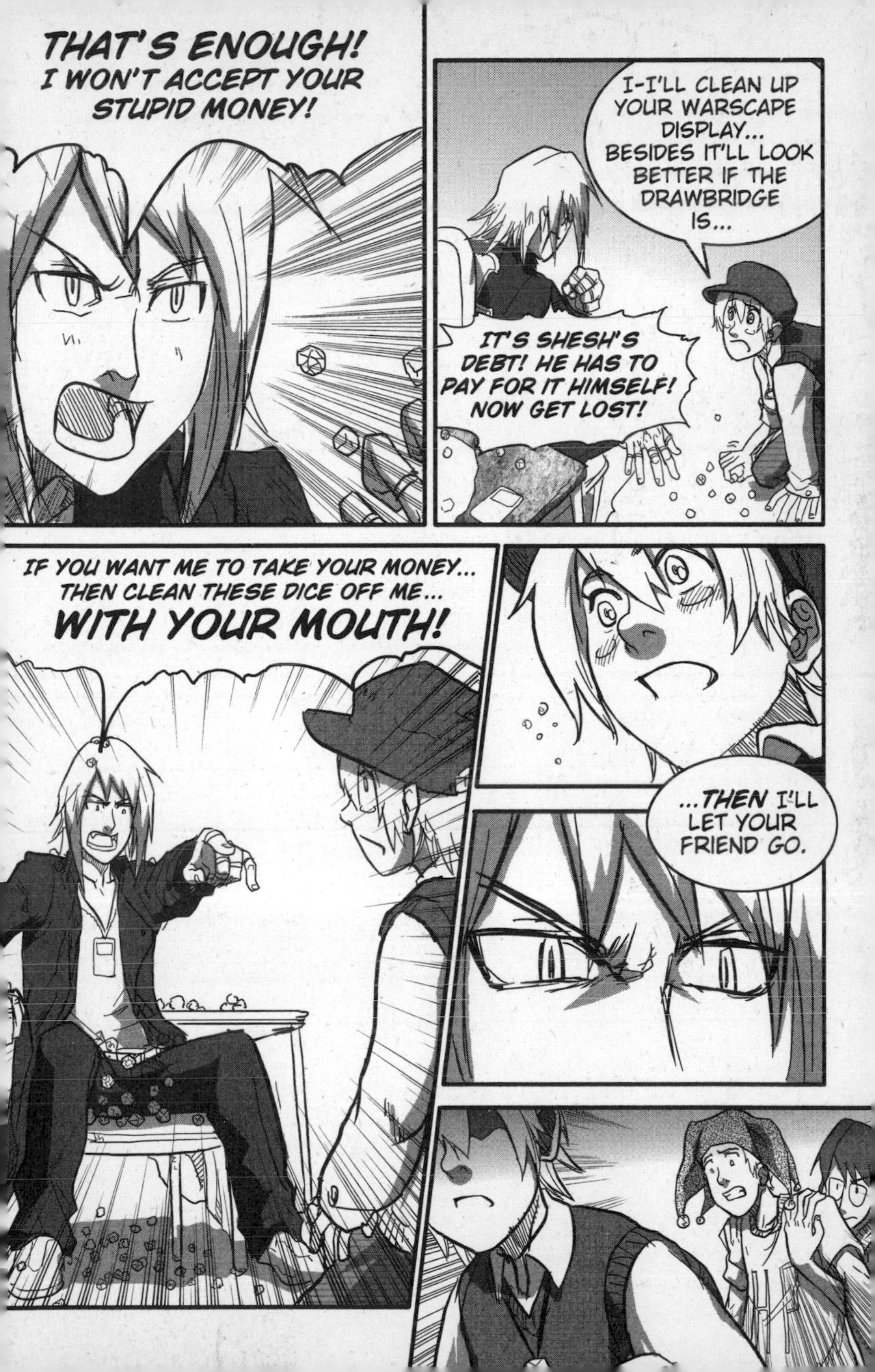
THAT'S ENOUGH! I WON'T ACCEPT YOUR STUPID MONEY!
I-I'LL CLEAN UP YOUR WARSCAPE DISPLAY... BESIDES IT'LL LOOK BETTER IF THE DRAWBRIDGE IS...
IT'S SHESH'S DEBT! HE HAS TO PAY FOR IT HIMSELF! NOW GET LOST!
IF YOU WANT ME TO TAKE YOUR MONEY... THEN CLEAN THESE DICE OFF ME... WITH YOUR MOUTH!
...THEN I'LL LET YOUR FRIEND GO.

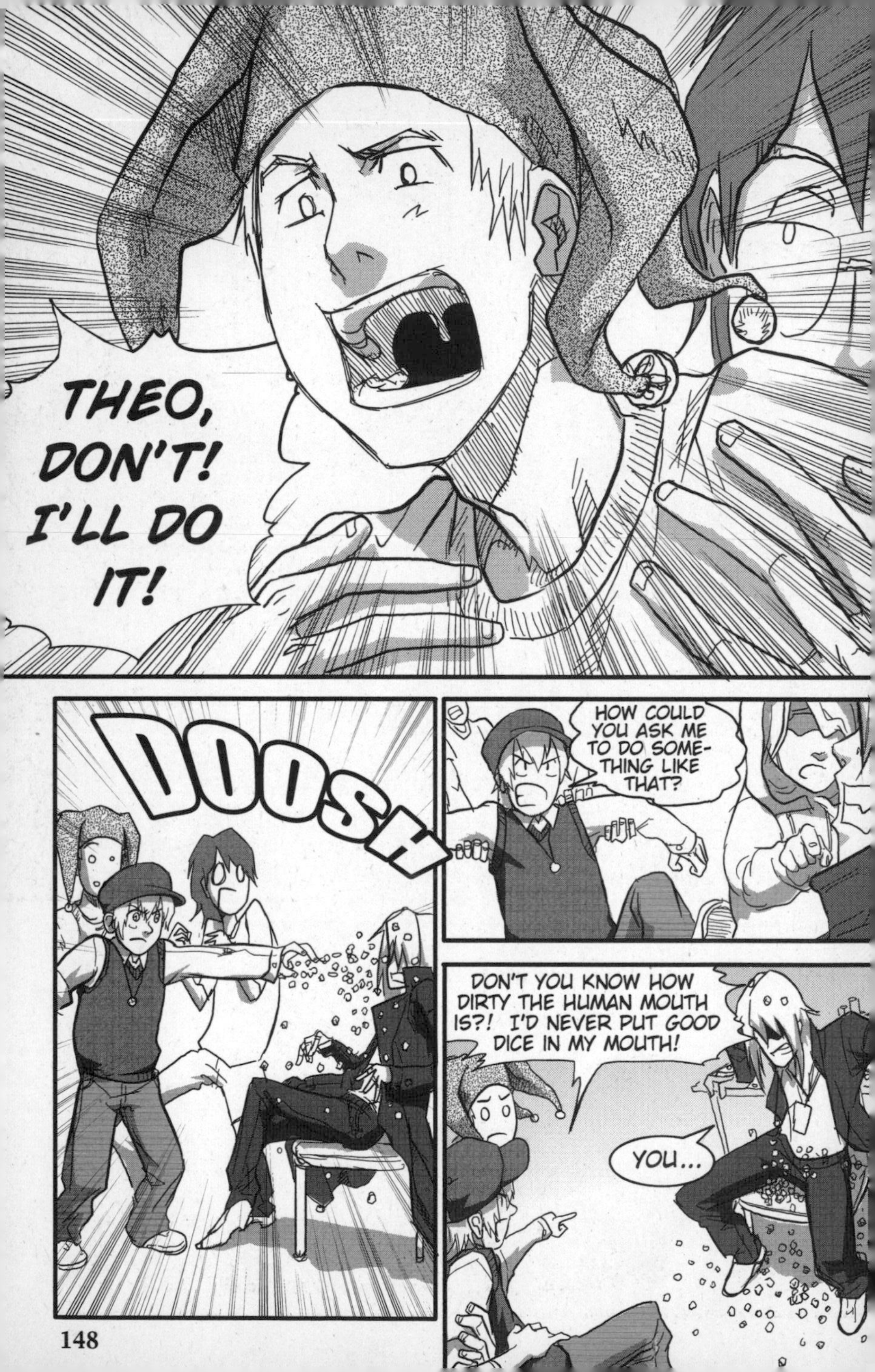

THEO, DON'T! I'LL DO IT!
DOOSH
HOW COULD YOU ASK ME TO DO SOME-THING LIKE THAT?
DON'T YOU KNOW HOW DIRTY THE HUMAN MOUTH IS?! I'D NEVER PUT GOOD DICE IN MY MOUTH!
YOU...

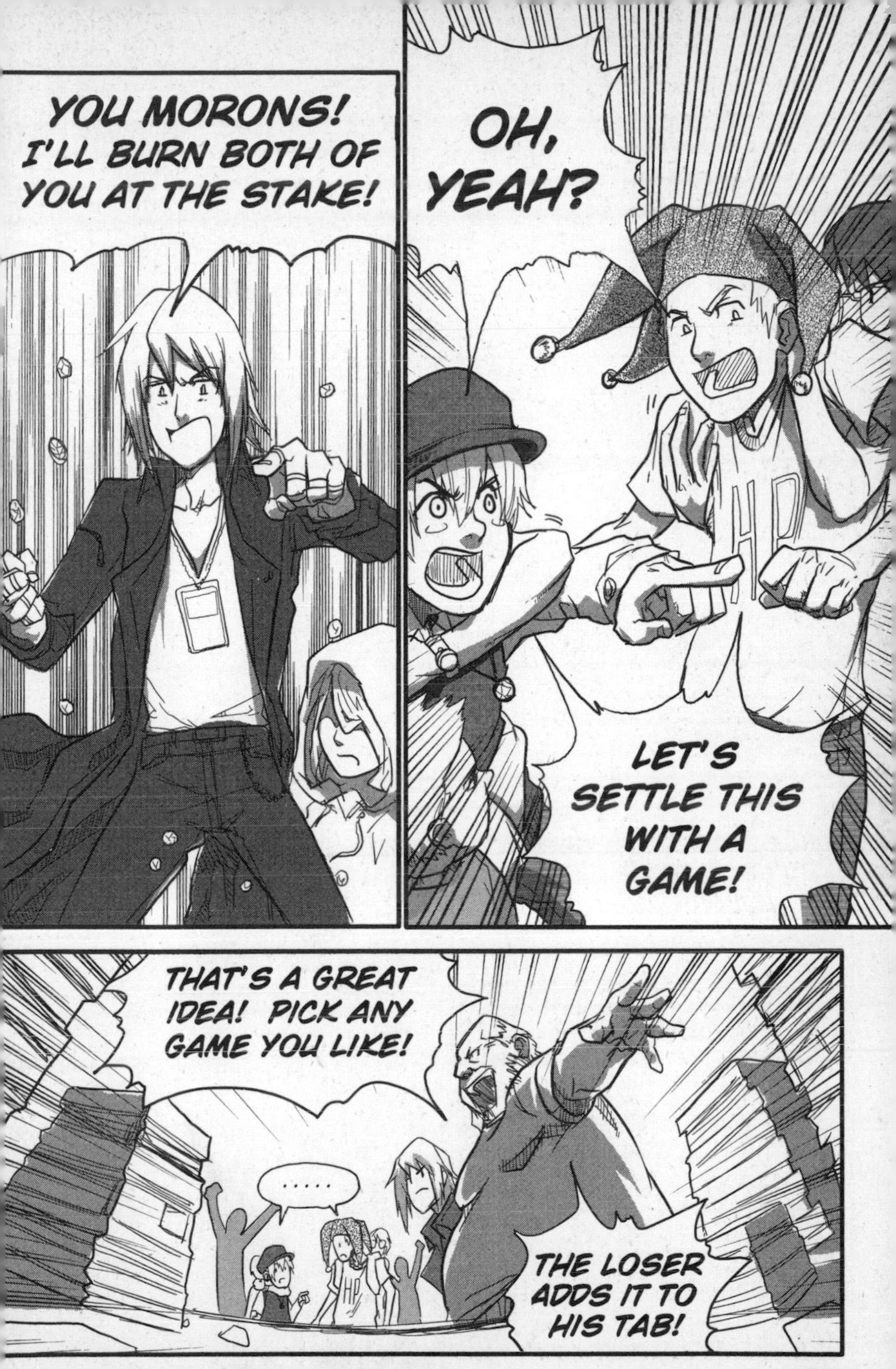
YOU MORONS! I'LL BURN BOTH OF YOU AT THE STAKE!
OH, YEAH?
LET'S SETTLE THIS WITH A GAME!
THAT'S A GREAT IDEA! PICK ANY GAME YOU LIKE!
.....
THE LOSER ADDS IT TO HIS TAB!

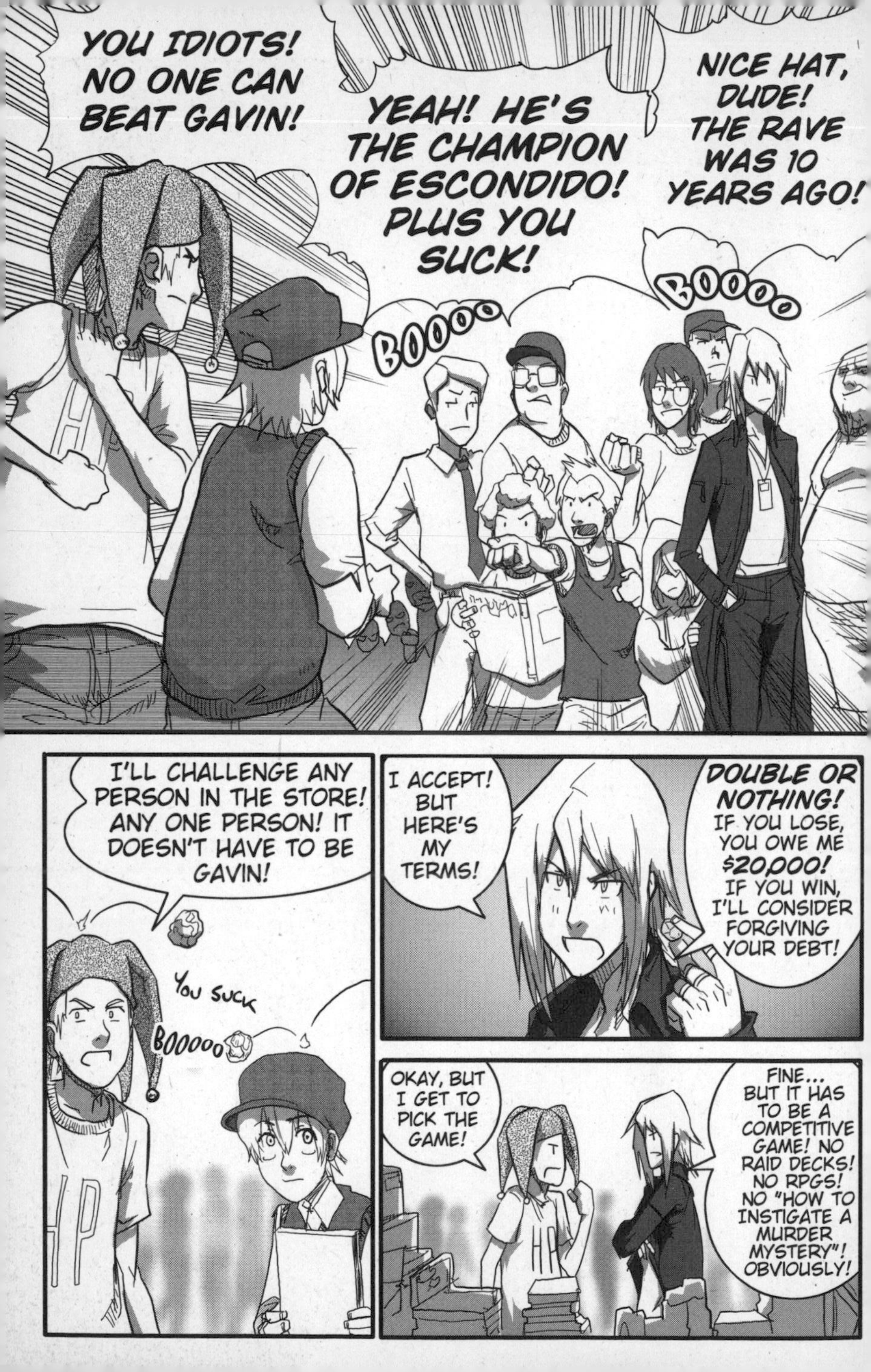
YOU IDIOTS! NO ONE CAN BEAT GAVIN!
YEAH! HE'S THE CHAMPION OF ESCONDIDO! PLUS YOU SUCK!
NICE HAT, DUDE! THE RAVE WAS 10 YEARS AGO!
BOOOO
BOOOO
I'LL CHALLENGE ANY PERSON IN THE STORE! ANY ONE PERSON! IT DOESN'T HAVE TO BE GAVIN!
YOU SUCK
BOOOOO
I ACCEPT! BUT HERE'S MY TERMS!
DOUBLE OR NOTHING! IF YOU LOSE, YOU OWE ME $20,000! IF YOU WIN, I'LL CONSIDER FORGIVING YOUR DEBT!
OKAY, BUT I GET TO PICK THE GAME!
FINE... BUT IT HAS TO BE A COMPETITIVE GAME! NO RAID DECKS! NO RPGS! NO "HOW TO INSTIGATE A MURDER MYSTERY"! OBVIOUSLY!

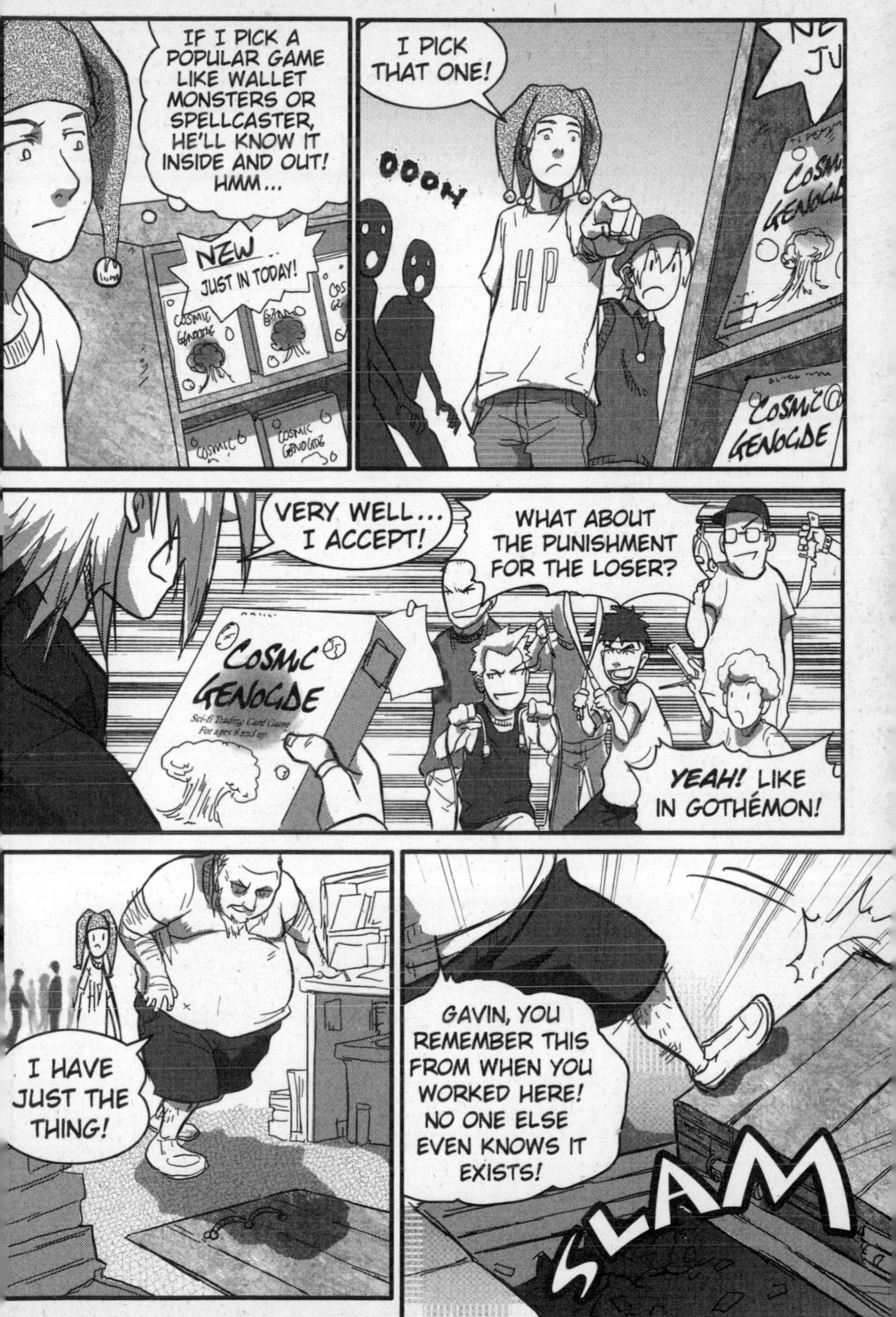
IF I PICK A POPULAR GAME LIKE WALLET MONSTERS OR SPELLCASTER, HE'LL KNOW IT INSIDE AND OUT! HMM...
NEW... JUST IN TODAY!
COSMIC GENOCIDE
I PICK THAT ONE!
OOOH
COSMIC GENOCIDE
VERY WELL... I ACCEPT!
WHAT ABOUT THE PUNISHMENT FOR THE LOSER?
COSMIC GENOCIDE
Sci-fi Trading Card Game
For ages 8 and up
YEAH! LIKE IN GOTHÉMON!
I HAVE JUST THE THING!
GAVIN, YOU REMEMBER THIS FROM WHEN YOU WORKED HERE! NO ONE ELSE EVEN KNOWS IT EXISTS!
SLAM

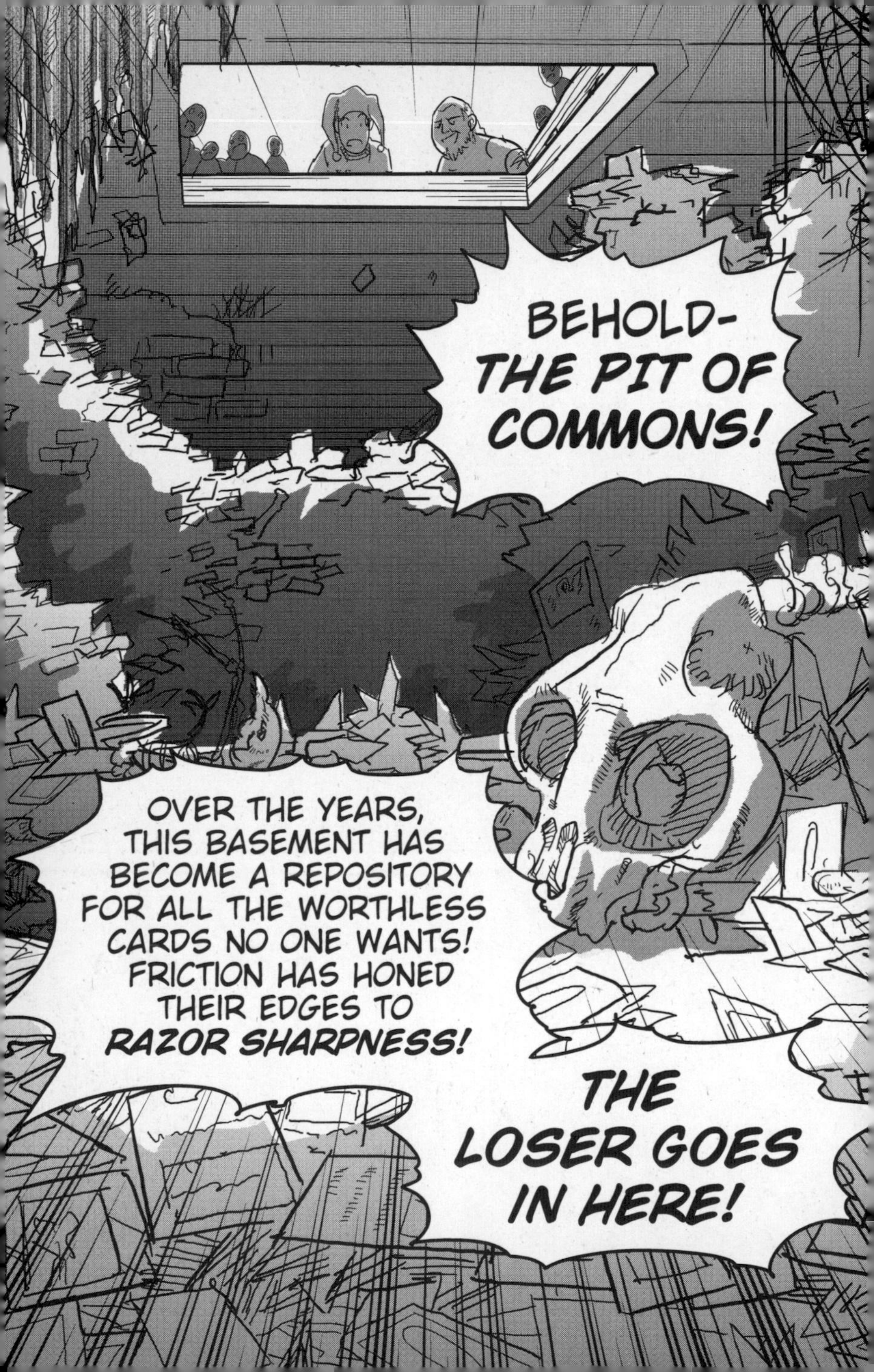
BEHOLD- *THE PIT OF COMMONS!*
OVER THE YEARS, THIS BASEMENT HAS BECOME A REPOSITORY FOR ALL THE WORTHLESS CARDS NO ONE WANTS! FRICTION HAS HONED THEIR EDGES TO *RAZOR SHARPNESS!*
THE LOSER GOES IN HERE!

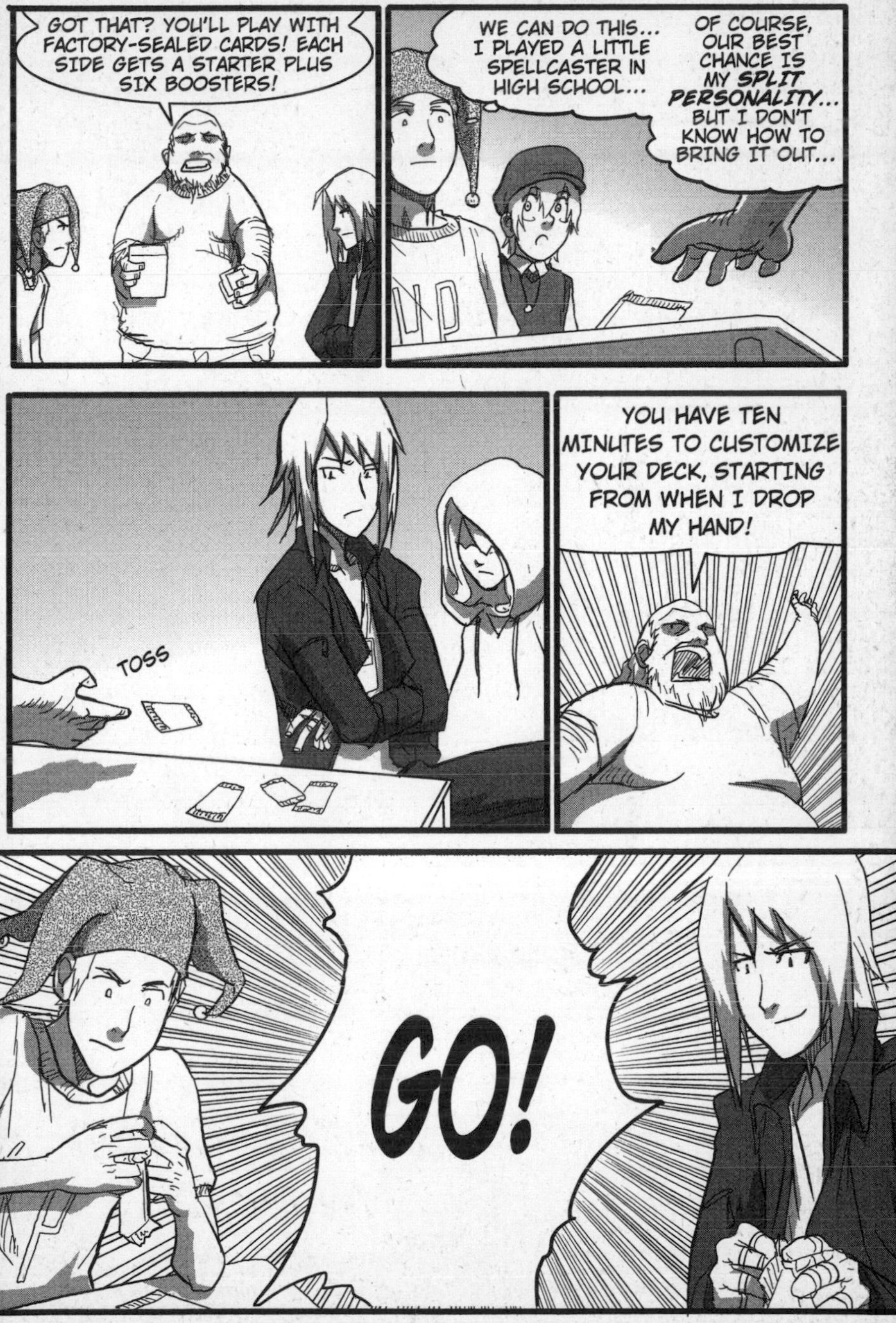
GOT THAT? YOU'LL PLAY WITH FACTORY-SEALED CARDS! EACH SIDE GETS A STARTER PLUS SIX BOOSTERS!
WE CAN DO THIS... I PLAYED A LITTLE SPELLCASTER IN HIGH SCHOOL...
OF COURSE, OUR BEST CHANCE IS MY SPLIT PERSONALITY... BUT I DON'T KNOW HOW TO BRING IT OUT...
TOSS
YOU HAVE TEN MINUTES TO CUSTOMIZE YOUR DECK, STARTING FROM WHEN I DROP MY HAND!
GO!

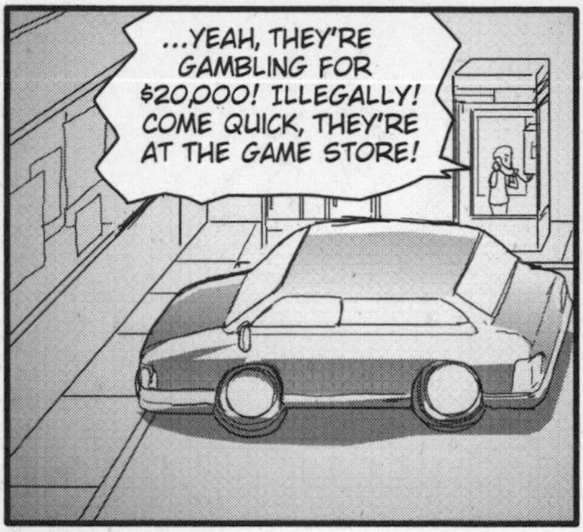
...YEAH, THEY'RE GAMBLING FOR $20,000! ILLEGALLY! COME QUICK, THEY'RE AT THE GAME STORE!
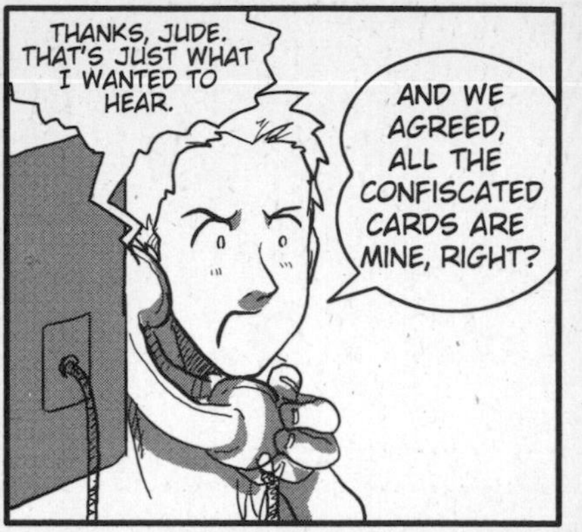
THANKS, JUDE. THAT'S JUST WHAT I WANTED TO HEAR.
AND WE AGREED, ALL THE CONFISCATED CARDS ARE MINE, RIGHT?
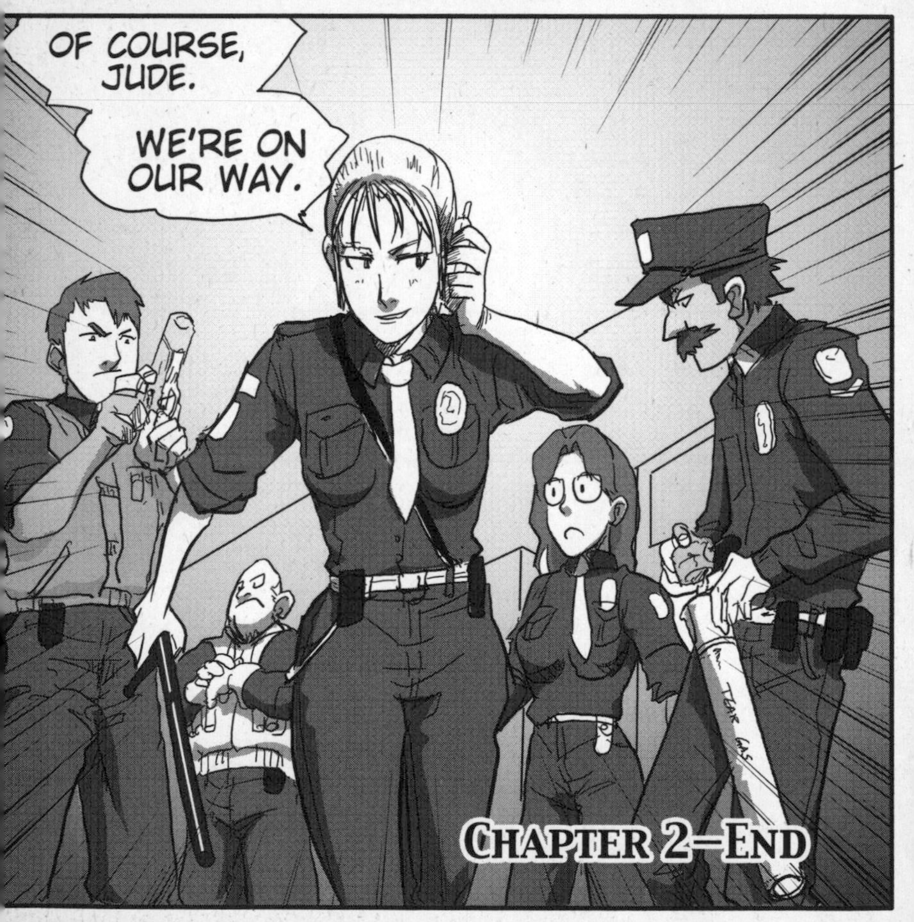
OF COURSE, JUDE.
WE'RE ON OUR WAY.
TEAR GAS
CHAPTER 2—END

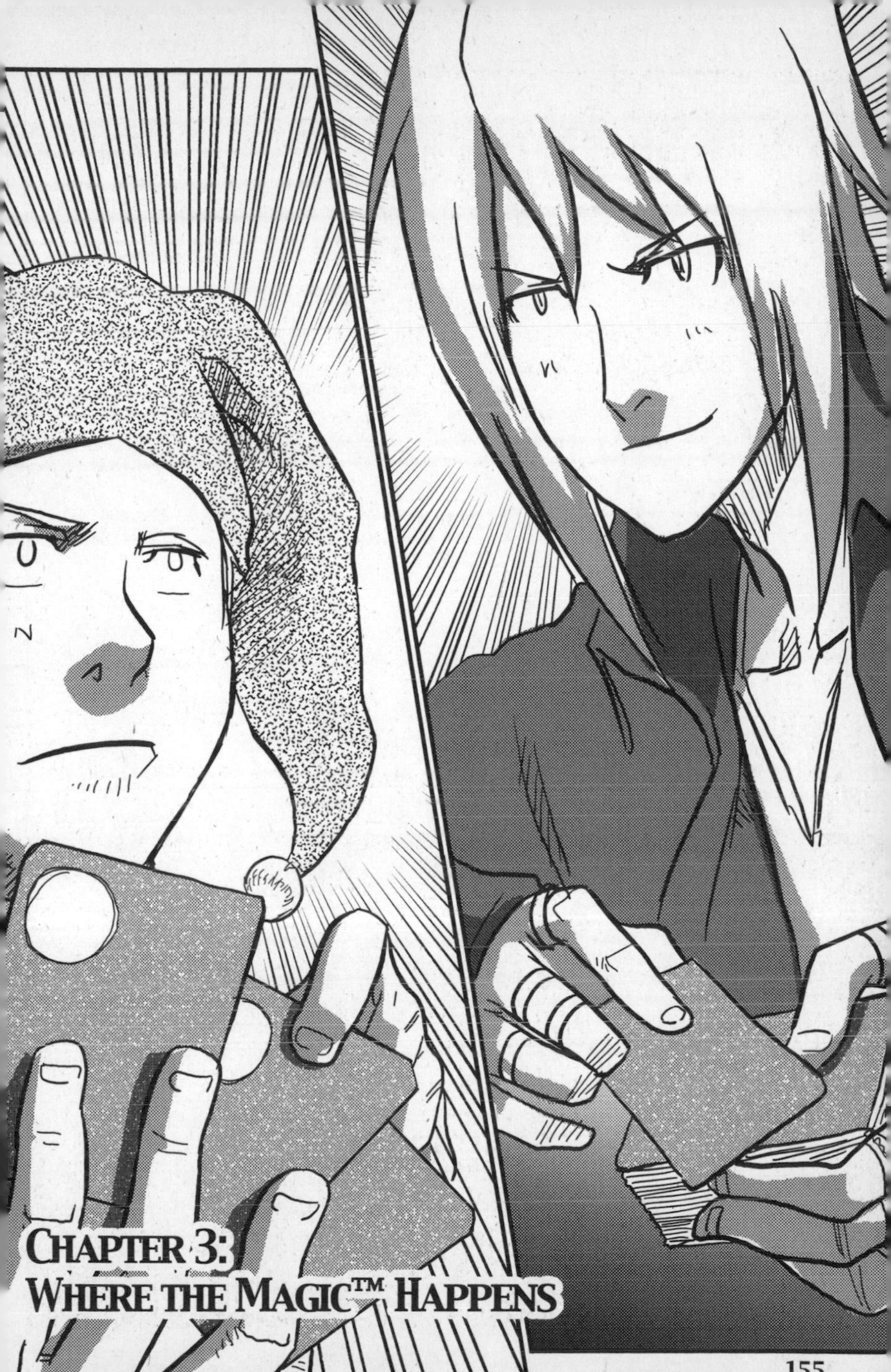
CHAPTER 3:
WHERE THE MAGIC™ HAPPENS

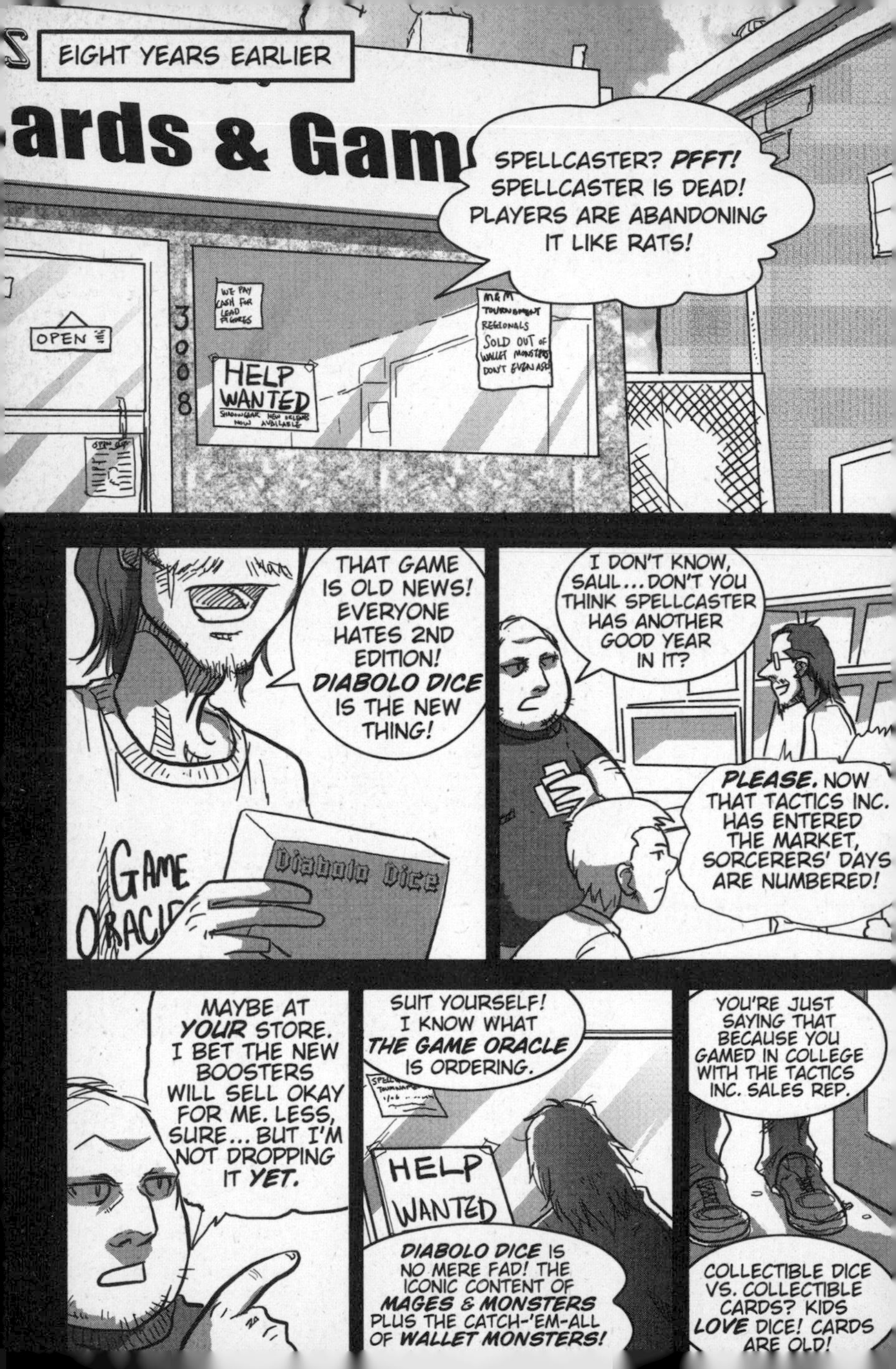
EIGHT YEARS EARLIER
SPELLCASTER? PFFT! SPELLCASTER IS DEAD! PLAYERS ARE ABANDONING IT LIKE RATS!
WE PAY CASH FOR LEAD FIGURES
M&M TOURNAMENT REGIONALS
SOLD OUT OF WALLET MONSTERS DON'T EVEN ASK
OPEN
3008
HELP WANTED
SHADOWGEAR NEW ORLEANS NOW AVAILABLE
THAT GAME IS OLD NEWS! EVERYONE HATES 2ND EDITION! DIABOLO DICE IS THE NEW THING!
GAME
Diabolo Dice
I DON'T KNOW, SAUL... DON'T YOU THINK SPELLCASTER HAS ANOTHER GOOD YEAR IN IT?
PLEASE. NOW THAT TACTICS INC. HAS ENTERED THE MARKET, SORCERERS' DAYS ARE NUMBERED!
MAYBE AT YOUR STORE. I BET THE NEW BOOSTERS WILL SELL OKAY FOR ME. LESS, SURE... BUT I'M NOT DROPPING IT YET.
SUIT YOURSELF! I KNOW WHAT THE GAME ORACLE IS ORDERING.
HELP WANTED
DIABOLO DICE IS NO MERE FAD! THE ICONIC CONTENT OF MAGES & MONSTERS PLUS THE CATCH-'EM-ALL OF WALLET MONSTERS!
YOU'RE JUST SAYING THAT BECAUSE YOU GAMED IN COLLEGE WITH THE TACTICS INC. SALES REP.
COLLECTIBLE DICE VS. COLLECTIBLE CARDS? KIDS LOVE DICE! CARDS ARE OLD!

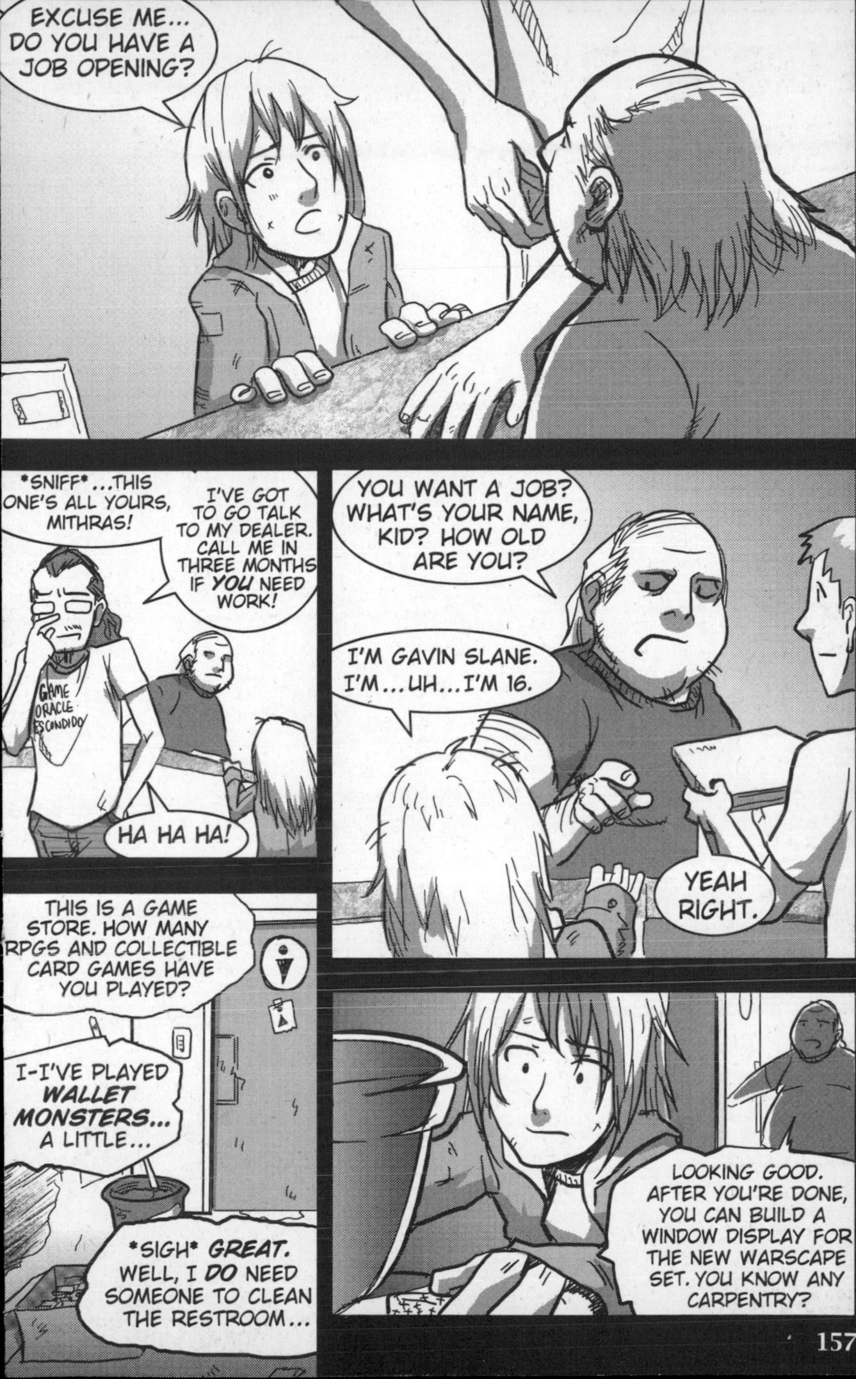

EXCUSE ME... DO YOU HAVE A JOB OPENING?
SNIFF ...THIS ONE'S ALL YOURS, MITHRAS!
I'VE GOT TO GO TALK TO MY DEALER. CALL ME IN THREE MONTHS IF **YOU** NEED WORK!
GAME ORACLE ESCONDIDO
HA HA HA!
YOU WANT A JOB? WHAT'S YOUR NAME, KID? HOW OLD ARE YOU?
I'M GAVIN SLANE. I'M... UH... I'M 16.
YEAH RIGHT.
THIS IS A GAME STORE. HOW MANY RPGS AND COLLECTIBLE CARD GAMES HAVE YOU PLAYED?
I-I'VE PLAYED ***WALLET MONSTERS...*** A LITTLE...
SIGH ***GREAT.*** WELL, I ***DO*** NEED SOMEONE TO CLEAN THE RESTROOM...
LOOKING GOOD. AFTER YOU'RE DONE, YOU CAN BUILD A WINDOW DISPLAY FOR THE NEW WARSCAPE SET. YOU KNOW ANY CARPENTRY?

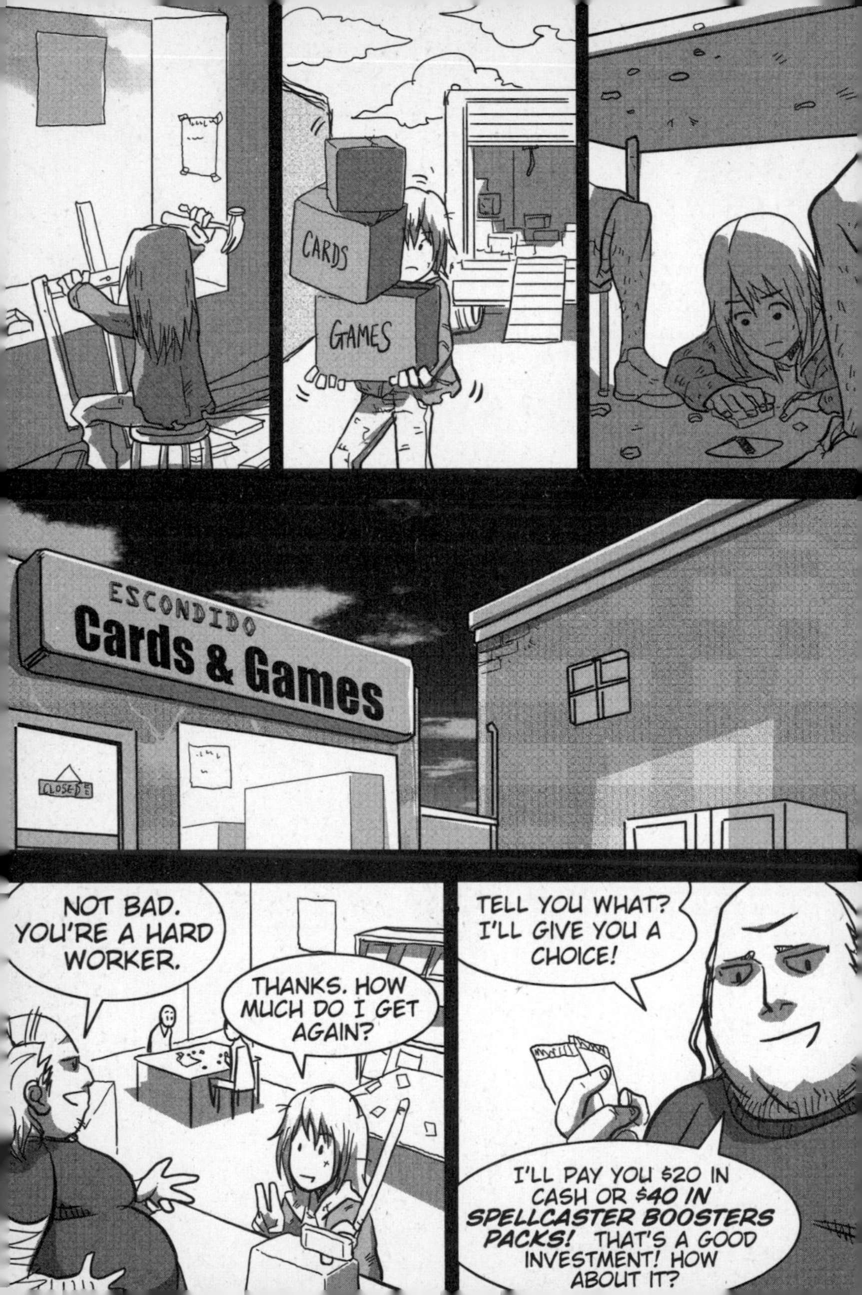
CARDS
GAMES
ESCONDIDO
Cards & Games
CLOSED
NOT BAD. YOU'RE A HARD WORKER.
THANKS. HOW MUCH DO I GET AGAIN?
TELL YOU WHAT? I'LL GIVE YOU A CHOICE!
I'LL PAY YOU $20 IN CASH OR *$40 IN SPELLCASTER BOOSTERS PACKS!* THAT'S A GOOD INVESTMENT! HOW ABOUT IT?

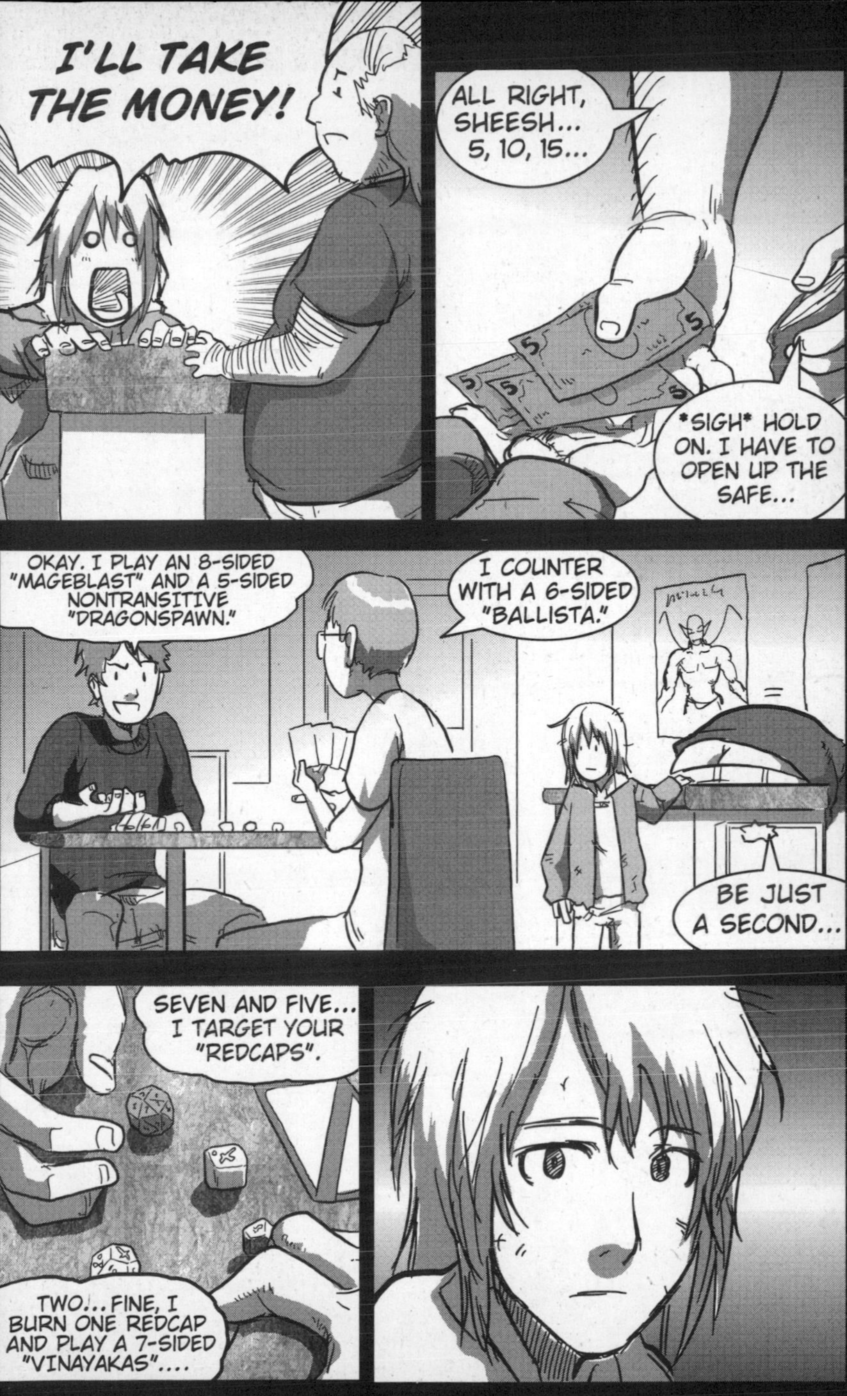
I'LL TAKE THE MONEY!
ALL RIGHT, SHEESH... 5, 10, 15...
SIGH HOLD ON. I HAVE TO OPEN UP THE SAFE...
OKAY. I PLAY AN 8-SIDED "MAGEBLAST" AND A 5-SIDED NONTRANSITIVE "DRAGONSPAWN."
I COUNTER WITH A 6-SIDED "BALLISTA."
BE JUST A SECOND...
SEVEN AND FIVE... I TARGET YOUR "REDCAPS".
TWO!...FINE, I BURN ONE REDCAP AND PLAY A 7-SIDED "VINAYAKAS"....

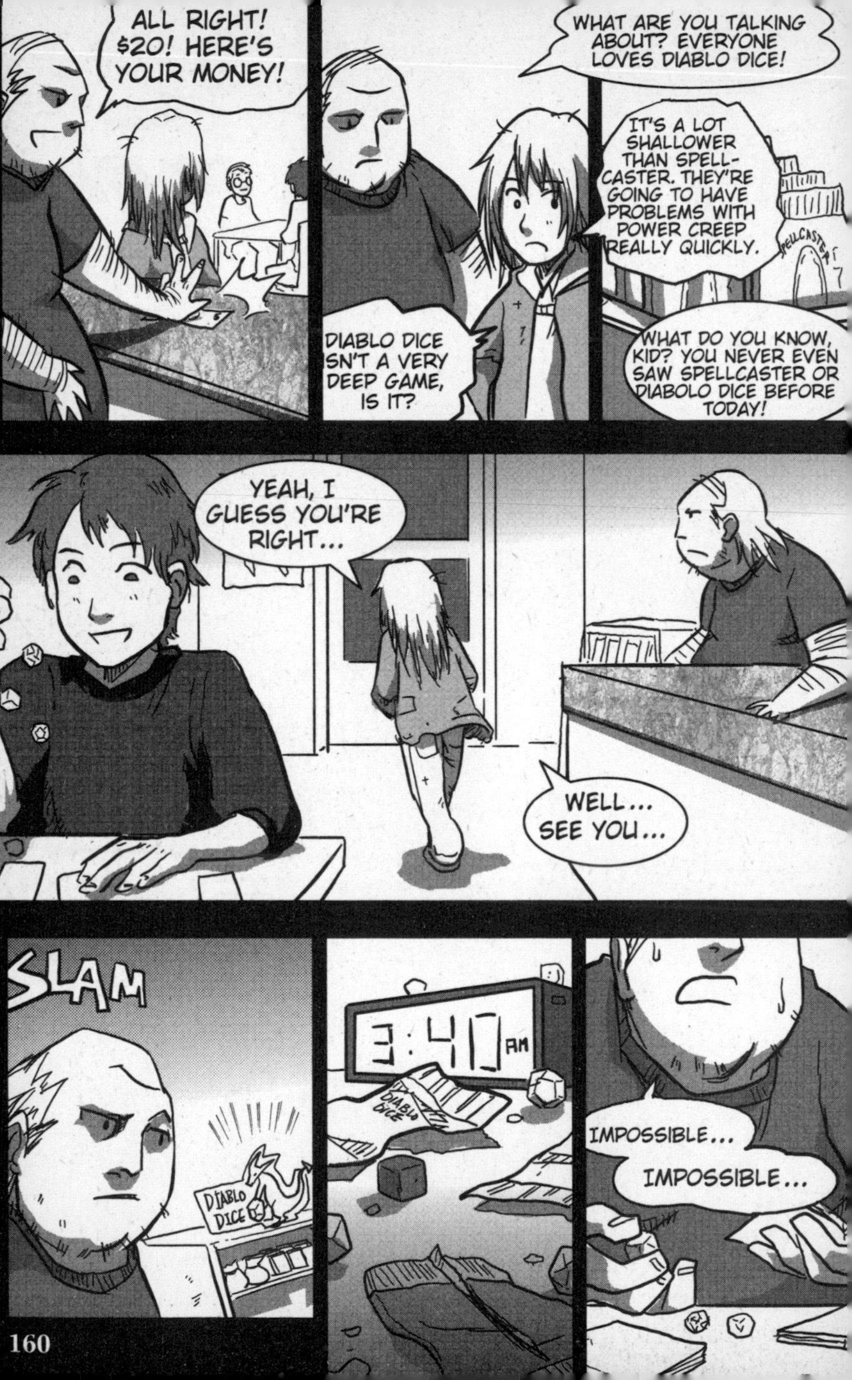
ALL RIGHT! $20! HERE'S YOUR MONEY!
DIABLO DICE ISN'T A VERY DEEP GAME, IS IT?
WHAT ARE YOU TALKING ABOUT? EVERYONE LOVES DIABLO DICE!
IT'S A LOT SHALLOWER THAN SPELL-CASTER. THEY'RE GOING TO HAVE PROBLEMS WITH POWER CREEP REALLY QUICKLY.
SPELLCASTER
WHAT DO YOU KNOW, KID? YOU NEVER EVEN SAW SPELLCASTER OR DIABOLO DICE BEFORE TODAY!
YEAH, I GUESS YOU'RE RIGHT...
WELL... SEE YOU...
SLAM
DIABLO DICE
3:40 AM
DIABLO DICE
IMPOSSIBLE...
IMPOSSIBLE...

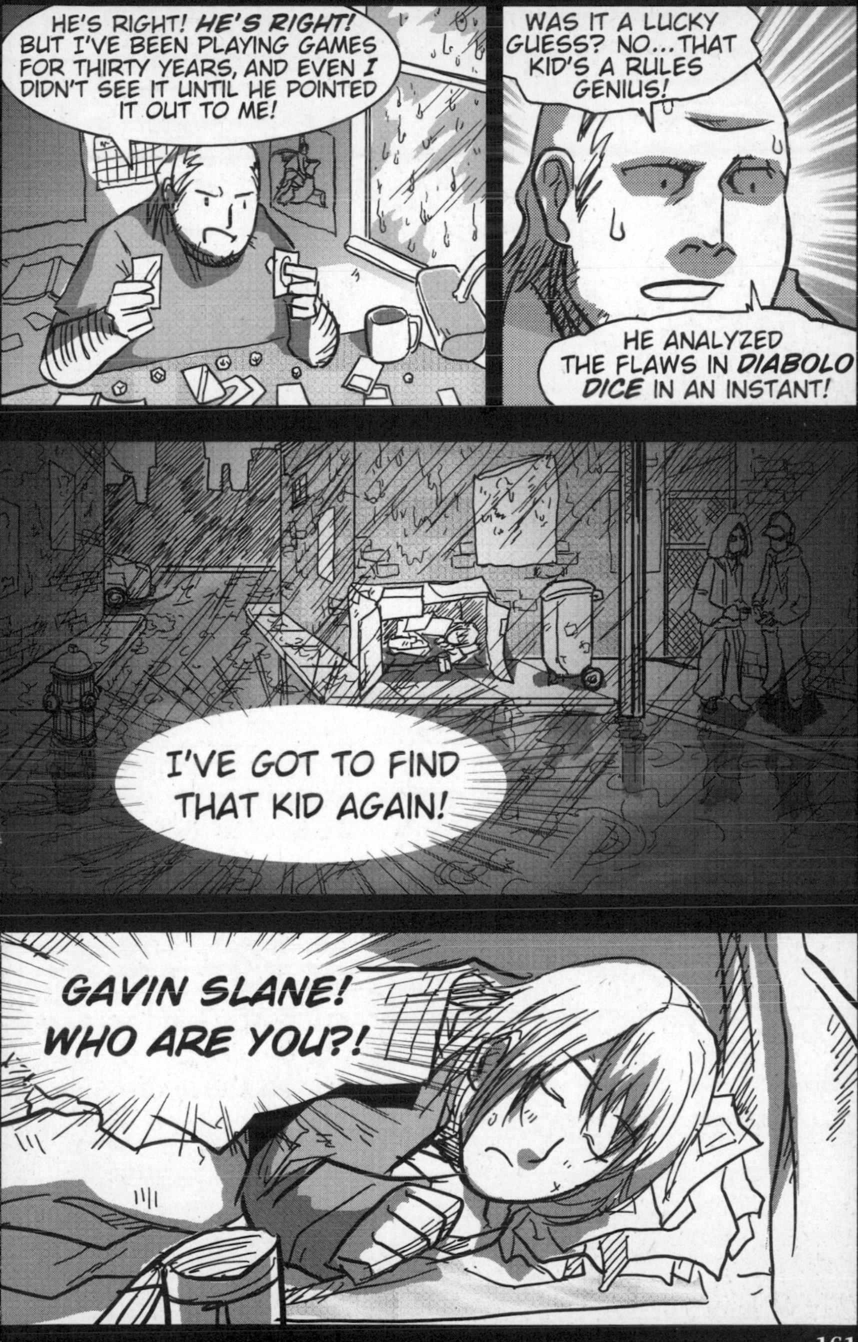
HE'S RIGHT! HE'S RIGHT! BUT I'VE BEEN PLAYING GAMES FOR THIRTY YEARS, AND EVEN I DIDN'T SEE IT UNTIL HE POINTED IT OUT TO ME!
WAS IT A LUCKY GUESS? NO...THAT KID'S A RULES GENIUS!
HE ANALYZED THE FLAWS IN DIABOLO DICE IN AN INSTANT!
I'VE GOT TO FIND THAT KID AGAIN!
GAVIN SLANE! WHO ARE YOU?!

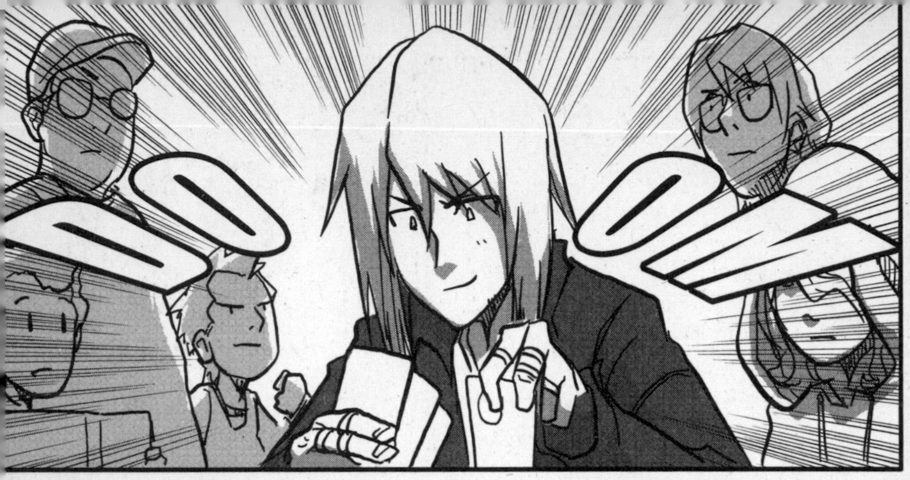

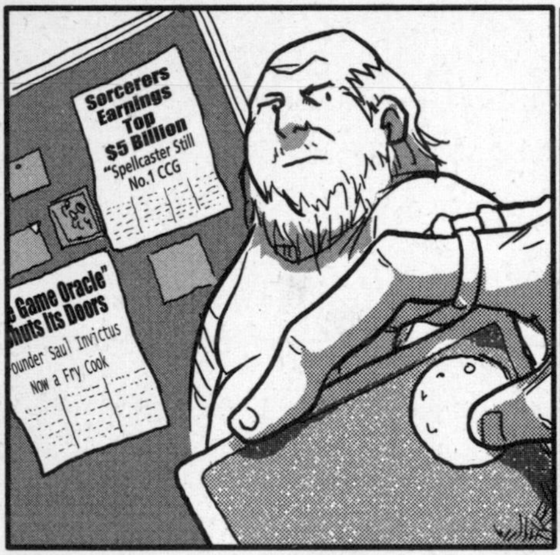
Sorcerers Earnings Top $5 Billion
“Spellcaster Still No.1 CCG
Game Oracle” Its Doors
Saul Invictus Now a Fry Cook

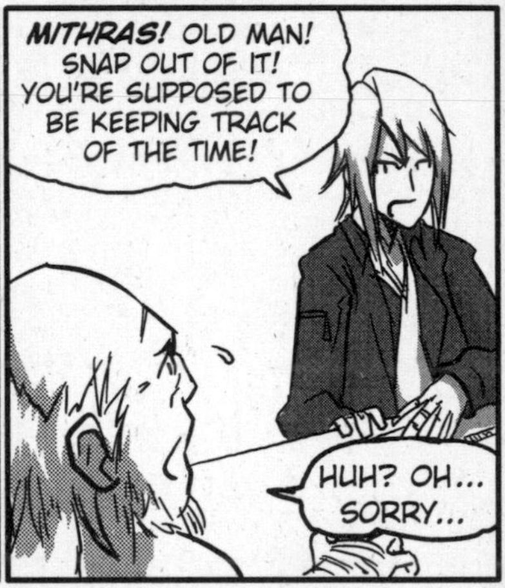
MITHRAS! OLD MAN! SNAP OUT OF IT! YOU'RE SUPPOSED TO BE KEEPING TRACK OF THE TIME!
HUH? OH... SORRY...

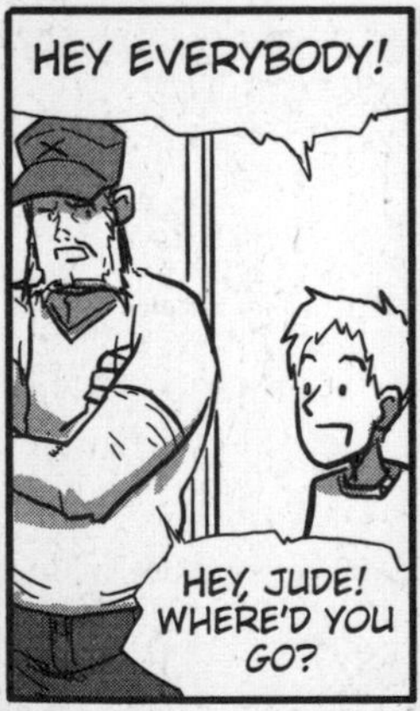
HEY EVERYBODY!
HEY, JUDE! WHERE'D YOU GO?

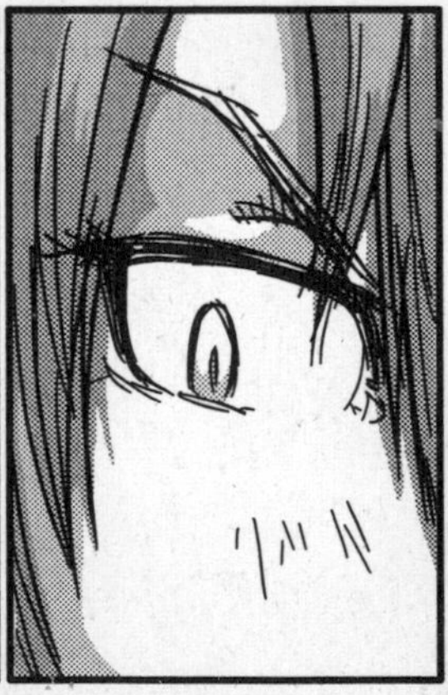

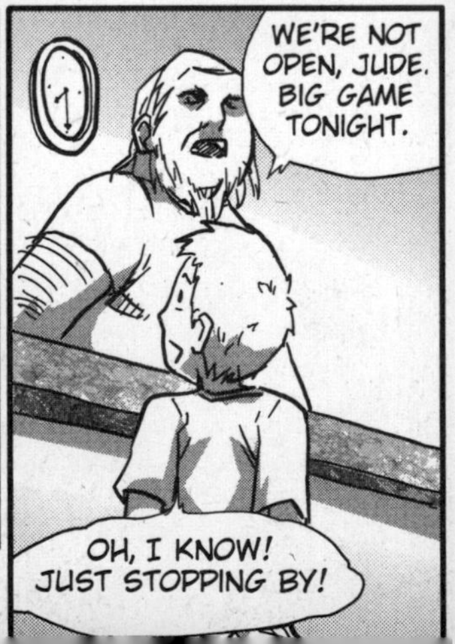
WE'RE NOT OPEN, JUDE. BIG GAME TONIGHT.
OH, I KNOW! JUST STOPPING BY!

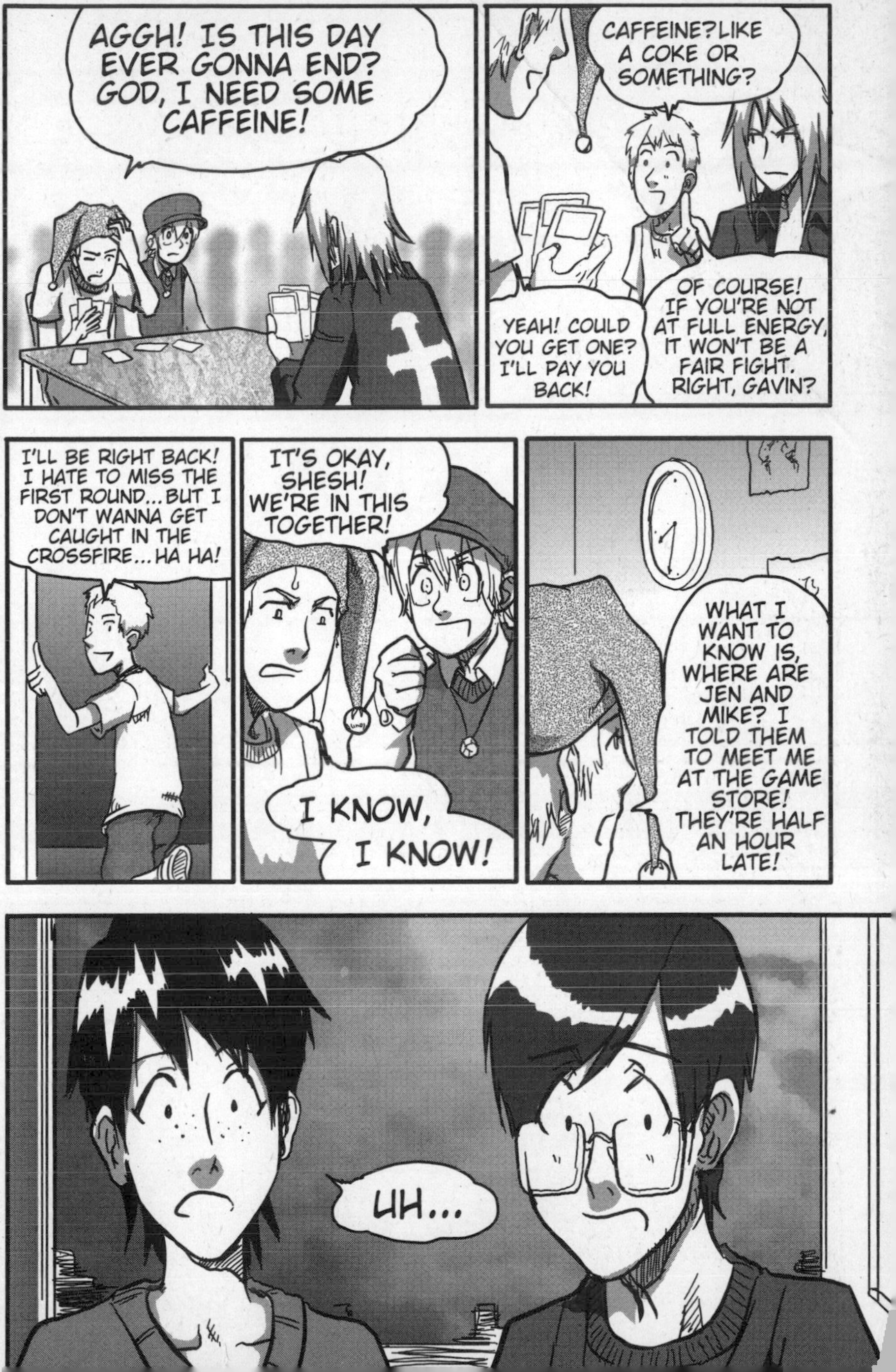
AGGH! IS THIS DAY EVER GONNA END? GOD, I NEED SOME CAFFEINE!
CAFFEINE? LIKE A COKE OR SOMETHING?
YEAH! COULD YOU GET ONE? I'LL PAY YOU BACK!
OF COURSE! IF YOU'RE NOT AT FULL ENERGY, IT WON'T BE A FAIR FIGHT. RIGHT, GAVIN?
I'LL BE RIGHT BACK! I HATE TO MISS THE FIRST ROUND... BUT I DON'T WANNA GET CAUGHT IN THE CROSSFIRE... HA HA!
IT'S OKAY, SHESH! WE'RE IN THIS TOGETHER!
I KNOW, I KNOW!
WHAT I WANT TO KNOW IS, WHERE ARE JEN AND MIKE? I TOLD THEM TO MEET ME AT THE GAME STORE! THEY'RE HALF AN HOUR LATE!
UH...

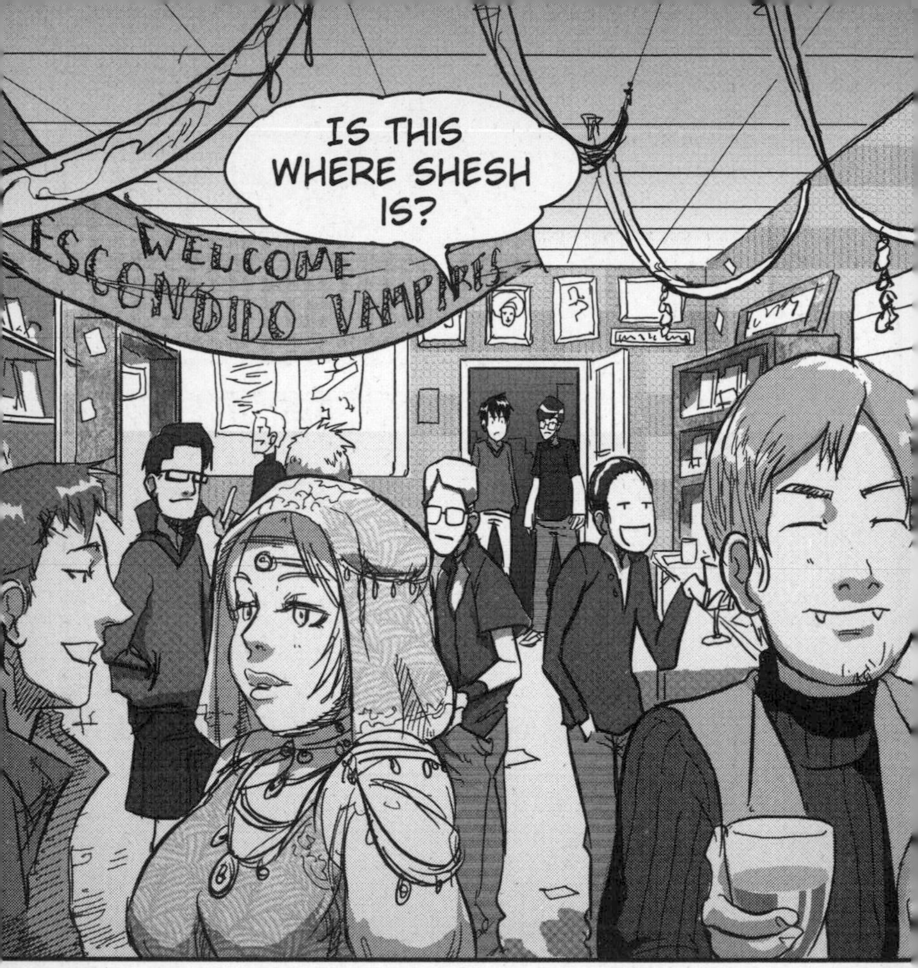
IS THIS WHERE SHESH IS?
WELCOME ESCONDIDO VAMPIRES

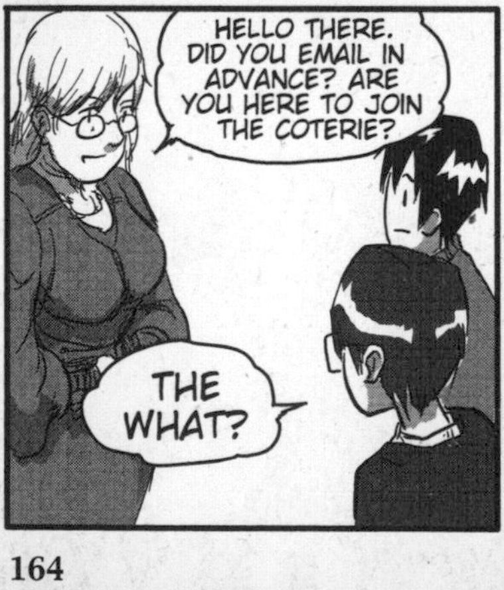
HELLO THERE. DID YOU EMAIL IN ADVANCE? ARE YOU HERE TO JOIN THE COTERIE?
THE WHAT?

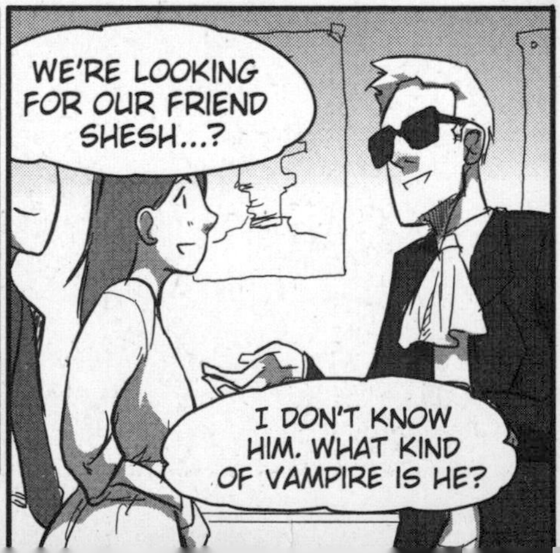
WE'RE LOOKING FOR OUR FRIEND SHESH...?
I DON'T KNOW HIM. WHAT KIND OF VAMPIRE IS HE?

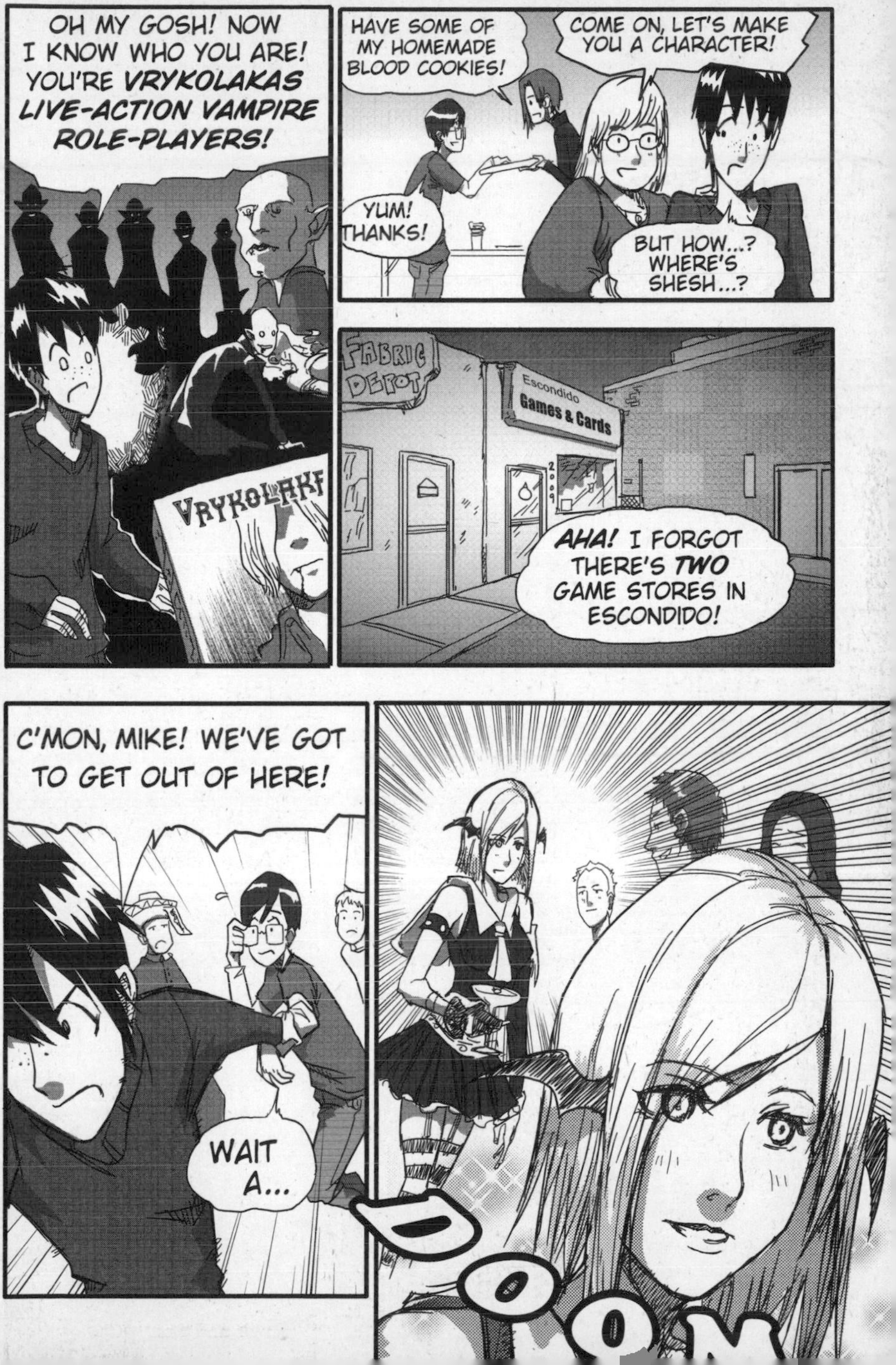
OH MY GOSH! NOW I KNOW WHO YOU ARE! YOU'RE VRYKOLAKAS LIVE-ACTION VAMPIRE ROLE-PLAYERS!
HAVE SOME OF MY HOMEMADE BLOOD COOKIES!
COME ON, LET'S MAKE YOU A CHARACTER!
YUM! THANKS!
BUT HOW...? WHERE'S SHESH...?
FABRIC DEPOT
Escondido Games & Cards
AHA! I FORGOT THERE'S TWO GAME STORES IN ESCONDIDO!
C'MON, MIKE! WE'VE GOT TO GET OUT OF HERE!
WAIT A...
DOOM

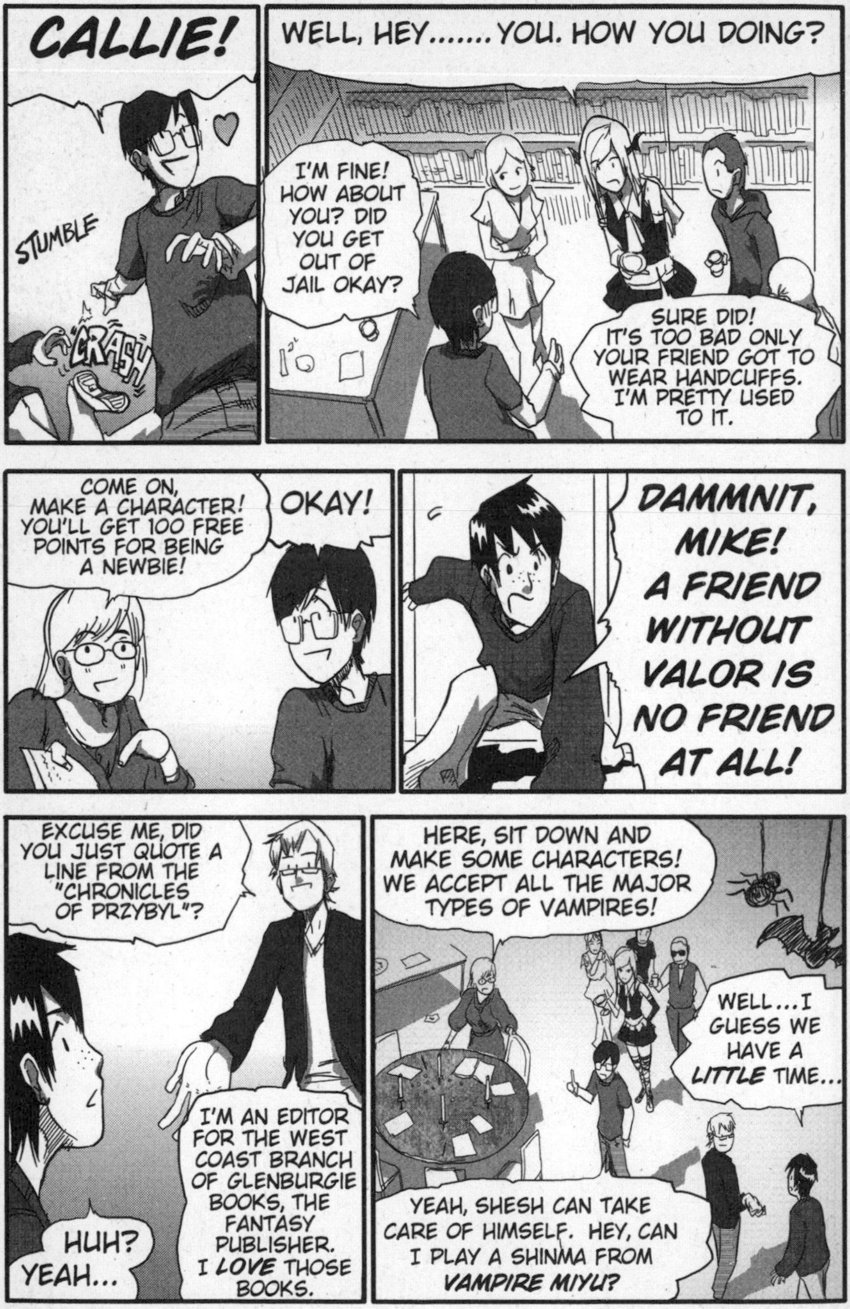
CALLIE!
STUMBLE
CRASH
WELL, HEY.......YOU. HOW YOU DOING?
I'M FINE! HOW ABOUT YOU? DID YOU GET OUT OF JAIL OKAY?
SURE DID! IT'S TOO BAD ONLY YOUR FRIEND GOT TO WEAR HANDCUFFS. I'M PRETTY USED TO IT.
COME ON, MAKE A CHARACTER! YOU'LL GET 100 FREE POINTS FOR BEING A NEWBIE!
OKAY!
DAMMNIT, MIKE! A FRIEND WITHOUT VALOR IS NO FRIEND AT ALL!
EXCUSE ME, DID YOU JUST QUOTE A LINE FROM THE "CHRONICLES OF PRZYBYL"?
HUH? YEAH...
I'M AN EDITOR FOR THE WEST COAST BRANCH OF GLENBURGIE BOOKS, THE FANTASY PUBLISHER. I LOVE THOSE BOOKS.
HERE, SIT DOWN AND MAKE SOME CHARACTERS! WE ACCEPT ALL THE MAJOR TYPES OF VAMPIRES!
WELL...I GUESS WE HAVE A LITTLE TIME...
YEAH, SHESH CAN TAKE CARE OF HIMSELF. HEY, CAN I PLAY A SHINMA FROM VAMPIRE MIYU?

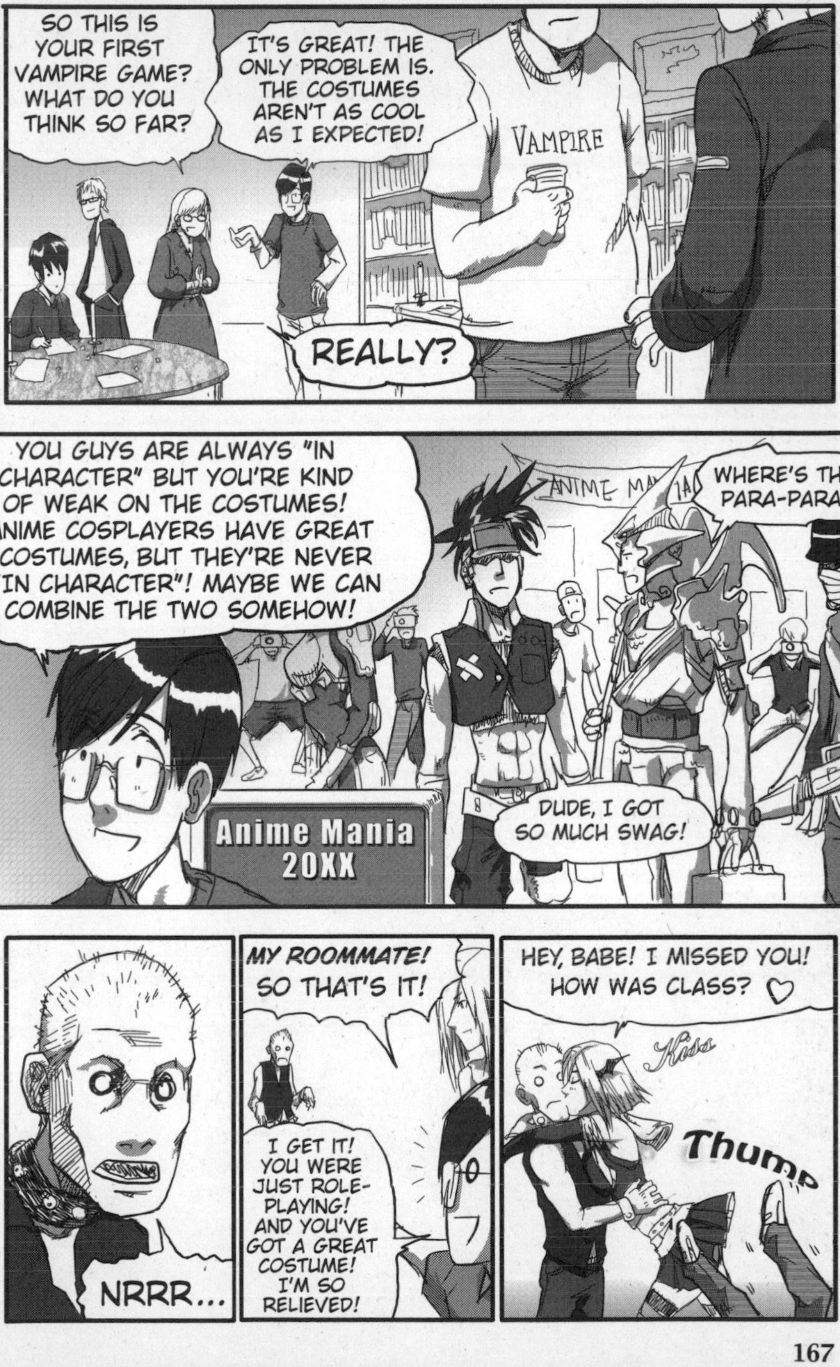
SO THIS IS YOUR FIRST VAMPIRE GAME? WHAT DO YOU THINK SO FAR?
IT'S GREAT! THE ONLY PROBLEM IS. THE COSTUMES AREN'T AS COOL AS I EXPECTED!
VAMPIRE
REALLY?
YOU GUYS ARE ALWAYS "IN CHARACTER" BUT YOU'RE KIND OF WEAK ON THE COSTUMES! ANIME COSPLAYERS HAVE GREAT COSTUMES, BUT THEY'RE NEVER "IN CHARACTER"! MAYBE WE CAN COMBINE THE TWO SOMEHOW!
WHERE'S THE PARA-PARA?
Anime Mania
20XX
DUDE, I GOT SO MUCH SWAG!
NRRR...
MY ROOMMATE!
SO THAT'S IT!
I GET IT! YOU WERE JUST ROLE-PLAYING! AND YOU'VE GOT A GREAT COSTUME! I'M SO RELIEVED!
HEY, BABE! I MISSED YOU! HOW WAS CLASS? ♡
Kiss
Thump

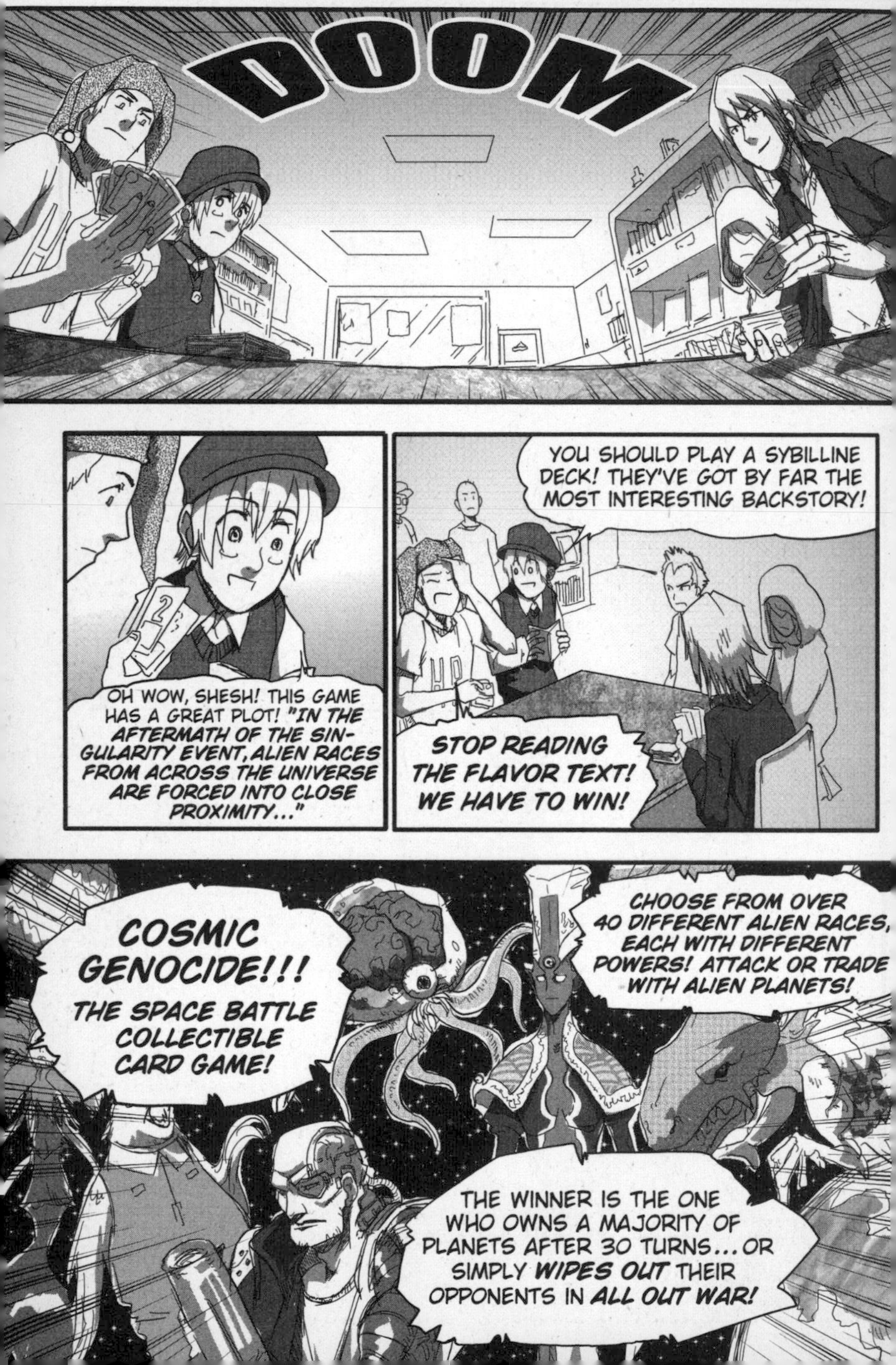
DOOM
OH WOW, SHESH! THIS GAME HAS A GREAT PLOT! "IN THE AFTERMATH OF THE SIN-GULARITY EVENT, ALIEN RACES FROM ACROSS THE UNIVERSE ARE FORCED INTO CLOSE PROXIMITY..."
YOU SHOULD PLAY A SYBILLINE DECK! THEY'VE GOT BY FAR THE MOST INTERESTING BACKSTORY!
STOP READING THE FLAVOR TEXT! WE HAVE TO WIN!
COSMIC GENOCIDE!!! THE SPACE BATTLE COLLECTIBLE CARD GAME!
CHOOSE FROM OVER 40 DIFFERENT ALIEN RACES, EACH WITH DIFFERENT POWERS! ATTACK OR TRADE WITH ALIEN PLANETS!
THE WINNER IS THE ONE WHO OWNS A MAJORITY OF PLANETS AFTER 30 TURNS... OR SIMPLY WIPES OUT THEIR OPPONENTS IN ALL OUT WAR!

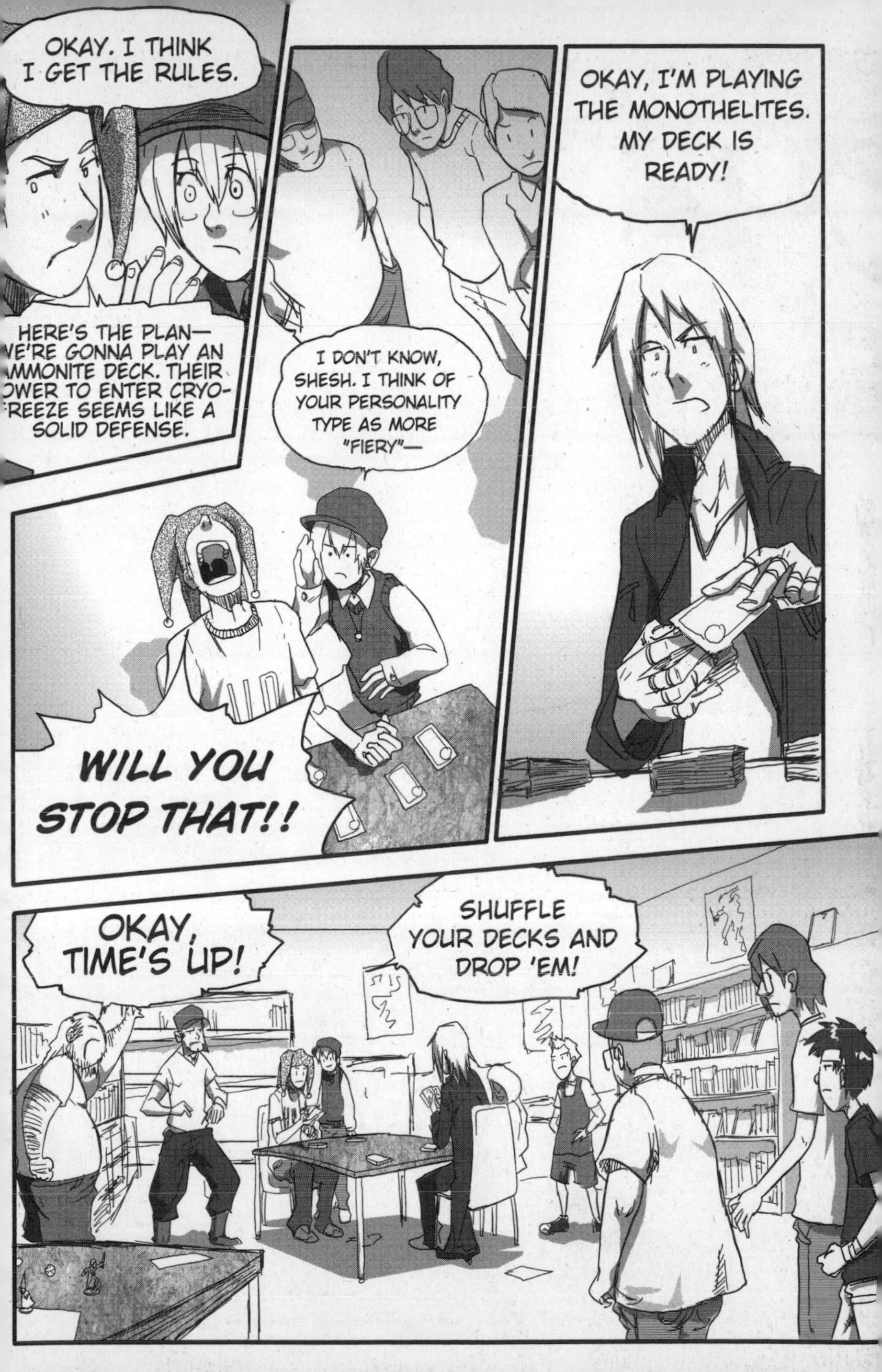

OKAY. I THINK I GET THE RULES.
HERE'S THE PLAN— VE'RE GONNA PLAY AN MMONITE DECK. THEIR OWER TO ENTER CRYO- REEZE SEEMS LIKE A SOLID DEFENSE.
I DON'T KNOW, SHESH. I THINK OF YOUR PERSONALITY TYPE AS MORE "FIERY"—
WILL YOU STOP THAT!!
OKAY, I'M PLAYING THE MONOTHELITES. MY DECK IS READY!
OKAY, TIME'S UP!
SHUFFLE YOUR DECKS AND DROP 'EM!

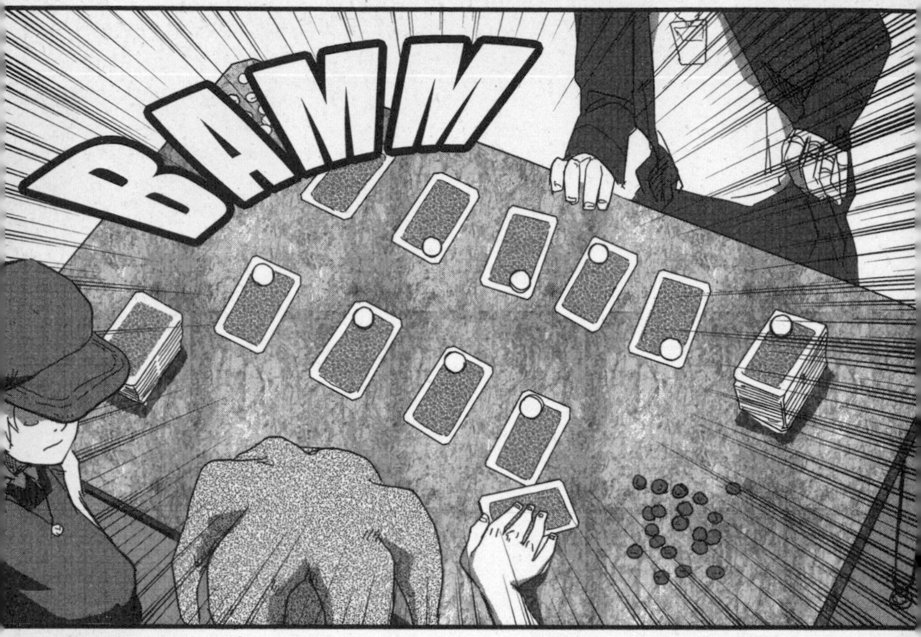
BAMM

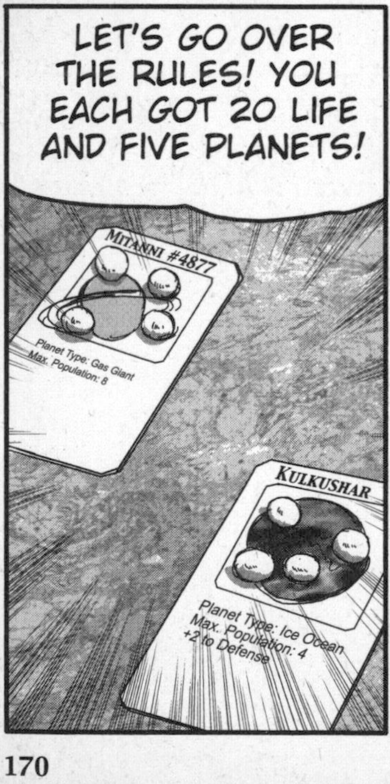
LET'S GO OVER THE RULES! YOU EACH GOT 20 LIFE AND FIVE PLANETS!
MITANNI #4877
Planet Type: Gas Giant
Max. Population: 8
KULKUSHAR
Planet Type: Ice Ocean
Max. Population: 4
+2 to Defense

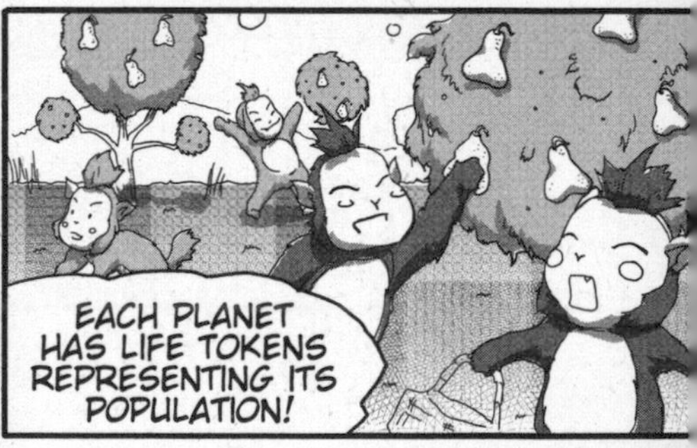
EACH PLANET HAS LIFE TOKENS REPRESENTING ITS POPULATION!

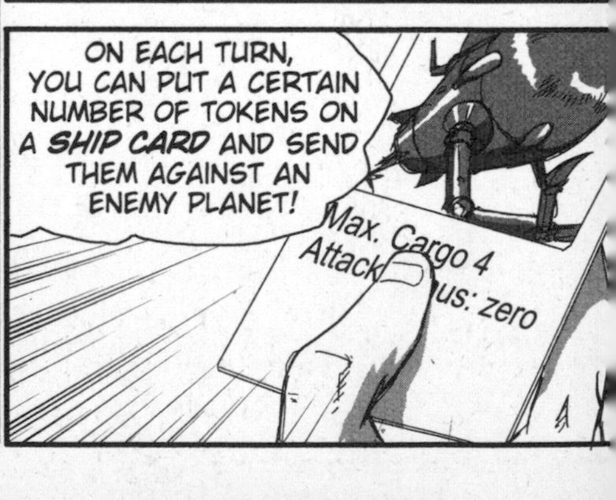
ON EACH TURN, YOU CAN PUT A CERTAIN NUMBER OF TOKENS ON A *SHIP CARD* AND SEND THEM AGAINST AN ENEMY PLANET!
Max. Cargo 4

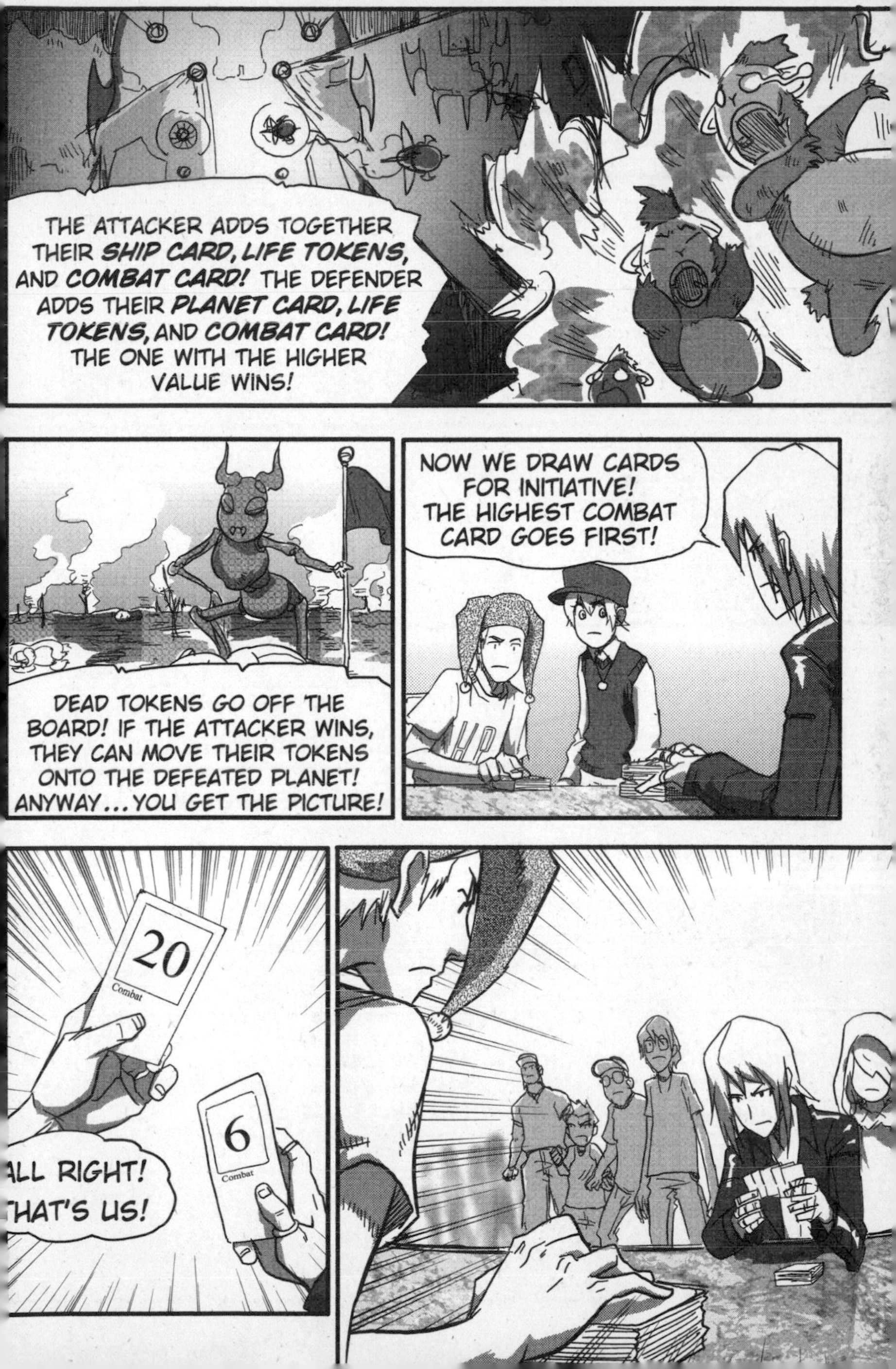
THE ATTACKER ADDS TOGETHER THEIR SHIP CARD, LIFE TOKENS, AND COMBAT CARD! THE DEFENDER ADDS THEIR PLANET CARD, LIFE TOKENS, AND COMBAT CARD! THE ONE WITH THE HIGHER VALUE WINS!
DEAD TOKENS GO OFF THE BOARD! IF THE ATTACKER WINS, THEY CAN MOVE THEIR TOKENS ONTO THE DEFEATED PLANET! ANYWAY... YOU GET THE PICTURE!
NOW WE DRAW CARDS FOR INITIATIVE! THE HIGHEST COMBAT CARD GOES FIRST!
20
Combat
6
Combat
ALL RIGHT! THAT'S US!

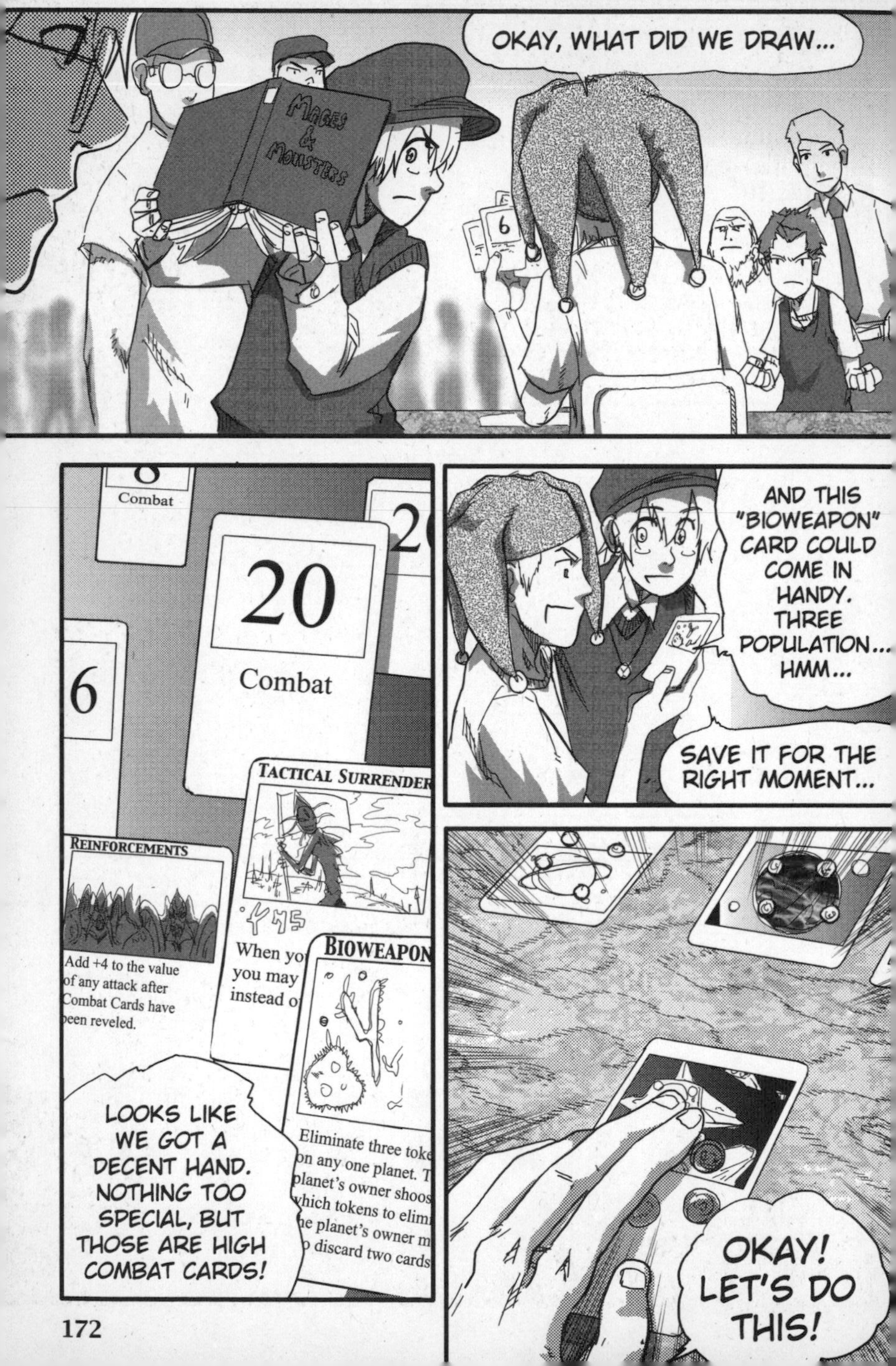
MAGES & MONSTERS
OKAY, WHAT DID WE DRAW...
6
Combat
20
Combat
6
TACTICAL SURRENDER
When yo
you may
instead o
REINFORCEMENTS
Add +4 to the value
of any attack after
Combat Cards have
een reveled.
BIOWEAPON
Eliminate three toke
on any one planet. T
planet's owner shoos
which tokens to elim
he planet's owner m
o discard two cards
LOOKS LIKE WE GOT A DECENT HAND. NOTHING TOO SPECIAL, BUT THOSE ARE HIGH COMBAT CARDS!
AND THIS "BIOWEAPON" CARD COULD COME IN HANDY. THREE POPULATION... HMM...
SAVE IT FOR THE RIGHT MOMENT...
OKAY! LET'S DO THIS!

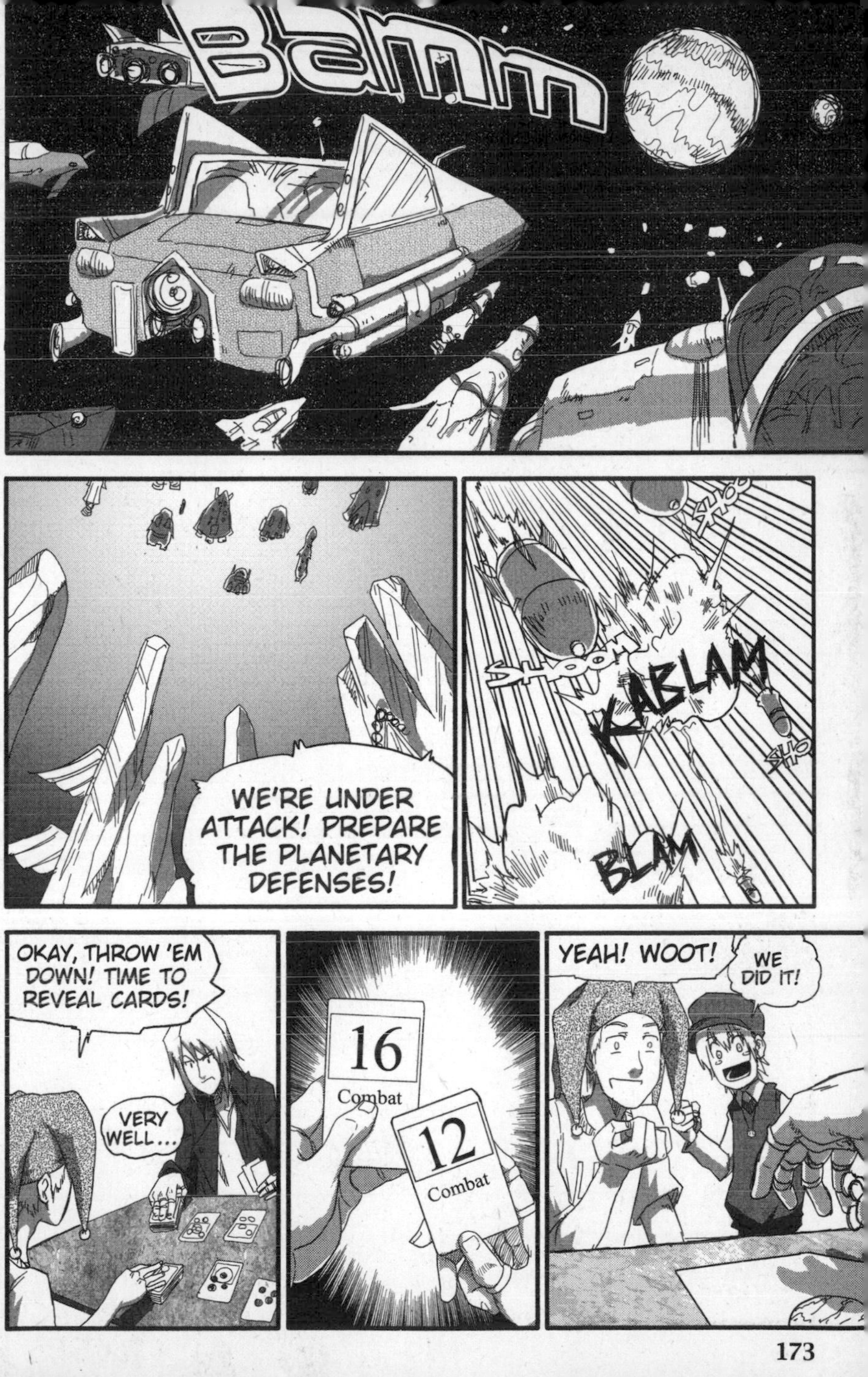
Bamm
WE'RE UNDER ATTACK! PREPARE THE PLANETARY DEFENSES!
KABLAM
BLAM
OKAY, THROW 'EM DOWN! TIME TO REVEAL CARDS!
VERY WELL...
16
Combat
12
Combat
YEAH! WOOT!
WE DID IT!

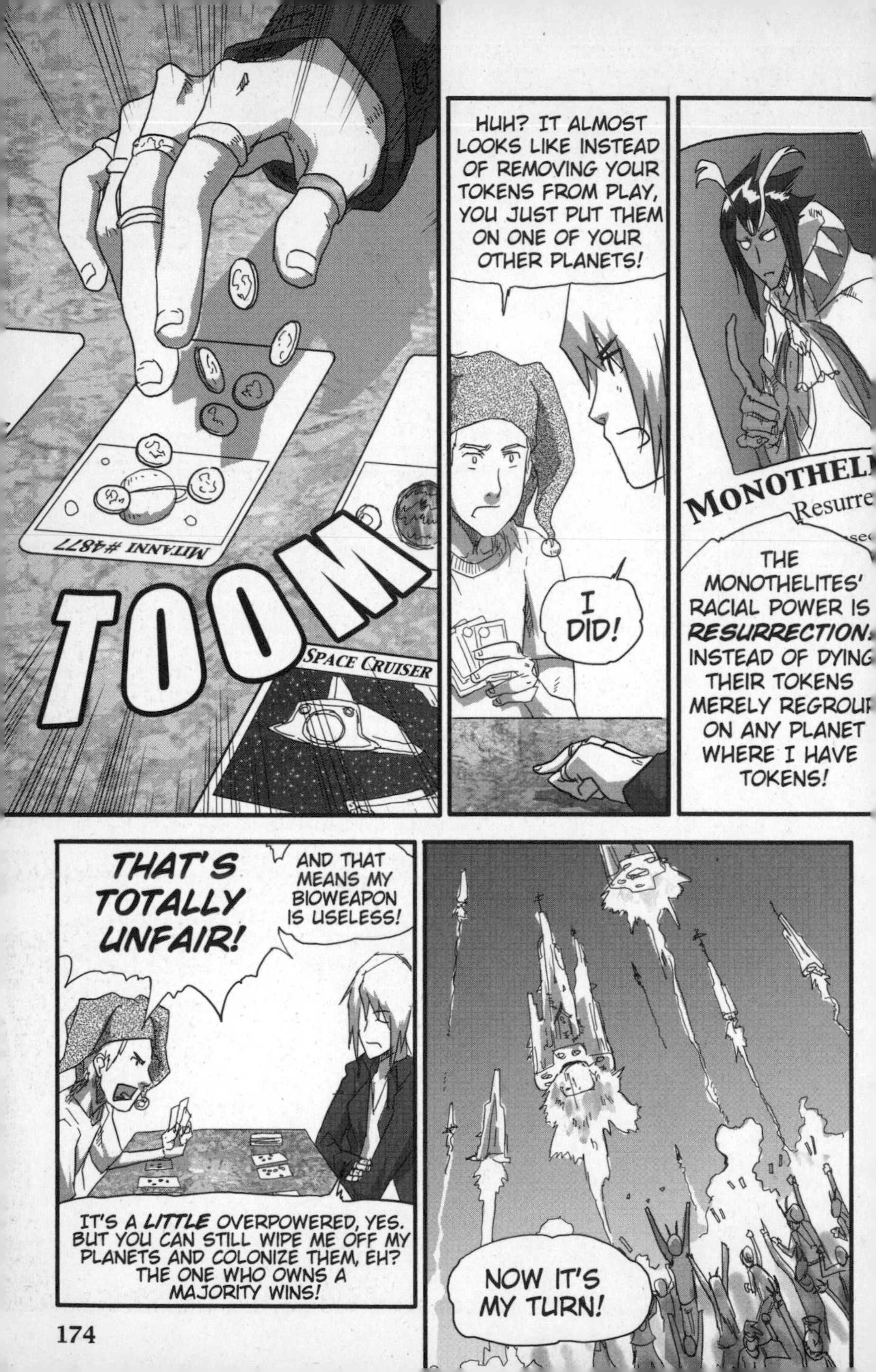
MITANNI #4877
TOOM
SPACE CRUISER
HUH? IT ALMOST LOOKS LIKE INSTEAD OF REMOVING YOUR TOKENS FROM PLAY, YOU JUST PUT THEM ON ONE OF YOUR OTHER PLANETS!
I DID!
THE MONOTHELITES' RACIAL POWER IS *RESURRECTION*. INSTEAD OF DYING THEIR TOKENS MERELY REGROUP ON ANY PLANET WHERE I HAVE TOKENS!
THAT'S TOTALLY UNFAIR!
AND THAT MEANS MY BIOWEAPON IS USELESS!
IT'S A *LITTLE* OVERPOWERED, YES. BUT YOU CAN STILL WIPE ME OFF MY PLANETS AND COLONIZE THEM, EH? THE ONE WHO OWNS A MAJORITY WINS!
NOW IT'S MY TURN!

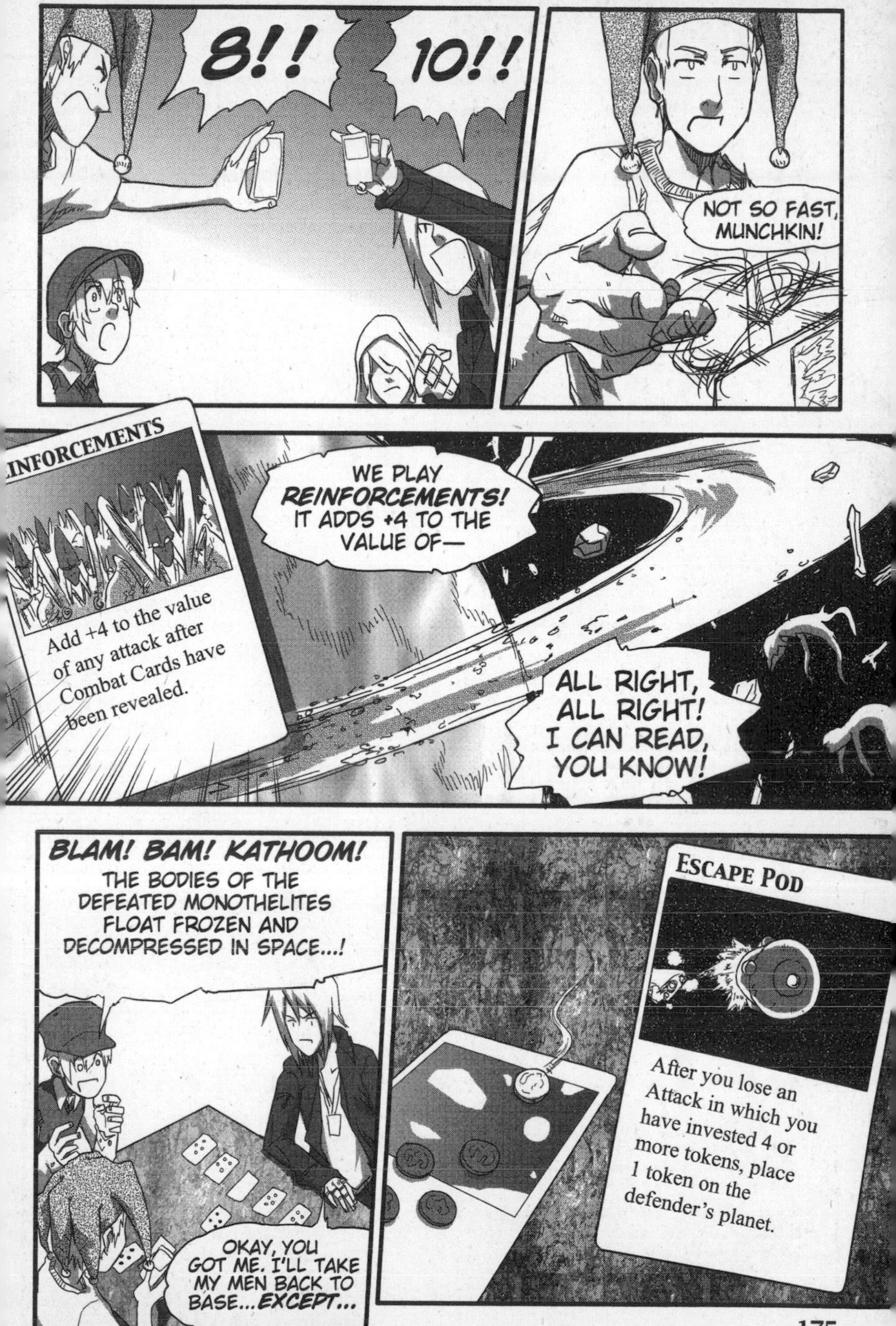
8!!
10!!
NOT SO FAST, MUNCHKIN!
REINFORCEMENTS
Add +4 to the value of any attack after Combat Cards have been revealed.
WE PLAY REINFORCEMENTS! IT ADDS +4 TO THE VALUE OF—
ALL RIGHT, ALL RIGHT! I CAN READ, YOU KNOW!
BLAM! BAM! KATHOOM!
THE BODIES OF THE DEFEATED MONOTHELITES FLOAT FROZEN AND DECOMPRESSED IN SPACE...!
OKAY, YOU GOT ME. I'LL TAKE MY MEN BACK TO BASE...EXCEPT...
ESCAPE POD
After you lose an Attack in which you have invested 4 or more tokens, place 1 token on the defender's planet.

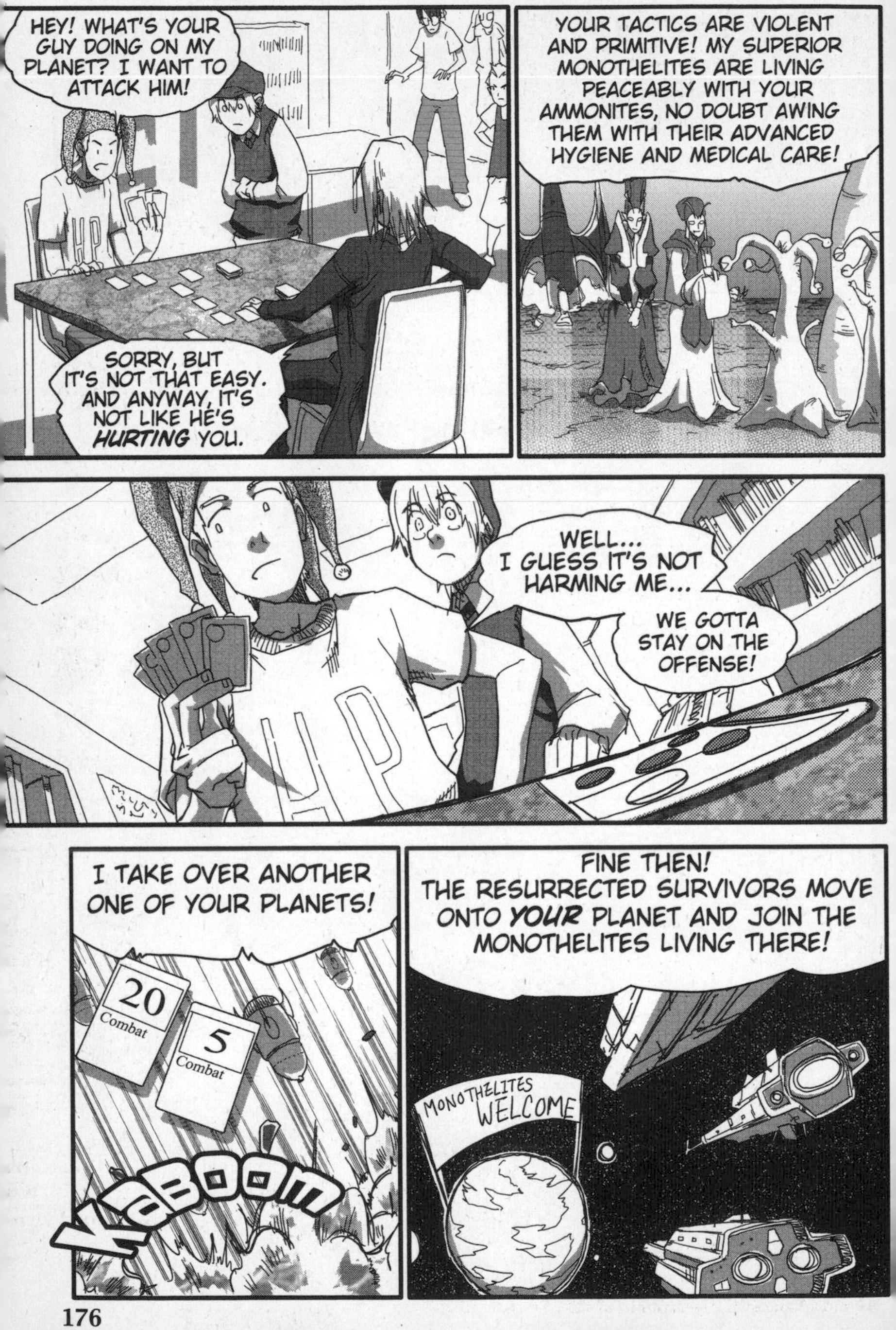
HEY! WHAT'S YOUR GUY DOING ON MY PLANET? I WANT TO ATTACK HIM!
SORRY, BUT IT'S NOT THAT EASY. AND ANYWAY, IT'S NOT LIKE HE'S *HURTING* YOU.
YOUR TACTICS ARE VIOLENT AND PRIMITIVE! MY SUPERIOR MONOTHELITES ARE LIVING PEACEABLY WITH YOUR AMMONITES, NO DOUBT AWING THEM WITH THEIR ADVANCED HYGIENE AND MEDICAL CARE!
WELL... I GUESS IT'S NOT HARMING ME...
WE GOTTA STAY ON THE OFFENSE!
I TAKE OVER ANOTHER ONE OF YOUR PLANETS!
20
Combat
5
Combat
KaBOOM
FINE THEN! THE RESURRECTED SURVIVORS MOVE ONTO *YOUR* PLANET AND JOIN THE MONOTHELITES LIVING THERE!
MONOTHELITES WELCOME

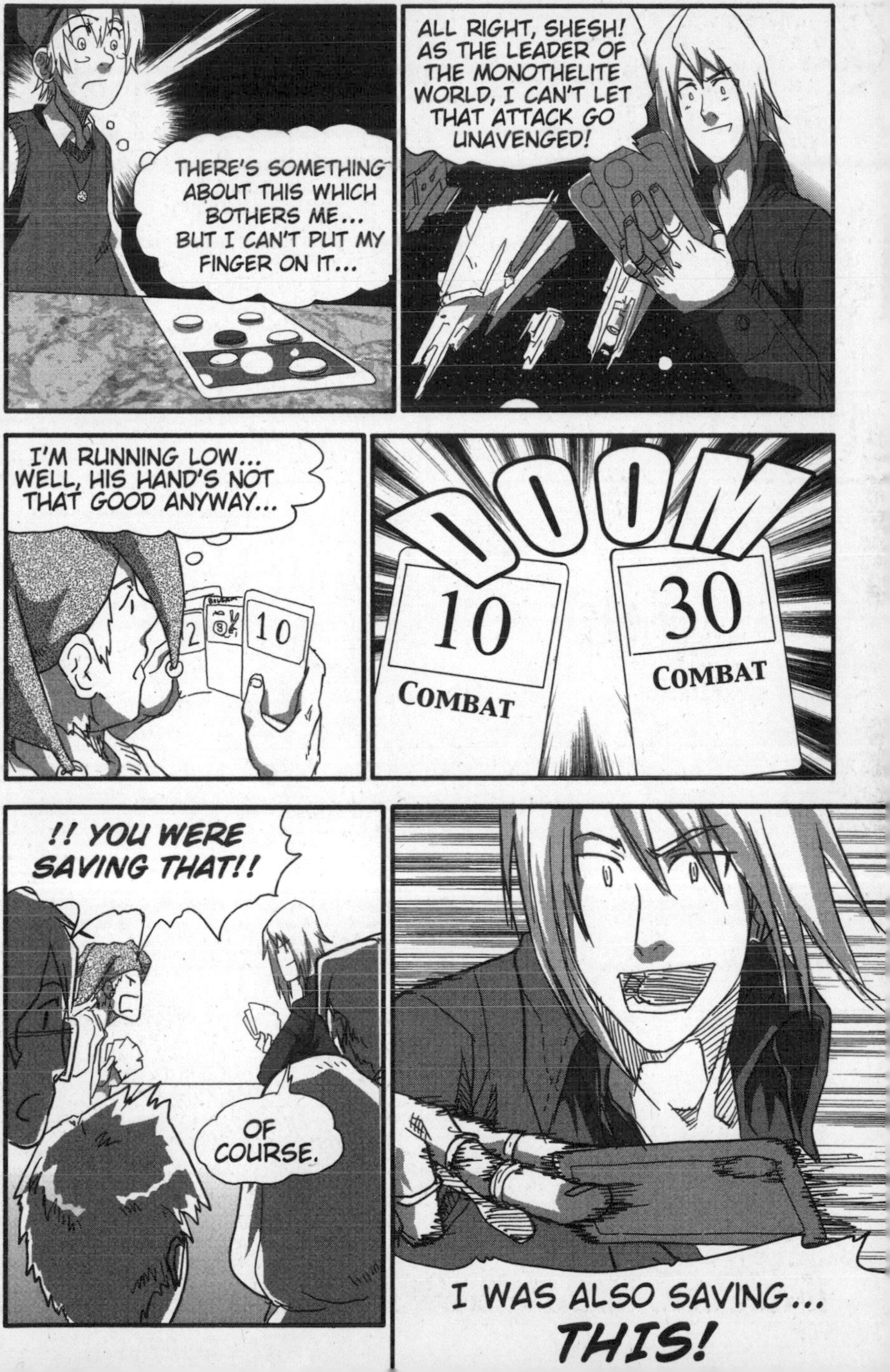
THERE'S SOMETHING ABOUT THIS WHICH BOTHERS ME... BUT I CAN'T PUT MY FINGER ON IT...
ALL RIGHT, SHESH! AS THE LEADER OF THE MONOTHELITE WORLD, I CAN'T LET THAT ATTACK GO UNAVENGED!
I'M RUNNING LOW... WELL, HIS HAND'S NOT THAT GOOD ANYWAY...
10
DOOM
10
COMBAT
30
COMBAT
!! YOU WERE SAVING THAT!!
OF COURSE.
I WAS ALSO SAVING...
THIS!

NEUTRON MISSILE

After a successful challenge, do not invade. Instead, eliminate up to eight tokens on the defending planet.

MISSILE SPLITTER X4

X4

When a card allow you o eliminate tokens, you ay divide the damage ong up to

A COMBO! NEUTRON MISSILE AND MISSILE SPLITTER!

I'LL BOMB FOUR OF YOUR PLANETS AT ONCE!

DON'T BOTHER LANDING ON THE PLANET! JUST ANNIHILATE THEM!

ZZT

ZZT

SHOOM

SHOOM

SHOOM

SHOO

OH NO! THAT'LL LEAVE YOU WITH ONLY A HANDFUL OF TOKENS!

WHAT NOW, SHESH?

NOW IT'S *YOU* WHO DOESN'T KNOW *MY* RACIAL POWER! THIS IS WHAT *CRYO-FREEZE* IS MADE FOR!

AMMONITES

RACIAL POWER: CRYO-FREEZE
ong since expelled from
planet, the mercantile An
eloped the ability
nments by

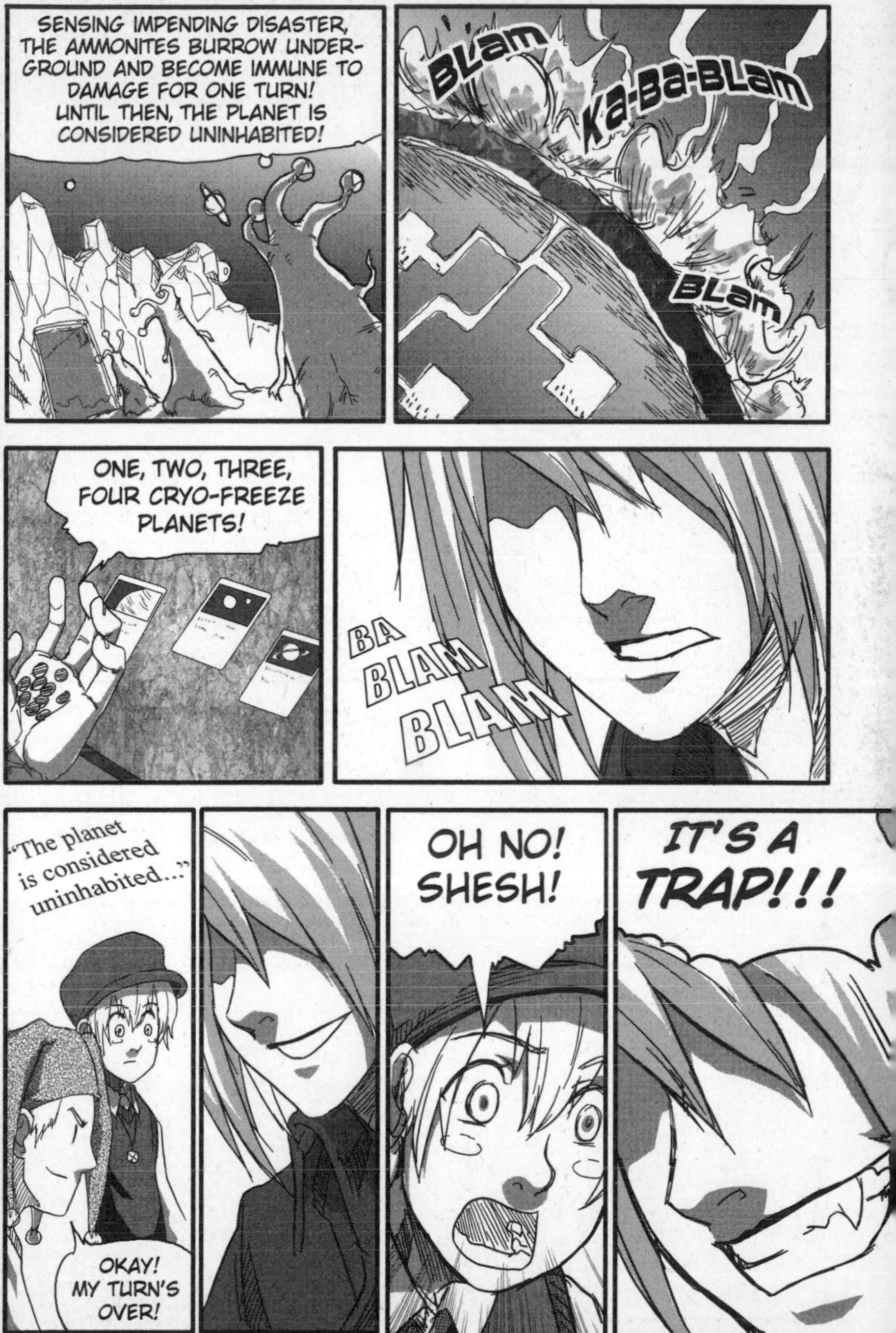
SENSING IMPENDING DISASTER, THE AMMONITES BURROW UNDERGROUND AND BECOME IMMUNE TO DAMAGE FOR ONE TURN! UNTIL THEN, THE PLANET IS CONSIDERED UNINHABITED!
BLAM
KA-BA-BLAM
BLAM
ONE, TWO, THREE, FOUR CRYO-FREEZE PLANETS!
BA BLAM BLAM BLAM
"The planet is considered uninhabited..."
OKAY! MY TURN'S OVER!
OH NO! SHESH!
IT'S A TRAP!!!

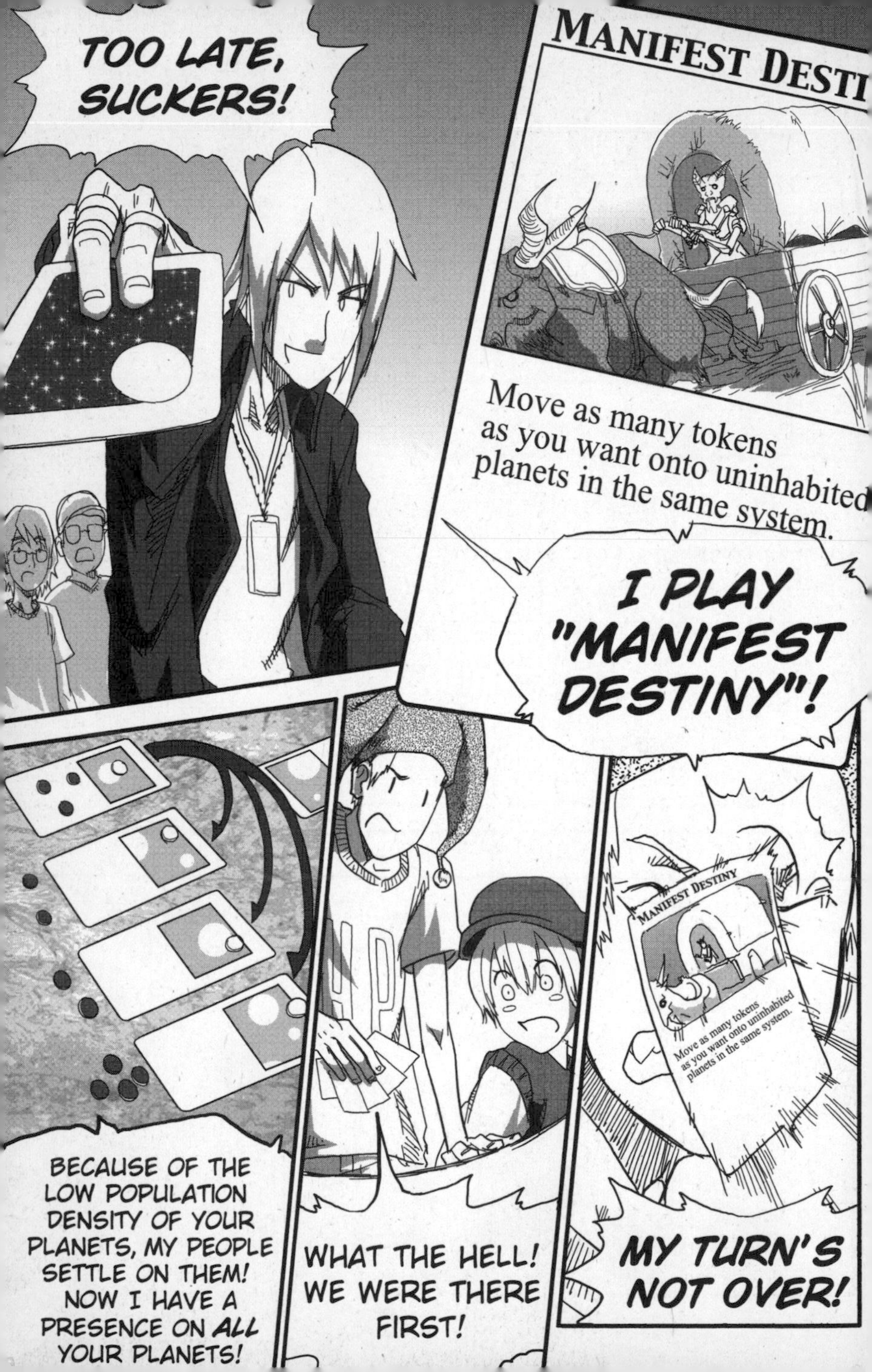

TOO LATE, SUCKERS!
MANIFEST DESTI
Move as many tokens as you want onto uninhabited planets in the same system.
I PLAY "MANIFEST DESTINY"!
BECAUSE OF THE LOW POPULATION DENSITY OF YOUR PLANETS, MY PEOPLE SETTLE ON THEM! NOW I HAVE A PRESENCE ON *ALL* YOUR PLANETS!
WHAT THE HELL! WE WERE THERE FIRST!
MANIFEST DESTINY
Move as many tokens as you want onto uninhabited planets in the same system.
MY TURN'S NOT OVER!

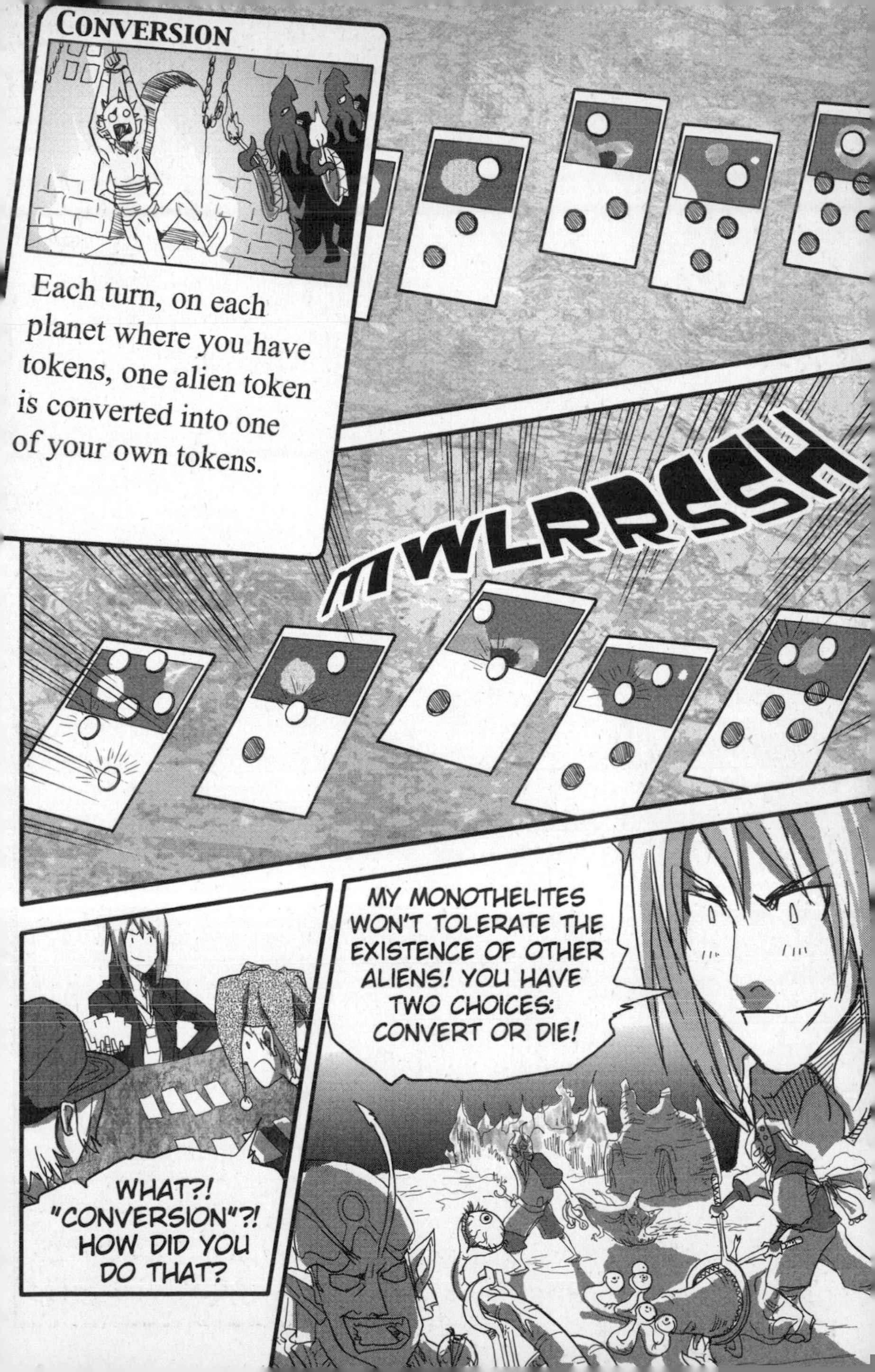
CONVERSION
Each turn, on each planet where you have tokens, one alien token is converted into one of your own tokens.
WLRRSSH
WHAT?! "CONVERSION"?! HOW DID YOU DO THAT?
MY MONOTHELITES WON'T TOLERATE THE EXISTENCE OF OTHER ALIENS! YOU HAVE TWO CHOICES: CONVERT OR DIE!

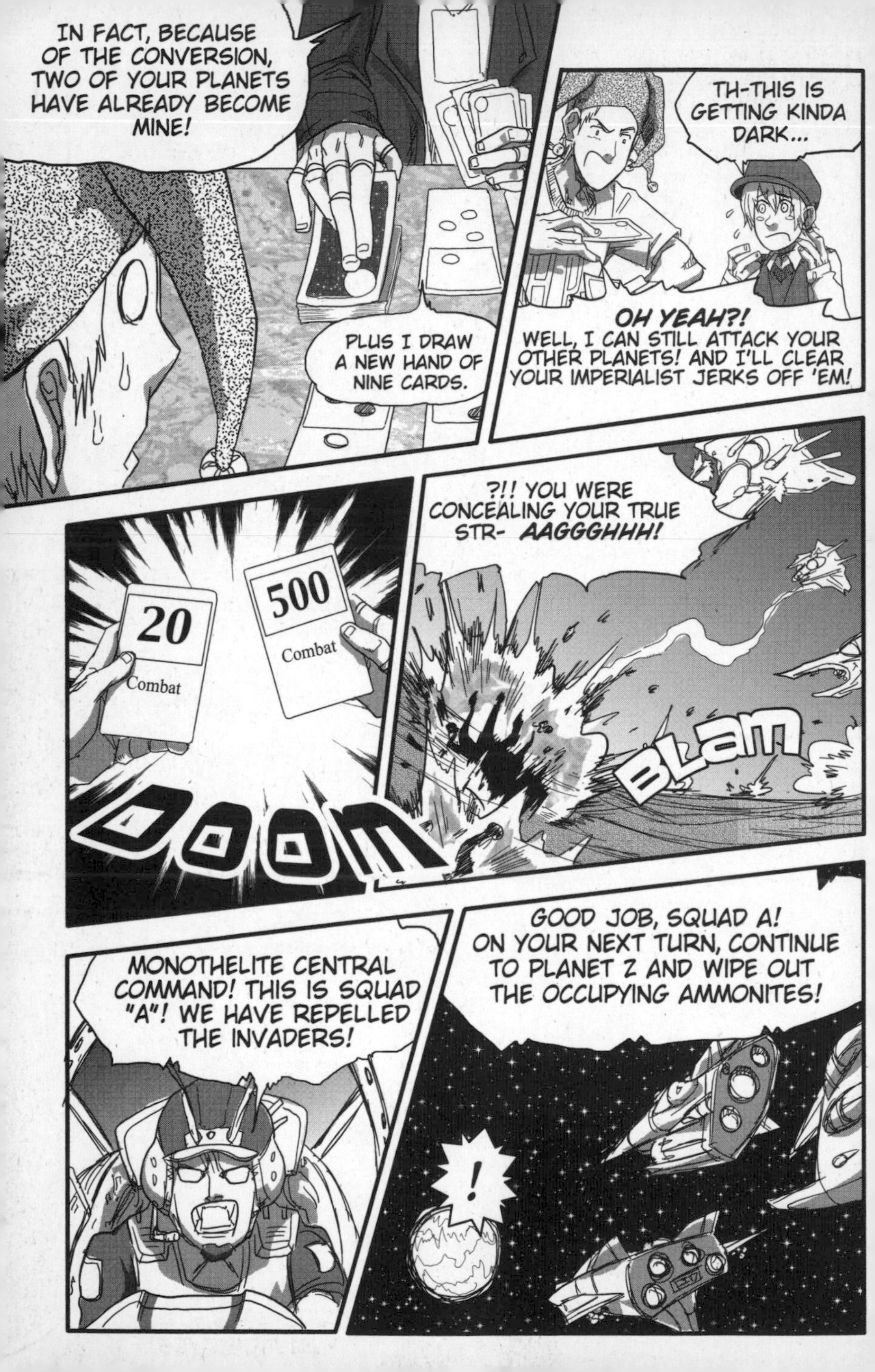
IN FACT, BECAUSE OF THE CONVERSION, TWO OF YOUR PLANETS HAVE ALREADY BECOME MINE!
PLUS I DRAW A NEW HAND OF NINE CARDS.
TH-THIS IS GETTING KINDA DARK...
OH YEAH?! WELL, I CAN STILL ATTACK YOUR OTHER PLANETS! AND I'LL CLEAR YOUR IMPERIALIST JERKS OFF 'EM!
20
Combat
500
Combat
DOOM
?!! YOU WERE CONCEALING YOUR TRUE STR- AAGGGHHH!
BLAM
MONOTHELITE CENTRAL COMMAND! THIS IS SQUAD "A"! WE HAVE REPELLED THE INVADERS!
GOOD JOB, SQUAD A! ON YOUR NEXT TURN, CONTINUE TO PLANET 2 AND WIPE OUT THE OCCUPYING AMMONITES!
!

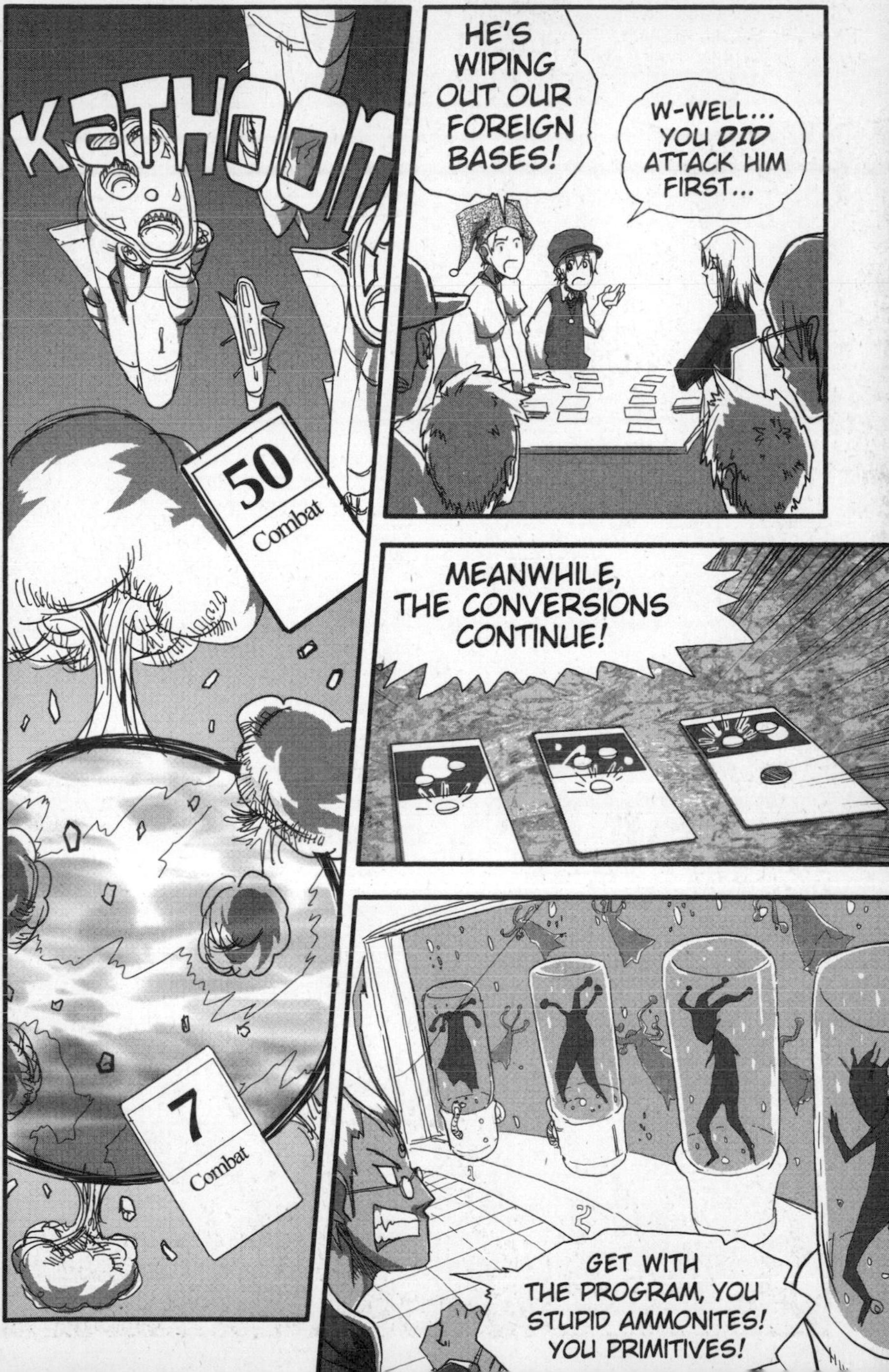
KATHOOOM
50
Combat
7
Combat
HE'S WIPING OUT OUR FOREIGN BASES!
W-WELL... YOU *DID* ATTACK HIM FIRST...
MEANWHILE, THE CONVERSIONS CONTINUE!
GET WITH THE PROGRAM, YOU STUPID AMMONITES! YOU PRIMITIVES!

GODDAMN IT!

SLIIIDE

@#$%! WHY IS HIS DECK SO GOOD? WHEN DO *I* GET TO DRAW NEW CARDS?

Y-YOU HAVE TO USE ALL YOUR COMBAT CARDS FIRST...

WELL IN THAT CASE I'M *SCREWED!* AND EVEN IF I SURVIVE THIS TURN, WHAT DO I DO?

3

ombat

Eliminate three tokens on any one planet. The planet's owner chooses which tokens to eliminate. The planet owner must discard for their choice.

When you are defending, you may play this card instead of a combat card. Preserve one of the conquered tokens on the conquered planet. Then other tokens we eliminated as usual.

HIS TOKENS KEEP REGENERATING! I CAN'T KILL THEM! IT'S JUST LIKE IN THE *MAGES & MONSTERS* GAME WHEN WE FOUGHT THE SLIME KRAKEN!

E-EXCEPT YOU CAN'T DO A TRACHEOTOMY SNEAK ATTACK...!

YOU LET A FIRST LEVEL ROGUE ATTEMPT A TRACHEOTOMY ON A SLIME KRAKEN?

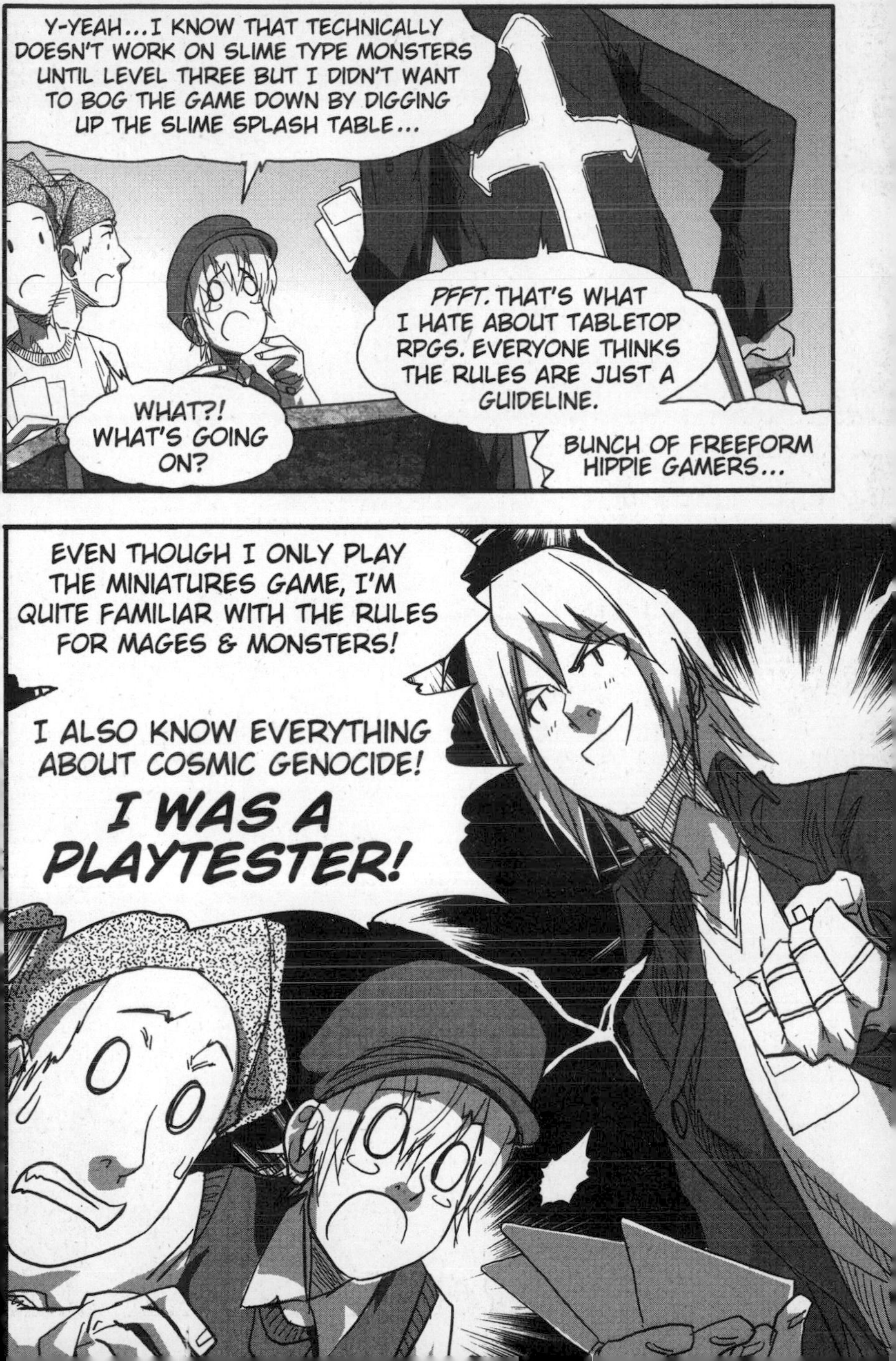
Y-YEAH...I KNOW THAT TECHNICALLY DOESN'T WORK ON SLIME TYPE MONSTERS UNTIL LEVEL THREE BUT I DIDN'T WANT TO BOG THE GAME DOWN BY DIGGING UP THE SLIME SPLASH TABLE...
PFFT. THAT'S WHAT I HATE ABOUT TABLETOP RPGS. EVERYONE THINKS THE RULES ARE JUST A GUIDELINE.
WHAT?! WHAT'S GOING ON?
BUNCH OF FREEFORM HIPPIE GAMERS...
EVEN THOUGH I ONLY PLAY THE MINIATURES GAME, I'M QUITE FAMILIAR WITH THE RULES FOR MAGES & MONSTERS!
I ALSO KNOW EVERYTHING ABOUT COSMIC GENOCIDE!
I WAS A PLAYTESTER!

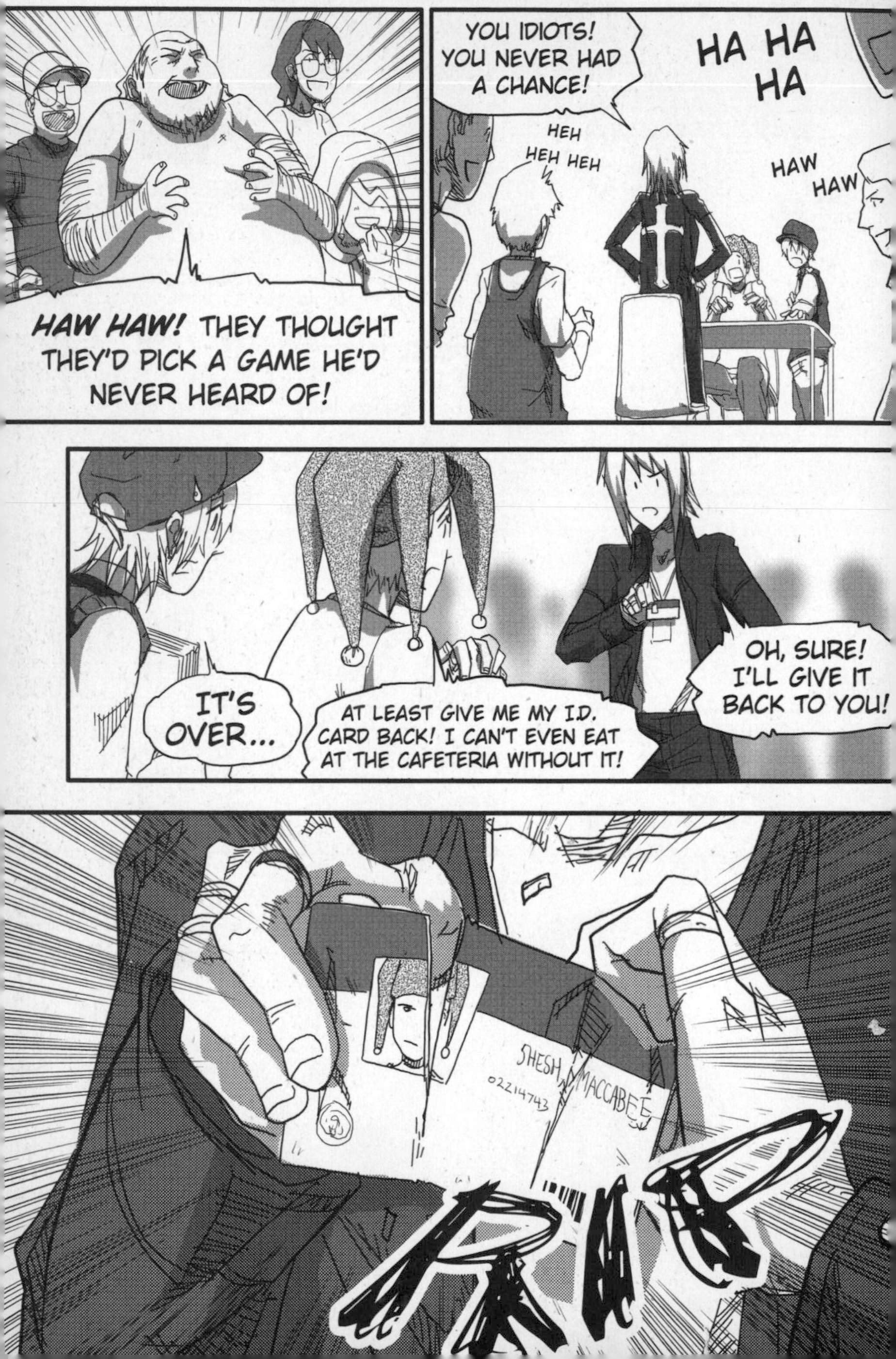
HAW HAW! THEY THOUGHT THEY'D PICK A GAME HE'D NEVER HEARD OF!
YOU IDIOTS! YOU NEVER HAD A CHANCE!
HA HA HA
HEH HEH HEH
HAW HAW
IT'S OVER...
AT LEAST GIVE ME MY I.D. CARD BACK! I CAN'T EVEN EAT AT THE CAFETERIA WITHOUT IT!
OH, SURE! I'LL GIVE IT BACK TO YOU!
SHESH MACCABEE
02214743
RIP

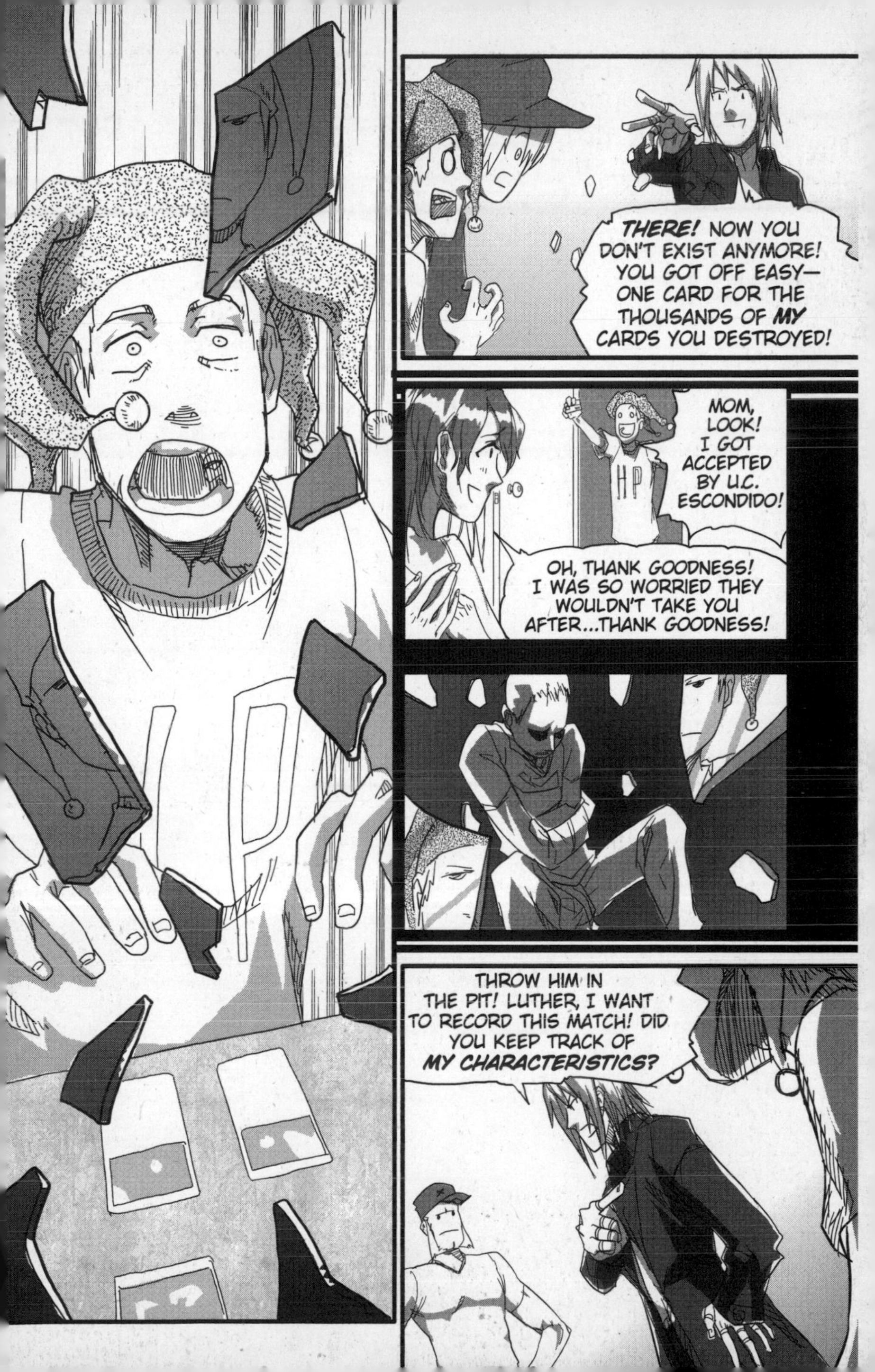
THERE! NOW YOU DON'T EXIST ANYMORE! YOU GOT OFF EASY— ONE CARD FOR THE THOUSANDS OF MY CARDS YOU DESTROYED!
MOM, LOOK! I GOT ACCEPTED BY U.C. ESCONDIDO!
OH, THANK GOODNESS! I WAS SO WORRIED THEY WOULDN'T TAKE YOU AFTER...THANK GOODNESS!
THROW HIM IN THE PIT! LUTHER, I WANT TO RECORD THIS MATCH! DID YOU KEEP TRACK OF MY CHARACTERISTICS?

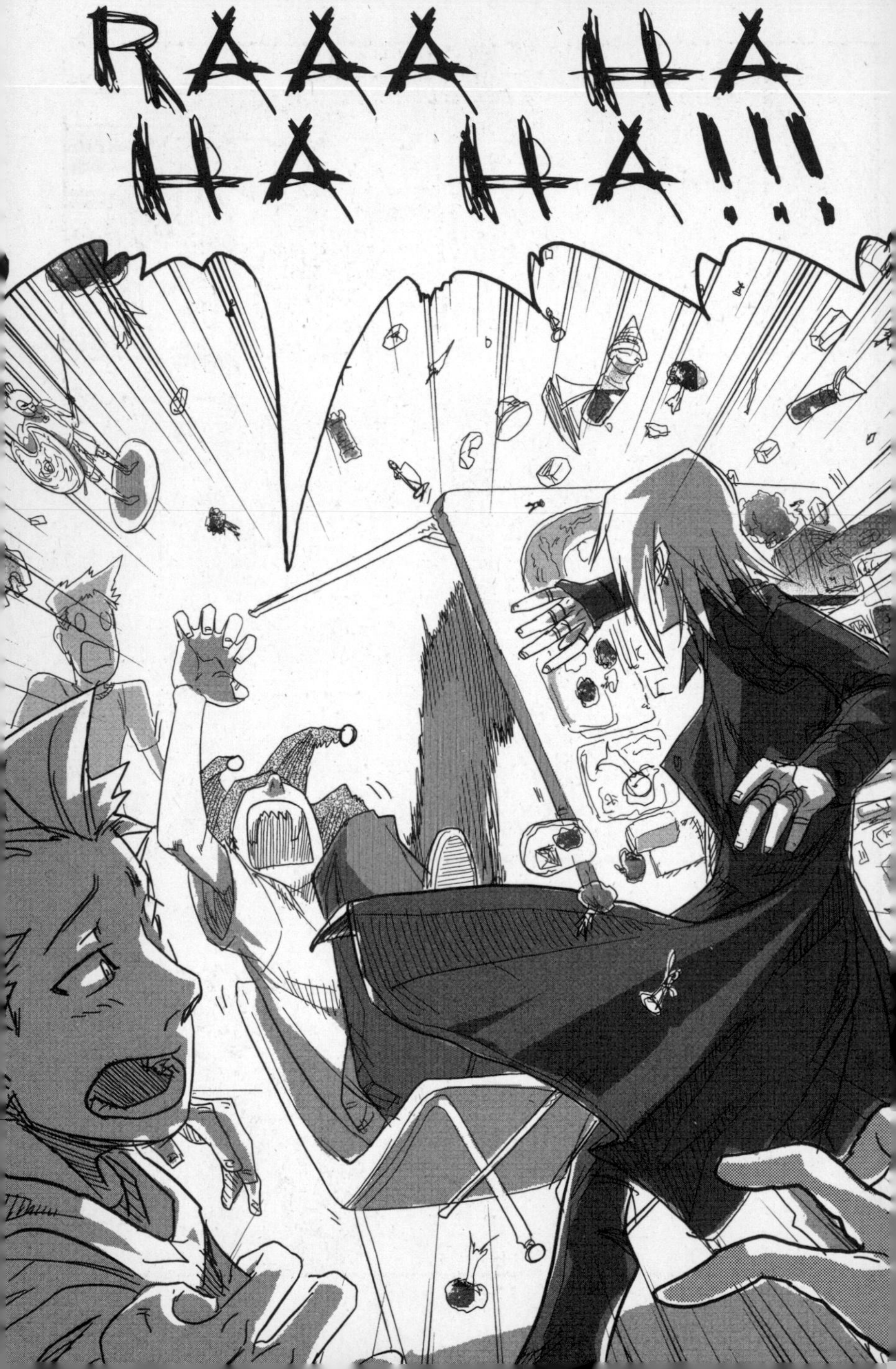
RAAA HA HA HA!!!

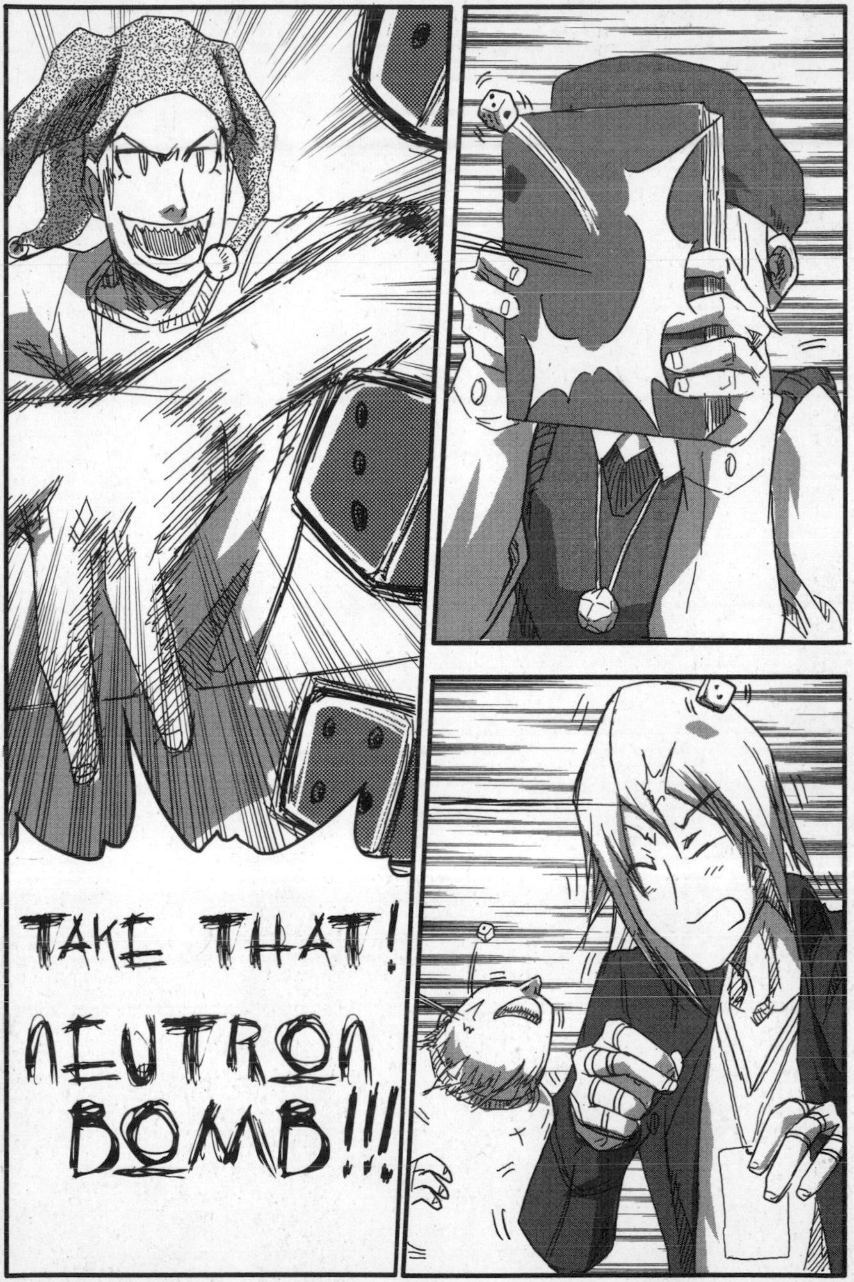
TAKE THAT!
NEUTRON BOMB!!!

NOTE: DON'T EVER DO THIS IN REAL LIFE.

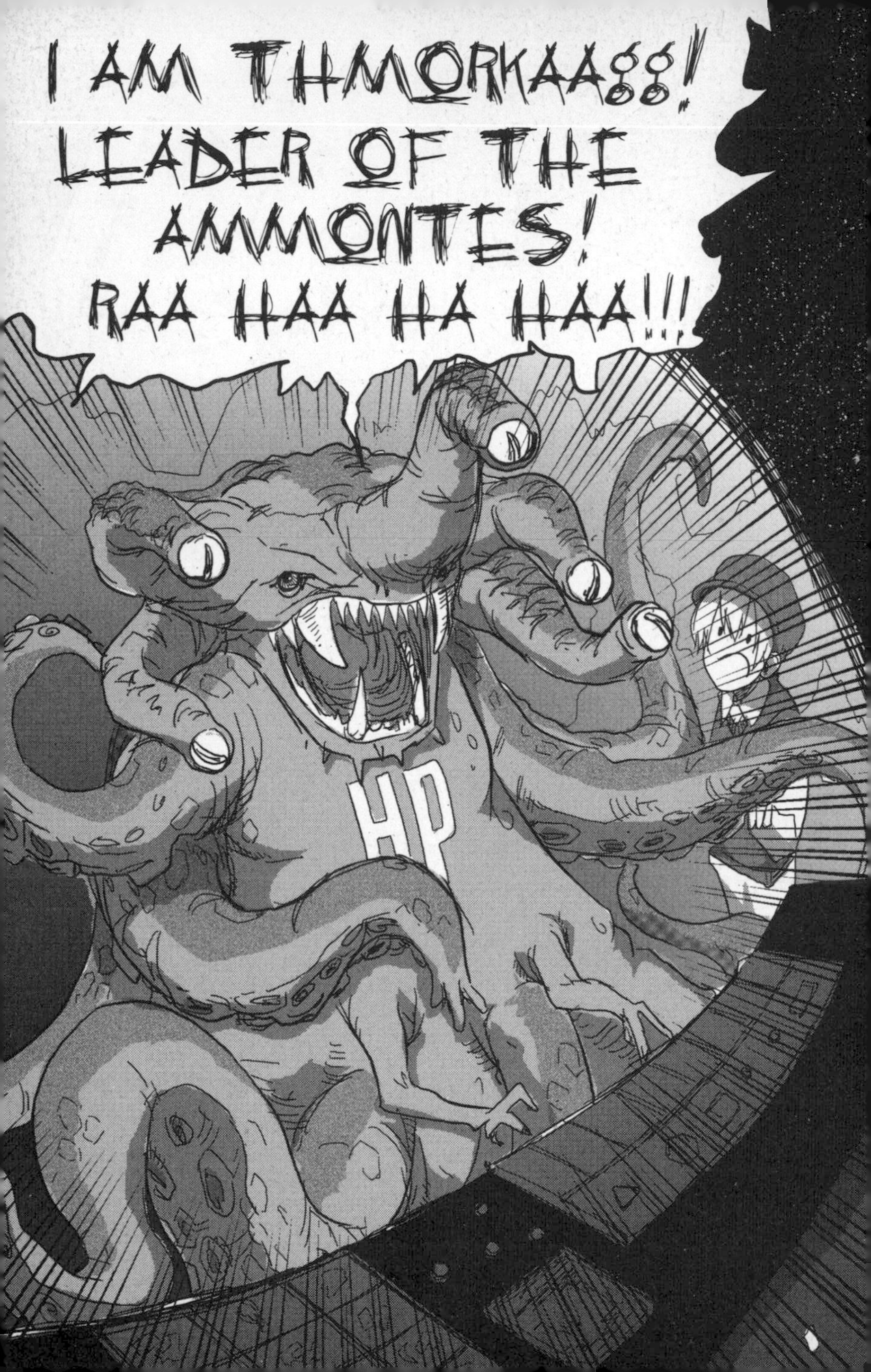
I AM THMORKAAgg! LEADER OF THE AMMONITES! RAA HAA HA HAA!!!
HP

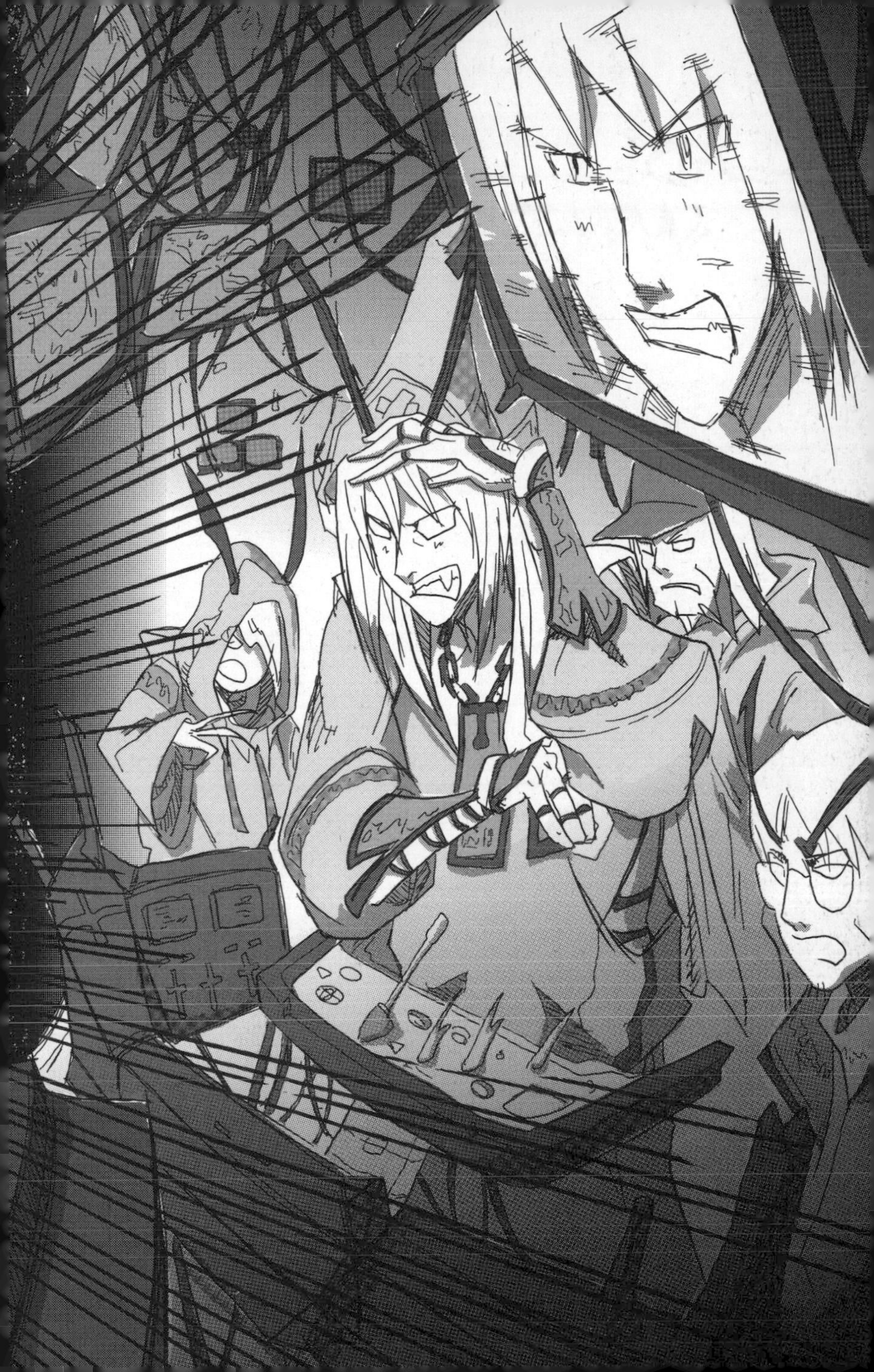

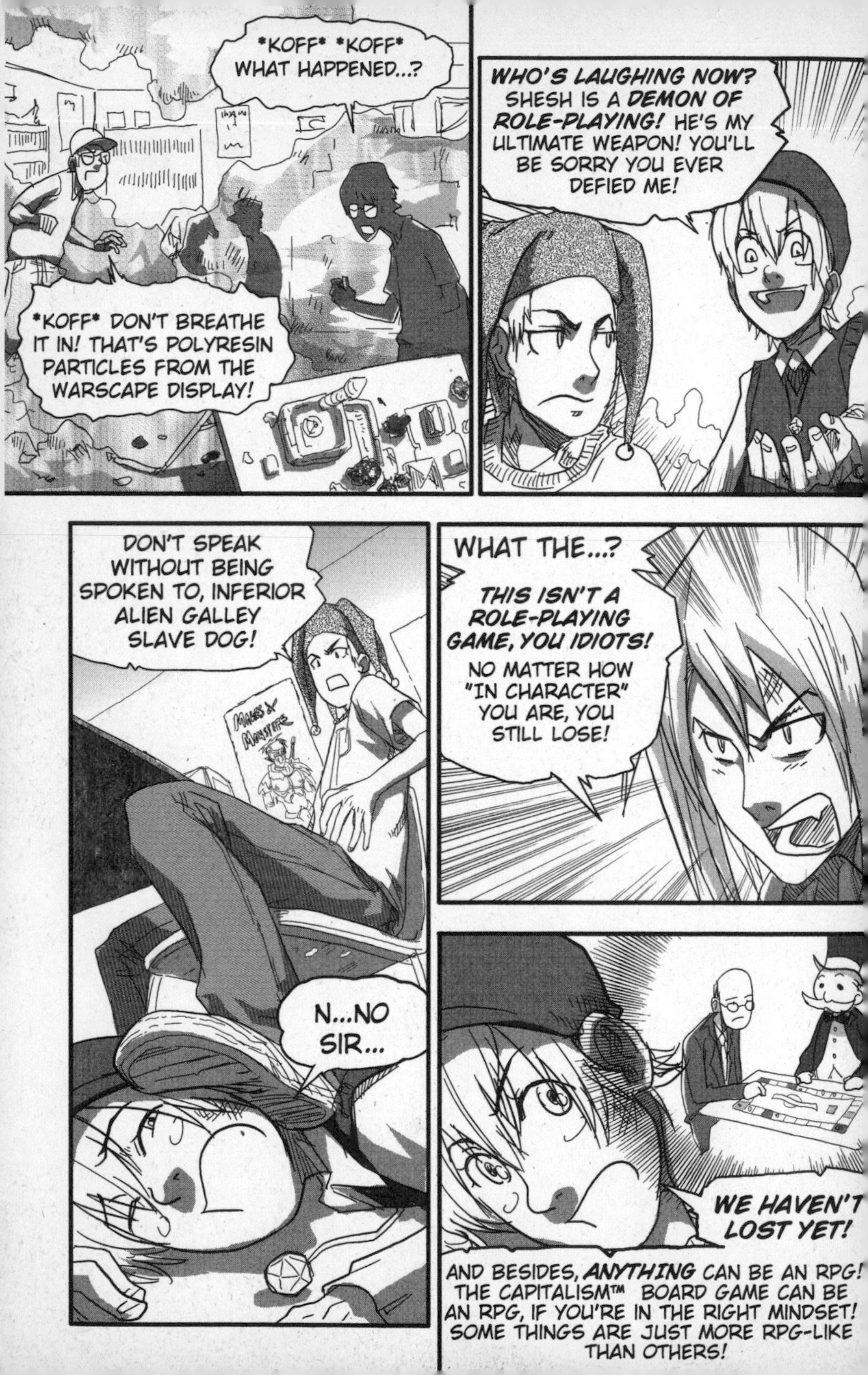
KOFF *KOFF* WHAT HAPPENED...?
KOFF DON'T BREATHE IT IN! THAT'S POLYRESIN PARTICLES FROM THE WARSCAPE DISPLAY!
WHO'S LAUGHING NOW? SHESH IS A DEMON OF ROLE-PLAYING! HE'S MY ULTIMATE WEAPON! YOU'LL BE SORRY YOU EVER DEFIED ME!
DON'T SPEAK WITHOUT BEING SPOKEN TO, INFERIOR ALIEN GALLEY SLAVE DOG!
N...NO SIR...
WHAT THE...?
THIS ISN'T A ROLE-PLAYING GAME, YOU IDIOTS!
NO MATTER HOW "IN CHARACTER" YOU ARE, YOU STILL LOSE!
WE HAVEN'T LOST YET!
AND BESIDES, ANYTHING CAN BE AN RPG! THE CAPITALISM™ BOARD GAME CAN BE AN RPG, IF YOU'RE IN THE RIGHT MINDSET! SOME THINGS ARE JUST MORE RPG-LIKE THAN OTHERS!

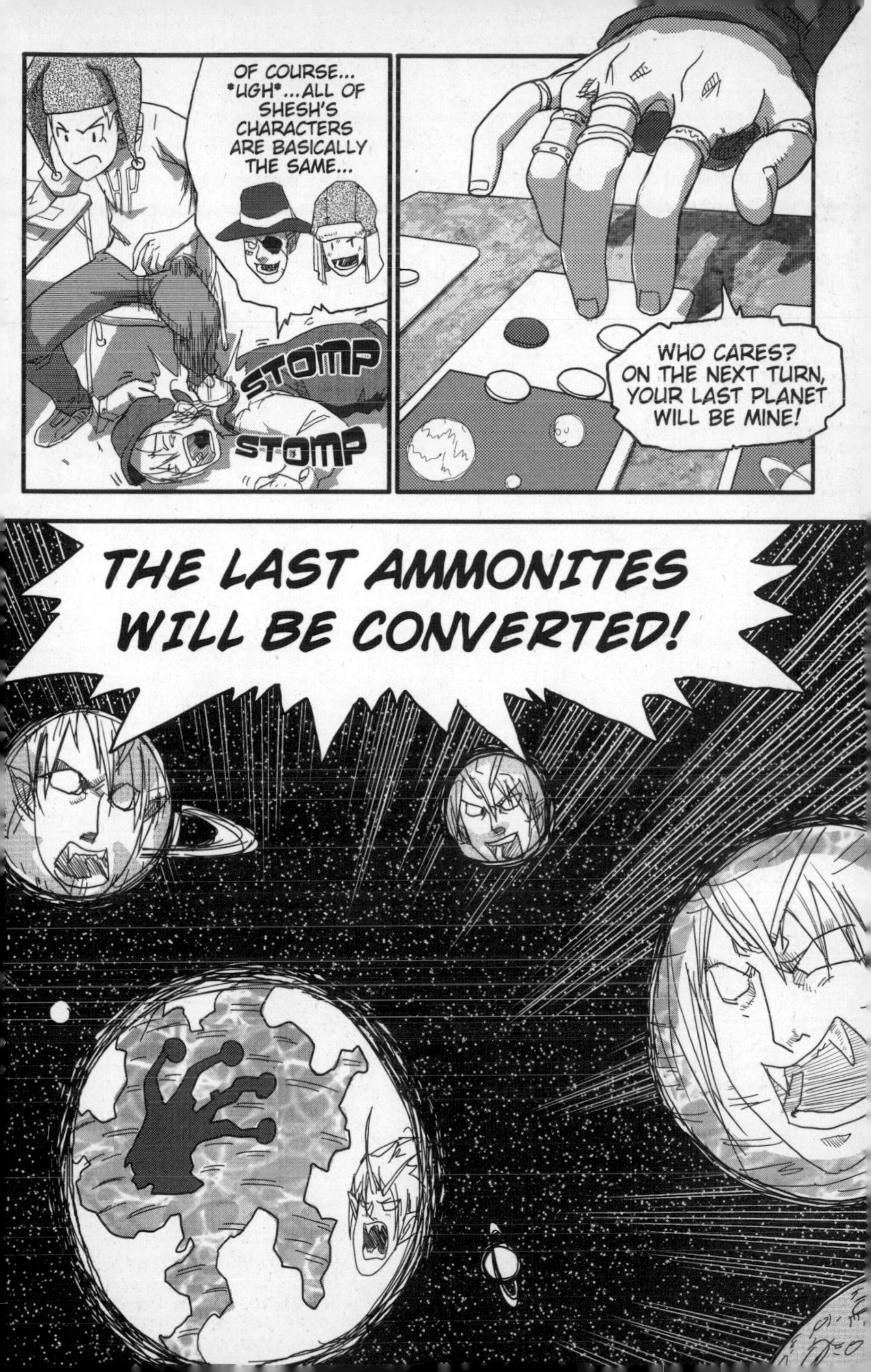
OF COURSE... *UGH*...ALL OF SHESH'S CHARACTERS ARE BASICALLY THE SAME...
STOMP
STOMP
WHO CARES? ON THE NEXT TURN, YOUR LAST PLANET WILL BE MINE!
THE LAST AMMONITES WILL BE CONVERTED!

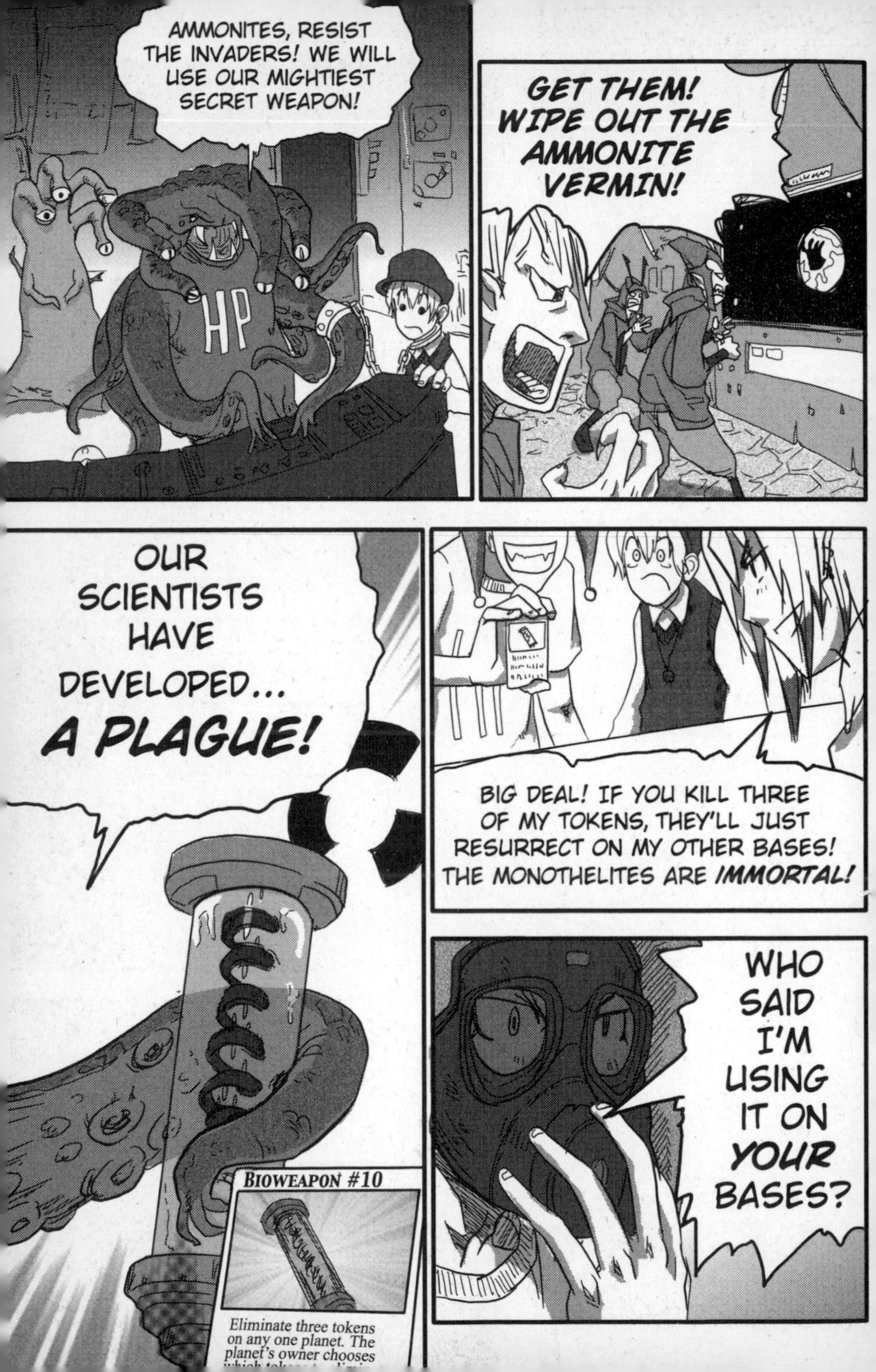
AMMONITES, RESIST THE INVADERS! WE WILL USE OUR MIGHTIEST SECRET WEAPON!
HP
GET THEM! WIPE OUT THE AMMONITE VERMIN!
OUR SCIENTISTS HAVE DEVELOPED... A PLAGUE!
BIOWEAPON #10
Eliminate three tokens on any one planet. The planet's owner chooses
BIG DEAL! IF YOU KILL THREE OF MY TOKENS, THEY'LL JUST RESURRECT ON MY OTHER BASES! THE MONOTHELITES ARE IMMORTAL!
WHO SAID I'M USING IT ON YOUR BASES?

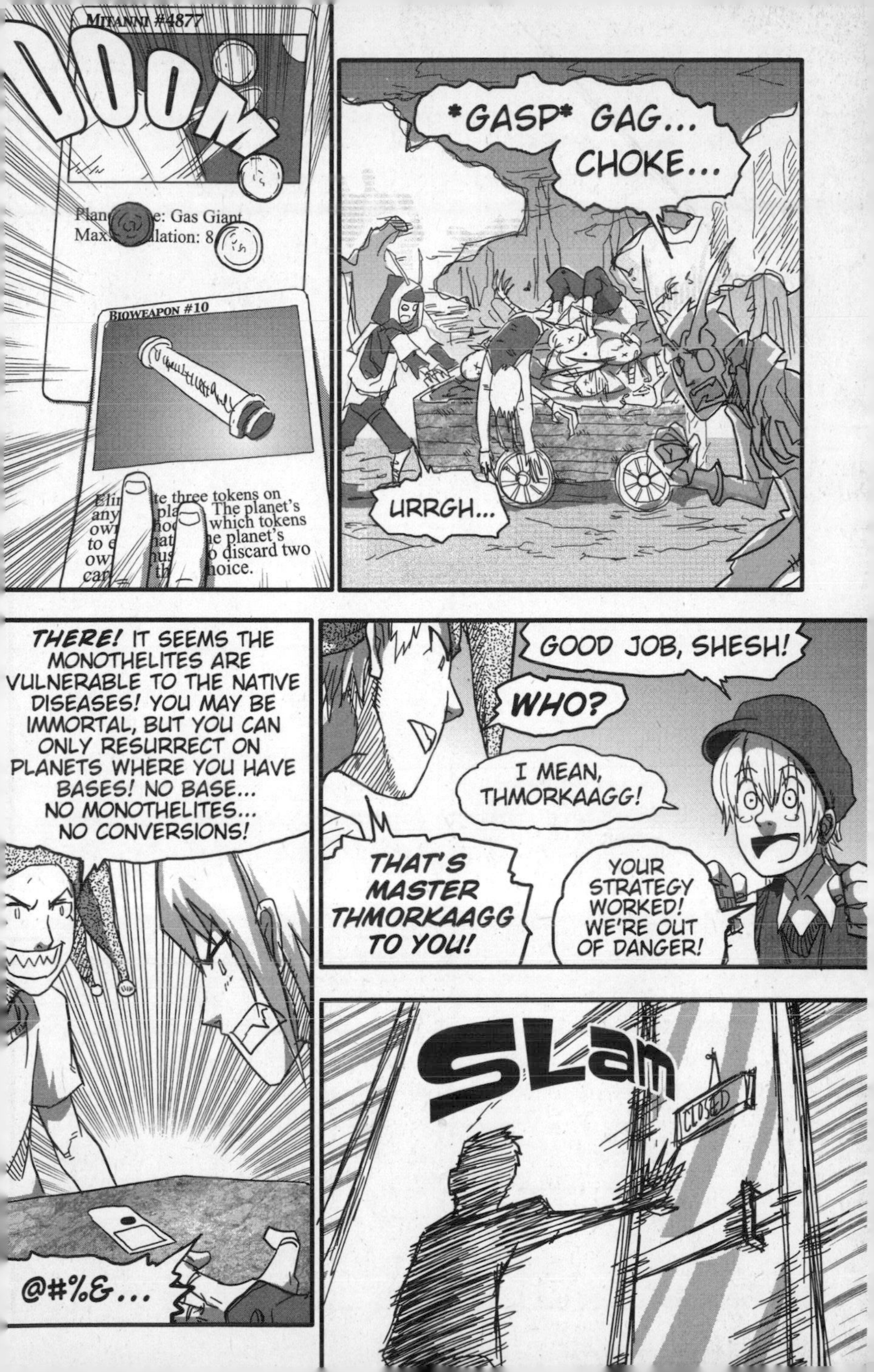
MITANNI #4877
DOOOM
BIOWEAPON #10
GASP GAG... CHOKE...
URRGH...
THERE! IT SEEMS THE MONOTHELITES ARE VULNERABLE TO THE NATIVE DISEASES! YOU MAY BE IMMORTAL, BUT YOU CAN ONLY RESURRECT ON PLANETS WHERE YOU HAVE BASES! NO BASE... NO MONOTHELITES... NO CONVERSIONS!
@#%&...
GOOD JOB, SHESH!
WHO?
I MEAN, THMORKAAGG!
THAT'S MASTER THMORKAAGG TO YOU!
YOUR STRATEGY WORKED! WE'RE OUT OF DANGER!
SLAM
CLOSED

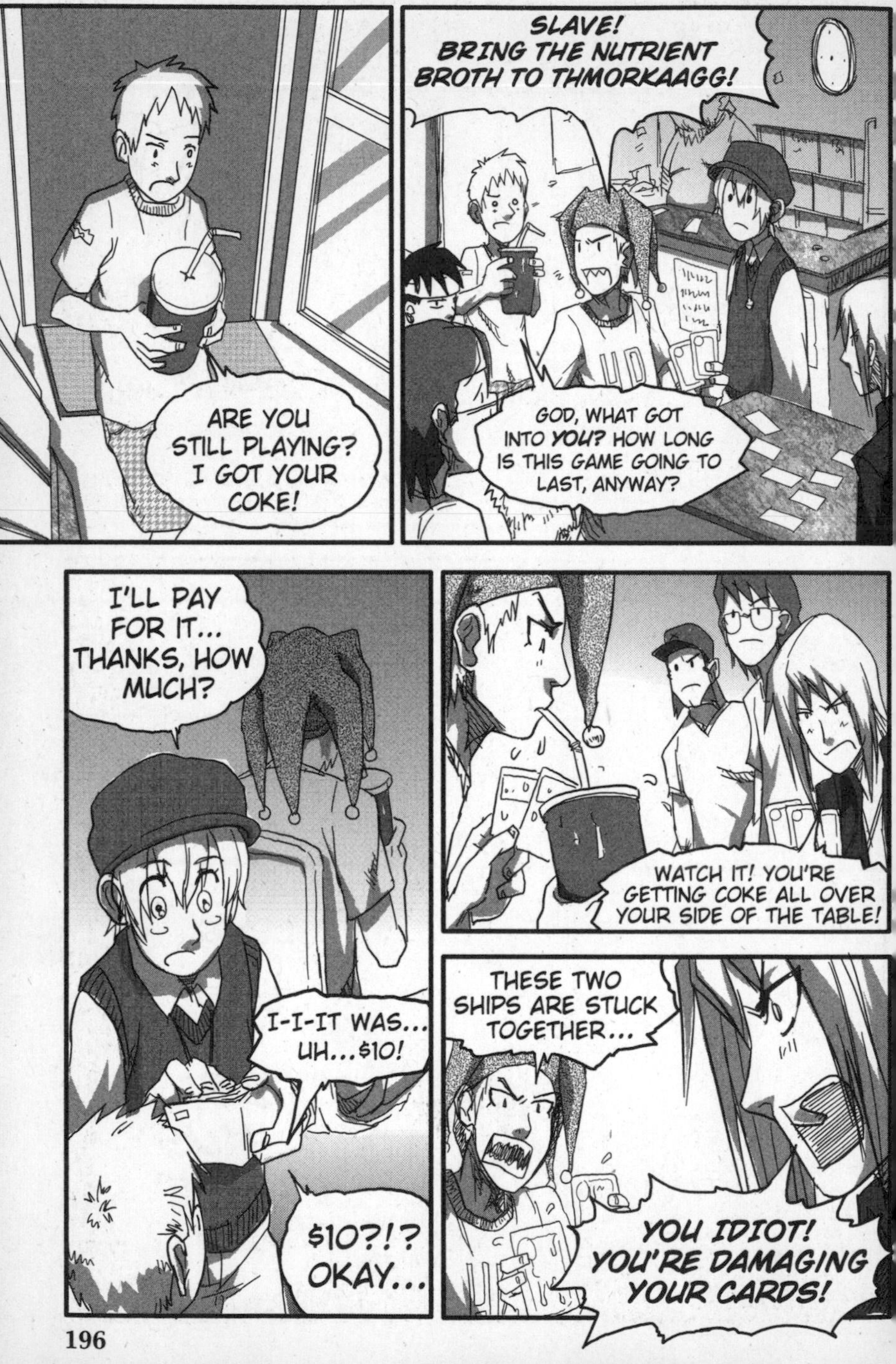
ARE YOU STILL PLAYING? I GOT YOUR COKE!
SLAVE! BRING THE NUTRIENT BROTH TO THMORKAAGG!
GOD, WHAT GOT INTO *YOU*? HOW LONG IS THIS GAME GOING TO LAST, ANYWAY?
I'LL PAY FOR IT... THANKS, HOW MUCH?
I-I-IT WAS... UH...$10!
$10?!? OKAY...
WATCH IT! YOU'RE GETTING COKE ALL OVER YOUR SIDE OF THE TABLE!
THESE TWO SHIPS ARE STUCK TOGETHER...
YOU IDIOT! YOU'RE DAMAGING YOUR CARDS!

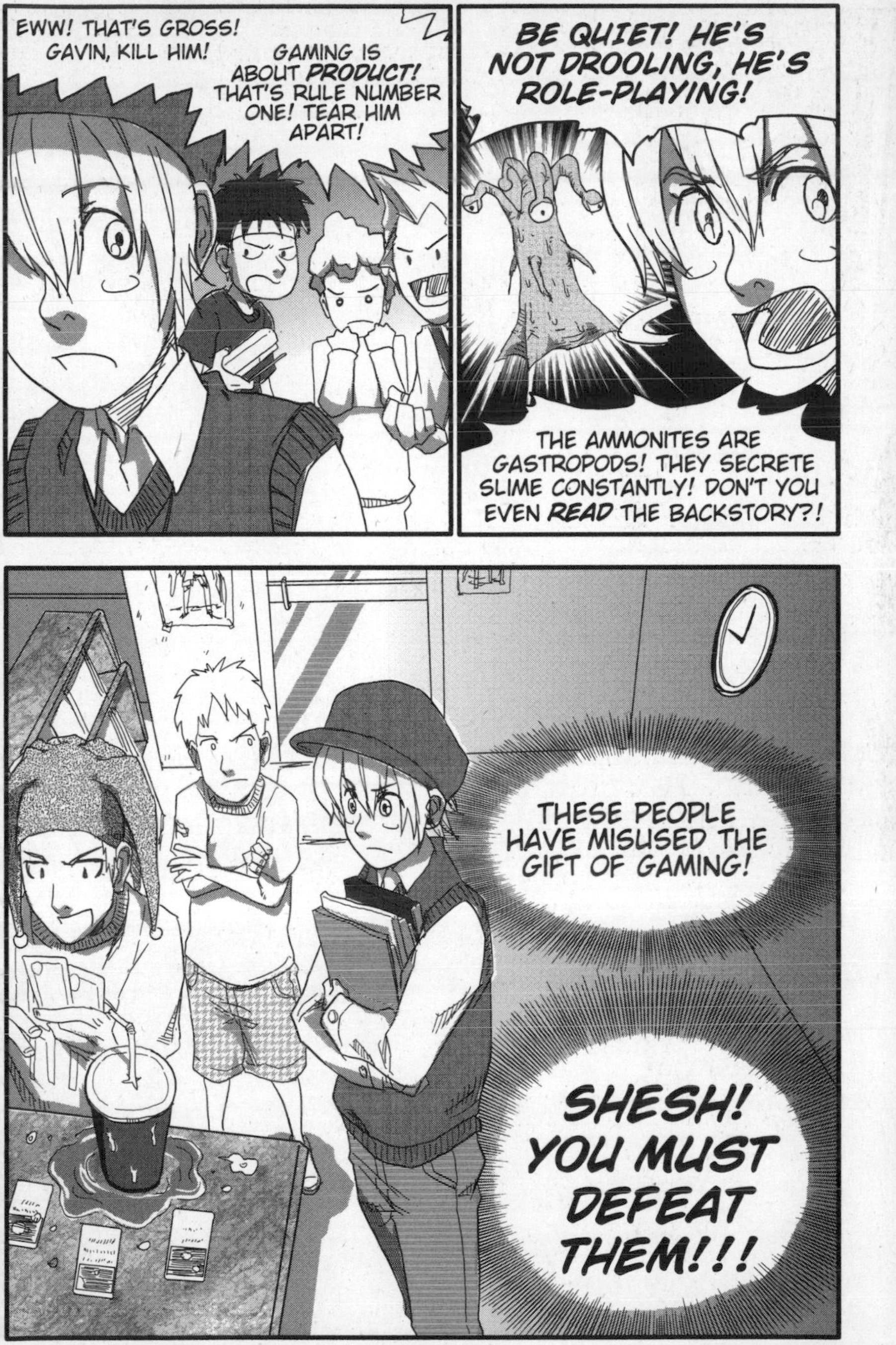
EWW! THAT'S GROSS! GAVIN, KILL HIM!
GAMING IS ABOUT *PRODUCT!* THAT'S RULE NUMBER ONE! TEAR HIM APART!
BE QUIET! HE'S NOT DROOLING, HE'S ROLE-PLAYING!
THE AMMONITES ARE GASTROPODS! THEY SECRETE SLIME CONSTANTLY! DON'T YOU EVEN *READ* THE BACKSTORY?!
THESE PEOPLE HAVE MISUSED THE GIFT OF GAMING!
SHESH! YOU MUST DEFEAT THEM!!!

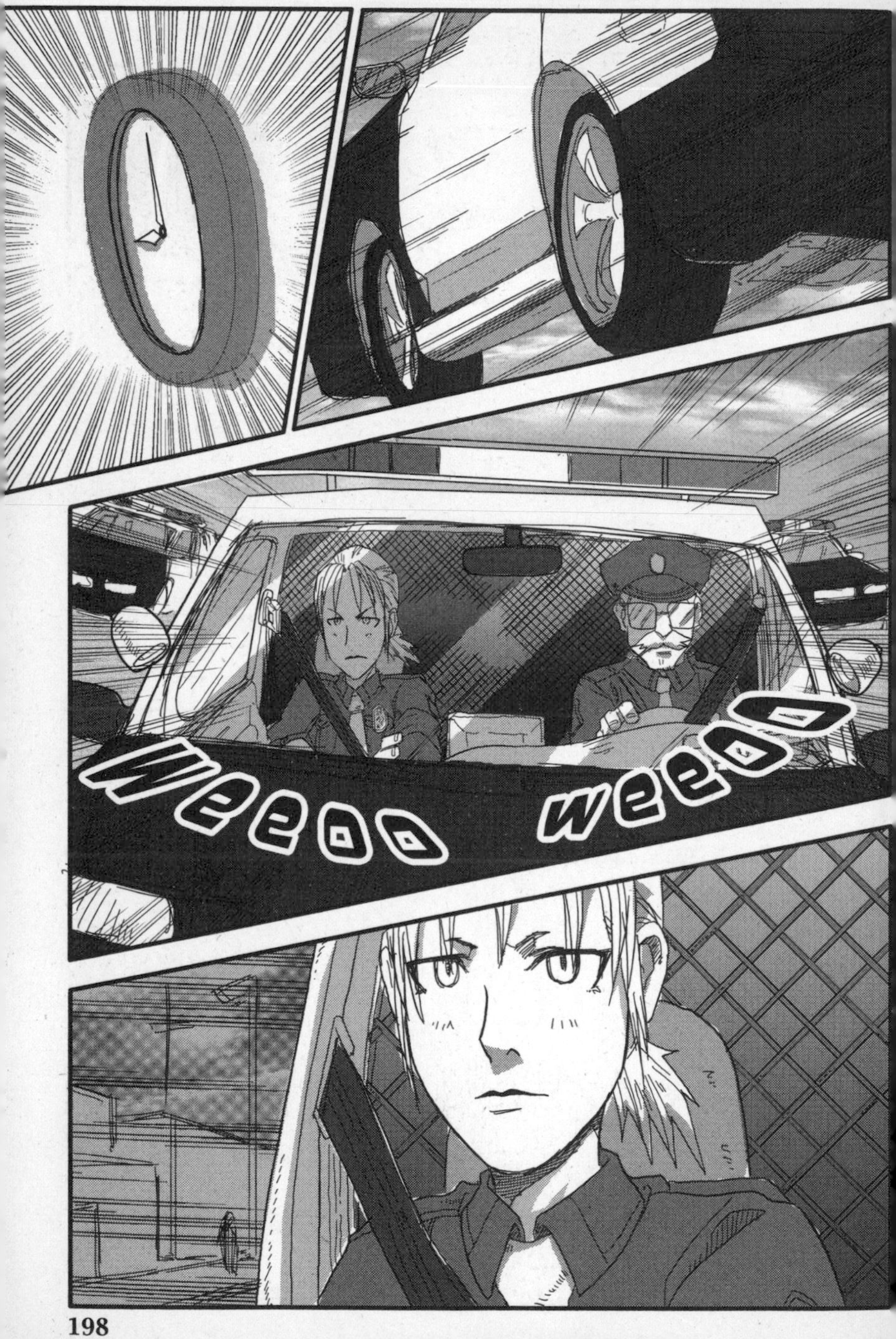
WEEOO WEEOO

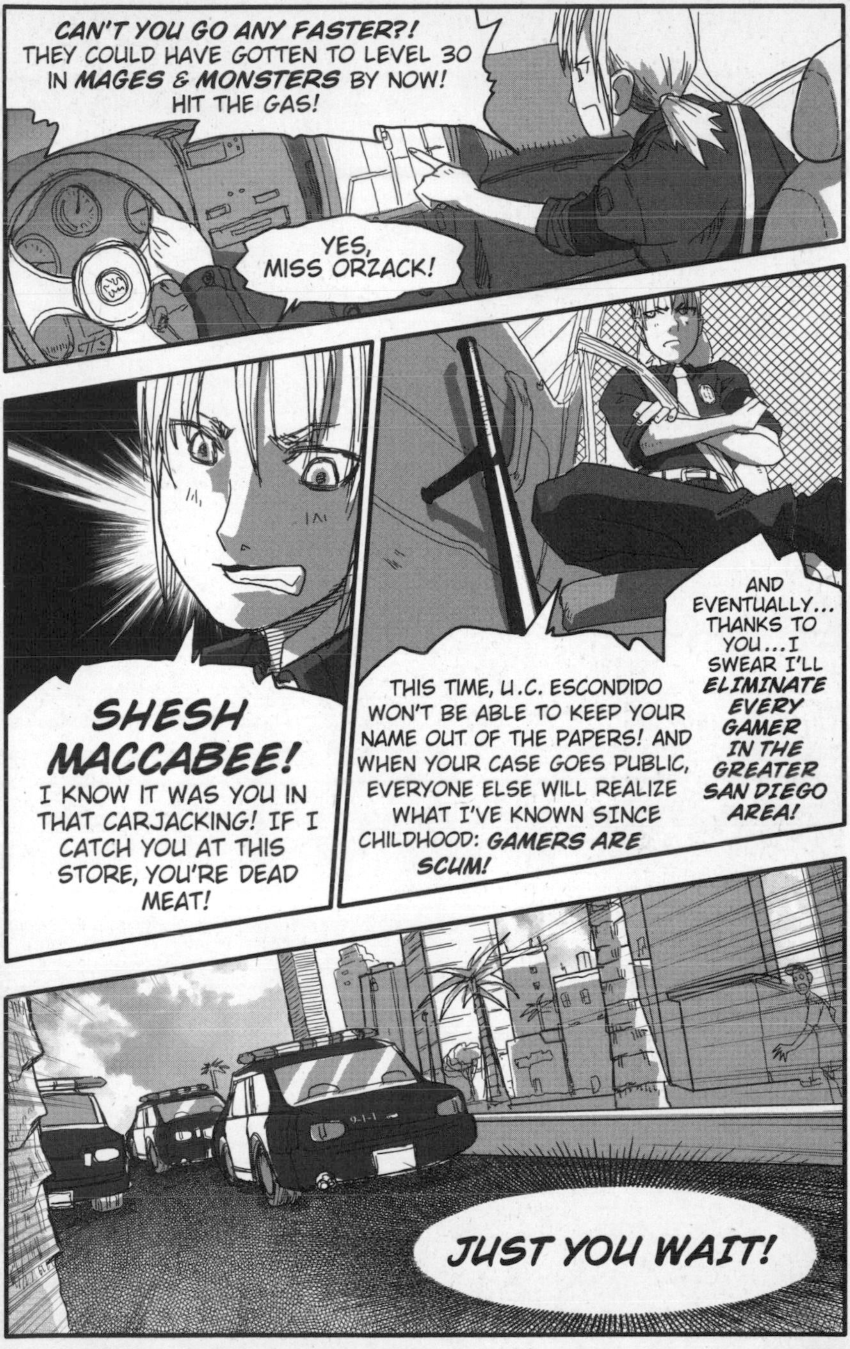

CAN'T YOU GO ANY FASTER?! THEY COULD HAVE GOTTEN TO LEVEL 30 IN MAGES & MONSTERS BY NOW! HIT THE GAS!
YES, MISS ORZACK!
SHESH MACCABEE! I KNOW IT WAS YOU IN THAT CARJACKING! IF I CATCH YOU AT THIS STORE, YOU'RE DEAD MEAT!
THIS TIME, U.C. ESCONDIDO WON'T BE ABLE TO KEEP YOUR NAME OUT OF THE PAPERS! AND WHEN YOUR CASE GOES PUBLIC, EVERYONE ELSE WILL REALIZE WHAT I'VE KNOWN SINCE CHILDHOOD: GAMERS ARE SCUM!
AND EVENTUALLY... THANKS TO YOU...I SWEAR I'LL ELIMINATE EVERY GAMER IN THE GREATER SAN DIEGO AREA!
JUST YOU WAIT!

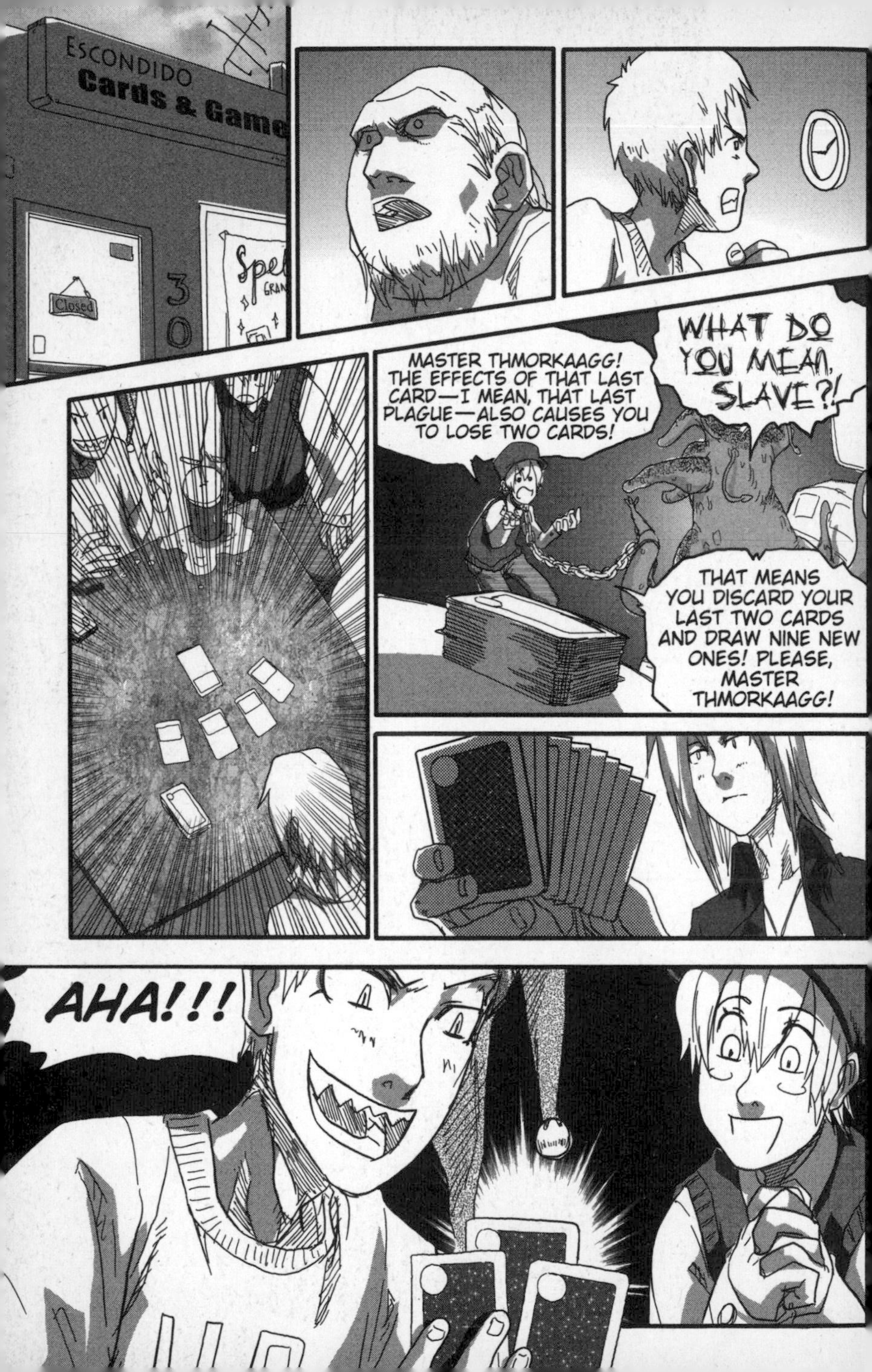

ESCONDIDO
Cards & Games
Closed
30
MASTER THMORKAAGG! THE EFFECTS OF THAT LAST CARD—I MEAN, THAT LAST PLAGUE—ALSO CAUSES YOU TO LOSE TWO CARDS!
WHAT DO YOU MEAN, SLAVE?!
THAT MEANS YOU DISCARD YOUR LAST TWO CARDS AND DRAW NINE NEW ONES! PLEASE, MASTER THMORKAAGG!
AHA!!!

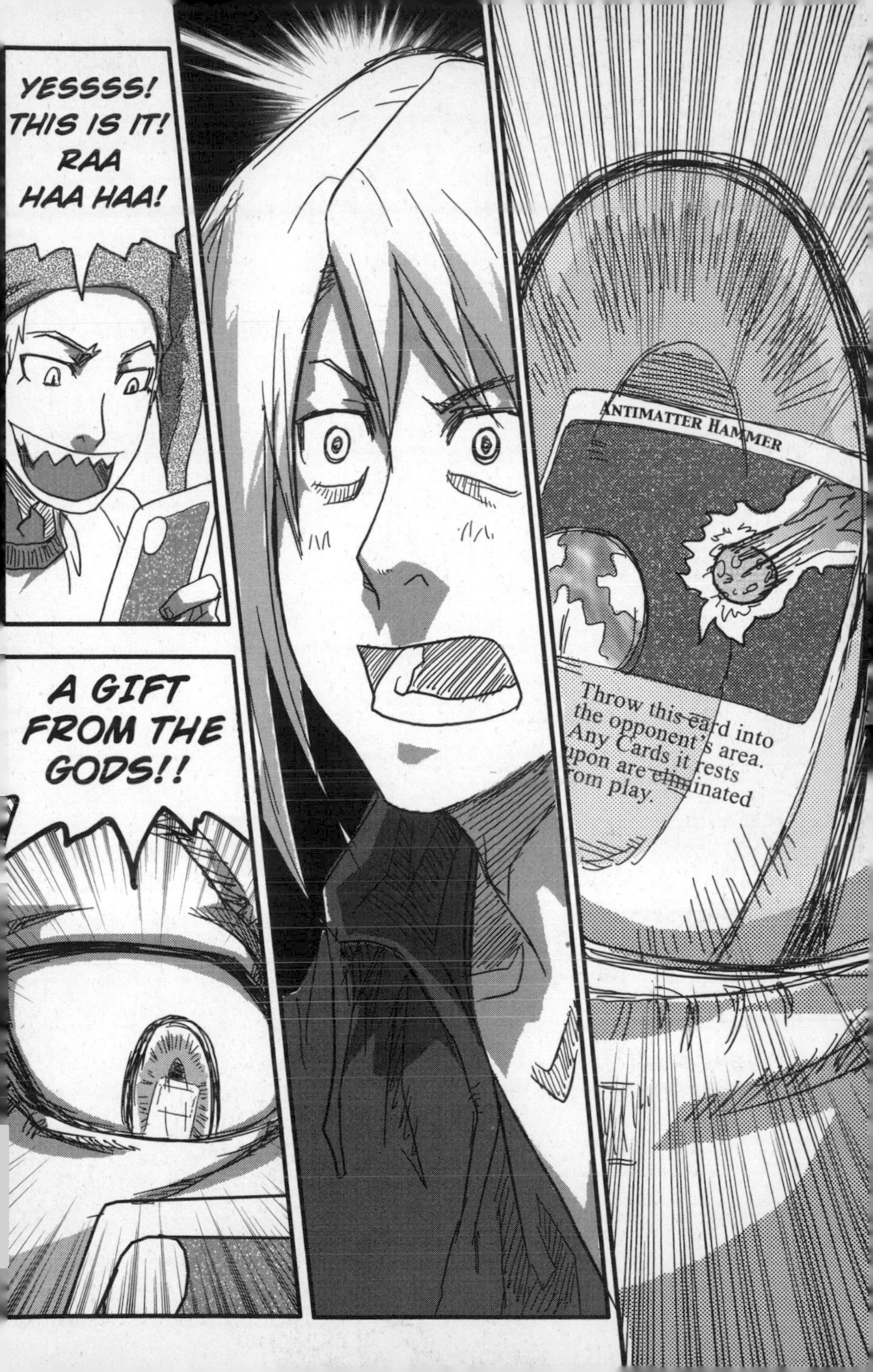
YESSSS! THIS IS IT! RAA HAA HAA!
A GIFT FROM THE GODS!!
ANTIMATTER HAMMER
Throw this card into the opponent's area. Any Cards it rests upon are eliminated from play.

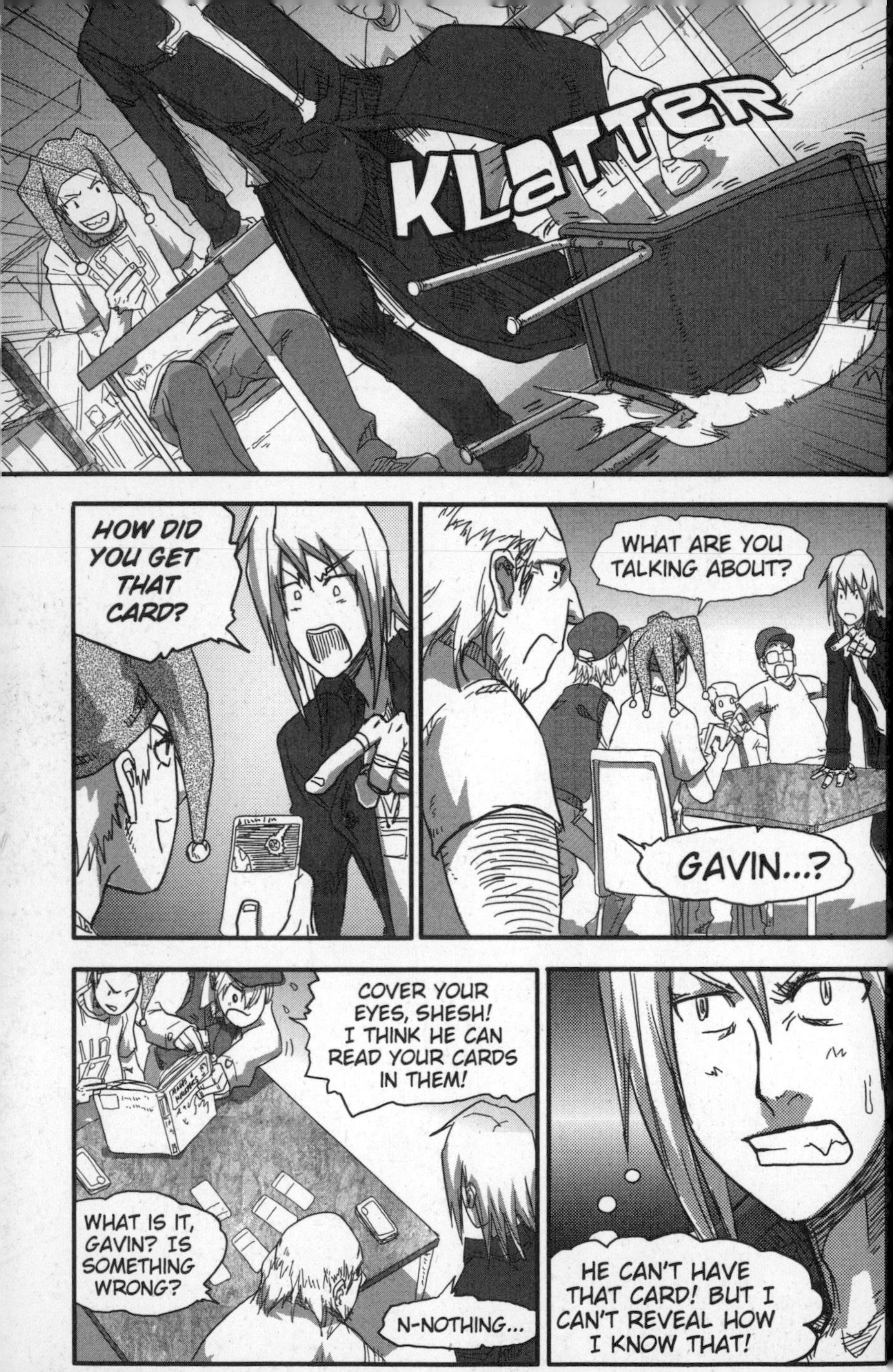
KLATTER
HOW DID YOU GET THAT CARD?
WHAT ARE YOU TALKING ABOUT?
GAVIN...?
COVER YOUR EYES, SHESH! I THINK HE CAN READ YOUR CARDS IN THEM!
WHAT IS IT, GAVIN? IS SOMETHING WRONG?
N-NOTHING...
HE CAN'T HAVE THAT CARD! BUT I CAN'T REVEAL HOW I KNOW THAT!

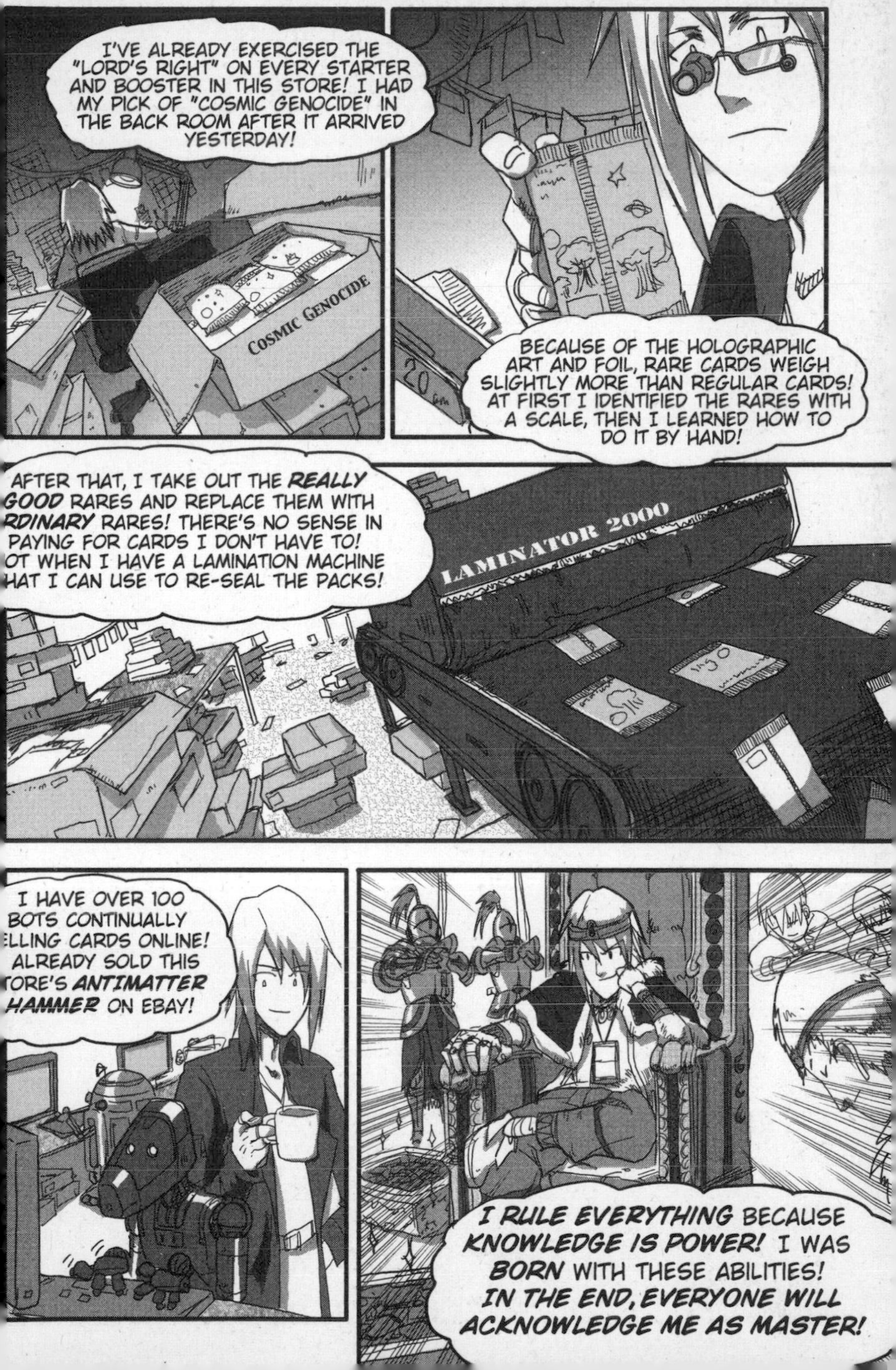

I'VE ALREADY EXERCISED THE "LORD'S RIGHT" ON EVERY STARTER AND BOOSTER IN THIS STORE! I HAD MY PICK OF "COSMIC GENOCIDE" IN THE BACK ROOM AFTER IT ARRIVED YESTERDAY!
COSMIC GENOCIDE
BECAUSE OF THE HOLOGRAPHIC ART AND FOIL, RARE CARDS WEIGH SLIGHTLY MORE THAN REGULAR CARDS! AT FIRST I IDENTIFIED THE RARES WITH A SCALE, THEN I LEARNED HOW TO DO IT BY HAND!
AFTER THAT, I TAKE OUT THE REALLY GOOD RARES AND REPLACE THEM WITH RDINARY RARES! THERE'S NO SENSE IN PAYING FOR CARDS I DON'T HAVE TO! OT WHEN I HAVE A LAMINATION MACHINE HAT I CAN USE TO RE-SEAL THE PACKS!
LAMINATOR 2000
I HAVE OVER 100 BOTS CONTINUALLY LLING CARDS ONLINE! ALREADY SOLD THIS ORE'S ANTIMATTER HAMMER ON EBAY!
I RULE EVERYTHING BECAUSE KNOWLEDGE IS POWER! I WAS BORN WITH THESE ABILITIES! IN THE END, EVERYONE WILL ACKNOWLEDGE ME AS MASTER!

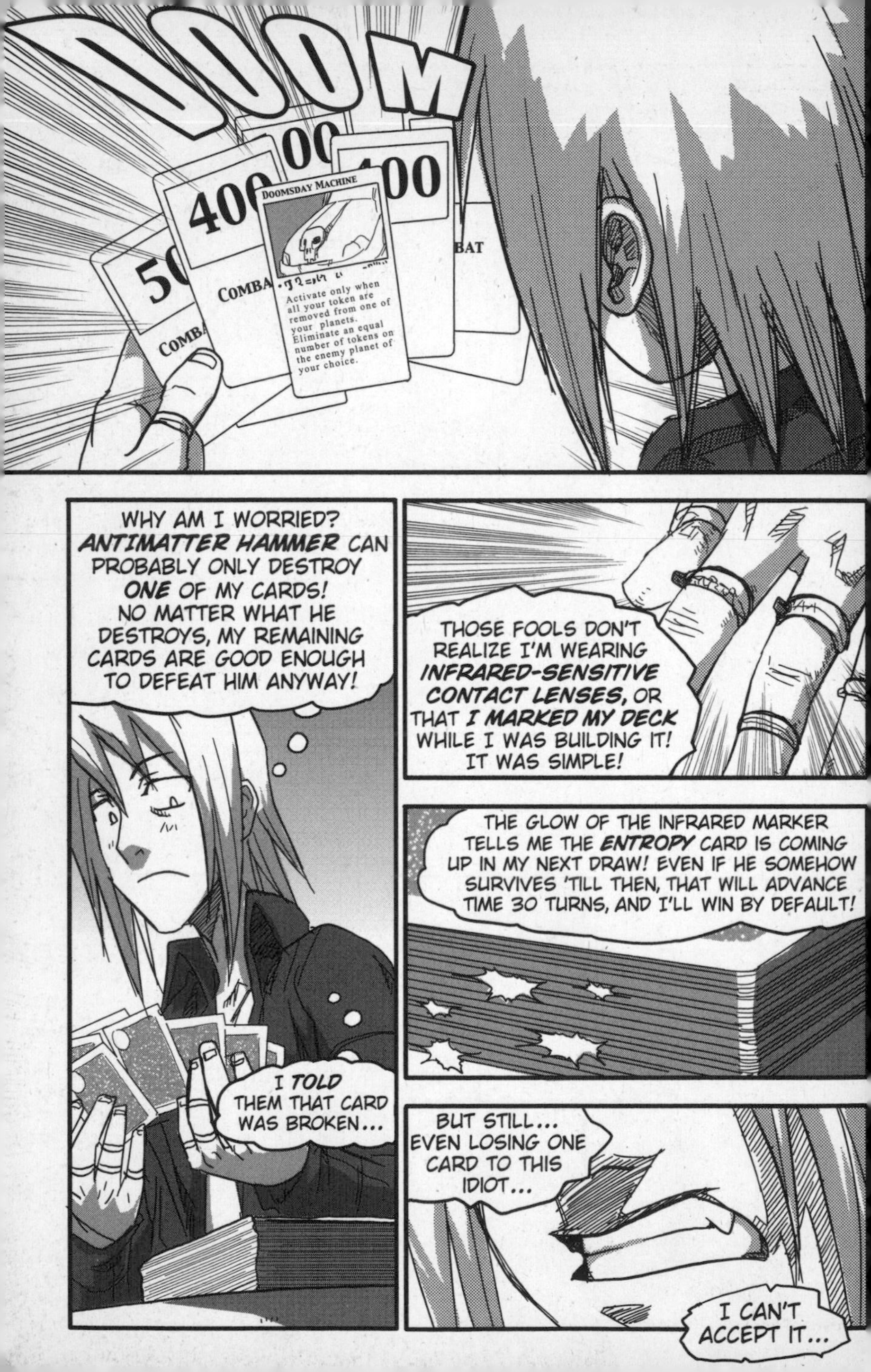
DOOOM
DOOMSDAY MACHINE
Activate only when all your token are removed from one of your planets. Eliminate an equal number of tokens on the enemy planet of your choice.
WHY AM I WORRIED? ANTIMATTER HAMMER CAN PROBABLY ONLY DESTROY ONE OF MY CARDS! NO MATTER WHAT HE DESTROYS, MY REMAINING CARDS ARE GOOD ENOUGH TO DEFEAT HIM ANYWAY!
I TOLD THEM THAT CARD WAS BROKEN...
THOSE FOOLS DON'T REALIZE I'M WEARING INFRARED-SENSITIVE CONTACT LENSES, OR THAT I MARKED MY DECK WHILE I WAS BUILDING IT! IT WAS SIMPLE!
THE GLOW OF THE INFRARED MARKER TELLS ME THE ENTROPY CARD IS COMING UP IN MY NEXT DRAW! EVEN IF HE SOMEHOW SURVIVES 'TILL THEN, THAT WILL ADVANCE TIME 30 TURNS, AND I'LL WIN BY DEFAULT!
BUT STILL... EVEN LOSING ONE CARD TO THIS IDIOT...
I CAN'T ACCEPT IT...

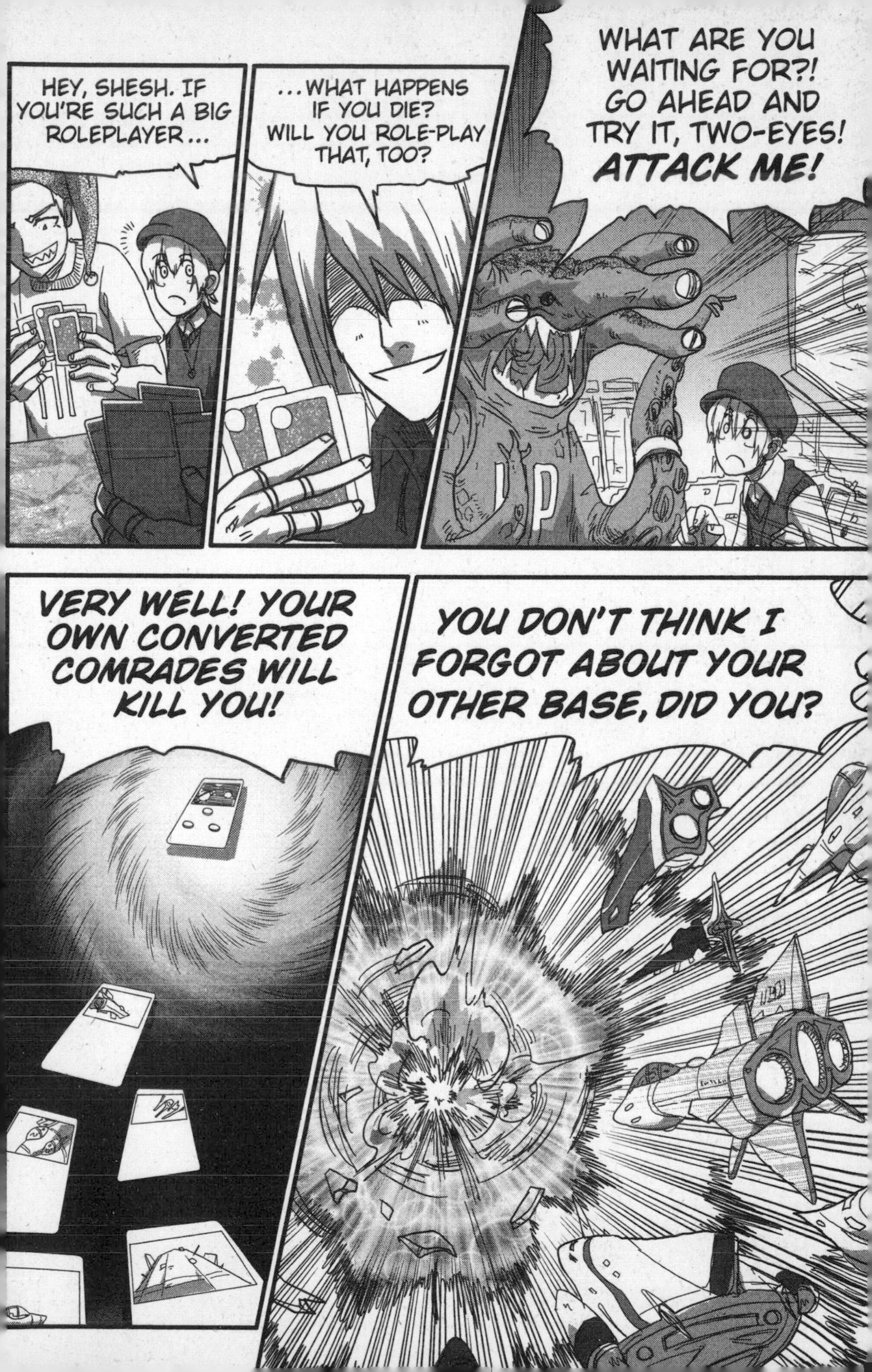
HEY, SHESH. IF YOU'RE SUCH A BIG ROLEPLAYER...
...WHAT HAPPENS IF YOU DIE? WILL YOU ROLE-PLAY THAT, TOO?
WHAT ARE YOU WAITING FOR?! GO AHEAD AND TRY IT, TWO-EYES! ATTACK ME!
VERY WELL! YOUR OWN CONVERTED COMRADES WILL KILL YOU!
YOU DON'T THINK I FORGOT ABOUT YOUR OTHER BASE, DID YOU?

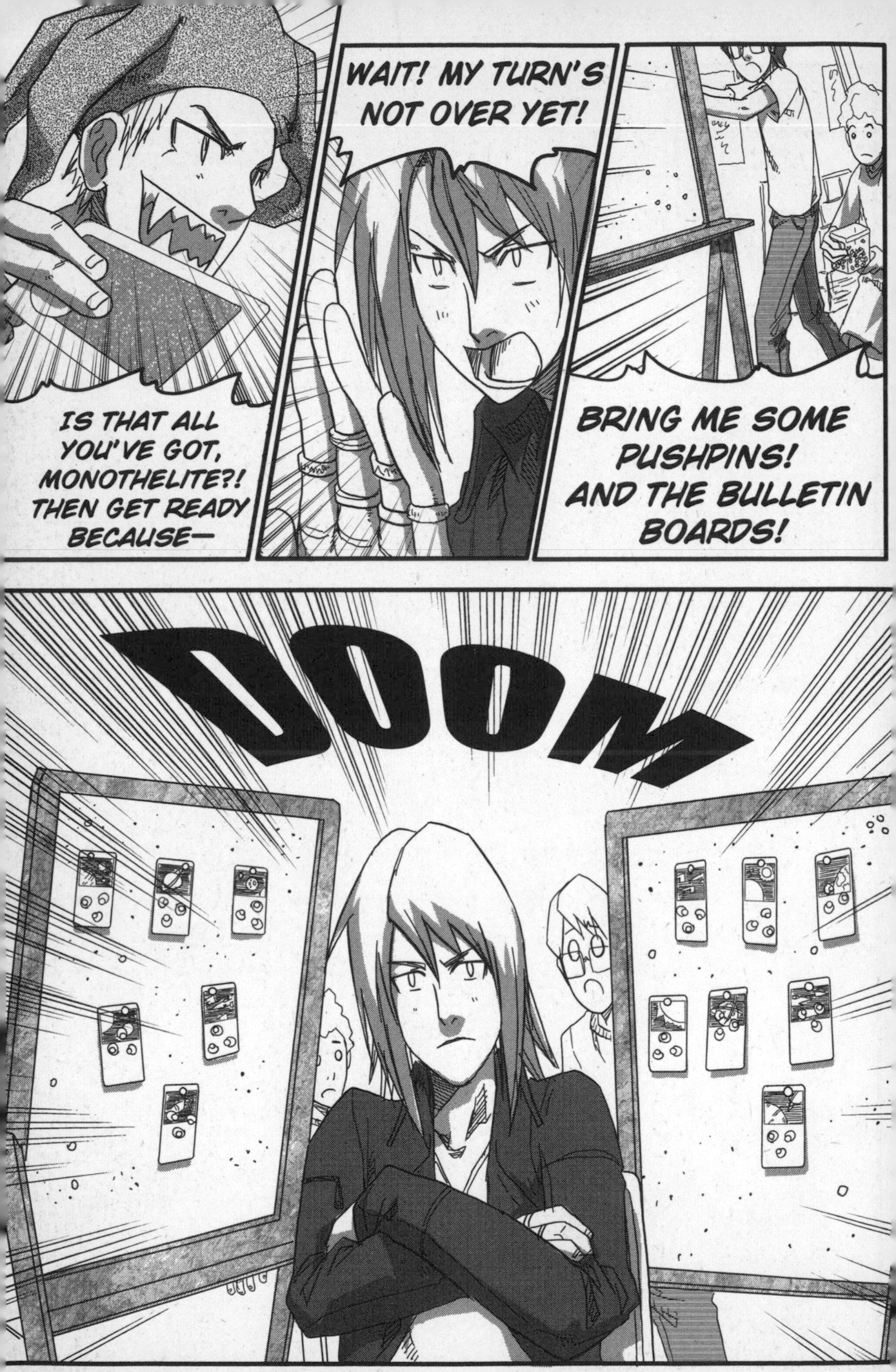
IS THAT ALL YOU'VE GOT, MONOTHELITE?! THEN GET READY BECAUSE—
WAIT! MY TURN'S NOT OVER YET!
BRING ME SOME PUSHPINS! AND THE BULLETIN BOARDS!
DOOM

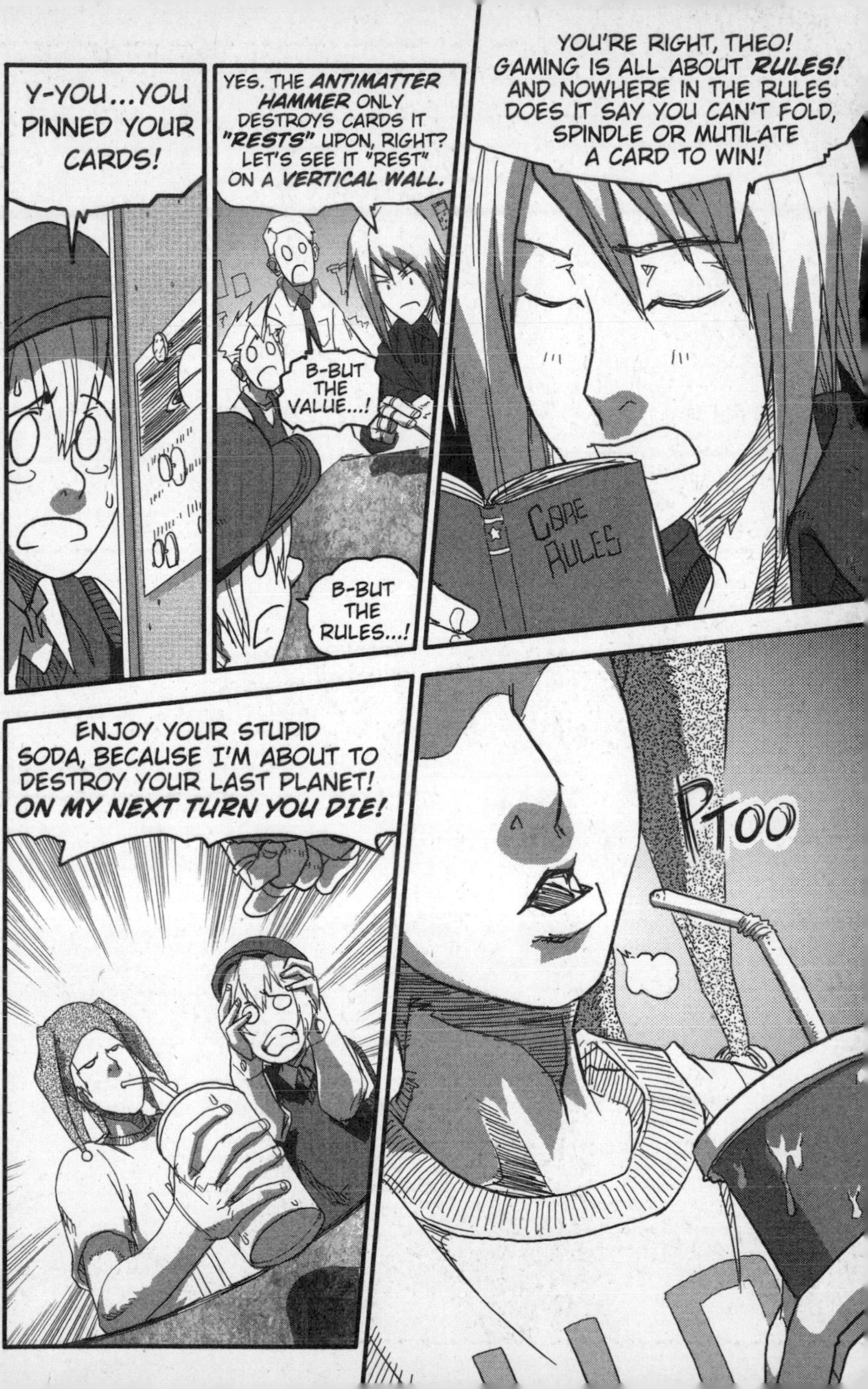
Y-YOU...YOU PINNED YOUR CARDS!
YES. THE ANTIMATTER HAMMER ONLY DESTROYS CARDS IT "RESTS" UPON, RIGHT? LET'S SEE IT "REST" ON A VERTICAL WALL.
B-BUT THE VALUE...!
B-BUT THE RULES...!
YOU'RE RIGHT, THEO! GAMING IS ALL ABOUT RULES! AND NOWHERE IN THE RULES DOES IT SAY YOU CAN'T FOLD, SPINDLE OR MUTILATE A CARD TO WIN!
CORE RULES
ENJOY YOUR STUPID SODA, BECAUSE I'M ABOUT TO DESTROY YOUR LAST PLANET! ON MY NEXT TURN YOU DIE!
PTOO

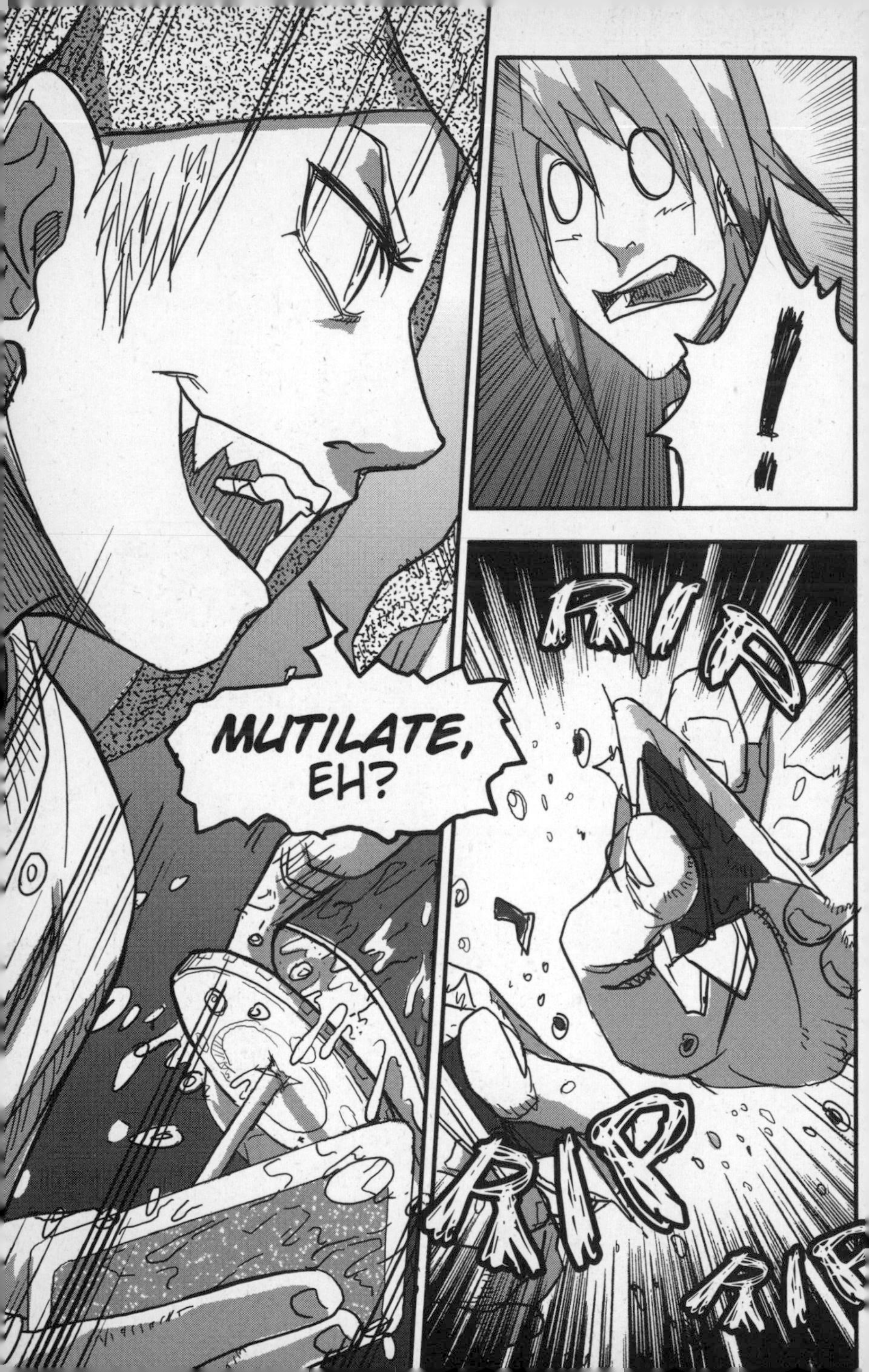
MUTILATE, EH?
!!
RIP
RIP

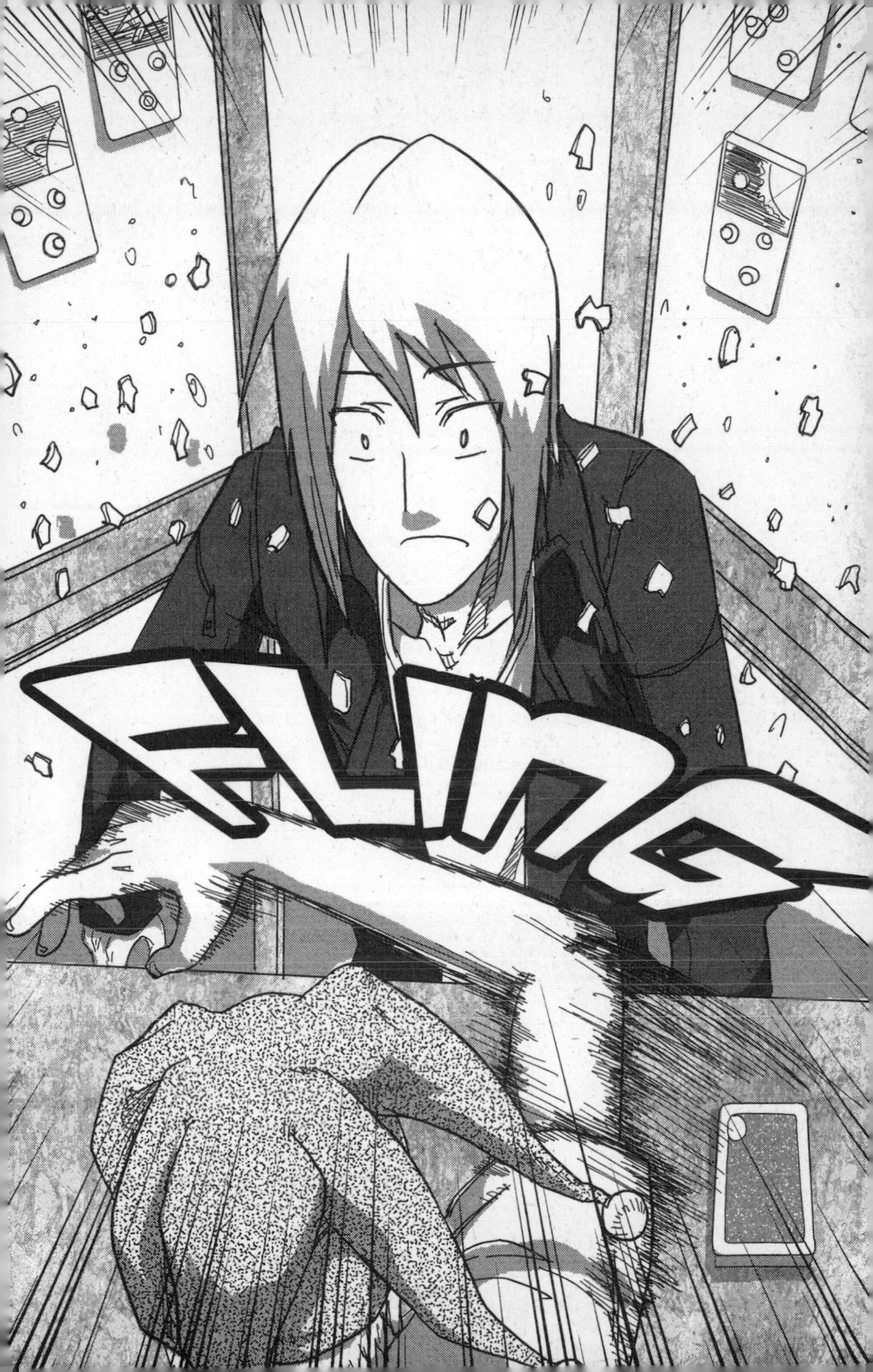
FLING

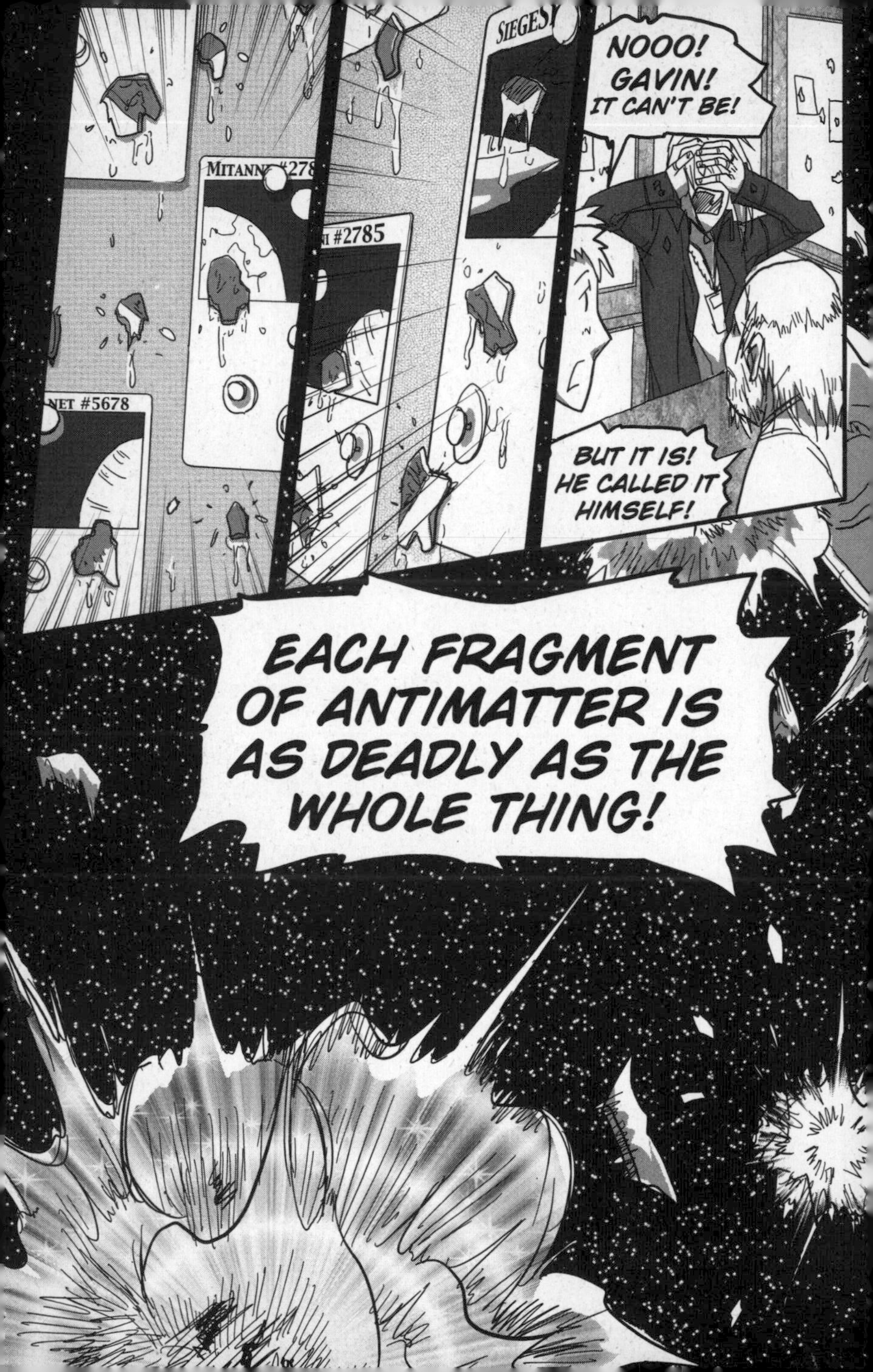
MITANN #278
NET #5678
NI #2785
SIEGES
NOOO! GAVIN! IT CAN'T BE!
BUT IT IS! HE CALLED IT HIMSELF!
EACH FRAGMENT OF ANTIMATTER IS AS DEADLY AS THE WHOLE THING!

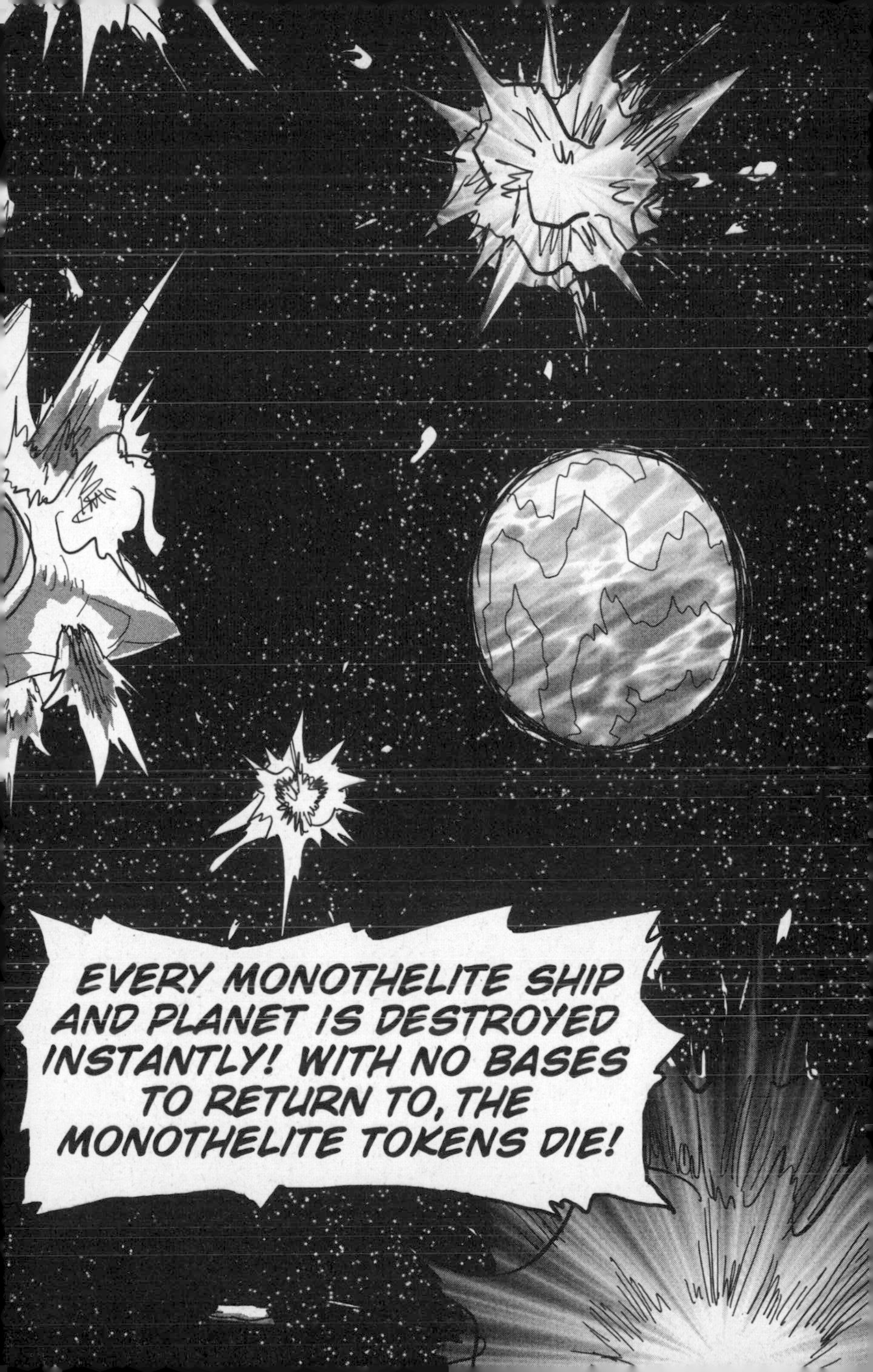
EVERY MONOTHELITE SHIP AND PLANET IS DESTROYED INSTANTLY! WITH NO BASES TO RETURN TO, THE MONOTHELITE TOKENS DIE!

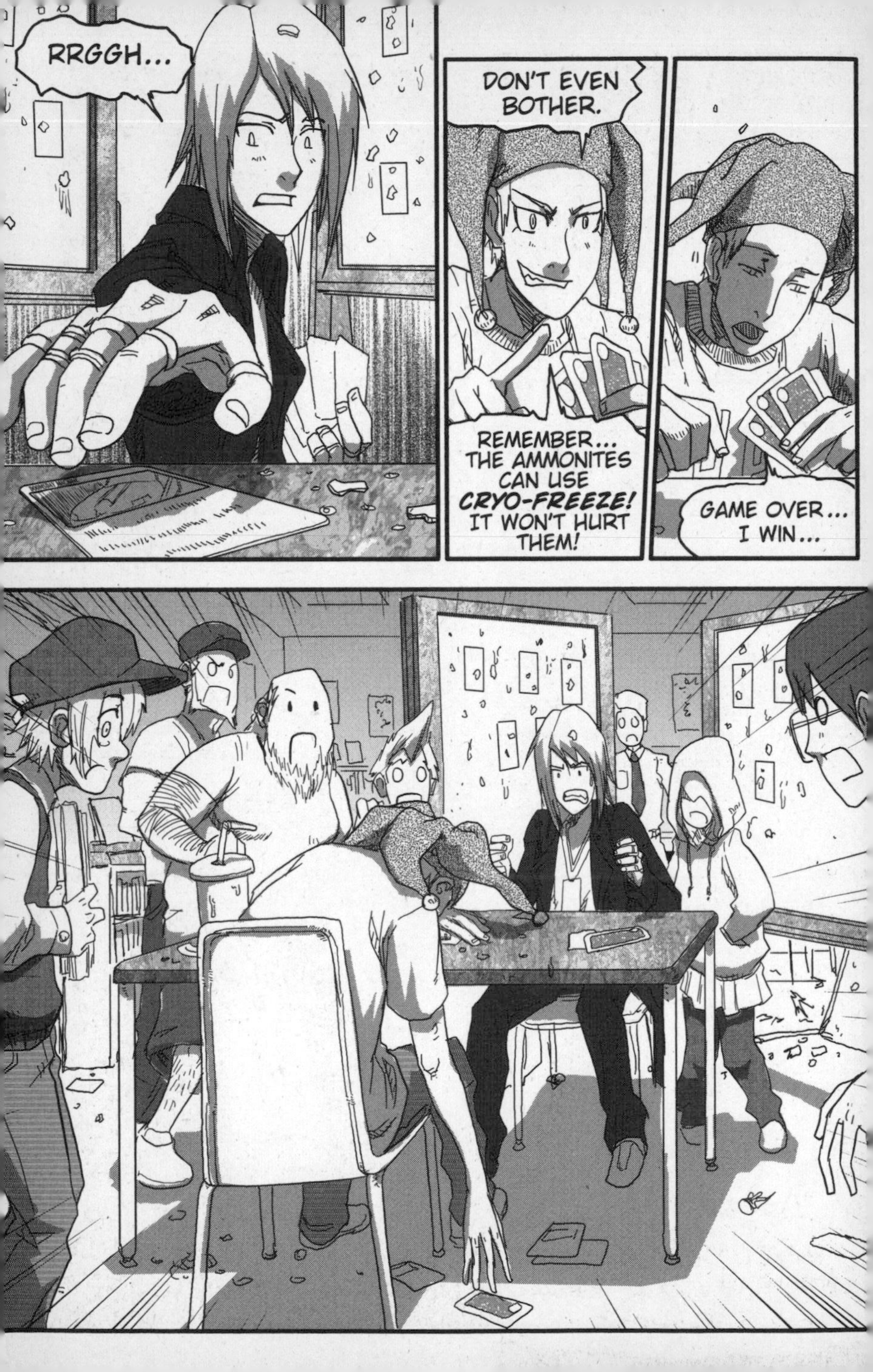
RRGGH...
DON'T EVEN BOTHER.
REMEMBER... THE AMMONITES CAN USE CRYO-FREEZE! IT WON'T HURT THEM!
GAME OVER... I WIN...

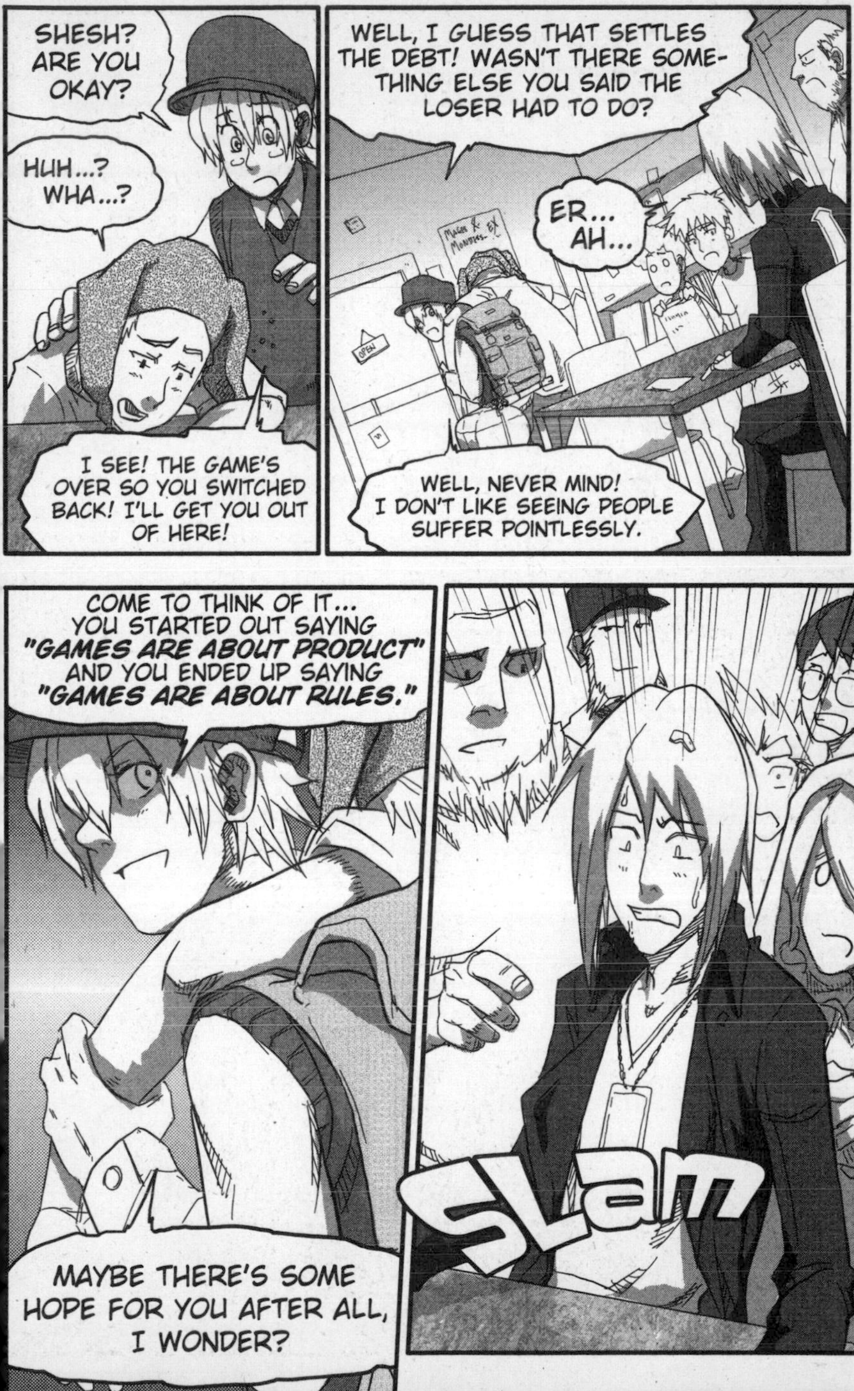
SHESH? ARE YOU OKAY?
HUH...? WHA...?
I SEE! THE GAME'S OVER SO YOU SWITCHED BACK! I'LL GET YOU OUT OF HERE!
WELL, I GUESS THAT SETTLES THE DEBT! WASN'T THERE SOME-THING ELSE YOU SAID THE LOSER HAD TO DO?
ER... AH...
WELL, NEVER MIND! I DON'T LIKE SEEING PEOPLE SUFFER POINTLESSLY.
COME TO THINK OF IT... YOU STARTED OUT SAYING ***"GAMES ARE ABOUT PRODUCT"*** AND YOU ENDED UP SAYING ***"GAMES ARE ABOUT RULES."***
MAYBE THERE'S SOME HOPE FOR YOU AFTER ALL, I WONDER?
SLAM

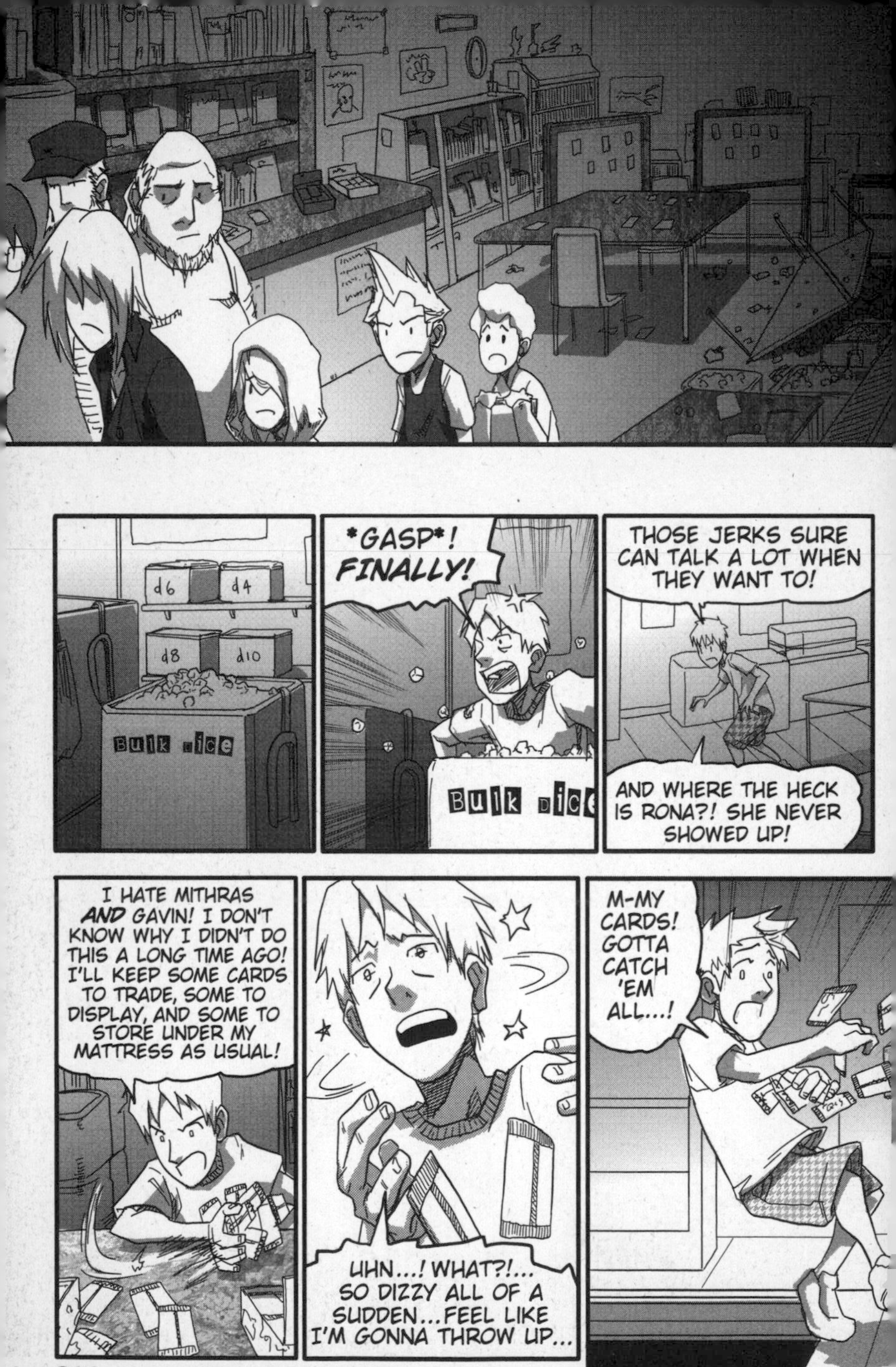
d6
d4
d8
d10
GASP! FINALLY!
THOSE JERKS SURE CAN TALK A LOT WHEN THEY WANT TO!
AND WHERE THE HECK IS RONA?! SHE NEVER SHOWED UP!
I HATE MITHRAS AND GAVIN! I DON'T KNOW WHY I DIDN'T DO THIS A LONG TIME AGO! I'LL KEEP SOME CARDS TO TRADE, SOME TO DISPLAY, AND SOME TO STORE UNDER MY MATTRESS AS USUAL!
UHN...! WHAT?!... SO DIZZY ALL OF A SUDDEN...FEEL LIKE I'M GONNA THROW UP...
M-MY CARDS! GOTTA CATCH 'EM ALL...!

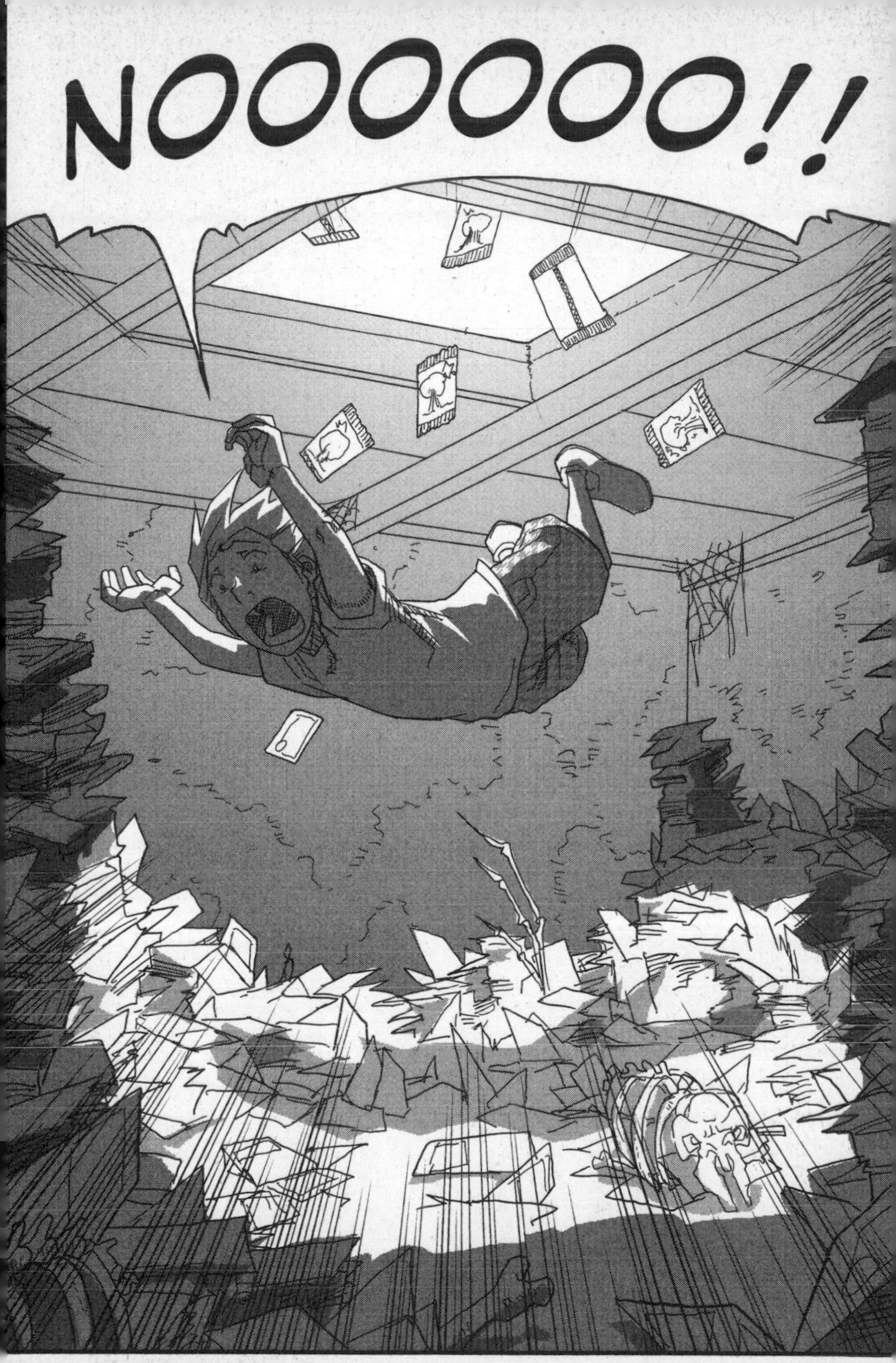
NOOOOOO!!

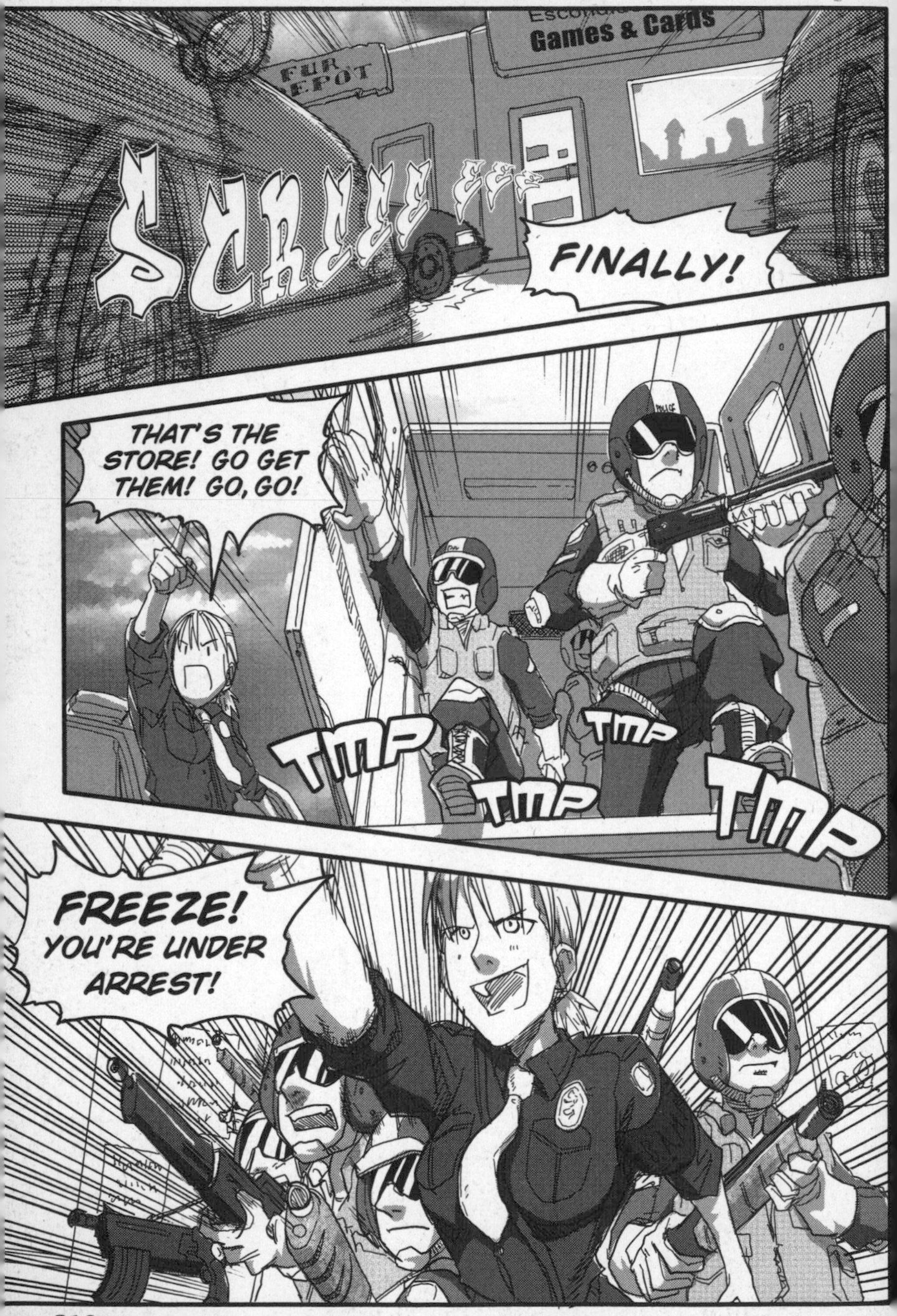
FUR
Games & Cards
FINALLY!
THAT'S THE STORE! GO GET THEM! GO, GO!
TMP
TMP
TMP
TMP
FREEZE! YOU'RE UNDER ARREST!

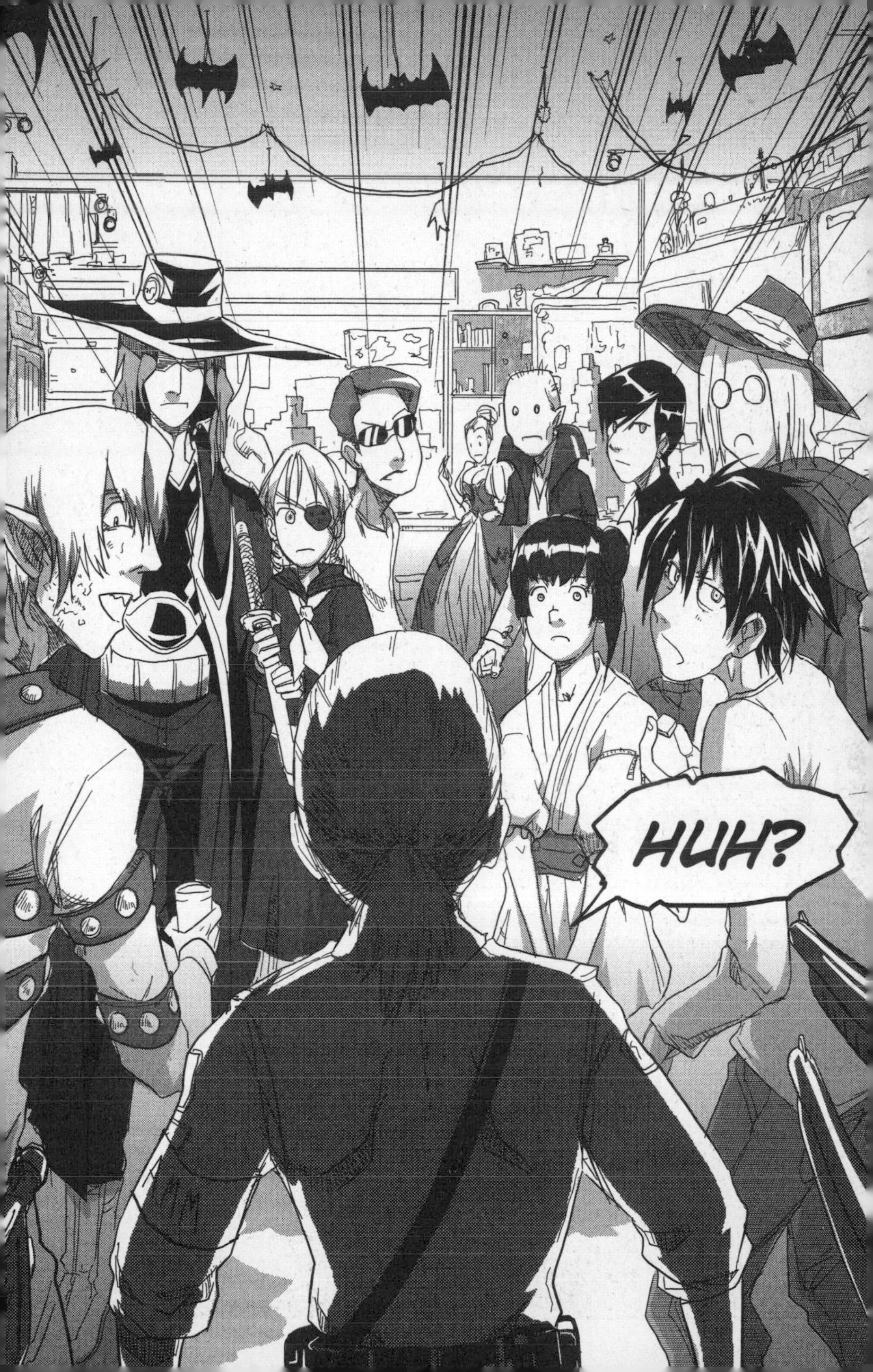
HUH?

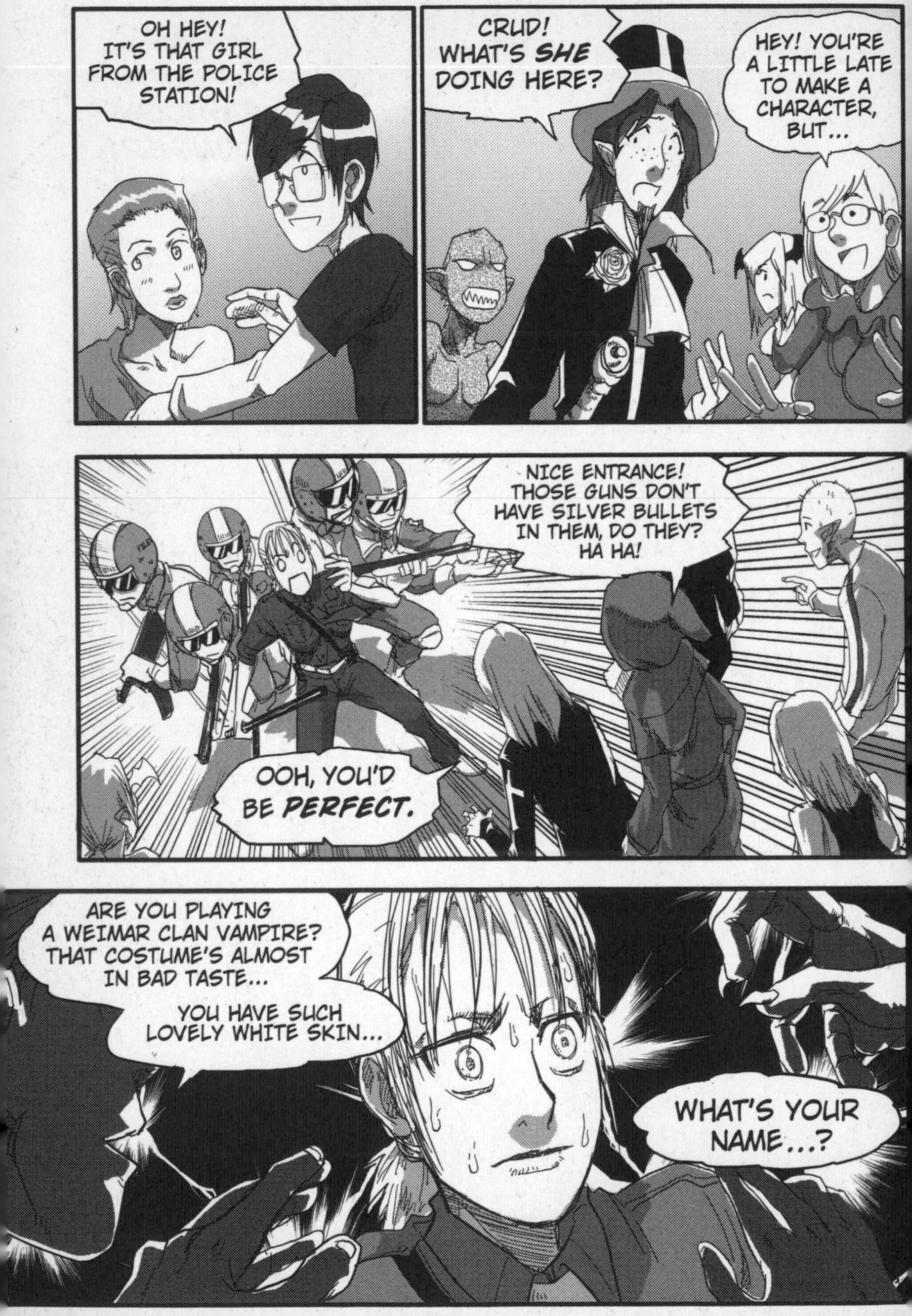
OH HEY! IT'S THAT GIRL FROM THE POLICE STATION!
CRUD! WHAT'S *SHE* DOING HERE?
HEY! YOU'RE A LITTLE LATE TO MAKE A CHARACTER, BUT...
NICE ENTRANCE! THOSE GUNS DON'T HAVE SILVER BULLETS IN THEM, DO THEY? HA HA!
OOH, YOU'D BE *PERFECT.*
ARE YOU PLAYING A WEIMAR CLAN VAMPIRE? THAT COSTUME'S ALMOST IN BAD TASTE...
YOU HAVE SUCH LOVELY WHITE SKIN...
WHAT'S YOUR NAME...?

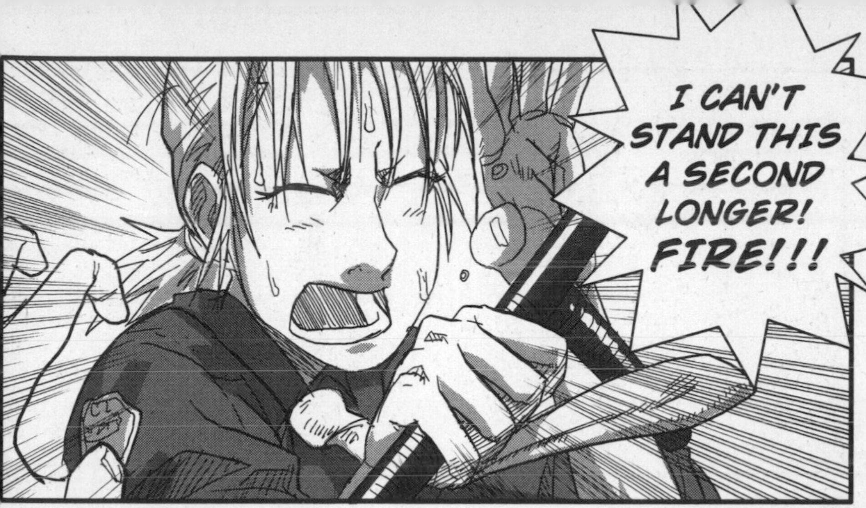
I CAN'T STAND THIS A SECOND LONGER! FIRE!!!

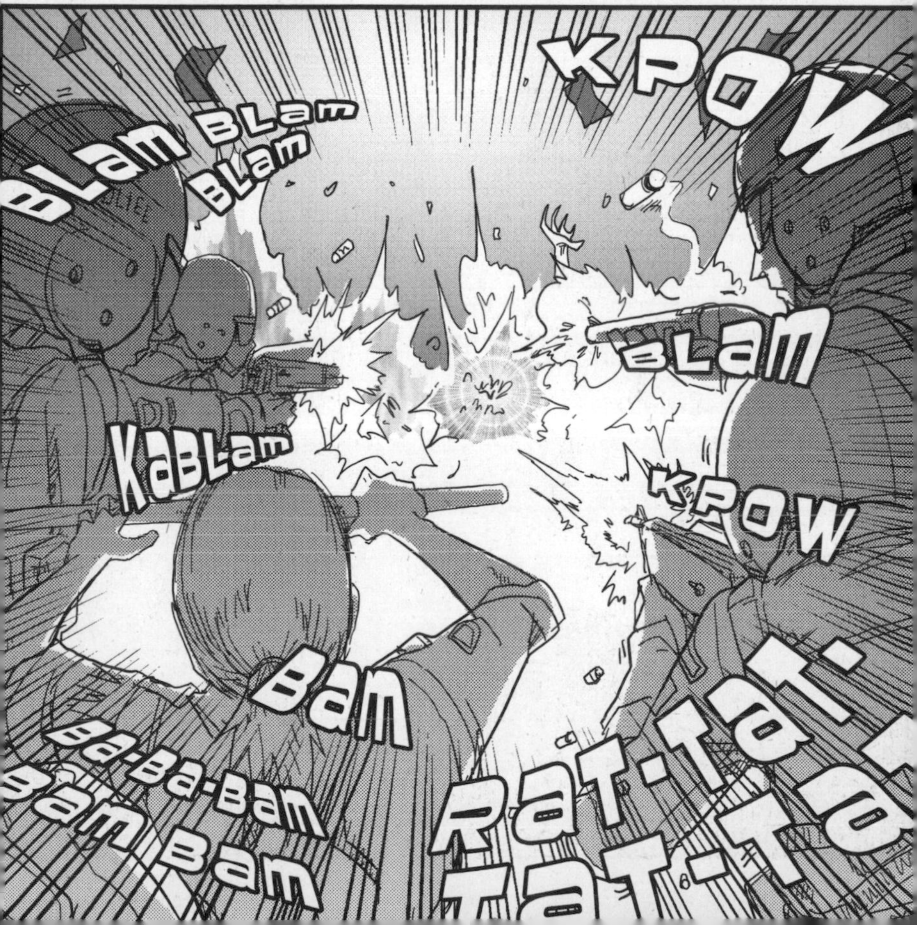
BLAM BLAM BLAM
KPOW
BLAM
KABLAM
KPOW
BAM
BA-BA-BAM
BAM BAM
RAT-TAT-TAT-
TAT-T

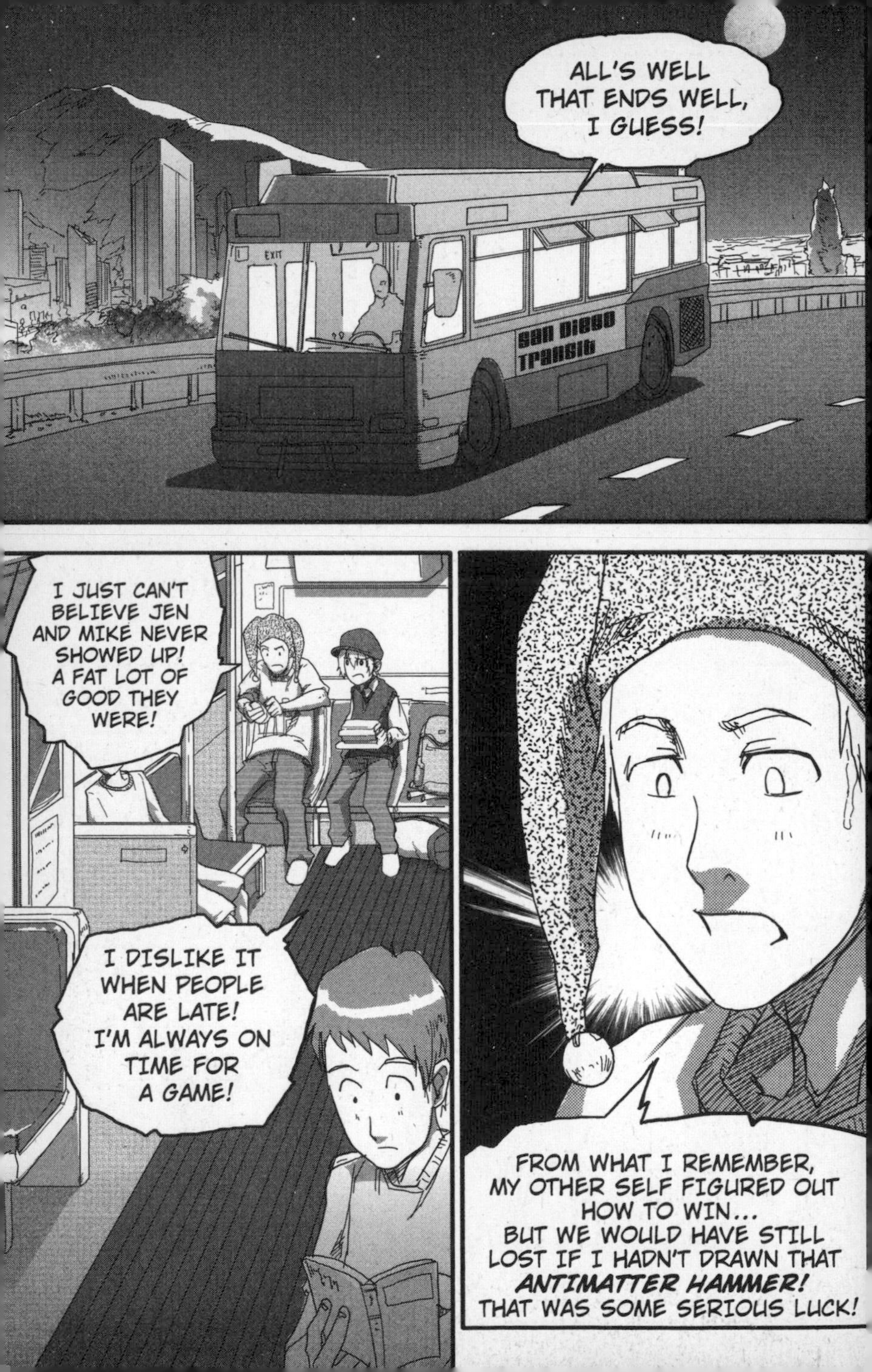
ALL'S WELL THAT ENDS WELL, I GUESS!
SAN DIEGO TRANSIT
I JUST CAN'T BELIEVE JEN AND MIKE NEVER SHOWED UP! A FAT LOT OF GOOD THEY WERE!
I DISLIKE IT WHEN PEOPLE ARE LATE! I'M ALWAYS ON TIME FOR A GAME!
FROM WHAT I REMEMBER, MY OTHER SELF FIGURED OUT HOW TO WIN... BUT WE WOULD HAVE STILL LOST IF I HADN'T DRAWN THAT *ANTIMATTER HAMMER!* THAT WAS SOME SERIOUS LUCK!

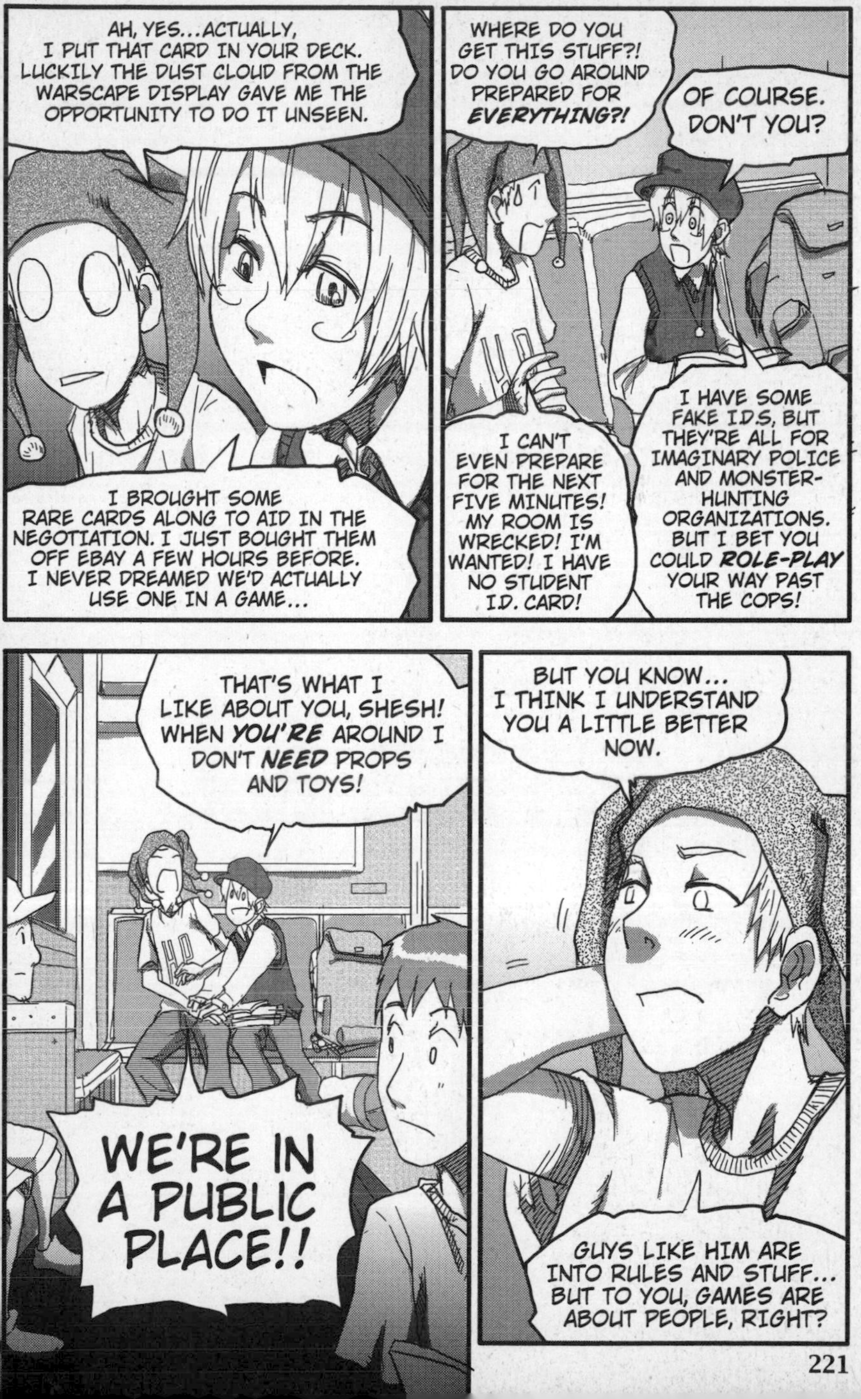
AH, YES...ACTUALLY, I PUT THAT CARD IN YOUR DECK. LUCKILY THE DUST CLOUD FROM THE WARSCAPE DISPLAY GAVE ME THE OPPORTUNITY TO DO IT UNSEEN.
I BROUGHT SOME RARE CARDS ALONG TO AID IN THE NEGOTIATION. I JUST BOUGHT THEM OFF EBAY A FEW HOURS BEFORE. I NEVER DREAMED WE'D ACTUALLY USE ONE IN A GAME...
WHERE DO YOU GET THIS STUFF?! DO YOU GO AROUND PREPARED FOR EVERYTHING?!
OF COURSE. DON'T YOU?
I CAN'T EVEN PREPARE FOR THE NEXT FIVE MINUTES! MY ROOM IS WRECKED! I'M WANTED! I HAVE NO STUDENT I.D. CARD!
I HAVE SOME FAKE I.D.S, BUT THEY'RE ALL FOR IMAGINARY POLICE AND MONSTER-HUNTING ORGANIZATIONS. BUT I BET YOU COULD ROLE-PLAY YOUR WAY PAST THE COPS!
THAT'S WHAT I LIKE ABOUT YOU, SHESH! WHEN YOU'RE AROUND I DON'T NEED PROPS AND TOYS!
WE'RE IN A PUBLIC PLACE!!
BUT YOU KNOW... I THINK I UNDERSTAND YOU A LITTLE BETTER NOW.
GUYS LIKE HIM ARE INTO RULES AND STUFF... BUT TO YOU, GAMES ARE ABOUT PEOPLE, RIGHT?

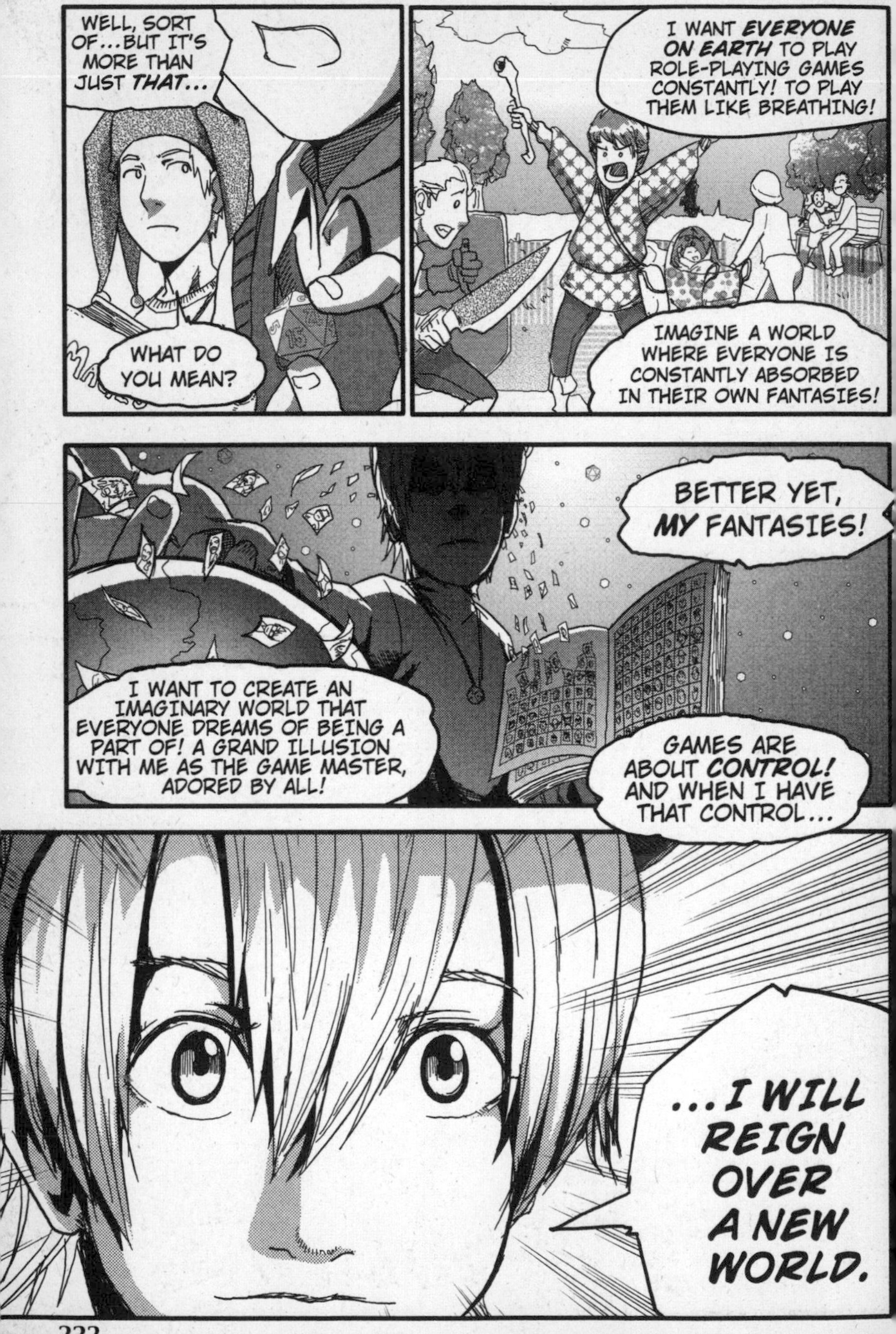
WELL, SORT OF... BUT IT'S MORE THAN JUST *THAT*...
WHAT DO YOU MEAN?
I WANT *EVERYONE ON EARTH* TO PLAY ROLE-PLAYING GAMES CONSTANTLY! TO PLAY THEM LIKE BREATHING!
IMAGINE A WORLD WHERE EVERYONE IS CONSTANTLY ABSORBED IN THEIR OWN FANTASIES!
I WANT TO CREATE AN IMAGINARY WORLD THAT EVERYONE DREAMS OF BEING A PART OF! A GRAND ILLUSION WITH ME AS THE GAME MASTER, ADORED BY ALL!
BETTER YET, *MY* FANTASIES!
GAMES ARE ABOUT *CONTROL!* AND WHEN I HAVE THAT CONTROL...
...I WILL REIGN OVER A NEW WORLD.

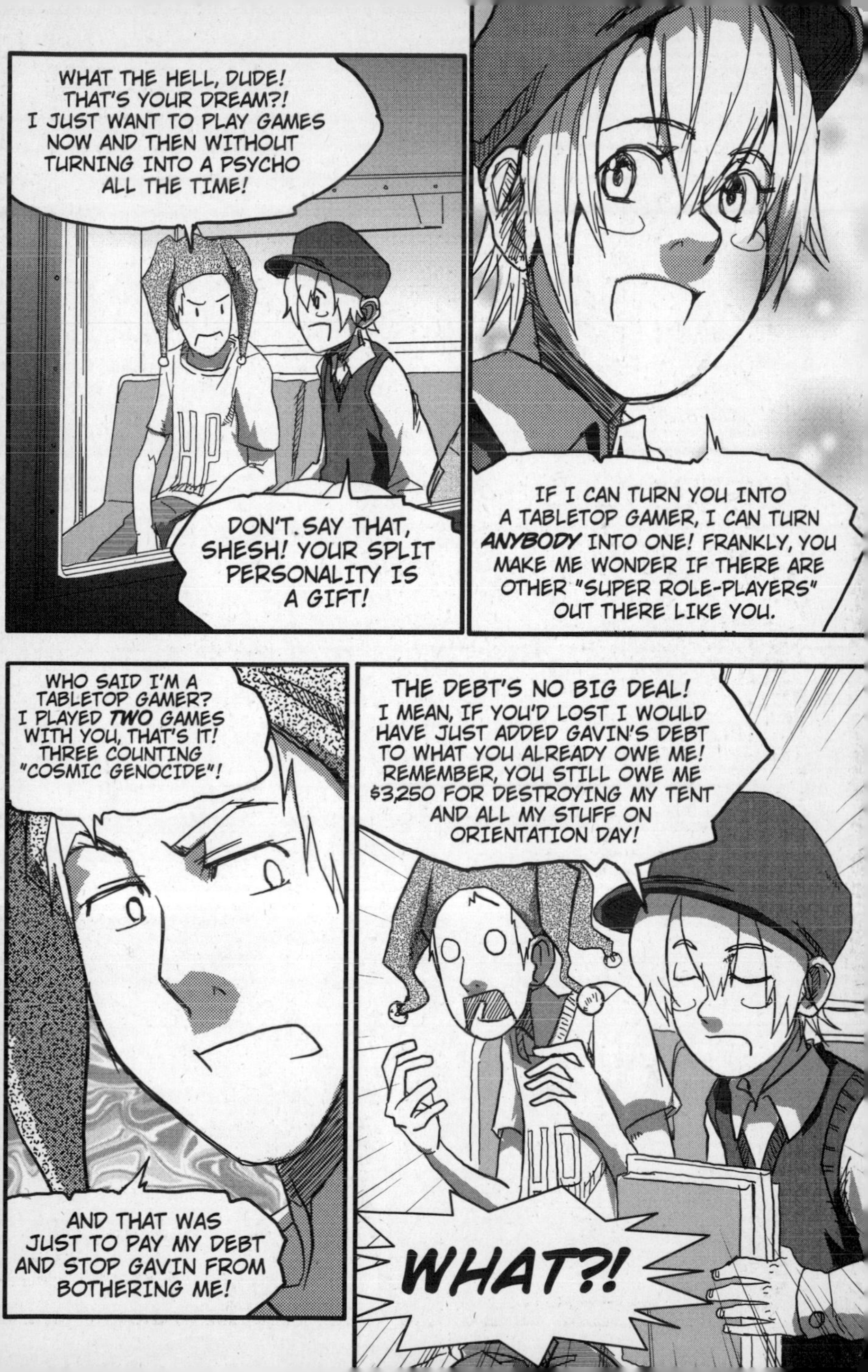

WHAT THE HELL, DUDE! THAT'S YOUR DREAM?! I JUST WANT TO PLAY GAMES NOW AND THEN WITHOUT TURNING INTO A PSYCHO ALL THE TIME!
DON'T. SAY THAT, SHESH! YOUR SPLIT PERSONALITY IS A GIFT!
IF I CAN TURN YOU INTO A TABLETOP GAMER, I CAN TURN ANYBODY INTO ONE! FRANKLY, YOU MAKE ME WONDER IF THERE ARE OTHER "SUPER ROLE-PLAYERS" OUT THERE LIKE YOU.
WHO SAID I'M A TABLETOP GAMER? I PLAYED TWO GAMES WITH YOU, THAT'S IT! THREE COUNTING "COSMIC GENOCIDE"!
AND THAT WAS JUST TO PAY MY DEBT AND STOP GAVIN FROM BOTHERING ME!
THE DEBT'S NO BIG DEAL! I MEAN, IF YOU'D LOST I WOULD HAVE JUST ADDED GAVIN'S DEBT TO WHAT YOU ALREADY OWE ME! REMEMBER, YOU STILL OWE ME $3,250 FOR DESTROYING MY TENT AND ALL MY STUFF ON ORIENTATION DAY!
WHAT?!

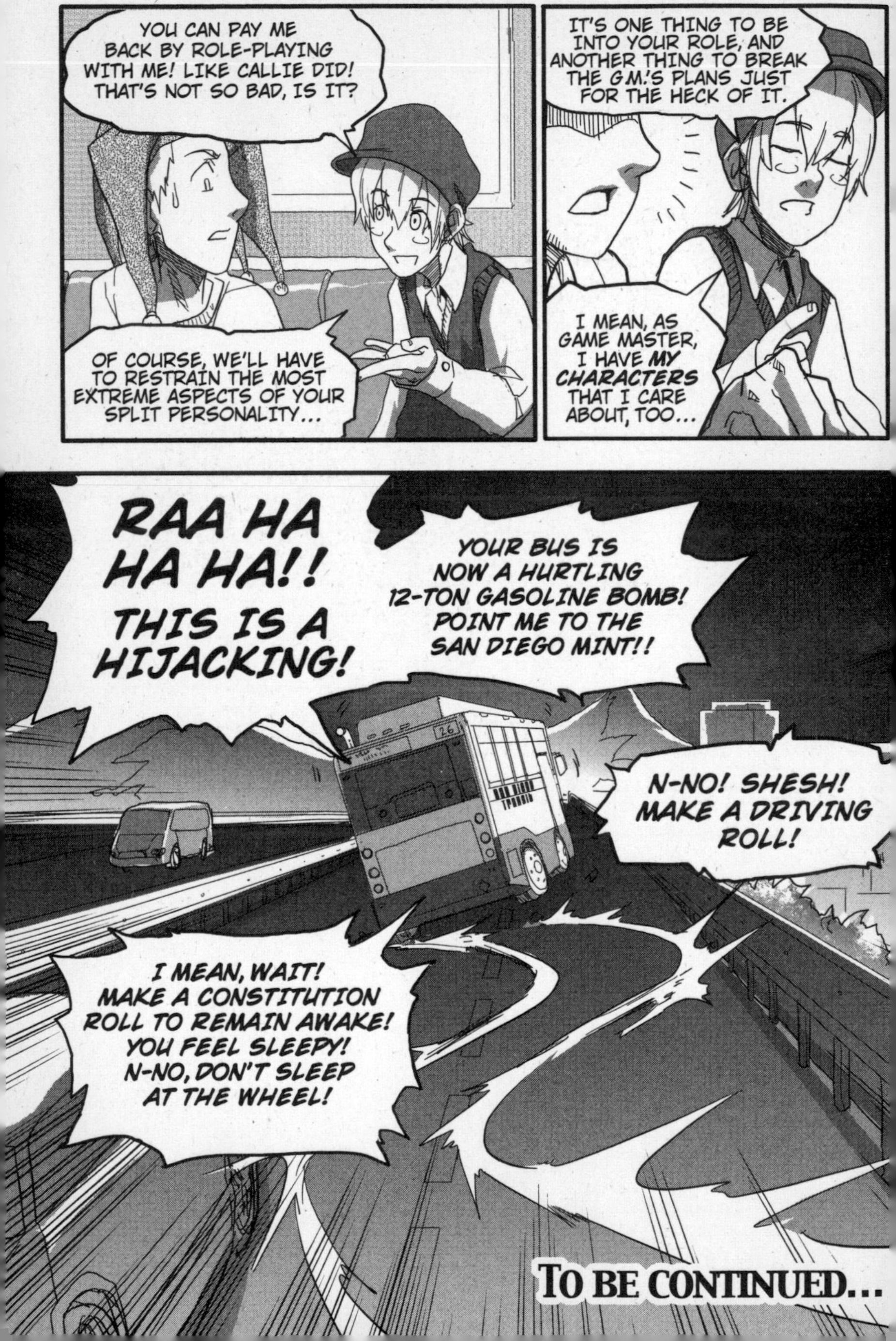
YOU CAN PAY ME BACK BY ROLE-PLAYING WITH ME! LIKE CALLIE DID! THAT'S NOT SO BAD, IS IT?
OF COURSE, WE'LL HAVE TO RESTRAIN THE MOST EXTREME ASPECTS OF YOUR SPLIT PERSONALITY...
IT'S ONE THING TO BE INTO YOUR ROLE, AND ANOTHER THING TO BREAK THE G.M.'S PLANS JUST FOR THE HECK OF IT.
I MEAN, AS GAME MASTER, I HAVE MY CHARACTERS THAT I CARE ABOUT, TOO...
RAA HA HA HA!! THIS IS A HIJACKING!
YOUR BUS IS NOW A HURTLING 12-TON GASOLINE BOMB! POINT ME TO THE SAN DIEGO MINT!!
N-NO! SHESH! MAKE A DRIVING ROLL!
I MEAN, WAIT! MAKE A CONSTITUTION ROLL TO REMAIN AWAKE! YOU FEEL SLEEPY! N-NO, DON'T SLEEP AT THE WHEEL!
TO BE CONTINUED...

KING OF RPGs

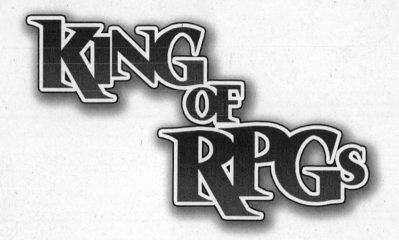

TRIBUTE ART GALLERY

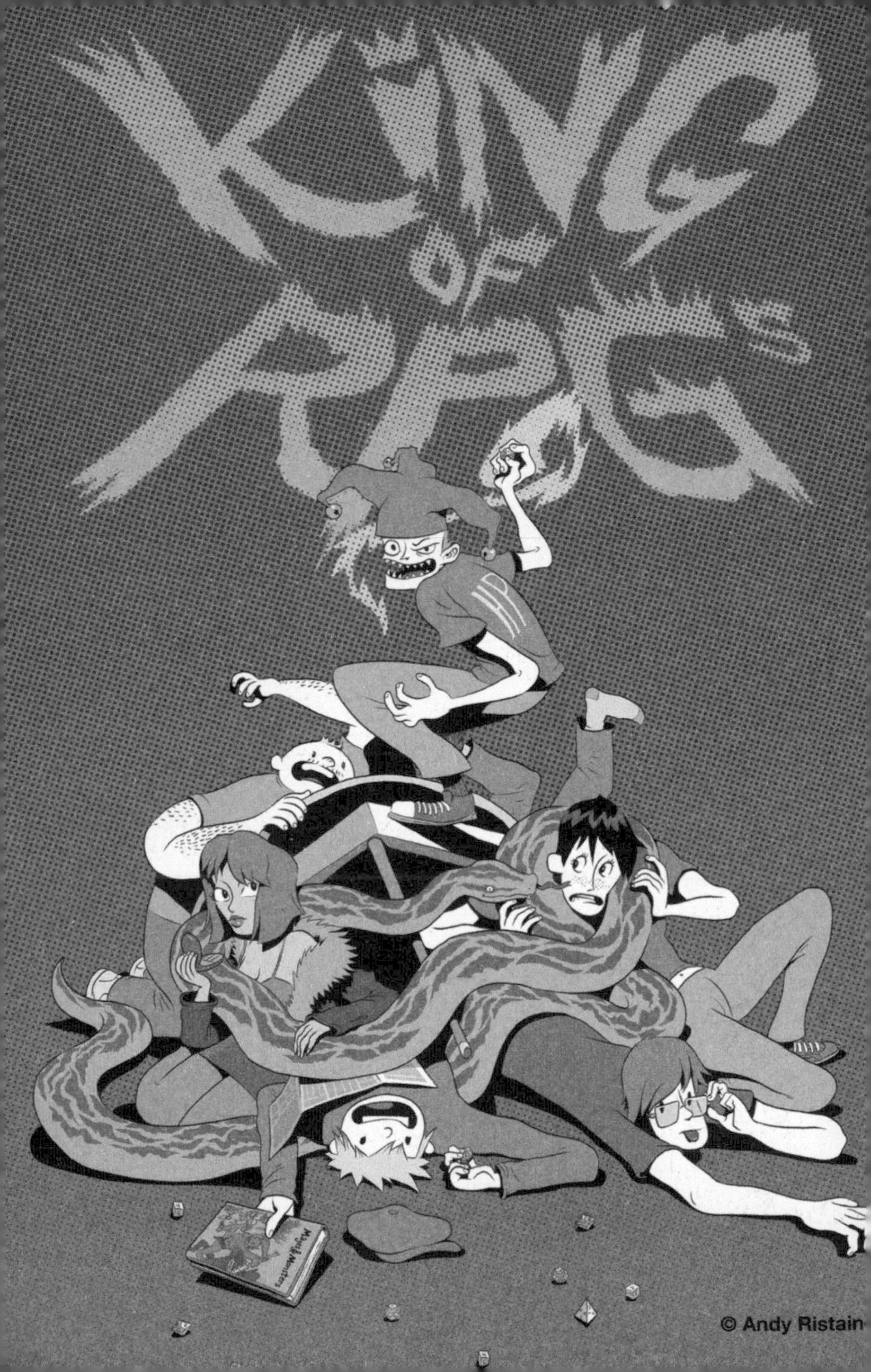
KING OF RPG
Mighty Monsters
© Andy Ristain

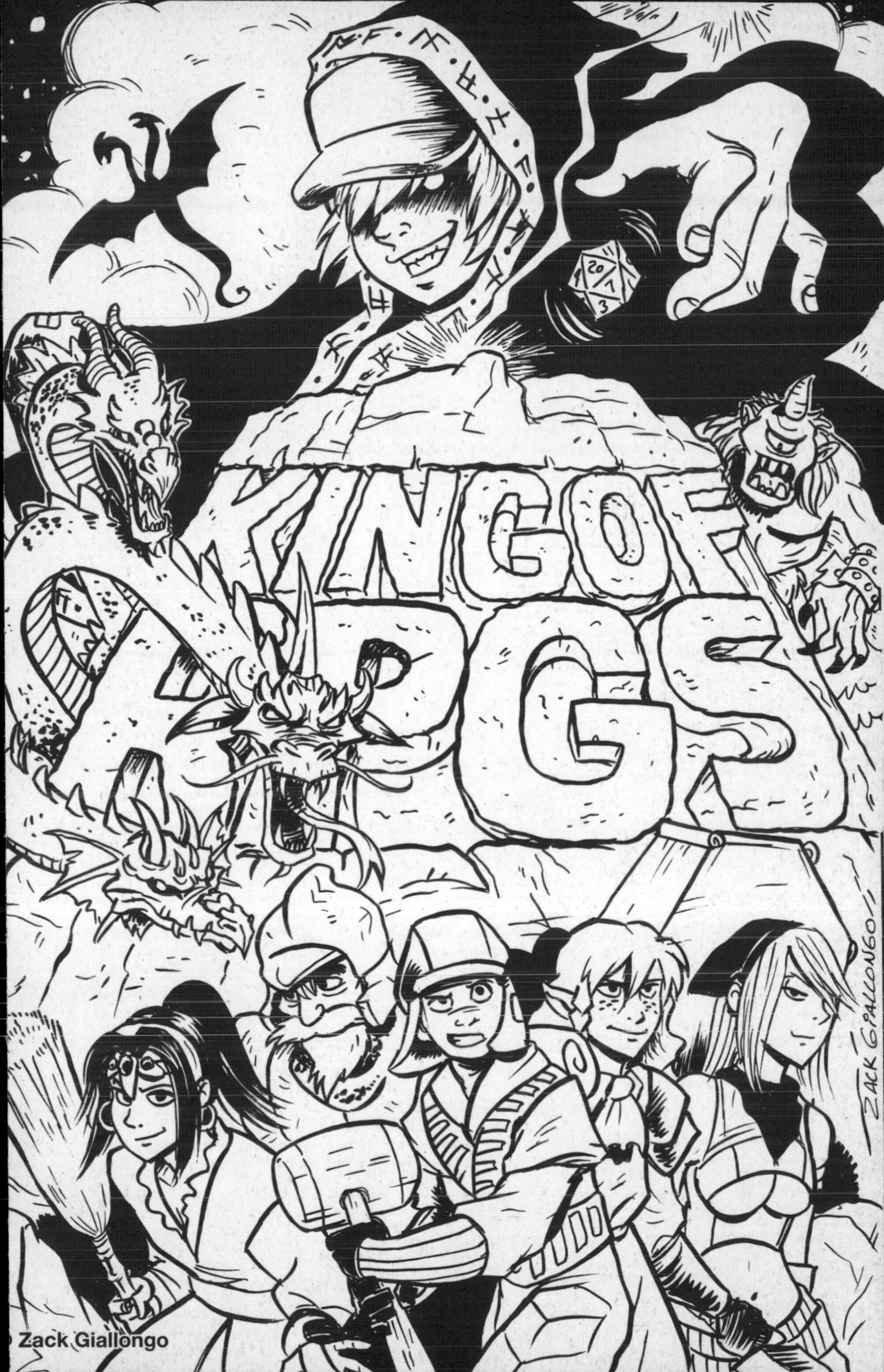
ZACK GIALLONGO
© Zack Giallongo

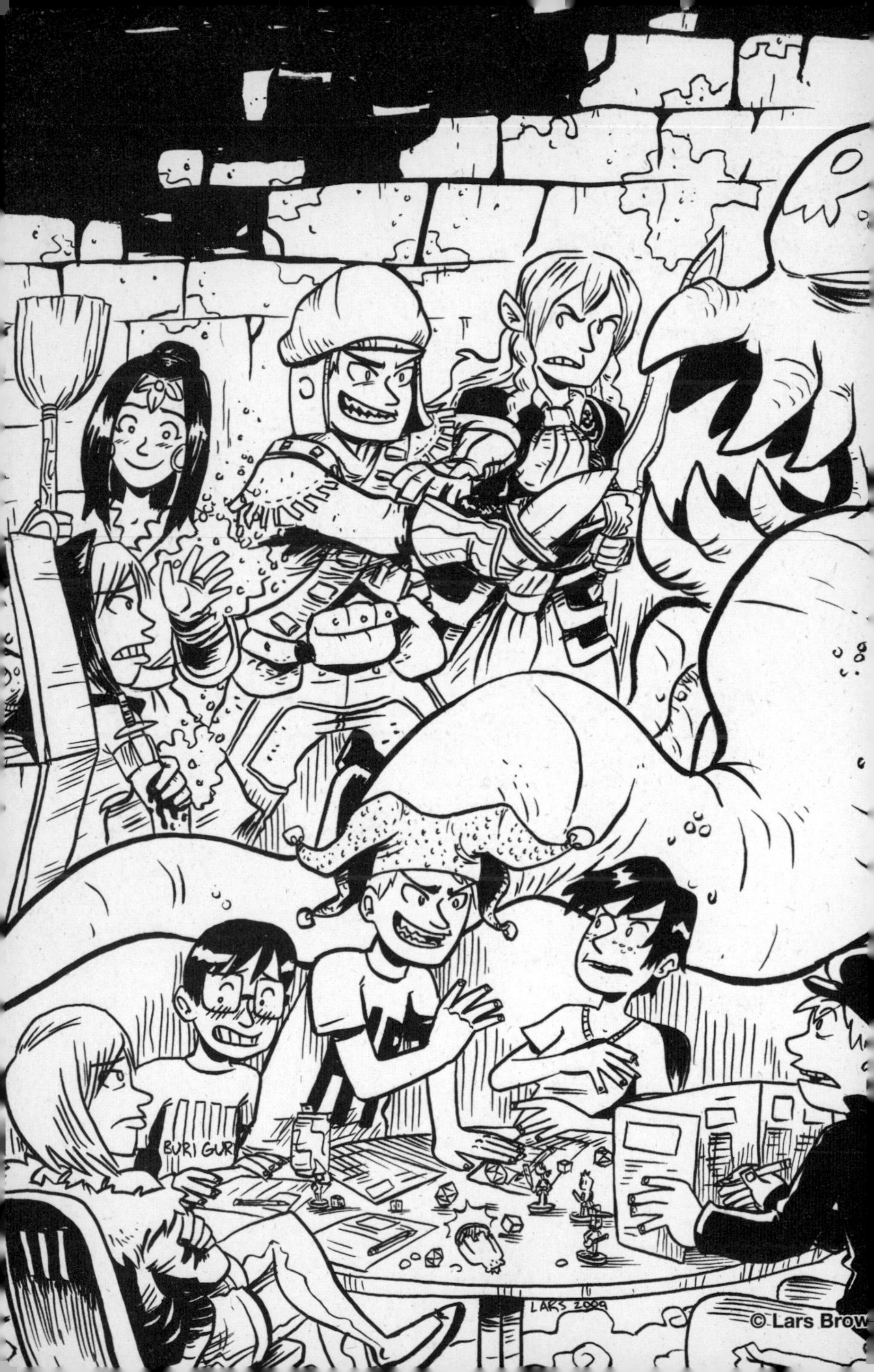
BURI GUR
LARS 2009
© Lars Brow

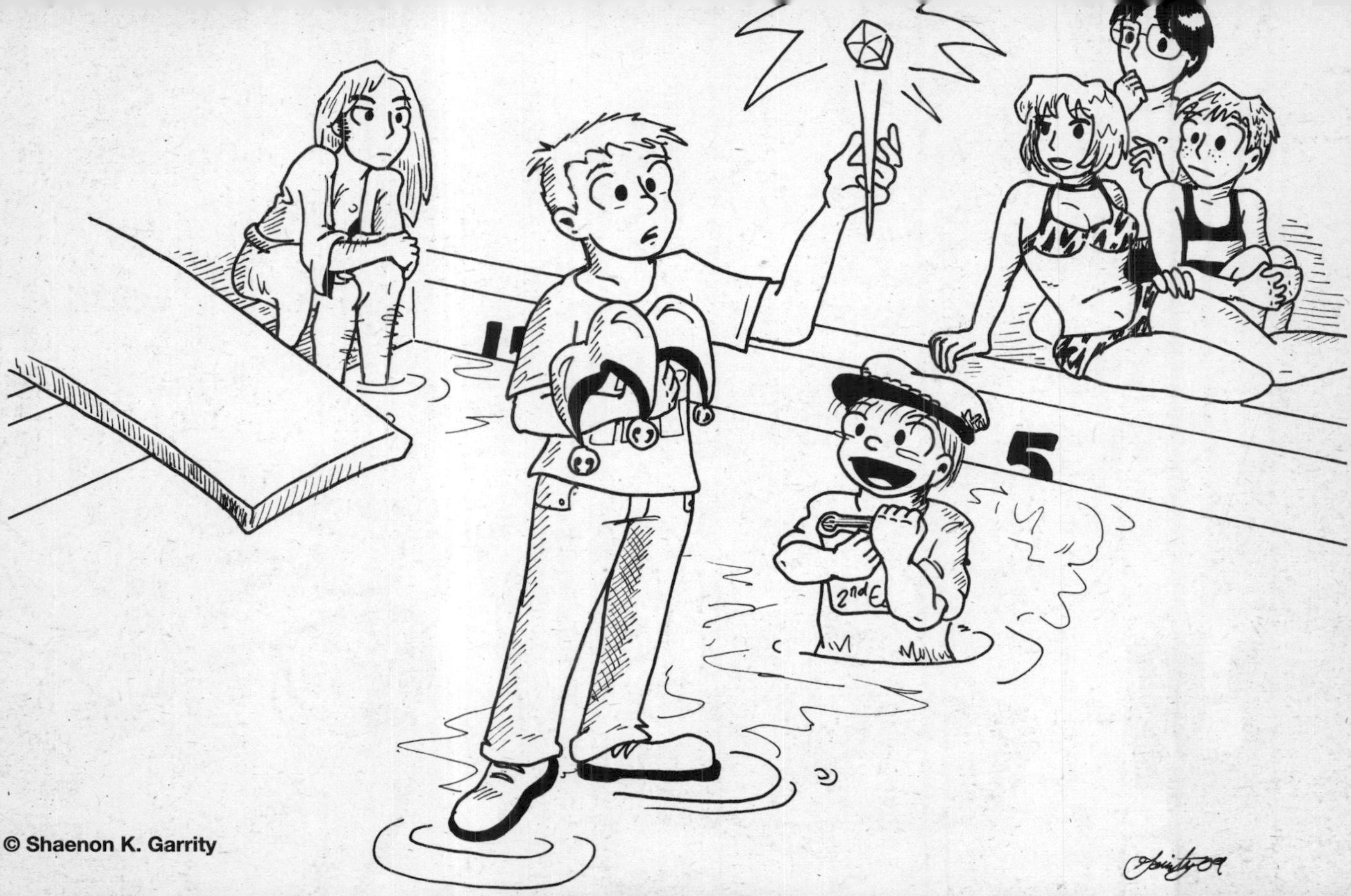
5
2nd E

ABOUT THE TRIBUTE ARTISTS

Lars Brown is the author of the graphic novel series *North World* from Oni Press. He spent a year working on Myst Online as a moderator where he was essentially role-playing a tour guide in a video game. www.north-world.com

Shaenon K. Garrity is the creator of such webcomics as *Narbonic* and *Skin Horse,* all at www.shaenon.com.

Zack Giallongo is a cartoonist living in the smallest state in the U.S. He is currently drawing a book titled *Broxo* about a boy barbarian for First Second books. www.zackgiallongo.com

Andy Ristaino is the creator of several books for SLG including *The Babysitter* and *Life of a Fetus* and has had stories in numerous anthologies such as *Meathaus SOS* and the upcoming *Popgun* volume 4. You can look at more of Andy's works at www.skronked.com

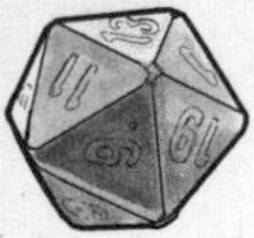

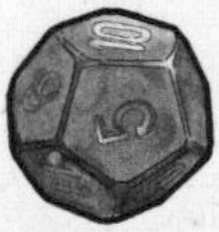

ABOUT THE CREATORS

Jason Thompson has edited the English editions of many manga, including *Naruto, Fullmetal Alchemist, Yu-Gi-Oh!, Dragon Ball Z, Hana-Kimi, One Piece, Shaman King, YuYu Hakusho, Uzumaki,* and *Sayonara, Zetsubou-sensei.* His book *Manga: The Complete Guide,* an encyclopedia of over one thousand manga reviews, was nominated for a 2008 Eisner Award. His writings on manga have appeared in *WIRED, SHONEN JUMP, Otaku USA, The Comics Journal,* Comixology .com, Suvudu.com, and other sites and magazines. He also draws and writes his own comics, which can be seen at his homepage, www.mockman.com.

Throughout **Victor Hao's** life, he knew being a creator was his destiny. He just didn't know that it would lead him toward the doors of manga. So he lives his lifelong dream of becoming a rock star in Rockband while bringing life to his animations and drawings in his apartment. Victor currently resides in San Francisco and has an addiction to MMORPGs and Facebook games. (www.victorhao.com)

A NOTE FROM THE CREATORS

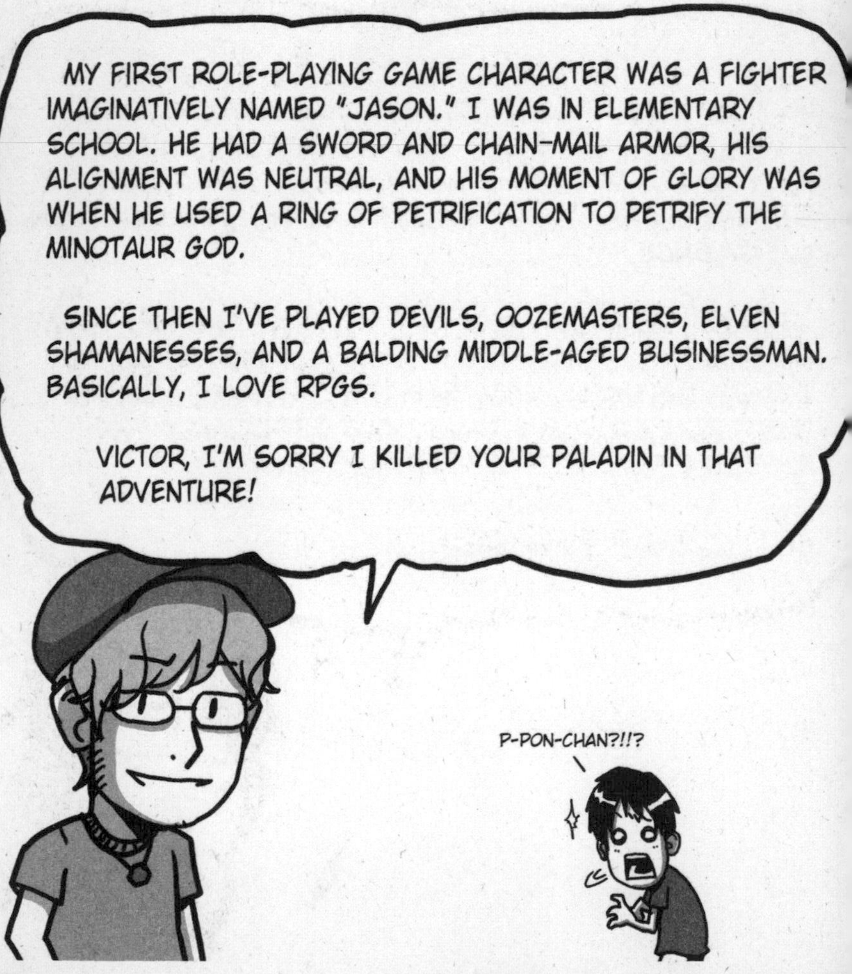
MY FIRST ROLE-PLAYING GAME CHARACTER WAS A FIGHTER IMAGINATIVELY NAMED "JASON." I WAS IN ELEMENTARY SCHOOL. HE HAD A SWORD AND CHAIN-MAIL ARMOR, HIS ALIGNMENT WAS NEUTRAL, AND HIS MOMENT OF GLORY WAS WHEN HE USED A RING OF PETRIFICATION TO PETRIFY THE MINOTAUR GOD.
SINCE THEN I'VE PLAYED DEVILS, OOZEMASTERS, ELVEN SHAMANESSES, AND A BALDING MIDDLE-AGED BUSINESSMAN. BASICALLY, I LOVE RPGS.
VICTOR, I'M SORRY I KILLED YOUR PALADIN IN THAT ADVENTURE!
P-PON-CHAN?!!?

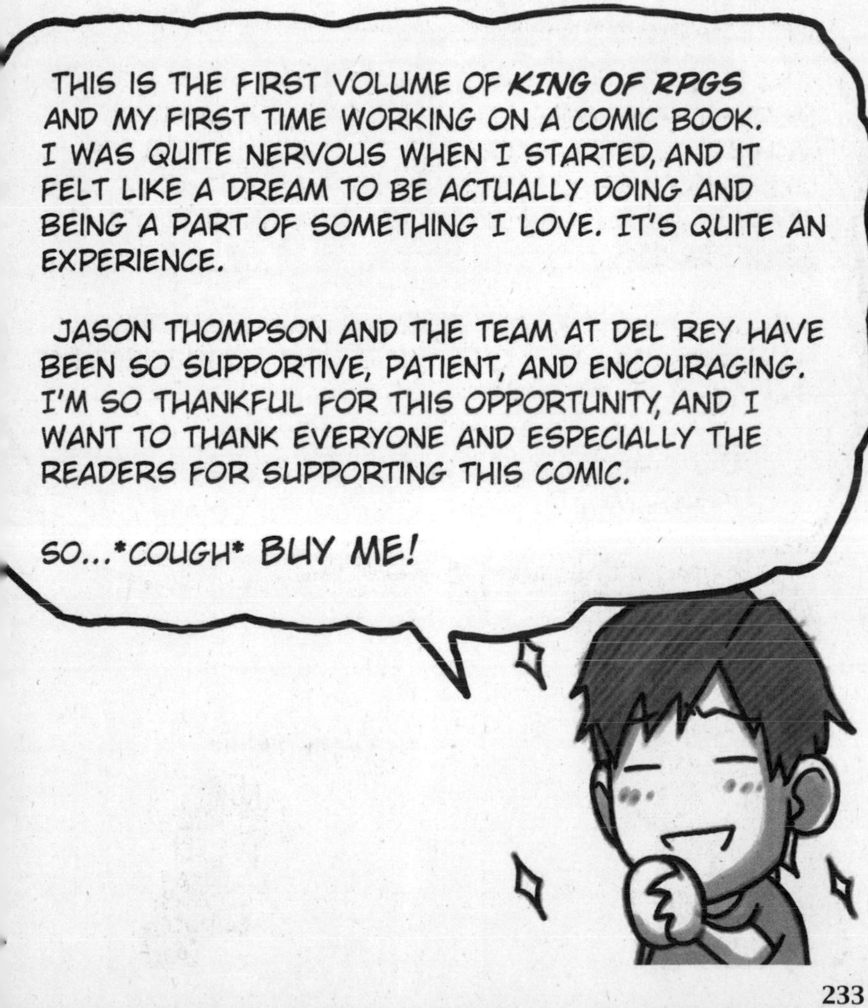
THIS IS THE FIRST VOLUME OF *KING OF RPGS* AND MY FIRST TIME WORKING ON A COMIC BOOK. I WAS QUITE NERVOUS WHEN I STARTED, AND IT FELT LIKE A DREAM TO BE ACTUALLY DOING AND BEING A PART OF SOMETHING I LOVE. IT'S QUITE AN EXPERIENCE.
JASON THOMPSON AND THE TEAM AT DEL REY HAVE BEEN SO SUPPORTIVE, PATIENT, AND ENCOURAGING. I'M SO THANKFUL FOR THIS OPPORTUNITY, AND I WANT TO THANK EVERYONE AND ESPECIALLY THE READERS FOR SUPPORTING THIS COMIC.
SO...*COUGH* BUY ME!

Be on the lookout for volume 2,
coming soon from Del Rey Manga!
Check out delreymanga.com for details.